KAFKA'S ROACH

Praise for *Insect Dreams*

"Get ready for a highly imaginative ride through the cultural frontier of the early twentieth century. A colossal book of characters and events that inspires tears of laughter and sadness in its rich blend of clever metaphor and unsettling facts, this book promises to become a pivotal literary landmark. Highly recommended."
—*Library Journal* (starred review)

"Written in a crisp, entirely absorbing style, describable only as inescapably intriguing ... Gregor reflects profoundly on where humankind is going. ... Few texts of philosophy can deal with such a subject with the same honesty and clarity of this work... *Insect Dreams* is beyond essential reading, it is essential thinking."
—*Historical Novels Review*

"Inventive, puckish Marc Estrin has produced a novel -- a first novel as it happens—that stands apart from business as usual in contemporary fiction. . . . His storytelling -- loose and expansive, historical and imagined, funny and sad—is a seriously ambitious work of art as well as a fine entertainment... He asks how the world between 1915 and 1945 might look to Gregor Samsa, the ultimate outsider, and follows the track of the possibilities that present themselves. This nonmethod gives the book its feel of spontaneity and life, its energy, its freedom from the deadening conventions of ordinary fiction"
—*The World and I*

"(A] remarkably assured debut . . . Estrin's achievement is to make Gregor not merely a mouthpiece or even a symbol but an expression of humanity testing itself against the darker forces of science and technology over which it appears to have lost control. *Insect Dreams* meets that test in the mordant tradition Kafka himself might have applauded."
—*The Raletgh News and Observer*

"Hefty and heartbreaking . . . What Estrin has done should not only be commended, it should be contemplated."
—*The Cleveland Plain Dealer*

"An inspiring read in which the strange life of a cockroach brings daily relevance to humanity's greatest ideas and aspirations."
—*The Bloomsbury Review*

"The joy of this astonishing book—apart from its wit and its true erudition—is the tenderness with which the author treats even the least, and least worthy, of his characters. *Insect Dreams* is the kind of book you finish and immediately begin rereading, to see if it was really *that* good. It is."
—Peter S. Beagle

"A grand comic opera starring a meditative cockroach scuttling through the corridors of power at the fulcrum of the twentieth century. An impressive debut, notable for a generous sense of fun that never detracts from the serious historical and existential implications of all that it so entertainingly depicts."
—*Kirkus Revieus*

"An intellectual tour de force that portrays with manic wit and tireless detail twentieth-century history as seen through the eyes of its most famous arthropod ... Estrin's mind games conceal a profound caring for people, their extraordinary creativity matched only by their ability to destroy. Those tireless readers who make it through the roller-coaster ride of Estrin's encyclopedic imagination will doubtless still be analyzing his complex, challenging first novel as they wait in great anticipation for the next."
—*Richmond Times-Dispatch*

"With its crazy-legged imagination, darting insights, and twitchy wit (*Insect Dreams*] is a creation that defies any sourpuss Raid to kill it dead"
—Tom *Robbins*

KAFKA'S ROACH:
The Life and Times of
Gregor Samsa

Marc Estrin

Being the original version of
Insect Dreams: The Half-life of Gregor Samsa

For FR
with thanks for his faith in metamorphoses

Contents

Washington, DC

Los Alamos, New Mexico

The twentieth century – still our century in spite of the turn of calendar – birthed two wildly different pathogens, both symptoms of erupting cause, and cause of much to follow.

The first appeared in 1915, with the hatching of Gregor Samsa, man-turned-insect -- from Franz Kafka's skull. Marx had written about human alienation in capitalism's industrialized work, while Weber had discussed the consequences for human consciousness. But never before had such a concentrated image, such a devastating symbol as Gregor been loosed upon the world. His presence has affected and afflicted modern literature and thought since then. "Realism" was no longer real enough when men woke up as vermin.

The second pivotal birth, of course, was that of the atomic bomb.

Prologue

As Gregor Samsa awoke one morning from disturbing dreams, he found himself transformed in his bed into an enormous cockroach.

This, the most famous opening sentence of modern literature. And this, the most famous closing sentence of modern thought:

What we cannot speak of, of that we must be silent.

Between the two, there passed a life, Gregor Samsa's life. It was not the life many suppose — a short life, a filthy life, a gathering of dust, a festering wound, a dessicated death. Franz Kafka knew only what he knew, and his famous 1915 report disclosed all it could. But Kafka's early death not only deprived us of a gifted writer; it also kept him, and all of us, from knowing the full story of Gregor Samsa, a life stranger than fiction, and worthy of contemplation.

****

From May of 1943 until July, 1945, Gregor, or G, as he preferred to be known, lived in a refurbished chicken coop behind my bungalow up on the mesa at Los Alamos. Both of us being bachelors, and neither of us involved in the technical demands of the project, we spent many long evenings talking, musing, and finally, plotting G's path to transcendence.

I use the word advisedly; it was his word, the theme which had emerged for him ever more clearly in three countries, over two world wars, through multiple careers. Together, we nursed his wound ("the unhealing wound", he called it, "the hidden wound that will not hide" , the "dolorous stroke". He was referring, of course, to the place in his dorsal carapace, just over his heart, which his father had damaged so long ago with a fiercely hurled apple. It still oozed brown liquid, staining his clothes — causing him much embarrassment.) He understood his mission as a species of quest. The object: the Holy Grail of transformation, a global urging of consciousness from bestial to human. A metamorphosis. Who but he would be better placed to break the spell on those of us wandering in the Waste Land?

The years since his death have not been encouraging. As grail hero, G was an utter failure. But as a person, a human being, if I may dare name him so, he profoundly affected me, and everyone with whom he came into deep contact. I have waited all this while to tell his story because I thought there were surely others more qualified to do so. But more importantly, I hoped that the passage of time would prove G correct, that his sacrifice would help restore the land, and free the waters of human kindness. By now it seems that if we, as a species, are to learn kindness, we will have to learn it from the unkind, in repellent pedagogy. But of G himself, how many of us were struck by

> *...that best portion of a good man's life.*
> *His little, nameless, unremembered acts*
> *of kindness and of love.*
> No matter that that good man was a cockroach.

****

My name is John Aschenfeld. I am a professor emeritus of History at Princeton, specializing in the History of Science. It was my good fortune to be asked by my friend and colleague, Harry Smyth, to be "present at the creation," as it were, to be on his team, researching and writing the "Smyth Report: Atomic Energy for Military Purposes," the official History of the Manhattan Project. Creation? More like Destruction. Had I really been present at the Creation, I would, like Alfonso X, King of Castile, have offered up some useful hints for the better ordering of the universe.

I will describe G's role "on the mesa" at the appropriate time. Let me deal first with the obvious objections of those readers literate enough to remember Franz Kafka's so-called masterpiece, *Die Verwandlung, The Metamorphosis.* By using the term "so called," I in no way mean to impugn this marvelous work, a narrative which shocked a generation, and initiated, even defined, what is fondly remembered as "the modern age" in literature. But an author can write only about what he knows, and as sensitive and insightful as Kafka was, it turns out that he, like many others, was taken in by a scheme more masterful than his own, a plan issuing from the great heart of a transformed Gregor, and effected through a remarkable *Putzfrau,* whose cleanup was more than professional.

By G's report, Anna Marie Schleßweg was 63 at the time of his *Verwandlung.* But for him she might easily have passed for 40 when shoving her way through a crowded market, or for 140 in the swarming shadows of *Walpurgisnacht.* What kind of a person, he wondered, could open the door of a man's bedroom, a room she had been cleaning weekly for four years, open the door, not find the room empty as usual, but occupied by a five and a half foot bug, what kind of a person could take in this scene, with the thing rushing about frantically, crashing into furniture, and finally secreting itself under the couch, what kind of a person could merely stand there, calmly, with her arms folded?

Gregor still cherished this early impression of true magnificence.

There is an injunction in the *Yi Ging,* the ancient Chinese Book of Changes: "The Superior Man sees many things, but lets many things pass." And its determinant: "The Superior Man displays the highest virtue by embracing all things."

Anna Marie, G asserted, was a Superior Man. She listened and she watched, but she did not let *everything* pass. She heard, for instance, how piteously G's sister Grete wept, and saw Herr and Frau Samsa paralyzed with denial. It was her great wisdom to leave the door to Gregor's room ajar as much as possible, so that worlds might intermingle, so that an uncanny convection might agitate the air and find some resolution.

3

And Gregor then listened carefully at the slightly open door, and heard frequent sobbing. He heard slow, dragging footsteps. He heard his father say, "If he could understand us, then perhaps we might come to some agreement with him. But as it is..." followed by a long silence. And then, sister Grete: "He must go. That's the only solution, Father. You must try to stop thinking that this is Gregor. That's the root of all our trouble. How can it be Gregor? If it were Gregor, he'd have realized long ago that human beings can't live with such a creature. He'd have gone away of his own accord." So much did she love him. So much did she trust him. So much, in fact, did she know him.

From that moment on, the thought of disappearance became G's ideé fixe. "*Wahnvorstellung*", he called it. His crazy notion. He would simply go of his own accord. He would make it his decision. He would spare them the agony and guilt of such a verdict.

But how to do it? Here his astute Jewish thinking did inform against him. Were he to announce his decision to the family, they would think they had forced him out, and feel searingly guilty. Were he simply to disappear, they would spare no effort to find him, and failing that, he would be a permanent wound in their hearts, even in his father's heart, the wounded heart of the wounder. Confused, he was. But Anna Marie had an answer to his neurotic debates: after listening to him while sweeping and straightening up his room, she sat her old bones down on the floor, leaned against the wall, and addressed him under his couch.

" It's simple," she said. "Play dead."

G was amazed he'd never thought of it. "It's easy," she explained. You just lie there."

****

Here was her initial plan: She would discover him "dead", there would be mourning for a month, a year, then all would be able to get on with their lives. They would not be the only family in Prague to have lost a son, especially since the War.

"But they would bury me," was G's obvious objection. I'd suffocate." And plan "dead" dead-ended there.

But only for a while. For shortly after their discussion, Sebastian Kramar, Bruno Klofac, and Matthias Soukup were allowed to move in as paying guests, *Zimmerherren*, roomers — an attempt by the family to bring new life into the morbid atmosphere, and to replace Gregor's salary as the mainstay of the family income.

It did not take long for Anna Marie to see a possibility in the new situation: the three men had been recently let go from the same failed business, all were looking for work, and after two or three months, all would be desperate for money. Would they like to help the Samsas out, and earn some money besides? How could they say no? What else did they have to do? Did they know about the thing in the (now) locked room?

"What thing?" they asked her.

"Come, I'll show you."

Kramar, Klofac, and Soukup reacted as one might expect — with surprise, then horror, then fear. It was only Anna Marie's calm that kept them frozen in G's presence. Without explaining the genesis of the situation, she, with Gregor's assent and support, was able to make a clear and convincing case for action. And G's behavior was reassuring: he would not hurt them; he needed their help.

As predicted, a combination of empathy and self-interest prevailed, and the following complex plan took shape:

— Gregor would act sicker and sicker, and eventually, convincingly, would play dead.

— But just before T-day, (T for "Tod" — "death" in German), Anna Marie would leave his door open, and Gregor would venture out of his room to the feigned surprise and shock of the roomers.

— Horrified, they would announce their imminent departure, and threaten to sue the Samsas for emotional damages. This, Gregor assured me, would have made his parents wary of pursuing any leads as to their future whereabouts.

— On the next morning, Anna Marie would arrive early, before G's parents were out of bed, and would announce his death in a simple, if brutal, fashion. Half awake, and thoroughly shaken, the parents, and sister Grete would view the body, and collapse in emotional disarray. And so they did.

— Anna Marie would then "dispose" of the body, while the roomers would inappropriately demand breakfast.

— Herr Samsa would in all likelihood throw them out immediately, and they and Gregor would all disappear at the same time, for seemingly unrelated reasons.

Quite the plot! The insect and the Putzfrau were proud of their play-writing. When the parents were out, Anna Marie would move Gregor into a damaged crate left out on the balcony, and would lower it into a waiting wagon borrowed from Klofac's brother-in-law. From Prague, it was only a day's journey to Vienna, where a potentially remunerative situation had been rumored.

Well. Hindsight can be arrogant, and as one who has got the story straight from the roach's mouth, I have little right to pontificate. Still, acute readers of Kafka will be able to judge for themselves where his report is thin and his characters' motivation doubtful. G's own story explains the oddities at the end of Kafka's story: why his door was so often left ajar; why Kramar, Klofac, and Soukup were so united in their behavior; and not as shocked on seeing Gregor "for the first time" as one might expect; why Klofac's indignant speech to the Samsa's seemed so prepared, so final, and so calculated to discourage further contact; why Anna Marie's "discovery" of Gregor occurred so early in the morning, and her presentation was so brusque and almost comedic. These people were not actors; they played their roles with little finesse. Pathetic smiles and unexplained "fits of humility" were the best they could come up with in performance. Rude mechanicals. Yet it was enough to confuse Franz Kafka.

Please forgive my pocket-sized excursion into literary criticism. It is not my field of expertise.

1. Blattidae

Before relating the remarkable events which followed, I must clarify, once and for all, the question of Gregor's entomological identity. Kafka, supreme artist that he was, labeled him only an *"ungeheueres Ungeziefer."* Only! What concentrated literary power in that naming! What frisson in the etymology! *Un...un...* the awful pounding rhythm of not-ness, of linguistic negation, of separation (tragically true!) , darkness and void. Gregor is nothing familiar. His life was an effort to make himself known.

The adjective *ungeheuer* means "giant," "enormous," "immense" — but with unearthly overtones: *das Ungeheuer* is a monster, some frightening or dreadful thing of all genders. And *Ungeziefer* is a generic term denoting all sorts of undesireables — pests, plague, vermin — deriving from the late Middle High German *ungezibere, unziver,* which originally meant an "unclean animal not suited for sacrifice," a beast surrounded by taboo. The idea of "vermin" connotes something parasitic and aggressive, something that lives off human beings and sucks their blood, and on the other hand something possibly defenseless: inmates in a concentration camp, something that can be stepped on and crushed.

"Ungeheures Ungeziefer": what a curse for the translator! How can one possibly capture in a few words the profound and frightening weight of this description? Notwithstanding, people have tried: Gregor has been called an "enormous bug," "a monstrous kind of vermin," "a gigantic insect." The facts, however, speak for themselves: he was a cockroach.

Scale, of course, makes a difference, and brings us quickly to the world of *"ungeheuer."* Would not the appearance of even a baby bunny, twelve feet long, drive us to meditate or seek protection? How much more so with an already repulsive beast. Identity is transformed by simple size, and it is not easy to apply normal thought to abnormal dimension.

Still, and nevertheless, Gregor was a cockroach, clearly a cockroach, in fact, simply a giant version of *Periplaneta americana.* How do I know this? Simple. One rainy afternoon up on the mesa, we keyed him out in a standard reference work, P. B. Cornwell's excellent *The Cockroach,* Hutchinson, 1938:

Kingdom: Animal — G laughed, since he so often felt himself to be vegetable or even mineral.

Phylum: Arthropoda — jointed legs. I, too, have jointed legs, but his are more jointed, and more obviously so.

Class: Insecta — no one has ever questioned that.

Order: Blattaria — thick, leathery forewings, grasshopper-like mouth parts, incomplete metamorphosis. The last we could only assume, given his unique history.

Family: Blattidae — from the Roman notion of a light-shunning insect, certainly true in G's case.

Allowing for the difference in size (1mm = ~ 1"), we made the following excursion:

— Tegmina (hardened outer wings) reaching just beyond abdomen, more than 6-7 mm wide. (G's was approximately 17 inches.)

— Tegmina not mottled or with dark lines in the basal area. (G's were a deep and beautiful burnt umber.)

— Last segment of cercus (the sensory structures extending posteriorly from abdomen) twice as long as wide. (Quite a bit less useful when wearing pants, which Gregor did. In nature, cerci are able to sense minute air movements, giving cockroaches the ability to flee from potential danger within 0.05 second. G's were almost exactly 10" long and 5" at the base.)

And thus we arrived at our goal in the key: *Periplaneta americanus* — the American cockroach. It was a hilarious session. I had never seen G so gay. "I, too, am classified material!" he crowed.

You may think it odd that, with his initial appearance in Prague, Gregor would be "American". The fact is that the names of cockroach species are completely misleading, a consequence of erroneous assumptions about origins by early systematologists. It is admittedly insulting for science to intrude and reduce Kafka's "*ungeheueres Ungeziefer*" to merely an outsized *P. americanus*. But there are levels and levels, and the story to be told will not stint on import.

Let me be more specific in describing my friend, Gregor Samsa, Risk Consultant to the Manhattan Project at Los Alamos. He was 5' 4" from the top of his head to the tip of his tegmina, not counting his cerci, which, because of the need to wear clothing, were most often strapped to his abdomen underneath. That is, he was a "normal" size person, if a little short for a male. He "stood" anywhere from 20 inches to six feet. It never ceased to be an issue whether to stand on all sixes, or to try to ape human verticality. As a six-footer, he was a bit awkward, somewhat tentative in his gait. Vertically, he could function well at cocktail parties or at meetings, seated in a chair. However, at home, or among close friends, he preferred the horizontal, more natural for his anatomy, and on six legs, could scamper on the mesa or the mountains far ahead of Fermi or Feynman or even Ulam.

His most striking features — at least to strangers — were his eyes, two huge compound eyes, seven inches across, of 2,000 lenses each, with a simple eye at the base of each antenna. In faintest light they would glisten, iridescent, ever-changing. Vision for those with compound eyes, is both less — and more — exact than for those of us with mammalian organs. While the overall image is somewhat blurry, a mosaic of soft focus, like the surface of a Seurat, the perception of motion is vastly more acute. As an image traverses from lens to lens, it ticks a sensor at each border which registers precise direction and speed. Peripheral vision is immense. The irony is that Gregor was judged legally blind. But were the roads to be filled with Gregors, there would be far fewer traffic accidents. Nevertheless, G's eyes were his most upsetting feature to strangers, even should he choose not to meet their gaze.

His other insect features could be concealed, for the most part, under clothing. But 4,000 simultaneous stares were admittedly disconcerting. Consequently, he early on took to wearing large sunglasses, specially made for him by Zeiss. His mouth was far more adept than our own, with hard, chitinous jaws for chewing from side to side, maxillae with both soft and stiff bristles for grooming his antennae and legs. And even though he was capable of eating a wide range of food, from prime rib at the Sans Souci, to rotting garbage in the dumpster behind it, he was equipped with both maxillary and labial palps to ascertain edibility — before taking anything unhealthy into his body.

Keeping antennae and limbs spotless was not just good breeding: his smell and vibrational senses would have been compromised otherwise. His ears, so to speak, were subgenual organs located in each knee joint, so sensitive, when he wore shorts, that he could detect the footfalls of other, normal size roaches, and distinguish earthquakes as small as 0.07 on the Richter scale.

Clothing created difficulties: without special gussets of netting, G would have been unable to breathe. As was normal for his species, he had eight pairs of spiracles at either side of his abdomen, and two additional pairs on his thorax. A rational approach would have been to dress G in something like tails, covering his back and legs, and leaving his abdomen free and open to the air. But such is human prudery that people found his bare teregites and sternites and, worst of all, his protruding cerci, offensive. No matter that they were covered with solid, seamless chitin, gleaming and waterproof with veneers of oil and wax as lustrous as the dashboard of a Rolls Royce. Still, they were his "backside" his "tush", some said, and they needed covering. He had more than once been determined to go to Tahiti, or Borneo, where he could walk around unfettered, able to breathe and excrete as the Good Lord intended. But his sense of task was unyielding, and the awkward arrangements necessary to pursue it had simply to be suffered.

It is with some reluctance that I speak of his wound, an extremely sensitive subject to G. It was about two thirds of the way down the middle of his back, just over his heart. Kafka's description of the young boy's wound in "A Country Doctor" was actually a description of G's, which, for some reason, the author chose not to include in his earlier tale: *An open wound as big as the palm of my hand. Rose-red, in many variations of shade, dark in the hollows, lighter at the edges, softly granulated, with irregular clots of blood, open as a surface mine to the daylight. That was how it looked from a distance. But on a closer inspection there was another complication. ... Worms, as thick and as long as my little finger, themselves rose-red and blood-spotted as well, were wriggling from their fastness in the interior of the wound towards the light, with small white heads and many little legs.*

That was it, exactly. The "worms", of course, were larvae. What might become of them were they left to molt was anybody's guess. The possibilities were so frightening that G spent much time and emotional energy extracting them and eating, or otherwise destroying them. There may have been some that dropped off unnoticed. It is the stuff of nightmares. The wound was simply unhealable, both cross and salvation. It required intense, continuing care, it led to endless embarrassment, it was a source of chronic mid-level pain — but it allowed G to stay on task, to ever remember the Grail of his quest: that he might catalyze the ultimate healing of humanity.

VIENNA

2. Tails Of Hoffnung

Over many star-drunk nights, Gregor's thoughts would emerge from his giant neurons, filling my ears with accounts of his transformed life, I madly scribbling shorthand with poor pad and pen and the zeal of a historian. His post-Prague existence began and was formed on the outskirts of Vienna:

Zirkus Schwänze Hoffnungs. The Tails of Hoffnung Circus. What could it possibly mean? Clearly a macaronic pun, German/English, a reference to the Tales of Hoffman (though *Erzählungen* in German), but there quite clearly "Tails", possibly even "Tails of Hope". How did the name reflect the mind-boggling collection of freaks and oddities there assembled? Were they the cast-off "tailings" of otherwise normal production? Or were they really extrusions, extensions of hope, a smattering of otherness in a fallen world? Was this a circus at all? Where were the trained beasts, the clowns and acrobats, the death-defying trapeze artists to titillate and awe the crowd?

On this issue, Amadeus Ernst Hoffnung was scornful and corrosive. "No trapeze acts!" he would bluster, and under this emblem he would subsume all other parodies of human freedom. "A family of acrobats high in the roof, balancing, swinging, rocking, springing, catching, hanging by the hair from their children's' teeth! What a betrayal of humanity, what a mockery of holy Mother Nature! Were apes to witness such a spectacle, no theater walls could stand the shock of their laughter!" And here, he himself would break into uncontrollable fits of narrow, sharp squawking, convulsions far louder than might be expected from his 5' 2" frame. How many times had he put this image to himself? How many times had he broken down until, eyes watering, he had to gasp for breath and sink down onto chair, or couch — or even floor? What was it about that image that so enraged him, and did he imagine his own exhibits might better depict the joys and labors of Mother Nature?

After 1919, when Albert Einstein became a household word, "the smartest man in the world", Amadeus Ernst Hoffnung began to refer to himself as "A.E., the Einstein of Possibilities". He ordered his staff, from cleaning ladies to star attractions, to address him as simply "A.E.", a pseudo-deferential nod to the revolutionary democracy of those early post-war years. But when Anna Marie, leading Kramar, Klofac, and Soukup — and their broken-down crate — behind her, first approached him in 1915, he was Herr Doktor Professor Hoffnung, though what exactly he professed was anyone's guess.

****

Zirkus Schwänze Hoffnungs had begun as *"Wunderkammer Hoffnungs"*, the hobby of a diminutive, shy adolescent. His "Cabinet of Wonders" had begun with his childhood rock and insect collections, his autographs of singers from the Vienna State Opera, "paintings" made by three generations of his cats, and what was clearly the largest ball of string ever imagined by his otherwise scornful cohorts. He would invite girls to come see his collections, and the few who did were duly impressed — but that's all. The idea that his collection could become a business was far from the thoughts of this lonely, needy child until one day in 1907 his parents bought a Victrola, the very model pictured on "His Master's Voice."

"Parsifal! Can we get Parsifal?"

"It hasn't been recorded. It would take too many records — they'd fill a whole room. But you can see it again next year when we go to Bayreuth."

His father was concerned that he grow into a fine cultured gentleman.

"No, I want it in my own house, to hear whenever I want."

"I'm sure there'll be more and more recordings. You can start saving for your own record collection. I'll add a crown a week to your allowance, and you can put it away for music."

"A crown a week? It would take years to save for Parsifal when it comes out. And then there's The Ring, and Giovanni "

"Why don't you charge people to see your collections?"

And so began young Amadeus' quest for gold. He saved his weekly crowns, and rummaged the thrift stores and flea markets of Vienna. He haunted antiquarian bookstores, and roamed the alleys behind the mansions of the well-to-do. His collection grew: some Indian beads, and an African necklace; a moth with an eight inch wingspan, a turtle shell of splendiferous colors, the skull of what had likely been a cow, an ivory tusk, a miscellany of odd, outlandish amulets for a "talisman" collection; a nail, said to be from Noah's Ark (oh, the credulity of a 14 year old!); a hand mirror rimmed with portraits of its owner from birth to seventeen (the last two frames empty), a mandrake root in the shape of a man; a music-box that played the Ode to Joy; a small Chinese vase painted with graceful characters and mysterious mountains.

Still, he was not prepared to open to a cash-paying public — until he found the most staggering item of all: a fossil cockroach from the upper carboniferous rocks of the Sosnowiec coalfields in southern Poland. Three hundred and fifty million years old, he was told, and not by the person who sold him the Ark nail, but by a professor at the *Technische Hochschule*. Three hundred and fifty million years. That was old! He could feel its age weigh heavily in his hand. He could sense the three inch insect ready to crawl, even without the last segments of its abdomen. Amadeus had invested three years and 300 odd crowns, and now, with the coming of the roach, he was ready to begin. In 1910 he hung out his shingle: *"Wunderkammer Hoffnungs, 1. Mark Eintritt"*.

June 28, 1914 was an important day. A Bosnian Serb, Gavrilo Princip, put a bullet in the heart of the Archduke Ferdinand in Sarajevo, and in the very same hour, 400 miles to the North, the Magyar leviathan, Anton Tomzak, walked into the Wunderkammer Hoffnungs in Vienna. Or rather, waddled in: Tomzak weighed 614 pounds without his shoes.

He had an interesting proposition. What would Herr Hoffnung think about his exhibiting *himself* as part of the *Wunderkammer*? He proposed to construct, at his own expense, a curtained off area in the space adjoining the main exhibition room and at specific hours to be available for display. He would begin working for nothing more than meals on the days he was present (oh, but what meals!), and if, after three probationary months, Herr Hoffnung's attendance were up, especially on the two days a week Tomzak exhibited, they would then arrive at some fair remuneration and a plan to further publicize his appearances.

A living soul in his Cabinet of Wonders? At 21, Amadeus was grizzled and wrinkling. What had seemed mere shortness and hairlessness was playing out more and more clearly as Werner's Syndrome, a rare disease of premature aging and hypogonadal function. Should he, a probable freak among men, become a proprietor of freaks? Even as a child, recursive irony had always been his favorite trope. Anton Tomzak's appearance now held a mirror up to his life, like the one in his collection, rimmed by his own successive portraits. A freak show. A wondrous freak show. Why not?

And especially since, after advertising for the first few weeks, Amadeus found Tuesdays and Thursdays packed for Tomzak's afternoon and evening shows. Each of his many pounds cried out performer. He joked and jibed, he performed bizarre strip teases with tear-away garments specially constructed by his sister. Audience members were invited to estimate his waist and thighs, and then to measure. Strong looking men were challenged to arm wrestle. Trios were summoned on stage to try to lift him. But where to grab? Small children came again and again and brought their parents to see them riding, fifteen at a time, on his head and shoulders, strung out along his arms, clinging to the clothes on his back and front, or with toeholds in his belt.

An article appeared in the *Neue Freie Presse,* featuring Tomzak, of course, but describing in great and loving detail the other artifacts and oddities of Amadeus' collection. And the crowds grew so large that groups had to be scheduled at half-hour intervals, as in the busiest of restaurants.

After a year of war, many Austro-Hungarians, especially the Viennese poor, were wandering the streets. During the last decades of the monarchy, the standing joke was that the situation was "desperate, but not serious." But now that big brother Germany had entered a war to "support" Austria-Hungary, the internal struggle among Germans, Austrians and Hungarians escalated, and many innocent people lost jobs to those of other nationalities or cultures. In spite of the requirements of a war economy, unemployment soared, and confusion reigned as a century of placid national existence fell to pieces, or was forcibly dismantled. Karl Kraus thought Vienna "a proving ground for world destruction," and the "differently abled", once supported by their families, or the social system, were crucified first. As houses and theaters were destroyed by acts of war, the streets and parks became homes for the unfortunate, and people not usually seen in public became the object of stares and whispers.

Eight months after Tomzak's appearance, Clarissa Leinsdorf and her daughter Inge showed up at the museum. The mother was 38 years old and stood 18" tall. Her daughter was seventeen, the spitting image of her mother, but two inches shorter. Who might have impregnated Clarissa, and how, was beyond imagining, yet there they were, standing in the rain, asking, in grating twitters, to be let in. Ten days later, Violetta the half-girl arrived, pushed in a wheelchair by her father. She had no arms or legs.

And so, within the course of a few weeks, the entire ambiance of *Wunderkammer Hoffnungs* became radically changed, and, with the closing of music halls and theaters, the crowds increased so much that Amadeus had to rethink his entire operation. It was still a Cabinet of Wonders, but of wonders that would burst the seams of any cabinet.

In short order, Amadeus became manager to Katerina Eckhardt, a beautiful Swabian woman whose wide skirt covered a second body protruding from her abdomen. Her attractiveness was not so compromised as to prevent her from giving birth over the next decade to four girls and a son, the last from her secondary body. Such are the confusions of war and inflation. After Katerina, there was the armless Milena Silovec, who could type 50 words a minute with her toes. Beside being on display, she became secretary to the burgeoning Hoffnung operation. On February 9th, 1915, a large cloth bag was found at the museum door with a note: "Plese give home to my poor babie." In the bag a jar, and in the jar, a 30 pound — fetus? — pickled in brine. No eyes, no nostrils, huge ears, and a tail. And who found this gift while knocking at the door? Yet another applicant, one George Keiffer, 8' 6", rejected by the Austrian army because of his size and dismissed from a French prison camp because he was too big to feed.

He could pick up an entire horse or canon — and he did — to the great delight of the ever expanding crowds at Hoffnung's.

And so the *Wunderkammer* became a circus, the *Zirkus Schwänze Hoffnungs*, a assembly of walk-through wagons, each featuring human anomalies, pathetic, astonishing, and willing. Leo Kongee, the "Man with No Nerves" rammed hatpins through his tongue, and pounded spikes into his nose. Godina and Apexia, the "Pinhead Sisters", joked with horrified viewers about the angels dancing inside their skulls. Gerda Schloss, "the Homliest Woman in the World", flirted with men and teased their female companions about their sexual competence. Herr Rauchenruck could inhale from a cigarette, and puff the smoke out a hole in his back, commenting all the while on the day's news and the course of the war. Then there was Josef/Josefina: Man or Woman, Who Is To Say?, and Serpentina: The Girl With No Bones. *Glotzäugiger* Otto could pop both his eyes right out of his face. And *Steinkopf* Bill charged 10 groschen for souvenir rocks broken on his head.

But December 17, 1915 brought Amadeus more to celebrate than just Beethoven's 145th birthday. In the semi-darkness of the four o'clock hour a quartet of humans pulled its wagon into the cluster of wagons now inhabiting a huge empty lot in Vienna's Meidling district. The trailer marked "*Buro*" was lit by lantern light, and this was the scene Gregor recalled and reported:.

Anna Marie knocked resolutely.

"Ja. Come in."

"Herr Hoffnung?"

"Ja. Und?"

"Do you have a moment?" Four of them peeked through the door. "We'd like to show you something."

"I don't need it. I don't need any more. I have enough problems. *Basta. Genug.* But come in already nevertheless, and close the door. It's cold out there."

"What is that awful noise?" asked one of the men from well behind.

"Herr Klofac!" scolded Anna Marie, their doughty leader.

"That, my impolitic, but honest friend, is what a deaf man hears inside his fortress skull." Amadeus removed the needle from side four of the *Grosse Fuge*.

"I'm sorry. You don't have to take it off."

"It's my little birthday celebration. I play it every year."

"Happy Birthday!"

"To Beethoven. Did you sing Happy Birthday to him?" Amadeus switched off the Victrola, his master's voice.

"No. We drove all the way from Prague..."

"Without singing Happy Birthday to Beethoven?"

"We didn't..."

"Did you sing Happy Birthday to him yesterday?"

"I thought today was..."

"Today and yesterday. He has two birthdays."

"He was born twice?"

"Extraordinary people do extraordinary things. That's what *Zirkus Schwänze Hoffnungs* is all about. What have you got to show me?"

"I thought you said you had enough."

"I like you. I'll make an exception. I like honest, boorish people."

"The men will bring in the — thing."

And Kramar, Klofac, and Soukup clomped out the door, down three wooden steps into the darkness.

"How old are you, madame?"

"Sixty three."

"Good. What's your name?"

"Anna Marie Schleßweg."

"And how old am I?"

"I don't know. Fifty?"

"I'm twenty-two."

"I don't believe you."

"Fifty is a good guess. More than half way. Werner's Syndrome people live to forty, plus or minus."

"I'm sorry."

"Why be sorry? I'll take you on a tour of my collection. Then you can *really* be sorry."

Crashing and grumping, the three ex-roomers ground the crate against the door frame.

"Easy does it, boys. I just finished paying off this trailer."

"Sorry, Herr Hoffnung. Soukup, tip this way a little. Klofac, lift. OK, now up...easy. Where shall we put it down?"

"Here, I'll move these chairs."

"Watch your fingers, Kramer."

"There it is."

"It looks like a crate to me."

"A crate with air holes. Soukup, open it."

"Not me. You open it."

Amadeus stepped in.

"I'll open it. I'm used to surprises."

But not like this one. He was stunned. 350 million years swirled up at him from the bottom of the crate. His roach. His Sosnowiec roach come to call. The Great, secret Joy of his recent, and long-departed youth. *O alter Duft aus Märchenzeit!* I feel a wind from other planets. He had to grip hard on the edge of the crate.

"He don't smell too good."

"What is he?"

"I dunno. Some kinda big roach, I think."

"Is he alive?"

"He was, last we looked. Hey, Gregor, Gregor, wake up. Say something."

"He talks?" Amadeus had regained his composure.

"Good and proper. I think he wasn't always a roach. "

"He just became a roach."

"He was a man. Young. Early twenties," Anna Marie announced.. "A salesman. He lived with his parents in the Zeltnergasse."

"And with us."

"In Prague."

"How did he —"

"He just...one day —"

"We moved in after it happened."

"Is this some kind of joke?"

"Here, lift him out. Kramer, grab his butt. Soukup, reach in and get him under his chest."

"Thorax, my friend," Amadeus corrected.

"Thorax. In the middle. Here, I'll help."

"It's ok. Just leave him in there."

"No, no, you have to see for yourself. He'll respond. He's just shy."

Four pairs of hands reached down into the crate.

"Careful of his antennae. They break." Anna Marie, ever solicitous.

"Up...up...swing him over this way. Now down. Can we put him on the couch?"

In a brown flash, Gregor jumped off the blanket and scrambled instinctively under the couch.

"He likes to be under couches," said Anna Marie. "He was always under the couch when I came in to clean his room. I took care of him before he decided to leave. He always hid under the couch."

"Thigmotaxis, my dear," Herr Professor Hoffnung explained. "Roaches are thigmotactic. From the Greek, *thigma*, touch and *taxis*, a reflex movement toward one thing or another. Roaches love to be touched all around."

"That's disgusting."

"Disgusting, but true."

It was ten o'clock before plans were completed and negotiations settled. As Kafka so trenchantly describes, Gregor, in his depression, had lost a lot of weight. And even an exoskeleton can appear strikingly dehydrated. With the accumulated dust, hair and bits of old food stuck to his back and sides, he was a shocking sight indeed. But his mad escape, his freeing his family from their burden, his larval sense of adventure had all lifted his spirits — and when he heard the talk of exhibiting him as "The Hunger Insect", he whispered hoarsely from under the couch.

"No."

Five *homo sapiens* at the table whirled around to the couch.

"He talks."

"What did you expect? He was a traveling salesman. They have to talk."

"What's his name?"

"Gregor. Gregor Samsa," Anna Marie assured Herr Hoffnung.

"Is that your name?" he asked. "I said, is that your name?"

Silence.

"He stopped talking."

"Maybe his name has changed."

"I don't want to be 'The Hunger Insect'," Gregor croaked. "I want to eat. Whenever I want to. And I want to think. I want to read and think."

"He always had a lot of books in his room," Anna Marie confided to Herr Hoffnung.

"People won't pay to see a cockroach read and think." Soukup, the Cynic.

"What if I tell them what I'm thinking?" Gregor asked.

"It might not be interesting."

"I don't think people will care what a cockroach thinks."

"Gentlemen! And Madame! Quiet. Our friend Gregor may be old hat to you, but I assure you that whatever he does — if he just sits there and stares — he will be a sensation."

"If he doesn't do something, they'll think he's stuffed."

"I'll move around. I'll get books off the shelf."

"Now he wants a shelf."

"How many books do you want?"

"What kind of books?"

Klofac, promoting the sale: "The shelf will come out of your salary."

Gregor's first book, chosen right from Amadeus Ernst Hoffnung's glass-enclosed book case, was Johann Gotthelf Fischer von Waldheim's *Zoognosia: tabulis synopticis illustrata, in usum praelectionum Academiae Imperialis Medico-Chiurgicae Mosquensis,* an immense leather-bound volume, with tables and illustrations of every known species of animal. He wanted to make sure he had something unique to offer.

3. Small Riot On The Western Front

It is curious what small effect world-shaking events can have on a large cockroach, well-housed and -fed in an Austrian circus. On battlefields, poison gas wafted to unsuspecting lungs. In the seas, torpedoes swam toward unsuspecting hulls. Machine-gun bursts riddled the trenches, and those inside them. And on the home front — starvation. Anna Akhmatova wrote

In the west, the fading light still glows
and the clustered housetops glitter in the sun,
but here Death is already chalking the doors with crosses,
and calling the ravens, and the ravens are flying in.[1]

G's problem was different, less world-shaking: it is hard for a cockroach to read. Yet such was his major objective: to try to understand himself and his transformation, and the huge changes going on in the world. It would be almost five years before the first radio station sent its signal springing into space from Pittsburgh in 1920. Until that time, G had only hearsay, conversation — and books. But how to read them?

Amadeus Ernst Hoffnung was nothing short of munificent in this regard, as he was in all things touching G. His father, too, that good man, Karl Maria, was fascinated with the circus' new attraction. It was a stroke of

1 Of the many gifts Gregor gave me, the revelation of Anna Akhmatova's poetry was one of the greatest. Unlike him, I could not read Russian, and she was largely unknown in the west.

fate that his engineering firm had recently made use of the services of Karl Zeiss and Co., in Jena.

In 1846 Zeiss had opened a shop to produce microscopes and other optical instruments. There, with the help of physicist-mathematician Ernst Abbe, who developed the optical theory, and the chemist Otto Schott, who invented a hundred new kinds of optical and heat-resistant glass, Zeiss was able to build an operation still, to this day, the leader in its field. While industry in most of western Europe was driven by the ideas of isolated individuals, in Germany a carefully planned effort was made to exploit the advances of science. By 1900, Zeiss and Co. had established laboratories employing hundreds of people.

One of them, fortunately, was Max Lindhauer, a lens-maker and amateur astronomer who, even through the hardships of the war, was able to continue working — at least to a degree — on his fanatical project, the "Zeiss Projector" for a planetarium which debuted in 1923 at the Deutsches Museum in Munich. What a breakthrough in design!

But I digress. Occupational hazard of aging historians of science. The point is that Max Lindhauer, working with his client, Karl Maria Hoffnung, was able to design a pair of glasses to solve G's problem. I say "a pair", but the device actually encompassed two sets of three small lenses for each huge eye, each of the lenses re-focusing the light of one cockroach corneal lens through a crystalline cone, to more accurately focus on one rhabdom, the minute rodlike structure in the retinulae of the arthropod compound eye. Out of 4,000 ommatidia, Lindhauer chose six, and instead of perceiving a soft mosaic. G was able to sharply scan a line of type with a slight curving movement of his head. Many lines of type. As locusts devour vegetation, G devoured books. I don't mean he ate them, excuse me, I mean he read many books. He didn't eat any of them — though he could have. Book paste is a cockroach gourmet delight.

You might think G's lenses would have to be exactly adjusted, and just the right ommatidia located in the maze. But that was the beauty of Lindauer's scheme. Because the ommatidia in each section of the large compound eye are so alike in diameter, and have such similar focal lengths, there is actually a wide latitude of application: plus or minus four on either side. When the masking which held the actual lenses was snapped medially to the ring at the base of each antenna, just a slight tap would adjust lens and ommatidium into perfect alignment. What excellent use of the discarded projector lenses for sixth magnitude stars!

Still, it is hard for a cockroach to read. The first four months were a period of adjustment, G plagued with headaches and neck pains, trying to determine the least fatiguing position and the most efficient means of page turning. Amadeus, of course, was a great help, bringing him books and journals, seeing to his material needs, and engaging him in relaxing, stimulating conversation.

What didn't they talk about! Mice and men and history and destiny. Funny people in the audience. Amadeus' rogue tomcat peeing in G's cage. Oh, cage.... Yes, cage! G was put in a cage. Or rather, he and Amadeus thought a cage might be best during visiting hours, to reduce spectator fear, and keep little children from snapping G's antennae. What was Gregor's "act"? It evolved over time. Originally billed as A Visitor From The Early Carboniferous (perhaps *"Vomfruhesteinkohlzeitbesucher"* seems less awkward in German), he gave short talks about the steaming interior marshes of the then single landmass of North America, South America, Africa, Australia, Asia, Eurasia, and Antarctica. But this soon seemed canned and phony, and Amadeus wondered if some in the audience might think he was some kind of lifelike automaton. So G went on to giving advice. The Advisor From The Early Carboniferous. People would ask questions about business or personal problems, or what books to read or (while the cinemas were still open) what films to see. Once a child asked, "Are there really Angels, and do they bring the Christmas presents, or do parents bring them?" What did he answer? He couldn't recall. But finally, who could take seriously advice from a cockroach, wise though it may have been? Perhaps children might.

On May 13, 1917, three illiterate children reported seeing the Virgin Mary outside the tiny Portuguese village of Fatima. The Virgin told them who she was, and that she would like a chapel built for her on the site of her appearance. As if this weren't enough, a few months afterward one of the children gave more details: what the Virgin had actually said was "I shall come to ask for the consecration of Russia to my Immaculate Heart.

If my requests are heard, Russia will be converted, and there will be peace. If not, she will spread her errors through the entire world, provoking wars and the persecution of the Church. But in the end, my Immaculate Heart will triumph."

Though Lucia dos Santos' recent political sophistication sounded suspicious to some, it didn't take much for this story to color public perception of the Petrograd events of October. In February the imperial government had been overthrown, and the Bolsheviks came to power. The Russian economy was hopelessly disrupted, and food riots broke out in the capital. Austrians, also hungry, began massive strikes, demanding bread and peace, and openly opposing the government. In January and February, 1918, the government succeeded in suppressing the antiwar demonstrations, though the national opposition movement gathered momentum.

All this time, G was inventing and re-inventing his act, trying to discover a formula which would be both satisfying to an audience and stimulating to him. He went from advice to political commentary, and when that became too divisive and cynical, to reviewing books.

German language publishers had been hard hit by the war. Paper was rationed at 3/5 of prewar consumption, while at the same time hundreds of thousands of soldiers wanted light, distracting reading. So although the cost of paper rose to eight times prewar level, sales of inexpensive books increased. The principal publishers were able to stay in business by publishing literary schlock on appalling paper with fall-apart bindings. Gregor's self-assignment was to keep the light of literature alive, to publicize the hard-to-obtain work by the great authors of the extraordinary decades around the turn of the century.

From his own bookshelves, and those of his father, Amadeus kept G supplied with a stream of brilliance: Hugo Hoffmansthal, Artur Schnitzler, Karl Kraus, Robert Musil, Hermann Broch, Thomas Mann, Hermann Hesse, Franz Wedekind. G was especially pleased with gifts from his beloved Prague: Franz Kafka, Werfel, Brod, Meyerinck, and his favorite — Ranier Maria Rilke. For several months, he did nothing but recite the latest to appear of the *Duino Elegies*. Under the New Mexican sky, I was privileged to witness a report and approximation of his performance of the famous Eighth Elegy:

With all its eyes the creature-world beholds the open.[2]

And he would take off his glasses, and show the audience his many eyes. Invariable oohs and ahs. Once a child cried.

> *But our eyes, that is, your eyes,* he would say,
> *as though reversed,*
> *encircle it on every side, like traps*
> *set round its unobstructed path to freedom.*

"The open," he would prompt, "your eyes *obscure* the open. Can you understand that with only two?" And here he would display his face, so often hidden, display it, sans lenses and masking, display it so slowly, that some tried to see themselves in the mosaic's rainbow reflections, while some wondered if there were not cameras behind, filming.

> *for while a child is quite small we take it*
> *and turn it round and force it to look backwards*
> *at conformation, not that openness*
> *so deep within an animal's face. Free from death.*

"Can you imagine? In the midst of this war? Free from death?"

And here he would drop to all sixes from the lectern which held up book and self, and begin to pace slowly, reciting from memory, and commenting impromptu. In this position he became more frightening to the crowd, and though those in the rear strained on tip-toe to see, there was always a general movement away from the cage, and toward the back wall.

> *You never have, no, not for a single day,*
> *pure space before you, such as that which flowers*
> *endlessly open into –*
> and then, he would stop and spin to the front:
> *always world, and never nowhere without no –*

a strange triple negative, algebraically positive, but dizzying to the beholder —

---

2 He performed it, of course, in German. For non-German speakers, I substitute an insightful version by J. B. Leishman and Stephen Spender

In his first readings, he would move up to the bars and reach out toward the nearest child, placed in front to be able to see:

A child sometimes gets quietly lost there, to be always
jogged back again.

The first two times — extraordinary — both children reciprocated and put their hands on him, once on his left claw, once on his right tarsus. And each was snatched back by a fearful parent, afraid of what such openness might attract. A third time, the child, a lovely, dark little girl, shied and cried, hand into mouth; her father grabbed her up and pushed his way out of the crowded room. G thought his reaching out was perhaps not worth the gamble.

Our own being — he pointed to himself, implying all the animals —
is infinite, inapprehensible,
unintrospective, pure, like its outward gaze.

Did he really believe this? At the moment, or yet to come?

Where you see Future, we see Everything,
ourselves in Everything, forever healed.

By the fourth time he said these words, he understood his calling, his mission, his goal.

And yet, within the wakefully-warm animal

(He, of course, was only as warm as the ambient temperature.)

within the wakefully-warm animal
there lies the weight and care of a great sadness.

G had great difficulty holding back tears, and many times, his view was blurred, turning his gaze further inward. It was not only parents of war-murdered children whose eyes were wet.
Here all is distance,
there it was breath.
The long pause accentuated the breathing in the room. Always a few wept, quietly.

But you, spectators always, everywhere,
looking at, never out of, everything!
A step toward the lectern.
It fills you. You arrange it.

Another step.

It decays. You re-arrange it, and decay yourselves.

A slow cross to the lectern, and a methodical climb back to upright position.

Who has turned you around like this, so that you always,
do what you will, retain the attitude
of someone departing?

Silence.

…you live your lives, forever taking leave.
Stunned silence.

Then Gregor would close the folder of poems…
"Thank you."
…drop to the ground, and walk slowly off to the curtained part of the cage, off-stage.

It was a phenomenal performance. Though his voice was creaky, his presence, the full fact of his Otherness created ten minutes of high uncanniness. High but deep, soul-shiveringly deep. Which might explain the lack of public response. Amadeus waited in vain for a jump in attendance, but the public leveled off, even fell slightly, and the critics, if any had attended, were silent. Godina and Apexia, the "Pinhead Sisters", came to every performance they could, timing breaks from their own, and clapping politely and too-long at the end. The Dog-Faced Boy, and the Alligator-Skinned Man, and Jana, The Monkey-Girl all came and wept. G saw them there repeatedly. They never spoke to him about it. In confounded perplexity, Amadeus asked Gregor to change the act, to find something new.

Well, he thought, if people won't respond to the deepest voices of their own artists, what about the exotic? What about a "Voices of the Enemy" series, readings and interpretations of the American "barbarians"? That would be sensational — if he could get away with it. Would the censors silence a cockroach?

I hope my readers will not think it Princeton chauvinism if I say that President Wilson, to this point, had played a shrewd game. Elected on the slogan "He kept us out of war", by the beginning of 1917, America was opulent from "neutrality". Its balance of trade surplus, less than $700 million in 1913, had soared to $3 billion three years later. There were 8,000 new American millionaires, and massive exports to the Allies far outweighed any exports lost to the Central powers. Bankers rejoiced: the Allies were forced to rely on large American loans to finance their American goods. At home, boom conditions created a prosperous middle class ready to absorb an increasing supply of books. The number of publishing houses grew and American authors found a world market.

However, in 1918, the combined Hoffnung libraries held only two works of American literature, Ida M. Tarbell's *The History of the Standard Oil Company,* and Theodore Dreiser's *The Genius,* a sprawling semi-autobiographical chronicle censured by the New York Society for the Suppression of Vice. No one could understand how the latter ended up on Karl Maria Hoffnung's bedroom shelf. He read English poorly, and there were no illustrations.

G, however, gloried in these dusty volumes. He would learn English, the language of the enemy. He would translate them, and develop in his audiences a deeper understanding of the American people, the likely winners of the Great War. They were not really the enemy. No, they were mere tools of financiers, *nicht wahr?* By the end of 1916, the Allies owed the Americans $2 billion. America had to join the war to shore up its bank loans. If the Central Powers were to win, a vast American investment would... Surly they could understand. He would even teach his audience English — as he learned it. Teach them words, common expressions. Was this disloyal?

Amadeus put the kibosh on the notion. G could study English if he liked — Amadeus would even supply the grammars and dictionaries. But it was simply too risky to be perceived as aiding and abetting the American financiers, and now the soldiers destroying our land and slaughtering our sons.

****

These were agonizing times for Amadeus. As a child, he had loved all change, family trips, new dwellings, even changes of scenery at the Opera. But now change was the enemy. At the beginning of the war, officers' swords were still being sharpened by the regimental armorer, and soldiers were making grenades from empty tins of jam. And now, only four years later, they were advancing behind a shield of tanks, protected by air cover directed by radio from the ground. Change. And personal change: Amadeus' disease was advancing exponentially. Muscle weakness, joint pain, periods of incontinence, loss of memory. At 25, Amadeus Ernst Hoffnung, was medically in his late sixties. He would die at 31, like his beloved Schubert — but unlike Schubert, he would die an old, old man.

The source of Amadeus' greatest pain was his responsibility for the growing number of beings crouching in a circle of wagons, horses pawing and snorting, tied to each, huddling in an empty lot on the outskirts of Vienna. In the early years of the war, there had been some — a little — money for an audience to spend on entertainment and the kind of spiritual challenge a museum and freak show might evoke. But now, spare marks were needed for food and clothing, if not for oneself, then for family or friends. Those knocking at Amadeus' door for work were ever more bizarre and pathetic, and at the same time, he needed ever stronger displays to attract a weary audience, leery of parting with any money at all. These two movements — odder attractions and a need for odder attractions — enabled him to continue, but at great cost to his ethical being, his image of humanity.

There came the end of the war, on the eleventh hour of the eleventh day of the eleventh month, and with it, the dissolution of his country: a tiny Hungary, and a bereft and broken Austria. But the even the New World Order was far more orderly than the crew of *Zirkus Schwänze Hoffnungs* – for Amadeus had taken on some decidedly questionable "acts".

A "Giant Moleperson" was exhibiting himself between two glass walls in a kind of "ant colony" display. He would dig his way through the dirt, some-

33

times disappearing into the interior, but most often at least partially visible as he dug towards one of the array of small holes in the glass which were his only source of air. He was naked except for swim trunks which came to mid-thigh, and his body was scratched, his hands bleeding from the gravel he encountered within the finer sand and moister clay. He was fed once a day through a small door from the outside into his "pantry", a portal ostentatiously locked from the outside, that was opened for the 4PM feeding by a uniformed guard. He had no name; he never, at least to G's knowledge, came out. He was "real": what you saw was what was there. How he got there, only Amadeus knew, and he wasn't telling, even when asked.

G, of course, was "real" too. But he had a life. He did not do irrational things like dig in dirt. He read, he studied, he interacted, he had goals. When he wasn't on stage, in his cage, he was chez Hoffnung, talking, sipping wine, staying abreast of world events. At night, he would go for long walks in the suburban Austrian darkness. In a sense, he was "acting" when on display, and so was perhaps less "real" than The Giant Moleperson. But he was decidedly more real than some of the exhibits, tricks and participatory machinations Amadeus had been reduced to.

The circle of wagons grew larger. In, and among them, were the dregs of homo sapiens' storehouse, the most uncomfortable inhabitants of the human condition, a gruesome crew which Amadeus called "my apology for the world." How else could one understand such offerings as Fu Hsi, a man of obscurely oriental origins, evidently with some kind of neurophysiological disorder, who lay in a coffin, "undead", with no perceptible heartbeat, yet who discoursed, with staring eyes, in accented German, about his death while building the Great Wall 23 centuries earlier? Or Emil, the Hunger Artist Gregor refused to be, gripping the bars of his cage, staring dumbly with his great, sunken eyes, blind to the sign which was changed daily — 125th day, 126th day — the implied command to the dwindling crowd: Be Sure to be Present at This Man's Self-Inflicted Death.

Such exhibits invited their onlookers down slippery moral slopes. Children, no doubt with the urging, or at least permission, of their parents, would vie to tickle, hurt, torture the coffin man with their most ingenious childish means. If their parents could not hear heartbeats through the stethoscope, perhaps little Hans or Anneke, could expose him with a straw up a nostril, or a finger nail in an eye. Or perhaps the Hunger Artist would eat some horse dung, freshly picked, if it were smeared on his face, over his mouth. The adults, too, had their ways, less crude perhaps, but therefore more cruel. Grown men and women would volunteer to leave their beds and the warmth of their partners to stay up all night, watching at Emil's cage, so that no well-meaning guard or street person might offer him food that he, in the hiddenness of night, might eat.

Amadeus knew of these adult activities, and they weighed on his increasingly arrhythmic heart. But for him, they were no more blameworthy than the more hidden lust for death exhibited by "normal" circus audiences, come to see — maybe, if things went well, and they got more than they paid for — the dashing out of a falling aerialist's brains. Less blameworthy, if anything, because more honest. But blameworthy nonetheless.

There was Rotpeter, the orangutan, named for his colorful bottom, who had been trained to type, on command, a line from Nietzsche's Zarathustra: `"MAN IS A ROPE - TIED BETWEEN ANIMAL AND SUPERMAN - A ROPE OVER AN ABYSS; A DANGEROUS CROSSING, A DANGEROUS LOOKING-BACK, A DANGEROUS SHUDDERING AND STOPPING."` The typewriter was set on "caps lock" because for all the thousands of hours of his training, Rotpeter could not master holding down the shift for capitals.

The insanity behind such a project! The cost, the feeding, the frustration, the perseverance! Human ingenuity gone mad. The ape's trainer and keeper, Fritz Denkmann, was a quiet, short man with thick glasses and few social skills. In firmer times, he might have been a professor of linguistics or philology. Yet now, this was how he had to earn his living. Astounding.

In G's opinion, Amadeus' own shoes were muddy from the slippery slope. Why else would he choose to place a glass case of pythons right next to Emil's cage so that crowds might watch them eat while the other starved? Small animals breathing out their lives in herpetological embrace, eyes bulging, like Emil's. Doubtful. Most morally doubtful.

And was Amadeus above sheer theatrical smoke and mirrors, a Barnum of Vienna for the suckers made, if not born, each minute? What was going on with the Blumfeldlichten, two little balls of ghostly greenish light, six inches in diameter, who would dance with spectators, following their turns and traverses with accurate response? Amadeus' latest gramophone was engaged to play the "Tales from the Vienna Woods", poor by our standards of fidelity, but state-of-the-art at the time. And each night, after dusk, men, women, couples, groups, would step (for a price) onto the small wooden dance floor laid out in the midst of mud and straw, to see if they could discover the secret of the lights. The first minutes were invariably spent trying to figure them out through trickery, and unexpected maneuvers. But the lights responded as masterfully as Rogers to Astaire (though the clodhopping was hardly similar to his), and without exception, the dancers, once skeptical, ready to pry and expose, spent their last minutes in the sheer joy of movement with such uniquely winsome, graceful partners.

But how did Amadeus do it? Are we to believe that these two little lights approached him to propose an "act"? Were their circumstances so straitened by the war that they were reduced to displaying themselves to paying customers? The laser hadn't been invented; there were no holographs. Neither G, nor the inquiring press had been able to detect any projection equipment in line of sight from the balls' domain. Besides, they toured as did all the others, playing outdoors in a wide variety of circumstances and weather, and no workmen were ever seen setting up any extraordinary electrical equipment. Each night they were brought on by Amadeus himself in a lead-shielded wooden box (a hint there?). A simple pitch inviting dancers — the exposé aspect was left entirely implied — the needle was set on the *Wienerwald* platter, the top of the box opened, the lights jumped out, and the waltz began. In the space between ten minute showings, the lights returned to their box, Amadeus closed the lid, and they rested. Or whatever they did.

What was Amadeus up to? Never mind how he did it — that secret he took with him to his early grave. Was this some *technologische Spaß* — his prophetic joke about man and machine? What was going through the aging mind of this visionary dwarf with its accelerated view of history?

And what was he trying to draw out of his audience? Why the machine, the tattoo machine, the tattoo machine in the blood pressure cuff. which, for 10 groschen would prick the double headed eagle of the Austro-Hungarian Empire in your arm, along with your name, or any saying fifty letters or less, you might desire. For an extra 25 groschen, it could employ ink, so that their souvenir would consist not just of fleeting blood and quickly sloughed scabs, but of semi-permanent blue. "It's a remarkable piece of apparatus," Amadeus would dryly observe. When the war was over, he lost interest, and discontinued the exhibit.

I must remind the reader I am only relating the stories G told me. From such remarks, you might conclude that Amadeus was going mad, that the chaos of his crumbling biology, of Austria itself at war's end, coupled with the insanity of his personal space — his room full of squeaking and yowling and croaking and cheeping — was taking its toll. But when he would enter his room, he had only to strike the table with his fist and yell: "Quiet!" and the monkeys climbed quickly atop the four-poster bed, the guinea pigs scurried under the stove, the raven fluttered onto the circular mirror, and only the black cat, the soiler of G's cage, unperturbed by his master's entrance, would remain calmly as he was, and start to groom. Perhaps the cat was deaf. In this taut silence, alive to animal being, Amadeus would sit, and smoke, and think. Sometimes he would repair to his shop to work on a new display. When he re-entered the world of his humanoid colleagues and creatures, he was rational, affable, even charming. No madness apparent — only method.

But in the world of his humanoid colleagues, there was little method – it was more like madness.

4. The Decline Of The West And Other Issues

1919 was Spengler-year in German-speaking lands. Everyone was reading him, debating his message, wondering who this prophet was, with his furrowed brow, his dark, fierce eyes, his great domed head. Oswald Spengler, man of mystery, an unknown, retiring schoolmaster, with no friends in normal academic or literary circles. How his weighty tome had exploded into public consciousness!

And it wasn't only philosophers and historians reading *The Decline of the West*. Never before had a huge philosophical work been such a bestseller, invading serious academic seminars and drunken beerhall banter, concerned church groups and flippant cocktail parties, political meetings left and right. Within eight years of its publication, it had sold 100,000 copies — and this at a time when families were hurting for food and housing, and books were low priority.

One can understand its appeal to the Germans and Austrians, the "losers" of the late conflagration. They were prepared to listen and hear. All right, they said, we may have lost the war, but you, you so-called winners, you have also lost. As triumphant as you may appear right now, we are all going down together. Sour grapes, perhaps, sour grapes of wrath, but yielding a wine that was, for a while, intoxicating.

But it was not only the losers who snatched up the work. The "winners", with more ebullience, and more money to spend, and especially the Americans with their intact publishing houses and huge economic surpluses, were also enthusiastic readers. People, it seems, like to read bad news. More recently, we saw the same masochistic, voyeuristic curiosity making Paul Kennedy's *The Rise and Fall of the Great Powers* a worldwide bestseller. Though 500 pages are devoted to the history of various cultures, back as far as ancient China, browsers at Waldenbooks would salaciously seek out the "good parts" — the twenty pages at the end on contemporary America. How will it come out? What's coming up? — the same public motives that drive the *National Enquirer,* newspaper astrologers, and the publishers of the Prophecies of Nostradamus.

Upstaged professors screamed out in a chorus of academic scorn: Spengler is a charlatan! The speculation is shallow! The book is riddled with errors of fact! The analytical methods are incompetent and unsound! But still the public kept reading. Academics who for years avoided one another came together to publish a book denouncing Spengler and his crudities. Economists felt that "Spengler's understanding of economic events remains that of a helpless dilettante." And still the public kept talking.

And so it was not as outrageous as it sounds now, in these anti-intellectual times, for Gregor to try, as his first post-war act, his sequel to the *Duino Elegies* Performance Piece, a public seminar, facilitated by a survivor of the early Carboniferous, a seminar on Spengler's *Decline of the West*. It was also an act of high courage; like a triple somersault with two and a half turns on the high trapeze without a net — such a feat had never been performed. School was one thing: motivated, cream-of-the-croppy students anxious to please professors of authority, fired by controversy. In such surroundings, Spengler might catalyze both heat and light.

But in a circus wagon with a cage at one end? With an unruly crowd, free to leave at any time? With children whining, dogs barking, and competing acts that might also be worth seeing? It was a brilliant tour de force on G's part. True, he had been a good student in his former life, but had had to leave the university to help support his family. True, being a traveling salesman had honed his communications skills — but teaching experience? He had none.

Yet for the last half of 1919, and early into 1920, his ongoing Spengler seminars became the "in" thing to do in Vienna. Be there, or be square, as they say today. While some circus-goers simply stumbled upon them, there was also a constant stream of seasoned debaters from all circles involved in the discussion: here were the students and their professors, the beer-bellied philosophers, the concerned clergy and the chosen of their flocks, the *haute-monde* and the *demi-monde*, the communists, socialists and proto-fascists. It was quite a debate. And good for Amadeus' bottom line.

From this distance, it's hard to believe, I know. Unimaginable in our time and circumstances. First of all, what author could provoke such lively and universal debate? Danielle Steele? Second, how is one to get people out to public events anymore when they're all at home, glued to their sets — soon to be high-definition, as if low-definition weren't bad enough? And third of all, who would be guided — facilitated, as we say — by a cockroach? Deep ecologists, perhaps, but they are few and far between. No, these days, the blow-dryer is the *sine qua non*. If you don't look like Vanna White, or Peter Jennings, it's hard to command a crowd. Yet G did so.

Early on, he included an introductory section, going over the basics of Spengler's thesis for the mix of spectators, most of them familiar with it — at least through hearsay — but some, not at all. Quite soon, though, he realized an introduction was unnecessary, that all the themes would come up on their own, at all levels of sophistication, in the inevitable shouting match that would follow. Well, not always shouting. Sometimes there would be sustained intellectual debate. But more often shouting. It was a disturbing subject, and it aroused public passion.

I'm afraid that now, almost four score years later, I shall have to do some exposition for most of my readers, even if it delays somewhat the story of my friend. A fickle public, combined with runaway inflation, worldwide depression, the rise of Nazism and the ensuing second chapter of the Great War, soon enough sent Spengler back to the oblivion from whence he had come. His name is absent from the index of our current history books. Even Paul Kennedy, so much in his debt, ignores him. As a historian, I think this is scandalous, but it represents a common failing of academics — any imperfections in the trees make the forest invisible. Yet, details aside, I would submit that Spengler got the larger picture right. More than right. Prophetically right. The course of world history has clearly vindicated him. We have merely filled in details for the outline he so presciently sketched. What did he say?

He opens thus:

In this book is attempted for the first time the venture of forecasting history, of following the still untraveled stages in the destiny of a Culture, and specifically of the only Culture of our time and on our planet which is actually in the phase of fulfillment — the West-European American.

"Forecasting history". What a bold assertion! History had heretofore concerned itself with the past. There were no Departments of Future Studies. Vico's 18th century *ricorsi* had not yet been incorporated into Western thinking. Toynbee's Study was 15 years down the road. Spengler was out there all alone. In order to forecast history, he had to discover, inductively, a grand pattern, an "inward form of History", repeating through all recorded time, and in every major culture — and it was this:

For everything organic the notions of birth, death, youth, age, lifetime are fundamentals…

He saw all cultures he studied come into springlike being, youthful and vigorous, flower in their summery, unique ways, and then autumnally decay. Their winters were frozen into rigid, petrified forms, and these forms he called "civilization". Our Western culture had been born around the tenth century, flowered in the gothic and the Renaissance, became "civilized" in the eighteenth century, and in the nineteenth century, with the industrial revolution, had begun the process of spiritual decline. The upcoming death of Western Culture was as certain as that of any other living organism. History was Destiny, unfolded through the cycle of human cultures, all of which shared a common rhythm and pattern. We cannot choose our destiny, we cannot alter it. We have no choice but to make the best of our historical situation.

Stark. Dramatic. No wonder it attracted so much attention. In this wintertime essay, he drove his metaphor hard. When the freezing point of a culture is reached, like water, it expands and can shatter its container. Though spiritually exhausted, it gathers the technical and material capacity for outward reach, desperately grabbing at life. And so begins what he called an Age of Caesarism. He accurately predicted the coming of a totalitarian state, not by looking at the social movements around him, but by taking the longest possible view. He predicted a coming age of imperialist wars in which nations would complete their spiritual death, and finally fall to pieces, yes, like Rome, but also like every other culture, finally succumbing to the invasion of new forces, alien, hostile to the old, full of springlike, spontaneous creativity and religious devotion. In the inevitable final battle between civilized engineers and God-inspired barbarians, the engineers would go down clutching their pens and pencils. Artists would also succumb: this was not a time for soul. Art would be frustrated by society's rejection, or corrupted by its licentiousness and power — a spiritual vocation gone astray. The Zeitgeist is inevitable, a time of perverted men in a hopelessly perverted age. Politics would consist of liars calling liars liars.

Gregor would be sure to emphasize this radical notion of "civilization". For us, the apogee of achievement, the targeted ideal, the goal toward which we stick and carrot benighted races. But for Spengler, the prelude to death and decay, with imperialism the typical symbol of the end.

At the time, G could hardly appreciate the uncanniness of Spengler's predictions. Writing as early as 1911, he had spoken of the endless repetition of the "already-accepted", of standardized art, of petrified formulas which would ignore and deny history. "Events," Spengler predicted, would become "the private affairs of the oligarchs and their assassins," and would arise from administration, not society. Even before the evidence of the war, he foresaw professional armies operating with an entirely different morality than civilian society. In 1917, he noted, "In a few years, we have learned to virtually ignore things which before the war would have petrified the world." Had he not died in '36, he might have seen more than even he could imagine.

Spengler clearly imagined "Generation X" and the couch-potato "End of History", the age of TINA (There Is No Alternative):

With the arrival of the Age of Empire there are no more political problems. People get along with the situation as it is and with the powers that be. In the age of the Embattled States, streams of blood reddened the walls of world cities to transform the great truths of democracy into reality and achieve rights without which life did not seem worth living. Now these rights have been won, but not even punishment can move the grandchildren to make use of them.

Gregor was far ahead of me. Had I known then what I know now, I might have helped him distribute these words on the mesa. I still have a yellowed copy of his leaflet:

> *If values are unreal and if humane purposes chimerical, then even scientific technique must finally become subservient to brute force: the need for rational restraint and self-discipline of any kind disappears. Technicism leads directly to irrationality, and the cult of barbarian power salvages the technician's otherwise growing sense of frustration and futility. It is no accident Germany produces both the most mechanized type of personality in its robot-like soldiers and civilians, and the most unrestrained reaction against humane discipline, in the form of an exultant sub-animality. America beware.*

The text was too long to be placed over the main gate, but it was G's ironic version of *ARBEIT MACHT FREI*.

****

This, in general. But there was one particular notion of Spengler's that intersected deeply with G's quest — that of Faustian Man in a Faustian Culture. You'll forgive me for the non-inclusive language. It was Spengler's, and surely the language of the time. It was the term G used. Further, if one were to strive for strict accuracy, even "Faustian People" or "Faustian Humanity" would not cover G's participation. So let it be "Faustian Man", with appropriate apologies. By Spring of 1919, the term was well known to the German-speaking public, and the circus seminars could proceed without explanation. For us, now, it is not as obvious.

The contemporary person on the street, if asked to define the adjective "faustian", might, if he recognized it at all, refer to the "deal with the devil", the nature of Faust's bargain. But that was not Spengler's central thrust. Faustian culture, for him, was simply the latest of the three cultures which had inhabited and defined "the West".

The worldview of Classical culture, according to Spengler, (and his generalizations have caused him much grief), was centered in the statically present: its paradigmatic expression was plane geometry's eternal truths. Then, Magian culture, a term invented by Spengler, basically that of early Christianity, but (and this enraged the pigeonholers) also including Arabian and other Muslim cultures. Its primary image was the struggle between good and evil, light and darkness, God and the devil, creation and destruction. Its representative mathematics was the more dynamic algebra, variable qualities and quantities jostling each other in changing relation.

Our own Faustian culture, the latest condition of the West, is driven by tense striving toward aims and goals, each limited in themselves, but collectively pressing toward the infinite. Our history is an unfolding of that unchecked thrust. The whole course of Western mathematics can be seen as as "a long, secret, and finally victorious battle against the notion of magnitude", symbolized by the Faustian embrace of the infinitesimal calculus, the development of probability theory, and now, after Spengler's time, its universal application in quantum mechanics. Nothing less could satisfy the Faustian soul than deep, eternal simultaneous striving towards the infinitesimal and the infinite. Ever restless, ever longing for the unattainable. Endless vistas, limitless space. Faustian man, Faustian culture.

One could sense it early on in the upward thrust of the gothic cathedrals, their spires disappearing into the mist. One could follow it in the perspective studies of the Renaissance, the astounding capture of an infinite vanishing point on a two dimensional surface. Global exploration, abstract, "pure" music, machine after machine, driving, aspiring. The Reformation claiming the infinite capacity of individual souls.

Spengler develops his history with great lyric intensity. The Baroque striving for infinity, dissolving traditional forms into bewildering concatenations of curves and structural deceptions; painters like Caravaggio and Rembrandt pushing perspective and shadow to the farthest limits and metaphysical depths. The young movement for free inquiry and scientific speculation.

And then came autumn. The 18th century, according to Spengler, was the autumn of the Faustian soul, and there we find the last and most exquisite creations of its fully-realized forms. The infinity of Mozart, peering out in the finale of the G minor Symphony, out into interstellar

12-tone space. Kant, Goethe, the conclusive formulations of the deepest speculations of the age.

And finally winter, the "civilization" phase of the Faustian spirit. Our winter. Middle-class values reign, even among the ruling class. And thus the general formlessness, rejecting any standards of taste for a mindless, insouciant individualism, and a need for unrestricted freedom. Wide, meaningless fluctuations of style, and now the "post-modern" piling on of incongruous detail, no end of "experiments", life as life-style. Spengler predicted the inevitable end of masterpieces: the spiritual possibility of creating great paintings or music was simply exhausted.

Political forms, for Spengler, were similarly meaningless. The so-called democratic forms of parliaments and congresses were hollow masks obscuring the basic political reality — the triumph of money. Everything was structured to yield to the power of financial speculation: constitutionalism, democracy, even socialism. Politicians of all stripes had no choice but to become paid agents of financiers. How Spengler would laugh at the current posturing around campaign finance reform, the emptiness of our rhetoric helplessly reflecting the inevitability of late Faustian dynamics.

His predictions were grim, as end-talk tends to be. They have, in their broad forms, come to pass. Before his death, Gregor Samsa encountered the most intense of them; we, his survivors, have also experienced the most pervasive.

Spengler's scenario was one of national Caesars competing in an age of great, perpetual war. The pride of "blood and soil" would be harnessed by the state, and exploited by the rich, as devoted militaries struggled for mastery of the world. Eventually one Caesar would win out, and establish a universal imperium. But long before that, all political ideologies and parties would have lost any semblance of meaning. Life will have coalesced into the general uniformity of monoculture. Large cities will become the only places that matter, their populations obedient to any leader who keeps them fed and amused. Life will be a meaningless repetition of mechanical tasks and mechanical values, while R&R will consist of vulgar, brutal diversions, and credulous acceptance of escapist, supernatural phenomena. It is not hard to recognize the present in Spengler's formulations eighty plus years ago. As you might imagine, they were quite compelling when hot off the press.

45

The success of Gregor's seminars were a surprise even to him, and certainly to Amadeus, who thought he had a realistic view of the illiteracy which stalked the wasteland. After the *Duino Elegies* flopped, G was trying to imagine a new, more down to earth, act. He previewed a kind of entomological strip-tease to Ravel's Bolero — which one might think would be compelling — but was poorly received. "Bad taste", commented the *Neue Freie Presse*. (I have the clipping. I will spare you the review.) Though little children seemed fascinated, parents were horrified. It never made it to the main stage, and this was probably just as well, since G was less than enthusiastic about it. A claw-puppet version of Capek's *Insect Play* met a similar fate. Neither Amadeus nor the critics saw much point to G's hiding behind a curtain, operating fake insects.

The solution was unexpected. It was July 4th, 1919. America was busy celebrating its birth, and G, the new Spenglerian, was busy contemplating its death. As a contribution to his language study, Amadeus had given G a gift subscription to "Le New York", the new Paris edition of the Herald Tribune. With relish he devoured not only the words, but the energy behind them, the optimism of a nation of winners, the idealism of President Wilson and his Fourteen Points. A League of Nations! Imagine! He marveled at Jack Dempsy and the Cincinnati Reds, at the dance crazes and marathons: all this energy in the midst of a flu epidemic which would kill 400,000 Americans. (Austria's flu had also carried off many, but produced only despair.) Most of all, Gregor was awe-struck at the audacity of prohibition, a legal overthrow of the ancient God of the Vine. King Pentheus was dismembered for less — by his own mother.

G had been reading Spengler for the last several months when, on that Thursday, he experienced an epiphany:

This too, he thought, this, here, is also part of the physiognomic of world-happening. The pin-heads and the dog-faced boy, and the people who come to stare at them. Hoffnung's accelerated aging, the emergence, here, in the midst of his collections, of more and more inexplicable, indefensible displays. We need to study ourselves, here, now... And the idea of the Spengler seminar was born.

Amadeus was doubtful. But open. He would make his own Spengler available to the crowd, chained to a stand at the back of the wagon. G would use his to quote chapter and verse. The sign outside the wagon was repainted in garish letters: THE DECLINE OF THE WEST: ARE YOU READY?

All worry was unnecessary, all doubt misplaced. At the very first session half the adults were already reading it; several had finished the first volume. Their comments drew in the innocents — even the older children, and as the innocents were initiated, G found his expository work mostly done. He had simply to move the discussion on when it was stuck, call on those who had trouble breaking in, and continually focus on people's own, local experience. A population of war-weary survivors was not prone to intellectualize, and the stories and feelings flowed easily and with great intensity. At the end of the show, G hastened over to Amadeus' office to dictate his impressions. Until he bought his first typewriter, in America three years later, he would need such help, as his claws lacked the fine motor skills of a writing human hand.

By his third "performance", word had spread even to the academic community, and the temperature rose accordingly. The historians came to defend their history, the economists, their economic theories. Normal classroom decor was decidedly absent in this small, cloth-covered wagon with its two lecterns and a cage full of straw at one end. Though people were crammed shoulder to shoulder, and all could hear perfectly from any corner of the room, there was commotion and shouting, and louder shouting trying to overcome it. Gregor could command silence only by expelling air forcefully through all his spiracles, emitting a spine-tingling hiss. Because of his clothing, it was not apparent where the noise was coming from, but the crowd quieted nonetheless. Over the months, the discussions deepened, as basic concepts became well-known, and seminar aficionados continued their regular attendance.

5. Metamorphosis II:
Möglichkeits Roach: an Insect With Qualities

At the close of a Friday evening seminar in November, still 1919, Gregor answered the door behind the curtained, off-stage area of his cage. He knew it was Amadeus from his signature knock, the first five notes of *Death and the Maiden*. But standing with the *Zirkusmeister* was a small, wiry man with a high, radiant forehead, and razor-sharp nose, a cigarette between his lips.

"May we come in?" Gregor heard. A deceptively polite beginning.

"Certainly. Uh...would you mind putting out the cigarette? All this straw... and the spiracles...."

He indicated his axillary line. The man descended the four wagon steps, muttering, stubbed out his smoke, and returned.

"Gregor, this is Robert Musil, the..."

"THE Robert Musil of *Young Törless??*"

"Yes. This came out what, a dozen years ago?"

"It was one of my crucial books."

"Thank you. It's rare that one's work is appreciated."

"Are you working on another novel?"

"Yes. I am working on something — something dreadful. But it keeps me restfully rich in dreadfulness."

"Doctor Musil was at your seminar tonight."

"I can't see into the crowd. Did you say anything?"

"Don't call me Doctor, Herr Hoffnung, please. One of my many pet peeves: respected professors and denigrated writers. Professors have achieved their highest public standing since the world began, and writers are now being called "men of letters," which, I suppose, means people prevented by some obscure infirmity from becoming competent journalists."

Amadeus objected, "What about Thomas Mann, Herr Musil, the great Thomas Mann?"

"Oh, Mann. Mann is too tolerant a human being, too much in tune with his times to ever achieve true unpopularity. He likes the world as it is too much, and is loved by the world in return. Whereas I like hardly anything. Mann writes for people who are here; I write for people who are not. At least not yet. I'm autistic, negative and fanatical. That's what they say. I have no warmth, except occasionally for Marthe, my wife. Contrariness is my metier, and repugnance toward life. I'm a man out of my time, Herr Hoffnung. But I like you, Herr Samsa. I like what you're up to. You are also a...being...out of your time."

A loud knock at the door of Gregor's wagon. Amadeus reached over to open.

"Ah, there you are, Herr Hoffnung. They told me you were here."

Anna Marie Schleßweg stood on the wide top stair, her white hair blowing in the wintery night.

"We're busy now. Can I see you later?"

"Herr Hoffnung, you haven't paid us our fee for the last two times. My son comes tonight. I need to buy food..."

"Let's talk about it later."

"I need it now. For tonight. I know times are hard, you told me, but they're hard for me, too..."

"How much do you need for tonight, my good woman?" the writer asked.

"Herr Musil, no..."

"How much?"

"Ten marks would do."

"Here."

"Thank you, kind sir."

"Just close the door. It's cold."

49

"That woman saved my life," Gregor explained. "She saved the lives of my family. She and her friends brought me here..."

"Kidnapped you..." said Amadeus

"At my request..."

"For their profit..."

"And my own. And everyone else's — including yours..."

"Gentlemen, please," Musil appealed.

Amadeus changed the subject.

"Herr Musil and I came to invite you for dinner chez moi, and a post-seminar seminar."

"My favorite," said the roach, and out they went.

The wind had stilled, and Orion was blazing low in the November sky.

"There's no corner of the heavens without its wonder," Musil began, "but the darkness in Pegasus and the brightness in Orion are its poles. Black emptiness in summer, light in winter, yin in yang and yang in yin."

"Of all the constellations," Amadeus observed, "Orion has the most clearly human, even conscious, presence. It's as if Nature acknowledges our shape and gestures, enthroning them in the sky."

"While astrophysically, the Great Hunter is a set of randomly associated events accidentally available to the particular plane of our solar system in the galaxy." Musil, the Devil's advocate. "Only we can see it; only we create the glyph. Does knowing such facts destroy your pleasure, Herr Hoffnung?"

"Actually, yes. I usually keep them in a separate compartment."

"Why not fuse them: exactitude and soul? Then what?"

"Then..."

"Then," Gregor jumped in, "we can understand the phenomenon of apparent rationality."

"As in society?", asked Amadeus.

"As in human consciousness," Musil suggested.

The three crossed the freezing mud to the other end of the lot, and climbed the steps to Amadeus' office wagon. It was the largest of the motley collection, almost a box-car on huge wooden wheels. The door creaked open, and the black tomcat ran among the legs of the guests, out into the night. Musil stubbed out his cigarette and followed the others into a well-lit room. The monkeys stopped grooming, and scampered to the top of the large bookshelf, while the raven walked with determination behind Amadeus' great reading chair. *"Ewig, ewig,"* he croaked from his offstage venue. Evermore.

"Have a seat, gentlemen, and give me a few minutes to prepare a humble board." Amadeus went to the woodstove at the far end of the wagon, poured water from pitcher to pot, and set it to boil. From the ice chest, he pulled a string of blood sausage, placed them in the water, and began to sharpen a knife for the cutting of bread.

Musil and G settled into the remaining armchairs, whose substantial cushions had supported much previous talk. And here began for Gregor a most fateful conversation:

"I've been to three of your Spengler seminars."

"You never said anything?"

"The primary job of the writer is to observe."

"And what did you observe?"

"A crowd of suckers, bamboozled, as usual, by fame."

"Spengler's?"

"And yours. Genius on genius. They'll do anything you want."

"I — a genius? I don't say anything. I just ask questions, get them to talk."

"You're not out there when they pour down the steps. I stand and listen, and take down their comments. 'Genius'. I haven't done a word analysis, but I can assure you 'genius' is the winner."

"But I..."

"You don't have to do anything. If race horses can be geniuses without even talking, so can you. 'Genius, genius.' Nothing but genius in the world. Just leaf through the newspapers — you'll be truly amazed at how many profoundly moving, prophetic, greatest, deepest, and very great masters appear over the course of a few months, how often the best novel of the last ten years is written. A few weeks later hardly anyone can remember them."

"You're saying Spengler is just a fad?"

"He certainly is a fashion," Amadeus called over from the kitchen. "And I worry how long your act will be able to hold. Did you ever re-encounter a play or a novel which just a while ago grabbed on to your soul, and the souls of many others, but now the sparkle is gone, the importance has disappeared, and dust and moths fly off at your touch?"

"This won't be true with Spengler," Gregor asserted. "His thrust is right into the immediate future, and out to the long range."

"Spengler is a fashion," Musil averred, "a current, war-weary fashion. And fashions are marked by two characteristics: one, that in retrospect, they seem ridiculous, and two, that as long as they last, you can hardly imagine taking seriously anyone who is not as engulfed as you are."

Amadeus brought plates of sliced bread, steaming Würste, and brown mustard, and three steins of beer.

Musil continued while his sausage cooled. "Reflect on the much ridiculed absurdities of fashion, which one year make us fat, then skinny the next, sometimes wide on top and narrow on the bottom, sometimes narrow on top and wide down below, which now prescribe that everything be combed upwards, and then that everything be combed downwards. If we consider it all from a wholly unsympathetic standpoint, my favorite one, fashion in clothing offers us an astoundingly limited number of geometric possibilities, among which we alternate in the most passionate way. If we likewise include fashions of thought, feeling and action, about which practically the same can be said, then our entire history must appear as nothing but a corral within whose confines the human hoard stampedes senselessly back and forth. And how willingly we follow "leaders" like Spengler, who themselves merely charge ahead of us out of terror. And what joy grins back at us in the mirror when we connect with the fashionable norm, looking, talking, thinking exactly like everyone else, even though everyone looks, talks and thinks differently than they did yesterday! Why do we need all this?! Perhaps we fear, and rightfully so, that our character would scatter like a powder if we did not pack it into a publicly approved container."

G had taken advantage of this extended tirade to devour his meal. In general, he did not like eating in front of others. It was one thing with Amadeus; Gregor's food behavior had ceased to elicit staring. But Robert Musil was a stranger, and worse, a famous writer known for his merciless eye. Nevertheless, it had been a long day, and this was G's first meal since noon.

"I find Spengler quite original", Gregor replied, his buccal cavity still full of bread and sausage. "I've never before..."

For anyone else, it might have been unnerving to be addressed by a chewing cockroach: in order to bring his mouthparts into functional position, not tucked against his coxae, G had to tip his head backwards, so that his great eyes stared at the ceiling, and not at his interlocutor. Musil was unfazed.

"I can hardly expect you to take seriously what I say, Herr Insect. Nor can I expect you to operate by the norms of human table manners. But while chewing with an open mouth, perhaps you might reflect on the conclusions one might draw from the strange unpleasantness of looking at old fashions..."

He took a tentative sip of beer. Aside from G's quiet mastication, a pensive silence hung in the room.

"*Ewig, ewig,*" came the word from behind the chair.

"Clearly," Musil asserted, "there is no other conclusion except that we become unpleasant to ourselves the moment we gain some distance from what we were. This, I would submit, also accounts for Spengler's over-dressed pessimism."

What was there to say? Neither Gregor nor Amadeus had ever encountered such knife-like opinions or dark force of expression. Amadeus, the skillful host, tried to break the silence:

"So I take it you did not enjoy Gregor's seminars?"

"On the contrary. I've said how much I like you, Herr Samsa, how much I enjoy what you are up to."

"What am I up to?"

"A very Spenglerian activity: playing out the Faustian man, or in this case, the Faustian Roach — you are a roach are you not?"

Gregor nodded.

"The Faustian Roach on his infinite quest."

"And what is that quest?" G inquired

"Am I wrong about the quest?"

"No."

"Then you tell me. What is the quest?"

"I'm not sure. It has to do with the war. And with my — privilege, I suppose — to stand outside humanity to see...

"To see what?" Amadeus moved to the edge of his armchair. This was important information he had been unconsciously seeking for the last four years. G sat silently.

After a long minute, Musil quietly offered,

"Let me help. The war. A good place to start. You will agree the war demonstrates a profound failure of all experiments, both personal and collective, to find a right way of living."

"At least in the West," said Amadeus.

"All right, let's grant him the West, though I can assure you the East follows hard upon. The synthesis of soul and reason has failed. That is the center. We hold Orion the Hunter and Orion the galactic accident in separate portions of our minds. That leads, had led, will lead — directly to war."

"If we could see — if we could feel the connections.."

"Precisely, Herr Cockroach. And while everyone has been searching for the factor that would summarize and unify all aspects of life, the unifying event of warfare has found and swallowed them all. There's little left for the individual or the nation but a final flight into sexuality and war."

"You sound like Spengler."

"But for me, there is hope."

"What is the hope?" asked Amadeus.

"Our six-legged friend over here, with the unhealing wound in his back."

"How did you know about that?" Gregor asked, surprised and oddly offended.

"It is the writer's job to listen and observe."

"I told him," Amadeus admitted. "I'm sorry."

"How am I the hope?"

"You are uniquely equipped to discover and model a new man for a new society."

"How is that?"

"Ontogeny recapitulates phylogeny. You are the first known throwback in the phylogenetic chain. Somehow, God bless, your ontogeny took a step back towards a more larval state.

"I am not a larvae."

"Cockroaches, as you surely know, demonstrate incomplete metamorphosis. You are as larval as you can be, not worm-like, but comparatively larval nonetheless."

"And so?" Amadeus sensed the writer was onto something.

"And so, unlike Western humanity, which both you and your friend Professor Spengler might agree is 'finished', you, Herr Samsa, are unfinished...."

"Like the symphony," observed Amadeus.

"Like the Schubert Eighth, yes. But unlike our unfortunate composer, consumed by spirochetes, you are healthy and alive, albeit with a wound that keeps you going. *You* can write the later movements. You, as one of the great larvae, are here to reveal ontogenic transitions as you claim your true identity."

"I'll never change back," Gregor insisted. "This is it. I know it."

"We don't need you to change back. We need you to go forward. But forward from the larval state, from a unique place which carries the capacity for real change."

"Let's say I do. Let's say I do go forward. How will that affect others? They're already finished."

"Ah, but *society* is not finished. Society, too, is in a larval state. What it needs is a larval model to lead it onward, upward, and out of the corral. With an inspiring model, even human pathology might be turned around..."

"I thought you said humans were already finished."

"But there are interesting contours to their pathological surface. Have you noticed that human experiences have recently made themselves independent of human beings? Who today can say that his anger is really his own, with so many people butting in and knowing so much more about it? There has arisen a world of experiences without anyone to experience them. Soon we will no longer experience anything at all privately, and our personal responsibility will dissolve into a system of formulae for potential meanings..."

One monkey leapt to the back of Musil's chair.

"Don't feed him."

"Perhaps I should stop talking and eat."

"No. Go on. But watch he doesn't steal the bread."

"Where was I?"

"Free-floating experience," Gregor reminded him. "The larval state."

"Ah, yes. There are men without qualities, and qualities without men. But people are poised on the edge of becoming Possibilitarians, our salvation as a race."

There it was, the word, the first time uttered, the word that Gregor, like Moses, lacked, and would henceforth become the tag and totem for his life: 'Möglichkeitsmensch' – Possibilitarian.

"People," Musil continued, "conduct their lives on interim principles: there are life-components, but no firm pattern, facts seem totally interchangeable. A whole man no longer stands against a whole world, but rather a human something moves in a diffuse culture medium. People are detached from ideas as well as emotions."

"So what is a Possibilitarian?" asked Gregor.

"A Possibilitarian does not say, for instance: Here this or that has happened, will happen, must happen. He uses his imagination and says: Here such and such might, should or ought to happen. And if he is told something is the way it is, he thinks: Well it could probably just as easily be otherwise."

"This is our salvation?" Gregor asked.

"If the sense of possibility is the capacity to think how everything could 'just as easily' be, and no more importance is attached to what *is* than to what is *not*, the consequences might be remarkable, wouldn't you say?"

"I would imagine," said Amadeus, "that Possibilitarians would get on everyone's nerves, condemning things people admire, and allowing things others prohibit..."

"Or more likely Possibilitarians would be detached, indifferent to either...," added Gregor.

"That's the danger. Reflection, not action. But think of the creative space Possibilitarians would open, living in a finer web, a web of haze, imaginings, fantasy... "

"I am not a Possibilitarian," Gregor murmured.

"Listen to me!" Both Amadeus and G jumped with surprise at Musil's sudden ferocity.

"We can't go on like this. Agreed?"

A rhetorical question. He continued without their assent.

"You, Herr Larva, are in a position to lead us back to a larval state from which we may rechart our course. You are the larval man of possibility, the unfixed man in all your ambiguity and ambivalence. Your open wound will continually remind you of the urgent need to heal, of the absolute necessity to steer us, Faust-wise, toward a conscious utopia. Your otherness, your intellectual mobility, will allow you to see life as a laboratory, to contemplate the union of opposites we need if we are not to slug out war after war. You, you, my friend, are the answer to Spengler. Get it?"

Musil circled his sausage with his bread, and took his first bite.

"Without you, they are all a bunch of sheep! With fangs."

He chewed disconsolately.

Amadeus, tentative: "We view sheep as stupid. But God loved them — he often compared men with sheep. Was He completely wrong?"

Musil answered with a glance of scorn.

"I admit," Amadeus added, "that their finely chiseled expression of exalted consciousness is not unlike the look of stupidity."

Musil kept chewing, and took a swallow of beer.

"Maybe Nature is not all healthy. Maybe she is downright mentally disturbed," Gregor mused.

"Is that what you think of yourself?" asked Musil.

"I don't know what to think of myself."

A loud banging at the door made Amadeus jump.

"Yes?"

"Telegram."

Amadeus exchanged glances with the others, and opened the door."

"Herr Hoffnung?"

He nodded.

"Sign here, please. Thank you."

Amadeus put the yellow envelope in his jacket pocket.

"Aren't you going to open it?" asked Gregor.

"I'll read it in private."

"We're here to help," said Musil, in an unexpectedly relaxed tone.

"No, I'll..."

In a flash, the monkey leaped off Musil's chair, snatched the contents from his master's pocket, and climbed whooping, to the top of the bookshelf to offer it to his companion. Esmeralda pulled the message from the envelope, and held it out in front of herself, looking as if she were about to do a public reading. Then she stuffed it in her mouth.

"No you don't, Esmerelda!"

In a flash, Amadeus rushed up the stepladder, and ripped the paper from the beast's mouth.

"Message still intact?" Musil inquired.

"Well-salivated, but whole," came the verdict.

"Clearly this was meant for public consumption." Musil settled back to listen.

Amadeus perused the telegram, and looked up at his friends.

ACCUSATIONS OF FRAUD CONCERNING ROACH STOP
ROENTGEN ACCEPTS OFFER TO X-RAY NOVEMBER 22 STOP
WILL YOU ACCEPT CHALLENGE STOP TAGEBLATT WIEN

"What's that all about?" Gregor raised his mouthparts from his beer stein.

"Oh, I didn't want to bother you with it. At your last Tuesday's show, some six-year old came out saying you were just a man dressed up in an insect suit."

"An inverted Emperor's New Clothes. How hilarious!" Musil smirked.

"He was overheard by some reporter, who figured this angle might get him a by-line. Called me that evening. I told him he was being preposterous."

"The wonders of journalism" exclaimed Musil. "So now he's convinced his editors to go with it, and they've paid old man Roentgen to trek down from Munich, lugging his equipment..."

"Poor old guy," Amadeus commented. "He must be 75 by now."

"Anything for science. And profit and fame."

"No, he's not like that. He's a sweet old man. Refused a patent, or any profit. I read he just lost his wife. This is his grieving work. We should accept if for no other reason."

"Like, for instance", Musil observed, "free publicity, a battle you know you will win, crowds cheering on their genius."

"It's a winning hand all around," Amadeus explained. "And we'll honor the poor child as a young scientist, skeptical, as well he should be, of inexplicable phenomena. We'll give him a year's free tickets to *Zirkus Schwänze Hoffnungs*. What do they call it in America, Gregor? A boo-boo prize?"

Gregor shrugged.

"He'll love it."

"Eleven fifteen," Musil observed, checking his pocket watch. Late tram into town stops when?"

"Midnight."

"Well, gentlemen, it's been a pleasure. I hope I wasn't too abrasive. But I did intend to be forceful. Herr Samsa, some have greatness thrust upon them. I'm afraid you've been chosen. If there's to be a new society, there has to be a new man, a different type of individual. And with this new man must come a new morality for the West, synthesizing reason and mysticism. Orion the hunter and random aggregate both — together. You, Gregor — may I call you Gregor? — you are the search, the possibility of newness. You are the redemption of the Faustian quest. I can only write about how *not* to live, about what I oppose, whom I disdain. It's not enough. Goodnight, gentlemen."

"Goodnight."

"Goodnight."

"Oh, you did hear the news today?"

"What news?"

"Eddington announced the results of the eclipse expeditions last May. Einstein's predictions were correct. Space is curved, Newton is dead."

And Musil walked out under the blazing sky, Orion now high above, club raised, sword dangling between his legs, the second sword-star a fuzzy haze of glowing, formative gas, pregnant with eons to come: the Great Nebula, Messier 42.

Amadeus pushed on the door. The latch clicked.

"*Ewig, ewig,*" the raven croaked.

6. X-Ray Interlude:
The Faustian Roach Is Not A Hollow Man

November, 22, 1919. On this date, 44 years later, John Kennedy would be assassinated in Dallas. But way back then, at least at *Zirkus Hoffnungs*, all was festivity and happy end, a demonstration of authenticity in a often-fraudulent world. The Viennese sky sparkled with an early winter brightness we no longer know in our smog-fogged cities, and the spirit of Science, as yet only mildly tainted, made the air electric with anticipation.

It was a Saturday morning. By ten, it seemed as if half the city were at the *Zirkus*. Why were they there? Because their neighbors were. Because the kids demanded it. Because it was distracting, inexpensive entertainment. Because it was such a sunny day. Because it was the thing to do. Some — primarily adults — were there to test the *Tageblatt's* charges.

For The Vienna *Tageblatt*, a sensationalist tabloid, the event was yet another extravaganza to increase its already considerable circulation. A sideshow made out of a sideshow — its editors loved the recursive. Vienna could stomach only so much of peace negotiations, balance of payment deficits and economic indices. Let *Neue Freie Presse* readers marinate themselves in economic and political theory, the *Tageblatt* would snag the others, all the many others, with less global, more pressing concerns — like whether they were being defrauded at a local circus by a man in a cockroach suit.

True, it had merely been the passing thought of a curious, imaginative child, destined, no doubt, for some blip of middle-level success. But the possibility of exposing a local, successful fraud was just the meat the Tageblatt loved to chew, and they pursued it vigorously, with pictures of Gregor on the front page in the days preceding, Inquiring Photographer interviews with People on the Street (evenly split in their opinions), a long, "scholarly" piece on the history of Roentgen and his Rays, and an artist's conception of how Gregor might look on the screen, should he be operated by a hidden man. In short, Amadeus could not have bought such publicity for any fee. It was, as they say now, a win-win situation, and, as he knew the result, Amadeus was not above exploiting it for his own ends.

ZIRKUS ATTACKED!;

WITNESS THE TRUTH FOR YOURSELVES - 22/10, 10h!;

SUPPORT YOUR LOCAL ARTISTS - 22/10, 10h!;

EXPOSE THE FALSE ACCUSERS! - 22/10, 10h!; F

OR TRUTHFULNESS IN JOURNALISM! - 22/10, 10h!:

Huge painted signs circled the lot on all sides during the preceding week. Lots of exclamation points.

Gregor would have none of this, of course. He refused all interviews, and patiently put up with occasional taunts from that week's audiences. Let Amadeus have his fun; for G, this was just one more lens on the late Faustian world.

Early on Saturday, Amadeus gathered his crew for a briefing. Was it all right with them to have the day off — with pay, of course, and with an equal division of the box? Cheers. Would they mind sitting on stage as witnesses, or perhaps offering themselves as demonstrations of the wonders of Roentgen Rays? Apexia wanted to know if the rays were dangerous for pinheads. Great laughter and applause. She was assured otherwise. Serpentina had a serious concern about her career. She had billed herself as "The Girl Without Bones", and what if it turned out that she had some? She didn't feel as if she had bones, and she twisted her arm as if to demonstrate. But what if there were actually bones in there, peculiar bones, perhaps ("Funnybones!" yelled out Leo Kongee, the Man with No Nerves), but bones, nevertheless? Would she have to change her name or her act? The meeting agreed she would be wisest to avoid Roentgen's machine, if possible. Should she be demanded by the crowd — well, they'd cross that bridge if they came to it. In any case, Gregor was the main event. The crew returned excitedly to quarters to get dressed in their Sunday best — no circus silks and spangles, but in the serious street clothing of serious citizens, as if for jury duty on a crucial case.

Amadeus expected Roentgen at 10, and what with setup and introductory activity, imagined that the big event would occur somewhat before noon. He had been given to understand that the demonstration would require complete darkness, and a fairly constant electrical source, so all the wagons were removed to the periphery of the lot to make room for the huge canvas touring tent. The seams were stuffed with straw wherever they leaked light, and the walls were staked all around. Outside the tent, two of the strongest and most faithful horses were harnessed to a generator via a twenty foot pole. When they trotted in a circle, which they were trained to do, they would generate a 60-80 volt current at 5 amps. Wires from the generator led to the small stage at one end of the tent. It was not entirely clear how Roentgen would be coming, or what he would be bringing with him, but Amadeus felt he had held up his end of the admittedly sketchy plan. He imagined Roentgen pushing heavy pieces of delicate equipment through the streets, or arriving with a crew from the railroad, unloading shipping crates of gear.

How surprised he was when, at ten minutes to ten, a fine Mercedes van arrived at the lot, and an old man in black frock coat and top hat descended, with help from his driver, from the passenger side. On the truck was written SIEMENS GMBH, ELECTRICAL AND X-RAY EQUIPMENT. Yes, of course! Why hadn't Amadeus realized? A medical x-ray van from the military. A complete unit, generating its own electricity. Better than horses by far.

There were introductions all around: Roentgen had been driven over from Munich by Prof. Willy Wien, his younger colleague at the Physical Science Institute, and winner, by the way, of the 1911 Nobel Prize for his work on black body radiation. With them, was Arnold Sommerfeld, Wien's graduate student, later, of course, world famous for his atomic model, the first to explain the fine structure of spectral lines, but here today because of his strong back and laughing spirit. Quite a crew!

Amadeus introduced himself and his contingent: here to help carry were 650 pounds of Anton Tomzak, MC for the event, and George Keiffer, the jolly pink giant, who announced that if he could lift a horse, he could certainly lift the x-ray equipment without hurting his back. Also quite a crew. Taken together, they spanned the male spectrum.

But not much lifting, shoving or even intelligence was necessary. The Siemens engineers and Mercedes designers had thought of everything: a rolling unit of Coolidge tube, shielding, generator and induction coil lowered pneumatically to the ground, as was an excellent wheeled unit with seat, baffle and adjustable barium platino-cyanide screen. A child could have rolled them from the truck, though George was useful in pushing them up the ramp to the stage. Wires ran from an elaborate panel in the rear of the van out to the equipment. Amadeus had originally thought to place the generator at the front of the tent as a dramatic visual, but cable length constrained the van to the side, next to the stage. The setup, running off the engine, could deliver a steady 30 amps at 150 volts.

Coolidge tube, induction coil, barium platino-cyanide. I'm sorry to be so assuming. Let me fill in some basics.

On a dark November afternoon, 24 years earlier, a younger Wilhelm Conrad Roentgen had been working in his laboratory at the Physical Institute of the University of Würzburg. Along with many others, he was exploring the properties of the newly discovered cathode rays — streams of energy which emanated from excited wires in semi-vacuum tubes known as Crookes tubes, named after their inventor, the English physicist, William Crookes. Bendable by magnetic fields, they seemed to be made up of electrons jumping off the metal, penetrating through glass and a few centimeters through the air.

On the afternoon of November 8, 1895, the slim, elegant, bearded professor had placed such a tube in a light-tight, black cardboard box, to contain its glow and better concentrate its energy and effects. When he activated the current, he noticed a faint purple-green glow in the pitch darkness of the room. Thinking there might be a leak, he turned on the lights, and checked the integrity of the box. Satisfied it was flawless, he darkened the room again, and flipped the switch. Again the glow, on a paper screen covered with barium platino-cyanide, a material which fluoresces — gives off light — when struck by various energy sources. What was exciting such fluorescence? Could it be the cathode rays? But the paper was several feet away from the tube, much farther than cathode rays were able to travel through air. He couldn't move the glow with a powerful magnet, so the rays did not consist of charged particles. What was going on? He didn't come home for supper.

The next weeks were spent exploring the properties of this odd radiation. He found the rays could create fluorescence up to six feet away. And most unsettling of all, he found they penetrated most opaque material. He knew they penetrated black cardboard. He tried to block them with a deck of cards: no go. He placed a thousand page physics text between the tube and the screen. It was as if the book were not there — merely a weak shadow. The rays went through a wooden plank, and various thicknesses of aluminum. He finally discovered something that would stop them: lead. They could not penetrate even a thin sheet.

Then came the moment that changed the history of the world. Roentgen was fairly sure that he was dealing with a particle stream: it seemed to travel in a straight line and cast a sharp, regular shadow around the lead sheet. To further examine the nature of the shadow, he cut out a small lead disc, and holding it carefully between his index finger and thumb, he positioned it between the Crookes tube and the fluorescent screen. To his amazement, he saw not only the sharp shadow of the the disc, but also the distinct outline of the bones of his hand. He shut off the current.

Roentgen was — as we would say now — spooked. It was a horrifying sight to this somewhat straight-laced man, his own skeleton encased in living flesh, a sight never before seen except under traumatic or surgical conditions. Accompanying his sense of awe were grave doubts about what it might mean for his career, should he tell the world. He could be snarled in controversy, ostracized from the world of respectable physics, all of his previous work discredited.

Paranoid, you may say, how could that be? This was a great discovery, why not trumpet it out? But we, in the world of Oprah and Geraldo, have entirely lost contact with the decisive force of bourgeois "respectability" in the days when professors wore black frock coats and top hats: this was a real issue for Roentgen. Scientist that he was, he continued his work — but in strictest privacy, keeping all his observations perfectly secret. Replacing the screen with a photographic plate, he meticulously imaged every possible variation of penetration and shadowing. He photographed a box of lead weights: the weights were visible right through the wood. He made studies of his wife's hand: the gold wedding ring hung eerily around the bone. After assuring her he meant no harm, he brought his shotgun into the lab and photographed it — and was able to see the lead shot right through the barrels.

Finally, convinced that he had reproducible results, he submitted his researches to the *Physical-Medical Society Journal* for publication. The paper, "A New Kind of Ray, by Dr. W. Roentgen" is a model of clarity and humility. It is still worth reading, a classic example of 19th century science, and is contained as an appendix in the several biographies of its author. Buried in the text, almost as an aside, is the single sentence, "If one holds a hand between the discharge apparatus and the screen, one sees the darker shadow of the bones within the slightly fainter shadow image of the hand itself."

Such is the stuff of discovery. As a historian of Science, I experience over and over the thrilling elegance of powerful observation, and clearly designed questioning. Mendel's pea experiments — nothing short of gorgeous! Fleming's recognition of the importance of a mold-contaminated petri dish. How many deaths would have resulted had he just said, "Damn!" and tossed the plate in the garbage? Galileo, William Harvey, *The Origin of Species,* Einstein's 1905 papers — Roentgen's 1895 paper has illustrious company. What a gift to work with such material!

But I'm getting carried away. Forgive me for digressing.

Within a few minutes, a state of the art radiology unit had been set up on a wooden stage in a canvas tent on an empty lot in a northeastern suburb of Vienna on a splendorous winter morning of November 1919. The Zirkus crew was assembled earlier than expected, with Gregor still backstage. Reporters and photographers from all the local papers, and several from Germany were given privileged seating in the first row. Only Emil Kahn, the child who had started it all, was missing. A late arrival, unexpected, but warmly welcomed by Amadeus, was H.V. Kaltenborn, European correspondent for *The Brooklyn Eagle*, a future pioneer in radio news, whose broadcast commentaries would play so large a part in Gregor's destiny.

At eleven, Emil arrived with his parents and took his place at the center of the crowded stage. Gregor and Roentgen were still outside in back,

Tomzak was out front, barking the crowd, and Amadeus was scurrying back and forth, ushering, helping seat people, making accommodations for the old and disabled. On stage, what an array was to be seen! Sitting properly, even formally, in their most conservative clothing, was a group which reflected Mother Nature's wildest, most radical fantasies. So great was the press of irregularity that the "normal" looking trio of Emil, Greta and Karl Kahn seemed almost deformed, odd in the extreme. Furthest stage right sat Fritz Denkmann, with Rotpeter, the typing orangutan — presently in diapers — on a short chain. He had chosen to sit at the edge, in case Rotpeter acted up. Next to this pair, Katerina Eckhardt, looking elegant, her second body concealed under a long, dark skirt. Propped next to her, on high chairs, the little people, Clarissa and Inge Leinsdorf, staring stiffly out, not knowing exactly what to do, and next to them Gerda Schloß, the "Ugly Lady", straining at the leash of propriety, occasionally calling out lewdly to select audience members. Lying on the floor in front of the high chairs, on a blue cushion, was the other Emil, the Hunger Artist, now in his 204th day of fast, close to death. Towards the center of the stage were Josef/Josefina, and Leo Kongee, the Man with No Nerves, without his pins and spikes, looking like your next door neighbor — if your next door neighbor looked a little strange. Child Emil and his family were in the center, and to their left, *Glotzaügiger* Otto, popeyed, but not frighteningly so. To his left, Koo-koo the Bird Girl, and lying in front of her, symmetrical with the Hunger Artist, the rather more perky Serpentina, who had resolved not to be x-rayed. Filling out stage left were the often-together trio of Dog-Faced Boy, Alligator-Skinned Man and Monkey Girl. Behind the seated row, Herr Rauchenrücken supported the upended coffin of Fu Hsi, the "undead' Chinaman, while George Keiffer, the giant, stood next to the case of the "Giant Moleperson", who peered out from a cleared space behind his glass wall. Without more formal clothing than his swimsuit, he had chosen, for this event, to show only his face. Seated on the floor, in front of the Kahns, were Godina and Apexia, the Pinhead Sisters, holding the Blumenfeldlichten as best they could. Shortly before the event, reminded about the need for absolute darkness, Amadeus walked on stage to box up and remove the dancing lights. When the crowd started to applaud, he hushed them, and left the stage, box in hand.

At 11:15, Tomzak made a grand entrance down the center aisle, lifted his huge weight up the two steps to the stage, and addressed the crowd in his delightful stentorian voice.

"*Meine Damen und Herren, Mesdames et Messieurs, Signorine e Signori, Pani i Pane,* Ladies and Gentlemen!"

He was emphasizing the purportedly world-shaking nature of the event, though there were likely no French or Italian speakers in the crowd, and only one English speaker, Kaltenborn, who also spoke German. Czech, perhaps. But Tomzak liked the feel of the foreign words on his tongue.

"I'm sure most of you know what all the fanfare is about. It's been in the papers, and on our end, we have leafleted the local community. But somehow the news has gotten farther than our little Viennese circle. I'm told we have journalists from as far away as Munich."

"Brooklyn, New York," shouted Kaltenborn in his soon-to-be-famous voice.

Spontaneous applause swept the audience, though why an "enemy" reporter should be cheered was not quite clear. Perhaps they felt they should applaud his coming so far.

"Because there may be some of you who merely wandered in, or were swept in by the crush of the crowd, I'd like to introduce the little man who started it all, Emil Kahn."

More applause.

"Emil will tell us exactly what happened. Emil?"

The little boy walked to the front of the stage. He'd not been warned he was to speak, but he was not shy, being raised by parents who thought his every word a treasure, and who applauded his every performance. He wore short pants and knee socks, though it was November, and a blue blazer embroidered with the double-headed eagle of the former Austro-Hungarian Empire.

"Well, I was just looking at the big cockroach, and even though he was standing on his skinny legs, I though maybe there was room for a little man inside who might pull levers or something and talk out the mouth...."

Tomzak jumped in.

"I'm sure you're not the only who has thought that way, Emil. In fact — here he was pandering wildly to building dramatic tension — there are several of us right here in the circus, the cockroach's fellow artists, who have had similar thoughts. How many of you up on stage have had such suspicions?"

Only Gerda, the "Ugly Lady" raised her hand.

"It's hard to say bad things in public about your friends," Tomzak confided in the audience, "but I can assure you, I have heard people among us say so. And you out there — how many of you have seen Gregor Samsa's shows at the *Zirkus Schwäntze Hoffnungs*? Stand up." Fully 2/3s of the seated audience rose from their folding chairs. Of those already standing around the back and sides, we can assume the same percentage.

"Now...stay standing...of those who have seen Herr Samsa, how many think he may be a man in a cockroach suit? You stay standing, the others sit down."

Most of the standees sank back into their chairs, leaving a dozen mostly professor-looking types on their feet. Tomzak was prepared for any survey result.

"See how many of you he may have taken in! If he is a fake, a fraud, as Emil suggests, how many of you have been naive enough to have the wool pulled over your eyes! What does this say for the future of our country? What does this say about the effects of our cultural inheritance, here in the city of Mozart, Beethoven, Schoenberg?"

The Schoenberg reference was unnecessary, used only to impress the professors.

"Well, *meine Damen und Herren,* this little child's suspicions — you may sit down, Emil — may shine some light on the critical problem of authenticity in our post-war world. But a strange light it is that will be needed to solve the question. And here to tell you about it, all the way from Munich, courtesy of the *Tageblatt Wien,* the Siemens Corporation, and Mercedes Benz, is the inventor of this strange light, the very first recipient of the Nobel Prize in Physics, *meine Damen und Herren,* we are pleased and honored to have with us today, the very great professor of Physical Science at the University of Munich, the one, the only, Herr Doktor Professor Wilhelm...Conrad...Roentgen! Give him a big hand, *meine Dam...."*

But before he could finish, the audience was up on its feet, cheering and stamping and whistling.

It warms my heart to think how honored scientists were among the older generation. What scientist today could claim the same applause? Who even knows the names of the physicists of today? Truly a Golden Age, it was.

Tomzak quieted the crowd.

"Professor Roentgen, Professor, you can come out now..."

A tall, somewhat stooped 74 year old man walked sprightly from the stage right wings.

"Professor Roentgen, would you care to explain your apparatus to those in the audience who have never experienced Roentgen or X Rays?"

He pronounced the "X" as if it were an word of holy power, the same implication of magic that shows itself today in naming cars "XL4", or "Tri-X Turbo". In a very quiet, humble voice, the Nobel laureate began:

"*Meine Damen und Herren*, it is a great pl..."

"Louder," prompted several at the back of the tent.

"*Meine Damen und Herren*, it is a great pleasure for me to ..."

"Louder," the voices urged, more loudly.

At this point, Amadeus walked on stage lugging a different box, a heavy one, trailing a wire to the Mercedes. It was an amplifier and loudspeaker, one of the first in Vienna. From his bulging jacket pocket, he pulled a large microphone, uncoiled the wire, plugged it into the black box, and handed Roentgen the microphone. Either because he was a physicist, or because he had used them before, Roentgen accepted it naturally, with a grateful bow. Again the crowd cheered, for the resilient professor, for Amadeus saving the show, for the wonders of technology — who knows?

If I may be allowed yet another slight digression from the tale at hand, I must say a few History-of-Technology-type words about the impact of amplification on the human condition. The philosopher Ivan Illich tells a story of visiting his Grandfather, in 1926, on the island of Brac off the coast of Dalmatia. On the same boat which brought him, there also arrived the first loudspeaker on the island. Few people on Brac had ever heard of such a thing. Up till that point everyone spoke with equally powerful voices. Shortly afterwards, the life changed: only those with access to loud-speakers were heard. To this day we suffer the consequences.

Sorry. But what are History of Science professors for?

Roentgen spoke with assurance into the microphone. "May we have the machine, please?"

Leaving his post at the Giant Moleperson's case, George Keiffer joined Anton Tomzak in wheeling the fluoroscope on stage. It came out from stage right in profile, and, as they were about to turn it 90 degrees, up and down stage, Roentgen stopped them.

"Leave it like that for the moment. Thank you so much. Let me just point out to you the components of this machine. Here, on the left, is the x-ray generator itself. Inside this box — let me open it — is a Coolidge tube, a decided advance over the Crookes tube with which I made my discovery. By the way, I am not the inventor of Roentgen rays, as our master of ceremonies too generously announced. I did discover them — by accident, I may add, and it took me a while to even believe in my own discovery. God invented them."

Thank goodness there was no applause for God.

"The electricity generated by our marvelous truck outside comes in this wire here, and heats the filament on this end. The electrons shooting off the heated filament bombard this target here — tungsten — and the tungsten emits the radiation. The harder, the faster we bombard it, the more intense and penetrating are the x-rays which come off. The heat from bombardment is run off into this copper radiator which dissipates it into the room. By aiming the tube appropriately, we can direct a stream of x-rays at any target. "

"Is everybody following?" Tomzak asked the crowd.

Reassuring nods and mumbles. Roentgen continued.

"We will direct these rays at this fluorescent plate over here." And he spun the chair assembly round so that the audience could see a 12" X 18" glass plate in a lead frame.

"Between these two pieces of glass," — he tapped either side — there is platino-barium cyanide — the same material that I found glowing in my laboratory 24 years ago. When hit by x-rays it will give off a greenish-purple light."

"Everybody still with the professor?" Tomzak asked.

More murmurs. A little child started to cry, and was shortly removed. Swinging the screen/chair assembly back around to profile, Roentgen continued.

"Now, if we place an object between the tube and the screen, the rays will either pass through the object, or they will not. We have found that the rays will pass easily through aluminum, but not at all through lead. Let me demonstrate."

"What about the cockroach?" yelled out a child in the second row.

"Patience, patience," Tomzak cautioned.

Meanwhile, on Roentgen's cue, George had reoriented the entire machine so that the tube was upstage firing straight down at the screen, which was closest to the audience.

"Let me see if I have the switch. Yes. All right, you may turn out the lights."

The tent went almost dark. A little light leaked in under a few feet of the west wall. An audience member stepped on the canvas to seal it off. Now the tent was pitch black. Over the quiet hum of the Mercedes engine, one could hear the *Blumenlichten* whining in their box, wanting to see the demonstration, too. Amadeus' whack on the top quieted them down.

Flicking the switch in his right hand, Roentgen set the Coolidge tube firing, and the screen glowed with eerie phosphorescence.

"Now," he said, "I will hold a sheet of aluminum between the rays and the screen."

In the weak green light, the audience could see a 12" x 12" sheet held by a wooden clamp between source and screen. But the screen remained glowing as before.

"As you can see, even though we try to block the rays, they pass through the aluminum to excite the screen. Now let's try some lead."

As Roentgen interrupted the beam with a sheet of lead, the screen went dark, and the room went black again. A murmur went through the crowd.

"Now let me show you what I saw when I held a small piece of lead in front to the screen to test its shadow."

Roentgen pulled from his pocket a circular lead disc the size of a quarter and held it with his left hand between source and screen. No murmurs now, but a definite collective gasp! A skeleton of a hand, a marriage band loosely circling its fourth finger, came close to holding a quarter-sized black circle. The deathly apparition began to wiggle its fingers, and a second skeleton hand entered the shadow to make what many would swear was the head of a horned and bearded devil.

"Lights please."

Roentgen turned off the rays. The audience adjusted its eyes.

"The image you saw was quite clearer than the one I saw twenty four years ago. The exigencies of three wars have perfected our technology. You can imagine how much easier it is for a surgeon using this equipment to extract a bullet from a wound, or set a bone correctly. If you haven't already seen it, you may afterwards inspect the marvelous portable x-ray wagon developed by Siemens and Mercedes-Benz. It is out behind the tent here on my right."

"And now," Tomzak stepped forward, "before the main event, the decisive testing of the charge of fraudulence, let's just see what this machine can do with the human form. Who in the audience wants to be a subject?"

No one came forward.

"Oh, surely, you're not afraid to having some death rays pointed at you?"

Little did he know how truly he spoke.

"All right, then, how about our company on stage? Which of you would like to be a guinea pig?"

"Me! me!" squealed Apexia and Godina in spontaneous duet. "Look at our pin-skulls, look at our pin-skulls!"

Roentgen sat Godina sideways in the chair between the Coolidge tube and the screen.

"If she screams you'll stop immediately?" inquired Tomzak with exaggerated concern.

"She won't feel a thing. Lights please."

In the darkness, Roentgen switched on the rays, and an image of a tiny skull with a largish jaw, and tapering crown flashed on the screen.

"Move your mouth."

And the skull performed a grotesque biting motion, like a strange, carved puppet. The audience laughed. Then it was silent.

"Me next," demanded Apexia, as she felt her way along the floor and up along the chair, and jammed her head up against her sister's. The two skulls were more than twice as frightening as one alone. The audience remained still.

"Lights, please."

The sisters returned to their places on the floor.

"Anyone else?"

Rotpeter had had enough, and practically dragged his diminutive trainer off the stage, whining loudly till he was returned to his cage.

Tomzak: "Perhaps he's changed his opinion about humanity." Snickers from the cast.

"Anyone else?"

"I'll do it," said Katerina Eckhardt, and walked in stately manner to stand in front of the screen.

"Where would you like to be x-rayed?" asked Roentgen, suspecting nothing.

"Here."

The professor adjusted the screen on its rack until it was several inches below her billowing skirt, and the ray gun to hit it.

"Lights, please."

And this time it was the professor who let out a gasp as he saw the extra pelvis and hanging legs and feet."

"My goodness," he said.

"Lights," called Katerina, and walked, stately, back to her chair.

Tomzak took over.

"Has everyone seen enough to believe that if Herr Samsa were in reality a man dressed up in an ingenious cockroach suit, Professor Roentgen's rays would see through his imposture?"

No response.

"Is there anyone who does not believe this?"

No response.

"Good. Then we're ready for the main event, the Trial by Radiation. *Meine Damen und Herren*, let me now introduce to you the center of the controversy, a being many of you are familiar with, a being whose being has raised some concern. You know who I'm talking about, our very own Visitor from the Early Carboniferous, Herr Gregor Samsa!"

Was the crowd tired? Were they simply holding off approbation until the charges were proved or disproved? Was all this becoming too much for them? Whatever the reason, the applause was thin as Gregor walked on stage, on all sixes, dressed in a new bathing suit in a style made popular by Harry Houdini.

Tomzak inquired, "Herr Samsa, is there anything you'd like to say before we begin?"

"This is a remarkable piece of apparatus."

"Thank you, very much," said Roentgen. "I am hardly responsible for its technical excellence."

"May I ask a question?" H.V. Kaltenborn raised his hand from the front row.

Tomzak replied, "Our American friend steps in where angels fear to tread. Certainly. Go ahead."

"Where is Herr Hoffnung in all this? He scurries back and forth toting equipment, playing the usher. Surely he has something to say."

Amadeus stepped out from the wings.

"I can say only that I am looking forward to the results of the investigation. I have complete faith in my friend and colleague, Herr Samsa, and complete trust in Professor Roentgen and his physicist colleagues to interpret the results for us. I hope you will report this event to interested parties in your own country."

"There is no hype in this event?"

"What is hype?"

"Public relations, showbiz."

"Herr Kaltenborn, are you already certain as to the results?"

"Not completely."

"Then why don't you just sit back and relax? Professor, will you proceed?"

The chair of the previous demonstrations was replaced by a modular tilt-table, which was set perpendicular to the floor. Gregor crawled up against the table to his full height of 5'10", and Tomzak strapped him on the tabletop to take the weight off his hind legs. Staining through the tank top, his moist wound glistened.

"Are you ready?" asked Tomzak.

"Yes," said Gregor.

"And you, Professor?"

"Ready."

"Lights, please."

Roentgen allowed the tent to remain black until the audience's eyes attained maximum sensitivity. Then he threw the switch. The screen had been at the level of Katerina's second body, and thus revealed a 12x18 inch section of Gregor's abdomen. Those who doubted stared with mere curiosity. But those who already knew had a more complex response. As even an innocent person will send polygraph needles flickering when asked a key question, so these individuals in the know — including Amadeus and Gregor himself — experienced an irrational moment of fear. What if it *was* a hoax? What if I *am* a hoax? Such doubts are of short duration, but great depth, rising up out of one's *ontos* itself. What if knowledge is unreal? What if existence itself is a sham, a universal illusion?

"Emil," asked Tomzak, "would you describe what you see?"

Emil crawled carefully around to the front of the stage.

"I see a bug. An empty bug. With some guts in there, and what's that? Is that your heart all the way down there in your back? It's beating. Is that your heart?"

Gregor was silent.

"Is there anyone else who wants to comment?"

A voice from the back: "Move the screen up and down, so we can see all of him."

Roentgen slid the screen along its track, while Tomzak adjusted the beam to follow. All of Gregor was examined.

"Are there further requests or questions?"

Dead silence in the purple green blackness.

"Lights, please," called Roentgen. And he switched off the beam.

It took a few minutes before the spectators made their way outside, shielding their eyes against the blinding sunlight. On the way out, one little girl was heard to say, "Maybe he wrapped his bones in something so you couldn't see them."

But no reporter picked it up.

7. Interlude II:
Praise Him With Drum And Dance. Praise Him.

H.V. Kaltenborn went home. It is interesting to note that "home" would still not tolerate his name — Hans von Kaltenborn. Though born and raised in Minnesota, he was still a potential victim of the red-blooded American hatred of all things German. At least he wasn't black. Or Jewish.

He reported his experience at the *Zirkus* in a two part article for the *Eagle*, the first dealing with the test event, the second with the phenomenon of Gregor himself. The articles drew a bit of attention, some from the newly emerging public relations industry, and some from professors, including a long query from Sir Julian Huxley concerning G's behavior, a letter he kept as one of his treasures.

It wasn't until his Third of July radio broadcast in '22, ironically, and inadvertently, on Kafka's 39th birthday, that American interest in Gregor took off. And take off it did! We don't know who was listening, or who initiated the idea, but within a month of the program, "The Gregor" was beginning to give the Charleston competition as the hottest dance craze, with its attendant music, consumer spin-offs, and advertising tie-ins. It may have begun as just another dance, but it soon began to take on the social and political overtones of an early ecological, collectivist movement. The Charleston was a dance of mad individualism, flappers flapping, flappos (or whatever the male equivalent was called) flailing, each dancing basically alone. In contrast, The Gregor developed as a team dance, attracting left-wing communitarians who wanted to have fun after Study Group. Upper-class flapping (or at least would-be upper-class) vs. the Salt of the Earth, men and women committed to proletarian purposes, dressing down, if necessary, to further contrast the choreographies, embracing and glorifying the lowest of the low — and what could be lower than a cockroach? The Gregor planted the seed of an incipient animal rights movement, with some dancers going so far as to boycott and even picket the corporate offices of FLIT. "Bzzzzzzzz, bzzzzzzzzz, bzzzzzzzz. Quick, Henry, the FLIT." No! Amscray! There were better ways, insects are our brothers and sisters, there were screens. Children were paid a penny a bug to harmlessly transport six-legged intruders outside. Besides, what was the effect of all that FLIT on our lungs, on our children's lungs? Rachel Carson was 15, but her movement was birthing.

All of which led American Cyanamide, in a brilliant pre-emptive move, to sponsor a series of dance contests specifically focused on The Gregor, and for all the political sophistication of the young Old Left, many dancers bought into it — to the scorn and dismay of erstwhile comrades. Gregor Contests sparked one of the earliest, and fiercest splits in the progressive movement, with Gregor dancers picketing Gregor Contests with a degree of enmity often reserved for family affairs. But "Use Their Money Against Them" seemed right enough for many, and the contests multiplied, sweeping many youngsters up into their first principled activities — on either side.

By the fall of 1922, the National Association of Gregor Dancers and Coaches (NAGDAC) was in place, and local contests coalesced into regional ones, with winners demanding a national Gregor "Olympics", to be held at Madison Square Garden. Because of the underlying leftist thrust of the movement, the first prize was to be split — half for the winning team, and half for Gregor himself, in the form of a first class, round trip on the *Mauritania*, to the good old U. S. of A. They would have their hero to behold.

G, of course, was not consulted, so great was the dancers' zeal. In fact, he knew nothing about it. While teams were competing on 39th St. from noon to six, Gregor, seven hours ahead, was having a simple dinner alone in his wagon, reading *Midsummer Night's Dream* (in English! — with

Schlegel's marvelous translation as a pony), and when the winning group was crowned at nine, G was halfway through a night of peaceful sleep, dreaming of a rude mechanical (*ein lumpger Handwerksmann*) turned into an ass. His dream did not predict the next day's telegram, informing him of the contest and its results, instructing him to apply for a travel visa, and to pick up his ticket at Cook Travel on the Ringstrasse. Enthusiastic American presumptuousness. It has its not-so-charming side.

The reader may be interested in the performance of the winning team. This, a clipping from the *New York Daily News*.

LONE STAR STATE SHINES IN BUG EVENT

Associated Press

The Brownsville Blattae, three energetic dancers from southern Texas, squeezed out the Petaluma Periplanets 43-41 to take the gold at the First Annual Gregor Olympics last night, here at Madison Square Garden. For those readers unfamiliar with the contest, some basic information: The event, sponsored by American Cyanamide, and emceed by H.V. Kaltenborn, was host to the semi-finalist winners of five regions across the country, the winners from a field of 375 teams, each sponsored by local business. The magnificent Cyanamide prize was $10,000, to be split equally between the winning team, and Gregor Samsa, the human roach, to support his fan club tour of the U.S.

Points were given for the most ingenious and technically accomplished dance steps imitating roach behavior. Basic locomotion, which all teams must master, is difficult enough. Cockroaches, as insects, have six legs. Three are always on the ground, providing the bug with a constantly stable triangle. The alternate three reach out ahead (see diagram). The three dancers, with legs 1&2, 3&4, and 5&6 must therefore move 1,4 &5. then 2,3&6, alternatively. With speed, coordination is almost unworkable. The initial event or the Olympics is a 100 yard sprint, with negative points awarded for gait infractions. After that, teams are on their own to evoke, as beautifully as possible, the spirit of their model.

The Blattae's twenty minute routine, performed to a medley of tunes by the Benny Goodman Quartet, guest artists for the finale, consisted of the following routines:

1. The Grooming: A high-class roach prepares for a night on the town. Antennae and legs are sensuously cleaned to "Body and Soul", with its sinuous clarinet solo by Mr. Goodman.

2. The Vibes From End to End: Mouthparts and cerci are wiggled and shaken, as an extended thrill runs through the creature. Mr. Hampton explores the farthest acoustics of his machine in "Vibraphone Blues".

3. The Train of Events: Taking liberties with the normal pattern of alternate stepping, the creature begins a wild, zigzagging ride through the world. Surprising variations on "Take the A Train" by the whole quartet.

4. The Gaze: Through the Ages: a review of selected millennia of the creature's race. Imitations of giant ferns, flying reptiles, and early mammals. Starting small, the creature goes through five molts getting larger at each, to the provocative strains of "Melancholy Baby".

5. The Crevice: An improvised search in the great arena for dark cracks in which to snuggle while the band offers "Whispering". Hope you like snuggling with a cockroach!

6. The Omnivorous: Audience members will have a chance to share food with their favorite six-legger, while "Lady Be Good" invites their generosity.

7. The Dead. To the tune of "Heaven, I'm in Heaven" the creature rolls over and over, and winds up, legs in the air, dead. A tour de force of team control.

Upon being awarded the Golden Roach, Carol Braun, thorax and team captain said, "For Duane and Alan and me, this is the greatest moment of our lives." Alan Torney, abdomen, said, "I just want to say a big thank you to Gregor Samsa for making all this possible. We'll see ya soon." Duane Babbit, head, nursing a facial abrasion, declined to be interviewed.

The event was picketed by RAG, the Radical and Anarchist Gregors, because of its corporate sponsorship. American Cyanamide is the manufacturer of RAID, a popular roach killer.

Telegram in hand, G was perplexed. America. He could become fluent in English. He could get to know a culture which had imagined the Fourteen Points — open covenants, freedom of the seas, arms reduction, marvelous! And he might meet someone... On the other hand, he had his niche here. He knew what he was doing. People accepted him. He didn't have a terrific act at the moment — people were getting tired of "Thinking Together About Einstein" — so he'd have to find something else. But he had friends here. Amadeus, he wouldn't want to lose him. How much longer till Amadeus dries up and dies? Maybe he should visit after that. But it might be lonely in America. Sure, he'd be some kind of hero, but fame is fleeting, and a dance craze is — a craze, a fad, nothing to count on. On the other hand, he wouldn't have to stay all that long. He'd be treated like a king, it sounds like, then maybe he'd do a little traveling. One thing he was sure of: he wouldn't do any ads for American Cyanamide. But what if they made things easier for him? What if they paid him? But still... What if he got seasick? He'd never been on anything but the ferry to Sweden. And that was when he was a person. He's still a person, of course, but even then he threw up. But if he didn't try, how would he ever... But it would be a terrible place to get stuck. But he'd have his return ticket. But what about the quest? The quest should be here. But a quest should be in a new world. But this, but that, but this, but that. But, but, but. But, but.

He looked at the telegram again and became so confused and frustrated, he did something very unusual: he ate it.

8. Suffer The Little Children[3]

"Herr W., Herr W., here he is!"

"Herr W., Emil, Epi, c'mere!"

Four blond, blue-eyed urchins came charging up to Gregor's cage to join their friends as G was taking the sun on a warm April morning. Behind them strolled a thin, sandy haired man in a green cardigan.

"And how do you know he is a he, Herr Schiferl?" the man asked.

The children studied G for a moment, who turned his amused attention on the conundrum.

"Because he doesn't have long hair," said Alois Schiferl.

"Because he's supposed to be smart," said Fritz Heer, for which he received a smart Wittgensteinian knuckle on the side of his head.

"Hey! Why don't you ever hit the girls?"

"Their heads are too soft. I pull their hair."

"I think he's a he because he's wearing a man's jacket," Elli Rolf offered.

"Is he a man, then, a human?" Herr W. asked.

"Maybe he's a puppet like the other ones, but bigger." Epi Schlüsselberger always had strong opinions.

"Like what other ones?" Gregor asked.

"He talks!" Karl Gasser shouted,

"Of course I talk. What other puppets? We don't have a puppet show."

3 This and the following encounter assembled from notes of G's recollections, and my own meetings with LW during his visit to Cornell in the summer of 1949.

"Oh, yes you do."

"Right down there."

"Over by the fat lady."

"And the lady without bones."

Herr W. interrupted. "Forgive me, Mr. Samsa, is it? My name is Ludwig Wittgenstein. I teach at the elementary school at Puchberg-am-Schneeberg..."

"Where is that?" asked Gregor.

"About 40 km west."

"Ah."

"My class was reading about Dr. Roentgen and you in *Current Events*, and they wanted to see you in person."

"Yes," Eugenie chimed in, "and only six of us could go, so we drew lots out of Herr W.'s cap..."

"And we won."

"May I introduce these traveling scholars?"

"It would be a pleasure."

"Alois Schiferl, Fritz Heer, Karl Gasser."

The boys clicked their heels and nodded their close-cropped heads.

"And Eugenie Pippal, Elli Rolf, and Epi Schlüsselberger."

The girls curtsied. Epi pushed her braid back out of her face. "Can we ask you questions?" she inquired boldly.

"You can ask all you want — if I get to ask one first."

They all agreed.

"I already asked it. What was the puppet show? I didn't think we had one."

"Punch the Jude." Two or three answered together.

"You mean Punch and Judy?" asked Gregor.

"No. Punch the Jude. You give him a punch. Herr W. says that means *Stoß* in English."

"With your fist."

"Ah, I see. *Faust*, too. So who was the Jude?"

"He was a Jew, and he had a big nose, and he wore a black gown and a black little hat."

"And he wanted to kill a little baby."

"Was it his baby?"

"No, his wife brought it to him. She was taking care of it."

"Why did she bring it to him if he wanted to kill it?"

"He wanted to grind it up into flour to make... to make..."

"Matzohs," Epi coached.

"Matzohs," Fritz acknowledged. "I forgot the word. It's a kind of bread Jews eat."

"It wasn't for flour," Epi said, "it was for the blood to make the dough. Jews need the blood of Christian children to make special matzohs for their holidays."

"Oh, that's right. It was for the blood."

"So did he kill the baby?" Gregor asked.

"He tried really hard. But the man doing the show came out and said that if we would punch him really hard, and get him to drop the baby, we might be able to rescue it."

"And what happened?"

"Well, different people tried to punch him and get him to drop the baby, but he ran all over the stage, and he was hard to catch 'cause it was so high up."

"And then, he called for his friend the Devil, and the Devil came and tried to protect him, and he pushed away everybody's hands."

"And his wife helped too. She was pushing away everybody's hands."

"But then a big, fat kid pushed them all aside, and he punched the Jude right in the face, and he dropped the baby, and the kid grabbed it, and everybody cheered, and the man came out again, and he said about how Jews were trying to hurt us..."

"And they made us lose the war..." Franz was incensed.

"And how we needed to protect our country..."

The children quieted down. Gregor was astounded.

"I need to see this for myself." He began to open the door to his cage.

"Oh, he's not there anymore. He just let the stage down and left."

"What do you mean, 'let the stage down'?"

"It was like he was wearing a big skirt. He would lift his skirt up over his head, and that would be the stage, and the puppets would come up over the top of the skirt."

"Ingenious. And then he just ran away?"

"Somebody told him to stop."

"A tiny little man with a squeaky voice and a huge fat man."

"I think they were the circus owners," said Herr W. "They asked him who he was, and who gave him permission to do the show."

"What did he say?"

"He actually threatened them. He didn't give his name, but he said they'd be hearing more from him and his friends. And he walked off, holding his skirt up out of the mud. I trust you *will* hear more from him."

"Aren't you Jewish, Herr Wittgenstein?"

"My parents were, until they weren't. How do you know?"

"You're Jewish, Herr W.??" Epi Schlüsselberger of the sharp ears. Wittgenstein shushed her, and walked a few paces away from the kids. Gregor followed him behind his bars.

"I just finished your book. If you can ever be finished with such a book. And I asked Meister Hoffnung about you."

"But it hasn't appeared yet."

"Annalen der Naturphilosophie, 1922."

"But cockroaches don't read philosophy journals."

"The world is all that is the case. Ludwig Wittgenstein."

"You've got it memorized?"

"A striking opening sentence."

"Where did you come up with the *Annalen*?"

"That little man with the squeaky voice subscribes. He loaned me his. Thought I'd be interested."

"And were you?"

"Let's talk about it later. There are six fourth graders over there waiting for whatever they're waiting for."

Wittgenstein motioned them over. "What are we here for?"

"To see the big bug," was Eugenie Pippal's plan.

"To get out of school," was Karl Gasser's.

Epi Schlüsselberger wasn't about to let go: "Are you a Jew? Herr W., are you a Jew? You didn't tell us you were a Jew."

"*Kleine Damen und Herren*, we are here today to discuss a tremendously difficult problem, one which more than ever engages — and eludes —the greatest minds of our time."

"What is it?" Elli Rolf was all ears.

"What does it mean to say something — or someone — is human?"

Ten minutes ago, the children would have laughed at the stupidity of such a question. But here, in Gregor's presence, laughter was not so easy.

"A human looks like a human," offered Alois.

"Remember those two who kicked out the puppeteer? Did they look the same? The tiny guy and the huge fat man?"

"But they sort of do. They both have two arms and two legs. And a head."

"What about the woman with no arms and no legs?" Is she human?"

"Yes," the children admitted.

"How do you know?"

"Cause she talks."

"What if she didn't talk?"

Gregor joined the discussion. "I talk. And I read books, and I walk around, and I eat lunch. Am I human?"

"No." The children all agreed.

"Why not?" asked Herr W.

"Cause you have bug eyes and six legs."

"So?" asked Gregor. "Did you see Katerina Eckhardt? No? Go see her. She has six legs. And Otto can pop his eyes right out of his head. Can you?"

The children were getting uneasy. What could be so hard about this question?

Wittgenstein was reveling in his Socratic element. "How do you know Herr Samsa isn't a puppet?"

"Cause nobody is working him. And the newspaper said there was no one inside."

"The x-rays." Karl Gasser was a good student. "Don't you remember?"

"Indeed I do," said Herr W. "and how do you know he's not some kind of marvelous machine that can move around and talk like a radio?"

"But there are people talking that make the radio talk."

"How can you tell that isn't the case with Herr Samsa?"

Although the question of human-ness, its definition, and implications were profoundly important to him, Gregor was charmed and amused by the intensity of the childrens' struggle.

"Maybe," said Elli, "it has to do with how people — well, you know, beings, I mean people-like beings — act. Maybe it isn't what you look like or how you are made, maybe it's how you act."

"How do humans act?" asked Herr W., gently pursuing his checkmate.

"They say hello, they're nice..."

"We are made in God's image." Alois at catechism.

"My father isn't so nice, especially when he's drunk. He hits me with his belt."

"Jews kill babies and grind them up for blood."

"And they drop bombs on us."

"Do you do that?" asked Gregor.

"We don't have bombs."

"But are you mean and cruel?"

"Sometimes," admitted Eugenie.

"I am. Especially to my little brother." Alois at confession.

"Hold on," said Herr W. "You think the definition of human is to be mean and cruel?"

No one agreed. On the other hand, no one disagreed.

"Let's get back to Herr Samsa here. Is he mean?"

"No."

"Does that mean he's not human?"

"No."

"If he's not not-human, is he human?"

Silence.

"Why don't we ask him what he thinks?" Fritz Heer, the social scientist to be.

"Yeah, he ought to know."

"Are you human?" asked Epi.

"I'm Jewish," said Gregor.

The children, all but one, burst out laughing. "A cockroach can't be Jewish!"

Epi: "Why not? Jews are vermin, right, and isn't a cockroach vermin?" Her formal logic was impeccable.

Gregor and Wittgenstein exchanged inchoate glances. Frightened? Confused? Impotent?

Herr W. took control. "Let's go see more of the circus. Let's see the lady with six legs, and we can talk more about this question when we have lunch. Then I'll take you into the city, and we can look at architecture, and go to the zoo and draw animals, and St. Stephen's, and the museum, and we can get settled in the hostel. Herr Samsa, may I come visit after the scholars are asleep?"

"What time will that be?"

"Say ten? We'll go out for a drink."

"Better to stay here if we want to talk. Just knock."

"Good. Come, Kinder. Let's let Herr Samsa relax before his first show."

And, indeed, the lot was starting to fill up with rowdiness. From where he stood, G thought he could see a puppeteer just off the circus grounds, gathering a crowd.

Relaxation was out of the question. In the course of ten minutes, Gregor had gone from easy amusement to quasi-despair. He knew Wittgenstein was just trying to get the children to think and reason, perhaps even, as in his book, to get them to understand there are some things that resist thinking, reason and discussion. The notion that there was a fixed, definable, human nature had gone out with the Renaissance, when the radicals proclaimed the essence of man's nature was having no nature, that human behavior was not bound by the laws of other creatures, that man, unlike the animals, the plants, the rocks, was capable of taking responsibility for his own actions. Such was the corollary of free will: no fixed human nature.

But if human character is infinitely plastic, what is to stop these children from being entirely sculpted by the strapping and pommeling of their elders? He carried one such wound in his own back, unhealing, a permanent crater in his soul. The Jews killed Christ, so why not babies? And won't revenge be sweet when the baby-killers are themselves ground to flour and blood, and eaten communally on some grotesque, high holiday of the future? G wasn't frightened for himself, or even for the future victims; he was aghast at the potential for the race — autonomous individuals "making" themselves and their children, independent of ancient "laws" of nature and human nature, building history from malignant scares and the scars of the woodshed.

Ten minutes until the first show. His talk on Einstein would never do, that ebullient, funny, optimistic man. What was pounding in his ganglia was the verse he studied yesterday for English, a new poem by Robert Frost, just published, and newly presented to him by Amadeus, the seductive schoolmarm.

Some say the world will end in fire,
Some say in ice.
From what I've tasted of desire
I hold with those who favor fire.
But if it had to perish twice,
I think I know enough of hate
To say that for destruction ice
Is also great
And would suffice.

He had looked up "suffice": *genügen*, "to meet or satisfy a need". What was the need? What was the great need for destruction, for self-destruction? Was autonomy, the power to exercise free will, the trigger? Was humanity nursing the infant perception of the need for its own demise?

The audience was gathering. From the floor of the cage he watched them assemble, glaring at chest level, trying to see into the hearts of the adults, staring at head level, trying to peer into the skulls of the children. He saw them as Roentgen might have seen them, a greatsmall shuffling of pulsing, shadowy interiors. He glared and he stared. His many eyes roamed the crowd, trying to recognize something, somebody. Nothing. Nobody.

Gregor looked at the clock, walked slowly over to the lectern, raised himself up, and gripped the top with his front claws. He looked for a long time out into the audience — and said nothing. The crowd waited. A child said, "Mommy, when is it going to talk?" and everyone laughed. And they waited again. Gregor scanned the room. Is he sick? What is this? A few people at the back began to leave. Then — very slowly — he said his poem, the one about fire and ice, and crawled back to his private space.

9. Tractatus Logico-Philosophicus

The knocking woke him. Thick darkness over all the land. Even darkness that might be felt.

"Come in."

The cage door creaked. Dark.

"Herr Samsa, are you all right?"

Lantern light. Deserted lot.

"Who is it?"

"Wittgenstein. Remember? From this morning?"

"Yes. The children. I fell asleep."

Gregor pushed himself up, and put on his crimson robe.

"There was a sign outside, NO SHOW TODAY DUE TO ILLNESS."

"Who put that up?" Gregor asked.

"I don't know. I thought you did."

"Maybe I did. I don't remember. Come in."

"I can't see in the dark."

"So frail a thing is man. Here, I'll light the lamp."

Gregor crept over to the table, found the matches, and lit the kerosene lantern. Wittgenstein made his way through straw over to the single chair in the room, a wicker rocker, the Guest's Chair.

"May I sit down?"

"Please. Coffee?"

"I'd prefer tea if you have it. Cambridge, you know."

"I'll put up the water. What brings you?"

"You invited me. There was a lot unsaid after Fräulein Schlüsselberger's Satanic syllogism."

"Ah, yes." G's consciousness was returning. " Jew human. Gregor Jew. Therefore, Gregor human."

"I believe the predicate object was 'vermin'."

"Vermin. Human. What's the difference?"

"That *is* the question, isn't it?" Gregor took a glass from the cupboard, and cut a slice of lemon.

"What did you all come up with over lunch?"

"We came up with an appropriate amount of confusion." Wittgenstein struggled out of his brown leather jacket, and hung it neatly on the back of the chair.

"Are you enjoying yourself up there in the mountains?" Gregor asked.

"No." The schoolteacher sat down, and crossed his legs. "It's entirely disagreeable."

"How is that?" Gregor brought the tea.

"May I have some milk, please? The other teachers, the parish priest, almost everyone is completely hateful to me. My 'colleagues' are unbearably pretentious with their so-called learning, and with how much more they know about teaching than I. Virulent, bogus intellectualism stuffed into stuffed shirts. Old school and New school..."

Gregor brought a small pitcher of milk. "What's 'new school'?"

"Oh, you know — Glöckel's reform tactics: 'The child is an active being whose mind is more than an bucket to be filled with information.' Of course it's true, but there's nothing like some boxing of the ears or pulling of the hair to motivate them. They whine and yell, but they like it. And they learn better."

"You're not a hit with the gentle reformists, I can tell. You'll get in trouble hitting children these days. "

Gregor settled his length down on the floor in front of his guest.

"The worst are the parents, hardly reformists. They love it when we're strict, and they don't complain about corporal punishment — except when *I* do it."

"You must strike them as odder than most. Odd People hitting children *verboten*." "

"They don't give a damn about their children. Want them to be farm hands, period." Wittgenstein placed his tea precariously on the arm of the rocker.

"So how did you finesse this trip to the big city? There's a hit song in America right now — *'How you gonna keep 'em down on the farm, after they've seen Paree?'*"

"Precisely. My star pupil, Oskar Fuchs…"

"He wasn't with the group…"

"His mother didn't want him to go to Vienna with 'the crazy man'. And Emmerich Koderhold's father doesn't want him to become 'an intellectual'. So they're not here. Then there's Gruber. I was giving him private lessons after school. The boy is a gifted mathematician."

"I know. His parents thought it was more important for him to be home helping with the milking." Wittgenstein gestured to indicate the obvious.

"Do you mind if I smoke?"

"Yes. The straw. My spiracles…" Wittgenstein put his pipe back in his jacket pocket.

"Any attempt I make to take the children beyond customary expectations is completely misunderstood and resisted. They think I'm a monster for keeping their children — those who are willing to stay — after school, or calling them back at night for astronomy lessons."

"It sounds frustrating."

"These people are loathsome worms, not human at all, half animal, half human."

"You sound angry."

"Odious and base."

"What about the children? You seem to get on well with them."

"I work well with the gifted ones, and they with me. But I'm a bit of a tyrant with the slow ones. I know ruthless honesty can seem cruel and sadistic, particularly when I offer it uninvited. But I just can't see why they're not interested in anything, the blockheads! The world is so fascinating. And hilarious. Trying to fathom it with our pitiful thought is such a comical spectacle — David sans slingshot vs. Goliath triumphant."

"But they're not interested…or amused?"

"Some are. A few. Fuchs, Koderhold and Gruber make it worthwhile. Somewhat worthwhile."

"Why do you continue?"

"You'll laugh. To help the peasants improve themselves, enrich their inner lives and better cope with the disaster. To lift them out of the muck."

"Tolstoy and his serfs."

"They're not my serfs, but Tolstoy, yes, definitely. Look, here." The visitor pulled a small, ragged volume from his jacket.

"Tolstoy's 'Tales for Children'? You carry them around in your pocket?"

"Bedtime stories. We read and discuss them. I carry them when I travel. They protect me."

"From what?"

"From stupidity, callousness, impetuosity, elegance." He placed the book on the floor. Gregor leafed slowly through the pages.

"Nice drawings. What's this one: 'How Much Land Does A Man Need.'?"

"James Joyce — you've heard of him?" Gregor nodded.

"Joyce thought that story was the greatest piece of literature in the world."

"What's it about?"

"What are all great stories about? Over-reach. Greed. The idiot hero is offered as much land as he can walk round in a day."

"Say no more. But why elegance?" G pursued. "You said Tolstoy protected you from elegance."

Wittgenstein took a sip from his cooling tea. "My family is still one of the richest in Europe."

"I had heard that."

"From?"

"Amadeus."

"Who is he?"

"The owner of the circus."

"Ah, Hoffnung, he of the great hope."

"I find him less and less hopeful. He's dying, you know."

"So are we all. What is he dying from?"

"Something called Werner's Syndrome, a type of premature aging. Not understood. No cure."

"I suffer from something similar."

"You? You look fine."

"You can't see my brain. Or my soul. I'm stupid and I'm rotten. May God help me! I'm barely awake enough to know I'm dreaming, and I can't wake up any more. I try hard, my dream body moves, but my real one doesn't stir. Decent people like you wouldn't understand such a fundamental deficiency."

"Why don't you go back to philosophy? Why is someone like you teaching grade school in a tiny provincial village with tiny provincial minds?"

'I've said everything I have to say. I'm bored now, my mind is no longer flexible. I can't write any more. And I hate philosophy books and philosophers. A waste of ink and paper and time and air. I just want to work as a gardener, or a nurse's aide, or something useful like that. I know it sounds queer, but my spring has run dry. Werner's Syndrome of the soul, I suppose. It's the way things are. I had three brothers commit suicide. " He picked up a blade of straw at his feet, and examined it carefully.

"And you?" asked G.

"Will I join my brothers? I'll let you know."

"6 comma 43." Gregor's response.

"What?"

"6 comma 43: 'The world of the happy man is a different one from that of the unhappy man.'"

"You *have* got the damn thing memorized! Well, 6 comma 431! Take that!"

"'At death, the world does not alter, but comes to an end.'" Gregor's giant neurons firing away. Wittgenstein was astonished. "I don't have the book memorized," said G, "but I went over the final sections quite carefully. And since I'm a slow reader, things burn in. The last few pages seem far more important to me than the preceding sixty."

"Of course."

"Of course? I'll bet it's not obvious to a lot of people. The science-above-all-ists will jump on the first 5/6ths and ignore the end. You're going to wind up king of a most foreign country. You wait and see."

"Most of the book is my careful building and slow climbing of a ladder which gets me up to the view at the end. Then I kick away the ladder, and..."

"And the world snatches it up and casts it in gold-plated concrete — to worship. 'What we cannot speak about we must pass over in silence'. You know how that's going to be interpreted? 'Mystics shut your traps, and stop wasting our precious time with nonsense.'"

"I'll be sorry if that's the way it turns out. It's all I could come up with. On the other hand, what does it matter? Solving philosophical problems achieves very, very little, nothing of importance. You know what's important? Austerity, manual labor — humanly useful work, and music. Maybe heart will understand, even if reason is ignorant and speechless. It's all beyond my strength."

"I know this is presumptuous — I hardly know you, after all, and I'm only an insect — but I think it's exactly your strength. You have a unique gift for examples, and for posing pregnant puzzles. But the *Tractatus* as it stands will set up science as the supreme authority of knowable truth. Why not rethink it in looser terms? Get beyond scientific propositions the way Einstein went beyond Special Relativity. How does everyday language work? What we're talking now. Are there different kinds of facts — and not just 'fact'? Surely there's some kind of truth in the huge gap between rigorous-proposition 4 comma 3621 and your "unspeakable", some kind of truth in the sky, the soil, the bed, in the broader forms of life."

"I'm not up to it. It's too tricky. Shifting. No cage. Lions bite your head off. I'm tired. I can't do it." Wittgenstein got up and began pacing. Gregor had to turn to follow him.

"Why aren't you up to it? There are different ways to know. Music is one of them. You said it was important. Work on that."

"Music is unspeakable."

"So? Does it have meaning?"

"Yes."

"How does it mean?"

"It's another species."

"I'm another species. Is there meaning for me?"

Wittgenstein sat down, and stared at G.

"I don't know," the fourth-grade teacher said. "Answers usually show up as questions. What are your questions?"

Silence. Gregor pondered while his guest stared at the iridescence of his eyes.

"I have only one question:" said Gregor. "Why are humans more bestial than beasts?" Wittgenstein waited. Gregor: "Rilke says it's because they're always outside, looking in."

"And you, the non-human?"

"I feel like I'm inside looking out."

"But your view is blocked."

"And blurred."

"By what?"

"I don't know. Hybrid. Vestigial. Something. And whenever I try to get that view, the hole in my back begins to ooze and burn. Look."

Gregor lifted the back of his robe. The brown stain in the gauze dressing was slowly expanding.

"Perhaps you shouldn't try."

"Yet another thing to be passed over in silence?"

"There's lots to be passed over silence! Almost *everything* should be passed over in silence. Silence deep as death."

"Then how would you change..."

Wittgenstein jumped up out of his chair. The glass of tea fell off the arm, and crashed to the floor, one more spreading brown stain.

"Forgive me. I'm sorry."

"Straw on the floor. A marvelous, if primitive, invention. It will dry."

"Look," said the reluctant philosopher, "you're clever enough to see the pattern. Knowledge brings pain. Period. It's done so since Eve and the apple. It killed Dr. Faustus — the real Faust, not Goethe's apologistic hodge-podge. It destroyed Dr. Frankenstein, and did in Dr. Jekyll. Doctor, doctor, doctor! Doctors are supposed to heal! There's enough pain in the world. We don't need more doctors to make it worse. Insatiable greed for knowing everything, for explaining, for predicting and manipulating. Unrestricted quest for knowledge, unbridled imagination, unlimited investigation with inadequate language, incomplete tools, scant preparation."

"The Sorcerer's Apprentice."

"Exactly. The myth of our time. The word. What is the magic word, the spell that will turn things off once we've turned them on?" He was pacing excitedly now, kicking the straw in front of him. "This war. Not just the *technos* of it — the so-called thinking behind it. The management of mass destruction..."

"You sound like your friend Russell."

"God save us! Russell! A World Organization for Peace and Freedom! I'd rather establish a World Organization for War and Slavery, just so it could be better thought out, more consistent with the little we know, and not get in the way of Justice."

"I see."

"You don't see. You and your quest. Curiosity will kill the roach — and perhaps a lot of others."

He sat down hard, as if in the hyper-field of his own gravity.

"May I get you some more tea?"

"Yes, please. No. Forget it. I'm already too excited."

"As you will."

"I'll predict for you how it will go, this cultural death-wish we are enacting in our ineluctable attraction to apocalypse. We seek to know, we seek some kind of absolute liberation, even suspecting it will lead to absolute destruction. It out-Spenglers Spengler: this cycle will have no successors. This is the final decline — of the west and the east and the north and the south, the physical, moral, spiritual torture and death of the totality of beings. You laugh. But we're coming to see that our only real, predictable tool — reason — is simply and totally inadequate. And our Faustian search for transcendence, yes, will send us beyond the delusion of reason — but directly into the sphere of total violence. "

"It's possible," Gregor allowed.

"It's certain. And the most reasonable will produce the most violence. Mark my word. There will be scientists who, in the calm and cool of seminar rooms will hatch the egg of world destruction. And you, dear Chitinous Apprentice, will see it come to pass. Do you know the poet Thomas Stearns Eliot? Has your diminutive Mentor fed you any of his poison? He has a new poem in which he asks, 'After such knowledge what forgiveness?'"

"I have it, I think. I remember that line. I haven't studied it yet." G scuttled back to his bed chamber and returned with the latest issue of the *Times Literary Supplement*, a subscription gift from Amadeus. "Here it is. Page 37. "Gerontion", correct? What is "gerontion"? I'll look it up."

"You won't find it. Here, read this part."

Think now
History has many cunning passages, contrived corridors
And issues, deceives with whispering ambition,
Guides us by vanities. Think now
She gives when our attention is distracted
And what she gives, gives with such supple confusions
That the giving famishes the craving.

"What is 'craving'?"

"*Gieriges Verlangen.* Greedy desire. Gluttonous demand."

"I know it."

"I'm sure you do."

Gregor walked to the kitchen and poured himself a glass of milk.

"What does it mean? The poem."

"What do you think it means?"

Gregor put down his milk, and walked behind the curtain. He returned with a yellow envelope.

"I seem to have won tickets for a trip to the United States."

"Maybe you should go. Large cockroaches are suspect enough here, and large Jewish cockroaches...You are Jewish, I assume."

"Jewish enough for Fräulein Schlüsselberger to recognize me: 'Jews are vermin, and isn't a cockroach vermin?'. Remember?"

"I do indeed."

"Do you think I should go? And if I like it, should I stay? Leave Europe?"

"Look, Herr Samsa..."

"Call me Gregor, please."

"I'm not comfortable doing that."

"Herr Samsa then."

"The Grand Plot Menu consists of only two major items: Column A: Jewish-Classical-Christian. Column B: Darwinian. There are no others. Which do you choose?"

"What has that got to do with going to America?"

"If you choose Plot A — the naked rule of power eventually transforming to Justice under Law, recognizing the dignity of all persons under a benevolent God, an emergent morality of altruism — if you believe that story in the face of the last ten years, then stay. You'll be cared for and rewarded. On the other hand, if you subscribe to Life emerging out of primal slime and fighting its way upward via fittest dog eat less-fit dog, then perhaps you should make yourself scarce — you will be crushed and eaten. If you believe the Great War was a mere catharsis of the ascending spirit, a purgation toward health, then stay. If you believe it was an pathognomic sign of moribund corruption..."

"I don't know what I believe."

"I don't know what I believe either. But for me, it doesn't matter; I'm finished either way. You on the other hand — perhaps you should decide. Is going to America part of your quest?"

"Who knows? Maybe everything is part of my quest."

"Incurable. Another unhealing wound."

Wittgenstein stood, put his glass on the stove, and put on his leather jacket.

"You're going?"

"Shepherding nine-year olds is a taxing affair for this vessel of iniquity. They'll be swarming in five hours. Thanks for your advice on my work. My ex-work. And good luck. Give my regards to Broadway. And Apprentice Samsa, remember one thing in your quest."

"And that is?"

"Pray for ignorance."

And Wittgenstein walked down the steps, and out into the night, trailing straw from his immaculate cuffs.

10. Go West, Young Roach, Go West

Cockroaches have no eyelids. If you had no eyelids, could you sleep? Sleep well? Sleep, he assured me, was a problem for Gregor. It had been a problem when he was a fabric salesman in Prague, and it continued to be a problem in his second career. The new electric street lamps, recently installed by the City of Vienna, made things worse, shining their bright modernity into his cage.

In insects as in humans, light has a kinetic effect, stimulating movement and heightened consciousness. Gregor's 5 million year old nervous system had not evolved to deal with the output of incandescent tungsten. The light made him nervous, and nervous roaches have a hard time sleeping.

Do roaches sleep? you ask. Of course roaches sleep. Roaches are human. I mean, this roach...

Time out. Forgive me. It's late, and I myself am sleepy. Let me go get a cup of tea.

Back again. I feel better. Roaches. Sleep. To sleep, perchance to dream.

Granted, G was special, the mother (father?) of all hybrid phenomena. Still, his new life was at least partially governed by the constraints of his new anatomy and physiology. Roaches do sleep, if you will grant that periodic states of resting inactivity constitute sleep. Indeed, G and I, in our time together on the mesa, did some experimentation to try to compare human and blattid sleep. It is surprising that such work had not been done before by the large community of entomologists. A search through the indices of approximately 400 insect books at the University of New Mexico library yielded only one reference (Wigglesworth, *The Principles of Insect Physiology,* J. Wiley, 1934, p.313): a half page section on "Reflex immobilization, hypnosis, &c", clearly inadequate to describe Gregor's nightly experience.

Cockroaches, of course, are most often nocturnal, and urban species especially so, in their adaptation to the living patterns of their human hosts. In a natural sequence of light and dark, *Periplaneta americanus* undergoes a marked increase of activity around dusk, five or six hours of intense foraging, and then gradual quiescence until the next nightfall. The extended light of modern urban life shifts the biological clock until "lights out", at which time the same rhythm begins, but with a shorter recovery period. Such a shift, I'm sure is difficult enough, inducing a kind of permanent jet lag and fatigue. But how much more difficult was Gregor's task of actually reversing normal rhythm: eighteen hours of activity and six dormant, instead of the other way around. Imagine being required to reduce your sleep by two thirds — chronically. That way lies psychosis.

Gregor performed heroically in his new role, but he needed deep sleep when he could get it. To that end, Lindauer's eyeglasses performed their second, and perhaps more important, function: they masked the light from all but six of his 4,000 odd ommatidia, greatly reducing sensory input, and allowing for deep, restorative sleep characteristic of a non-REM, stage four condition.

Our Los Alamos experiments yielded some fascinating, entirely unexpected results: REM — rapid eye movements — are, of course, out of the question given the structure of the insect compound eye. Occasional gross head twitching does not signal the same neurophysiological state, and could occur anywhere in G's sleep cycle. But, as some rough electroencephalography showed quite clearly, REM or not, there was a 90 minute cycling period of low-voltage, mixed-frequency EEG patterns, at least superficially similar to those of wakefulness, accompanied by a higher respiration rate, increased blood pressure (as indicated by an impromptu sphygmomanometer rig around the abdomen), and more bodily movement. In the interest of Science, G gave me permission to report another characteristic typical of REM sleep: commonly full or partial penile erection.

In short, Gregor exhibited all the objective characteristics of REM sleep — without human eyes. Previous insect physiology, when it concerned itself with insect sleep at all, had identified only a kind of reflex inhibition secondary to thigmotaxis, pressure of certain hairs triggering a quieting response, or akinesis, occasionally functioning as thanatosis or death-feigning, so as to be overlooked by predators. One particularly sadistic experimenter — these were the days before the animal rights movement — actually cut such thanatosic insects in half at mid-thorax, and found the posterior fragment quickly recovering its activity, while the anterior fragment remained in catalepsis. He concluded that such nervous control resided in the brain, and proudly published his discovery in the *Australian Journal of Entomology*. How *he* slept at night, I don't know.

Gregor's, however, was no simple reflex, but a complex physiological state which, as in REM sleep, entailed elaborate dreaming. Although he spent many hours describing his fascinating dreams, there is one particular dream which I must report here.

It was on the night of May 1st, 1923, twelve days after his encounter with Wittgenstein. Gregor remembered this date clearly, because every May 1st since childhood, he had read (or had read to him) Anderson's marvelous story, "The Old Oak Tree's Last Dream." He read it yearly in commemoration of the May fly in the story, whose entire life encompassed only one day, who was intimately familiar with death, but happy, almost joyous, nevertheless. Even as a child, that attitude had struck him as a heroic achievement, something to be memorized deep within, and practiced when his own time would — inevitably — come. There had also been workers parading in the streets, shouting and waving red flags.

Throughout the ages, dreams have fascinated dreamer and hearer alike, have been understood as divine message, as predictive announcement, as cure for disease, as fantastic extension of the waking state, and as "the royal road to the unconscious" — as the good doctor from Berggasse 19 so often insisted. But Gregor's May Day experience may have added another category to the understanding of the dream state. Maybe, maybe not.

It was 11PM on a Wednesday. He had been reading Russell on Einstein, hoping to find a new pedagogical angle to liven up his deteriorating act. The Oak Tree's flying dream lay open after his earlier annual re-read. It would take him a while to fall asleep, and as was often his habit in warm weather, he went out into the beauty of the night to walk the dark, quiet streets of the Meidling district. When he turned the corner of Niederhoffstrasse, he experienced a sensation difficult for him to describe. He, of course, did not have the comparison, but it seemed to me similar to how those of us who frequent modern airports feel when we walk along at normal pace on a moving beltway, and the world whizzes by us, as if we were wearing seven league boots. When we step from the rolling rubber to the marble floor, we experience a jolt in time, a radical, always unanticipatable de-acceleration, spacetime dragged in friction. It takes a dozen or so steps before our world resynchronizes with the world around.

The first time it happened, G though he might have had too much to drink. But a bottle of Zipfer Dunkle had never affected him before. Perhaps it was an ear infection. But he had no ears. The second time it happened, he became afraid: what if this were the first sign of some degenerative disease, a subject he had thought a lot about since meeting Amadeus. Though he did not know the physiology, these were thoughts well taken. Hyperreactivity of the giant abdominal ganglia, hypersecretion of acetylcholine by the corpora cardiaca, or of serotonin from the CNS — recent work on *Periplaneta* has shown the power of minute neurohormone concentrations to create profound physiological changes — even in mammals.

By the fourth episode, he began to play with the sensation. It seemed to come and go — could he control it? He found he could bring on the phenomena at will by performing a kind of Valsalva maneuver, contracting his abdomen as he did to hiss an audience to silence, while at the same time shutting down his spiracles to prevent the egress of air. Within a few seconds, the world began to speed by, and his own spacetime seemed expanded and slow. Expansion.

Easy speed. Flight. Why not flight? He had wings...why not use them? But he never had done so. They were folded under his hard external wings, the chitinous tegmentum which ran the length of his back. He loosed the cape from around his neck, extracted his front legs from his jacket and wiggled out of the diaper-like affair he wore so as not embarrass his human public. Naked, he was, in the Viennese night. A warm, late spring breeze. The pleasure was overwhelming. He took a huge breath of the Daphnescented air, and valsalva'd himself into a state of electrifying dizziness. As long as he did not move, neither did the world. And his abdominal exertion opened a saggital split along his back, loosing the apex fold and anal lobe of his virginal hindwings. The wind had picked up from the west, blowing over the gardens of the Schönbrunn Palace, drying the delicate lace of his newly unfolded parts. G crossed the Ruckergasse intersection and stood, facing the broad western view. Could he fly? He would try a run down toward the palace. If, once aloft, he had to make a crash landing, it would be better to come down in the softness of the gardens than in the potentially lethal traffic of Wienzeile Linke. Taking another in-breath, he bore down hard against the closed sphincters of all 24 spiracles, began to trot, then to canter; his wings began to hum. The world roared by in fierce, thrilling distortion. Liftoff! It was easy! With a two foot wide body, and four foot wings, his wingspread was a full ten feet, as wide as that of the largest condor, but carrying only half the body weight. The superior leverage of internally attached muscles lifted him easily, farther than he had intended. By using his lower abdomen as an aileron, he was able to lower himself to a altitude of a hundred feet or so, cruising over the park, its statues, its fountains and zoo. "West," he thought, "I'm headed west, the land of evening, the direction of decline. West. Quest."

Although they are strong flyers, roaches are not particularly good navigators. Actually, Gregor was heading north. And a good thing, too, for after some minutes of confusion, he saw the Danube below, a silver streak in the moonlight, beginning its great, unmistakable curve to the west at Klosterneuberg. At Tulln, the broad and placid river narrowed into a restless twist of currents, and between Krems and Melk lay the legend-haunted valley of the Wachau, the historic, often-contested corridor between east and west, with its castles and fortresses, monasteries and abbeys at every bend of the river, its wine-growing villages and forested slopes spread out left and right below as Gregor flew, now southwesterly, upriver towards Linz. The struggle between water and rock had begun early in creation. In the Wachau, the contest continued mightily, with hidden granite hurdles bringing forth great liquid leaps, and bays and inlets colonizing would-be land. The Wachau by moonlight. Had life ever been more beautiful?

Gregor was without fatigue or fear. Why turn back? Why not go all the way? But where was all the way? America. To the west. He looked around and saw Polaris behind him, to his right. He banked, lifted his tail, and began to climb with greater velocity, ever upwards, into Minkowskian space. Geodesics. Great circles. Gravitational bending of spacetime. Einstein had imagined it; Eddington had proved it; Gregor would harness it. He was free, victim no more of the profound, once-absolute embrace of gravity's prison. With no force "pulling" him, but only free trajectory in the mass-induced curvature of space, he would use his wings against it, he would hook his claws into spacetime, and as climbers hook crampons and picks into vertical walls of ice, he would navigate his own terrain. Free will! If humanity was too confused to understand, let a Blattid lead the way! Newton's determined universe was no more, "objective" states were unmasked as the illusions they were. Reality was determined by the observer, by him, by Gregor, and Gregor alone. Above the atmosphere, he peered out at red-shifting galaxies, beckoning him on. More of space, less of time, more of time, less of space, Machian stars structuring spacetime merely by existing. The dark backward and abysm of time, Shakespeare called it. Back to the primordial ylem.

Across the Arctic Circle he flew, elliptical, tireless, inspired, rolling along the non-Euclidian structure of spacetime, past and future simultaneously present, equivalent, indeterminable. Greenland, then Baffin Island below, slightly off-course, as is usual for a roach, but crashing into nothing other than his own sense of awe. The moon was no more, northern Quebec an unbroken darkness. He drew his head upwards, shielded many of his eyes under his pronotum, and hurtled, almost blind, into the Riemannian space of the earth's atmosphere. The lights of Quebec City called him back. The fading glimmer of Montreal, the Adirondacks and the Greens framing daybreak over Lake Champlain. Was that Albany to his right? He was weak on smaller American cities. But there, ahead, what did he see by the dawn's early light? Manhattan Island. And the Long Island. He had studied the maps. It was New York!

"I may be like a marble rolling along a curved rubber spacetime surface," he thought, "but unless I do some fancy navigating here, I'm going to be one squashed Periplaneta." Cautious with his new skills, he maneuvered himself over the broadness of the Hudson, between Nyack and Tarrytown.

He spread his wings, lowered his tail against the wind, and as he stalled, his velocity cut to 75 mph, he swooped down into active flight over Yonkers and the West Bronx. The clock on the Times Tower said 5h30. Gregor needed a place to land, but was wary of the streets with their early morning traffic and unpredictable culture. Even though New York had hosted the Gregor Olympics, New Yorkers had never actually seen a 5' 10" cockroach. And G had heard that in New York, roaches were considered "a problem", the same as Jews at home.

He looked around for the tallest building he could see, and there it was, on 23rd St and Madison Ave. He didn't know it was on 23rd and Madison, but he saw it clearly all the same, a tall skyscraper, the recently completed 50 floors of the Metropolitan Life Insurance Building, the tallest building in the world, modeled after the Campanile of San Marco in Venice. He had seen pictures of it. Or were they pictures of the Campanile of San Marco in Venice?

G eased down on the diagonal green brass roofing, taking the impact smartly and evenly on all six of his powerful legs. Was he here? In New York? Or was this a dream? He looked east toward the sun, and saw the Long Island stretching away into the distance. He looked west, and saw the mighty Hudson, and north and saw the great Central Park, just a few miles away. Being on the north side of the building, he couldn't see south. While he sat for a few minutes, crouched on the roofing, resting, thinking, a bi-plane circled in for a closer look.

What did he think? He couldn't remember. He was not thinking in words. He was not thinking in images. He heard no music in his head. It was as if he had left a mass of intellectual energy behind in the heavens, energy which was only now reloading in his brain in no discernible sequence, soaking his nervous system all at once, the way a spill might fill a sponge. And all of a sudden he felt tired, exhausted, hollow. He hooked his foreclaws into a seam in the brass, and passed out.

Gregor told me about his May Day dream on May Day, 1945, two and a half months before Trinity. He called it a dream; I accepted it as such. But later that year, as executor of his papers, I discovered an envelop of train tickets, Vienna-London-Vienna, and a first class ticket on the *Mauretania*, London-New York-London — all unused.

NEW YORK

11. Metamorphosis III: The Roach American

Some four centuries before the birth of Christ, the Taoist sage Chuang Tzu wrote of a famous dream:

Once Chuang Tzu dreamt he was a butterfly, a butterfly flitting and fluttering around, happy with himself and doing as he pleased. He didn't know he was Chuang Tzu. Suddenly he woke up and there he was, solid and unmistakable Chuang Tzu. But he didn't know if he was Chuang Tzu who had dreamt he was a butterfly, or a butterfly dreaming he was Chuang Tzu.

How charmingly malicious. Even its author objects: "Between Chuang Tzu and a butterfly there must be some distinction!" But no, he concludes, there is no distinction. The dream is told in a chapter "On Making All Things Equal."

The principle theme of Chuang Tzu's classic is, simply put, freedom. How can one live freely in a world dominated by suffering, chaos, and absurdity? Many Chinese sages proposed social reforms, political changes, new ethical norms to cure humanity of its ills, to free its inhabitants for creative, mutually beneficial lives. Such was Gregor's nebulous plan, made compelling by his general condition, and urgent by his wound. Chuang Tzu would have shaken his head and chuckled. For G was in exactly his dreamer's situation. Was he Gregor Samsa the cockroach, or Gregor Samsa the fabric salesman dreaming he was Gregor Samsa the cockroach?

Kafka's original report comes down firmly on the matter. Nowhere does he state that Gregor was dreaming, hallucinating, or mad. Nor are G's family or other witnesses presented as anything but normal individuals confronted with a decidedly abnormal phenomenon. There is no dream-like pre-logic in his report. Indeed, Kafka goes so far as to tell us, unequivocally, right at the beginning, "It was no dream."

But Kafka was wrong before, as G's subsequent story has shown. His opinion on the matter is therefore little more valuable than yours. The question remains — the question of home — at all levels. Who is home? What is home? When is home? Where is home? Why is home? Or as Heidegger might ask: What is it to dwell?" And as he might answer: "Dwelling is the manner in which mortals are on the earth."

Of Heidegger, more — much more — later.

G was mortal, presumably, and on earth, and was thus perturbed by these matters. Together, we spent much time investigating them. Our discussions (could it be because I am a historian?) often took place inside a triangular corral whose posts and vertices were Santayana, Marx, and Nietzsche. Or rather three related, gnomic notions of each, to wit:

1. "Those who cannot remember the past are condemned to repeat it."

2. "... all great world-historic facts and personages appear, so to speak, twice... the first time as tragedy, the second time as farce."

3. "Eternal recurrence". Nietzsche asks how we would tolerate the infinite repetition, without the slightest change, of each and every moment of our lives. Most of us would find this horrifying; we would all like to edit and patch what was false and broken. A person who could accept eternal recurrence without self-deception or evasion would be an *Übermensch*, an "overman" whose distance from the ordinary man is greater than the distance between human and ape.

By the time we met, Gregor's life was replete with remarkable foreshadowings. The Equal Rights Amendment drive of 1923, and that of our own time. The Scopes Trial, and our current bouts with "Creation Science". Wittgenstein's Turing Test and Turing's own, a quarter century later. A hundred thousand earthquake deaths in Tokyo, in 1923, and the repeat body count of Hiroshima.

More fascinating than looking backwards was the guessing game of how this or that as-yet-unrepeated event would show up again. As condemnation? As farce? As changeless and unbearable? Gregor, with his European sensibilities, was responsive to each nuance of irony, to every shade of recursiveness and repetition. He scouted out every pattern of history, every Spenglerian mini-cycle in his reading and his life. Was he to be *Übermensch* or *Üntermensch*, conquerer or victim? Or was he doomed to be just *Nebenmensch*, neither above, nor below, but standing always to the side, unable to join or affect the human throng?

I have in hand a shabby, accordion-fold filer in which my friend, ignoring the alphabetical divisions, put his notes, photos, clippings and other chronological memorabilia of his American incarnation. These records begin with a letter home — or at least a letter to the friends left behind. It was never sent. Why, I'm not sure. Possibly because the scratchy, almost illegible scrawl was embarrassing to him. It was written on hotel stationary, and reads (in German)

The Occidental Hotel

243 W. 43rd St.

New York 36, N.Y.

(here his hand writing begins)

3 August 1923

Dear Amadeus, Anne Marie, and Mr. Kramar, Mr. Klofac, and Mr. Soukup:

It is now one week since my disappearance, and the thought of your confusion and perhaps disappointment has been weighing heavily on me hour by hour day by day, and so I...

[Here the German breaks off, and the letter begins again in English, on the same paper, now clearly a draft]

Dear —

Now is pass one week since I am disappeared, and I am expecting your confusion and maybe disinpointment [sic.] very heavy, even sad. So on this one week education of me in sad America, of Mr. President Harding [illegible] and unexpectd sick. I will to ...

Here the page breaks off. These fragments are interesting only inasmuch as they show the humble, guilt-laden origins of what became his extraordinary compilation of two decades of "the American experience", seen through the compound eyes of a stranger doubly foreign. It will be a while before he comments on the legacy of Harding and his friends.

The next document is typed in capital letters on yet another sheet of letterhead:

10 MAY 1924 EXCELENT MACHINE NOT HARD TO OPERATEING. LONG TIME TAKING TO FIND LETTERS, BUT I GET BETTER QUICKLY ALREADILY. DEAR AMADEUS, ANNE MARIE NO I WAIT UNTIL IS EASIER THAT I CAN WRITE A GOOD AND INFORMATION LETTER.

This is the last we hear of G's intentions to write home. Perhaps he simply wrote a letter and sent it, although a year before his death, as he prepared to join the Alsos Mission, he was wondering about re-meeting Kramar, Klofac, and Soukup without ever having contacted them. Amadeus and Anne Marie would by then have been dead. In any case, at this point, the file finds its purpose; it becomes a looseleaf diary of Gregor's thoughts and experiences. The next ten pages are taken up with his language studies. Some selections:

SWELL, CUTE - TERMS OF PRAISE (PRIMA, NIEDLICH, SUESS?)

SHUT UP - DISMISSNG, KEEP YOUR TRAP SHUT, BUTTON UP YOUR LIP TELL IT TO THE MARINES (MARINES HERE, GRANDMA BEI UNS!)

BOOZE=DRUGS?

DOPE=GOSSIP, BUT ALSO DRUGS.

DISMISSING - DUMBBELL (LKE EXERCISING MACHINE)

SKREWY, NUTS, A RUBE, A SUCKER (SAUGEN???)

....

MANY WORDS FOR MONEY: DOUGH AND BREAD, TWO BITS (OF WHAT?) SAWBUCK

(NOT IN DICTIONARY), MAZOOLA (GOOD!), MAKE LOTS OF MAZOOLA

CORNY (MAIS-LICH?)

KEEP SMILING. (SOMETIMES HARD TO DO AND WHO WOULD KNOW?)

....

LIKING OF ANIMALS, NOT ALL INSECTS. BEES GOOD - BEES KNEES = SOME ONE IS EXCELLENT, PRIMA

ALSO LIKING OF CATS - CATS MEOW, CATS PAJAMAS (DO CATS CARRY PAMAJAS HERE? MAYBE IN RICH HOME, CATS WHISKERS, GLAMOR PUSS

```
BAD INSECTS BUG-EYE BETTY AN UGLY GIRL

MORE MONEY - SIMOLEON, SCRATCH, JACK

TARANTULA JUICE = HOMEMADE LIKER. (GOOD OR BAD?), ALSO HAIR
OF THE DOG???

NOTHING YET ABOUT COCKROACHES, THOUGH I HEAR THERE A MANY,
BUT NOT HERE IN HOTEL

BUTTERFLYS BOOTS = GOOD

MORE DEROGATION: JEW = KIKE, MOKKIE, NEGRO = DINJ, JIG,
JIGABOO, NIGGER, BOHUNK=SOMEONE FROM CENTRAL EUROPE SO I GUESS
THAT IS ME, GREGOR BOHUNK!

YOU'RE THE SNAKES HIPS ??   ELEPHANT'S EYEBROWS. YOU SAY
ANTYTHING HERE AND IT MEAN WHAT YOU WANT DEPENDING HOW YOU SAY
IT.....
```

By the way, I still have G's typewriter in a closet at work. It's past the junk stage, and is now appreciating in value as an artifact in the history of technology: a genuine 1877 Remington Model One — not to mention its having belonged to Gregor Samsa. Where he picked up a forty year old machine only God knows, but it was perfect — just what he needed. In the very next year Remington brought out the Model Two — featuring a shift-key — which would have created insuperable problems. As it was, he had to engage each key with his two front legs (raised key frames were helpful), and then snap up quickly on his hind legs to achieve the quick pressure that would spring the hammer-lever. He was far too large to use the now-famous "archie" method of springing down on the keys from the top of the frame. But for both archie and Gregor, typing was a major workout. It amazes me he wrote as much as he did, though as he aged he understandably wrote less and less.

```
21 MAY 1923 GREGOR SOCIETY NICE BUT SHALLOW. THEY ARE "FANS"
AND MEISTENS EMOTION IMMATURE AND POLITICAL IGNORANT. NOT SO
EDUCATED.
```

****

The loss of a language can be terribly debilitating, and the change from German to English all the more so for their similarities. If one relocates, in

China, say, or Japan, one abandons all attachment to a mother tongue, and languishes — or flourishes — in total otherness. But to hear speech you think you understand but don't, to use words and utter sentences which seem right but sound wrong — this is truly unnerving. Furthermore, what loss is here! German seems to speak another, more complex, order of reality. German case inflections and verbs maddeningly placed at ends of sentences (see Mark Twain's hilarious "The Awful German Language!") allow for truly complicated constructions, with subtle, mischievous, multi-layered relationships between words. That final verb can undercut or sabotage the entire thought structure which has preceded it, and layer irony upon irony, in a delicious mental/spiritual confection. Not so in English, especially American English, and especially in the 2500 basic words of the beginner. The expansive openness of the German sentence is replaced by a short, clipped, subject-verb-predicateness, at its best, perhaps, in Hemingway, but most often at its worst. The unbridled connectivity of compound German nouns, was exchanged for a hash of words of less than three syllables — not exactly "the bee's knees" of speech. An eternal language-Present, clouding any sense of embedded language history ("you say anything here and it mean what you want"). Clichés of certainty replace Talmudic complexity. Such was the price of Gregor's trade off. And with the post-war hatred of all things German, there was little sympathy for his accent or his mistakes, and certainly none for his thought patterns.

(In German:) INSANITY IS THE EXCEPTION IN INDIVIDUALS. IN GROUPS, PARTIES, PEOPLES, AND TIMES IT IS THE RULE. NIETZSCHE. (In English:) YES BUT ALSO N. WILL LIKE THE DIONYSIS ENERGY OF THE WET PEOPLE.

The "wet" people refers, of course, to those fighting Prohibition, either publicly, legislatively, or privately, with shutters drawn and bottle in hand. In G's experience, at this point, probably the latter.

3 JUNE FRANK S. CALLED TO OFFER OF JOB ON CHICKEN FARM IN NEW JERSEY - I WOULD LIKE MORE OUTDOORS AND HARD WORK. I TELL NO BECAUSE I AM LIKING CITY AND MEET INTERESTING POEPLE. I WILL PROBABLY TAKE JOB IN ULLA S HOTEL SHE OFFER ME.

****

Ulla's hotel was the Occidental, on 43rd Street, just west of Broadway. Ulla Ekelund, a robust, thirty-year old Swede, fifteen years in America, was the manager of the middle-sized, upscale hotel in the heart of downtown, and the likely source of G's typing paper. As secretary-treasurer of the Go-Gotham Gregors , she was there at the phone early on May Day when a good Samaritan dialed the number on G's slip of paper. Ulla commandeered a sleepy cabbie, picked up the disoriented stranger after his descent to 23rd St., and took him back to her rooms at the hotel.

G's telling of the first months of his celebrity was brief, and I thought muzzled. There had been a swirl of activity, as evidenced by the paucity of his notes, and he was torn between appreciation for his reception, and deep-seated distrust, even disdain, of celebrity itself. And of course, he was a victim of its brevity: a long 15 minutes, and no more.

As if to celebrate his arrival five days earlier, the American Association of High School Principals proclaimed a ban on the doing The Gregor in school gyms across the country. They decried a "younger generation on the rampage", women with bobbed hair, short skirts, and rolled stockings groping with athletic boys in striped tank tops. The Gregor was particularly offensive, because it violated the norm of a decorous couple. Teams of three seemed vaguely adulterous — polygamous or polyandrous. Unlike the competing Charleston, The Gregor's "motions" were animalistic rather than abstract, and both descriptive and suggestive. Not to mention the political level discussed above, and the Gregorites mouthing words of the hated Bolsheviks, words of community, teamwork and brotherhood.

Little did Gregor know what he was crawling into: two weeks after his arrival, the results of the Philadelphia Dress Reform Committee Survey were being compiled. A group of prominent citizens of the City of Brotherly Love had sent a questionnaire to over a thousand clergymen asking them their idea of a proper woman's dress. Based on the results, the committee designed a "Moral Gown" which was soon endorsed by ministers of fifteen denominations. Loose-fitting, sleeves just below the elbows, and hem within 7 1/2 inches of the floor, it was not quite the costume in which one might dance The Gregor. Fortunately (or unfortunately), outside of Philadelphia, the Southeast and Utah, sales were few, and the loosed libido flowed on, infecting the young, some of the middle aged, and frightening elders out of their wits.

I have a postcard of an ad outside a Broadway movie house: "Brilliant Men, Beautiful Jazz Babies, Champagne Baths, Midnight Revels, Petting Parties In The Purple Dawn, All Ending In One Terrific Smashing Climax That Makes You Gasp." Alas, the sign doesn't show the name of the film. And that was only the beginning. Within five years, the ante was up, as another postcard of a 1927 billboard shows: "Neckers, Petters, White Kisses, Red Kisses, Pleasure-Mad Daughters, Sensation-Craving Mothers — The Truth, Bold, Naked, Sensational!" Gregor arrived in the midst of this rushing river. It wasn't Old Vienna.

5 JUNE 23 I DECIDE TO TAKE ULLA S JOB OF ELEVATOR OPERATOR. SHE SAYS I WILL MEET MANY IMPORTANT PEOPLE THAT CAN DO THINGS FOR ME. SHE LETS ME STAY IN HER SPARE ROOM. I HOPE I WILL NOT BE TO HER A BOTHER (PEST?).

And here begins a tale which went entirely undocumented in his notes, but which G shared with me in late-night musings. Ulla's offer of a room seemed entirely altruistic, if slightly tinged with faddish hero-worship. But lying alone, in bed, at night, with only a thin, unlocked door between them, Gregor imagined he could hear her breathing. He certainly could hear her occasional moans. And the soft, lingering perfume of her unscented flesh made his antennae tingle.

The suggestive vibrations began on the very first night when they sat in her (now his) room talking late in the semi-darkness. Tomorrow was his first day of work, and he wanted to be as sharp as possible. But in spite of his stretching and yawning (granted, more difficult to interpret in an insect), she refused to leave. When the Swedish clock on the mantle piece rang out its twelve lovely chimes, rather than leaving, Ulla launched into a long story, full of sensual detail, about the clock, the one object salvaged from her relationship with Bjorn, her very first lover. Why was she telling him all this? Why did he need to know about Bjorn in bed? What was she trying to do? Why didn't she go to sleep? Was she waiting for something? Because it was her room, Gregor didn't feel he could ask her to leave. Was that how he would repay her generosity? No, he would trade a tale with her, the story of the most important clock in his life, the amazing clock in the Old Town Square in Prague. I have see it myself, have studied the relevant histories, and agree – it is phenomenal, a singular landmark in the history of technology.

To this day, each quarter to the hour, tourists gather to gawk at the magnificent fifteenth century creation of Master Hanus, a clock so marvelous that in the whole world there was none to compare. As a child, Gregor was drawn over and over to its huge double works, the upper, a twenty-four hour clockface in gorgeous blue criscrossed with golden arcs, and the lower, an astronomical calendar advancing at the stroke of midnight one day at a time across seasons depicted in 12 rural scenes. But the most fascinating part was the hourly dumbshow put on by Master Hanus' uncanny figures. Standing on pedestals at the upper face were the four threats to the city of Prague: a turbaned Turk, shaking his head with a slow "No" to the Christian city; a bearded Jew, some said Judas, with his moneybags (something for the little Jewish boy to think about); Vanity, admiring his reflection in a mirror; and finally, grasping his hourglass, Death, who reaches out to pull the cord which chimes the hour. Above these worthies, over the clock face, two small windows magically open, and the Apostles shuffle past, turning to their audience, and finally the figure of Jesus appears, hands raised in benediction. At the sides of the lower face stand four still figures of virtue, including a beautiful angel hoisting a fearful sword. Anticlimactic and almost comedic: a cock which pops out, crowing, flapping its wings to signal the end of the hourly show.

Quite enough to fascinate a Prague Jew-child, who had to pass it twice each day. But more riveting still was the legend of its builder, Master Hanus, which the five-year old was told by his all-too-frightening father. At the dedication ceremony, the learned University men had great praise for the clockmaker's pedagogy. For when studied carefully the huge upper face revealed the way the sun revolved around the earth, the positions and shape of the moon waxing and waning, the signs of the zodiac — six over, and six under the earth, and under what sign they were at any given time. It showed when the sun would rise and set on any particular day, where in the horizon the sun stood at any particular time, northerly in winter and southerly in summer. The lower face charted the days of the week, the months and the seasons, and labeled the holidays and saints' days for every day in the year. But with such information available, some professors grumbled, the populace might be distracted by the mechanical tricks of the apostles and the bell-pulling Death. Some pronounced them "foolish embellishments". But they were few.

Those who had the privilege of inspecting the inner works could only marvel that a single human mind had imagined and perfected the marvelous interlocking works, the absolute precision of all the weights, cogs and wheels, including the huge wheel of 365 cogs which required an entire year per revolution.. Only one man understood the whole system, and that was Master Hanus. At the opening event, one Janek Hrod, a competing clockmaker, asserted that the Master's clock was divinely inspired, and that if he, Janek, had to care for, or repair this machine, he would surely go mad. "I do not believe," he said, "that a more magnificent creation could be found anywhere in the world unless Master Hanus himself should build it."

If this were a Hollywood film, ominous music would have sounded at this line, for, hearing it, the Mayor of Prague and all his councilors shared one frightening thought: it could happen. Hanus could be hired by Budapest, or Vienna or even Brno to build a still more inspired clock, refining ideas and techniques gained in building this one. Perhaps Hanus was already at work on plans. Cutaway to the figure of Vanity, above. And even though Hollywood was half a millennium away, they set loose a most Hollywoodish plot, inspired by vanity, perhaps, but equally by greed for the tourists they might lose.

One moonless night, as Hanus was seated at his bench, three masked figures entered his workshop, and put out his eyes. The next morning his apprentices found their master bound, gagged — and blind. Though Prague was up in arms, Hanus had only one word for his avengers: "Stop looking. Though the culprits are near, they will not be found." He could have said more. But he simply sat in the corner of his workshop, sad, motionless, growing ever smaller, as dust gathered on his tools. So this was the reward for his accomplishment.

Daily he grew weaker, more sunken and gray; the end, he knew, was near. Late one Tuesday morning, he called on Joachim, his boy, to lead him to the clock. There were no friendly greetings as the once honored Master requested entry to the works. "I have a new idea on how to make the weighs slide more smoothly," he told the guard, and Joachim slipped 5 crowns into his burly hand, as instructed. He led his master to the complex center of the works, and they waited — Joachim in the dusty shafts of light, Hanus in the sunless dark. In several minutes, the first whirring began, then another and another. The first of twelve bells chimed out as Death worked his rope. The windows opened above, the Apostles began their greetings. But before the benediction of the Lord, Master Hanus thrust his bony fingers into the core of the works, groped around, and pulled out two small pins. The wheels began to rotate madly, roaring and squeaking — and came to a halt. The Apostles froze. The cock never crowed. The great machine stood motionless as Hanus slumped to the floor. Clutched in his hand was the last of the pins, but what it was no one knew. It went with him to his hole in the ground — outside the town walls, the dumping place for criminals. It took over eighty years for the damage to be successfully repaired.

Child Gregor did not really understand the story, but the glorious clock and its magical figures were mysteriously tinged with an impenetrable, barely understood darkness. Yes, there was the image of the blind clockmaker dead and shriveled among his works. Yes, there was a childish, primitive notion of revenge. But those were not the operative opacities. There was something else, perhaps some "undiscovered country" which aged him spiritually, and prematurely. It was as if being with the clock, twice daily, with that story in his heart, initiated him into a brotherhood of seekers, a fraternity of those who see darkness where others might see light, and who seek to illuminate that darkness with wild idiosyncrasies. It is pure speculation on my part, but if one were to seek the ultimate cause of Gregor Samsa's insect transformation, it might be his membership in such a sect. Others have tried to light human darkness with reason; some with unreason or anti-reason. But who before, in the history of the world, has had the courage to step entirely outside human existence so as better to understand and possibly change it?

In any case, as important to Gregor as the Prague clock may have been, it was not why he told its story late that first night in Ulla's apartment. He told it to end the conversation, for what could follow such a tale? He told it to express his sense of vague discomfort, his pre-fear that goodness might transform itself into its opposite. He told it to affirm his own center before retiring to a strange bed.

Ulla responded as he had hoped. Without comment, she got up from her chair, silently walked over to Gregor, gave his left antenna a long, soft stroke, and walked silently into her own room, closing the door behind her.

Gregor undressed, hung his clothing on a chair, and slipped between the cool sheets. He did his nightly yoga breathing, puffing up his abdomen, then contracting it sharply forcing air first through the right spiracles, then through the left, and wondered if Ulla was frightened by the sound. Inhale... exhale...rest. He lay there in the darkness, still feeling the touchsmell of her hand as a tingling came over his body. In the eight years since his transformation, he had not thought seriously of a woman, had not felt a need, an urge, to couple at any level, for his changes had taken much getting used to. His self-image was reconstructed daily. And then there was that awful wound in his back. Oh! He had forgotten to tell Ulla about it, and surely there would be brown stains on her sheets, even through the dressing.

As he lay in the dark thinking of Ulla, of her blond hair and shapely, muscular presence, he felt a wave of nausea rise from abdomen to thorax. What was this? Why this sense of vague disgust at external muscles, fat and flesh? How much neater he was, his soft parts packaged in hard glossiness. What a stupid idea, the endoskeleton. Why put softness on the outside, hanging there, vulnerable and gross? What kind of inane design was that? His sister Grete owned a good, nineteenth century violin. She put it in a hard case to protect it. Grete. He hadn't thought of her that way before. A bag of flesh hanging on bones. Flesh pads on bone touching strings. Inside-bones. Bones reaching for the cord which rang the bell....

Exhausted, he fell asleep. But the bed in Ulla's room was not ever to be a restful place. The moment the hardness of his back pressed into its sensuous softness, he began to think, or dream of women, of his hardness engulfed in their softness, enveloped in a warmth which only a cold-blooded creature can understand. Much pain was born in that bed. But more of that at the proper time.

7 JUNE VERY TIRED TO STAND WHOLE DAY LONG IN ELEVATOR. I PROP

MYSELF UP AGAINST THE SIDEWALL BUT STILL BACKLEGS ALMOST GIVE
UP. MUST HAVE HIGH CHAIR. I ASK ULLA.

****

Another history-making technology marker: Elisha Graves Otis, a laconic Vermonter, found himself in 1852 working in a new factory in Yonkers, N.Y. The Bergen Bedstead Co. had asked him to install its new machinery, and in the course of this operation, Otis designed the first "safety hoist", a rope lift with an automatic safety to prevent it from falling should the rope break. Up to that time, the poor reliability of braided hemp had made lifts too dangerous for passenger use. Things went slowly for Otis until, in 1854, he made a dramatic demonstration of his device at the Crystal Palace Exposition, riding a platform high into the air, then ordering his assistant to cut the lifting rope. His clamps engaged the guide rails as soon as the tension went out of the cord, while Otis stood there, suspended 75 feet in the air, waving to the crowd below. The Otis Elevator Co. was born.

The first passenger elevator, a tourist attraction, was put into service by the Haughwout Department Store at 490 Broadway two years later. It was driven by steam power, climbed five stories in less than a minute and was a pronounced success, more successful than Haughwout himself, who has faded into mercantile obscurity. By the mid-80s, electric motors were taking over from steam, and the first electric elevator, in the Demarest Building, coiled its cable on a winding drum in the basement. By the time Gregor took the controls in 1923, power was exerted from a rotor at the top of the shaft, and G's job was to accurately align the car with the exit for the safety of his passengers, and open and close the gate. The Occidental had recently installed, in two of its elevators, a state-of-the-art automatic leveler which took over when the operator shut off manual control within a certain distance from the floor, and guided the car to a precisely positioned stop. Alas, as the operator with lowest seniority, Gregor rarely got to run these units.

Still, he enjoyed being in command of his machine, precisely lining up door and floor, and working the gate with its shiny brass handle and curiously pleasing sound. The profession of the elevator operator was, for Gregor, far more substantial, even glamorous, than it would be ten or fifteen years later, when it became a vestigial anachronism in a technologically advanced world of self-service.

The Occidental Hotel dressed its elevator operators to fit the image of technical expertise and service. The boys wore red gabardine double-breasted jackets, with epaulets, four rows of brass buttons, and flat braid at the wrists. Below, dark twill trousers with a red satin stripe along the outer seam. Topping the uniform off, a red, pillbox hat emblazoned with the Occidental setting sun.

Gregor's case was a bit different. Though management was sympathetic to his peculiarities, giving him a modified stool to rest his tegmen on, and even pleased by his celebrity, no one was at all sure that guests would react the same way. In consultation with the hotel tailor, a decision was made to dress G so as to hide, as far as possible, his true condition. His hind legs were thrust into regular men's shoes and stuffed white socks, which were held in place by a garter-like device fastened under his pants to his abdomen. His middle legs were contained by a cummerbund, thus making him appear to be captain of the operators, rather than the lowest in the hierarchy. His front legs were fitted into a stiff jacket with white gloves sewed on the sleeve ends, stuffed with batting, except for the third and fourth fingers, into which Gregor inserted his claws. Because of the limited movement involved with manipulating the up/down lever, the illusion was fairly successful. All this would have been intolerably hot and stuffy for a human being, but Gregor's thermal regulation was not as demanding, and his breathing needs were nicely met by the red gauze stripe along his spiracle line. As usual, his compound eyes and long antennae demanded creative solutions. The first thought was to present G as a girl — the first female elevator operator in New York City — a girl with a huge mass of blond hair, which could be arranged appropriately to minimize his facial features. G himself rejected this notion, since he feared being teased by the other operators and bell-hops. He was, however, willing to wear dark glasses and a high ascot which concealed his mouth parts. He was open to a nasal prosthesis, but held off to see if he might do without one. Whether it was simply tactfulness on the part of his patrons, or their habitual silent staring straight ahead, as is common in elevators, he was never once confronted about his lack of a nose. Such is the estrangement in midtown New York.

The first week was the hardest, but Gregor grew into his new role with surprising grace.

12. The Lips That Touch Liquor Shall Never Touch Mine.

1 JULY 23 LETTER FROM EINSTEIN IN MY POST BOX!! I CAN'T BELIEVE.
HOW HE COULD HAVE HEAR OF ME AND MY TEACHING? INVITATION I MEET
HIM TOMORROW NIGHT.

And meet they did. Gregor and Einstein. Only it wasn't Albert. It was Isadore Einstein, the most famous and creative Prohibition Agent in the entire United States. Izzy Einstein, agent extraordinaire, master of the comic-opera disguise and capricious capture. Gregor had imagined the first name "Izzy" on the note as the physicist's American nickname.

In 1917, the United States Congress, in its wisdom, had passed a resolution for an eighteenth Amendment to the Constitution, and by 1919, 45 of the 48 states had ratified it, thirteen more than necessary for its adoption. On Jan. 29, 1920, it became the law of the land: *"The manufacture, sale, or transportation of intoxicating liquors within, the importation thereof into, or the exportation thereof from, the United States and all territory subject to the jurisdiction thereof for beverage purposes is hereby prohibited."*

The war had accustomed the nation to drastic legislation like price control and rationing, and people had become used to the Federal Government having wide, new powers. Prohibition slipped in on the war-time momentum which required saving of grain, and had turned public opinion against everything German — like the big brewers and distillers.

All had to be sacrificed to efficiency, production and health, and if a sober soldier was a good soldier, and a sober factory hand was a productive factory hand, the argument for prohibition was for the moment unanswerable. Only gradually did the public — and its servants — discover the hurdles involved.

The Volstead act, passed in 1919, was legislation designed to enforce the Eighteenth Amendment. It was framed so that it was legal to buy and consume alcohol, but illegal to transport or sell it — a sop to the civil libertarians. The government's task was to shut off the supply of liquor.

This was something of a problem. There was a land border of 18,700 miles, most of it unwatched. There was "Rum Row", the "booze fleet" of ships anchored just the other side of the 12 mile limit, ready to unload onto speedboats in the night. Thousands of druggists were allowed to sell alcohol on doctor's prescriptions, and for some reason alcohol suddenly became a cure-all. Ministers and rabbis could provide sacramental liquids to their congregations, and some of those congregations turned quite large and strange. Near-beer was still legal, but the only way to make it was to brew real beer, and remove the alcohol. A lot of removal problems here, and much additional slippage in denaturing industrial alcohol. Illegal distilling was ubiquitous: a commercial still could be set up for $500 to produce fifty to a hundred highly profitable gallons a day — instructions in any public library. For the less ambitious, a one gallon portable still cost $6.50 at any hardware store. And cops could easily be bought. In short, the problem of control was immense, and as the war faded into memory, and Americans sought "normalcy", the idealistic thrust behind Prohibition turned to widespread resentment and rebellion. Tired of serving noble causes, many wanted to just relax and enjoy themselves.

There raged a post-facto public debate: the "Drys" claimed Prohibition had created the new American prosperity. Just look at the mounting numbers of savings deposits. A large, much quoted, tool manufacturer alleged that on Mondays, he now found clear-eyed men with steady hands. Prohibition was credited with reducing deaths from alcoholism, emptying the jails, and diverting the working man's dollar towards the purchase of automobiles, radios and homes.

On the other hand, much like those who would legalize drugs today, the "Wets" saw Prohibition as creating a national crime wave — not only of illegal alcohol, but of protection rackets and gang murders: Al Capone was king of Chicago's liquor. With the crime wave came a general increase of immorality, and a skyrocketing of divorce as husbands were hauled off to jail, or lost family savings in confiscated alcohol. According to the Wets, Prohibition caused a widespread flaunting of law which endangered the very foundations of democratic government.

And of course the Wets thought the Drys were fostering Bolshevism with their fanatical, idealistic zeal, while the Drys thought the Wets were fostering Bolshevism by their cynical contempt for law. It was hard for a Bolshevik to get an even break, as the Palmer Raids so clearly showed. It was easier, and more politically effective, to denounce Bolsheviks than to appropriate funds for adequate enforcement.

But Izzy Einstein was a Roman candle in the darkness. Jewish Roman. His nutty, comical schemes netted thousands of unsuspecting suckers — hard, sophisticated, cynical, daring — but suckers all the same. Even the Wets enjoyed it when one of their own fell for Izzy's pranks. While one less bootlegger meant one less competitor, the laughter arose from real admiration of the cleverness of Izzy's traps. With all his ploys and disguises, this fat little man with the big cigar, the "incomparable Izzy", had made the grim game of Cops and Robbers into fun.

Gregor was lying in his room on a warm July evening waiting for his call, re-reading Einstein's own *Relativity: The Special and General Theory: A Popular Exposition* (in German — a book he had picked up for 10¢ on Fourth Ave.) so that he might not appear stupid to his honored guest, when the phone rang in Ulla's room.

"Gregor, it's for you."

"Ah."

He sprang up, and headed for the connecting door. An image of his first struggle to rise from his bed in Prague flashed through his mind, and he laughed to himself at the disappearance of what once seemed insuperable difficulties.

"Einstein on the phone," he said to Ulla. "For me."

"Really?" Ulla sat back down on the edge of her chair. "He has a Brooklyn accent."

"Hello. Gregor Samsa here. Yes. Mr. Einstein? We could talk up here? (Ulla, would that be all right?) Yes, we can talk up here. 17 B. Fine. I see you shortly."

"I would never have thought Einstein would have a Brooklyn accent," mused Ulla.

"I can't tell what is Brooklyn or Manhattan."

"Well, you two can speak in German. Don't mind me."

"Ja. Maybe we do that."

Silence, as Gregor and Ulla awaited the knock of the great man.

"Those elevators take a long time," Gregor remarked. They both laughed. And waited.

A loud rapping at the door, the kind of knock that some in our time have dreaded. Ulla Ekelund, manager, hostess, and inveterate groupie, leaped up to get the door. Two men in tan suits and fedoras stood puffing cigars in the hallway.

"Mr. Samsa, please," said the short, fat one.

"Come in."

Ulla was already blushing at the thought of meeting the great man. But where was he? Gregor rose from his chair, and extended a claw to each of the men, who took it, and shook it, with kind of rough ease.

"I'm Izzy Einstein. This is Moe Smith, my partner."

"Welcome," said Gregor, and began to shut the door.

"Might as well leave it open," said Moe. Fred will be joining us in a minute."

"Who is Fred?" G asked, stepping back into the room.

"One of our musketeers," said Izzy. "But a schvartza, so he couldn't use the elevator. He'll be up as soon as he climbs the seventeen flights."

"Schvartza is a colored person," Ulla told Gregor, who still seemed confused.

"You mean colored can't use the elevator?"

"What kind of an elevator operator are you?" boomed Izzy. "You can't read? A big sign over the call button."

Gregor would have blushed, but...

127

"Forgive, please. I am here only three weeks. I haven't notice."

"Don't worry about Fred," said Moe. "It's good for him. He's getting a little beer belly. Near-beer belly."

Fred arrived in the hall, quite out of breath, a tall, heavy black man in a brown suit, but with no fedora or cigar. Izzy did the introductions.

"Fred Johnson, this is Gregor Samsa, and, uh, I didn't get your name, Miss."

Ulla held out her hand to each man, and actually curtsied, an Old World nicety, completely out of place with proletarian servants of the law.

"Ulla Ekelund. I'm Gregor's roommate."

Eyes rolled in heads, as three Prohibition Agents looked at each other in masculine disbelief. There would be plenty of locker room banter on this one. They checked out the bed for single or double.

"Very pleased to meetcha," said Izzy. "Miss Ekelund, would you mind if we had a word with Mr. Samsa alone? Federal business."

"Oh, certainly," said Ulla. "Gregor, I'll meet you in the lobby when you're finished. You can come down with the gentlemen."

Gregor nodded, and she swished out of the room, aware of the seductiveness of her turn. Fred locked the door behind her.

"Shall we all sit down?" asked Izzy, and motioned each man and Gregor to their assigned places, as if it were headquarters.

"Excuse me," said Gregor, "but where is Professor Einstein?"

"I'm Professor Einstein! Prof. Isador Einstein, Professor of Tricknology. You've heard of me?"

"Actually not." Gregor squirmed. "But I'm very new, and all goes so quickly..."

"It don't matter, " said Moe. "We've heard of you."

"And we got a little business to discuss," said Izzy, chomping on his cigar. We represent the Federal Government, the United States Government, and as a person of foreign origin, German even…"

"I am from Prague, in Czechoslovakia…"

"Germany, Czechoslovakia, same thing. As a person of foreign origin, you would do well to cooperate with us. Understand me?"

"Oh, yes, yes," said Gregor, enthusiastically. "I'm honored to be here…"

"And if you want to stay," said Fred, "you'll help us with our little problem."

"But how can I help you? I'm just a foreigner. I don't speak..."

Izzy took charge.

"In two days you are scheduled to appear at the Gotham Gregor Dance Festival at the Hippodrome."

"Yes. Fourth July. America's anniversary."

"Afterwards, there'll be a party thrown by the Gotham Gregors for the winning team. Correct?"

"Yes. I am told."

"Do you know where the party is going to be?"

"I don't."

"We do," said Moe. "It's at Reisenweber's, Eighth Avenue and 58th..."

"A place so big and famous," Izzy interrupted, "no one thinks it can be touched. We're gonna touch it."

"What kind of touching?" asked the insect.

"Pinching touching," said Moe.

"I don't understand this word."

"It means when you catch someone and arrest them," Fred explained.

"Like Milizia? Arrest for what?"

"Mr. Samsa" Izzy began, "You are aware that we have Prohibition in this country? You are not allowed to sell or transport alcohol."

"I know," said Gregor. "I don't drink much, but it seems — you say featherbrainlike? — to me."

"It may be featherbrainlike, but it's the law. And we enforce it. Reisenweber's is serving all the liquor it served before the law, but no one has been able to catch them."

Fred explained: "You have to be able to actually buy a flask from them, give them money and they give you a bottle..."

"Or even a shot," said Moe. "Izzy has this system..."

Moe pulled open his jacket to display a small funnel in the pencil pocket of his vest. He tugged on it, and up came a rubber tube. "It goes into this little bottle in the lining. Here, feel it."

"I believe you," G said.

"We put the money down, pick up the glass, and we say 'Well, here goes,' or something like that. Meanwhile the bartender is turning around to the register, we empty the shot glass down the tube — and we got him."

"You got to have the liquor to show as evidence. You can't just drink it — you got to show it. "

"The waiters and the barmen at Reisenweber's are too damn careful, too damn smart. They won't sell unless they really know you. But you are going to help us get them."

"How? I can't..."

"You don't even have to be there, if you don't want," said Izzy. "I'm going to put on a cockroach suit, dress up as you for the big bash. Not a chance they wouldn't serve me. Actually, it'd be better if you came. I can't get my hands to look like yours. I'd look like a goofball in a roach suit. You be the real Gregor, and I'll just be a fan, a mascot at the party."

Gregor sensed he had little choice but to go along. The thought of being deported by an angry government when he had just arrived...this was no good. He might need the government — later — for permits or who knows what. Although he was repulsed by this American chicanery, he felt forced to play the game.

The occasion went off as planned. The revelers arrived at Reisenweber's as it was closing at 2. Even then, so late, occasional fireworks in the park lit up the sky. Forty or fifty humans had walked up from 46th Street, and two giant roaches, one of them with a big belly, the other with a heavy heart. Izzy decided to give the the party a little time before the bust — he wanted to have some fun himself. With Gregor there, his costume could be comically simple, not meant to deceive — just a large dark sac, a black face mask and helmet with long wire antennae taped on, long sleeves, white gloves, tights and black shoes. He was just another "Gregor" in the midst of the Dionysian frenzy.

The one break in the script came at the moment of the bust when Izzy, whiskey in hand, pulled off his helmet, poured his drink into his funnel, and announced to the accommodating bartender, "I'm Izzy Einstein, and you're under arrest." Izzy was used to a resigned "No!" or simple "Goddam!" But this bartender started crying, wailing, and then began to scream in Polish that Izzy was taking away his livelihood, that he had four children who would starve, that he was going to commit suicide, and wouldn't Izzy take his wife as a trade for not arresting him? Moe and Fred held him down while Izzy searched the back, found a concealed staircase to the roof, and there discovered 1200 bottles of gin, seven barrels of whiskey, and sixteen enormous cans of alcohol. "Twenty thousand bucks worth of hooch!" he crowed. "Call the 28th."

And six lethargic men dragged themselves out of the precinct house, arrived with dramatic but unnecessary lights and siren, and lugged the cases and barrels and cans down from the roof. The Gregor crowd, along with several late passers-by, watched incredulously as a torrential river of spirits was poured into the gutter, and disappeared down an Eighth Avenue drain, When they had finished their dully vindictive work, they booked Mr. Budzynski, the bartender, who every now and then offered up his wife for ransom, and sped him, cursing God and the government, off to jail.

But of all these events, Gregor seemed most disturbed by Agent Johnson's trudging up seventeen flights of stairs. In Europe he had heard of race prejudice in the south, but this was New York, the enlightened jewel of the north. Before his next entry, we find this clipping from the Amsterdam News, June 30, 1923:

WHAT I WANT TO BE WHEN I GROW UP

a paper by Julian Pollard, Class of 1923, P. S. 604 Manhattan,

to be read at Graduation Exercises

Honored mother, teachers, friends, and my father that got killed in France, I am going to write down in this paper the thing I would most want to be when I grow up. I would want to be a lawyer. When you are a lawyer, you can go in the court and argue for justice. There is a lot of people that want justice, and when you are a lawyer, you can help the people get it. Poor people want justice all the time, but they have not got the money to pay for it, and somebody else gets the justice. So when I was a lawyer, I would try to get the poor people justice free of charge.

That is what I want to be, but it is not what I am going to be. I am a poor people myself, so I am going to be something else, and I think I should write that down in this paper too. I am going to rack up balls in a pool-parlor, and I am going to shine shoes under a elevator-station on Eighth Avenue, and I am going to be a janitor, and a waiter, and a Red Cap, and a Pullman porter that has to sleep sitting up. I am not going to be a lawyer getting justice for poor people in the court. Somebody is going to have to get it for me, because I will be having my hands full being a dishwasher, and a window-cleaner, and a price-fighter, and a garbage-collector. Also, I will keep on being colored.

Yes, those are the kind of thing I am going to be, and I am not going to like it. I am not going to laugh about wanting to be something with honor and only get told A lauwyer! What's a matter with your head, boy? You crazy? I am not going say Yessuh and grin like Aunt Jemima. I am going to be mad. I am going to get in trouble. There is a sign in our classroom that says all men are created equal. It don't say anything about only being equal if you are white, so I am going to try and be equal whenever I get a chance, and they are not going to let me be equal, and I am going to get in trouble about that, and I know it.

That is all I have to write in this paper.

The yellowed newsprint is covered in drops of brownish stain, as if from the dripping of Gregor's wound.

13. Love, Oh Love, Oh Careful Love
– And Other National Sports

In purple dress and short-sleeved blouse, the frail-looking young woman, delicately colored and delicately made, stepped gracefully into the elevator at the sixteenth floor. Her head, her neck, her long slim arms, her little hands seemed cut from alabaster. Where had Gregor seen those hands before? The bones, the bones, ah yes, the bones in Roentgen's machine, an endo exo-skeleton! Her dense brown hair, scooping in great waves, dipping low on her forehead and massing into a great dusky bunch behind, looked almost too heavy for her long neck to support. She hugged the wall to Gregor's left, and made way for each of the passengers as they arrived, maintaining her place at the front, as if she were afraid to be suffocated. G could not help glancing, with each new entry, to see if she were still visible. At the fourth floor, after an au-pair with her two small wards had tucked themselves behind her, she smiled. Her huge eyes lit up like agates, and two dimples laughed out of once brooding stillness. It was only then that Gregor realized he'd been staring. He whipped his head around, gave a little cough, and focused on the rising wall for the rest of the trip to the lobby.

The passengers pushed out of the ornate cage, and though she was in front, the woman in purple and white allowed them to pass in front of her, pressing her thin frame against the wall. When the car was empty, she walked slowly out, and stood a few feet away, her back to Gregor, a lovely sculpture on the ornate carpet. The two were frozen in silence amidst the morning bustle.

Then the woman snapped her fingers, said out loud, "I knew I'd left something!" and spun around to get back on the elevator. For Gregor, it was a moment beyond calculation, courage or foolishness. He simply asked, with European politeness, "Is there anything I can get for you, madame?" This was a woman used to delegating tasks, and getting things done. But it was not that which brought forth "Why, yes. Thank you, sir." She was deeply struck by the authentic gentility of the question, and answered without thinking:

"I've left something important in my room. Do you think you might fetch it for me?"

"Certainly, madam. I'll need your key. What is it?"

"On the table to the left of the bed you'll see a stack of three journals called 'Equal Rights'. Could you bring them down to the lobby while I make a phone call? I'll meet you right back here at the elevator." Her voice was low and musical[4], in an almost plaintive key. *Erbarme dich. Ja,* he thought, *Erbarme dich, mein Gott!* When her words ceased, there was a moment of profound, almost hearable stillness. Quietness, stillness was her power. She looked G in the eye with a luminous glow. Her tiny hands fetched the key from her purse.

G's initial calm had passed. His palms would be sweaty if cockroaches had palms; his trembling white-gloved hand received the key. Remembering to bow, he turned to the elevator, got in, and closed the gate. Room 1600. Ugh. 1600 — Giordano Bruno burned at the stake. Is this an omen? No. *Dummheit.* Up he went, as fast as possible, ignoring the calls at Seven and Ten. Fourteen. Fifteen. Sixteen. And whipping the gate open, he made his way along the carpeted hall to 1600. It was a small room, with a window facing Broadway. From it, he could see out over the East River to — what was it? — Brooklyn or Queens? — three remarkable bridges, there to the right, the clock tower of Metropolitan Life, his first berth in the New World.

---

4 I can affirm this, having heard her testimony at a congressional hearing concerning women's rights as a possible amendment to the Civil Rights Act of 1964. G's account of their meeting was oiled by an uncommonly large intake of ethanol at one of Feynman's famous parties. A late-night lubricity of telling.

What was it she wanted? A magazine. Three magazines in a pile. Table next to the bed. The bed. Her bed, still unmade. Her body in there, her lovely bones, minimally endo-skeletal, caressed by the smoothness of white sheets. On the bed, a nightgown, neatly folded, but still a nightgown, a nightgown which had touched her nakedness. G could feel his tegmina starting to rise, involuntarily, his wings quivering underneath. His dorsal gland became slightly wet. No, no! This is silly. Dumb. Insane. Stop it. Journals. Bed table. There they are. "Equal Rights". "Alice Paul, Editor." Is she Alice Paul? Envelopes on the dresser. Yes, Alice Paul. Her name is Alice Paul. What a lovely name! Alice. Alice. And she's an editor, an important person.

Gregor tucked the journals under his arm, and stepped out of the room. Needing two hands to steady the key, he put the magazines down on the carpet. In the quarter minute it took him to lock the door, he began to swoon, and dropped down on four of his sixes in front of Alice Paul's door in the thankfully empty hallway. When his vision cleared, he saw the journals in front of his face, Equal Rights, Five cents, reflexively opened the cover with his mouth, and began to read the Declaration of Principles:

1. That women shall no longer be regarded as inferior to...

"Mein Gott, was tue ich?" he thought to himself, and scrambled his front legs up the wall until he was once again upright, leaving the journals on the rug. "Here need I a better more-easily-bending-body" he thought, still translating from German. Flexing his lower legs, (a task made more difficult because of the supports in his pants), his front legs on the wall, he succeeded in lowering himself enough for his middle legs to be able to reach the journals. But *Scheisse*!, they were all bound up under the cummerbund, which he could not loosen without losing his grip on the wall, and tumbling floorwards again. A well-dressed young man came out of 1610, and stopped in his path.

"Need a hand, bud?"

"Oh, yes, very much thank you, my back..."

"You hurt your back?"

"No, I...yes, my back. Backpain."

"Here, let me,,."

"Thank you. I just...If you could for me those magazines up off the floor..."

"Say, where do you come from, Charlie? Where's that accent from?"

"I am from Prague."

"That's not in Germany, is it?"

"No, no. Not in Germany."

"I didn't think the hotel would hire Krauts. Where is that, Prague?"

"In what is now called Czechoslovakia."

"Were they with us in the war?"

"Oh, yes."

"OK, here's your mags or whatever they are."

"One million thanks. I will take you down in elevator. You are going to the lobby?"

"Yeah, sure. Sure you can make it? Maybe you should ask for time off."

"No, I am fine. It was only bending to get the journals that was problem."

Gregor gestured the semi-good Samaritan into the elevator, closed the gate, and pushed the lever to the left. "How long have I been? Mein Gott, I've been keeping her waiting so long." He ran the elevator past callers on 11, 9 and 8, and at each of these floors there were shouts as he shot by. He opened the gate in the lobby, and thanked his savior yet again.

"Yeah, sure, any time. See ya. Don't take any wooden nickels. Oh, hey, want some tickets to a ball game? Here you go. Got another date. Use 'em or give 'em away. Princeton vs. Yale at the Stadium. Should be good."

"Wooden nickels," G thought. "What is that, wooden nickels?" But he had no time to go through his idiom list, for there, coming directly towards him from the bank of phones, was Alice Paul, his love. "Thank God I didn't keep her waiting!" But what was he to say? He'd give her the magazines, and she'd thank him, and he'd never see her again. His head sank in despair — but there in his hand, green on his white glove, were two tickets.

"Thank you so much, kind sir."

"She called me 'sir'", Gregor thought, "'kind sir', not 'boy', 'kind sir'!" He handed her the journals. Alice Paul smiled, and turned to go.

"Miss Paul?"

"How did you know my name?"

"Oh, I, uh, I, I am looking at the journal, and your name is on it. I just assume you are the editor. I'm sorry — forgive me if I mistake..."

"No, no. You're absolutely correct. I am Alice Paul, and I am the editor of *Equal Rights*, and I'm flattered you would take the trouble to look. It's very nice to meet you." Gregor's heart skipped a beat.

"Miss Paul?"

"Yes?"

"You probably tell from my speech, I am new in America."

"I did think so, yes."

"And just now, a nice man give me these two tickets to — I don't know what..."

"Here, let me see." Gregor extended his hand. "Two tickets — and they look like good seats — to the Princeton-Yale Championship Baseball Game this afternoon at Yankee Stadium." She handed them back.

"Miss Paul, would you, do you think could you...go with me to this baseball game, and explain it me? I know it is the national sport, and I feel I must know how it works, a baseball game. I am lucky to be give such tickets, not true?"

"Yes, you are lucky. And it's nice of you to ask me to come with you. But, kind sir, I don't know much more about baseball than you do. It's a man's game..."

"They don't let women?"

"No, I think they do. In fact, they advertise 'ladies days' with free admission. But it's just to attract more men."

"So you won't be able to go with me?"

"What time does it start?"

"Two PM, it says. That is 1400 hours."

"It might be fun. Interesting, anyway. I have a meeting now, which will probably include lunch. But I can be back by one. We can make it. I'll find out how to get there, and I'll meet you here in the lobby at one fifteen. Is that all right?"

"Oh, it is wonderful! Thank you so many times! I am finished at ten o'clock of a.m. Then I have work all night. "

"Then you'd best take a little nap. I'll see you at a quarter after one."

"Oh yes, a nap, a siesta — you say that here?— I take a nap and I see you at thirteen… I mean one and quarter. Thank you so much."

Needless to say, Gregor's attempt at napping was not entirely successful.

He finished his last twenty minutes of duty without repercussion from his passing calls by, and made his way excitedly to Ulla's apartment. She was out at a meeting with the wait staff. He plopped down on her bed, took off his hat, lay there for five minutes, then sprang up and plopped down on his own. He turned on the radio. He turned it off. He put on his eye shades, counted to 100, *eins, zwei, drei…*and took them off. "I have heard to say," he thought, "that no matter how fluent in a second speech, it is always in the mother tongue that one counts." So? Was this interesting? No. He got up, and paced the room, taking off his wig, allowing his antennae to uncurl to their full, glorious length. He sat down on the bed to clean them, pulling their length slowly through the brush-like palps of his mouth parts. The world smelled fresher and more good, he thought, the day blessed by possibility. He shut the green door to Ulla's room, took off the many layers of his uniform, and lay naked on his bed, kicking his legs above him, remembering Prague, and the picture of the woman in furs on his wall. Alice was far more beautiful, far more. And she probably didn't own furs; she didn't need clothing to make her look elegant. She had a long neck, many, many neck bones. And long, long hair if she would let it….The vision broke, and he fell asleep.

But not for long. A gentle but persistent knocking worked its way through his knees into his ganglia, and he rushed to pull a sheet over his nakedness.

"Yes? Come in."

"I'm sorry to bother, you Gregor. I know you're trying to sleep. But I've misplaced my key to the freight elevator. It's too embarrassing after last week, and I don't want anyone to know. I'm sure I'll find it, but meanwhile, can I borrow yours? I have linen to distribute. And also you left your hat on my bed."

"What time is it?"

"Eleven fifteen."

"Oh dear, oh dear!" G leaped out of bed, holding the sheet around around him. "I have to meet some one at one fifteen."

"You have plenty of time. Do you have the key?"

"No, I don't. Yes, I do — have keys. In my pants on the chair."

"What's up? You seem all excited. Anything wrong?"

"No, nothing. I have just an important appointment, and I don't know what to wear on it."

"What kind of appointment? I'll tell you what to wear."

"I go to my first baseball game in America."

"Oh, casual, casual. Any coat and tie will do."

"No, I have to look good. My best."

"What's up, Gregor?" Elsa teased, "Got a date with an angel?"

"An angel? No, no, not yet! What are you thinking? It's a woman is nice enough to be taking me to explain a baseball game..."

"You can still be casual..."

"No, no, I must impress her to like me."

"Gregor Samsa! Running after young ladies, and only six weeks in the country! And what's wrong with me? You never asked *me* to go to a ball game."

How could he explain to her, his benefactress and champion, that her buxomness — which others found so exciting — filled him with a vague nausea, bags of what could only be *Fett* hanging from her chest, her hips, her abdomen, how bizarre, how endoskeletal! There was *something* attractive about her — he could feel the vibrations when he lay in bed at night — but to go to a ballgame with her when he could go with Alice Paul, the thin, famous editor?

"All right, see if I care. I want you to wear that beautiful brown suit you wore for the Gregor Society Fourth of July bash. And your brown fedora. And I want you to tell your sweetie I picked out your clothing."

****

"Whoever wants to know the heart and mind of America, had better learn baseball." Thus Jacques Barzun, the distinguished historian, nine years after Gregor's death. The insight was exact. Recent changes in our decades of greed have been accurately reflected in our "national pastime": the wealth and avarice of owners and players, the angry factions, the language of "rights". In 1923, however, the game had a cultural freshness all the more sparkling for the recent scandal of the century, the "Black Sox" throwing a World Series for payoff. The country was quick to react, to wash its dirty laundry clean, and today the sun shown brightly on a newly-built and two-months-opened Yankee Stadium gleaming on the upper Harlem river, directly across from the Polo Grounds.

A cynic might complain that building the Stadium, itself, was a response to brutal manipulation by John McGraw, the owner/manager of the NY Giants, and landlord to the Yanks. Still, it is a story crowned in glory which opened an era of myth-making, splendiferous sport.

After Babe Ruth had been bought from the Red Sox in 1919, the Yankees, renting the Polo Grounds when the Giants were away, set a record for major league attendance, the first team to top a million — so great an attraction was the Babe. McGraw knew there were no longer any Manhattan lots available at any price. "If we kick them out," he said, "they won't be able to find another location. They'll have to move to the Bronx or Long Island, the fans will forget them. They'll be through." Today the man would be honored for his high sense of competitiveness.

Yankee owner Col. Tillinghast L'Hommedieu Huston (*quel nom!*) was not one to take eviction lying down. He devised a plan to build a stadium over the Pennsylvania Railroad tracks at Eighth Avenue and 32nd Street, and the Pennsy was willing. But just as the deal was about to be closed, the War Department stepped in and killed it: the space was to be reserved indefinitely for anti-aircraft gun emplacements. To defend Macy's and Gimbel's perhaps?

Forced off Manhattan Island, the good colonel finally located a 10 acre plot in the Bronx on a corner of the William Waldorf Astor estate, within view of the Polo Grounds just across the river. After spending more money than had ever been spent on such construction, the first three-tiered major league ball park, the first park to be called a "stadium", had its grand opening on April 18, 1923. John Phillip Sousa led the Seventh Regiment band, and Al Smith, the governor or New York, threw out the first ball.

The stadium was known as "the house that Ruth built," and before the game, Babe had told a reporter, "I'd give a year of my life if I could hit a home run in the first game in this new park." In the bottom of the fourth he smashed a savage home run into the right field bleachers with two men on. I was there, age 8, along with 72,000 others. I can assure you, that was the real baptism of Yankee Stadium, a total immersion in wildness and adulation.

On June 26, the Yankees were away at Chicago, and the new stadium had been rented to Princeton and Yale for their end-of-season play-off. Gregor and Alice made their way from the Woodlawn Ave. Elevated (an exciting trip!) to the north entrance, and through the tunnel on the third base side. G was unprepared for the explosion of green which greeted him. The cockroach eye is extremely sensitive in the green and yellow range (5000-6000 Angstrom units), and after his morning of muted interiors, and his afternoon of gray sidewalk and steel, the young Blattarian was overwhelmed by the intensity and hue. Green-how-I-love-you-green charged through his giant neurons, the American frontier, the myth of innocence, the "fresh, green breast of the New World". This was the perfect American day, in the perfect American place, the *mens sana* of universities in the *corpore sano* of sport, and here he was with his newly beloved leading the way, *das Ewig-Weibliche,* Democracy in America!

They wended their way down the concrete steps to their box seats on the third base line. Gregor was almost speechless with the beauty, excitement and joy of it all. A billboard for flypaper over the left center bleachers: *"Last year Whitey Witt caught 167 flies, but Ajax caught 19 billion, 856 million, 437 thousand, 665."* So excited was G by this paradise of green and brown — dropped in the middle of a city, surrounded by apartments, served by the "El"— that he laughed at the message, and did not shudder. Surely there was nothing in weary old Vienna to equal The Yankee Stadium in the Bronx, America.

"Why is there a pile of earth in the middle of the field? Will not the baseball players run into it?"

The only game G knew was soccer, with its vast, smooth field. Indeed, he had played, not well, but adequately, at his high school, the Altstädter Deutsches Gymnasium.

"I believe it's called the pitching mound," said Alice. "The players don't run across the field, they run around the bases. See them, the three bags? There's one right here in front of us. "

"Ah, yes. In the expanse without grass. Do they go around and around as long as they can?"

A vendor descended the steps toward them. "Hot dogs! Get your red hots! Hot dogs!" The Harry M. Stevens Company, even then, on the march. Some things never change.

"Mein Gott, ein Würstchen! Oh, we must have. You would like? Yes? Two plates, please, with brown mustard."

"We don't got plates, bud. Just buns. You wanem on a bun? Mustard we got. Yellow."

"How much do they cost?"

"Ten cents. For you, two for a quarter."

"Gregor, thank you, but I'll pay for my own."

"Please, Miss Paul, let me pay. It is I have dragged you here...Two, please, sir."

"You want sauerkraut? No extra charge."

"You speak German!" G was pleased and excited.

"German? I wouldn't even talk to a Kraut. Here's your dogs."

"I'll have one, too, my friend," said an older man in the next box. "My grandfather was German, and my grandmother was Austro-Hungarian. Will you still sell me a frankfurter?"

"Don't gimme a hard time, Charlie, I'm just tryin to make a livin like everybody else. Here's your dog. Mustard and sauerkraut."

"Vielen Dank." The man tipped his gray fedora.

Gregor leaned over. *"Sie sind Deutsch?"*

"No."

"But you have a German grandfather and Austrian grandmother...Oh, excuse, me this is Miss Alice Paul...and I am called Gregor Samsa."

"Charlie Ives. Glad to meet you. No, my grandfather and grandmother were American — both sides — and their grandfathers and grandmothers were American, all the way back. We came over on the Mayflower as they say. Practically founded the country. We did found Danbury, Connecticut."

"Why then you told the frankfurter man you were...?"

"He was being a jerk about not talking to Germans, standing there selling German products. Hell, Beethoven was German. Excuse me, ma'am. And Mozart was Austrian."

"You are a music person."

"Some might say so. Some would laugh. Here, I'll sing you a little song about hot dogs.

Oh the king held up his hot dog

Grover Cleveland — he was a president —took the king of Ethiopia to a baseball game in 1896.

and he faced it man to man...

And he fed him a hot dog, see..."

As he sang, Charlie Ives beat out the rhythm with both hands on the rail in front of him. His sauerkraut fell off onto the field.

"We don't believe in kings in America, and we don't believe in hating foreigners either because this is a country made of foreigners. So a guy like that really gets my goat."

"What is 'gets my goat'?"

Alice explained.

****

On June 26, 1923, Charles Edward Ives was 48 years old, partner and CEO of Ives and Myrick, the most innovative and successful insurance firm in America. He was also a visionary composer whose technical inventions and fearless imagination anticipated and inspired much avant-garde 20th-century music, for he, too, had had a transformational epiphany. As a child in Danbury, Connecticut, high in a church bell tower, he heard two marching bands rehearsing, each approaching the other from a distance, then marching past one another, playing different tunes in different tempos and different keys, not "fitting together" at all. What a sound! Most people would have dismissed this as transient noise. Not little Charley Ives. For him, that moment established the center of "real" music, "not for sissies!" The world has yet to catch up to him. But he had stopped composing.

"Sounds to me like you need a little orientation to the national pastime, son. Where you from?"

"I'm from Prague, a big city of what is now Czecho-Slovakia, and Miss Paul is from...?"

"Moorestown, New Jersey."

"Did you say you were Alice Paul? The Alice Paul? From the Nineteenth Amendment?" Alice nodded. "Miss Paul, said Ives, "I'm honored to meet you!" He tipped his hat. Gregor beamed with pride, though he didn't know the Nineteenth Amendment from the Ninth. "I'm planning to organize for an amendment myself."

"What is that?" asked Alice.

"The Twentieth Amendment. We need to get politics out of governing, and give power to the real people. We don't need any more of these skins-thick, hands-slick, wits-quick, so-called leaders with their under-values. Congress should be a simple clerical machine for the people. My amendment proposes a direct referendum beginning nine months before the election..."

Just then, the Princeton team burst out onto the field.

"We need to talk more about this. Here's my card. Will you come see me?"

"I live in Washington."

"Well, I'll come see you in Washington. Is that all right?" Alice nodded. "Do you have a card?"

"Just call the National Woman's Party."

Gregor chewed his hot dog, and listened in amazement. Who were these people? Who was this woman who lived in the Nation's Capitol? Oh, no, Washington. Is far away. How far away? Is there a train from New York to Washington? There must be. The Yale and Princeton megaphone men yelled, "Please rise and join in singing the Star-Spangled Banner!"

It would be eight years before the old song became the obligatory National Anthem, but the college boys were early on to something big.

"Do you know this?" asked Alice.

"I don't know all the words..."

"Just move your mouth," said Ives, "and hold your hand over your heart." Gregor was smart enough to put his claw on his left chest and not over the wound in his central lower back.

During the singing, Ives, with hat in hand, and stars in his eyes, sang out in a high, cracking tenor, the most remarkable obbligato to the awk-ward tune, like some drunken spider braiding a baroque filigree onto a poor praying mantis, a decoration of either death or transfiguration. He ended on a fortissimo, braying "brave", a convinced semi-tone above the tonic, and bowed, humbly, to the cheering of the crowd.

"Mr. Samsa, switch seats with Miss Paul, so I can explain what's going on."

"No. I want her to hear too so she can explain me again later."

"Do you even know who's playing? This isn't a regular major league game."

Exhilarated talk went on throughout the game, often yelled over the roaring throng: the history of Ivy League rivalries, baseball as American myth, man love vs. fairy love, Abner Doubleday and the fraudulent American origin of the game, hitting tricks, coaching strategy, fielding technique, pitching philosophy, advertising in the ballpark, comparison with the pros, baseball and the pursuit of innocence, the physics of curve balls, male bonding and its dangers, the new, harder ball, why the bull-pen is called the bullpen, likely trends of the coming post-Ruth era, the Common Law origins of the infield fly rule, the oppressive labor conditions brought about by the reserve clause, the Taftian origins of the seventh inning stretch, American transcendentalism, the segregation of colored players to the Negro leagues, and of colored fans to the bleachers, (to bleach themselves, perhaps in the unremitting sun), baseball idioms which have become part of everyday language: out in left field, three strikes, you're out, off-base, switch-hitter, wild pitch, in the ballpark, to throw someone a curve ball, to be unable to get to first base — with G furiously making mental notes.

Gregor asked amazing things like, "Why do the men just sit in the club-house?" (He meant dugout.) "Why don't they run out and try to stop them from catching the baseball?" A not unreasonable question. Or, "What would happen if the batter would run or to first base or to third base — whichever he wanted, and just make the same direction till he makes a home run?" What an addition that would be! Like three dimensional chess. What complex fielding it would bring forth.

Alice made anthropological remarks about the *anthropoi* on the field, their sexuality, their gestures, their politics, and about the *anthropoi* in the stands, their reactions, their sense of good and evil, their piggish eating behavior and slovenly treatment of the seating area, their "baseball Sadies", mindlessly along for the ride.

Ives contributed detailed information on technique (he was a pitcher himself), baseball history, anecdote and myth, insurance problems concerning large crowds and fast moving hard objects, balls and bottles, and also some speculation on crowd noise as a model of complex sound for symphonic composition.

Even twenty years later, Gregor remembered one thread of the discussion he found particularly enlightening, a theme he would encounter, significantly, to the end of his days. It began in the fourth inning when the plate umpire was hit and slightly injured by a fouled-back ball. The crowd went wild with cheering. G was puzzled as to why they should enjoy seeing someone hurt.

"It's not just 'someone'," corrected Ives, "it's the umpire."

Gregor didn't understand the distinction. "The American psyche," Ives continued, "is stretched between its love of law, and its love affair with lawlessness. "

"Ah, the outlaw-hero," observed G. "Billy the Kid", Jesse the James."

"Precisely. Americans are a legalistic people, and baseball has a far more elaborate set of rules than any other sport. We like it that way, and we memorize all the statistics that go with it."

"And the umpires are like judges. They wear special dark clothing like judges..."

"To give them transcendent authority. And like judges, some umpires are strict, others more flexible. Some will let players argue with a call, some will throw them out of the game at the first peep. But argue or not, the ump is always right. You can go through the motions, arguing with some umps, but you can't win. Ever. The ump is always right."

"Like men," said Alice. "You can argue, but they're always right."

"'Kill the ump!', Ives continued. We don't *like* transcendent authority. <u>We</u> want to make and interpret the rules. So the ump is a perfect target. He embodies the rules, but also enforces them. For this, the punishment is death. Oedipal father-*fortissimo-furioso*. Every damn batter and every runner a litigator. I wouldn't be surprised if baseball winds ups, twenty, thirty years from now, creating a land full of lawyers!"

"It is ironic," G observed, "that these despised villains are the guaranteers of *Unbescholtenheit* — do you say integrity?"

"In America, freedom is more important than integrity," said Ives.

"In America, freedom is more important than integrity."

Gregor would have cause, often, to remember these words.

It was a day of wonders — on the field and off. Despite the outstanding hitting and fielding of a Princeton shortstop named Moe Berg, Yale took the game 5-1 to win the Big Three title. Yalie Charles Ives was too nice a man to crow about it. His only post-game comment was "That Moe Berg is too slow for a shortstop. He should learn to catch." And he invited Gregor to come visit at Ives and Myrick if he got the chance. He gave him his card.

Gregor and Alice followed the crowd back to the El, and each stood quietly on the noisy ride south, straphangers recalling the richness of the day. Instead of taking the shuttle at Grand Central, they walked west along 42nd Street, the sun beginning to lower in the sky, many New Yorkers still out strolling in the cooling part of a lovely summer day. Gregor took a small detour to inspect the lions at the Public Library, and Alice thought he looked "quite heroic" standing next to them. They sat in Bryant Park watching children perform their elaborate jump rope routines.

"Are you hungry?" asked the being in the suit.

"Not for food," answered the being in the dress.

"For what then?"

"Those little girls over there...what kind of a world will they have to move into? When they get too old to jump rope, what happens?"

"The breasts will grow, and..."

"Even you...

"You jump before you know what I will say."

"Sex. Sex and sex. The prison of male desire."

"I begin to say that the breasts will grow, the hearts will grow underneath the breasts, the minds will grow above, and maybe — when there are more people like you — the voice will come out from between the mind and heart."

Gregor knew he was in dangerous territory, but his admiration for his bench mate, and the sexual energy he felt around her kept him going, his dorsal gland as wet as his wound.

"Tell me what you are doing."

"What I do?"

"In Washington. What you do in Washington."

"I sit in an office."

"What is it called?"

"The National Woman's Party."

"Are you what is called a femininist?"

I have to laugh when I think of G saying this. Asking Alice Paul if she is a feminist is like asking the Pope if he's Catholic. Alice Paul *was* feminism. She was the single person most responsible for achievement of women's suffrage. She was an untiring inspiration to a generation of politically, psychologically, liberated women. She was the general of the army, the chief strategist of the think tank, the first to be out on the streets, or hauled off to jail, the most convinced, the most forceful, the most articulate, the most clear-headed revolutionary currently walking the land. By 35, she had forever changed the governing of the United States, and now, three years later, she was aiming to change its very being. Did she laugh at G's question. No. She simply said,

"The word is 'feminist'. And yes, I suppose you could say I am."

"I thought so. I look at the contents of your journal."

"Would you like your own copy?"

"Oh, yes, very much, I do.

"I'll send one."

"But in the meanwhile, can you tell me simply what is a feminist?" Breasts. Heart. Mind. Voice. Breasts.

"I wish it were simple. There are people who think I don't know what the word means."

"Truly? But you are editing a magazine... You must explain me about your Amendment, as I was not here."

" The men went off to war to fight for Freedom."

"And your great president's Fourteen Points. I read them."

"And what do The Fourteen Points say about women?"

"I must think. I can't remember."

"That's because they don't say anything about women. Our children were killed fighting for Freedom, and not one woman in this country was free."

"You mean free to vote election."

"That's the first of all freedoms. From elected officials come Law, and from Law comes culture and behavior. This is a country run by men, for men."

"So is Czech Republic, so is Austria."

"Do you think this is right?"

"To tell the truth, I did not think."

"Exactly. This has to change — all over the world. We decided to change it. Nine years ago, my group began to picket — you know what that is? — to stand in front of the White House where the President lives, with signs asking President Wilson to help us get the vote."

"Surely he did, such a great man."

"Surely he didn't. At least not at first. So we placed more pickets, and put up more signs, and people just watched us, and thought about what the signs said."

"What did they say?"

"I can't remember the exact words. But something like We shall fight for democracy, for the right to vote." Or "governments derive their just powers from the consent of the governed." That's from our Declaration of Independence."

"Thomas Jefferson."

"Yes. Good."

"I've studied your history."

"As written by men. Things were fine, we were getting sympathetic newspaper and magazine coverage until the war fever began, and then we were attacked — by men in the streets, soldiers, sailors, little boys even, spitting, throwing bottles and stones. The police just stood there and watched."

"And President Wilson did not stop them — right outside his own house?"

"He ordered us to be put in jail."

"Why? What did you do? I thought in American you have a right to…"

"For blocking the street. We weren't blocking the street. The people attacking us were blocking the street."

"You really went to jail? You? This lovely woman sitting here?"

Breasts. Heart. Mind. Voice. Breasts.

"We kept coming back. 218 women from 26 states were arrested over several months. More than a hundred went to prison. Some for sixty or seventy days."

"You?"

"Seventy days."

"What did you do?"

"We went on a hunger strike."

"What is 'hunger strike'?"

"When you refuse to eat. You make the authorities — and everyone — decide if they are ready to kill you for blocking the sidewalk."

"Like a Hunger Artist."

"What's that?"

"In Vienna we had — I mean there was — a carnival with a man who would see how long he could go without to eat. There was a sign outside his cage how many days it was."

"Was he protesting something?"

"No. That was his art. To be able to go without food. To be able to survive longer than anyone else in the world without food."

"They *made* us eat. They couldn't take the responsibility, or the publicity, if we had died."

"How did they do that? Make you eat?"

"They held us down on a table, six big men, and they forced tubes down our throats into our stomachs and poured some horrible concoction in."

"Oh no..." Gregor's heart went out to this thin, pale, large-eyed woman. He spontaneously reached for her hand. She pulled it away. Then, guilty at offending a gentle soul, she put it lightly back on his.

"It felt...dreadful. I couldn't breathe. My stomach retched and I vomited all over myself. Each time. They put me in the psychopathic ward."

The sun shone red in the library windows, casting long shadows toward the east. Gregor's heart was so full of sympathy — sym-pathy, *Mit-leid*. with-feeling — he couldn't say a word. He covered her lightly touching hand with his other claw, and they sat together in silence, each absorbed in memory and special longing. A bedraggled man in a filthy blue suit paused on the path in front of their bench, and pulled a crumpled brown bag out of his pants pocket. He might have been forty — or seventy, his eyes draining pus, his unshaven face ulcered by the weather. Opening the bag, he threw a handful of bread scraps on the grass in front of the couple. First one, then three, then a huge mass of pigeons stormed out of the sky to fight amongst themselves for food. The man turned to the couple.

"Will you help poor Thomas buy more bread? For the birds? A dime? A nickel? The birds are hungry. Look how hungry."

Gregor took his claw off Alice's hand, and reached into his jacket pocket. Nothing. It was too difficult for him to search his pants.

"I have no smallmoney. Do you?"

Alice opened her purse.

"We say 'change'. And yes, I do. Here, Thomas. And some bread for you, too, all right?"

"Thomas blesses you. The birds bless you." And he continued his walk up the path, stopping in front of the next occupied bench to scatter his minimal feast. Gregor and Alice watched him go through the same routine with an elderly woman.

"Do you think he is a *shyster*?" Gregor asked.

"You mean a con-man, someone who tricks you? No. And, in fact, I do feel blessed."

"You are a beautiful person, Miss Alice Paul." Gregor could not contain himself. But then he did not know what to say. Alice stood up. "You are wanting to go?" he asked.

"Let's go back to the hotel. I'm getting chilly."

They walked the rest of the way in silence. While crossing Sixth Avenue, Alice took Gregor's claw to pull him along out of traffic's way. She held on for two long blocks, and did not let go until they had crossed Broadway, and stood in front of the Hotel. It was almost nine by the time this odd couple stepped into the ornate lobby. The bell-hops stared.

As you might imagine, Gregor was both wary and excited about what the night might hold. A line from Rilke, his beloved companion, kept running through his head:

Wie soll ich meine Seele halten, dass
sie nicht an deine rührt?

How shall I withhold my soul so that
it does not touch on yours?

I hesitate to continue the narrative. Prurient curiosity does not rate high on my list of demands to satisfy. Yet the events of that night had so many repercussions with regard to Gregor's self-image, his understanding of his place in the world, his mission and further world-line, that I feel it important to communicate at least some of what he shared with me on one of those long, starry nights on the mesa.

"You must go?" he asked.

"I should. I have a meeting tomorrow morning with the one man who resigned from President Wilson's staff over the way he treated us."

"Who is that?"

"His name is Dudley Field Malone. A successful lawyer, a good friend of the President's, managed his campaign. Wilson made him Collector of the Port of New York. Yet he publicly repudiated his good friend. A principled man. I appreciate his courage. We're putting our heads together about strategy."

G wasn't sure about putting heads together. A wave of jealousy ran through his thorax and thickened his throat. A desperate save:

"Would you mind telling me about strategies? It would help me better understand America. We can go in my room, and you meet Ulla, the manager of the hotel who lets me use her apartment..."

"It wouldn't disturb her?"

"No. I'm sure she will be interested."

"And I'd be interested to hear from a woman managing a large hotel. Let me go to my room first, change my clothes, get a little something to eat, and I'll come in an hour. Will that be all right?"

"Oh yes. Very all right. Come to room 2016, on floor twenty. I wait for you."

"Thank you, Gregor. I'll see you at ten."

There is a scene in Chaplin's *Gold Rush,* in which Charlie asks for a date with an attractive young woman. All is quiet and polite. When she accepts, he thanks her, bows, and they each go their ways, she to join her friends, he into his cabin. He closes the door behind him, pauses, then explodes into wild, abandoned joy, jumping on the furniture, bouncing off the walls, throwing pillows until one breaks, covering him, and filling the room, with settling feathers. Had he not been restricted by human clothing, G might have done a similar dance, crawling up the lobby walls and across the ceiling, whipping the chandelier into a chiming frenzy with his antennae, and dropping, unexpected, on the fur-laden shoulders of some incredulous upper-class matron. But, of course, he did no such thing. He contained his joy within his hard, brown carapace, rang for the elevator, tipped his hat to his colleague Frank, and proceeded with elevated heart rate to his room on the twentieth floor, in Ulla's empty apartment. He knew she would be away that night.

Ten o'clock. Fifty minutes to go. What to do? Fifty minutes, fifty years! He checked the dressing over his wound. Damp. He gave it a smell check with his right antenna. Better change it. He got undressed, peeled off the tape, and deposited the brown-stained bandage in the kitchenette trash. Ulla was used to this. But what was that wonderful, heady smell? Oh, no! His dorsal gland was starting again to drip pheromone in anticipation. G was becoming drunk with his own attractiveness. Was Narcissus ever so intoxicated? It may be a good thing that human noses are vestigial. Into the shower to counter secretions. Water, water everywhere, and let me take a drink. I'm hungry. Did I have supper? No! She went to eat. She's thin. My Alice of bones and skin. She needs to eat — to keep up her weight. She's had enough hunger. Soapy, soap, soap. *Da ist noch ein Fleck! Fort, verdammte Fleck, fort, sag' ich!* Mmmmm, that feels good! But careful around the wound. I do believe it's getting smaller. Less inflamed around the edges? Maybe not. Come out, little genitals. Let's wash the old tube, and clean off the hooks. Haven't seen much action lately. Lately? Where are we? 1923? Eight years! You still remember how? OK back into your sheath. Antennae, come here. Soap you down for maximum bouquet. Knee one, knee two, knee three, knee four, knee five, knee six. The better to hear you, my dear. Water off. The "His" towel....

Gregor re-dressed his wound, and wrapped himself in one of Ulla's bathrobes. Back in his bedroom, he surveyed the scene. 9:45. One bed, one chair. If I sit on the bed, then she takes the chair, and it will be hard to get her to the bed. On the other hand, if I take the only chair, and she is forced to sit on the bed, that will make her tense Maybe guarded. Well, let's see how it sorts out. I can always bring another chair from Ulla's room. Now, clothing. Greet her in this robe? Why not? No. Too pushy. Too scary. But casual. Slacks and an open shirt. And perhaps slippers, for just that touch of risqué.

He dressed, and slicked back his antennae. He sat down in the chair.

9:55. He stood up and retrieved his copy of Einstein from the bedside table. He sat down again. Nonchalant. Let her walk in and see me reading. 9:56. Nonchalant. This is an impressive book. Not everyone reads Einstein in the original. 9:56 and a half. Calm down, old man. *Auf die Frage: "Warum fällt ein Stein, den wir emporheben und darauf loslassen, zur Erde?" antwortet man gewönlich: "Weil er von der Erde angezogen wird."* She won't come early, I bet. If she comes right on time, does that mean she's anxious to see me, or that she is just punctual to all appointments? Like a business appointment. If she comes late, does that mean she's trying to tease me? Maybe she doesn't really want to come....

There was a knock at the door outside Ulla's room. I'll let her knock a second time. Make her wonder just a little bit. Come in? Come in! Gregor crossed his lower legs, and remained nonchalantly seated.

"Gregor?"

"Yes?"

"It's Alice."

"Oh, how nice. Come in. I'm in here, through the green door."

Alice stuck her head into Gregor's room. G rose to greet her, as slowly and gracefully as he could. The volume of Einstein clattered from his lap to the floor, losing its dust cover.

"Oh, dear," said Alice, and rushed to rescue the book. Gregor, remembering the recent retrieval problem at her door, allowed her to pick it up for him.

"Thank you. Do you know this?"

"*'Über die spezielle und die allgemeine Relativitätstheorie'.* No. I don't read German. But Einstein, yes, him I know. So does everyone. I didn't realize you were a scientist."

"Just an interested *Laie* — you say layman?"

She nodded. "I'm impressed."

"Have you been in Europe?"

"I did some graduate work in England — a long time ago."

"Now I'm impressed. May I call you "Doktor"?"

"Alice is fine."

"Come sit down. Here, I'll from Ulla's room bring a chair."

"Where is Ulla? You said she'd be here."

"There was emergency with the chambermaids. Not serious, but they have a meeting she had to be."

"Will she be back?"

G pushed a small armchair through the door.

"I think as soon as it is over." They both sat down.

"So." Gregor waited.

"You said you wanted to know more about our plans." As usual, Alice was quick to get down to business.

"Ach, ja," said G, "that is correct. I want to know why, first, some people think you don't know what is feminism. You, the famous Doktor and author."

"I'm here in New York because we just met at Seneca Falls to organize for a new amendment to the Constitution..."

"Another amendment! You and Mr. Ives. How things are quickly changing!"

"Mr. Ives, if I may say so, is a crackpot — you know what that is?" She banged on her head to demonstrate. "Our drive will be realistic — and successful. An amendment to guarantee equal rights for women."

"The name of your magazine."

"Precisely. I wrote the amendment text; it's simple: 'Men and Women shall have equal rights throughout the United States and every place subject to its jurisdiction.'"

"Who would have one problem with that?" Gregor drew his chair closer to hers, the better to hear her answer.

" No one, you would think. But people will, I assure you. The first hurdle will be protective legislation."

"What is that?"

"Right now, there are laws which restrict women's working too many hours, or working at night, or..."

"Is that because they want to give safety? Night streets are dangerous?"

"Then fix the streets. Don't keep women from working if they want to. What is a waitress to do? The dinner shift provides the best pay. Is it only for men?"

"I see."

"Do you? The reason men want minimum wages and maximum hours for women — while opposing it for themselves, I may add — is because it makes women less competitive. Men's altruism is a mask. They steal away women's jobs under the cover of chivalry."

"So your amendment would make it nothing different for women and men."

"Correct." Alice, soft but hard.

"Because they are equal."

"That's right." This discussion was not exactly what G had in mind.

"But women and men are not really the same," he said. Women are smaller and weaker, and often they need protection."

"It's men that need protection — from each other. Do women make war? It's men that mismanage a man's world.. Conflicts settled by violence, bloodshed, and militarism. When women are included in world affairs, things won't be that way."

"How do you know?"

"And, excuse me, 'protection'? Men's so-called protective instinct comes primarily from jealousy and self-interest. Women are 'good' if they are protected by a man, and 'bad' if they're not. Why the uproar now about unwed mothers? Because they defy male proprietorship, and act out their sexual freedom." Alice got up from her chair, looked at her host, and sat down on the bed. Gregor's knees perked up.

"You believe in sexual freedom?"

"I believe in a woman's right to determine what she does. Just like a man. Equal. Equal rights."

"There are women who don't agree with you. The ones who think you know nothing about feminism."

"Some women, especially the younger women now, the flappers — I don't know about the Gregorettes — but the flappers oppose our program because they still believe women were created solely for the comfort and glory of men. Older women oppose it because they think anything new is scandalous. Some, young and old, oppose it because equality for women affects their selfish interests. Some oppose it because they don't think polit- ically. They would rather play up-lifter to the weak than give the weak a weapon which would make them strong; but, for the most part those opposed or indifferent are opposed or indifferent because they don't know the facts and haven't been aroused to their responsibility to do justice. The

National Women's Party will do that. We did it to get the vote, and we can do it now." All this militant rhetoric was spoken slowly, in a gentle, deep voice. But Alice's eyes blazed dark fire.

"Do you mind if I tell you my reaction?" asked Gregor.

"No, surely not. I'm interested in a European point of view. Because this movement must be taken worldwide."

It wasn't clear to G whether, under these conditions, honesty was the best policy — given the tachycardia, and the wet pulsing of his dorsal gland — but he was already feeling guilt in his planned manipulation, and honesty here might be anodyne.

"It seems that all those who opposes you is or reactionary, or selfish, or do you say 'patronize'? — *gönnerhaft*, or just simply stupid. Maybe there is something correct about what they say, too. For example, do you have here the man pays the woman when there is a divorce?"

"Alimony. Yes."

"Do you think the woman should also pay the man, too?"

Alice was unflappable. "Some feminists want to do away with alimony."

"That will not be very popular with women."

"No. But instead of dropping alimony, the law could require that each pay the other an amount that would make up for earning capacity lost in marriage and family care."

"*Schlau*. The man does not get much, but yet the law is equal."

"The point is that equality under the law precedes all else. Everything will follow from that. We must be firm on this. That's what we decided last weekend.

Strange. Rather than pulling away from Gregor as a result of his honest critique, Alice felt closer to him. She began to recover that sense of connection which had developed during the day , especially in the park, but which had begun to wither in their current setting. Gregor sensed the warming immediately, perhaps with his antennae, perhaps with antennae more spiritual. He decided to press on with this new, seemingly successful, direction. Such are the uses of honesty.

"I am hearing a contradict. On the left side you say that women and men are equal, and on the right side that women are better."

"Even though women are in many ways superior to men, all we ask is that they be considered equal under the law. There's no contradiction."

"How are women superior?"

"Women value human life more, probably because they give birth to it. Last week in Wisconsin, a jury sentenced two youths to six years in jail — each — for stealing a watch. No woman would do that. Women should be allowed on juries."

"It appears you dislike men."

"I don't dislike men. I wouldn't go out with one, but I think the interests of all humanity are identical. Men just don't know how to further such goals."

"Even Dudley Feel Malone, or whatever his name is?"

"Most men are bad at it."

"And animals?"

"What?"

"Animals have interests, too.

"Yes they do."

"Even insects?"

"Of course."

"Even male insects?" Alice got up from the bed.

"Oh, Gregor, don't be silly." She put her hand on his tegmen. "Let's stop talking about this. I talk about it all the time. Let's go for a little walk on this warm summer night, and then I have to go to bed."

"Would you go to bed with me?" There, he said it! All or nothing. Whatever happens, happens. He was surprised by her response:

"Why?"

"You said you wouldn't go out with a man."

"And?"

"And I'm lonely. And I like you. And maybe you might like me."

"What about Ulla? Don't you sleep with Ulla?"

"Ulla?? No! Never. She lets me share her rooms."

"Why not — if you're lonely? Men will sleep with anyone."

"I can't explain. Or I do not want to."

"But she'll come back from her meeting. What will she think?"

"I lie to you. She is not in a meeting. She is at her uncle house in the Bronx, and will not be home tonight.

"Why did you lie to me?"

"I don't know. I told you she is here so you would feel safe and come. If you would not stay, you would not know I lie."

Alice stood facing him for perhaps 30 seconds, then sat down on the bed and took off her necklace.

And here, gentle reader, I must draw the curtain. The interactions of chitin and flesh are rare, and like many rare things — tropical orchids, Beauty's visits from the Beast, solitary woes — they are best left in darkness, unmolested. Suffice it to say that it was not a happy experience for either Gregor or Alice. Strangeness mixed with shame will spawn an unsound brew. Flesh is tender, chitin hard. How to play antennae with someone who has none? Some lips are made for kissing, others definitely not. Humans are the only mammals that mate face to face; one of our pair was not even a mammal. There are places for which hooks are not appropriate. The one good thing that can be said was that they did not have to worry about birth control.

14. Interlude For Scalpel And Piano

Some would-be lovers can brush off a traumatic night, or even a series of them. Some will try again, hope burning eternal in the sweating breast; some will seek couples' counseling, licensed or unlicensed; some will cast about for psychological, physiological, or pharmacological assists — or medical appliances. But this pair was too deeply wounded: she, because at 38, she had never imagined losing her virginity this way (she had never imagined losing it at all), and he, because for the first time, he had given great pain to someone he loved.

It's true he had sorely pained his family several years back, yet that was not his own doing — his cruelty had been thrust upon him. But now he had seduced this strange and lovely woman, manipulated her into his bed — and made her cry. Who was he? What did he want? Was he doomed forever to be out in the cold, his beak pressed against the window of humanity? Was he — doubly inhuman — up to his imagined task of helping humanize humanity?

He lay in bed, covered with her fluids — saliva, sweat, possibly blood. Worst of all — her tears. His own wound 175 through the dressing on his back; he lay, despondent, in a cold, brown pool. Alice had left his room at 2 AM, disheveled and dejected. When he called her at 8 to apologize, he found she had checked out earlier that morning.

24 JULY 1923 WITH ALICE LAST NIGHT VERY VERY BAD EXPERIENCE. GRAUSAM. I CAN NOT ENDURE THIS WAY, NOT SOMEONE FOR INTIMATE

HUMAN RELATIONSHIP. I MUST CHANGE!!! I SEE A PLACKARD IN THE
TROLLYCAR FOR PLASTIK SURGON. TOMORROW I GO TO LOOK ON TROLLYCAR
FOR TELEPHONE.

This must have been a desperate decision for Gregor, for in another context, he had told me of his disgust at the plastic surgery industry developing in Austria and Germany after — and even before — the War. Surgeons were becoming fabulously wealthy performing *Nasenplastik* — nose jobs — on rich Jews wanting to improve their images, their business prospects, their chances for intermarriage. Moishe Rosenbaum transformed into Martin Rose — Martin Rose of the aquiline nose. *Nasenplastik, Mammaplastik* — how scornful he was of this kind of chicanery, as if Mother Nature could be hoodwinked with a few thousand dollars and a scalpel. Yet here Gregor was, one more Jew in search of metamorphosis, reduced to scouring public trolleys for a referral. Where would the money come from? *That* he hadn't considered, so needful was he in his agony.

The doctor on the poster appeared to be about thirty-five, a blond, clean-shaven, square jawed, WASPy, but friendly-looking man in a white coat. Do You Have A Problem With Your Appearance? Free Consultation. Call HA6-9884.

Gregor made an appointment with a pleasant sounding receptionist for his first day off.

Morning thunderstorms having cleared out a week of oppressive humidity, it was a pleasantly cool afternoon in early August. Gregor took a cab from the hotel up to 999 Fifth Ave. Long walks on two legs exhausted him, and he was still unsure about scurrying along the streets of New York in horizontal mode. He hadn't realized what an expensive address 999 was, at 76th Street, just opposite the entrance to the Metropolitan Museum. But when the driver said, "Here ya go, bud," and he stepped out of the cab, he realized for the first time that he might be getting into something over his head. Well, the ad had said "Free Consultation", and he could always back out if needed.

Nine-ninety-nine was a large, gray townhouse sandwiched between two huge luxury apartment buildings. The door bell did not identify its occupant. Gregor checked the slip of paper in his jacket pocket: 999 — a hard number to read or write incorrectly. He rang the bell. The same pleasant phone voice greeted him: "Yes?"

"Gregor Samsa here. I have a four o'clock appointment."

"Yes, Mr. Samsa, we're expecting you. I'll buzz you in. Take the elevator up one flight, and I'll meet you at the door."

Doors were always hard for Gregor. It was difficult for him to manipulate American door knobs designed for hands, not claws, and especially when he had only the few seconds provided by a buzzer. But it seemed as if Dr. Lindhorst had had him precisely in mind, for this knob was actually a lever, as in Europe, which could be easily engaged. Yet what a lever it was! He felt it before he saw it, a grotesque brass head with a long, protruding tongue. While the outer aspect of the face was that of a normal, even handsome young woman, with her lovely right ear caressing the human palm, the inner aspect, closest to the door, was a horribly mutilated quasi-face, as if its subject had been half-eaten by the most ravenous cancer. Her tongue was hyper-extended, not as a convenience to Gregor, but in a cry of misery or repugnance. Strange, he thought, and shuddered.

A small, self-service elevator greeted our elevator operator, an ornate, mirrored cab with only one button, a sky-blue oval marked "HIGHER". Where was "down?" he wondered. There must be a separate entrance and exit, he thought, so patients will not have to be stared at. Clever. Thoughtful. He thinks of everything. Gregor pushed the blue button.

The elevator was completely silent, and extraordinarily, bizarrely, slow, taking perhaps two minutes to climb the twenty or so feet to the first landing. On the wall in front of the gate, the passenger could leisurely view a brilliantly-executed collage of faces and figures from Bruegel and Bosch, Leonardo's "Five Grotesque Heads", Durer's "Horsemen of the Apocalypse", each horseman scattered willy-nilly, among the madhouse of others — and all these multiplied, should one turn away, in what Gregor now observed to be subtly distorting mirrors. It was surely an extraordinary man who had planned such entertainment for his patients. He had never have imagined this from the bland face on the placard.

The cab stopped in front of a plain, paneled door. A lithe young woman with glowing skin, but strangely wrinkled hands, opened it, and gracefully pulled back the inner gate.

"Mr. Samsa, how nice to see you. Come in." Gregor stepped into a small antechamber, perhaps a waiting room. "I'm Miss Mozart." G's eyes lit up. "No relation, I'm sorry to say. Won't you have a seat? The doctor will be with you shortly." She disappeared behind one of the three doors.

Gregor paused before the only chair in the room, a carved oak masterpiece, probably from the 16th century, as singular as all the doctor's other artifacts: instead of the normal lion's paws, the arms of the chair ended in human hands, gripping globes, the globe on the left carved and painted with the map of the known world, on the right with the celestial spheres. Both featured monsters — of the depths and of the heights. On the middle digit of each hand, a ring with pearl of great price. The legs of the chair were shaggy, and ended in cloven hooves, though of what beast Gregor could not say. The tapestry on the seat depicted flowers, small and large, while that on the back was covered with a marvelous array of iridescent insects. He sat down — and felt a strange vibration course through his body, a sensation one might have if suddenly embraced by the hairy god himself.

The plant and insect theme was continued on floor and walls. In this relatively small room were thirty or forty framed exhibits of butterflies and moths, arranged by sub-species. The rug was a small masterpiece of oriental craft, a dazzling interweaving of stems, leaves and flowers. Set in pots and canisters were an assortment of plants Gregor had never seen before, in either the old world or the new. An epiphytic orchid hybrid was consuming a tree fern with muscular rhizomes, while cork-screw parasitic pods hung like ornaments from a mass of tendrils completely obscuring their woody host. The largest object in the room was a 9 foot tree in a huge golden pot on which all manner of shapes were shimmeringly reflected. At times Gregor thought he could see his own image, but he wasn't sure: whereas his own arms were steadying him against the pot, his possible reflection was reaching out, in longing. The tree's red-brown branches were studded with thorns, and put out clusters of leaflets and small yellow flowers. But most remarkable, the bark seemed to be crying: aromatic fluid, the color of Gregor's, was seeping from innumerable cracks in the bark, and hardening into decidedly tear-shaped globules which he could harvest, should he so desire. Several feet up, a split in the trunk revealed two bald labia, rimmed in bark, pushed apart by some pressure behind them. Were Gregor more sexually sophisticated, he might have recognized the animal image they formed. Pressing out from the core of the trunk, as if straining to escape was — there was no mistaking it — the shaped image of a reaching hand and fetus face — a human infant trying to grasp its way into the world. This was not a carving, mind you. This was an act of playful Nature, dancing among the categories, crossing her own uncrossable lines. Gregor got up to more closely examine this freak of sculpture. Five fingers on the hand. And the mouth open as if uttering its first cry.

"Mr. Samsa, how wonderful to meet you!" G jumped. "I've heard about you for years — good things, good things…"

A burly, stocky man, one human head shorter than Gregor, his dark red face haloed in white hair, his beetling eyebrows looming over piercing eyes, his enormous, blue-veined nose in colorful contrast, offered his huge, hairy hand to Gregor. He wore a gray European smock more suitable for a potter's shed than a medical office and which was, in fact, covered in streaks of clay.

"You must forgive me for keeping you waiting. I had to finish up a little sculpture — oh, it's nothing, a trifle, but one in which a patient is most interested."

"Who are you?"

"Dr. Lindhorst. Who did you think? Maxwell Lindhorst. This being America, you may call me Max, since I feel we are already old friends."

"But Dr. Lindhorst…"

"Yes? I said call me Max."

"But Dr. Lindhorst is — more young. And he has a white coat."

"*I* have a white coat. I just don't scare my patients with it."

"But the picture on the trolley car."

"Appearances, appearances. All you Americans ever think about. Excuse me, I know you are not American — you are Czech, correct? — but it is Americans, by and large, who read the ad."

"You put up picture of you that isn't you?"

"Who said it was me?

"The placard says, Dr. Lindhorst…"

"I beg to differ, my friend. The placard says, simply, 'Do you have a problem with your appearance? Free consultation.' You found my name only be calling the phone number."

"Well, ja, that is true."

"I cut the picture out of a toothpaste ad in the Saturday Evening Post. Dentists prefer Pepsodent, or whatever."

"You mean he isn't even a plastik surgeon?"

"He may be a plastic surgeon, for all I know, posing as a dentist. Appearances. We mustn't worship at the shrine of appearances. Come into my office and you can tell me what brings you here."

The doctor, if that is what he was, opened the remaining door — not the elevator door, nor Miss Mozart's, but a fourteen paneled, exquisitely painted affair.

"What are these figures on the door?" asked the roach, before walking through.

"Above, the Seven Deadly Sins: There's Anger , and this one is Greed, ugly little fellow, and here's Envy, yellow, not green, this is Gluttony, and can you guess this one? — Lust, and Sloth. Up on top, Thomas Aquinas' favorite, Pride. And down here we have the Four Cardinal Virtues: meet Prudence, Temperance, Fortitude, and Justice, a convenient summary of the teaching of the ancient philosophers and of the excellences at which they aimed. To these four, Christianity added the three theological virtues of Faith, Hope, and Love, sometimes called Charity, a poor translation of "*caritas*", itself a mere gloss on the Greek "*agape*". This classification was taken over directly from the Apostle Paul, who singled out Love as the chief of the three. Isn't she attractive?"

"But why are sins above, and virtues below?"

"That is for me to know, and for you to find out, Mr. Samsa. May I call you Gregor, since you will be calling me Max?"

Max Lindhorst ushered Gregor into his office, a high-ceilinged chamber, completely lined with books, many ancient, some to be reached only by ladder. He gestured Gregor to a large chair behind a combination desk and work-table, on which, lying on newsprint, was a clay mask of a noble male face, the carving tools beside it. The doctor took the only other seat in the room, the clay-dusty top of a small step ladder.

"Why am I behind your desk, and you sit on a ladder?"

"Because you are in charge, and I am your servant. This is sometime hard for a patient to understand, so I make it clear this way. Do you like the sculpture?"

"Who is it?"

"It is nobody yet. But it will be. It will be the face of a currently unfortunate young man lately too familiar with a pit bull named Isaac."

"It looks just like someone I know, a philosopher in Vienna..."

"By the name of Ludwig Wittgenstein?"

"How did..?"

"Do you think you are the only person acquainted with this man and his genius?"

"No. Of course."

"I choose this face to give to my unfortunate so that his cover may inspire his book, if only it worked that way. Appearances."

"How do you know of me?" Gregor asked.

"I first heard of you several years ago from my friend Kaltenborn."

"The reporter."

"Yes, and now radio announcer. He said he had seen your Roentgen act. Quite a piece of showmanship."

"It wasn't showmanship, if I understand that word. It was to demonstrate that..."

"It was to demonstrate that the owner of your circus could use the newspapers to drum up a bigger crowd. *Nicht wahr?*"

"I don't know. Perhaps."

"But that's not how I really know you. In the last few months, my daughter Olympia has written of nothing but you. Her team was the winner of a Gregor Dance contest in — coincidence — Olympia, Washington."

"Washington! Does she live near the Capitol?"

"Olympia *is* the capital of Washington."

"No, of the United States. America."

"Gregor. There is a state called Washington — all the way on the other side of the country. Then there is Washington, the city, which is the capital of the United States."

"And your daughter lives in the far away one."

"Unfortunately."

"Why unfortunately? You don't even know her."

"I have a friend in the capital of the United States."

"And?"

"I don't know. I thought maybe your daughter would know her."

"You sound sad."

"No. I just thought…"

"You are sad."

"I am not sad, but tired."

"From?"

"I did not sleep very good last night."

"Ah. This is no reason to visit a plastic surgeon."

"Dr. Lindhorst. This is but a consultation, correct? And it is free of charge?"

"Certainly. I never let money stand in the way of my patients' satisfaction. Besides, for you, the famous Gregor Samsa, all is free, everything. My compliments."

"You mean if we have an operation, I don't pay?"

"I am interested in your happiness."

"I don't pay?"

"You don't pay."

"You see, I have very little money."

"You don't pay anything. What can I do for you?"

There was a long pause. Strange as it may seem, Gregor had not previously considered an answer to this predictable question.

"Dr. Lindhorst, my situation is, do you say unique?"

"I know that, my friend."

"There are things about me, about my body, which stop me to do…"

He could not say out loud what he had so long held in secret: the name of his game, the title of his quest. It sounded too pat, simultaneously too megalomaniacal and too trivial: "I am come to help the human race." Oh, I see. Tell me another one. But if he could not be intimate with another human being, how then to do? Write a book? What would he write?

"Why did you sleep poorly last night?" asked the doctor, cutting to the quick.

"In my bed I think of…"

"The woman from Washington."

"How you know?"

"I'm paid to know. Or not paid, as the case may be."

"Doctor, do you think I can be more attractive when I have the right number of limbs?"

"What is the right number?"

"Four. Four limbs. Two arms and two legs. Like you."

"Maybe you need *more* legs, not fewer. Eight, perhaps. Or ten."

"That will only make it worse. Then they will never except me."

"Who?"

"Human people. A woman. If I had one to love me, it maybe would be I could do everything."

"A woman who could love you with four legs could just as easily love you with ten. Or twenty."

"Not true. Too many legs make difficult holding."

"You cannot sculpt your way to happiness."

"You don't know what is like to go all the day and wonder what everybody thinks. Everybody. I want you to take off my middle legs."

The doctor looked at Gregor long and hard. He took a silver cigarette case from his smock, opened it, and offered one to his patient. Gregor declined.

"No thank you. The smoke makes my spiracles to hurt."

Dr. Lindhorst snapped the case shut and slipped it back in his pocket.

"Do you see that little statue on the bookshelf over there?"

"My eyes are not too good at far away."

The doctor got up from his stool, brought the piece over to the table, and plunked it down under Gregor's nose. It was painted plaster of Paris, eight inches long, and showed a lovely, pink naked woman — "stacked", as they say — modeling for a sculptor. But the sculptor was a pig, also pink, and the statue he was molding was that of a pig, a lovely, pink, naked pig in the same seductive pose as the woman's. His model had two red nipples; his sculpture had eight. In bas-relief along the base, Gregor could make out the word "Pigmalion", nipple red on pale green.

"I won this at Palisades Amusement Park. It took me three tickets worth of ring-toss."

Gregor was familiar with the game from his own carnival in Vienna.

But he had never seen such a vulgar statue.

"Why did you want it?" He tried not to be judgmental.

"It reminds me of you. And of a lot of my patients who want to sculpt themselves in their own image."

"But you are the sculptor."

"As I said, I am only a servant, a pair of hands to do their bidding. Do you know the story of the real Pygmalion?"

"He was a sculptor who fell in love with his statue." Gregor had taken six years of Greek and Latin at the Altstädter Deutsches Gymnasium.

"And what happened to him?"

"I don't remember. But nor do I remember anything terrible, and if something terrible would have happened, I would probably remember."

"No, you're perfectly right. Venus answered his prayers, and turned his statue into a real and lovely Galatea who loved Pygmalion, her creator, with all her heart. Nine months later, they had a child. They both lived happily ever after."

"I thought you would tell me they were punished."

"Do you think they should be punished?"

"No, but..."

"No but yes. Why did you mention it?"

"Myths usually speak — you say transcressions, *vergehen*, to go estray?"

"Very good. What was the transgression?"

"Hubris." The Greeks, of course, had a word for such a thing: over-weening presumption, irreverent disregard of human limits, the sin to which the great and gifted are most susceptible. Faust before Faust.

"So," G wanted to know, "why weren't they punished?"

"Not every malefactor is punished — right away. Do you remember the rest of the story? Metamorphoses, Book Ten, the book of Venus Afflicted? Ovid, the egg of all changes? What was their daughter's name?"

"I think...I don't know."

"Paphos. She was so happy, they named a Greek island after her. And she had a son. He wasn't so happy."

"What was he called?"

"Cyniras. But his daughter Myrrha, called him 'sweetest, dearest father'."

"Why you say but?"

"Every father loves a doting daughter, but not necessarily a lusting one. When her mother was off on a trip, she weaseled her way into his bed, and seduced him three nights running. On the third night, he realized this wasn't just some three-night stand courtesan, but his own daughter. He grabbed his sword to kill the unnatural thing, but Myrrha managed to escape with his child in her womb.'

"You blame only her. But he was unfaithful to wife..."

"But this is not a story about unfaithfulness. It is a story about incest. *Blutschande*."

"Why you tell me this?"

"To help you understand the myth of Pygmalion. And of we Doctors Pygmalion — you and I. Our Greek sculptor friend didn't just fall innocently in love with a beautiful statue. He is guilty of narcissism, onanism, and incest."

"What is onanism?"

"Spilling your seed upon the ground."

"Ach ja, *onanieren* —to jerk off."

"My, my, your idiomatic English is excellent. Where did you learn that? "

"From a bell-hopper in my hotel. He is teaching me words not in my dictionary. But Pygmalion does not jerk off. I don't remember that."

With great delight, Dr. Lindhorst sprang from his ladder seat and retrieved a beautifully bound volume of Ovid from the shelf nearest his desk. "Let's see...here... *He gives it kisses*' — the statue — *'He calls her the companion of his bed, and lays down her reclining neck upon soft feathers...'* Do you think that statue came out dry?"

"That is very beautiful. Maybe I need such a statue who does not mind how many legs I have."

"Masturbation, narcissism — you know what that is — and incest — those are the clarifying echoes, two generations away, from Pygmalion's original sin."

"And you say if I ask you to sculpt me — to be my sculptor hands — then I am doing jerking off and narcissism and incest?"

"I just want you to think carefully about what you are asking. I am a doctor who dispenses dreams, and you, dreamer of dreams, must be prepared for what they bring. I am your servant. Are you your master?"

"What happened to the daughter? Myrrha is it?"

The doctor brought the book to Gregor, and laid on the table in front of him.

"Read it. There. Kaltenborn says you're a great actor. Show me how well you can read."

"But this is English. I am not so good. I am better at Latin. Or German."

"You're an American now. Read."

"'*Gods, I accept my punishment gladly, whatever it is.*' This is Myrrha talking? '*I offend the light and defile the darkness. I pray you, therefore, change me, make me something else, transform me entirely, clean me...*'"

"Excellent. Your accent leaves something to be desired, but very good. Here, I'll read you the rest: '*There must have been some god who heard her desperate petition and granted her prayer, for the earth now covered her feet, and her toes were rooting into the soil to support the trunk of her body, which stiffened as flesh and bone transformed themselves into wood, blood became sap that flowed up and into her branching arms, and skin became bark. Within her, under the wood, in her womb, a restless fetus moved, and the tree could feel it and grieve at the ruin of those fresh hopes that a baby's birth should imply. Tears flowed from the tree, miraculous fragrant tears of what we know as myrrh.*

And the child within her seeks a passage into the light, a way to be born and live. The tree is swollen and contorted, and although it cannot call out, it appears to writhe in its pain. Lucina...' — that's the goddess of childbirth — '*Lucina pities its tears and the plaintive sound of the wind in its groaning branches. She touches the wood with gentle hands. The tree cracks open, the bark splits, and the baby boy is born....*'"

"Moment. There is such a tree in the room out there..."

"I saw you inspecting it."

"Those drops on the bark were the tears. And there was a hand reaching out, and a face..."

"Adonis being born, a child, and then a youth, so handsome that Venus herself falls painfully in love."

"Ah, yes, Venus and Adonis."

"What happened with Venus and Adonis?"

"You must think I am stupid, but again, I don't.... It is all quite vague."

"You would do well to take these stories more seriously. They're all about you. Adonis may have been good looking, but he was a brat of little brain. A goddess in love with him? He'd rather go hunting."

"Maybe he was wise. Not to involve in a such unequal involvement."

"You mean a cross-species relationship? You may be right. But if he *was* wise, you'd never know it from the story. On the hunt, a wounded boar charged him and ripped his balls off with his tusks. He bled to death from the groin, poor fellow. Not a happy ending."

"So what you say is the looking-like-innocent acts of Pygmalion the sculptor carried much evil within them."

"Enough to make one cautious. " He put Ovid and Pigmalion back on their shelves. "Shall we still talk about amputation?"

"Yes."

"Really? Well then, let's talk about amputation. How will you support the middle of your body? I assume you still use six legs occasionally."

"They all come from my chest close together. It should not make such difference."

"Let me see you crawl with your middle legs folded."

Gregor walked and ran, and even jumped along the rugs of Lindhorst's office.

"How about crawling up the walls and along the ceiling. Do you still do that? You'll have only two thirds the stickiness."

"I still do it when I'm very happy."

"Are you ever very happy?"

"No...yes...not often."

"But you might be. Especially if your scheme works out. Give it a try. There's some free wall space between those shelves. Just don't knock down the moth."

Much to his surprise, G found he was shaky on a vertical wall. He did not dare the ceiling.

"Looks tentative, my hexapodic friend. Are you sure you want to give that up?"

"I know this must have a trading off. I do not need to walk on ceilings."

"Well, *I'd* like to be able to walk on the ceiling!" It had been a childhood ambition of young Max in the high-ceilinged apartments of Berlin. "What about back strain? Come over here." He put both hands on Gregor's back at the level of his still-folded middle pair of legs. "Let's take a short stroll." And he put his weight over his arms. They must have been a comical sight: the large cockroach with middle legs caressing his own thorax, and the short, thick, smocked doctor attempting to keep up, trying to maintain his downward thrust. They barely avoided knocking over the ladder. This went on for no more that thirty seconds before they were both exhausted.

"How did that feel?"

"Terrible. But you won't be doing that to me."

"Does your back hurt?"

"Yes. So would your back."

"I don't have middle legs," said the man.

"Neither would I," said the roach.

And that seemed to settle that, though the logic was somewhat faulty.

"What is the large insect I almost knock down?" Gregor pointed at the framed object on the climbing wall. It was a moth of some kind, the largest he had ever seen. Two six inch, broad, red-brown wings fastened to a minuscule body between them, giving the beast a wingspan of more than a foot. Gregor recognized the feathery antenna as scent detectors, able to locate a female miles away. What he did not recognize was the outsized black tube hanging from the abdominal tip, extending fully three feet down the wall. The whole display took a frame as large as a small human coffin.

"*Attacus atlas*, the giant atlas moth. A very poor dinner guest: he is born without a mouth or digestive system."

"So may be the perfect dinner guest for those without much dinner."

"A European observation."

"It is beautiful and impressive. But what is the long, tube thing?"

"In the ten days this being has to live, he need spend no time foraging or digesting. He has only one purpose, one activity: mating. That tube is penile hypertrophy."

"Who he could give baby with that? A horse? A cow?"

"You have inter-species sex on the brain, my poor friend. Not only could he not impregnate a moth, he could not even fly. He died sans issue, the only one of his kind."

"I have a friend in Vienna who loves to have that display."

"Who? Your circus owner? Hoffnung, is it? The Human Cape of Good Hope? Give me his address, and I'll send it tomorrow."

"I do not know if he still lives. He has a fast-to-age disease. Better you keep it. How did the moth become this way?"

"I take the credit and the blame. I wanted to see what would happen if I grafted a mouth and intestinal system from a related *Saturniid* moth. If it could eat, would it live longer, would it grow larger, would it change its behavior, and seek more lofty entertainment? It was an extremely delicate operation, using micro-tools I invented for the occasion. And, as are all my procedures, it was successful."

"And?"

"And the moth recovered in less than a day, and began to graze on the leaves in his aviary. Within twelve hours, he had stripped bare two small trees, and eight inches of penis trailed behind him. He could no longer fly, so I shoveled the ground full of fresh leaves from Central Park, which he roared through. It literally sounded like roaring. A low roar. At three days he was dead — like that. I have it all on film."

"Awful. Why you do hang it on the wall?"

"For your instruction. Do you still want to be drastically modified?"

"It may help me..."

Dr. Lindhorst stepped resolutely to the desk and pressed a button under the leg space. Miss Mozart stuck her blond head through the door.

"Yes, Doctor?"

"Miss Mozart, please prepare procedure T for Mr. Samsa here." Miss Mozart nodded both her head and eyelids in a gesture that sharply brought Alice to Gregor's mind. His residue of hesitance was washed away in the sweet ache that rose from heart to throat. Still, he was frightened at what he seemed to have committed himself to.

"All right, my friend, Maxwell Lindhorst at your service. Maxwell Lindhorst, who lacks the knowledge, the wisdom, and even the right to decide what is best for his patients. Many consider cosmetic surgery an act of vanity. Some see Pride there, or Envy, or Gluttony for praise, or Sloth finding the easy way around, or Anger taking a knife to self instead of other. In your case, I suppose, it is Lust in the driver's seat. But I do not judge — because only you can know. This will all be free, gratis, as I promised. I merely ask you sign this consent form. Don't worry. You don't have to sign in blood. I'm not interested in your soul."

The doctor took several sheets of paper from a desk drawer and placed them, along with a fountain pen, in front of Gregor. G drew his large reading glasses from his jacket pocket, and perused the pages. It was not clear what he actually understood: much of the document was in technical, medico/legal language.

"Can I die from this?"

"Of course. One can die from anything. Joy, for instance. Or love. However, it would be extremely rare."

Gregor took up the pen, but had trouble unscrewing the top.

"Here, I'll do that for you," said the obliging doctor. Miss Mozart knocked lightly, and again stuck her head into the room, this time from a door among the bookshelves which Gregor had not noticed. Her bun was gone, transformed into a stream of golden hair.

"The room is ready, Doctor."

"Thank you."

She disappeared behind the door.

"Shall we go?"

"Now? Right immediately?"

"There's no time like the present. Except the future. Except…the future."

Max walked to the bookshelf door, opened it, and beckoned his patient through. Gregor expected some sort of operating room, with huge lights over a surgical table, green tile walls and floors. Instead, he found a room more like a recording studio: a wooden chamber with acoustical tile and strategic baffling, in the middle of which a Bösendorfer concert grand faced the only seat in the room, a contraption quite like a dentist's chair, yet obviously far more comfortable.

Miss Mozart, now clad in an embroidered Irish robe, held a hospital jonny over her arm.

"Mr. Samsa, will you step behind the screen, remove your clothes, and put this on?" She handed him the jonny.

"All my clothes?"

"Please."

Gregor, truly embarrassed, backed himself behind the four-paneled Chinese masterpiece. He could have sworn it had depicted a serene and holy mountain. But now, from behind, the image had transformed into a fierce tiger, dismembering a small deer. He folded his clothes, dropped them neatly on the floor, and slipped into the skimpy covering.

"I can't reach to tie this behind."

"Come out," said Miss Mozart, "I'll do it for you."

Gregor didn't mind showing this beautiful woman the smoothness of his tegmen. He strode more confidently out, and presented her his open back."

"Oh!" She jumped back. He had forgotten his wound. With the day's already disturbing events, the bandage was more than saturated.

"What's the matter?" Dr. Lindhorst came quickly around to look. He held the jonny open at arm's length.

"Having a bit of a problem, there, Gregor? What's going on?"

"My wound, it..."

"What happened?"

"My father was frightened."

"And he threw an apple at you."

"Yes. How did you know?"

"I read about it. There's a book about you. Did you know that? I knew of you when you first came to be. Long before my daughter did. "

"I do not see this book. Do you have a copy?"

"In the story you die. The chambermaid throws you out with the garbage."

"That is *Dreckhaufen*. I am here. Oh, but perhaps the book was by my parents. They think I am dead. We trick them, Anna Marie and the *Zimmerherren* and I. It was not good my family must have me around. They must continue their lives."

"Many people think you're dead."

"Not the Gregor Dancers."

"The Gregor Dancers don't read German books. Anyway, that was, what, eight years ago? Why hasn't your wound healed? Mind if I take off the bandage? Miss Mozart, will you fetch some fresh dressing? Thank you."

This was the first time Gregor had ever shown his wound to anyone. It was the first time he had been asked about it. So here was an unexpected benefit of his visit to the surgeon.

"Rose-red, in many variations of shade, dark in the hollows, lighter at the edges, spots of blood, small necrotic areas...and...we've got to clean this out."

"I clean it twice a day."

"But there are maggots in it."

"Occasionally, there are maggots. They come and they go. They do not hurt me. I think this is the way it is —it will not get better."

"It will take a tegmental graft."

Miss Mozart returned with a tray of sterile gauze and saline, and deftly cleaned and dressed the wound while the doctor spoke.

"We may be able to do something about this later, unless it's a somatization of a spiritual wound, which would be a serious category error to treat. The immediate issue is the amputation. Can you concentrate on what I'm saying while Miss Mozart works?"

Gregor drew his attention back from the light playing in her hair. Yellow light attracts insects.

"Yes. I listen."

"You still want to go ahead, Mr. Pygmalion?"

Gregor nodded.

"When Miss Mozart finishes, I am going to ask you to lie in this chair, and get as comfortable as possible. Then I am going to ask you for a vow of silence — complete silence — for one hour. We will be going through a pre-procedure which brings our chances for success to almost 100%. Other surgeons have a range of results; I do not. You have chosen the right pair of hands, Gregor, and the right strategist behind them."

Miss Mozart was finishing the bandaging. A work of art.

"Are you willing to be silent for an hour, to concentrate entirely on what you hear?"

"I stay silent and listen."

"All right. Come lie in the chair. Miss Mozart will adjust it for you. Comfortable? Good. We're going to strap you in for your own safety."

There was a long silence during and after the buckling. An expectant tension filled the room. Dr. Lindhorst sat down on a small padded projection coming out of the chair, took hold of one of G's bare legs, and spoke quietly towards its knee.

"All cultures except our own western, sanitized and scientized one have understood the intimate connection between body processes and those of the soul. When the soul consents, its physical shell will follow. Without that consent, there is unpredictability and chaos. My surgical results are more successful than those of my colleagues because while they start by opening the skin, I begin — and end — by opening the soul.

The eyes may be the portals of the soul, but they are exit portals only. Seeing is an important, but finally trivial sense. Eyes can be opened or closed, objects can be visible or not, the world can be dark or light. Nature would not give a central place to such a contingent sensibility. No, the chiefest and deepest connections are made through the ear — which can hear at all times, in the dark, around corners, when eye is blind, which can hear aggregations of distinct vibrations — distinct pitches in chords — when the eye would average them into one. Blue and yellow becoming green — what loss is there!

Today we are going to engage your soul — through your ears. I'm fully aware that in your case, the word is metaphorical. Insects have no ears, I know. But they have fine hearing organs at the leg joints. That is one reason I am reluctant to amputate: we are talking about partial deafness, reduced acoustic acuity, closing one third of the doors into the soul.

Still I am willing to go ahead, Gregor Samsa, if, in your wisdom, you would so like. But I know there is much still unsaid between us, and many consequences of the unsaid. I am aware of your sleeplessness last night, your *Bettschmertz*, as it were. I am aware of your mysterious friend in Washington, D.C. , and of your wanting to be loved.

Gregor, Love is brother to his sister, Death. Eros and Thanatos, my friend. Longing always leads somewhere, and that somewhere is not always longed for. You must appreciate this — deeply — before you take an irreversible leap of mutilation in the service of love. If you understand and truly accept, your tissues will heal. If you do not understand, if you do not truly accept, you will carry yet another unhealing wound." He paused to let his words sink in. "Miss Mozart, you may begin."

The slim, intense woman took off her shoes, and sat down at the

Bösendorfer, barefoot. Reaching behind her neck, she encircled the long fall of her golden hair with her fingers, moved it from her gown, and let it drape loosely onto her half-bare back. Though Gregor could see every detail with his immense peripheral vision, he felt himself drifting back into a hazier space deep inside his cuticle. Long echoes of Lindhorst's hypnotic voice rippled slowly in circles of ever-softer sound.

Miss Mozart placed her right hand on the keyboard. The first gentle A reached up a plaintive minor sixth, and hung there, suspended in non-time, until its own weight eased it down to the supporting net of the note below — only to immediately fall through that net — oh surprise! — to the accented half step below, the awe-full D# of the Tristan chord, the chord of chords, that miraculous find of ambiguous, melancholy longing. Miss Mozart's left hand joined her right to urge the F and B below, while her right fourth finger struck the G# that would resolve upwards, and upwards again beyond what might have been its goal. The Tristan chord, F-B-D#-G#, a chord so extraordinary that one can search in vain through music to find its like. Search was its name, and its mode, and its function. Search. But for what? The beauty of despair? The despair of beauty? What trembling question was being asked by this voice in the night? In the long pause which followed, Lindhorst whispered,

"Be in the silence, Gregor. Let the sweet pain soak in at your soft joints." Then he signaled to Miss Mozart to continue.

The second phrase, a step higher, infinitely slow, exaggeratedly, tormentingly slow, left Gregor hanging as did the first, the *Sehnsuchtsmotiv*, the Leitmotif of Longing, calling him from the vast darkness of What. His wound began to weep into its new dressing. His dorsal gland began to moisten. The meat at his leg joints began to soften, as if to bid welcome to the knife.

"Something is dissolving, Gregor. What is it? Don't answer." He couldn't have.

A third time the phrase called out, higher still, and longer, reaching upwards by two more notes, as if its fingers were stretching from an already outstretched hand.

"It hurts, my friend, does it not?"

As if to answer, the phrase returned, the same last, rising pattern, an octave higher, and then only the last two notes, a half-step reaching upward, and once again, the two reaching notes, an octave above, harmonic tension so great as to be humanly unbearable. And yet it hung there, radiating, in the silence — until beginning again, it pushed beyond itself, and with a final leap, reached beyond itself, above and below, to a land that could be footed, an almost safe place — an accented chord of F-A-C — but with a B above, a skyhook which let gently go, and allowed the hearer — and the universe — to collapse down to the floor of an ever-rising, but graspable flow of molten melody, the Motif of Love.

"Now you can swim, Gregor. Your wings are beginning to spread." And indeed, G could feel pressure at his back, once associated only with sexual excitement, but now with something more mysterious, sexual in part, but as larger as the sea is to the teardrop. Miss Mozart's fingers called forth the Bösendorfer's magic, and the melody rang forth in quiet, sensuous richness, as if from twelve pianissimo cellos, though there was not a cello in sight.

The clock had ticked off ten minutes, but there were no minutes here, only an expanded, warping space-time, similar to Gregor's flight, but now colored with the depth of new emotional and spiritual dimensions. The labyrinthine melody rolled on and on, reaching ever higher, falling back and reaching again, a melody of melting and surpassing tenderness, sweeping up in its wake the mists of the sublime — that world so far beyond perceptual or imaginative grasp that our sense of its beauty is deeply mixed with dread. Alarming and reassuring both, it swept along, in ecstatic prolongation, immensely complex, dissolving tonal language — and any other — as if God himself were exuding enharmonics. Complex, yet beyond complex, and thus simple: exaltation, transformation, an intoxicating brew of idealism and lust, delirious forces striving to embrace, exchanging the Kingdom of Day for the Kingdom of Night.

Fingers flying, Miss Mozart piloted this extraordinary tone poem back to its unsafe harbor, the *Sehnsuchtsmotiv*. The Prelude to *Tristan and Isolde* sank down to its embers.

"After such love, why is there still longing?" Lindhorst whispered, tears in his eyes. Miss Mozart turned quietly to the very last pages of the piano score, and in hushed tones, began Isolde's song of Love's triumph over Death. *"Mild und leise,"* Gregor knew the words, *"wie er lächelt, wie das Auge hold eröffnet..."* She sang beautifully, as extraordinarily well as she played, and not having to overcome an orchestra, she was able to evoke the most delicate nuances of emotion and inflection as Isolde gazes upon her lover, transforming his death into eternal, living, life. In the intimate murmurings of the first serene phrases, slowly rising through unbelievable ascending passages of modulating sequences, wave upon wave, lyrical, rhapsodic, ecstatic, to climactic heights of passion and transfiguration, Isolde makes her decision to die, to melt with Tristan into ultimate ground of being, to leave behind the torment of the Finite doomed to infinite yearning. Together they will be at home in the vast realm of unbounded night, borne on high amidst the stars, and then down, down, to where there is no down

In dem wogenden Schwall,
in dem tönenden Schall,
in des Welt-Atems
wehendem All —
ertrinken,
versinken —
unbewußt —
höchste Lust!

Release! Death powerless against the Inextinguishable — love's vast, immeasurable redemption. Yet even here, after this inspired surging of metaphysical perception, even here, in the midst of yes, even here, appear the ineffable harmonies of the *Sehnsuchtsmotiv*, longing beyond longing, even in final exhalation — longing. Then silence. Profound silence.

Miss Mozart sat still, staring at the piano, her wrinkled hands in her embroidered lap.

"Gregor, are you still there?" Dr. Lindhorst checked his abdomen for the rise and fall of breath. "Gregor, listen to me carefully. This music is all very well and good, but it is a paean to annihilation. Do you understand that? There is redemption there, and transcendence, but it is transcendence of individuation itself. Do you want redemption from being and its torments, the most sinister kind of redemption?

Do you remember the Little Mermaid, Gregor? I'm not joking. Hans Andersen's Little Mermaid who wanted to be rid of her fish tail and have two props to walk on, like humans, so that the Prince would fall in love with her? She gave up her tongue for the Sea Witch's magic drink so her tail would part and she would gain what men call pretty legs. But every step she took hurt — as if she were treading on sharp knives. And in the end, the Prince marries someone else, someone with a tongue who can speak and sing, and the Little Mermaid's heart broke, and his wedding morning brought her death and dissolution to foam on the sea. Gregor, do you think this has anything to do with you? Are you prepared to dissolve for love like the Mermaid? Like Isolde? Do you want to be foam on the sea?

And treading on sharp knives? I trust you are acquainted with the phenomenon of the phantom limb? All patients have sensations seemingly localized in the amputated limb, often like muscle pain with the phantom feeling cramped or uncomfortable. But some patients suffer chronic, severe pain, unresponsive to therapy. Are you prepared to reach out to assuage your pain, and find nothing there to touch? Do you think you can swindle the Devil, escape from being meat?

And, Gregor, speaking of the devil, just what is your connection with his sulfurous realm? Have you ever asked yourself how you got this way? What crime you had committed? What deal you are pursuing? What are you? — an externalization of the beast in man? I know, I know, you're a nice person. They're all nice people. But why *you*? For this," here he rapped on the hardness of G's thorax, at the level of amputation, "why you? Don't answer. I'll tell you why you. Because you ask too many questions, and have too many quests. There's a composer named Charles Ives living up in Connecticut. Wrote a piece some fifteen years ago called "The Unanswered Question", for which, unfortunately, Miss Mozart has no score."

"I couldn't play it." She got up from the piano and disappeared through a black, heavily-paneled door.

"The Unanswered Question. You need to know this piece, Herr Samsa, and meditate on it. Do you read music? There are no recordings, and probably never will be. Mr. Ives sent me a copy of the score. I'll show it you some time. It's clear enough. Ives, too, is on a quest. He wants to banish the conflict between consonance and dissonance, between sound and silence, between questioning and answering, between finality and eternity. Why?

Why? What's wrong with these conflicts? I'd like to put all you questers in one large room, and photograph you weekly in your Unreal City."

Perhaps it was because Miss Mozart was no longer there, perhaps it was the stridency in Maxwell Lindhorst's voice, but Gregor was coming around from his mind-altering polyesthesia.

"Are you with us again?"

"You allow I talk?"

"Yes. You're such an obedient German."

"I'm Czech."

"German Czech. Gregor, a lovely woman has stooped to folly, but must you folly too? There are people in a burning building who will not come out unless the weather is just right. Must you be the one to rout them? There are many false grails, Gregor. Did you know Wagner was going to write an opera about the Buddha's last journey? I can imagine Schopenhauer coming out on stage, and lecturing the audience about salvation through renunciation. The greatest good is never to be born at all."

Dr. Lindhorst got up from his seat, grabbed the two handles protruding from the rear of the chair, and began to push Gregor toward the black door.

"But since, Herr Samsa, you are already born…"

"I'm not ready."

"What?"

"Don't take me in there. I'm not ready."

"You're not? I thought you were."

"I was. Now I'm not."

"But are you ready for a *modus vivendi asceticus? Noli me tangere?* Ethos of purity contra pathos of impurity? An anxious, neck-breaking game, continually on the edge of the impossible?"

"You mock me."

"Like hell I do."

"I want to get up. Please to unstrap me."

"With pleasure."

Gregor told me this story in great detail on Christmas Eve, 1944. I asked him what exactly in Lindhorst's oration made him change his mind, but apparently it was nothing Lindhorst said or meant. During the *Liebestod*, an image from Dante had flashed across Gregor's mind, a man who carried a light on his back to illuminate the way for others. But the only way to accomplish his task was to plunge resolutely into the darkness.

At the time G's vision seemed appropriate, even heroic. But shortly after his death, I began to wonder at Lindhorst's audacious perspicacity — as I still wonder at Germans and Germany, at the proximity of the great monuments of German culture at Weimar to the crematoria a few kilometers away at Buchenwald, burning fiercely day and night, unknown to us, even as we spoke under blazing Orion in the New Mexican night. Surely this is one of the great unanswered questions: the riddle of the Final Solution — to which the world will never have a final solution.

15. Klaxons

"To Dr. Faustus in his study Mephistopheles told the history of the Creation, saying:

The endless praises of the choirs of angels had begun to grow wearisome; for, after all, did He not deserve their praises? Had He not given them endless joy? Would it not be more amusing to obtain undeserved praise, to be worshiped by beings whom he tortured? He smiled inwardly, and resolved that the great drama should be performed."

It was with this quotation, somewhat strange, that Bertrand Russell, friend and mentor to Wittgenstein, a mentor of mine and teacher to generations, opened his essay, "A Free Man's Worship". With it, he continued his challenge to the faithless world. I was one of the disappointed — even horrified — expert witnesses at the 1940 court proceedings which annulled his appointment to a City College professorship. The shame of it! Lord Bertrand Russell, one of the mightiest minds and most courageous hearts of this century — not fit to teach American students! I won't go on. Even writing this short paragraph brings back memories which fill me with despair.

Suffice it to say that "A Free Man's Worship", though written in 1903, was one of the principle documents circulating and discussed during the war and after, succeeded in 1925 by his even more provocative *What I Believe*. Of the many writers on humanity's new place in a universe newly understood by science, Russell was without peer, an ever-flowing font of meditation on emerging thought and knowledge, and himself a profound influence on modern philosophy, one of the few truly seminal thinkers of the twentieth century.

Gregor became thoroughly attached to the man in reading his work. He remembered Wittgenstein mentioning him, but first encountered Russell in 1923, reading *The ABC of Atoms*. One small section in particular grabbed his attention. I have his copy — being recipient of his eventually extensive library — and find the following passage underlined, with triple exclamation points in the margin:

> *The theory of relativity has shown that most of traditional dynamics, which was supposed to contain scientific laws, really consisted of conventions as to measurement, and was strictly analogous to the 'great law' that there are always three feet to a yard. In particular, this applies to the conservation of energy. This makes it as plausible to suppose that every apparent law of nature which strikes us as reasonable is not really a law of nature, but a concealed convention, plastered on to nature by our love of what we, in our arrogance, choose to consider rational. Eddington hints that a real law of nature is likely to stand out by the fact that it appears to us irrational, since in that case it is less likely that we have invented it to satisfy our intellectual tastes. And from this point of view he inclines to the belief that the quantum-principle is the first real law of nature that has been discovered in physics.*
>
> *This raises a somewhat important question: Is the world 'rational', i.e. such as to conform to our intellectual habits? Or is it 'irrational', i.e. not such as we should have made it if we had been in the position of the Creator?*

A "somewhat" important question, indeed! For Gregor, it became a kind of urgent theme, but an ambiguous one, anchored on one side in "life", and on the other, in some larger realm beyond life, but including life, a realm he had recently visited in the swirling vastnesses of Wagner. Is the world rational or irrational? Could one think on things, and somehow improve them? Gregor's dream, vague, jejune as it was, was to somehow help "rescue" humankind, a task of supreme and pressing importance. Yet what if humanity were of little or no significance in the universe?

According to Russell, any modern thinker had to accept the fact

> *that Man is the product of causes which had no pre-vision of the end they were achieving; that his origin, his growth, his hopes and fears, his loves and his beliefs, are but the outcome of accidental collocations of atoms; that no fire, no heroism, no intensity of thought and feelings, can preserve an individual life beyond the grave; that all the labors of the ages, all the devotion, all the inspiration, all the noonday brightness of human genius, are destined to extinction in the vast death of the solar system, and that the whole temple of man's achievement must inevitably be buried beneath the debris of a universe in ruins — all these things, if not quite beyond dispute, are yet so nearly certain, that no philosophy which rejects them can hope to stand. Only within the scaffolding of these truths, only on the firm foundation of unyielding despair, can the soul's habitation henceforth be built.*

An accidental collocations of atoms destined for extinction. Why bother then? Roach, human, why bother? Yet Russell was able to exercise "a free man's worship", and oppose a vision of the good, in thought and aspiration, to the tyranny of outside forces. And as Russell, so Gregor, a disciple pummeled, yet inspired, by a new companion along the rocky path.

What did others make of these new modes of thought? As if by action/reaction, in the midst of all the scientific brouhaha, religion became a burning issue. People remembered clergy blessing the late declaration of war, and now, in hindsight, fled massively into agnosticism and doubt. And in reaction, from a world of psychoanalysis and behaviorism, of atomic and astronomical research, of speakeasies and dance contests, high skirts and low morals, corporate and gangland crime, from the "roaring twenties", a religious revival was born. Leading the charge, crosses raised high and flags waving, were the Fundamentalists.

By mid-decade, a quarter of the American population subscribed to various tenets of Fundamentalism. For every pamphlet of Bertrand Russell's and his modernist colleagues, there were twenty from wide varieties of fundamentalist organizations. Bible colleges were born and flourished. Many letters were written — to editors, schoolboards, library selection committees, radio stations, to every level of governing body. From hill and mountainside, from village and hamlet, from every state and every city, fundamentalist voices were heard, and not only in the South. They could fill Carnegie Hall whenever they wished — to vigorously denounce evolution. But it was not in the church community that fundamentalism made its largest impact.

In 1915, a few months after Gregor's metamorphosis in Prague, twelve men had huffed and puffed their way up to the top of Stone Mountain, Georgia, carrying gas cans, cloth, and timber. As the sun went down in the early winter evening, and families in Atlanta settled into Thanksgiving dinners, the sky over the giant monolith blazed in yellow, green and blue: a huge burning cross announced the rebirth of the Ku Klux Klan.

Previous nativity events: the birth of insect Gregor, and D.W. Griffith's *Birth of a Nation* that past summer. But while G's appearance created horror around him, the film had brought joy and celebration to millions of southerners; the Klan became the group hero of the silver screen, noble, idealistic, a modern-day version of the Knights of the Round Table, King Arthur, The Holy Grail. It took a while for the storybook aspects to develop into reality: five years later, it had only 2,000 members since not everyone was enthusiastic about sheeted rides in chilly or heat-oppressed nights. But by 1921, with new organizers, new cash incentives, and capitalizing on the Red Scares, there were well over one million members.

With patriotism drummed to hysterical levels following our entry into the War, the Klan became more militantly moralistic, scourging idlers, draft dodgers, prostitutes, and "laborers infected with the I.W.W spirit". It moved to vigilantism, a world of action, not words, with regional targets for pure-blooded Americans. In Texas, the Klan whipped up hatred of Mexicans; in California, of orientals, in New York, of Jews and other eastern European immigrants, in New England, of French Canadians, and most famously, in the South, of Catholics and Negroes. The whipping was both metaphorical and real.

Who joined the Klan? People with a need for camaraderie. People without much to do. People who loved parades and costumes, picnics, boat trips, debating contests, spelling bees. Middle-aged grade school graduates, oppressed by the advancing new world order, promoting the one thing they were sure of — their 100% pure-blooded Americanism, the single virtue they knew they possessed, one which could qualify them to be the guardians of American society. In flowing robes, night-riding on horseback or waving from open cars, any sense of inferiority was easily hooded.

But not only that. The KKK was not peopled by only pathetic specimens (labeled so by superior liberal historians). Real people joined out of a fierce, unschooled conviction that something was rotting in their states, people ready to act to protect pre-marital chastity, marital fidelity, parental authority, prohibition laws. capitalism, white supremacy. They were out there, putting themselves on the line to fight crime and crooked politicians, to counter the tepid unconcern of liberals, and the rabid proposals of foreigners with alien, un-American ideas. They were protectors of the American Dream as they had been given to understand it, and rescuing the American Dream might sometimes call for violence. Their fathers and grandfathers had fought the Civil War, and they themselves, the Great War. Was the onslaught of modernity not a threat even more profound? When a civilization goes wild and creates wildness within it, its feral beasts need punishment to keep them in line. As tar needs feathers, backs need lashing, and necks need lynching. Testicles on the rampage need the knife. And flooding oratory may need fire to quench it. While most KKKers shrank from such tactics, both the bravely committed and the cowardly confused moved to embrace them.

In Oklahoma, the Klan took on whores and their pimps, bootleggers and gamblers, criminals and scofflaws. In 1923, there were 2,500 floggings by "whipping squads" recorded across the state. In Marlowe, Oklahoma, a black man was lynched for "breaking a custom of many years' standing" that blacks must be out of town by sundown. So was the white hotel owner who employed him — lynched In Houston, Texas, a lawyer was tarred and feathered for taking on the "wrong kinds of clients." A Louisiana wife-beater was treated similarly, and a notorious ladies' man was kidnapped and flogged unconscious. Local police failed to arrest, and local juries failed to convict — and all the while Gregor was piloting his elevator up and down, naive and unaware.

Klan and Church were often intertwined. While black churches might be burned, white Protestant churches might be "visited". An entire klavern, perhaps 200 men in full regalia, would enter a church unannounced in the middle of a service, march gravely up the aisle, hand the minister an envelope stuffed with money, and leave as silently as they came. An anti-hold-up, dramatic, in broad daylight. No one inquired about the source of the funds.

Catholic churches, however, were beyond the pale. Catholics were assumed disloyal to the United States, in allegiance only to the Pope. Parents of every Catholic baby, so it was held, celebrated by hiding a gun and fifty rounds of ammunition in the local Catholic church. When the time came, all the little Catholics, now grown up, would be instructed to retrieve their lethal birthrights, seize power, and give the United States to the Vatican. In Kokomo, Indiana, a rumor spread that the Pope, having arrived to claim the United States, was pulling in on the southbound from Chicago. A mob arrived to stone him.

In September, 1921, the liberal *New York World* ran a series on the resurgence of the Klan. Gregor had seen these on first arriving in New York, but had no context in which to understand them. Amusing to the sophisticated, horrible to many others, the articles were a windfall for Klan organization, as 5,000 applications for membership arrived in each day's mail. Such is the power of the liberal press!

H.L Mencken drew what for him was an obvious conclusion: that the Invisible Empire of the Klan was coeval with the more visible empire of the America itself:

> *If the Klan is against the Jews, so are half of the good hotels of the*
> *Republic and three-quarters of the good clubs. If the Klan is against*
> *the foreign-born or the hyphenated citizen, so is the National*
> *Institute of Arts and Letters. If the Klan is against the Negro, so*
> *are all of the States south of the Mason-Dixon line. If the Klan is*
> *for damnation and persecution, so is the Methodist Church. If the*
> *Klan is bent upon political control, so are the American Legion and*

Tammany Hall. If the Klan wears grotesque uniforms, so do the Knights of Pythias and the Mystic Shriners. If the Klan conducts its business in secret, so do all college Greek letter fraternities and the Department of State. If the Klan holds idiotic parades in the public streets, so do the police, the letter-carriers and firemen. If the Klan uses the mails for shaking down suckers, so does the Red Cross. If the Klan constitutes itself a censor of private morals, so does the Congress of the United States. If the Klan lynches a Moor for raping someone's daughter, so would you or I. (Smart Set, 1923)

The single value linking Klansmen and their supporters coast to coast was intense xenophobia. This was their country, built by their ancestors, presumably for them: they weren't about to have it snatched from under their noses. But by 1920, Cleveland, for instance, supported newspapers in 21 non-English languages. Rage was brewing in eastern and midwestern cities where up to three quarters of the population was foreign-born. Many whites felt cornered by Saccos and Vanzettis, surrounded by languages they couldn't understand, subjected to ideas they couldn't, and didn't want to, fathom. And rather than confronting such feelings, certain aspects of contemporary science supported them. Reputable scholars were convinced that race mixing could bring only disastrous results. At my own University, two noted psychologists, Bill McDougall and Carl Brigham, produced *A Study of American Intelligence (Princeton, 1923)* which contended that "the intellectual superiority of our Nordic group over the Alpine, Mediterranean and negro groups has been demonstrated." Henry Osborn, the biologist heading the American Museum of Natural History, publicly expressed his fears that the United States was being "mongrelized." Foreigners were stupid people who did poorly on gross intelligence tests, scoring far below native speakers of English. One should not be surprised then, that being without the intelligence, quick wits, self-reliance, energy and mechanical aptitudes of the native born, and being only a generation removed from serfdom, foreigners were attracted to lazy ideas such as socialism or anarchism. Immigrant populations were rife with paupers and insanity — there were statistics to show it — and though they arrived poor, unlike earlier immigrants from Northern Europe, the new ones stayed poor, and insisted on propagating their culture of poverty in Chinatowns, Little Tokyos, "Lower East Sides", "barrios" and Little Italies around the once-pure land. And so foreigners were being dragged from their homes and beaten, their belongings destroyed, their houses set on fire.

None of this bode well for Gregor, an alien many times over: dark-skinned, with a heavy east-European accent, and improving but poor grammar, born in Czechoslovakia (our old enemy), and most recently of Austria (our old worse enemy), whose native tongue and thought patterns were those of the greatest enemy of all. Not to mention his claws and compound eyes.

In 1921, the new Harding Administration signed into a law a National Immigration Act, bringing totals down from approximately one million per year, to 350,000, with quotas set at 3% of the already-present said population. Thus the "majority" groups were selectively favored. In 1924, Congress reduced the number to 100,000, creating chaos at the nation's ports. On the last day of each month, ships crammed with immigrants would bunch up at harbor entrances like marathoners at a starting line. They would rev up at a few minutes to midnight, and, dangerously crowded, would race to "get in" at the beginning of the month so they could unload their immigrant cargo within that month's quota. Latecomers might have their entire haul of immigrants declared ineligible for entry if the quota had been filled — with doleful consequences for ship and cargo alike. Spirits of tragedies twenty years in the future were already haunting the docks.

Ellis Island was a chaotic hell. Designed to handle 1,700 immigrants a day, it was empty for four weeks, and then attempted to process 40,000 during the first two days of the month. White, English-speaking, first-class immigrants were whisked on through, while the huddled masses yearning to breathe free felt even more homeless and "tempest-tost", jostled around in unspeakable crowding, and subjected to humiliating health exams. It was a good thing Gregor had not arrived through normal channels.

****

As the roach — with all his legs — was leaving 999 Fifth Ave. in the early evening of August 2, 1923, a first bulletin was streaking its way across the lights on the Times Building. By the time he arrived at 43rd St., the crowd in the Square had grown to hundreds. Gregor was too exhausted by his recent ordeal to even wonder what the commotion was all about. The next morning's headlines told the story: "'PRESIDENT HARDING DIES SUDDENLY; STROKE OF APOPLEXY AT 7:30 PM; CALVIN COOLIDGE IS PRESIDENT." The *Times* story was bordered in black:

The Chief Executive of the nation, and by virtue of his office and personality, one to the world's leading figures, had passed away at a time when his physicians, his family, and his people thought that medical skill, hope and prayer had won the battle against disease.

Yet Gregor, tutored by cynical bell-hop colleagues, was "in the know" about other possible explanations: that the President had been poisoned by his wife, insanely jealous of his lover, Nan Britton, and their illegitimate daughter, his wife who had been alone with him at the time of death, and who would not permit an autopsy; or that he had been murdered by his "friends", the legatees of the Teapot Dome and Veteran's Bureau scandals, and of fiscal shennagins around a German Metals Company after the War. The KKK believed that Harding had been poisoned by Catholics.

Millions of Americans lined the tracks to catch a last glimpse of "Uncle Warren" as the funeral train made its stately way from San Fransisco, through Chicago and Washington, and finally to his home in Marion, Ohio. People wept and sang hymns. Meanwhile "the little fellow", as Harding privately described his vice-president, Silent Cal Coolidge, stepped forward from his home in the woods of Vermont, to lead the nation from "normalcy"[5] to prosperity. Five years later, in his valedictory State of the Union Address, he told the nation that

No Congress of the United States ever assembled, on surveying the state of the Union, has met with a more pleasing prospect than that

---

5 A presidential malapropism which, by virtue of coming from on high, has since attained the status of "normality". I am amused by the overabundant rhetoric in which it was birthed. Harding, campaigning in 1920 against the commotion of Wilson's presidency, announced, "America's present need is not heroics, but healing; not nostrums, but normalcy; not revolution, but restoration; not agitation, but adjustment; not surgery, but serenity; not the dramatic, but the dispassionate; not experiment, but equipoise; not submergence in internationality, but sustainment in triumphant nationality." Not exactly – except for the last — what Gregor would encounter.

which appears at the present time... The great wealth created by our enterprise and industry, and saved by our economy, has had the widest distribution among our own people, and has gone out in a steady stream to serve the charity and the business of the world. The requirements of existence have passed beyond the standard of necessity into the region of luxury. Enlarging production is consumed by an increasing demand at home and an expanding commerce abroad. The country can regard the present with satisfaction, and anticipate the future with optimism.

Famous last words. Nine months after that, the country began its slide into the abyss. The "roar" of the twenties had been hollow.

Yet as Gregor sat on his bed on that August night in '23, with all his eyes, his creature-world beheld the open. If, as the new president was soon to announce, "The chief business of America is business," it was true for Gregor, too. He would get on with his business — *Möglichkeit* — a different business, much at odds with America's major thrust, yet as crucial to its welfare. And Alice? Dear Alice. May she heal and thrive. She was a good person. Strong. She would do fine. He would write her soon to apologize.

Up and down, up and down. The elevator paced out the sine wave of events, of men's fortunes, of human aspiration. Before elevators, the poorer patrons had huffed and puffed up the stairs to their sixth and eighth floor rooms. Now, the rich commanded views from new twentieth floors, and the richest, from the thirtieth. Every elevator trip demonstrated the finest gradation of the American class system. By the end of the month, Gregor felt he could tell a 23rd floor person from a 26th floor one if both were standing in a crowded lobby. And because he could continually test his hypotheses, he soon became quite accurate. People-watching in elevators as a technique for class analysis. He could have published a paper.

Shortly after 11 on August 31st, Gregor left the hotel for a post-shift, night time stroll. As he turned the corner onto Broadway, he noticed a small crowd gathering in the street, reading the Times bulletin. His first thought — he didn't know why — was of a presidential assassination. Some anarchist or socialist had murdered President Coolidge, and the police were swooping down on all progressive people. Let it not be, let it not be. But no — as he focused his ommatidia on the moving lights, he discovered that Japan had been hit by a devastating earthquake, and that Tokyo and Yokohama were incinerating in a great fire. He turned back immediately, took the elevator up to Ulla's, let himself in, and headed straight for bed without even nodding to his hostess. As he was undressing, she knocked on his door.

"You OK?"

"Yes."

"You look white as a sheet. Well, tan anyway."

"I don't feel well. You have heard about the earthquake and big fire in Japan?"

"Yeah. It was just on the radio. Is that what's upsetting you?"

"Yes. I think so."

"It's sad, but what's it to you? You got relatives over there?"

"No — not really."

"Can I get you anything?"

"No. I'll be fine in the morning."

But he wasn't fine in the morning, for the next day's *Times* reported, in great detail, the story of the "worst natural disaster in history". A hundred thousand dead, another hundred thousand seriously injured. Fifty thousand missing, a million and a half homeless, 60% of Tokyo and 80% of Yokohama completely destroyed. A population grown indifferent to the daily shivering of seismographs had learned the bitterest of lessons.

It had been a hot and muggy Saturday in Japan, and office and factory workers were waiting for noon, impatient to get home for the weekend. A hundred thousand housewives had fired up hibachis to prepare lunch. The new Imperial Hotel was readying its grand opening that afternoon, an experimental building by Frank Lloyd Wright, challenging the Japanese idea that structures must rest on solid ground. Instead, Wright had sunk his piers into seventy feet of mud, a "floating" approach to earthquake safety, unacceptable to local architects.

At 11:58 a monstrous roar engulfed both cities. Buildings toppled, thousands of people were crushed in narrow alleyways, oil tanks burst into flames. Yellow dust blinded and choked those who survived. Then the larger tragedy struck: 100,000 hibachis had scattered their glowing coals into 100,000 houses of paper and wood. The flames grew and devoured entire neighborhoods. Bridges and rails melted, and threw twisted trains off cliffs and trestles. Water lines burst, gas lines exploded, and repair was impossible because of the heat. Masses gathered in "safe" open spaces only to be suffocated as the firestorm consumed all oxygen.

Is it cruel, colonialist, scientific, to say? — When all was done, amidst the gruesome rubble of downtown Tokyo, Wright's Imperial Hotel stood tall, undamaged, creative engineering the final and only winner.

As he lay in bed the night before, Gregor knew none of this, yet still he was nauseated and could not sleep. Why? *Did* he have relatives there, perhaps from a former life? What was Tokyo to him, or he to Tokyo?

And then he recalled an object belonging to Amadeus, a carved 16th century dagger, some eleven inches long, consecrated to one use only: *seppuku, hara-kiri,* ritual suicide. As a young adult, G had gone with a school friend (actually, a "date") to see *Chushingura*, the most popular play in the Kabuki repertoire, performed at the Stadttheater in Prague by the first touring Japanese company. It was based on a true story about a lord unjustly forced to perform *seppuku*, and the revenge taken by his retainers. Gregor had found the scene of ritual suicide not so much horrifying as infinitely intriguing, and he read voraciously on the subject.

In addition to the act itself, often calmly performed, with expressions of gratitude for opportunity to enact such an honorable deed, two other details fascinated him. Early in the history of the tradition, the performer alone was responsible for his death; the killing stroke had to be his alone. In addition to the abdominal tear, more painful and symbolic than instantly lethal, he had also to cut through his spine or, later, his carotid artery. Before so doing, he would tuck the ample sleeves of his white kimono under his knees, so that when he fell, he would fall forward, in an honorable direction, and not backward, displaying his ghastly wounds to his superiors. Gregor would often meditate on this moment of tucking in. Being a fabric salesman, he would imagine particulars of his own kimono, and such detail would draw him into the mental and spiritual state of the wearer in a most personal way. What would he, Gregor Samsa, do, think, feel, hear, see at this moment? It was a thought experiment which left him metaphysically gasping.

Another element which gripped him was the role of the assistant, or *kaishaku*. As the tradition evolved, it became important for the *seppuku* performer who, no matter what his crime, was in this act an honorable man, to be spared as much pain as possible. Consequently, responsibility for the coup de grace no longer fell on him, but on his assistant. After the performer drew the knife through his own abdomen, the *kaishaku* would decapitate him with one clean blow. Because the condemned had initiated the sequence, the beheading was understood as more honorable than the simple beheading of a common criminal. The *kaishaku* was often a friend of the condemned who, once requested for the role, trained assiduously for the fatal stroke. Only already accomplished swordsmen were eligible, but even the most accomplished secretly studied his friend's neck and practiced on various kinds of mockups. Imagine this practice, thought G. He couldn't decide which was more courageous, the act of the performer or that of his aide. Both were almost incomprehensible to his western mind. Even now, in the late 20th century, executioners fire as a team, or push an array of buttons so that no man knows who has taken the life — of even a despicable stranger. But here, friend to friend, I will do this for you. Thank you.

And the details! It was considered best not to cut the head entirely off with one stroke, but to leave a layer of uncut skin and muscle at the front of the throat, so that the head would not roll offensively away, but rather fall forward, hang down, and conceal the face. The technique was called *daki-kubi,* or "retaining the head", and was a mark of the most excellent swordsmanship. It was this that required the most study and practice. Awful. And awesome. The product of lifelong Buddhist/Samurai training. How far we are from this, ritual suicide, the thoughtful, thankful, courageous embrace of Friend Death.

Yet here was this horrible earthquake. making all irrelevant, doing an end run around the vast mental and spiritual training of the race. Of all people the Japanese — Buddhists aware of contingent existence, so capable of conscious, mindful choice — how ironic, how horrible for that fine discrimination to be overwhelmed by the brutality of earthquake and firestorm. What an injudicious waste of sensibility — *that* is what nauseated him. What was the use of any attainment if it was to be swept away by incomprehensible, uncomprehending forces? This was not the end of the world á la Russell, engulfing human civilization in the fire of the exploding sun tens of billions of years hence. This was a puny shifting of the earth, here and now! And the irony of those hibachi coals, lit with love and caring by faithful partners, igniting mass death...

He recalled Jewish weddings in Prague, the bride and groom under the chupah, in holy space, and their final act: crushing a fine wine glass under the heel. Jews! That Jewish vision, based on so much dreadful experience, that even in the happiest of times, even in sacred space, surrounded by relatives and friends, the universe can simply shatter. Shatter in violence. In earthquake and firestorm. Jews! Japanese!

With an ache in his heart, he fell into restless sleep amid disturbing dreams.

16. The Trial

U p and down, up and down. One of Life's great mysteries is that after only a few up-and-downs, a year has passed, and then more than a year. Gregor had done much reading, much people-watching, had made a few appearances at dwindling dance contests (a fad is a fad, and the Charleston and the Red scares had for the moment won out). He had sampled the cuisine at every inexpensive restaurant and hot dog stand in a 10 block radius. He loved it all. Cockroaches are devotedly omnivorous.

Two months after the Japanese disaster, G was up in his room, quietly weeping at the foot of the radio. Another earthquake? No.

Texaco, in Saturday generosity, had been presenting *Parsifal*, live from the Met. Dry-eyed for four hours, Gregor found himself weeping at the final scene, *Erlösung dem Erlöser*, redemption for the redeemer. Why weeping? Why weeping at triumph? This story of a guileless fool, who knows not who he is, or from whence he comes — this story had obvious resonance for Gregor. Keeper of the grail. But what could that mean for *him*? A simpleton attaining spiritual goals impossible for wiser men. Was this his path? And the wound, Amfortas' unhealing wound. Amfortas. *Infirmitas*. This was no trauma from a thrown apple. This was ... what? The wound from the spear that wounded the Savior. The stigma of love become desire. What was his own wound to that? Was Alice his Kundry awakening him from sleep to sin? Or was he rather her castrated slavemaster? Where was Redemption in such twisted relations?

As if in response to his swirling confusion, the phone rang:

"Allo, Gregor Samsa here."

"Gregor, it's Alice. Paul. In Washington." A long silence. "Alice Paul — do you remember me?"

"Yes."

"Is this a bad time to talk?"

"Yes. I mean no. I have my shift in quarter hour."

"It may seem strange to call you out of the blue, but..."

"You didn't answer my letter..."

"What letter?"

"I send a year ago a letter."

"I never got a letter. Gregor, you can't trust the mail in America — it's not like in Europe. If it's important, you have to send a telegram, or call on the phone. Was it important? "

"I was thinking of you now before you call."

"Good thoughts?" Pause. "Bad thoughts? I've thought about you, too. But good thoughts, good thoughts."

"I am listening *Parsifal*.

"I don't know it."

"Then never mind. Why you are calling me?"

"Gregor, you sound angry."

"No. Really. I am just surprised to hear you. Why you are calling me?"

"Your English is better. But you have to say, 'What's up?'".

"What's up? I will remember that."

"What's up is this. Do you remember Dudley Malone?"

"This is your friend, the lawyer, in Washington?" G could feel his jealousy organ irrationally starting to glow.

"Yes. I told you about him. The man who publicly resigned from President Wilson's staff."

"I remember."

"Something intriguing has come up, and you may be able to help. I can tell you about it briefly, and if you're interested, perhaps we can all meet and talk further."

"Yes? Go ahead. What's up?"

"There's a high school teacher in Tennessee named John Scopes who's just been indicted for..."

"What is indited?"

"Charged with a crime."

"I see. What is the crime?"

"The crime is teaching his students about Darwin's Theory of Evolution."

"This is a crime in America?"

"It's a long story. I can tell you later. Last year Tennessee passed a law against it — political grandstanding. No one thought it would ever be enforced."

"But someone enforced it?"

"It was actually Scopes' friends. They thought the law was stupid, and they wanted to test it, so they persuaded him to get arrested..."

"He wants to be in jail?"

"He's not in jail, but he's scheduled to go to trial next summer."

"I still don't understand why someone would want to..."

"That's the way the system works here. Legislatures make laws, and if they're bad laws, they're tested by someone breaking them, and then arguing the case in court."

"Why don't they think them better before the hand?"

"Beforehand. You can't always think of everything. It's not a bad system, provided the courts do their job, which is not always the case."

"So it's not a good system either."

"Gregor, you have to go to work in five minutes. Here's the point. Dudley has been asked by the ACLU..."

"ACLU, what is that?"

"Sorry. The American Civil Liberties Union. Dudley's been asked to take Scopes' case, and argue it in court in Dayton. Tennessee. We were talking this morning..."

"You were visiting him? Where are you?"

"I'm in Washington. At home. We were talking on the phone."

"Yes?"

"We were talking about evolution, and I mentioned my friendship with you...are we still friends?"

"Yes."

"And we hit on the idea of your being a witness in the trial. Does that interest you?"

"What I witnessed?"

"It's not what you witnessed. It's what you are. You're material evidence."

"Alice, I must go. We talk about it later."

"But are you interested?"

"I don't know. Yes. I need more information. How long it takes. What I do..."

"Certainly. I'll be in New York next week. We can go to Dudley's office together and talk about it. I'll call you when I get in."

"I am going to see you next week?"

"If that's all right."

"Good. Yes. Very all right."

"Then I'll call you Thursday. It's nice to talk to you. Happy Halloween. Boo!"

"What is boo?"

"Boo. I'm a ghost. From the past. Ghosts say 'boo'."

"Ein Gespenst? Ein Ghost?"

"Never mind. I'll see you Thursday. Bye-bye."

Gilbert Murray, the distinguished humanist and Regis Professor of Greek at Oxford, once called the Scopes Trial "the most serious setback to civilization in all history." Yet in public memory, the "Monkey Trial" was a simple icon, open and shut. In an hour and half of sometime sadistic questioning, Clarence Darrow reduced William Jennings Bryan — three time Democratic presidential candidate, ex-Secretary of State under Wilson, beloved Populist — to intellectual rubble, made him the laughingstock of the intelligentsia, and the whipping boy of "real" Fundamentalists, for whom his wavering on the six days of creation was liberal heresy.[6] At the same time, Scopes, Darrow, Malone and their team lost the case. The jury judged Scopes "guilty" after eight minutes of deliberation — as well they might, since he had admitted teaching evolution, and that was the only question Judge Raulston allowed. Yet the trial was far from simple, and its echoes continue to reverberate today in ever louder, more insistent voices, on both legal and scientific levels.

---

6 This aspect of the trial has been so well covered, both in original reports and in the fictionalized drama *Inherit the Wind*, that the reader may consult the record him or herself.

On the surface, the trial was about John T. Scopes, a high school science teacher and football coach at the Rhea County High School, in Dayton, Tennessee. Was he guilty of breaking a law — the recently passed Butler Act?

> *Be it enacted by the General Assembly of the State of Tennessee that it should be unlawful for any teacher in any of the universities, normals and other public schools of the State, which are supported in whole or in part by the public school funds of the State to teach any theory that denies the story of the divine creation of man as taught in the Bible, and to teach instead that man is descended from a lower order of animals.*

Yet for both prosecution and defense, the trial was about much bigger things. Bryan was quite clear about the prosecution's concern: should not a people be able to determine what is taught to their children, in their name and with their money? The good people of Tennessee, who had had the wisdom to pass such an act in the first place, were Scopes' employer, and as Bryan noted, the real question is whether he can misrepresent his employer and demand pay for saying what his employer does not want said. He also demands that his employer furnish him with an audience while he says what his employer does not want said.

The very same thrust now brings forth enthusiastic liberal approval when raised as "community control of schools", or freedom to teach "Afrocentric history". But when Tennessee farmers and small businessmen demanded the same in 1925, or when their descendants now demand creation theory be taught alongside evolution, they are greeted with derision. The problem remains unsettled, a question of state and local rights.

The defense was focused on a different target, the constitutionality of such laws. Florida had passed a similar one; Mississippi and Arkansas were about to adopt one (even after Scopes), and Kentucky had recently defeated such a measure by only one vote. The ACLU was concerned enough to put time and money into Dayton. It felt that though the State might legitimately prohibit the teaching of biology in public schools, once having committed to teach biology, it could not be taught in a way inconsistent with the practice of the science. And above all, the State could not legislate the Bible as the criterion of truth.

Judge Raulston, the onlookers (most of the town), and the politicians who passed the Butler Act had still a third obective: to resist the onslaught of "modernism" against the sacred ways and truths of tradition. The KKK had no foothold yet in Dayton, but its citizens held similar beliefs. Were the simple faiths of ordinary people to be legislated away by intellectuals, "sophisticates" and outsiders? Bryan was the people's champion, defending popular Democracy against the impositions of the educated few.

While it is generally accepted that even in "losing", the defense was the real winner, such was certainly not the case in their own minds. From the beginning, the defense strategy was to lose the case, pay a small fine, and then appeal, all the way to the Supreme Court if necessary, to establish a constitutional ruling. Their first tactic was a move to quash the indictment on constitutional grounds. But Judge Raulston did not find anything unconstitutional about the law passed by his friends in the legislature. The defense then shifted strategy: they tried to introduce such testimony into the record as to provide grounds for a higher court to overturn, expert testimony about evolutionary theory and its rela-tion to Biblical tradition, and Christian faith. Dayton had never seen such a collection of world-famous scholars as that moving into its few rooming houses. But Judge Raulston would not allow expert witnesses to testify, since their opinions had no bearing on the only question at hand — whether or not John T. Scopes had broken the law. The judge did allow written affidavits to be included in the trial record, and the defense thereby had some handle on an appeal. But for the conduct of the trial, there was only one last-ditch alternative, a radical one: call-ing Bryan himself, the chief lawyer for the defense, as a witness. Judge Raulston immediately saw the impropriety of the request, and would have dismissed it had not Bryan himself made a plea to accede. It was to be his finest moment, his chance to confront the unbelievers who would lead the current generation astray, his golden opportunity to lay the specter of evolution to rest. It was also sheer, unprepared, arrogance — and he paid heavily for it, perhaps with his life. The international furor raised by Bryan's appearance prompted Judge Raulston to exclude all press — as well as the jury — from all subsequent argument and testimony, including that of Gregor Samsa.

204

After Bryan's "defeat", and Gregor's appearance, the jury was called back, Scopes was found guilty, fined $100 (paid by the ACLU), his jail sentence suspended, and the trial was "put behind us." The defense appealed on the basis of its written affidavits, but the Supreme Court of Tennessee reversed the original decision on narrow technical grounds — that all fines over $50 had to be set by the jury, not the judge — and the state's attorney dropped the case, thus frustrating the ACLU's plan to take it to the Supreme Court. As the Chief Justice of the Tennessee Supreme Court wrote in his opinion, "We see nothing to be gained by prolonging the life of this bizarre case." The Butler Act stayed on the books until its repeal in 1967.

Gregor's short, but significant, appearance has itself left little mark on history. With the courtroom cleared of all attendees except the principles, with no radio or telegraph reports, no news photographers clicking and crackling away, the final moments of the trial were largely invisible to the public, recorded only in the archives of the American Civil Liberties Union and, with inconsistencies, contradictions and exaggerations, in the correspondence, diaries and notes of the few people remaining in the courtroom.

Mrs. William Jennings Bryan was one of them. Carried up the steps into the courtroom in her wheelchair each day, she sent "bulletins" to family at home — interesting, if somewhat partisan, accounts of the trial's events. The reader will perhaps be interested in her final message, which I will footnote with additional commentary. Again, I ask your indulgence for using such scholarly apparatus, a habit three-quarters of a century old. It has been well said: for the man whose only tool is a hammer, every problem looks like a nail.

DAYTON, TENNESSEE

July 25, 1925

BULLETIN NUMBER THREE

Papa is recovering well after fainting in court this morning. It was probably the heat, and the exhaustion from yesterday's "duel to the death" with Mr. Darrow, but I was a little frightened when I saw him clutch his chest and slump down.[7]

---

7 Hindsight, of course, shows how wrong she was. Bryan was dead four days later. Even after twenty years, Gregor was convinced he had contributed to the man's death.

Yesterday there was a great alarm about the floor of the courthouse;
it was cracking and some people said the walls were trembling under
the great weight of the crowd. The judge, therefore, adjourned court
to the courthouse yard, where a stand had been erected and seats of
lumber were provided. The change from the hot stuffy courtroom was
a very agreeable one.[8]

The first dramatic incident of the day was the apology which
Darrow made to the court. He had been cited for contempt at the
previous session and was very humble in his apology. The judge
replied that he would forgive him. I was very pleased to see him
jerked up and would not have wept if he had spent the night in jail.
He has been so bitter and venomous all the way through.[9]

Yesterday afternoon was when Papa was called as a witness by
Darrow and questioned by him in a most abusive manner. Papa
stood by his guns very manfully, and, while his answers made him
appear more ignorant than he is, he did not give Darrow any oppor-
tunity to catch him, and stumped that gentleman considerably by
asserting that he did not think the word "day" in Genesis meant a
twenty-four-hour day but could be just as easily translated as period.
Darrow was not expecting this and it evidently disappointed him.
Darrow's questions were purely technical such as no one could possibly
know. For instance, how many people lived on the earth at the time
Christ was born? and similar queries. When he asked a question
about the Bible, Papa forced him to read the passage; he would not

---

8 It must have been agreeable, too, that right behind the platform was a huge painted
sign which said "READ YOUR BIBLE DAILY".
9 While Darrow is generally accounted "the winner" in the contest with Bryan, it is
true that many people were put off by what seemed personal vindictiveness toward
his opponent. While he had philosophical and political reasons for his fervor, the
encounter seemed more like flaying a trapped animal. Bryan, on the other hand,
maintained his personal dignity, and was saddened by Darrow's performance. "Mr.
Darrow says he is an agnostic. He is the greatest criminal lawyer in America today. His
courtesy is noticeable — his ability is known — and it is a shame, in my mind, in the
sight of a great God, that a mentality like his has strayed so far from the natural goal
that it should follow — great God, the good that a man of his ability could have done
if he had aligned himself with the forces of right instead of aligning himself with that
which strikes its fangs as the very bosom of Christianity."

permit him to quote it in his own language. This was gall and worm-wood to the gentleman. The whole thing was entirely out of place and in the night the judge decided it was irrelevant and had the proceed-ings expunged from the court records.[10] But, of course, it went out all over the country. It had the further injustice of not giving Papa a chance to question Darrow. He was loaded for him and would have made an excellent shot had he had the opportunity.[11]

Feeling ran quite high during the encounter between Papa and Darrow, and on Monday night the attorneys came up to the house and gave us a bit of unwritten history which will interest you. It seems there were in the audience some of the mountain gunmen, and just at the close of the debate when Papa had said, "You have no interest but to scoff and sneer at the Bible," and Darrow had replied, "I have no interest except to explode your fool opinions which nobody believes." — at this interesting juncture the judge let fall his gavel and court was dismissed. But, as I was saying, the lawyers told Papa that night that the gunmen in the audience thought Darrow was about to lay hold of Papa in the heat of the debate and one of them had his hand on his gun, saying afterwards that if Darrow had taken hold of Papa Darrow would never have left the platform alive.[12] This threat came to the ears of the judge and alarmed him

10 Even before the interrogation began, Judge Raulston had dismissed the jury. They may have been the only people in the entire town who had not witnessed the outdoor trial.

11 Darrow had procedurally outwitted Bryan. Had Bryan had a chance to cross-ex-amine Darrow as Darrow had cross-examined him, he was planning to explore Darrow's assertion in the Leopold and Loeb case that Nietzsche had corrupted the murderers. If Nietzsche corrupted Leopold and Loeb, could not Darwin corrupt the school children of Tennessee? But since Darrow was not called as a witness, Bryan was not able to put such questions.

12 A similar situation had developed with respect to the arrogant and locally detest-ed H.L. Mencken, darling critic of the urban intellectuals. For a week he had been reporting on the Dayton "peasants", "yokels", "morons", and "hillbillies" who never knew anything and never would." On Friday, July 17, he had been visited by "some of the boys", who informed him that "we've decided that this here climate ain't too healthy for you. There's a mighty strong tree in the courthouse yard, and we'll give you two hours to leave town." Mencken let them know that that was one hour too long, and left immediately, taking a taxi 40 miles to Chattanooga, and then the train to Baltimore.

*because he knows the temper of the mountaineers and he resolved
to return to the courtroom and risk the unsafe walls. This morning,
fortunately, it was raining, which gives a good excuse for not going
outside, and the court was held upstairs.*

*When the judge brought the court to order, the second dramatic event
occurred. Mr. Malone, whose morals I wrote about in my last letter[13],
requested to put a new witness on the stand. When questioned, he admitted this to be an "expert witness", and the judge ruled that unless the new
witness could testify to details concerning Mr. Scopes, his expert testimony
was irrelevant, and should, like the others, be committed to writing and
entered in the record. The defense went into conference, and Mr. Malone
changed his request to something he admitted to be unorthodox — that the
new witness be presented and entered into the record as "evidence." Papa
looked at me quizzically, and even Judge Raulston seemed confused, but
when promised that it would not take very long, he dismissed the audience,,
the jury and the reporters, and gave permission for the new witness or evidence to be presented. (Only those of us on the "teams" — I was considered
on Papa's team! — were permitted to remain.) A man walked in from the
lobby dressed in coat and hat in spite of the great heat. Mr. Malone wanted
to seat him in the witness chair, but the judge ruled that he should stand at
the table with the other evidence, the various copies of the Bible, the written affidavits, etc. At a signal from Mr. Malone, the man removed his hat
and coat, and looked to be some kind of large insect, perhaps a remarkably*

---

13 From BULLETIN NUMBER TWO, July 20, 1925: "Then appears Dudley Field Malone, very round bald head, and an exceedingly alert expression. As you children will remember, he was one of Paps' under-secretaries in Washington. He now has the proud distinction of being a divorce lawyer in Paris. When we knew him in Washing-ton he was the husband of one of the daughters of Senator O'Gorman of New York. He later became infatuated with Miss Doris Stevens of Omaha, Miss Stevens being a prominent member of the National Party which was responsible for all the picketing done in front of the White House. The National Party has been a great annoyance to the regular suffrage association. Malone left his wife for the sake of Miss Stevens, and finally got a divorce from her, although a Catholic. I understand he has been excom-municated from the Catholic Church. He has been married to Miss Stevens, so they say, although she still calls herself Miss Stevens, being one of the generation of women who does not care to take the name of her husband. She also wears no wedding ring and is here, very tall and slim and bobbed-haired, to witness the trial." [And of course, to be with her ex-comrade-in-arms, Alice Paul.]

overgrown waterbug. This was when Papa fainted, and of course the whole
court was immediately taken up with that. After a few minutes, Papa was
fine, drinking cold water, and proceedings began once more. I had thought
perhaps this person, a Mr. Gregory Samsa, was some unfortunate, suffering
from a rare disease, like people who develop elephant skin. But no, appar-
ently, if one is to believe Mr. Malone, Mr. Samsa was a perfectly normal
human being, a fabric salesman living in Prague, Czechoslovakia, who one
day evolved[14] (or unevolved, as Papa says) into an insect. He took off most

---

14 It may have been biologically naive of the defense, but Gregor was presented as evidence that life forms can change from one kind of entity to another, and were not fixed at the moment of their creation. On the other hand, this was a proposition far ahead of its time, one hotly debated today.

Darwin believed that the formation of new species was always slow and gradual, the result of natural selection on many tiny, random, genetic variations over long periods of time. In the last fifteen years, this classical view has been challenged by paleontologists who have put forth a contrasting account of "punctuated equilibrium". Darwin maintained that the gaps in the fossil record would be filled in to create a continuous account of the evolution of life forms. Stephen Jay Gould and his followers argue instead that the evidence of the fossil record does not support slow gradual evolutionary change only, but often shows great numbers of organisms persisting with little or no change over long periods of geological time — suddenly punctuated with periods of abrupt change and appearance of new forms. Gould et al. argue that the record should be seen not as lacking in completeness, but as adequate evidence for this pattern of "punctuated equilibrium" — long persistence interrupted by rapid change.

From whence these changes? Consider the contrast between the evolution of frogs and that of mammals. The numerous species of frogs have remained morphologically and functionally stable over the eons, while in the same time span, mammals have evolved into widely diverse forms, with many adaptations to wide-ranging environments. But at the same time, the number of point mutations in their respective DNAs differs little. This would suggest that major genetic change, and formation of new species, are associated with larger alterations and rearrangements of the genes, rather than Darwin's slow accumulation of point mutations. Gregor's personal transformation, while extraordinary and striking, is not entirely inexplicable, being of the order of magnitude of "normal" change of larvae, say, to butterfly, a change brought about by the incompletely understood "turning on and off" of gene sequences.

A first question might be, "Where did the cockroach genes come from?" The most likely answer is that they are already present in our 95% "junk" DNA — sequences with no obvious current function. If ontogeny recapitulates phylogeny, those sequences must be programmed in individual genomes, able, at some point, to express themselves. If entire genomes of successful species "hidden" within "junk" DNA are able to emerge under extraordinary circumstances, the evolutionary significance is huge.

Our recent ability to analyze gene structure at the molecular level has revealed DNA's amazing plasticity. Investigators have found nucleotide sequences that can move from one position on the chromosome to another, often carrying neighboring

of his clothing, and displayed his insect parts in a manner most convinc-
ing, though I suppose it could have been a human in a cleverly designed
costume. At any event, the strategy backfired on Darrow, Mr. Malone, and
his friends since Papa maintained, and the judge agreed, that Mr. Samsa,
whoever and whatever he is, could as easily be explained as an act of God as
an evolutionary event, and these last proceedings were also stricken from the
record.[15]

---

sequences with them, thus rearranging the genome. These "jumping genes"— known as transposons— have been found in both nucleated and non-nucleated cells across the animal and vegetable kingdoms. In the higher mammals, including humans, they are the source of the tremendous diversity necessary for antibody production. Some forms of cancer may develop as a result of these rearrangements.

It is conceivable that Gregor's transformation was related to a massive rain of such transpositions, a first thrust of Nature towards greater success for the human species, for surely, the class *Insecta* is the most successful in the history of animal forms. Insects account for about five-sixths of all animal species so far described; in addition to the nearly one million insect species known, entomologists estimate one to four million yet to be described. Evolutionary "progress" may not always be in the direction of the new; it may be reversion to earlier, more stable forms. The well-known resistance of cockroaches to radiation is surely a valuable trait in a world of ozone holes and nuclear waste, not to mention nuclear Armageddon. While Mr. Bryan characterized G as being "de-evolved", he may have been the atavistic advance garde of the future.

The debate over evolution was not put to rest at Dayton. Indeed, it rages more furiously than ever — both between scientists and fundamentalists (now calling themselves "creationists"), and among scientists themselves. (See the furious fight between Gould and Daniel Dennett described in the *New York Review*, 12 June/August 14, 1997.) The fight itself has given new courage to contemporary creationists. If Gould's assertions about punctuated equilibrium are correct, then, *contra* Darwin, the evolutionary process must be seen through a lens of discontinuity, thus opening the door to saltationism. Darwin states four times in the Origin that "*natura non facit saltum*" (Nature makes no jumps). But discontinuity to the point of saltation would indicate otherwise. Gould himself opposes saltationism, and sees punctuated equilibrium as a mere variation on Darwin and not as a changed, repudiatory paradigm. Nevertheless, the creationists are out to exploit the eddy of debate with their own spin: if evolution is discontinuous, there is both doubt about Darwinian orthodoxy, and room for a playful God.

The seeds of this contemporary controversy were present at Dayton more than seventy years ago. Both prosecution and defense were correct in seeing Gregor as evidence for their respective positions.

15 Mrs. Bryan's summary does not do justice to Gregor's effect on the trial itself. It is true that audience, jury and reporters were out of the room during his appearance, but the judge was clearly shaken, as was the prosecution team. As I have already mentioned, the shock of seeing Gregor may have precipitated a medical event which led, within days, to Bryan's death. The old man was clearly distracted enough to forfeit his

*Then the lawyers on both sides went into conference and decided
to permit the jury to come in and be charged by the court with no
speeches from either side.[16] After a number of preliminary motions
the press and the audience were admitted, and the jury filed to their
places, having been shut out for days. The judge then charged them,
rendering his opinion in a rather sing-song tone, but very clear
minded as to the point involved. The jury retired and were out of the
room about five minutes, returning with a verdict of "Guilty," but
left it to the court to determine the fine. Court then placed a fine of
one hundred dollars and bail was fixed at five hundred dollars —
the Baltimore Sun, the awful Mr. Mencken's paper, offering to be
responsible. Scopes then appeared and recited a little piece which had
clearly been taught him by the defense layers about his feeling that
the law was unconstitutional and that he would resist it as long as
possible, etc. When he had finished, he cast a sheepish eye at his counsel to see if he had said all that was required.*

****

La commedia è stupenda. On the evening after the trial, students at RCHS
held a dance in Darrow's honor. The 68-year old man came, danced and
"even smoked cigarettes with them" according to Arthur Hays, a lawyer on
the defense team. Adulation and second youth made for a heady evening.

Bryan, too, was honored — in the four days he had to live. While
Darrow was doing the Gregor and the Charleston in a smoky gymnasium
on that warm, moonlit evening, the old populist was walking with friends
in the hills at the edge of town. He stopped, rammed his cane into the

---

opportunity (see note 11 below) to make a summation to the jury, and thus recoup
his lost authority. Judge Raulston, too, was rattled enough to exceed his authority in
assessing the fine, and thus to have his famous case overturned on appeal. Even the
defense team was moved by G's dignified demeanor, and John Scopes was motivated
to do some research on genetic mechanisms which, unfortunately came to little.

16 Again, the defense team outwitted the prosecution. Darrow, realizing that Bryan
might make a comeback with as summation speech to the jury, pleaded Scopes guilty
and waived the defense's right to a closing address. Under Tennessee law, the prosecution was also deprived of the right.

earth and suggested that up there, on the top of that hill, there be built a Boy's School. The students would wear uniforms of blue and gray, symbolizing the reunion of this great country, and they would read the Bible of their fathers to keep that union ever knit. If Dayton would go ahead with the project, he would pledge it $50,000 — a huge sum —then and there. Money was raised in collaboration with a scores of evangelical orders, prohibitionist societies, and peace organizations for "a school whose stones would be quarried from the hills of Rhea County, and whose curriculum would be quarried from the Bible." A year later, the cornerstone was laid by Gov. Peay for William Jennings Bryan University, a single story building built, in part, by the muscle and sweat of its own students, young men who did not smoke.

Alice and Gregor left before the various festivities. They were both on the late afternoon bus to catch the evening train to Washington. Because of Gregor's color, they sat in the rear, so as not to attract the driver's attention. Alice did call forth furtive stares from passengers black and white, with her weary paleness standing out among the dark faces rear of the wheels.

Gregor spent the next month sleeping under the couch in her apartment on Capitol Hill. The last event in his Washington education was watching a parade on Pennsylvania Ave. It was August 8th, 1925, and 40,000 hooded Klansmen marched the broad thoroughfare from White House to Capitol celebrating their victories in the recent election – Coolidge re-elected, Bob LaFollette soundly defeated — and their faith in America's future redeemed.

17. More Disturbing Dreams

Handcuffed. Front and middle legs. The strap squad walks him briskly down the corridor, through a heavy door, and into the execution chamber.

A massive piece of furniture. Dark, shiny oak, elementary school smell, heavy, angular, functional, wide arms, ladder back, vertical wooden slats for headrest, two hefty legs behind, two narrow ones in front. The timbers of justice. Tiny room, white walls, white ceiling, white shiny floor, the better to mop you up from, my dear. All dominated by the chair, THE CHAIR, a weighty sculpture in a small, bare gallery.

Union electrician, long leather gloves, fastening electrodes, easier without those gloves, should I mention it to him? Headpiece, aach — cold sponge against chitin

If the warden were to order this man to crawl under the chair, as if into a kennel, and bark, he would gladly obey the order.

Who are you, why are you here? All you people in suits and ties. You with the notebook, what are you scribbling? Who are you? I don't know you. Are we going to be introduced? Why are you here?

A sudden, violent shortening of every muscle in the client body: inner flesh become as steel. Back pulled tight, head wrenched back, hooks and hairs clutching inward, splaying out. The current runs a cycle, from very high voltage to more moderate voltage, and as voltage abates, the body sags ever so slightly. Then — with a distinct click! — the cycle returns to maximum current, and the body in the chair jumps again, like someone dozing, awakened by the phone.

I know this. Circus. Magic Act. The volunteer is bound and gagged and strapped into place, a mask over his eyes. Everything has the quality of a stunt, culminating in a mystical, improbable cloud of steam, a thin column of smoke rising from the headpiece. Electrical contraptions in cheap side-shows. Step right up, ladies and gentlemen. The extra-special thing about this act is that the deaths are real. Oh, ladies and gentlemen, bring your sadism, only 2 marks. The repercussions are incalculable. .

The crowd, the white room crowd, fascinated by the Spectacle of the Burning Parcel, easy prey for pickpockets circulating among them. So much for deterrence.

"Hey, Greggo the Last, wanna take a look? C'mon. Know thy enemy."
11:11.

"Now here's how we'd improve it — first of all, it needs a more comfortable backrest, don't you think?"

"I would double up the gauge," Klofac observed. "Wires won't get so hot."

"What about a drip pan?" Kramer suggested. "Make the cleanup easier."

"Besides," Soukoup observed, "they could use the fat in the kitchen. Present company excepted, of course. No fat on this boy."

"I think two leg grounds would be better than one, don't you? In at the top, whoosh out through the bottom."

"And I'd put Jell-o on the patient's head, not just a sponge. You like Jell-o, Greggo? Cherry Jell-o?"

Kleagle waxed poetic, as usual: "Ah, the gloss of technical precision on the savagery of mutilation unto death. Humane approaches to inhumane acts — the great accomplishment of the Enlightenment! *Ave*, civilization. *Ave*, Westinghouse *ad dexteram Teslii. Ave*, alternating current, *gratia plena*.

And Kaminer, his suckup amanuensis: *"In heisse Lieb gebraten..."*, and the three of them crooning in chorus, *"IN HEI-SSE LIEB GE-E-BRA-A-AAA-TEN!"*

"Maybe it would be kinder to tell them they were just going to have a treatment for head lice. Would that be better, Greggo? A surprise? From the government?"

But Greggo was focused on another issue: "Why a chair? Why not a bed?"

"Oh, but it's not a chair, Greggo, it's a throne, a royal throne. You're going to be the king of the dance. Kings don't lie in bed. They're busy, busy, busy saving their people, busy making the deserts bloom. I hope you know how to dance. Oh, how silly of me. You *are* a dance."

"But don't you think the blade should be slanted, or at least convex?" Klofac asked.

Dr. Kramer to the rescue: "That would solve the problem posed by overlapping vertebrae. Cutting instruments have little effect if the stroke is perpendicular. When examined microscopically, they are seen to be saw-blades, which can operate only by sliding across the body they are intended to cut."

The clock rang the quarter hour. Death pulls his rope. The moon throws the guillotine's long shadow far along the cobbled street. *Stabat mater dolorosa.*

"Field trip over. Time to go back home."

Down the slowly sloping hill, past warehouse doors, locked or chained. A sickly girl stood at a pump in her dressing gown, gazing at Greggo while the water poured into her bucket. The guards talking quietly among themselves.

"There really must be good continuity at the electrodes if you want to keep flesh burning at a minimum."

"That's right. I would think if you overload — say more than six amps — you'd broil the meat on the body."

"It'd be like an overdone chicken — the meat'd come off right in your hand."

"Not the thing cosmetically. We do return the body to the family, don't we? Returning cooked meat would be in poor taste."

They all guffawed.

"I don't think this one has a family. Hey, Greggo," his voice raised, "You got a mom and pop? Got a seester, meester?"

"I have a sister."

The isolation cellblock was reached by stone steps rising from the guttered street. Beyond the staircase he could see in the courtyard three other flights of stairs climbing to balconies and a little passageway which seemed to lead into a second courtyard. A thin column of smoke was rising from a building partially invisible.

"I'm likely to be pardoned. My advocate is working on it. He's optimistic."

"A man can't be too careful," observed Soukoup. "Even while they're pronouncing the pardon the Judges foresee the possibility of a new arrest."

"And old Greggo here isn't a man, anyway. A man can intervene, make a plea for himself. But this one here, he's just a thing waiting to be done by the hangman. Human life should be sacred…"

"The lesson of the gallows is that a man's life is no longer sacred when it is thought useful to kill him."

Kleagle the historian: "After walking eleven hours," a traveler of the early centuries relates, "without having traced the print of human foot, to my great comfort and delight, I saw a man hanging upon a gibbet. My pleasure at the cheering prospect was inexpressible, for it convinced me I was in a civilized country."

Klang. Klick. Klop. Death row cells are narrow, close, toilets small and cramped, little more than metal pipes wedged in the floor. They hardly flush, you can't clean them. The cells always smell like shit.

"I have something to read to you," says the warden — but the piece of paper in his hand, bordered in black, speaks for itself. Curiously bloodless: one dry "whereas" after another culminating in a businesslike "therefore." "Please sign here. Any special requests for a last meal?" What a curious thing to ask.

The sun had risen on a living Greggo. Executioner Sanson, Warden Henry, and ten official witnesses enter the death chamber through a side door. Sanson puts a blood red outer garment over his neatly pressed clothes. He had napped well enough in the afternoon. Greggo walks down a narrow concrete path to the door behind which twelve men are sitting to witness his death. The wiry warden, salt-and pepper hair cut short, gold rimmed glasses accentuating his sharp facial features. The death chamber is painted white with an electric light blazing hot in the ceiling. G-man is pale. His upper legs are lashed to arm rests, his middle ones bound tightly around his thorax, his lowers are strapped to the chair legs, and his body to the chair so tightly that his thoracic-abdominal junction is like to snap.

The electrician comes into view on my right. He attaches one of the electrical jacks to the metal plate inside the leather strap holding my right tarsus. Too thin for good contact. I wiggle around to show him. He clips my sensory hairs with wire-cutters, and moves the electrode to mid-tibia. He reaches behind me for the sponge-covered death implement sitting in saline solution, and slips the screw post into the death cap, specially fashioned to enclose antennae and sit tightly on the epicranium. What they don't know is that if I press my elbows tightly against the wood, I can hear ravishing, humming vibrations, and I will concentrate so strongly on these that when my head falls, I may even be in doubt as to the event, feeling nothing more than a slight sensation of coolness at the back of the neck.

Sanson steps up behind me; I feel a cold sponge in the space between my eyes. I sense the man moving in front of me to fasten the death cap under my chin. Careful with the mouth parts, please. Thank you. You're welcome. I nod and smile — but cringe away as he stuffs cotton in my mouth, to trap any blood which I suppose might gush from my brain. He steps back quickly. Silence. What are they doing? I press my elbows hard against the chair.

"Greggo, it ain't like the old days. In the old days people was put to death for little things. Who wouldn't steal some bread to feed the wife and kids? I would if I had to. I mean it was easy to put myself in your shoes."

11:19

"But today, all you guys on the Row are like animals. You deserve all the shit we give you. OK, boys, cuff him up. Both sets of hands. It's time for the final walk." Chief guard Kludd.

"This guy ain't so bad. He's for the little man, the workin' people. Like us." Socially conscious Spinks.

Emil, "The Professor" Knecht: "All social questions achieve their finality around the executioner's thrust. Mr. Samsa, did you know that electrocution was introduced in New York State, our brother to the west, as a merciful improvement to the centuries-old practice of hanging?"

"Leave him alone. He don't want to hear no lectures now."

"No, please. It will help me get through."

"The process by which this judgment was arrived at is instructive. You see, no one really knew for sure whether electricity would actually kill humans or merely stun them into a death-like state that, while having all the outward appearances of departed life, would not satisfy the legal and moral requirements of the public conscience."

"He ain't a human, he's a animal."

"Shut your mouth."

"A cat and a dog, followed by a horse, had been killed in this manner as well as an orangutan the size of a small human male (although the animal's long hair caught fire and charred his exterior), and that seemed to be enough to convince members of the New York Legislature that electrocution would be a more humane form of execution compared to hanging."

"It's a ugly experience, Greggo. Just think about the insides of your body, you know, how the organs are burned, you know, thousands of high volts. Think about the precious brains in your head, you know, think about your eyes. Those great big eyes. What will your eyes do with all those volts being ran through your body? Who the hell knows?"

On its way up the hill, the little parade disturbed many children playing in the courtyards and on the stairs. They looked angrily at Greggo as he shuffled slowly through their ranks. The eyes of a group of youngsters were so tensely fixed on G that for a moment he stopped, and stood silently, looking at them.

"C'mon Sluggo, get moving!" Kludd yanked on his chain. Someone in the crowd clapped his hands high in the air and shouted Bravo.

The bright red tumbrel moving at a walk through five locked gates to the outer edge of the prison. The outer edge and yet the depths. My death workers, my escorts, Kludd, Knecht and Spinks, all in their ill-fitting black suits, with all sorts of pleats, pockets, buckles, and buttons, and belts. Eminently practical, no doubt, though it's unclear what actual purpose the pleats and pockets serve. And now: "Everything ready. Proceed with execution." Immobilize head with harness and chinstrap.

Chair always visible — a giant yellow structure embraced by thick black straps, connected by tubes of wire to an unseen generator, and crowned with a prominent circular sign on which is inscribed in bold red letters READY. Stark presence of the Terror. How am I going to react? Will I go crazy on the way down? I can't walk smiling, acting calm, too hard, not natural. I can't.

Official tests of the chair, the noise and vibration heard by inmates on the Row. "That baby's working real good today." At noon the warden tests the reserve generators. The guards come by with their sticks and poke at you:

"Naked.
Open yer mouth
stick out yer tongue.
Wear any dentures?
Lemme see both sides of your hands.
Pull out that dong.
Don't got no foreskin?
Lift it.
Turn around
bend over.
Spread your cheeks
Bottom of yer feet
Get dressed."

From the Last Night Cell to the Execution Room. Let's go. You gonna cry tears in your eyeballs. Last supper — a fine treat for the likes of you. We'll add a little dirt for you, killer bastard, a little soap in the soup.

11:23

The guards who came and took me to the death room acted as if they were going to a party. Great pleasure and joy. The children blew kisses, but one woman spit. The guards, the death workers full of sexual fulfillment; their faces gave off enough light to get us through the evening mist. A bent old man and his student walked alongside the wagon. Old to young:

"Such sights are frightfully painful. The blood flows from the vessels at the speed of the severed carotids, then it coagulates. The muscles contract; their fibrillation is stupefying; the intestines ripple and the heart moves irregularly, incompletely, fascinatingly; the mouth puckers in a terrible pout. It's true: the eyes are motionless with dilated pupils; their transparency belongs to life, but their fixity belongs to death. All this can last minutes, even hours in sound specimens. Death is not immediate: every vital element survives decapitation. We doctors are left with the impression of a murderous vivisection, then premature burial."

On the last day at 8 AM the death squad comes and sits facing you, oh Greggo, watching every move you make for the rest of the day. At noon you get your last meal. At 10:30 PM you are given a shower and the execution clothes, then moved to the end cell which is completely empty except for a toilet. PRE-EXECUTION CHAMBER NO SMOKING, NO SPITTING. At 10:55 the entire death crew comes in to escort you to the chair. Two officers for strapping you in. The stomach and chest straps go on first, then the arms and wrist, then the legs. Once attached to the plank, you become part of the machine. The wire to the left leg is connected and the head piece is fitted in place. The warden asks if you have any last words, then the leather mask is placed over your face. You sit and wait.

Sunday, Aug 28. Six thousand begin to march, twenty-five abreast, with fifty thousand falling in behind. South to the crematory! Two hundred thousand watch the March of Sorrow along six miles. Irish jeering FURRINERS GO HOME, police charge out of control, anyone with a red armband "Remember Justice Crucified, August 22, 1927" is specially targeted. Heavy rain as if to wash Boston clean — how many people willing to get soaked for the sake of two anarchist wops! Their last sight, the marchers: a thin column of smoke rising from the crematory chimney. A thin column of smoke rising from the central chimney, dark and straight against a sullen sky.

"Removed from this place...close custody...thence taken at such time to the place of execution, there to be hung by the neck until dead." There was a low whine and a short loud snap, as of huge teeth closing. Greggo's head flew back and his body leaped forward against the straps. Almost at once a thin column of smoke rose from his head and left wrist, and was sucked into the ventilator overhead. His body churned against the bonds, his mouthparts ceased trembling, turned red, and slowly to blue. Moisture appeared in the cuticle and a sizzling noise was heard. (Executions were finally hidden behind prison walls not so much because they offended public taste, but because the public liked them too much.) The smell of burning flesh grew heavy in the air. Greggo was being broiled in the shell. After two minutes the current went off with a distinct clap and Greggo slumped back into his seat, head hanging forward in an honorable direction. No one moved. The public loves to come and see. They laugh and laugh at turkey-red flesh. Gobble gobble. The doctor steps forward to listen, but moves back again, shaking his head. A second charge, and more smoking and sizzling and broiling, chitin melting around the straps. The doctor listens carefully and raises his head. "I pronounce this man dead," he says, and coils up his stethoscope. *Stabat mater dolorosa.* Five minutes of rational technology for Greggo, five minutes proposed, invented, and exonerated by the medical profession.

Policemen signal traffic to break into the procession, cars force their way a few feet amid our cat-calls and screams; one policeman forces a seven-ton truck into the crowd and we attack the driver with umbrellas. When the cop tries to club us, we sweep him aside. Coming into Jamaica Plains I think, and now the police have orders to break up the march, period, no matter what. A small army charges us with clubs. One cop attacks in a police car, running people down, while others climb into demonstrator-friendly cars, club the drivers, and drive the cars off-street. Persons riding on running boards are pulled off and beaten. By this time, most of the marchers are in flight toward Boston, pursued by a line of police — clubbing men, women and children.

I am being beated and my hat fell off, and when I try to pick it up, the sergeant kicks it out of my reach, yelling, "Welcome to America, rube!"

What would Mama think? Greta? On Execution day the radio is completely shut off from the death house.

> As the switch is thrown, the body leaps.
> *His vision is grown so weary*
> *from the this bar and this one and this*
> *that he sees no more.*
> *To him it seems there are only bars*
> *and beyond the bars no world.* [17]

No executions on Sundays. But a minute after midnight, it's not Sunday, and four guards escort you from your cell down the Row to a small room, the Preparation Room, a place for the dead-to-be. You are strip-searched, then hustled next door to the Death Row shower.

---

17 Gregor often referenced Rilke's poem, *Der Panther*, as he did when telling here his disturbing dream — perhaps because it reflected the sense of imprisonment that haunted him.

Padding circling, back, around,
turning, repeating,
strength orbiting a center
in which a great will stands.
in stupefaction.

Stupefied, you shower and put on the cheap suit.

Langone's Funeral Parlor at the foot of Hanover St. Two red-draped coffins amidst banks of flowers. A hundred thousand people file through over three days, cracking marble floors. Huge floral pieces in borrowed shop windows up and down Broadway. Lines outside half a mile long, women in black weeping for their beloved Rodolpho Alfonzo Raffaeli Pierre Filibert de Valentina d'Antonguolla, the beloved that never came. They seat you, dazed, while Kullich and Kirko quickly pinion arms and legs and torso. Your eyes follow the feverish activities of the men fumbling at the straps. *Are people to say of me that at the beginning of my case I wanted to finish it, and at the end, I wanted to begin it again? If it had not been for this thing, I might have lived out my life talking at street corners, haranguing scorning men. I might have died, unmarked, unknown, a failure. Now we are not a failure. This is our career, and our triumph. Never in our full life could we hope to do such work for tolerance, for justice, for man's understanding of men as now we do by accident. Our words — our lives — our pains — nothing! The taking of our lives — lives of a good shoemaker and a poor fish-peddler — all! That last moment belongs to us — that agony is our triumph.* Someone in the audience whoops and shouts "Encore!"

Kerko holds a a carved 16th century dagger, some eleven inches long just above your head, and you now see clearly — you are supposed to seize the knife yourself, and plunge it in. But your arms are bound.

The hood is adjusted, the final act of preparation. A slim, gray-haired gentleman approaches the chair with nervous tread. He bends low to examine the right leg electrode, makes the final adjustments of the hood and steps rapidly away to the instrument panel, ten feet to the rear.

In the year of the Lord 1927 it is considered and ordered by the Court that you, Greggo Samsa, and you, Alice Paulo, suffer the punishment of death by the passage of electricity through your bodies within the week beginning on Sunday, the 10th day of July , in the year of our Lord 1927. This is the sentence of the law. Dogs are brought in to slake their thirst. Electrons subside, another examination... a voice is heard: "Warden, I pronounce this thing dead." Victims of the crassest plutocracy the world has known since ancient Rome, America and the Commonwealth of Massachusetts have killed you. Judge Thayer :"DID YOU SEE WHAT I DID TO THOSE ARNYCHISTIC BASTARDS?" In the year of the Lord, 1927?

Power is the capacity to transform a living person into a corpse, that is, into a thing.

11:33.

We must bow to the inevitable. Anus stuffed with cotton, mouth taped against vomit, we must be cosmetically acceptable.

How will I act? Most prisoners, they say, walk to their executions with surprising calm, in a state of dreary despondency, resigned, stars in a drama pandering to public fear and lust for vengeance, sometimes called Justice. But some fall apart during the last walk and have to be dragged kicking and screaming to their deaths. Which? Which one?

Greggo, Klingsor and Kluge, connected at the wrists, trudged along the steeply rising streets. All waved to the policemen stationed at corners along the way. In half an hour, the cobbled path gave way to open fields, and a small stone quarry. The moon shone down with that simplicity and serenity which no other light possesses.

What should I do? How shall I behave? It's strange that a man rarely faints during his final seconds. On the contrary, his brain is terribly alive and active, racing, like a machine at full speed. Imagine how many thoughts must be throbbing together, all unfinished, some of them irrelevant and absurd: That man staring has a wart on his forehead, and, here, one of the executioner's buttons is broken. And at the same time he knows — there is one point that cannot be forgotten, and everything turns around it, around that point. And to think that it must be like this up to the last quarter second, when his head is already on the block, and waits, and — knows, and suddenly he hears the iron slithering down above his head. *Stabat mater dolorosa.*

The executioner gets $250 per victim. Just for throwing a lever. He gets it in cash — no record in a checking account — plus traveling expenses, round trip from New York. Strange, the odd submissiveness in the condemned at the moment of execution. We have nothing more to lose. We could play our last card, choose to die of a chance bullet, or be hung in the kind of frantic struggle that dulls the faculties. This would be dying freely. And yet, with few exceptions, we passively walk toward death, and the journalists write "the condemned man died courageously," meaning that we made no noise, we accepted our status as a parcel, and everyone is grateful to us for this. Hundreds of persons offer to serve as executioners without pay.

This prison is built in the form of a cross. Old Charlestown. The form of a cross. They'll drive the nails through my wrists to muzzle the medial nerve. The crucified die of suffocation, but praise be for spiracles. My whitewashed little room with its two heavy iron doors, my tiny window above a prayer bench, my simple wooden cross. A cross for Jews...

11:42

A temporarily living thing.

All evil grows from fear of our own liberty. Living here, without liberty, we enter the larger sphere of The Lie — of order and strategy and terror, at the same time our daily bread and our guards' bread as well. But The Lie is everywhere. For someone who has seen what prison can do, it's most discouraging to see what free men are also able to do. How horrifying it is to see such cowardice facing Lies big and small, such brutal distortions of truth in the shuffling of power. The Lie In Freedom is man's most extraordinary invention. Between its sometimes benign game and its often malevolent perversity there opens a vast human terrain... Warden, will you make sure this letter gets to my father in Prague?

11:45

The warden, with plump round face and little black mustache and narrow slits for eyes; a well-known Boston surgeon; the prison physician; the Surgeon General of the Massachusetts National Guard, who looks like a college professor; the medical examiner of Suffolk county, who looks like a romantic poet with tousled hair; the Sheriff of Norfolk County, a stern-faced old Puritan, who had had Greggo in charge for seven years, and Alice off and on — one of those who had piled Judge Thayer's desk with flowers on the day that learned man delivered his charge to the jury, explaining the nobility of being loyal. One reporter — William Playfair of the Associated Press, chosen by lot to represent the Fourth Estate. Playfair! ¡Presente!

The witnesses ranged themselves along the wall. In the center of the room, under the glare of the overheads, stood the chair, straps hanging. Executioner Elliot took his place behind the screen that hid the switch but not his head. What an advance — that no man's blood is shed by the often unsteady hand of his fellow, but that murder is executed by an instrument without life, insensible as wood, infallible as iron, enthusiastic as the body electric.

Another screen concealed the stretchers. In Paris, executions took place at the Statue of Liberty, a gift from the United States.

A distant clock struck midnight as saints processed. Alice walked to the chair unaided, with the simple dignity she had in worst of times. As they began to adjust the straps she sat bolt upright, casting wildly about with her eyes until she saw the screen with Elliot's face peering over it. Then she called out in Italian, "Viva la feminisma!", and with that grew calmer and added more quietly in English: "Farewell Greggo and all my friends." Only then did she seem to become aware of the witnesses. "Good evening, gentlemen," she said. The guards had finished with the straps and the headpiece and electrodes, and one of them now slipped the mask over her face. Warden Henry nodded and the executioner's hand moved behind the screen. "Farewell, Madre!", and 1900 volts at 6 amps charged through her slim frame.

Sacrum sanctam Guillotinam. Do not forget to show my head to the people: it is worth seeing.

The lights dimmed. When the guards came to G's cell he knew she was dead. Greggo Samsa stepped firmly, head erect, gray denim prison pants flapping slightly from the slits in the sides. Just inside the door he paused near Warden Henry and said with great precision: "I thank you for everything you have done for me. I am innocent of all crime, not only this one, but all, of all. I am an innocent man."

With that he shook hands with the wardens, the doctor, two of the guards, then took his place in the chair. As the guard on the right knelt to adjust the contact pad to his bare leg Greggo spoke again, his eyes covered. "I now wish to forgive some people for what they are doing to me." 1950 volts would suffice for this dreamer and man of words.

In the darkness he can now perceive a radiance that streams inextin-guishably from the door of the Law.

With panther-like poise, with dignity, standing before the observers, self-possessed, calm, in command of the situation, Greggo looked at the crowd before him, and said slowly and clearly:

"I wish to say to you that I am innocent. I have never committed any crime — some sins perhaps — but never any crime."

A hundred million workers knew that you and Alicia had died for them. Black and white, brown and yellow and red; men and women of a hundred nations and a thousand tribes, prisoners of hunger, victims of neglect, the wretched of the earth — all experienced in your annihilation the awesome beauty and terror of the sublime, the mystic process of blood-sacrifice, which through the ages has brought salvation to a weary world! More light!

The warden was scarcely able to pronounce the required formula: "Under the law I now pronounce you dead, the sentence of the court having been carried out." Into thy hands I commend my spirit.

The audience came to life again and were analyzing the situation like experts.

What arrangements do you want to make for your body?

And when sometimes the eye expands
and holds all still, suspended —. Then an image enters,
passes through motionless limbs —
and in the heart flicks out, extinguihsed.

11:51

"Some of the other guys...well, they said,...I mean...will I mess on myself? I don't want to be embarrassed...." The human condition comes down to a question like this.

The black door. Tell them the black door is green.

There is a feeling you have left something undone.

Unstrap the body, hose him down, remove his clothing and bag it for incineration.

11:56

The warden walked up the iron stairs into the Death House, dressed in a starched white shirt, with very thin bow tie, puffing on a pipe, blowing wisps of aromatic smoke around him. Pity me, Father, for I know not what I do. His hands were gnarled, with rough and callused palms. "I'm sorry, but it's my painful duty to tell you you have to die tonight. Now." Three tall, husky guards quietly approach the cell, and with the rattle of a key, swing open the door. No word is spoken. At a nod from the leader, the prisoner rises. A guard bends down, carved knife in hand. With a deft stroke he slits the right trouser leg. Silently the march begins. Thirteen steps.

A door opens and we are in the execution chamber. Someone in the audience waves his hands high in the air and shouts Bravo.

18. Aliens And Sedition

Gregor Samsa was given to disturbing dreams, it's true. But in August 1927, disturbing dreams ran rampant over five continents. On the night of the 22nd, a tremor of panic shook the world.

— In Boston, machine guns on the prison roof were trained on uneasy crowds in streets below. Firemen prepared to open high-pressure hoses. Police boats patrolled the Charles to check an attack by sea. Searchlights caught the glint of steel from fixed bayonets in the street. Three hundred marchers en route from Bunker Hill, but eight hundred police charged and broke them up. More than two hundred demonstrators arrested while trying to picket the State House, Gregor Samsa among them. Civil rights are playthings for quiet days, not for a day of death.

— In NYC, from the afternoon on, the entire police force was mobilized, and several companies of soldiers on Governor's Island, fully armed, waited for a signal to cross the river into the city...

— In London, shortly before 5 AM, the Death Watch walked in closed circles — coal miners, textile workers, longshoremen...

— In Rio, a little before two in the morning, crowds at the US embassy shouted so loud, they thought they might be heard in Boston...

— In Moscow early morning crowds swarmed around wall newspapers. What time is it now in Boston?"

— In Paris, workers howled nightlong at our Embassy...

— In Warsaw, daylight was breaking, and demonstrations were broken up even as illegal posters appeared, calling upon Poles to make a final effort to save them...

— In Sydney, it was mid-afternoon. Longshoreman went on strike. They marched to the American embassy chanting...

— In Bombay, mill workers lay down their tools for an hour of silence and prayer...

— In Tokyo, at midday, police attacked workers in front of the American embassy...

Never before in all human history was there a thing like this: these floods of tears so widely shared, so inclusive of people across the planet.

Mr. Fairplay, the AP witness, spoke to a smoky room of a hundred reporters chomping on cigars.

"No, they didn't confess. Just grandstanded with more Anarchist propaganda. ("The little infant Jesus! Ain't they lambs, these Reds?") He said — the correspondent consulted his notes — he said he forgave everybody — no, it was "some people."

After the execution, there was rioting in Paris, complete with barricades in the streets, a potentially revolutionary insurrection.

In Geneva, placid Geneva, mobs roamed the streets, overturning American cars, sacking shops displaying American goods. gutting theaters showing American films. One rioter was killed when troops with fixed bayonets moved in.

A marcher was killed in Leipzig, in Hamburg a number of demonstrators were wounded and a policeman and a worker killed...

Forty protesters were hurt in a riot in London, and a hundred in Oporto, Portugal, when police broke up the demonstration in front of the American Consulate...

In South Africa, racist South Africa, the American flag was burned on the steps of the Johannesburg City Hall.

In the U.S., nothing comparable occurred in the six days between executions and funeral. People seemed exhausted — or relieved. A *Boston Herald* editorial summed up the establishment stance:

The time for all discussion is over. The arrow has flown. Now let us go forward to the duties and responsibilities of the common day with a renewed determination to maintain our present system of government, and our existing social order.

So as not to disturb the apparent calm, radio networks and newspapers downplayed reports of world reaction. Newsreel companies, too, took part in the conspiracy of silence. Here is an article Gregor clipped and folded into his diary, along with the editorial:

The Exhibitor's Herald, Sept 3, 1927

The Sacco-Vanzetti case is closed, and that means as far as newsreel pictures of the events which terminated with the execution of the pair.

The case is closed on the screen voluntarily. Executives of the newsreel companies were unanimous in their decision to eliminate all reference to the matter in their releases.

The announcement was made following conferences with representatives of Will H. Hays, after receipt by the Hays Organization of requests from overseas that the motion picture industry do its share in bringing the case to an end by ignoring it on the screen. Films in the vault will be burned.

It was clear to Gregor, and to those who participated with him in the struggle, that what they had been through was not a miscarriage of justice as was widely alleged. By 1927, G had seen enough of America to understand that *this* was justice here, class justice, in action. He vowed to help change it.

At that time, in the city of Boston, there was a club known as the Athenaeum, a club for Boston Brahmans, for university presidents and judges, a club which no foreigner, no first-generation rabble rouser, no Jew or Negro, had ever penetrated.

On August 23, 1927, the morning after the execution, a slip of paper was found inserted in every magazine and newspaper in the reading room. On each slip were the following words, typed in capital letters on an old Remington Model One:

ON THIS DAY, NICOLA SACCO AND BARTOLOMEO VANZETTI, DREAMERS
OF THE BROTHERHOOD OF MAN, HOPERS IT MIGHT BE FOUND IN UNITED
STATES, WERE DONE A CRUEL DEATH BY CHILDREN OF THOSE WHO FLED
LONG AGO TIME TO THIS LAND OF HOPE AND FREEDOM.

Someone in the audience, clap your hands high in the air and shout
Bravo.

19. Like A Sick Eagle

"Good morgen, Mister Chollie."

"Hey, mornin', Mistah Gregor. How you are dis fine Monday on Wall Street? Now I don't want you jumpin' outta no windows today. Lookee heah, the Times say WALL ST. READY FOR HEAVY TRADING AS ORDERS POUR IN. Things is lookin' up. 'Sides, gotta vote for Norman Thomas tomorra. Every vote count."

"I have no stocks, so I am not jumping out of windows. Besides, I can fly if I really want to."

"Oh, yeah, you a card, Mistah Gregor. But you gotta also watch out fo' other people flyin who *ain't* got no wings. Dey fly right onto yo' head, you jus' as dead. Like dem two las' week." Dese hea streets too narrow for dat kinda monkey business."

"I take my *Times*, and my *Vorwarts*."

"It always maze me some people kin read dat Jewish writin'. Look like chicken scratchin' to me."

"I come from chicken land. Everybody reads it in the old country."

"You all chickens."

"Every final one."

"Well have a good Monday mornin, Mistah Gregor. No suicidin' please, and you be sure to vote tomorra. Mistah Thomas, he our man. He gonna make things betta."

"Where do I vote?"

"Where you live?"

"Here, in New York City."

"But where heah in New York City? Mornin, Mistah Milgram. Heah yo *Times*."

"I live in... different places."

"Well you got to have a registid address. You got a registid address?"

"What is that, a registid address?"

"You go to you closest courthouse, an you tell em where you live, and they write it down, and they tell you where you kin vote."

"I will do that."

"I don' know if you might be too late fo' tomorra."

"I go at lunchtime and see."

"OK, Mistah Gregor, you be good, you heah?"

"You must also be good, yes?"

"Ahm always good. Cain't be bad, even effn I try. Be shu to vote for Mr. Thomas, effn you can vote."

"I will."

Gregor walked the three blocks to Cedar, feeling the heaviness of towering granite in the early morning November gloom. He glanced at the front page of the Times: yes, WALL ST. READY FOR HEAVY TRADING AS ORDERS POUR IN. Well, maybe things *would* pick up. He didn't really understand the market, but knew enough to know that when prices were low, people would buy, and prices would rise. Orders pouring in? That sounded good. Not even the main headline. Just one column. The big news — TAMMANY SEES BIG VICTORY. LA GUARDIA IN FINAL PLEA ASKS FOR THOMAS VOTES. Maybe there will be upset. He wished he could vote. On the bottom of the page, a two column spread: ELEVATED TRAIN STOPS FOR DOG, RAMMED FROM BEHIND. EIGHT PERSONS HURT. Monday, November 4, 1929. New York. Would a train stop in Prague — or even Vienna? *Weiß nicht.* In America it stops — and is punished. Poor country, sick from its own strengths. The land of opportunity, everybody can get rich. And everybody can jump out of windows. Sick country. Like a sick eagle. Like a sick eagle looking towards the sky.

He thought of Mr. Ives' song. Mr. Ives was so nice to give him a signed copy of his book of songs. "To Mr. Gregor Samsa, my prize student. March,

1929. Ch. E. Ives" That was his favorite, "Like A Sick Eagle" — he could sing it just the way Mr. Ives would like it. Even better. Mr. Ives wanted quarter tones, but Gregor could easily do eighth tones, sixteenth tones if he were careful.

I love this song too. It was how G and I discovered our friendship. We must have been the only two people on the mesa who had even heard of Ives, much less knew this song, this tiny masterpiece, a one-page study in descending tones, short phrases with weary, chromatic pauses between them. The score is marked, "Very slowly, in a weak and dragging way", shining exhausted light on Keats' disheartened poem:

The spirit is too weak;
mortality weighs heavily on me
like unwilling sleep,
and each imagined pinnacle and steep
of Godlike hardship
tells me I must die...

"like a sick eagle," Gregor sang, *"like a sick eagle looking towards the sky."*
Ives wrote it, I believe, while his new wife, Harmony, was in the hospital, undergoing the hysterectomy that would render them childless, with an unhappy, adopted daughter. What a way to start a marriage!

"What a way to run a country," thought G.

46 Cedar St., Ives & Myrick, the foremost insurance agency in America, perhaps the world. Gregor worked on the sixth floor, at a desk in a long room with a high ceiling and huge windows with dark, oaken frames. Mr. Myrick's desk was right up front, along with all the others'. But the shy and messy Mr. Ives had a private office in back, behind frosted glass, with its own elevator entrance, and its own unique chaos. Most of the time, the door was closed.

Gregor walked into the building lobby, and began his trek up twelve half-landings. He had had enough of elevators. He liked that there were twelve half landings, like the twelve half-tones Mr. Ives was always raging at for being "unnatural limitations of sissified ears" that just liked to "lie back in their easy-chairs." G loved the image of those ears relaxing with their hands behind their – ear? — on some kind of lounge chair, perhaps at a sanatorium at Kierling or Davos. Today he would play the game of contrary motion, rising slowly up the stairs, singing (if you can call it that), as the chromatic line went downward. Each step up would be a sixteenth tone down. For G, it was fun, his *Musikalischer Spaß*, a gay, if forgetful way to avoid thinking about the confusing chaos around him. Monday, he knew, was the day of the week with the most suicides.

By the last half-landing he had reached the "…gle" of "eagle" an upward flat fourth leap (Mr. Ives called it "a demented fourth") as the eagle looks upward towards the sky. The four upwardly rising tones at the end is the only relief to the brooding heaviness, the sense of inexorable doom, the inevitable end of all mortal beings.

Only in the upward movement of the last four diatonic tones is there a faint glimmer of hope — and Gregor saved the last four steps for them — one whole tone each: "towards"… "the"… "sky"… and then he jumped up onto the last landing — free, light, his own man, Gregor Samsa, insurance adjuster-in-training, at the prestigious firm of Ives & Myrick.

The reader is no doubt curious as to how Gregor got this job. In fact, looking back over my manuscript, I see that, detoured by an abysmal wound in history, we last left the economically self-sufficient elevator operator going off to Dayton, Tennessee in the summer of 1925, four and a half years previously. To Dayton he did go, then to Washington for a month chez Alice, and then back to New York, too embarrassed to apply again for his job at the Occidental. He had told Ulla about his plan to join Mr. Scope's defense team, but she was sure that Mr. Klamm the headwaiter, his direct supervisor, would not permit him to go. A day or two vacation maybe, but a week or more? Never. The other boys would be stretched too thin. Service would suffer.

So Gregor simply left — without notice. Ulla made some excuse for him, a dying grandparent in the South, urgent need for help, but Mr. Klamm was as angry as she had imagined, and a replacement was hired the very next day. Klamm himself had to pick up part of G's shift, a detail which did not lighten the furious atmosphere. Gregor was back in New York on August 9th, a date which, twenty years later, would live in infamy, though he would not know it. Maybe. Maybe he does not know. Maybe he does.

He snuck up the back stairs to Ulla's apartment, the images of the great Klan march still pulsing in his ganglia. It was obvious he couldn't stay, but Ulla did agree to keep his clothing and few possessions until he found another job, another place to live.

And thus began what G would refer to as his "hidden years". It took months for him to open up to me about this time, but when he did, he narrated it with a kind of glee absent from his normal discourse, normally so heavy with his quest, his wound, and toward the end, with his plans for self-destruction. Up against the wall of New York, a city unforgiving even in boom times, he was forced into a conceptual leap in order to survive: he had to become — once more — a cockroach. A cockroach in New York City, a home as welcoming as Rome to the Pope, as the outback to the aborigine. Yes! A New York City cockroach — what could be easier? His size might make for some hardship, but Gott, ja! what could be more obvious?

It was summer, a hot and muggy August, and lodgings were a minor problem — if necessary he could sleep out in any number of parks, alleys or dark empty lots. Food was the primary issue: what do cockroaches eat if they're not sitting at table? Darn near anything, that's what. "Bark, leaves, the pith of living cyclads, paper, woolen clothes, sugar, cheese, bread, blacking, oil, lemons, ink, flesh, fish, leather," wrote the British scholar I. A. C. Miall in his 1886 edition of *The Structure and Life History of the Cockroach*. And in 1925 it was even easier: the last decade had seen a proliferation of the newly-invented dumpster. At first, Gregor explored the back alleys of his old neighborhood. Lindy's, at Broadway and 51st, had a huge output of half-eaten food. No pith of living cyclads for him when he could feast of the remains of pastrami sandwiches, cheesecake and apple strudel. Every once in a while, when he had a yen to play the European dandy, he would head up to the Russian Tea Room at 56th and Seventh, and nibble, ever so daintily, on smears of caviar, or shards of sturgeon, perhaps from the very plates of Igor Stravinsky and his gaggle of *émigré* princesses. Late one evening, he was walking the alley behind Reisenweber's at Eighth and 58th, just as a huge load from the kitchen was being delivered unto the night air. But Jewish guilt kicked in, along with the thundering voice of his father: "Are you going to take food from the very place you betrayed? Have you forgotten the poor Polish bartender, Mr. Budzynski, probably languishing in jail, his four starving children crying at home, all because of you, you, you? And you want to take food from this dumpster? The wages of sin, my son, the wages of sin is death!" He passed it by, and avoided the alley thereafter — putting only the smallest dent in his movable feast.

At the end of September, the air began to chill, and he set about looking for a place to stay. But why one place? Did he have to pay rent? Why not two, three, four places, one for every mood? He had to stop thinking like some poor human immigrant, and start thinking cockroach. What freedom! No rogue and peasant wage-slave he. He had a small, cozy flat in an empty brownstone on W. 61st, a loft on 49th and Tenth Avenue, and a fantasy-space in an abandoned Chinese restaurant around the corner at 49th off Ninth. No pockets, no keys. He could slip through the cracks in slightly open windows, or in at the bottom of mal-fitting doors. He had his choice.

Food and shelter checked off, he turned his attention to winter clothing. What a relief it was to know that, as a cold-blooded animal, he had no need to maintain any particular body temperature. True, the colder it was, the slower he became, and should he reach "chill-coma" temperature, he would be completely immobilized. But as November came on, he found that intentionally exposing himself to lower and lower outside temperatures, he could acclimatize, and reduce the temperatures at which activity was still possible. He knew there must be some cold death point at which his internal liquid would fatally freeze, but in a civilized city, in the north temperate zone, such extremes could be easily avoided. In case of severe hypothermia, could always bury himself deep within the composting heat of any dumpster.

With the basics of food, (no) clothing and shelter taken care of, Gregor could afford to take in the city in all its cultural glory, a bohemian roach-about-town. One evening at the end of January, 1927, shortly before becoming involved with Sacco and Vanzetti, he was approached on W. 43rd Street by a fur wrapped, over-rouged woman.

"Hey, Mister..."

"No, thank you, I..."

"I'll give you a good deal."

Should he, or shouldn't he? His last sexual encounter, well over two years ago, had been disastrous; he had felt de-sexed ever since. The thought of a woman's soft flesh had become repulsive once more. He didn't know this person. He could get a disease. She was vaguely attractive, but... Wasn't this illegal? What if he were caught? Without papers, he could be deported... Still...

"They're great seats. Fourth row, center."

"What?"

"Fourth row, center. We have an extra ticket."

"Ticket for what?"

"Oh, forgive me. I thought you were heading for the box office. You were reading the poster."

And, in fact, Gregor had stopped to puzzle out the poster in the Town Hall display. "Pro Musica International Referendum Concert." What sort of referendum? Wasn't that when you voted on something? Music to vote by? Vote for what? He couldn't vote, he thought, but still he was interested. He had just stepped away from his myopic inspection when the woman...

"Debussy, Ives, and Milhaud. You never get a chance to hear this music."

He had never even heard of Milhaud...but Ives?

"Ives?"

"Charles Ives. The insurance genius-composer. You've heard of him?"

"Is he about two meters tall, and he is writing an amendment for your Constitution?"

"I haven't met him, but it sounds like it could be."

"I think I have met him. Does he like baseball?"

"That I do know. My husband and he played on the same team at Yale."

"Yale. That was the team at the game."

"Then it was probably Charlie Ives. Don't you want to hear some of his music?"

"Yes. I would like to. But I have no money at the moment."

"Oh. Too bad. We do need to get something for the seat."

"I'm sorry."

"That's all right. I'll tell you what. If I can't sell it, I'll leave it under your name at the box office. Can you check back in an hour or so?"

"Thank you. That's very nice of you. Gregor."

"Just Gregor?"

"Samsa. Gregor Samsa."

"S-a-m-s-a." She, writing it on the back of a chewing gum wrapper from her purse.

But Gregor did not check back. He didn't want to sit next to this woman. For one thing, her afternoon perfume was already making his antennae itch even in a mid-winter breeze. What would it be indoors, with a fresh dose? For another, he couldn't really sit front and center at some international Town Hall voting with the shabby clothes he had taken to wearing in his new metamorphosis into freedom. He might go to Ulla's and retrieve his good suit for the evening. But, no, he couldn't just breeze in and out, and there wasn't really time to talk before eight — he hadn't seen her for several months. But all this did not quench his curiosity about the insurance genius-composer who was writing a Constitution amendment. Nor did it stop him from going to the concert.

In the last months, G had become expert at slipping in and out of buildings unnoticed, of caressing the shadows, and being caressed by them. He knew the midtown alleys like the claw of his pretarsus. He knew the back doors of Town Hall. He knew the ushers stood in them pre-concert, in the coldest weather, to smoke. He had a black overcoat and a flute case for such occasions. Walk in quickly, authoritatively, nod the head, flash the flute case nonchalantly. They had never challenged him before, and wouldn't now. What usher wants to be dressed down for hassling some distinguished international musician? Then, up to the second floor via the stairs at the back of the hall. Slip into the auditorium as the usher seats another customer, and wait behind the curtain on the back wall. What a wonderful thing to be flat. Even six feet tall, Gregor could get behind an arass without making a noticible bulge. In the dark, with two stick-like tarsi protruding slightly at the bottom, he was so far undiscoverable. He had only to edge over and stick his knee outside the tapestry for excellent acoustics — even if he couldn't see.

He would go to the concert. Then afterwards, he would visit Ulla, take some time, share the last months — and say, he might retrieve that card Mr. Ives had given him at the ballgame. Hadn't he given him a card? It must be in the pocket of his jacket. He was wearing his brown suit, wasn't he? Ulla would remember. She was his clothing consultant for his date with

Alice. Yes, he'd get the card, and if he liked the music, he would call up Mr. Ives and tell him.

And so it happened. Gregor arrived at the back door of Town Hall at 7:25, walked right by two ushers finishing up their Camels, and found his curtained place at the back of the orchestra. Not fourth row, center, but it would do. There was his reluctant patroness in Row D. That little man is her husband? Well, she didn't say "husband", did she? He wondered if she had sold the ticket. He'd look at intermission to see if a seat either side of them was empty. For now, the soft darkness. He hooked his front claws into the curtain for support.

****

This concert of January 29, 1927 was a courageous love-labor of E. Robert Schmitz, a French pianist who had shown up at Ives & Myrick looking for insurance. When the conversation turned to music they were startled — both. Ives had discovered a brilliant pianist and promoter, and Schmitz a fascinating and undiscovered talent most generous with money. The night's concert was to be played by 50 musicians from the N.Y. Philharmonic under the baton of Eugene Goosens, an up-and-coming conductor-composer. It had been originally proposed to premier the whole Fourth Symphony, but the "Comedy" movement took up so much energy, there was no time left for rehearsing the even more demanding last movement: only the first two would be played. Besides, Goosens couldn't make head nor tail of the music, and thought his men would be lucky if they could just get through it. He didn't tell Ives — whom he had found personally impressive and charming.

Charles and his wife, Harmony, had come to all the rehearsals, but, in their typically bashful way, hid themselves in the green room where they could hear scarcely anything. Goosens had to come backstage to consult, so scared, they were, to come out and face "the men."

Ives was last on the program, which began with Debussy's late, elusive cello sonata, a strange, other-worldly work in which the cello, chameleon-like, metamorphoses into violin, into flute, into even mandolin. The house was half-full, but the applause for Pierre Fournier, the intrepid young French cellist, was thunderous. Gregor loved this 1915 work, and regretted he had not heard it in Europe — though it had appeared in the same year as he, himself.

He was less impressed with the second work, Darius Milhaud's incidental music for Aeschylus' *Eumenides*. Whips and hammers were used in the orchestration, and a small chorus was required to groan, whistle, and shriek in several keys at once. Too much striving for too little effect. The audience seemed to share his view, the applause being barely more than polite.

Gregor stuck his head out during intermission, but decided to remain hidden, and not mingle with the crowd. He saw a dark portly personage down front slowly make his way to the rear among a small circle of reporters. That must be Mr. Milhaud. He knew what Debussy looked like. Besides, wasn't he dead? After the hall was almost empty, he spotted Mr. Ives and his wife sitting anonymously in the right rear, near the exit, positioned, he thought, to flee. Gregor was curious what he might hear.

The hall lights blinked, and the audience returned to its seats for the largest work of the evening, the opening two movements of Ives' last symphony, finished thirteen years earlier, at a time when sideshow Gregor was performing Rilke for his own questionable audience. From the opening challenge of cellos and basses, he didn't know what hit him. This fierce question gave way to a distant choir of strings, flute and harp, whispering fragments of the hymn, "Bethany', *"Nearer, my God, to Thee"*. Gregor didn't know the words, of course, but the feeling of intimate divinity was patent, all the more telling for the preceding, striding immensity. *"E'en though it be a cross that raiseth me..."* It would have been good for him to know the text. *"Still all my song shall be nearer, my God to Thee."* Maybe it was too soon for him to know this, the cross. It gives me the shivers, though, to think of G behind the curtain with such thought-forms broadcast by so many transmitters seated in the hall:

Though like the wanderer, the sun gone down,
Darkness be over me, my rest a stone;
Yet in my dreams I'd be
Nearer, my God, to thee...

Or, thinking of his to-this-day-impenetrable immigration:

Or if, on joyful wing cleaving the sky,
Sun, moon, and stars forgot, upward I fly,
Still all my song shall be,
Nearer, my God, to Thee.

A small group of players continued Bethany's shimmering veil throughout the first movement, independent of their colleagues, a hidden spiritual presence revealed only when the larger orchestra quieted. Had G been able to see, he would have been assured of their existence, but his insect-fine sensibilities could still detect them, lyric, meditative, behind the acoustically looming foreground. Ives must be on a quest, too, he thought, a quest for wholeness, a way to bring such diversity together. This was a work of high mystery.

A solo cello sang a drawn-out melody based on "Sweet By and By" — where Father waits "over the way" in a dwelling place on the beautiful shore. Gregor would learn more of this that pre-election morning. Not three minutes in, behold! a choir, out of nowhere, asking the question Gregor had been feeling:

Watchman, tell us of the night,
What the signs of promise are...

Gregor could hear the words, understand them. What about the night? And the answer:

Traveler, o'er yon mountain's height,
See that Glory-beaming star!

Yes, but it is so distant, a mere pinpoint in a universe of darkness... The chorus, too, was skeptical:

Watchman, aught of joy or hope?
But the answer, unequivocal:
Traveler, yes, it brings the day,
Promised day of Israel.
Dost thou see its glorious ray?

All this within a rich fabric of orchestral sound woven from fragments of other hymns, gently polyrhythmic, polytonal — as is the world. And in

242

less than five minutes, the movement was over, evaporating in the question, *"Dost thou see its glorious ray?"* Dost thou, Gregor Samsa? Dost thou? Yes. Yes, I do.

But what now? Do we see the glorious ray? See it in our ears?

What followed was one of the most extraordinary events in western music, probably in all music — ever. Maestro Goosens, when questioned afterwards about it, was quoted as saying, "My dear boy, I didn't know what happened after the downbeat."

What happened was all that ears could possibly hold, the damndest racket ever to come out of an orchestra before or since. It's not clear how much Gregor "got", standing behind the tapestry at the back wall of Town Hall. But the main thrust was clear: there was a tiny voice which kept appearing, a hymn-singing, delicate voice. It would lift itself up in frailty, and harmonized in shifting quarter-tones, would make sincere attempts at hymnody. But each time — it would be smashed, crashed, bashed, trashed by ever-greater pandemonium, massive musical agglomerations of dizzy-ing, polyrhythmic marches, ragtime piano riffs, secularizations of other hymn tunes, jingoistic clear-the-way for America, America on the march — even a foreigner, a less-than-legal immigrant could hear that.

And when America marched, it was in a confusion of keys and meters, with tens of different rhythms going on at once, and half a dozen tonal cen-ters at the same time — appropriate in a country where everyone seemed out for himself. Awash in a maelstrom of competing keys, the total effect was far beyond tonality, an utterly complex shaping and clashing of sound masses. It was the sound of our twentieth century, as even Gregor could understand, the roar of our cities and factories, the clash of our people, races, cultures, a satanic bellowing-out which added up to sheer madness. In such a context, old tunes seemed transformed: "Columbia, the Gem of the Ocean", once a song of joy, now roared monstrous power, mon-strously applied; the old Stephen Foster tune — *"Down in the Cornfield, hear dat mournful sound"* seemed here not about massa's death, but about the travesty of White supremacy in the racist south — and north. In short, the movement seemed a nightmare crushing of the inner sounds of yearn-ing, hope, and vision, an intimation not of immortality, but of eternal punishment.

Poor little tune in the solo violin (it was *Beulah Land,* which G did not know) — out there all alone, waiting for the inevitable, singing with your head in the guillotine. Why are you there? What are you doing in company such as this? You — fragile, sentimental, but undaunted, with your somber accompaniment and strange quarter tone noodlings. Did you come only to be trampled under our heavy industrial feet, crushed by the venalities of our small-town Babbitry with its blaring booster bands? Or is your presence ironic, a sweet reminder that religion shares complicity in our tragedy? Or are you just there, as truly you are, nine-hundred-lived, watching, waiting for the racket to die out on its own? At the end of the movement, Gregor did not know.

He did know he was shaken. He knew he had been present at a miracle of pedagogy — Mr. Ives was trying to tell him something about his new country, about himself, about his quest. He knew he would go see him, as he had been invited to, six and a half years earlier.

He watched the Iveses sneak out amidst the booing. He heard the following exchange in the lobby: "Is Debussy dead?" "Yes." "Is Ives dead?" "No, but he ought to be." He knew Charles Ives would be his teacher.

And G's teacher he was, not least of all about the philosophical basis and loving nature of life insurance. Gregor went back that night to Ulla's room — not home...had she gotten herself a boyfriend? — let himself in with his key, and rummaging in the left hand pocket of his good brown suit — there it was, the card:

CHARLES E. IVES
IVES & MYRICK
The Mutual Life Insurance Company of New York
46 Cedar Street
Telephones, John 3663 - 3832

He called the next day, was put right through, and was amazed and flattered that Mr. Ives remembered him.

"'Course I remember you, sonny. How many people have never seen a baseball game before? And the lady with you, Miss Paul. She never did get in touch..."

244

They made an appointment for February 2nd, at the office. The talk ranged from philosophy to music. Ives was particularly interested in Gregor's experience of the Great War. He had never had a chance to speak at length with "the enemy". Together they bewailed man's inhumanity to man, and Ives showed G a draft he was writing on One World Government which said — wait, I have the finished pamphlet here, stuck in Gregor's file —

> There is one thing in their work which the People's World Nation
> Army Police shall not do under any conditions — forever and ever
> — in any way whatsoever — and that is to use aeroplane bombs.
> Anyone who does shall be stoned to death — not buried in graves but
> in swill piles — and any man who ever says that bombing is right
> will be beaten on the jaw until the door bell to Hell rings them in!

Gregor, of course, couldn't agree more, and supplied Ives with heart-rending details of the aftermath of Allied bombing in Vienna. He was as good as hired. But when Ives popped the question, "Who's your favorite composer?" and Gregor answered shyly, but truthfully, "Until last week, Gustav Mahler, but now, if you will forgive me...you," the die was cast. Ives called him a lolly-gagging suck-up, but was secretly flattered, and when Gregor described his experience at Town Hall, the old man was convinced he had met someone perceptive, visionary, courageous and humane, someone worthy of working in life insurance. G would start training the very next day. Before he left, Ives handed him a copy of "The Amount To Carry", a pamphlet he had written to help his agents understand "the innate quality in human nature which gives man the power to sense the deeper causes..." Gregor quite whistled and danced his way down twelve half-flights of stairs.

But in early November, two years and eight months later, things seemed darker, gloomier, like a sick eagle — more portentous. When Gregor opened the gabled door to IVES & MYRICK, he found the other early arrivers away from their desks, gathered towards the rear of the great room, some ten feet from the door to Mr. Ives's office. He made his way up the center aisle.

"What is happening?" he asked Kathryn Verplank, Ives's personal secretary, whose desk was the center of conglomeration.

"We don't know," she whispered. "Mr. Ives is in there. I think he's alone — he has no appointments. There's talking and yelling — I think it's just him, though. Today is always difficult for him, the anniversary of his father's death. But it's never been like this before..."

Gregor joined the crowd of 10 or so straining to make sense of what was going on behind the frosted glass. He heard heavy furniture being dragged, and Ives calling out, "Stick to the end, Charlie, don't stop when it gets hard." Then, in a slightly altered voice, "If you know how to do things the right way, I'm willing to have you try the wrong way — well. But you've got to know what you're doing and why you're doing it." More furniture noise. "But Father, why can't a feller, if he feels like..." Some grunting, toot-tooting, then loudly, but as if the voice were being projected out into the street, the song,

"Jump, jump, jump, the boys are jumping,
Jump, jump, jumping here we go..."

This was enough for Gregor. He pushed his way out of the crowd, and with both his claws turned the knob and pushed open the door to Charles Ives's private office. The old man was standing on the floor leaning out the tall window, wide open to the cold, November air. Snaking behind him, like some great tail, was all the furniture in the room, desk, three chairs, table, two small bookshelves, and a compact safe on wheels — in which he kept his manuscripts. He was still in his hat and overcoat, though he had been in the office for at least an hour.

"Excuse me, Mr. Ives...

"Come in,. Samsa, come in. Close the door behind you. It's a little cold out there. *Come in to my Lord, oh come in...*" he sang.

"It is cold, Mr. Ives. Here, let me close the window," said Gregor, making his way quickly between his employer and the open space six floors above the sidewalk. "There. Better. It will warm up in a short while."

"Tell me about the defenestration of Prague, my lad. Do you know about the defenestration of Prague? It's a wonderful phrase, 'the defenestration of Prague.' Worthy of a short song, don't you think?"

"Why did you do this to the furniture?"

"Oh, you wouldn't know this, but today's my father's birthday, I mean deathday, and he and I always have some sort of party. Today we're playing trains like we used to. The old Ives Brothers Railroad. Tell me about the defenestration of Prague."

"Let's sit down, and we talk about it." Gregor arranged two of the chairs as far away from the window as he could. "Here, I'll take your hat and coat."

"Thank you, Mr. Samsa. You know, a man who tries to hitch his wagon to a star and falls over a precipice, wagon and all, always finds something greater than the man who hitches his gilded star to a mule who kicks him back into a stagnant pool, where he lives forever in ecstasy, safe and sound in his swamp, splashing mud on mankind."

"That is surely true, Mr. Ives."

"Defenestration."

"Yes. This is something we must memorize in grade school, so I still know the date: 23 of May, 1618."

"Was it a lovely spring day?"

"I don't know. Prague is often beautiful in May, with the castle gardens blossoming."

"Did they defenestrate into the blossoms?"

"The castle nestles close to a huge stone wall which drops into a deep, deep moat. I imagine they fell out into tall treetops."

"Who?"

"Ah. Slavata and Jaroslav."

"Fell or pushed? Or jumped?"

"Definitely pushed."

"Jumping is more manly. Why pushed?"

"For ordering Protestant chapels being closed. This makes the beginning of the Thirty Years' War."

"The peasants against the Hog-Mind. Good for them."

Gregor took Ives's hat and coat to the coat rack.

"Were you going to jump?"

"Where?"

"Out the window. Just now."

"No."

"You were singing about jumping. That is why I come in."

"I was thinking about jumping, so I started singing about jumping.

Think-sing. But I wasn't going to jump."

"Were you thinking about jumping for yourself, or about jumping in abstract, like the men who jump together last week on William Street?"

Ives finally sank into his great leather desk chair.

"I'm not doing well, Mr. Samsa. I'm in a bad spell that won't say uncle."

"What uncle?" G interrupted.

"Say uncle. That means you give up. It won't give up. The spell. I don't know where the expression comes from."

"Ah."

"The doctors say I have to go slow, I'm having a general running down, some kind of depression. My arms hurt so much, I can't touch the piano. My hands shake so much, I just leave snake tracks on the paper. Harmony and Edie have to rewrite my letters for me. Charlie Ives, hiding behind the ladies, will you get a load of that! You know why I grew this beard? To play Santa Claus? No. It's because my skin hurts too much to shave. It's my heart, polyrhythms, it's my diabetes kicking in hard, going for the extra point."

"You can still work on your music..."

"I can't even see the damn music! It's like little green dots crawling all over the page. I've got no energy to compose. Haven't written anything real in years. Not since the Concord. Not since the Fourth. I've just been cleaning house. And I'll tell you it needs some cleaning. If you think my desk here is bad..."

"Maybe you should take a vacation from work. You travel hours every day on the train. What if you just stayed home? We handle things here. Lots of good, intelligent people. And Mr. Myrick can help us stay in touch with you..."

There was no response.

"Mr. Ives?"

"I'm thinking about it. Throw in the towel. Why not? I'm finished. Just taking up high-rent space."

G pondered his next move.

"Mr. Ives?"

"Yes?"

"You know how in your symphony the chorus asks the watchman about

248

the night? What comes after the night?"

"Watchman, tell us of the night."

"Yes. What does the watchman say?"

"There are no signs of promise."

"He says that there is a mountain to climb, and above the mountain is a glory-beaming star. He says to hope and make joy, because the night brings the day..." And Gregor started to sing. In trembling, otherworldly tones, scarcely audible, but perfectly pitched, he sang ,

Promised day of Israel.
Dost thou see its glorious ray?

"Stop it! yelled Ives. "That's stupid. You want *real* watchmen? Check Mendelssohn's *Lobgesang. 'Hute, ist die Nacht bald hin?'*

"'Watchman is the night going away soon?'"

"Yes. And you know what the answer is?"

"I don't know the piece."

"You should! The watchman says

'Wenn der Morgen schon kommt,
so wird es doch Nacht sein..."

"Even though morning comes, the night will come again.'"

"Right. And that's not the worst:

wenn ihr schon fraget, so werdet ihr doch wiederkommen
und wieder fragen: Hüter, ist die Nacht bald hin?

"If you ask, you will come back and ask again, Watchman, is the night going away soon?"

"Right. Over and over –it never ends."

"That is a different story, Mr Ives. Maybe it's the Mendelssohn German story…"

"Isaiah!"

"… but you are American. The *American* story is what you wrote."

"The American story is the eternal struggle against Hog-Mind! What do you think is happening out there? It's the hog-mind of the minority against the universal mind of the majority."

Ives got up and started pacing, working his way up and down the train of furniture.

"Mr. Ives, sit down and rest..."

"Hog-mind slowing down human progress. Hog-mind with its pride — its pride in property and power. Got to get rich, got to own our famous city of Destruction, got to drive down the stock, take your profits, the bankers and leaders, Hog-Mind leaders. But even those thick-skins are beginning to see now that they're *not* the leaders — so they're jumping out of windows. You hear me, Mr. Samsa? Movement is the leader, progress is the leader — they're only clerks, underaverage men, thick, slick, and quick with their undervalues — otherwise they wouldn't be leaders. Under-leaders. Leading us under — all of us. But the day of under-leaders is closing — the people are beginning to lead themselves, and they have been since before the Hohenzollern hog-marched into Belgium fueled by the world's greatest idiot — brute force — the group-hog of the minority!"

"What is hog-mind?"

"Hog-mind! Hoggy-mind, the self-will of the Minority! Hog-mind and all its sneak-slimy handmaidens in disorder — superficial brightness, gallery thinking, fundamental dullness. Spreading suspicion, cowardice, and fear, then weapon-grabbing. *Schweingeist.* It's all a part of the minority, the Non-People, the politicians, the bankers that own them, the antithesis of everything called soul, Spirit, Christianity, Truth, Freedom, insulting us — those cowardly, material-minded, chronic fault-finding, suspicion-swill-feasters who so clog up their narrow mental lanes with the Tweeds, the Kaisers, and the Herods that the Lincolns, the Savanarolas, and the Christs pass unnoticed. Look out there." He threw up the window again. Gregor jumped to close it. "Look in that stupid *New York Times* you have. You want to learn something? You want enlightenment? Stop reading the damn paper, making America soft with its commercialism, with its mechanization, its standardized processes of mind and life, touting conventional, ineffective ways, platitudes, dogmas, headlines, half-truths which confuse every issue and every ideal. Where's my chair? Mr. Smooth-It-Away, read all about it, Mr. Live-For-The-World, Mr. Scaly Conscience, damn pet slants of some old bosses, sneak-thieving medieval-minded dictators with their underhanded, dark-age bossy gouging tricks displacing the direct will-of-the-people way! Emasculating America for money! Breakfast and death are a little too easy these days, wouldn't you say? Is the Anglo-Saxon going pussy? — the nice Lizzies — the do-it-proper boys of today — the cushions of complacency — the champions of bodily ease — the plaaaaay-it-pretty minds — the cautious old gals running the broadcasting companies — those great national brain-softeners, the movies — the mind-dulling tabloids with their headlines of half-truths and heroic pictures of the most popular defectives, and the *Times* is no different — the ladybirds — the femaled-male crooners — the easy-ear concert-hall parlor entertainments with not even one "god-damn" in them — they're all getting theirs, and America is not! We're losing our manhood! The Puritans may have been everything the lollers called them, but they weren't soft. They may have been cold, narrow, hard-minded rock-eaters outwardly, but they weren't goddam effeminates. Where's my hat and coat? Oh, you hung them up. The majority of Americans own something — a few, too much; everybody knows that. But whatever they own, for the most part they've worked for it hard with their hands and their brains. And if some Minority bandit should sneak down the road and try to take away those Americans' homes, shops, farms, whatever they've laid up for a rainy day, for their children, a new version of the lion and the mouse will be staged and the Minority Hog would be too groggy to applaud many of the scenes. And let some hog-minded, self-willed Minority agent try to take away any of their natural rights or freedom he'll find himself on the canvas from a blow which'll be heard on Mars."

"Mr. Ives?"

"What? You wanted to know what hog-mind is!"

"Mr. Ives, you're so angry."

"Damn right, I'm angry. You know what I saw on the train this morning? Editorial saying, 'Not one in a million is troubled with a conscience.' 'Not one in a million is troubled with a conscience!' Hog-mind hog-wash! Of the world's greatest lies, this is the greatest. Can you get me a glass of water? That would mean no distinction between human life and life in the most luxurious pig-sty. It would mean that Man has grown so bitter morally that his growth can hardly be measured. It would mean death was his only hope — and death without a god, or even a poor substitute for one."

"Here's your water. Here, sit down in your chair."

"Thank you. Mr. Samsa, the mind of chronic Suspicion is the greatest enemy of human progress in any form, the great Trojan warhorse of Suspicion, every fiber reeking with Suspicion — Suspicion in its hundred forms, passionate Suspicion of everything and everyone — a river of cowardice. But Mr. Samsa, if there is one ideal value social evolution's got to have, it's belief in the innate goodness of mankind. Innate goodness. That's why we sell insurance! If the majority want to put themselves in the timid hog-mind class for a while, all right. But a few man minority on Wall Street can't have the right to determine the quality, the courage, the generosity of the People. If Suspicion ever gets the lead, it's all over with the world. It's all over with me."

"Are *you* suspicious?"

"Me? No. I believe in the Majority. The People.

The Masses are singing, are singing, singing,
Whence comes the Art of the World,
The Masses are yearning, are yearning, are yearning,
Whence comes the Hope of the World...

Excuse my damned crotchety warble, but I wrote that song, I wrote that text, my wife and I wrote it..."

"I'm not suspicious either. In this very office there are three not-suspicious people."

"You and me and...?"

"And your glorious Mr. Thoreau you showed me last month. Your green leather Thoreau, there, on your desk. I read the book about his pond. Now I know you better and do a better job with you."

"He was a great musician."

"So are you. Do you remember how he ends the book? Do you remember the story of the strong and beautiful insect which came out of a table sixty years, maybe a hundred years, after its egg..."

"Of course I remember."

"The farmer heard it gnawing away for a long time, trying to get out. Do you hear any gnawing? Listen."

"I hear gnawing."

"What is it?"

"I don't know. Gnawing."

"It's the winged life in you. It's still there, already hatched, gnawing. It will come. At unexpected time it will come. Don't give up. Just wait."

Ives sat quietly in his chair, listening. Then,

"I will. Wait."

"Do you remember the very end?"

"Of what?"

"Of the pond book."

He reached over to his desk.

"Only that day dawns to which we are awake. There is more day to dawn."

"There is more day to dawn."

"The sun is but a morning star."

"Does that remind you of anything, watchman?"

"Promised day of Israel."

"Dost thou see its glorious ray?"

"But after the day the night comes — again."

"So?"

Gregor helped him on with his coat, took Ives out, and walked with him, slowly, silently, all the way up to Grand Central, where he put him on the train for West Redding. Ives officially left his Agency on January 1st, 1930, but remained available, at home, for consultation. He spent his days hatching the insect egg within him.

20. A Short Excursus Away From The Light

"A bagel. I want a bagel. I *need* a bagel."

Gregor put on his new camel hair coat on this frosty Ides of March, and scuttled down two flights of stairs into the morning sunshine. Eighth and C. The fabled Lower East Side, more than its image, less than its myth.

Once he was a salaried employee again, the Roach About Town had decided to settle in, gather his belongings under one roof — his own, and concentrate on building a life. True, the Wall St. crash had clouded things somewhat, but the mood at Ives & Myrick was upbeat, reflecting, perhaps, the sunny personality of Mike Myrick, and the hibernation of the confused and depressed Charles Ives. Gregor's $35 a week was more than ample for room and food — provided he live frugally in a low-rent neighborhood.

The Lower East Side was the obvious choice. For a being so dedicated to life, L'chayem, this was the core and center, the bubbling ur-soup of real-life life, tenement canyons and courtyards hung with laundry, bed-clothes, people up and down fire escapes, bodies, always bodies leaning out windows, talking, calling, yelling. Inside, outside, the rhythm continued, the streets always alive with pushcarts and junk bells, cats yowling and beggars singing, dogs whining and babies crying, men, women, children talking, talking, always talking up a storm. Even the parrots could curse, constantly — in Yiddish. Talk, talk, talk, Jewish talk, up and down the airshafts, semitic surf and symphony, untiring counterpoint to the rattling of dishes, the squeaking of clothes-lines, the plop and splat of peelings and fish heads tossed from above. On the street corners, soapboxes, seers and rebels, prophets and cranks, shouting God's fire and America's woes unto the sky. In Yiddish! Yiddish! A language he could understand without translation, words he could speak without accent. The Old World in the middle of the New — at last he belonged.

He belonged among the children who owned the streets and every smallest corner of alley or lot, every found piece of twisted junk, every stick of lumber, wheels off rusty prams, old clothing, who rejoiced in even the find of a dead, half-rotting squirrel, somehow escaped from Tompkins Square. The children! How beautiful these children. Like little animals with yarmulkes and braids, scouring the world for the few pennies they needed for a hot dog, or a cup of chocolate, halavah, knishes, pickles, or fifty kinds of candy, playing tag and tops and kites and stickball, skelly and ringeleveo. Swarming.

The children and the aged. The nobility of these gaunt, gray-bearded men, shuffling in black coats and hats to schul and synagogue, the same as in Prague. The same clothing, the same bentness, the visible, invisible weight of learning and dedication. The peddlers, old timers — and new ones forced from their stores by the crash, managing the streets, filling them with infinite variegations of the material world. The "I cash clothes" man, the old and dignified scissors grinder with his huge, wheeled, grindstone. Gregor loved to watch the sparks fly, fire from friction, swords into plough-shares. He loved hearing the names of angels and demons from every corner, seeing the babushkas and old fur hats, the riot of banana peels on gray pavement; he loved even the smell of urine. To a blattid, urine smells of life.

The sights and sounds, the tastes and smells of the Lower East Side were a continuous, multi-sensorial madeleine, bringing our six-legged Proust back to his bipedal youth in Prague in the decade before the "sanitiza-tion" of the Jewish quarter, Josefov. Though his upwardly mobile father had moved from ghetto to square several years before Gregor's birth, still, the square backed right on to the ghetto, and young G spent much of his non-school day exploring the crooked alleyways, the dark tunnels with their "spittoons of light" as he called them, leading to interior courtyards of houses named "The Mouse Hole", or "The Left Glove", or "Death". Like the Lower East Side of the thirties, Prague's Jewish Quarter of the previous eighties had suffered an exodus of the better-to-do. The more prosperous families had moved out of Josefov, leaving only the poorest of poor Jews, soon joined by multicultural ranks of the underprivileged: gypsies, beggars, prostitutes and alcoholics. By the time Gregor's father, he of the apple, moved out of the ghetto, only 20% of its inhabitants were Jewish in this, the most densely populated area of Prague. The malodorous neighborhood was seen as a blight upon the city, in the words of Meyrink, "a demonic underworld, a place of anguish, a beggarly and phantasmagorical quarter whose eeriness seemed to have spread and led to paralysis." No wonder Herr Samsa wanted out. No wonder the city fathers wanted urban renewal. In 1893 they decided that Prague might become the jewel of the Empire, a beautiful, bourgeois world-city like Paris. And so the old neighborhoods came down and were replaced with block upon block of opulent art-nouveau buildings, decorative murals, doorways and sculpture. Along with gypsies and prostitutes, the Jews, too, were cleared out: the end of a community which had existed in Prague for a thousand years.

Given the Nazi occupation forty years later, we might expect there to be no trace at all of Josefov today. But truth is stranger than fiction: the remnants of the old Jewish quarter had their savior, one Adolf Hitler, who chose to preserve what little was left of the ghetto — the Jewish Town Hall and the Altneu Synagogue wherein sleeps the golem, the Old Jewish Cemetery, eternal home of the great Rabbi Lowe who created him, and five other synagogues with their contents — as the basic sites for an "Exotic Museum of an Extinct Race". Jewish artifacts stolen from all over central Europe were stored in these buildings, and now constitute one of the great collections of Judaica in the world. With friends like these...

Sorry for the diversion. I was making the point that the situation in the ghetto of Gregor's youth was much like that in New York fifty years later, and thus his new life had a deep and secret resonance which softened the edges of what someone more objective might see as desperation. For even the early days of the depression-to-come had led to many evictions, and forced ever greater numbers of families to crowd together in unheated quarters with aunts and uncles, cousins, grandparents, and friends.

Late October is no time for an economic crisis, for the winter comes hard upon, winter with its dripping walls and airborne diseases. Poverty in winter. Can you imagine the collective suffering of a hundred thousand tenements, grimy, windblown junkheaps of rotting lumber and cracked brick? And in them, thousands, tens of thousands of tuberculars and paralytics, hunger, fatigue, a world of rotting livers and breaking hearts, babies screaming until breath stopped, pneumonia, influenza, typhoid. Garbage trucks and hearses prowled the streets in ghastly competition. Multitudes were without work, and strikes, suicides, food riots pushed pious women to prostitution. The streets reeked with filthy slush, and the sun vanished in greyness behind the sky. Lower East Side winter, 1930.

Yet Gregor, eternal optimist (at the time), was wont to see the beneficent Janus face of adversity. Its precious jewel was that spirit of community where everyone knew everyone, complained and kvetched (a word G taught me), but were there for one another when chips were down — as they almost always were. If Schwartz summoned Goldberg to a call on the corner pay phone, he'd earn a penny or two. With any eviction notice came a collection from housewives up and down the block. Who could afford a physician? Yet people cared for one another, and the old witch doctor, Baba Schimmel, made her rounds, an ancient crone with huge varicosed calves, carrying philters in her knotted apron. The scene of children chasing a sightseeing bus, pelting it with rocks and garbage — and a dead cat – yelling "Go home, go back uptown!"— What else could G conclude but that there was some enormous vestige of neighborhood pride, a sense of strength among the surviving.

****

On a sunny March morning, Gregor put on his camel's hair coat to go buy a dozen bagels. He loved bagels — he always did. His mother used to make them, soft and warm and chewy. He would watch them rise from the dead in the boiling pot and float, triumphant, carving out a tesselate honeycomb of circles on the bubbling surface. Now that he was older, he recognized in bagels the great symbol of Buddhist Nothingness, and the joyous O of O, say can you see and O, what a beautiful morning. And having recently studied Sir D'Arcy Thompson's *On Growth and Form*, a copy of which he had inexplicably found in a trash can outside Tammany Hall, he was now aware of his brotherhood with the bagel, toroid to toroid, a solid mass surrounding a hole.

Perhaps even more than bagels, he loved going into Paddy's Bagel Bakery on Sixth St., off Avenue B. The name was improbable enough, but the large brown bagel hanging out front, growing out its intensely green four-leaf clover broke the bounds of all rational construction. And the sign was just the beginning of the outlandish Paddy experience. Gregor would descend a short flight of stairs to a basement level areaway piled with years of tossed-in trash, a genuine archaeological dig site. There was a narrow, almost clear path toward a door which over the years had carved a radial swing space in the mass of miscellany, and as G headed for his goal he thought — as we do today concerning four wheel drive — how lucky he was to have six legs, in case he needed them. He pulled open the door and was hit, full body, with a caressing blast of steam which felt um-um-good on a freezing Sunday. He closed the door behind him.

Once inside, he could see, as usual, absolutely nothing. The steam was thick, almost impenetrable, and the two 15 watt bulbs hanging from the ceiling served only to make it opaque as well. Remember, bagels have to be boiled before baking, and here in this low-ceilinged basement storefront sans ventilation, it was the steam from two great vats that took front and center — and above and below. And behind. Gregor knew that others were in the shop, but he assumed he was the only customer since all he heard was continuous nattering back and forth in a language of gibberish. It could have been a whole hoard of Niebelungen dwarves, or more likely a large cohort of leprechauns jabbering away in Gaelic. Shadows flitted and projected through the thick, atmospheric fog, but shadows of what — no one could tell.

"A dozen plain bagels, please," he shouted into the hubbub. He didn't know if he had been heard. He repeated his order, and waited, antennae alert, mosaic eyes moist with cloud. A hand appeared out of the mist, holding a brown paper bag. Whose hand this was, he'd never know, but he took the bag from it and replaced it with twenty five cents. The hand withdrew into the mist without so much as a thank you. He had turned to grope his way back into the street when the door swung open in front of him, and

258

G made out the form of a newsboy, silhouetted against the light, waving a paper. Or was he simply fanning away the steam?

"Whuxstree, whuxstree, read all about it, new planet called Pluto! Pluto the new planet!..."

Perhaps it was the shock of sudden light or the dizzying high of steam in the spiracles. More likely it was the stroke of that word: Pluto. Gregor sank down to the ground, and crawled, invisible, until he hit a wall, and pressed up against it. The newsboy, eliciting no customers, backed out, slammed the door shut, and G was left in the misty darkness.

"Pluto. Pluuuuto. I come from Pluto." The voice echoed deep inside him, reverberating off the inner surfaces of his chitinous shell. "I am from Pluto." Perhaps his earliest complex thought, trailing darkest clouds of glory. He would tell his parents, over and over, "I come from Pluto." His mother would say, "Don't be silly, *mein Schatz*," while his father would refuse to understand. And indeed, how could his parents understand, for the planet, with its chthonian name lay still in the darkness, outside the known reaches of the solar system. But not for child Gregor with his clear memories of long periods of overwhelmingly beautiful night, the sky half filled with a huge moon, looming through swirls of greenish gas. The strange, pale glow of a vastly distant sunrise. His movement lithe, half-floating in near-weightlessness. Cold. The cold. He remembered the cold, an intimate dwelling place among barely shivering atoms. He called it "Pluto".

The whole scene came crashing back on him now, again swaddled in darkness and faint mist, but this of the warmest, wettest kind. He lay on the floor under a dark shelf above, antennae quivering with a faint, paresthetic scent of sulfur. Where was it last he sensed that smell? Sulfur, oxygen's downstairs neighbor in Mendeleev's great table, aggressively sniffing out the world with its two electrons, and being sniffed, in turn. That smell...

If a doddering old History of Science professor may be allowed yet another intrusion, even into Gregor's interplanetary swoon...

The discovery of Pluto was one of the more remarkable stories in a science replete with same. When Herbert Hoover was sworn in as our thirty-first president on the 4th of March, 1929, he would have told you, if asked, that there were eight planets in our solar system, and being an ex-mining engineer, could have listed them, in order: Mercury, Venus,

Earth, Mars, Jupiter, Saturn, Uranus and Neptune. Perhaps he used one of the many mnemonics available to recall them: "My Very Educated Mother Just Served Us Noodles".

Yet at that very moment, there were two earthlings who could have assured him otherwise: Vesto Melvin Slipher, the world-renowned director of the Lowell Observatory in Flagstaff, Arizona, and Clyde W. Tombaugh, a 23-year old farmboy from Kansas.

The story begins even before there was a Kansas, back in 1781 — March 13th to be exact — when the British astronomer, William Herschel, became the first person in modern times to discover a planet unknown to the ancients. He called it Uranus after the personification of heaven, and like that personification of heaven, it proved to be a bit erratic, straying tens of thousands of miles off its mathematically predicted course. Some unknown force must have been distorting its path, and in 1845 (sixteen years before the state of Kansas) the French astronomer, Urbain Leverrier, worked out the likely mass and orbit of a hypothetical planet beyond Uranus. Given that roadmap, Neptune was found and named in the following year — but again seemed to pull away from a purely mathematical dance. And worse, its mass was too small to account for Uranus's meanderings. There was still something out there, invisible, sucking on those two huge spheres. But given the reach of contemporary telescopes, nothing else could be found. And as the resolutions gradually increased, so did the number of points of light. How many 17th magnitude dots can one analyze?

In the early part of our century, two Americans once again took up the search, an occasion for two of those extraordinary coincidences which seemed to decorate G's life like mysterious jewels. Percival Lowell, the literary, world-traveling scion of the distinguished Lowell family of Massachusetts, had been inspired by the discovery of "canals" on Mars to devote his life and personal fortune to studying the red planet. Because of the stillness of the air above, and the rarity of cloud cover, he had built a private observatory outside Flagstaff, Arizona and equipped it, at great expense, with the most advanced equipment available. At this site, he developed a theory, published in 1906 (*Mars and Its Canals* — still interesting reading), of intelligent life forms on Mars cultivating long rows of vegetation, using irrigation from annually melting ice caps. You may laugh at a theory which seems more appropriate to the *The National Enquirer* than to the *Annals of Astronomy*, but it was not until Mariner 4's 1965 fly-by that it was conclusively disproved.

Lowell moved on from Mars to an elaborate mathematical study of the orbit of Uranus. He attributed its irregularities to the gravitational pull of some unseen planet beyond Neptune, calculated its probable position, and organized a systematic search by his observatory staff, directed, after 1916, by Vesto Melvin Slipher. Fourteen years after his death, "Lowell's Planet" was discovered.

Coincidence number one: Percival Lowell was the brother of A. Lawrence Lowell, the president of Harvard, whose hidebound review put Sacco and Vanzetti to death. The Harvard brother was the leading member of a committee to advise the Massachusetts governor on the case, and had he or any member of his "Lowell Committee" failed to find the defendants guilty beyond a reasonable doubt, they would have been spared. They did not fail. Heywood Broun asked "From now on, will the institution of learning in Cambridge, which once we called Harvard, be known as Hangman's House?"

Coincidence number two: How is one supposed to compare field photographs of half a million stars? Lowell, whose plates over the years surely contained a faint image of his planet couldn't make out its slight traverse through the zodiac.

Do you remember Hans Lindauer, Zeiss designer of the planetarium projector and donor of lenses for Gregor's reading glasses? Hans Lindauer. Here he is again in our story – coincidence number three — the inventor of the Zeiss Blink Comparator. Vesto Melvin Slipher was wise enough to purchase the new device shortly after it appeared, and using it, Clyde Tombaugh "blinked" Planet X (as it was then called) into visible existence.

The Zeiss Blink Comparator was an ingeniously simple device. Photographic plates of identical sky fields from two different nights were put into the machine, which focused them into the same eyepiece. They were then "blinked", quickly alternated, into the eyepiece, and any celestial object which had changed place over several days would appear to jump back and forth, thus calling attention to itself. Hans Lindauer — a clever mind. Needless to say, there were technical difficulties to be overcome — precisely matching up star fields, allowing for slight atmospheric differences in visibility night to night, identifying defects in photographic plates, and so forth. But a determined perfectionist like young Clyde went through three quarters of the zodiac using the highest standards of patient, technical precision, and on February 18th, 1930, less than a year after he was hired to do this scut-work, the 23-year old tow-head with thick glasses and callused hands loaded the Blink Comparator with plates taken January 23rd and 29th, and out jumped Planet X from the star-dense constellation of Gemini, smack in the middle of the Milky Way, a 15th magnitude dim "star" that changed its position against a fixed background.

Clyde Tombaugh. Did he jump around like the star, and rush to announce his finding? Not Clyde. He put in two more weeks of patient work, searching for the image in intermediate and outlying positions, and only after he had proved its existence to himself, seen its slow, continuous inching through a 248 year course around the sun, did he go up to the director's office to nonchalantly announce, "Dr. Slipher, I've found your Planet X."

For the next few nights, Slipher, Clyde, and other lab staff checked and rechecked, and the director was ready to put his reputation on the line by announcing the discovery to the world. But when? With an astronomer's love of the calendar, Slipher chose March 13th, 149 years to the day from Herschel's discovery of Uranus, and, coincidentally, Percy Lowell's birthday, a date which the wily director knew would much please Lowell's widow — the observatory's continuing benefactress.

Announced on a Friday, along with a request for name suggestions , the news provoked a flood of telegrams to Flagstaff, one from the grandfather of eleven-year old Venetia Burney, of Oxford, England. Venetia was studying mythology in school and over breakfast suggested that Pluto, king of the underworld, might share his name with the new planet because it was "so distant, dark and gloomy".

After much sifting through suggestions, this was the one that stood out, partly because of its aptness, but largely because the astronomical sign for Pluto is ♇, the initials of Mrs. Lowell's beloved husband, and thus provoking more continued funding. The largest objection to be overcome was the name's possible association with "Pluto Water", a widely advertised laxative.

So "Pluto" it was, announced in the Sunday papers, the headline screamed out by the newsboy into the darkness of Paddy's Bagel Bakery.

One more word about Clyde W. Tombaugh. Through a mutual friend, I came to know him quite well in his later years. He became a quiet, sweet old man, twisted by kyphosis, one of the astronomical world's great punsters. I remember him talking about finding Pluto in his heyday: "It was like a coaxing a wheedle out of a naystack." He never learned to use a word processor, or even a typewriter. I received one of his detailed, long-hand letters early this year, just before his death. He spoke about the irony of his life spent working in cold and darkness in a desert world of blazing sun. It reminded me of Gregor.

Gregor, whom we last left pressed against the wall under the shelf, under the ground, in Paddy's wet darkness. Why had the mention of Pluto affected him so strongly?

I had never understood his original, terse story until one day he and I were getting ready for a soak at the Jemez Hot Springs, a favorite haunt of the Los Alamos community, where many new ideas have erupted during late night discussions infused with the stink of sulfur. I had already sunk down in the blissfully warm water: G was putting on his dry suit when suddenly he sank to the ground. I thought he had lost his balance trying to put his hind legs through the tiny holes in the garment. But no: he had actually become faint. I helped him into the pool thinking the healing waters would bring him around. He kept muttering "Smell, smell...", by which he could only have meant the sulfurous vapor. As he wasn't doing well, I bundled him into the truck and took him home. After a cup of chamomile tea, he related a very strange story, harking back fourteen years to the experience at Paddy's.

A cockroach's antennae — his organs of smell — are very long — a third again his total body length. Smell is an intense stimulant of the blattid sensorium. Were one to draw a distorted facial map on the sensory part of a cockroach brain, it would have a very big nose. The ghostly newsboy's cries had brought back an overwhelming olfactory incident from several winters previous, the memory of which had thrown him into a swoon similar to the last.

It was on day four of the five day blizzard of '27, and G had gone out in the blinding snow to forage for dinner. The wind-chill was intense, I imagine, though they didn't measure wind-chill in those days. What I do know is that after wandering around for half an hour in conditions of poor visibility, G had stumbled into a large dumpster in the alley behind Blinder's Cut-rate Bakery. His legs were starting to slow, and his thoughts were taking on an expansive quality that comes with intimations of crystallinity. Lowering himself into the offal — more to partake of its bacterial warmth than to forage — he was overwhelmed with the smell of hydrogen sulfide from a case of rotting eggs deep in the dumpster's south-east corner, now disturbed and venting.

Hydrogen sulfide is quite poisonous to humans, rapidly corroding and destroying lung tissue. But lungless cockroaches react entirely in the depths of their ganglionic webs, and being so close to the edge of this life, the combination of smell and toxin sent Gregor — he concluded — into a swirl of past life memories and chaotic impressions, astrological, astronomical, mythological, tragi-comical, intra-specific.

Even as he told me about them later, in the warmth of his chicken coop, a comforter over his abdomen, a cup of steaming tea in his lap, he went off into a kind of tangled rambling which I will try to reproduce from the deep impression it made upon me. If I don't get it exactly right, little matter: the connections seemed so loose as to be fluid and interchangeable.

"Sulfur," he intoned, "sulfur is breath of the underworld, Plutorealm, Plutospirit. I come from Pluto — under the light of the great moon."

(Let me remind the reader that all this happened more than a year before the discovery or naming of Pluto. And Pluto's huge moon, Charon — the ferryman of Hades, 40% Pluto's size, was not found until 1976, thirty one years after G's death!)

"Horror-rich wealth of the invisible," he continued, "I'm coming, I change. *Kein Tod, kein Verwandlung.* Sulfur sounds in emptyspace, metamorphosinvisible, the travelers, vultures and stars.., Pluto-born in winter land, and never live till spring. Abendland. West. Oooo-west. [I don't know if he was referring here to his original vision or to the recent experience at Jemez.] A Universe of ...Death...perverse, all monstrous, all prodigious things, abominable...inutterable and worse. [This I recognized from Milton. I hadn't realized G was involved with *Paradise Lost*.] There are songs still to sing... beyond human...

And here he began a halting *Sprechstimme* version of the last of Schubert's *Winterreise*, the song about the inscrutable hurdy-gurdy man, impervious to life's woes. He fell asleep, muttering, singing. I took the cup out of his hand, wrapped him more securely in his patchwork comforter, and left. To this day, I puzzle out that thought-web in the dark light of Gregor's destiny.

21. The Unexpected Always Happens

Gregor overslept on the Monday after Paddy's — a rare event. He awoke at 10:15, the morning sun streaming into his eyes over the chimney tops of Avenue C, "The Avenue," Galway Kinnell called it, "Bearing The Initial of Christ Into The New World." Christ the Jew.

He jumped into his clothes, did up his antennae as quickly as he could, pocketed a day-old bagel, whizzed down the stairs and hit the streets running. But at corner of Eighth and B, he was stopped short: a crowd of some sixty people were gathered around a little, 40-year old Jew and his wife, sitting at an enameled kitchen table, their four children around them, shivering in tattered clothing, the youngest crying pitifully, as if he could foresee what was abroad in the world. All their worldly belongings were piled around them — a shrine, a museum, a mausoleum of objects: an old, bedbugged mattress with protruding springs; a stained, embroidered under-stuffed chair; a lamp with a burned-through shade, (a burned Jewish lampshade!) Around the family and the furniture, the small objects that constitute a life: a washtub packed with dishes, a box of bedclothes, a broom. What broom, Gregor wondered, could sweep this journey clean? A seven year-old was idly rocking an empty carriage abandoned last month by her baby brother, a still valued possession to cling to in an uncertain world.

With heavy heart, the wife reached into the washtub, retrieved a tea glass and placed it on the table. Were they going to have tea? G wondered. Where would they boil water? A neighbor woman close by placed a penny in the glass and mumbled a Hebrew prayer, and the husband stared at his hands laid flat on the table. From a twelve year old, another coin — and then, from many, many. Rosie the prostitute pushed gently through the crowd and placed a dollar bill into the glass half full of nickel and copper — an act her judgmental neighbors knew not how to judge. Incredible. Indigestible. The crowd parted to let her back through, and heads turned to watch her walk back into her shameful building. The husband still stared at his hands. "We are not beggars," he cried out, as he lifted his head for the first time. "We are respectable people!" And he drew back into his humiliation.

Gregor was about to put his bagel on the table, next to two apples and a banana, when there was a stirring at the back of the crowd, and a voice called out,

"OK, the cops are gone. Furniture back in the house!"

A woman ordered, "Form a squad and block the doors if they come back!"

The Young Communists were calling for volunteers. Such a family was entitled to a place to live. And people responded. Not just the young and daring, but small boys and girls, frail, elderly men, women with young children clinging to their hems. Gregor picked up the lamp with the scorched shade, and marched it back into the apartment.

"Sheriff! Sheriff!" came the lookout voice, and a group of young men, well-practiced, ran round the corner to kick over ash cans and bang with fists on parked cars, diverting the police so the uneviction might continue.

The ten or fifteen people who had declined to take part stood aside, watching the action. Sensing a ready-made audience, a disheveled, gnome of a man appropriated the last kitchen chair, pushed it over to the bystanders, and jumped up on its cracked seat.

"My dirty thief of a cousin, Herman Rothblatt, may his nose be eaten by the pox, he stole my shop, he stole my shop away from me!"

Before he could elaborate, a muscular young cadre with no coat, his sleeves rolled up in the cold, pulled the chair out from under him and tossed it to a comrade in the uneviction brigade. Herman Rothblatt's cousin picked himself, dusted off his dishevelledness, and walked silently away. Before rounding the corner of Eighth St., he turned and yelled, "When

Messiah comes to America, he better come with a big car and a chauffeur and a full wallet, or people will think he's just another poor Yid, and he'll have to wash dishes in a restaurant!" G saw him throw up his head in pride, and disappear around the corner.

It was already eleven. He wouldn't be at work for half an hour. G thought of taking a cab, but in the midst of others' poverty felt ashamed to do so. He turned south, and walked quickly down Second Avenue to Houston and over toward the Bowery.

In his essay, "The Awful German Language", Mark Twain excoriates the German proclivity to pile word on word for compound conceptions. He is positively livid over such "alphabetical processions" as *Generalstaatsverordnetenversammlungen* — meetings of the legislature. "In the hospital yesterday, a word of thirteen syllables was successfully removed from a patient…" Yet sometimes such jugglings can create distinctions unavailable in English. On his quickwalk downtown, Gregor was playing in his heartmind with the paradoxes of the *Unterüberwelt* and the *Überunterwelt*. Gregor lived in the *Unterwelt*, an "underworld" not in the Plutonic sense, but in the way the "underdog" is under. Nevertheless, his neighborhood underworld was actually an overworld, superior — at least morally — to the district he worked in, and thus an "overunderworld". Wall Street, his destination, was the inverse, an "underoverworld" in which evictions, bankruptcies, and even suicides were private affairs, sometimes whispered about, but never collectively mourned. As he walked, he tried to feel the downward slope of moral descent on the absolute flatness of the physical path, and amidst the class-ascent of the taller and taller, resplendent buildings. Up, down and level, all at the same time, a mysterious Trinity pervading most human affairs. He arrived at work tense.

It didn't help that he was three and a half hours late. When Kathryn Verplank, once Mr. Ives's personal secretary, now general site manager, appeared at his desk, he feared it was all over. Caught.

"Mr. Ives would like to see you in his office."

Mr. Ives?? Why is he here? Did he come all that way to personally fire me? I can just leave without disturbing him.

"He has something for you."

"Yes, ma'am."

Gregor rose slowly and inched his way towards the room behind the frosted glass. Something for me. A tin watch to honor my less than three years of service? He can be frightful when he is mad. It was one spooked roach who knocked tentatively on the great man's door.

"Come in!" came a voice frighteningly firm, so unlike the last doddering hesitations Gregor had heard. Prepare for the worst.

"Mr. Samsa, how nice to see you!"

Ives got up from his desk and strode robustly across the room to shake Gregor's claw. What was going on? Isn't he mad I was late? Was this a trick?

"Well, I did what you told me."

"What was that?"

"Gave birth to the insect gnawing in the table. The table, that's me."

"You mean you wrote another Symphony?"

"Sonata, my boy, a sonata. For the old hammerklavier."

He went back to his desk and plucked a thick music manuscript from the top of a pile of unopened mail.

"Her you are. Take a look at the dedication."

SONATA NUMBER THREE FOR PIANO

THE INSECT SONATA

CHARLES E. IVES

"It's on the next page."

Gregor turned over the elegantly copied manuscript page.

To Mr. Gregor Samsa, Best Of Employees, For Conducting Me, Ma Non Troppo, From Mesto Rottenabile To Allegro Onceagaindo. With Deep Appreciation.

C. E. I.

Gregor was dumbstruck. What could he say? He turned over the pages. A lot of notes. A huge number of notes — and strange notation. First movement, CREATION; the second, REVELATION; the third movement, REDEMPTION.

"Thank you, Mr. Ives. I wasn't expecting... I mean to say I was expecting you to get better, but I didn't think I..."

"And here are two tickets to the premiere — April Fool's Day I've already rented the hall. That'll fool 'em as thought I was a goner. You'll come with Mrs. Ives and me."

TOWN HALL
APRIL 1, 1930, 8PM
"THE INSECT SONATA", by CHARLES E. IVES
NICOLAS SLONIMSKY, piano
The work will be played twice.

Gregor did not get his tin watch. He did not get fired. But he did get confused. How was it possible that he, a mere insect, could have helped bring such a thing to birth? Was this the first evidence that he was truly on the path, that his quest had a realizable goal?

He took his lunch at the usual time, but couldn't go back to work. Concentrating on numbers, budgets, probabilities — impossible. He became aware of the wound in his back It was not leaking but tingling — perhaps glowing. Dry. Electric. He called in sick from a pay phone on William St. He was sick — sick with The Sickness Unto Life, but this he didn't tell Mrs. Verplank.

G walked home slowly, out of the dark canyons of perplexed plutocracy, up the moral gradient, up Broadway to the Park, over to Center Street, up to Houston. Turning east, high *Überunterland* now, he realized he hadn't yet eaten and stopped into Yonah Schimmel's for a knish. Ah, the warmth of hot, spiced potato on a nippy day of not-yet-spring! He opened his mouth and allowed the knish to make smoke in the broad air. Now he was a fire-breathing dragon, a Fafner guarding the secret hoard. Hoard of what?

Crossing Houston, always dangerous, better concentrate, he turned north on Avenue A. Just past the courthouse, he felt a tug on his left sleeve.

"I know you from this morning. I see you standing there before you take the lamp into the house."

It was the gnome, the cousin of Herman Rothblatt, still disheveled.

"My cousin, may the worms find him, may he eat nothing but dry crusts, he stole my shop. He stole my umbrella shop. I own it myself. I work for myself. I live and laugh, I take him in as partner, he needs a break."

270

"You said that this morning."

"I didn't. I didn't say what kind of shop. I didn't say about partners."

Gregor sped his pace, so that the manikin had to trot to keep up with him.

"He stole my shop, and now I will die of starving. A curse on Columbus, the thief! A curse on America, the thief! We live... slow down! ...we live in a land where lice make the fortunes, and good people starve. May six and sixty six black years fall on them, the lices have ruined the world with greed! Liars and thieves everywhere, wars, murders, children killed by streetcars. When Messiah comes he will change all this, believe me. They'll be sorry."

Gregor stopped. They had reached Eighth Street.

"Do you need money?"

"Yes."

"Will five dollars be enough?"

"Ten."

Gregor pulled two five dollar bills out of wallet and handed a third of his salary to his swarthy companion.

"Here."

"Thank you. You are not a lice. You are a good man."

"I have to go now. Thank you for telling me about you."

"God bless you. You are a good man, not a lice."

In fact, this little colloquy had quite taken the wind out of Gregor's sails. He had started uptown breathing in the bracing gradient of poverty, that poverty of spirit that will be blessed with the kingdom of heaven. But now he was breathing plain old simple, wretched poverty, the poverty of theft and eviction and crafty, manipulative begging. He passed the corner of the morning's events, deserted now, eerily empty of its usual play. He reached his home — on the corner of Avenue C.

This God-forsaken Avenue bearing the initial of Christ
through the haste and carelessness of the ages.

High, then low. It was no accident that his gaze was drawn to that stone in the courtyard, an early gravestone, broken and discarded, which some enterprising landlord had used to fill a hole in the paving.

the 21th. 1719 Ag
ed 38 years
Here lies one wh
os lifes thrads
cut asunder She
was strucke dead
by a clap of thunder.

 Barely readable, but searing all the same.

Mr. Pinzer was chatting in the courtyard with Mrs Grossman as she hung the laundry.

"From the Talmud one can learn anything," he assured her. "For instance, it takes the Angel Gabriel six flaps of his wings to come down to earth. The Angel Simon, it takes four flaps, but the Angel of Death, him it takes only one flap of the wings."

It is wonderful to be learnèd.

22. The Insect Sonata

Looking for his reactions to the Insect Sonata, I found the following entry in Gregor's diary sheets, along with an unused Town Hall ticket.

TUESDAY, 1 APRIL 1930. TODAY WE HAVE DAY OFF TO PLAY TRICK ON SOMEONE TO HONOR OF MR. IVES. WE HAVE NOT DO THIS LAST YEAR. I THINK MR. MYRICK TRIES TO MAKE UP FOR MR. IVES. I DO NOT HAVE TRICK IN MIND. GO TO HEAR CONCERT TONIGHT. WHO I WILL ASK TO COME WITH ME? TILL EULENSPIEGEL.

Whatever did he have in mind? The last figure I would compare him to would be that scatological sixteenth century trickster. With the exception of his increasingly filthy bedroom existence in Prague, however needy G may have been in various phases of his life, he was always neat and polite. The idea of Till's defecating on this or that, of gratuitously killing animals, of stealing or tricking...the whole thing is too absurd. Perhaps he was referring sardonically to his occasional attempts to get a date. Giving a long-single male two tickets to a concert — well, as Gregor used to say, the gift is not as precious as the thought. But until I found this entry, I had not understood the context of the conversation which took place in the taxi en route to Town Hall.

Though Gregor had offered to meet the Iveses at the concert so as not to take them out of their way, they wouldn't hear of it: they would pick him up at 7:30 at the corner of 8th and C. Instead of plotting and pranking, G had spent the day being fitted for appropriate attire. Via a call to

Ulla, he had located a Jewish tailor from Krakow who, instead of following the migration north to the garment district, had established a tiny shop on Elizabeth St., in the heart of Chinatown. His sign read EMANNUEL PINSKY, ESQ. ELEGANT CLOTHES FOR STYLISH MENS, with translations in Yiddish and Chinese lettered below. Perhaps it was more grammatical in Yiddish. Gregor arrived at ten in the morning, and after telling Mr. Pinsky about the evening's affair, received an enthusiastic "Oi, have I got just the thing for you!"

Gregor was always hard to fit. It was no surprise that he didn't leave Pinsky's (famished) until 4:30, carrying a large white box containing a dark blue worsted tail coat, a pair of gray pinstriped wool trousers, with braces and cummerbund (the starry-eyed tailor reported that "pinstripes" were his invention, named after him), a pleated, pale blue linen shirt with a darker silk ascot, and to add a touch of what Pinsky called *"finésshe"*, a larger-than-life, red satin carnation. "You'll be the hit of the show," he assured his doubtful and embarrassed customer. But Pinsky knew America better than he, and was after all an acknowledged expert in stylish men's wear. So G went along with the enthusiasm of the master, and accepted the generous offer, "For you, special", to rent rather than buy.

He was overdressed. When he climbed into the cab, he found Ives in his usual gray overcoat, over his normal brown tweed suit and brown tie, his daily fedora perched far back on his head. Harmony looked a bit more elegant in her black dress and light fur piece, but still....

Charles, always truthful if not tactful, said "Mr. Samsa, you look like the winner of the Nobel Prize for Undertaking — Wouldn't you say so, dear?" Harmony thought Gregor looked just fine. Driving up Fourth Avenue, they were talking about April Fool's Day in America and similar Feast of Fools days in Europe when Ives burst out with an alarmingly accurate imitation of the opening horn solo from *Till Eulenspiegel,* making a heroic, if unsuccessful attempt at the final low F.

"What's that?" asked G, always ready to learn.

"When Strauss conducted the first rehearsal of that piece, he was assured by the first horn player that the Till melody couldn't be played."

"Till...Eulenspiegel?"

"Yes, of course. What else? Strauss charged through the orchestra,

274

grabbed the idiot's horn, and played it right off, standing in the middle of the horn section."

"I was thinking of Till Eulenspiegel this very today."

"Damn horn players want everything nicey-nice and easy."

"Charles, calm down." Harmony put her hand on his thigh.

"Why did you bring up Till Eulenspiegel?"

"We were talking about fools. Why were you thinking about Till Eulenspiegel?"

"I was thinking how he never has anything to do with women."

"No. He falls in love."

"He doesn't."

"'Till, the cavalier, exchanging sweet courtesies with beautiful girls'," and here Ives went into the romantic version of Till's horn theme. "It's marked *liebeglühend*, what more do you want? He's got it bad."

"And?"

"And she jilts him, what else? Who could put up with Till Eulenspiegel?"

"I think this is not in the stories. He uses his bed only to die."

"He dies in bed?"

"Of the plague."

"No. He dies on the gallows. You can hear him drop a major seventh: *'Der Tod!'*"

"I think this is not in the book. But it doesn't matter."

"Of course it matters if you die of the plague or on the gallows."

"Why? Dead is dead."

"One is murdered by Hog-mind, the other by...germs. One is an accident; one is principled suicide. It matters. Greatly. Strauss got it right, whatever the book says!"

The cab drew up on 43rd Street, and Harmony opened her purse to pay the driver. The three got out, two of them in the early-middle of a life and death conversation. They were an singular-looking trio.

The lights were going down. A young usher flashlit the route to their seats in the back row. There was a moment of rustling silence, and Nicolas Slonimsky — the extravagant Russian *émigré* pianist, composer and conductor with a passion for ultra-modern music — walked on from stage right. Perhaps staggered might be a better word, for he had done nothing but eat, sleep and drink this difficult work for the last three months, trying to get it into his brain and under his fingers. He had conducted several Ives premieres, and had the composer's trust. He was not a sissy. He drank strong samovar *chai*. Still, a man needs sleep.

But one can stagger and still be on fire, and Slonimsky, even punchy, was a force to be reckoned with. He bowed to the audience. Without a word of introduction, he walked upstage of the Steinway Concert Grand and returned with a large brick and two pieces of two-by-four, one 47 3/4", the other 45 1/2", the longer painted in white, the shorter in black enamel. He put the wood on the piano bench, and carefully leaned the cement block on the sustaining pedal. Climbing out from under the keyboard, he retrieved the wood, and placed the longer piece, narrow edge down, along the white keys, and the shorter one, wider side down, along the black. He was ready to begin the first movement: Creation.

Standing over the keyboard, the piano bench behind him, he took a huge breath, and crashed his whole body weight down, elbows first, onto the wood. Some in the audience gasped, most jumped. The piano let out a sound such as had never been heard on the planet. At no time, ever, had all eighty-eight notes of a Steinway Concert Grand been simultaneously publicly sounded and sustained.

The Boeing 747 is such a well-designed plane that, should all its engines simultaneously fail at 35,000 feet, the huge beast has enough wing-lift to coast for 600 miles before having to land. Similarly, the Steinway Concert Grand. Quadruple fortissimo to start, the opening ultra-chord took a full two and a half minutes to decay into nothingness, though the absolute end-point depended on each listener's distance and auditory acuity. Slonimsky stood above the keyboard, his eyes closed, and allowed his spirit to spread to the farthest physical and spiritual reaches of the expanding vibrations.

When he could hear no more, (he was the last in the hall), when what he would call his etheric body had reached its maximum distance and had begun to contract significantly, he removed the two-by-fours, replaced them upstage, reached under the piano, pushed the brick to the side of the pedal, and took his seat at the keyboard.

Before I continue, let me confess that I was not present at this historic performance. I am piecing this narrative together from Gregor's reports, from a study of the score which was finally published in 1967 by Universal, and from some recent listening to the only available recording, just released by Gilbert Kalisch on Nonesuch. (Even John Kirkpatrick, the only man to truly master the *Concord Sonata*, could not handle it.) And while I am digressing from the concert, let me say, too, that while it is nowhere indicated in the copious commentary in the score, it is clear that Ives's famous opening was also the first direct musical reference to the "Big Bang" theory of Creation.

This notion, now the leading cosmological hypothesis, had come in 1926 to the Belgian mathematician/priest Georges Lemâitre in a religious vision. It accounted for Hubble's red-shift findings, and explained the recession of galaxies in the framework of Einsteinian General Relativity. He published his theory in 1927 in an obscure Belgian journal *("Un univers homogène de masse constante et de rayon croissant rendant compte de la vitesse radiale des nébuleuses extra-galactique", Ann. Soc. Sci. Bruxelles, 47A, 1927, pp. 49-56)*, which, in 1930, was discovered by a graduate student of Arthur Eddington's — who then announced it to the world just a few months before the concert. The public loved its straightforward image of the "primeval atom", the "cosmic egg", containing all matter in the universe, whose explosion marked the beginning of time and space — which may explain the general acceptance of this cacophonous moment. Without being told, people understood that the opening of a movement called "Creation" might consist of some kind of big bang. The actual experience, apparently, was something else.

The big bang gives way to a world of vast, austere empty space. Out of silence, there appear atomic fragments of pre-melodies, one note, three notes, two, a gentle report of almost-vacancy. Beethoven had attempted same in the opening moments of the Ninth, but Ives takes this micro-macro view far further, developing not a larger, more convincing, musical phrase, but the idea of "phrase" itself, and the very conception of tonality — bi-, tri-, quadri-tonality — as the pre-melodies stake out their tonal grounds. The section is marked "In the Egg-Case, *Molto Adagio*", and in it we recognize the eggs of the Egg, streaming outward, developing the charged direction of their own contents. Punctuating the slow metamorphoses of individual capsules were quiet outbursts of tremolos at the seventh and ninth, creating halo-like shimmers of light. Since there are six such crescendo-decrescendos in the movement, I assume they clock the six days of creation, after which there is rest. On the fifth of such presumptive days, the day when God said, "Let the waters bring forth abundantly every moving creature that hath life," the music thickens markedly. It now has enough mass for rhythm to emerge, at first simple syncopations, and finally a poly-rhythmic cosmic dance, a combination of simultaneous musics, as Ives was wont to do, but here slower, softer, more anatomized, not the repulsing chaos of the Fourth Symphony "Comedy", but a far more inviting, massaging soundspace enveloping the listener in a finally friendly creation. On the sixth presumptive day, with the addition of "creeping things" to the bestiary, a clear, easily recognizable rhythmic figure, a quarter note, a rest, and quick pickup to the next quarter: the telltale rhythmic signature of of an insect heartbeat, gathering.

The middle section of this ABA movement is marked "The firmament walks up a mountainside to view the firmament", an odd, but evocative, piece of topology. We hear the slow, gentle, aggregation of kaleidoscope-massed chords and tone clusters, the total effect of which is to rough out, in strange harmonies, an accompaniment to a still absent melody. The bass tries out "Oh Maker of the Sea and Sky", only to have it fade away, incomplete. The tune returns again, "Creator Spirit, By Whose Aid...", and advances a few bars further, before dissolving in its own accompaniment. In this middle section, the overall serenity is occasionally pierced by inexplicable explosions, surprising, sometimes barbaric, leaps of tone sequences from one end of the keyboard to the the other, recalling George Ives's experiments with the humanophone — accenting in yet another way the pervasive feeling of spaciousness. Wisps of quotations — Handel's frogs and locusts, Mahler's lindens, Haydn's whales and worms, Beethoven's cuckoo, Ives' friend Carl Ruggle's lilacs, Saint-Saëns's, Tchaikovsky's and Sibelius's swans — make fragmentary appearances, a half a dozen notes, like the sprinkling of stars which form a constellation.

Then, as if from a different level of space-time, the first mood returns, now enclosed in a trinity of superimposed sets of perfect fifths, a pedal point pervaded by heartbeat, giving birth, as if from a resistant hardwood table, to a hesitant, but slowly complete, chorale setting of "Watchman, tell us of the night", the melody floating in and out of tonality, sober, *maestoso*, cognisant of the triple mysticism of its cloak of open fifths. "Watchman, tell us of the night" — here not an anxious question, but a humble entreaty, its feet washed in mystery.

With this, Slonimsky closed the movement, quietly, firmly, then placed his hands in his lap and waited the full three minutes requested in the score. For the first of these, the audience was completely silent, hypnotized by the evocation, "spaced-out", to use a contemporary expression in its most correct and literal sense. In the second minute, people grew uncomfortable. Some worried that something was amiss, while others gathered their suspicions of a put-on. A small flurry of whispering was shushed out by the faithful, and the silence cycled round again on a deeper level.

The pianist opened his eyes and once again placed the the brick on the sustain pedal. He stood by the side of the piano while two stage hands pulled pins from their hinges, and placed the huge piano lid against the wall, stage right. The performer now had in front of him, an enormous horizontal harp, ready to speak of "Revelation".

But not just a harp. A harp inside an enormously powerful, sophisticated structure, evolved over centuries, a structure capable of containing and supporting more than eighteen tons of amassed string tension. A structure of multiple strings in two overlapping fans. A structure of spruce and steel very like a coffin.

I am a poor pianist, and I leave all maintenance of the Yamaha to Emil, our most excellent tuner. But I have often been attracted, amazed, even thrilled by the technical genius of the modern pianoforte. And yet, each time I put my head under the lid, I feel strongly: *coffin*, an ominous, but somehow freeing impression nurtured and sweetened by the involuntary rush of the last Schumann song in the *Dichterliebe*, the one about "the old evil songs, the wicked, depraved dreams." Heine and Schumann want to bury them all in a large coffin, a coffin larger than the Heidelberg Cask, longer than the bridge at Mainz, a coffin so huge it must be carried by twelve giants and buried in the sea. A coffin for all those songs and dreams — and Heine's love, and Schumann's suffering. What better coffin, then, than a massive piano case? When I play the caressing postlude to that song, the end of the whole song cycle, my spirit is wafted under that black lid to be massaged and prepared for its final freedom. I wonder if Ives had any sense of this in writing the second movement, if all its boisterousness is ironically placed inside a tomb, and must be so understood.

In any event, the entire second movement, "Revelation", marked "*Scherzo* TSIMAJ", takes place inside the case, and requires of the performer an utterly unprecedented technique, and of the composer an extended notational system. It also demands a new vocabulary from the would-be reporter. Just as we have few words to describe taste or pain, or most of the 473 sounds cats can make, so the verbal lexicon is completely inadequate to describe the rich sound palette of an undamped piano harp in a sophisticated sound chamber, urged by fingers which can pluck and stoke, flick and scratch, flesh, bone, and nail, by fists that can bang, and palms that can slap, by forearms grazing and elbows jabbing, and even by hair brushing lightly, across or along the strings. Add to those the percussive sonorities of various striking objects: the metallic echo of wedding ring on harp bolt, the ticking or tocking of chopstick and toothpick, the liquid rebound of strings released by soft dough. And all this in a universe sympathetic with vibration, where each sound creates families of related sub-sounds, ripples upon ripples, slow beats after fast, high upon low upon high. No description can communicate such aural complexity.

Because a performer would quickly be lost in a forest of undifferentiated stringing, the strings were colored black and white to mirror the familiar keyboard; though paint had been lost over the hammers, and in areas of maximum vibrational displacement, the visual effect was still striking, and Gregor asserts that certain combinations of vibrating strings, though each only black or white, can create short flashes of color. I don't understand the physics of this; perhaps it occurs only for the blattid nervous system, or solely in mosaic eyes.

Even if I can't describe the sound in great detail, I can provide a roadmap to this extraordinary piece thanks to Ives's clear musical and extra-musical ideas and his detailed marginalia.

After the long silence of, I suppose, the Sabbath, the movement opens triple pianissimo, with a quietly pulsing, timeless, Eb, the same sustained note Wagner chose to represent the beginning of the world from abysmal depths. ("Mark my new poem well," he wrote Liszt (11 Feb. 1853): "it holds the world's beginning, and its destruction.") Most curiously, Ives notates the tone as F♭♭, for reasons which will later become clear.

All of a sudden, there is a loud, old-fashioned, short fanfare, the kind of musical cliché which would invariably be followed by "And now, Ladies and Gentlemen...", over which is written "Welcome to the Grand Old Opryetta", and the sound drops back to the F♭♭, now pulsing in the first movement's rhythmic cell of the beating roach heart. Suddenly, the note pushes unexpectedly off into the rising E♭ arpeggio of the hero theme from *Ein Heldenleben,* only to fall flat on its face as the sixteenth notes tumble down, splat, back to a more agitated pulsing. The manuscript then notes "In The Cage", and the F♭♭ pulse takes on the perturbed syncopations of the pacing beast in that short, 1904 piece — and then stops short, as the pianist begins the most banal version of "How Dry I Am", a tune well-known in those late years of prohibition. In the margin, "This song is in F♭♭ — and that's very flat!" The tonic pulsation is tailed in closest stretto by an E♭♭ echo while a ghostly soprano plucking plays out the maudlin Mother's song of two decades earlier, "Where's My Wandering Boy Tonight?", and the stretto adds a D♭♭ to produce a series of micro melodic fragments of three falling tones. Then, in a sonically amazing series of jostling overtones, the stretto organizes itself into a gradually emerging modulation in which F♭♭ is ghostily changed to F♭, and F♭ metamorphoses into F♮, dragging its stretto neighbors with it into the emanating tune F-E-E-D; F-E-E-D.

The music stops abruptly, and the new section is marked "Feeding Frenzy, *Allegro Scrupmtuoso*", as an increasingly agitated rhythmic figure is mixed into the more and more dissonant sonic halo and the performer begins what must be the most fiendishly difficult task in the repertoire. *"Antennae accelerando,"* Ives orders, and the music breaks out into quick-march version of "I Hunger And I Thirst", and "Come Thou, Font Of Every Blessing". Then, a clarion call from chopstick-struck strings: "Hark A Thrilling Voice Is Sounding", and the whole grand harp breaks into a Yale Football March, with a tapped out supra-melody of "Rush Down Boys". In the score is written, "All hands on deck!!!", and all hands are surely there, and knuckles and elbows too for a chaotic concatenation of barn dances, popular parlor tunes (with highly unpopular treatments), polka-dot polkas, cross-rhythmic children's songs and devilish ragtime, *"allegro (conslugarocko)* — wag those knees"*, all swirled together in stubbornly original juxtapositions, "wrong note" harmonies, and polychords. Ives writes "play adagio or allegro — very nice", so the performer has completely free choice about what comes out of the black box.

Slonimsky's manic disposition, fueled by months of caffeine, made this performance a never-to-be-equalled thrashing about in the cupboards of Americana and the annals of technical prowess. Honky-tonk whip-chords, sharp, unexpected jabs at irregular intervals, *"Presto con Blasto"*, *"Con Furyo-ffff"*. Again, an abrupt halt; in the manuscript: "Back to the hero — all good Opryettas got to have a hero." So, scratched out with fingernail on the thickly wound lower strings, we hear the belching song of an over-stuffed roach, the F-E-E-D theme now revealing itself as the second phrase of "Three Blind Mice" — "see how they run", mice in this case metamorphosed into roaches running in mighty molasses motion.

Then, crash! the fastest and most difficult passage of all, a long section of rapid, sprawling chromatic chords, out of which the left hand pulls quintuplet dances of jaunty wild demons, while the right hand slap-accentuates every fifth sixteenth note, and the entire raucousness comes to a vociferous climax in a repeated polytonal canon on "The Streets of Cairo", a belly-dance tune, which emerges to dominate the scramble. In the manuscript: "EVEN HERBERT HOOVER WILL GET THIS," — though I must admit I don't. Under everything, the now-identifiable eructations of our fat, sated hero belching out the Czech national anthem and a well-sauced version of The Moldau, accompanied by an ironic rendition of "Old Folks Gatherin'" from Ives's Third Symphony. "Ain't it a grand and glorious noise?" he writes, and only the most determined musical curmudgeon could disagree. He finishes up with a section entitled "Southpaw Pitching" a left-hand solo recitative of highly improvisational character which brings our modified hero face to face with his revelation.

But what is the revelation? A revelation most ambiguous. I must return the reader to the indication *"Scherzo* TSIMAJ" at the opening of the movement. We know from the Piano Trio (1911) that TSIAJ means "This *scherzo* is a joke". But what of the added "M"? "This *scherzo* is mostly a joke"? What is the non-joke meaning? That outside the egg there is thirst and boisterous life, hunger and frenzy and fight? The intent, I think, becomes clear in the inspired last movement, "Redemption". The stage hands fit the lid back on, and raise it to its full height.

"Bring Art into life and Life into art (no elite redemptive space!)" floats mysteriously above the movement title, in small letters at the right hand top of the page. Then, "III. REDEMPTION", that short phrase announcing a gift to humanity as full of import as the "6. *Der Abschied*" in Mahler's masterpiece, Gregor's beloved *Lied von der Erde*, the *Song of the Earth*.

It is unclear if Ives ever heard any Mahler. He may have during 1909-11 when Mahler conducted the New York Philharmonic. Ives said he avoided listening to new composers because it threw him off stride, as the old war-horses did not, but he probably heard more new works than he cared to admit. It *is* known that Mahler had discovered Ives. In 1911, just before leaving New York, he noticed a symphony score by some unknown, apparently untutored, American composer on the table at the Tams Music Office, and took it back to Europe with him for an intended performance. Had he lived to perform Ives's Third, the course of twentieth century music — and Ives's life — would have been quite different. But Mahler died that spring of the heart ailment he knew was hovering, the sickness that provoked *Der Abschied,* and the transcendent meditations of his Ninth. But how quick he was to recognize — in music that sounds so different — the commonality between them: that love of humble, commonplace melody, the project of incorporating "the whole world" in a musical work, transforming as needed, honoring the "bad old songs" and using their energy to invigorate and transform more complex "classical" genres. They were both great foes of Hog-Mind.

"Allegro fortissimo with marked energy". Back at the keyboard, the movement begins, with a complex clarity fresh to the ears after the misty vibrations of an unrestrained piano harp. Reversing the usual procedures, as he often does, Ives begins with the most complex statement possible, in which many subsequent motives appear — immediately, simultaneously, with four part polyphony growing to five parts by the third beat and nine by the fourth beat — of the first measure. There is enough germ material for an entire symphony here, all in one measure. While other composers might begin with a simple motive and develop its implications in the course of a

work, Ives starts out with multiple complexities that seem like late devel-
opments which, as the movement proceeds, become more and more open,
more clear, more straightforward. Another version of the Big Bang.

The second measure is still enormously complex, but even now a movement toward simplification begins. Like galaxies condensing out of the
initial explosion, patterns start to appear. The nine parts of the end of the
first measure form themselves into harmonic blocks, with the three lowest
voices shaping a bass chord, the four higher parts moving together into a
soprano-alto chord, and two tenor voices snaking interstitially between.
The three blocks move with so much variability and independence that
together they form a kind of hyper-counterpoint, with each block the
equivalent of a single contrapuntal voice. Thus does nine become three,
dissonant in a basically consonant way.

There follows an *animando* section, *crescendo*, with the upper choirs
rising and the lower ones descending until they each drop off into empty
space, extruding the tenor duet out in front to begin the second section,
an overlay of funeral marches incompletely metamorphosing one into the
other, as does the cockroach, to an irregular, discordant accompaniment
below that growls quietly in its own universe. The funeral march from the
Eroica changes its famous descending trochees (to be sounded so mov-
ingly at Gregor's death) into the steady, falling eighth note spondees of
the middle phrase of the Chopin funeral march, and from there transforms to the more familiar, haunting iambics of the last movement of the
Scriabin First Sonata. Accompanying this noble procession, like Sancho
alongside the Don, is a second line of more burlesque commentary, the
mock-funeral from the Mahler First, chirping along from above, while
"The Worms Crawl In, The Worms Crawl Out" rocks deep below, like an
ominous carved cradle. The F-E-E-D theme returns, the "See How They
Run Funeral March", in pendular motion, transposed back to $F\flat$ $E\flat$ $E\flat$ $D\flat$,
then easing down to $F\flat\flat$ $E\flat\flat$ $E\flat\flat$ $D\flat\flat$, that $F\flat\flat = E\flat$, the base note of the Earth,
extended out, its trailing afternotes appended behind it, twitching grace-
notes-after-the-fact, descending into the underground.

Silence.

Then shocking surprise: the fierce opening of the movement occurs
again, *"fortissimo possible"*, causing, I am told, several members of the audi-

ence to wet their underwear or worse. As before, the sound grows richer as the choruses form, as the contrary motion fills the space. But this time, the outer choirs do not fly off into upper and lower regions, but produce — a second, even greater, surprise — a voice.

This was Slonimsky's singing debut, for when are concert pianists ever asked to sing? "For God," he bellowed out, "is glorified in man," a line from Browning's long dramatic poem, *Paracelsus*. As Beethoven had needed the human voice to bring the Ninth to culmination, so Ives had transcended the limits of the piano sonata. Some wonderful singer might have been engaged to enter here, as a flute player does at the end of the Concord Sonata, but no. Ives specifically notates "No helpers allowed!" as if to demand that any performer demonstrate — in his or her own person — the ability to metamorphose and transcend.

I'm told it was an impressive performance. The vocal line and harmonies are such that standard technique would not have sufficed in any case — the premium was on musicianship and a sense of the dramatic — both of which Slonimsky possessed *in excelsis*.

He sang of Paracelsus, that German-Swiss physician and alchemist, a real-life Faust of the sixteenth century, who established the role of chemistry in medicine, a restless seeker after knowledge who would not stop until he discovered "the secret of the world." A proud man, brilliant but arrogant, "singled-out by God", he thought, "to be a star to men", Paracelsus was always at the center of controversy. He took no prisoners. He was deeply hated.

At the end of his life, he offered up a testament to the world, imagined and articulated by Browning in the long, inspired, final speech of his poem.

For God is glorified in man, he asserts,
And to man's glory vowed I soul and limb.

To man's glory — and to his own. But then, Paracelsus' final self-assessment:

Yet, constituted thus, and thus endowed, I failed:
I gazed on power, I gazed on on power till I grew blind
What wonder if I saw no way to shun despair?

285

The power I sought seemed God's;

So *that* was the meaning of the huge outburst at the beginning of the movement, the human counterpart and echo of the Big Bang: it was man trying to play God, a performance whose accompaniment must become a funeral march.

I learned my own deep error; Slonimsky sang, in a new section, *andante molto,*
> *And what proportion love should hold with power*
> *in man's right constitution;*
> *Always preceding power,*

What an admission for this power-seeking man! Paracelsus. Slonimsky. Perhaps Gregor? Was this old man Ives's warning to Gregor?

> *And what proportion love should hold with power*
> *in man's right constitution;*
> *Always preceding power,*
> *And with much power, always,*
> *always much more love.*

Those last, deeply reflective words, "al-ways, al-ways....much....more.... love. The two "always" drawn out in slow funereal iambs, the length and hesitation of "much" and "more", the final fall of a major sixth onto the long-held D of "love" — fallen, yet still a half-tone above E♭ — how similar the mysterious, immense space created is to that of *Der Abschied,* with its closing, hypnotic chant of *ewig.....ewig..,* a final testament of the greatest depth and wisdom.

From the Big Bang of Creation, through the complex Revelations of the manifested world, from the arrogance of the Seeker to the final simplicity — Love. I have heard the Dalai Lama explain, "My religion is very simple: my religion is kindness." This was Ives's gift to Gregor, the bug that crawled out of his table, his thank-you for being reminded of that glory-beaming star, the promised day of Israel.

The audience was rapt, enchanted, blessed. It took the hearers a full minute of silence to begin to tentatively applaud. In that minute, wherever their souls were, they were unaware of one detail, known at that moment only to Slonimsky and Ives: After the final note with its long fermata, after the double bar, was written, in small letters, *vers la flamme.*

Then, applaud they did, wildly, with Bravos!, stamping and whistling. One enthusiast actually yelled "Encore!", but the indignant stares he got soon convinced him otherwise. "But the ticket says..." The ticket was wrong. No encore was possible.

Gregor was transported; the Iveses were ecstatic. Slonimsky returned for a bow, and indicated the composer at the back of the house. Used to slinking out of concerts amidst the booing, the old man was not quite sure how to acknowledge such acknowledgment. Harmony nudged him: "Stand up. Take off your hat."

The applause lasted for two more Slonimsky exits and entrances. Musical history had been made. How surprised our trio was then to find that only a few people came up to greet them. The center of interest seemed to be elsewhere — around someone in a wheelchair sitting in the aisle, keyboard side, towards the front. Gregor couldn't see through the crowd who it was. The Iveses were about to go backstage to congratulate Slonimsky when the wheelchaired figure pushed his way through his admirers, up the carpeted slope and around the back of the hall to where Charles, Harmony and Gregor were putting on their coats. It was the Governor, the Governor himself, Franklin Roosevelt.

Mr. Ives! Mrs. Ives, I take it? And you must be the subject! He reached out and shook hands with each, moved, and moving, with genuine gratefulness for his extraordinary experience. Even G's outfit did not phase him: he grasped his claw.

Hold that shot, that handshake, that famous handshake, the handshake that would determine the rest of Gregor's life — and death.

23. RISQ

Gregor was a big hit at work. Kathryn Verplank, ever loyal, had posted the reviews on the bulletin board outside her old boss's office — the room still untouched, waiting for his fabled return.

The New York Times was approving, if somewhat supercilious (as was its wont). Olin Downs could not even get the composer's name right in his note "concerning the Insect Sonata of a Mr. St. Ives (sic)". Still, even that grand old man seemed moved:

> "The thing is an extraordinary hodge-podge, but something that lives and vibrates with conviction is there, a "gumption", as the New Englander would say, the conviction of a composer who has not the slightest idea of self-ridicule and who dares to jump with feet and hands and a reckless somersault or two on his way. It is genuine, if it is not a masterpiece, and that is the important thing."

But the *Herald Tribune*'s Lawrence Gilman was ecstatic:

> "The Insect Sonata is exceptionally great music — it is, indeed, the greatest music composed by an American, and the most deeply and essentially American in impulse and implication. But beyond American it is universal, wide-ranging, capacious, with a deep appreciation of the full scope of the world and its creatures. It has passion, tenderness, humor, simplicity, homeliness. It has imaginative and spiritual vastness. It has wisdom, beauty and profundity, and a

sense of the encompassing terror and splendor of all life and destiny
— a sense of those mysteries both sub-lunar and divine."

When Gregor walked in on Wednesday morning, he was cheered by the crowd at the bulletin board. He took off his hat (a brown fedora in shameless imitation of his mentor), made a deep, stiff-backed bow, and spent a few moments describing the work and audience reaction to his colleagues, none of whom, except the Myricks and the Verplanks, had attended. All were especially impressed by Gov. Roosevelt's reaction, and his actually shaking Gregor's claw. Enthrallment by celebrities was not invented by *People Magazine.*

His celebrity lasted about fifteen minutes, and then the office settled in to its daily routine, G plugging away at his desk along with the hundred or so others. For the month the clippings stayed up he was bathed in the ever more mottled light of Ives's masterpiece, and then it was simply gray again, as even the glorious spring was darkened by a tightening economic disaster. President Hoover kept up his optimistic announcements, but they rang increasingly hollow — so hollow, in fact, that they led Gregor to look more deeply into the abyss.

My friend Ken Kesey recently wrote, "...the reverberation often exceeds through silence the sound that sets it off; the reaction occasionally outdoes by way of repose the event that stimulated it; and the past not uncommonly takes a while to happen..." Gregor submerged himself in the reverberation, and allowed the past to expand its implications. He spent the next two years developing a project that would make his name famous, and catapult him into the highest ranks of policy-making.

It is not given to everyone to invent a totally new science: Galileo, Pasteur, Mendel, Einstein, Bohr, Wiener... the list would be a short one. And while G's seminal work on Risk Management is nowhere near as crucial as that of his predecessors, it has had much impact, and has saved countless lives in the six decades since its publication. More lives, ironically, than his real quest — for the grail of human kindness.

Yet he worked in obscurity. His colleagues at Ives & Myrick had no idea what he was doing with those stacks of government documents on his desk, or where he spent all that time out of the office. Mike Myrick knew, of course, and cut him a great deal of slack. Where did he spend his time? At the periodicals division of the Low Memorial Library at Columbia University, pouring through the Memphis *Commercial-Appeal,* the Jackson *Clarion-Ledger,* the Greenville *Democrat-Times,* the Chicago *Defender* and other black papers: the Pittsburgh *Courier,* the Baltimore *Afro-American,* the Boston *Guardian*, the Louisville *News*, the Norfolk *Journal and Guide.*

Irrational as anyone else, he preferred the Low Library to the even larger collection at 42nd St. because it reminded him of Rabbi Lowe, and their common home in Josefov. The Rabbi, you may recall, was that wise man — perhaps too wise — of the sixteenth century who created a golem out of clay to protect the Jews of Prague. Things did not turn out well: the rabbi lost control of his monster. As he had created him, so he had to kill him, a sacrificial act of great import. At this distance, it is easy enough to see the parallels with Gregor's own over-reaching. Yet at the time, it seemed a simple preference — to do his work at Low.

This is not the place to detail it, but I do want to give the reader an inkling of the scope of G's work. Until his re-thinking, the insurance industry was simply reactive, making do with elementary actuarial analysis, trying to match its underwriting commitments with statistical data on various types of loss. Gregor's breakthrough was to imagine a proactive role for the industry. Insurance payments did not really compensate for the loss of home, family, business, earning capability. Why could not an insurance company also help reduce the risk, operate preventively, saving itself money, and its customers untold grief?

The word "risk", Gregor discovered, comes from the Arabic *risq*, which signifies "anything that has been given to you by God and from which you draw profit". *Risq* has connotations of a fortuitous and favorable outcome. But as the notion migrated westward to Spengler's declining "evening land", it became more and more pessimistic. A twelfth century Greek derivative would appear to relate to chance outcomes in general and have neither positive nor negative implications. The modern French *risque* has mainly negative — but occasionally positive connotations, as for example in *qui ne risque rien n'a rien,* while in common contemporary English the word risk has only negative associations as in 'run the risk of' or 'at risk'. My Webster's emphasizes its negative aspects by reference to 'the possibility of loss, injury, disadvantage or destruction'. Gregor wanted to return risk to its earlier, eastern, more hopeful roots.

To do that, he needed an accurate analysis of negative risk potential, with regard to both its probability and its destructiveness, and also a structured approach to managing risk so as to minimize the likelihood of negative outcomes. His approach involved several ingenious means of risk identification, determination of areas of greatest concern, prioritizing risks that required immediate action, techniques to manage, control or eliminate the risks identified, and a system for evaluating the effectiveness of measures taken. Never before had such a complete analysis been made. Never before had such an inventory of potentially beneficial actions been assembled.

About halfway into his researches, G entered the swamp of human consciousness, the varied perceptions of and reactions to risk, and it is in this area he made the most crucial of his contributions. Until G's work, actuarial work consisted entirely of economic and statistical models. Gregor introduced — as a major factor — the human, psychological, dimensions of the problem.

Estimation of risk is a tricky business. Two hundred years ago Bernoulli observed that given the opportunity to play a game in which there is an equal chance of either winning or losing, say $1,000, the majority of people would not play. Furthermore, as the potential for loss — or gain — increases, the proportion who will not play increases. In general, humans seem to be 'risk-averse'. (Gregor was quick to discover that other species are similarly risk-averse. Given the choice between flowers containing a constant amount of nectar and flowers with a variable (but the same average) amount, risk-averse bumblebees prefer to visit flowers of constant yield. As for roaches — no experiments had been done.)

Human risk aversion has consequences for risk-related behavior. People tend to underestimate the likelihood of relatively undramatic and frequent events, but over-estimate the likelihood of those that are infrequent, but dramatic. Thus they will drive their cars without seat belts — but become tense as their airplanes take off or land. Such behavior patterns needed cataloging, and G was the first to do it as an important component of his *Scienza Nuova* of risk management.

An even greater problem centers around low-probability events. If the potential outcome threatens the very existence of the individual, organization or country, it cannot be ignored no matter how improbable it is. But what to do if the probability is "effectively zero", yet the potential loss is thought to constitute "an unacceptable risk"? No amount of rational analysis will resolve the issue of what is "unacceptable". Reducing risks for one group may increase risks for another — and *this* is what brought G to his fateful study of the 1927 Mississippi flood — a rich paradigm of complexities and mismanagement. Politics had reared its ugly head.

I call his subject matter "fateful", as fateful as his love of Low Library — for in this intersection of study and place, the last phase of his life was set in motion. The post-recital handshake was a premature entrance — like the too-early horn theme heralding the recapitulation of the *Eroica* — too early, but significant. This, however, almost exactly two years later, was the real thing.

****

It was the most beautiful of spring days in April, 1932. The trees on the Morningside Heights campus were in outrageous blossom, and so were the students, in shirtsleeves for the first time since the brutal winter. Gregor made his way through crowds of impossibly beautiful Barnard coeds into the cool dark of the huge library. Psycho-erotically, he was always poised on the edge — loneliness and longing vs. a natural disgust with soft external parts, and painful memories of his occasional mis-encounters, Alice chief among them. To get through the gauntlet of breasts and hips, of smiling faces and gay human flirtation, he would consciously push himself over the edge, concentrating on the nauseating jiggling and chirping, the insipid puerility of these couples — were they in for a fall — all of them! A little of that went a long way — far enough to get him to his isolated cubicle in the stacks, where he settled into his deeper default of hopeful, universal love.

At lunchtime, he brought back to the periodicals desk the huge stack of newspapers he had been accumulating all morning. Standing in line behind a foreign student with language difficulties and some complex problem, his thin arms were almost buckling under the weight when a deep

292

voice behind him said, "Need some help?" He turned and saw a handsome man in his mid-40s wearing an open-necked, white short-sleeved shirt, his pocket bristling with pens.

"I would be most grateful, thank you," he replied, and his new good Samaritan lifted half the stack from Gregor's arms, and perused the top front page.

"'Conscript Labor Gangs Keep Flood Refugees in Legal Bondage'", the *St. Bernard Voice*. What are you up to?"

"I am studying the flood from '27."

"Why?"

"I am seeing how it could be better managed."

"By Hoover?"

"Yes, but not just Mr. Hoover. It shows a breakdown in the system."

"How so?"

At that moment, the student ahead left the desk happy, and Gregor and his helper plopped their papers on the desk. The clerk checked them, and returned Gregor's library card. G turned to leave.

"Wait. Don't go. I'm interested in what you've found out. Do you have time for lunch?"

"I was just now going out for eating."

"Can we go together?"

"Surely. I go get my briefcase and I meet you here."

****

Let me remind you youngsters who don't remember much about the 1927 Mississippi flood: On Good Friday, April 22, one day after a huge crevasse opened just north of Greenville and threatened to flood the entire delta, President Coolidge named his Secretary of Commerce, Herbert Hoover, to coordinate all rescue and relief efforts. It was the chance of Hoover's life: fortunes were being undone, farms and families destroyed, and here he was, cast in the role of savior, able to call on Army and Navy, the federal treasury, every state's banks and businesses and National Guard — a no-lose situation for him, doing well by doing good.

He spent some sixty days in the flooded territory, touring with a railroad car full of reporters, issuing orders and press releases. He dominated the newsreels and radio waves. Every major metropolitan daily ran front page stories about his brilliance and heroism. "The Great Humanitarian" they called him, "The Great Engineer". And of course, in the afflicted midwest the story was even bigger.

Old Man River himself was offering Hoover a chance to realize his only unconquered frontier. At 27, the young Stanford engineer had helped find and develop fabulously profitable mines and became "the highest paid man of his age in the world". At 40 he owned a share of mines and oilfields in Alaska, California, Romania, Siberia, Nigeria, Burma, and Tierra del Fuego. What was left to achieve? Power. The power of the most powerful position in the world, the American presidency.

As if on script, the President did nothing: in spite of much pleading, he would never visit the devastated areas to help raise consciousness and funds. Coolidge did nothing — and Hoover did everything. For months, not a day went by without media images of Hoover saving American lives. Newsreels, magazine feature stories, Sunday supplements — his every word was news. There was virtually no criticism; though some might quibble with his self-serving statistics, any nattering was swept away in torrents of praise. Before the flood, he was a minor player in Republican politics. After the flood, he was inevitable presidential timber.

Hoover represented a new kind of man creating a new world order: he was an engineer. Not since the heyday of the early Enlightenment had there been so much faith in science. And engineering was more than just an academic discipline, spinning out theories from ivory towers. Engineering was cars and highways and bridges — and prosperity for all! Engineering was the new gospel, and Hoover was the priest par excellence, rich, respected, head of the American Engineering Council, "the engineering profession personified." The twenties were the age of Taylorism, "Speedy Fred" taking his stopwatch to the multifarious tasks of America: efficiency, planning and management control promised "an end to material scarcity". "The golden rule will be put into practice by the slide rule of the engineer." Hoover rode this wave for all it was worth.

No hisses and boos, please. This was no cheap villain, but a complex, driven man, a man with a plan. Perhaps he was disappointed and eventually corrupted by power. But early on he was a blazing visionary, calling for "abandonment of the unrestricted capitalism of Adam Smith," condemning "the ruthlessness of individualism", and attacking the "social and economic ills" caused by "the aggregation of great wealth". "No civilization," he said, "could be built or can endure solely upon the groundwork of unrestrained and unintelligent self-interest."

Coolidge, who truly *was* a limited man, called Hoover "Wonder Boy", and privately told his friends, "That man has offered me unsolicited advice for six years, all of it bad." Which is perhaps why he sent him, naked, into the flood – and the presidency.

One more word for you Yankees who have never seen a levee. A levee is big. It's not just a wall, a dike where Little Hans sticks his finger in a hole. In fact, a levee is a precisely engineered system — batture, barrow pit, berm on the river side, the levee itself, and a banquette buttressing it on the land side. The batture is the land between the river's usual bank and the levee, often more than a mile wide, usually forested to minimize damage from waves and scour. Ending 40 feet from the rise of the levee is the barrow pit, usually about 300 feet wide and 14 feet deep, a kind of dry moat which the river has to fill before hitting the wall. Then there's the berm, the ground between the barrow pit and the wall. And then the levee itself, thirty to forty feet of sloped earth, melded into a muck ditch beneath, with an eight to ten foot flat crown, with its support banquette landside. Hundreds of thousands of refugees camped on top of their levees. A thirty foot levee would be almost two hundred feet wide at the base. And all planted with thickly rooted Bermuda grass to hold the soil. You can imagine how enormous the force must be which can sweep such structures away.

"Where would you like to eat?"
"I go usually to the little café right here across the Broadway."
"Fine for me."

24. Into A Thickening Plot

"I'll have a BLT on toast."

"What is that, BLT?"

"Bacon, lettuce and tomato. Try it. It's good. It's American."

"I have usually egg sandwich. But I try BLT."

"Make that two BLTs. I'm Rex Tugwell."

"Ohhh — I've heard of you."

"I hope it was good. Probably not."

"I think it was good, but the person who say it probably not. You are 'Rex the Red'?"

"Professor Rex the Red, please. Tyrannosaurus Rex, subversive revolutionary"

"This is what people call you?"

"Ignoramuses. I'm actually a conservative trying to save their damn profit system. You can't succeed in the twentieth century with nineteenth century organization."

"I'm Gregor Samsa."

"I know."

"How you know this? I have never see you before."

"But I saw you. At a Town Hall concert a couple of years ago. You have a face that's hard to forget."

"Yes, forgive me."

"Nothing to forgive. Columbia has lots of strange folks around."

The waitress brought their BLTs.

"Look, Samsa," said Tugwell, "I'll get right to the point. I'm working with two other professors here on Gov. Roosevelt's campaign. Ray Moley and Dolph Berle, you know them? No? Anyway, you may have found some useful details about Hoover's handling — or mis-handling — of the flood relief. We want to gather up a lot of information and think through the issues, come up with alternatives, and get rid of Mr. President. We can't have a second four years of Hoover and his big business friends. So tell me what you've discovered about the Great Engineer."

"So far I concentrate on two big problems. I try to think how to managing risks better, so I am not precisely concentrating on Mr. Hoover."

"That's fine. What are the problems?"

"Wait. This is bacon. Jewish can't eat bacon.

"I told you it was bacon. BLT. Bacon, lettuce and tomato."

"Oh, I thought you were saying about baking lettuce and tomato..."

"Go ahead. God will forgive you. BLTs aren't in the Torah. Tell me what you've learned about Hoover.

"First is the treatment of black people, and how it make them not want to help."

"Was Hoover involved in that?"

"This is most delicious."

"See, I told you so. Hoover."

"I'm sure he must know about it, but I have not find him to do anything."

"What's the second problem?"

"Second is the sacrifice of the poor people below New Orleans — for psychology effect. There is no democracy. All is decided by the rich people for benefit of rich people."

"Tell me more about that."

"You know they break the levee in St. Bernard. Dynamite. The Army."

"Yes. "

"They did not have to do so. I am certain. They do it to show New Orleans will be safe for shipping and banks, with all levees breaking above up the river, spreading out the water so New Orleans is never in danger."

"They were *saying* there never was any danger — and there never will be."

"They say that afterwards. Before, they say they have to dynamite the poor people's levee to relieve pressure."

"Where is Hoover in all this?"

"I don't know yet details. He was perched on all information like a *Spinne* in his web, so he must know. Also they do not pay back any of the people they promise to pay when they flood the lands. I know the Hoover and the Red Cross refuse all responsibility. They say it is the New Orleans's business."

"They have too much faith in businessmen. And what about Hoover's treatment of blacks? He needs the black vote. We can take it from him."

"Again I am sure he know about it. Here. Wait. I copy a letter to him from the newspaper..."

Gregor shuffled in his briefcase for a moment.

"Here. *'Dear Mr. Hoover, It is said that many relief boats have hauled whites only, have gone to imperilled districts...'* What is 'imperilled'?"

"Districts that are in danger."

"Ah. *'... boats have gone to imperilled districts and taken all whites out and left the Negroes; it is said that mules have been given preference on boats over Negroes.'"*

"That's not the worst of it, Samsa. We have reports that National Guardsmen were rampaging through the camps, beating anybody who threatened to leave, raping the women, stealing money..."

"Yes. There was a guard, a Mr. Charlie Silas, who one say would all the time murder black workers, and throw them in the river."

"Ah, yes. Mr. Charlie. Camp owner, not National Guard, the son of a bitch. You have mayonnaise on your — what do you call that?"

"What?"

"Here, let me wipe it off. What do you call that on your face?"

"Mayonnaise? *Mayonnaise.* Same."

"No. That part of your face."

"Oh. I don't know. *Mundwerkzeug* maybe. Mandible *auf Englisch?*

"Mandible. Sure."

They spent the next three hours going through Gregor's notes and clippings, discussing details of the activities upriver at Greenville, and downriver below New Orleans. Tugwell wrote down each mention of President Hoover.

The scene at the levees had been generally this: At the beginning of the phenomenal rains of early spring, blacks had been hired with state and municipal funds at 75 cents a day to stack sandbags on top of the levees. It was backbreaking, dangerous work: each bag weighed 75-100 pounds, and the slopes were slippery with rain. The wages were less than those for picking cotton — but there was no cotton to be picked, and the spirit of a mutual community-at-risk was still present, or, as the white community saw it, everything was in its place. Mississippi Senator Leroy Percy wrote a friend, "nothing could be more interesting, so far as racial study goes, than to see five or six thousand free negroes working on a weak point under ten or twelve white men, without the slightest friction and of course without any legal right to call upon them for the work, and yet the work is done not out of any feeling of obligation but out of a traditional obedience to the white man."

Once the levees began to break, the story changed. Water tore out trees, splintered sharecropper cabins, crushed, undermined, then swept away houses and barns. And now it was landowners whose property was being ruined vs. tenant farmers who could take their labor elsewhere — with less risk of life and limb. Out came the shotguns. Every morning, in towns on both sides of the river, police ran patrols through black neighborhoods and grabbed black men off the street to work the levee. If they refused, they were beaten or jailed or both; some were shot. No white people shared the work. The feeding was almost nil in some places. Armed whites and National Guardsmen held the blacks at gunpoint, as Hoover looked the other way.

Thousands of blacks were working feverishly to salvage the levees at the time of their collapse. Many were swept away, out onto the flooded land, or into the raging river, where it was impossible to recover their bodies. No lives were lost among the white guards.

Hundreds of thousands — mostly blacks — were camping on the eight foot strip on top of the levees — the only dry land. Half of all farm animals were drowned, and as the waters withdrew over the next months, rotting carcasses became breeding ground for serious disease. There was mud everywhere, four to eight inches, mud giving off sick odors of sulfur and decay. Water supplies were contaminated. Dogs swarmed over the land, washed away from food and owners, barking, barking, turning wild, spreading rabies among animals and humans. Rattlesnakes, water moccasins, and frogs infested homes and public buildings. The smell of death was everywhere: the stink of dead fish and crayfish — tens of millions of dead crayfish — in every gutter and street.

But cleanup was "nigger work". Loading and unloading barges to feed hundreds of thousands of people and tens of thousands of animals — was "nigger work". Reloading onto smaller boats for distribution, preparing food, feeding livestock, sorting and distributing supplies, cleaning buildings, repairing the water supply, putting flooring under tents, all was "nigger work". The receding waters did not end the white community's need for reluctant black labor. The shotguns stayed loaded.

Northern Black newspapers ran headlines like "REFUGEES HERDED LIKE CATTLE TO STOP ESCAPE FROM PEONAGE", or "DENY FOOD TO FLOOD SUFFERERS; RELIEF BODIES ISSUE WORK OR STARVE RULE". Surely Hoover — who needed the black vote — had seen these. Yet the Great Humanitarian was silent. The Great Humanitarian denied federal aid.

The connection between government and individual welfare was still weak in the early thirties. Forty years before, a democratic president, Grover Cleveland, had vetoed a grant for Texas drought relief because the federal government had "no warrant in the Constitution to indulge a benevolent and charitable sentiment through the appropriation of public funds for relief of individual suffering in no manner related to public service." And only twenty years earlier, Teddy Roosevelt required a pledge from New Orleans banks before he would allow his Surgeon General to aid in fighting a yellow fever outbreak. Though the role of government had expanded considerably since then, it still stopped short of direct aid to alleviate suffering. And, whatever his private feelings, Hoover had his nose cocked to the political winds. No direct aid. Government should sway with examples of good leadership without coercion. The private sector must take responsibility for its own situation. "Strong men", community leaders — *they* were the men in power, and with firm federal leadership from a bully pulpit, they would use that power to alleviate suffering. Although the Treasury showed an unprecedented surplus that year, Hoover denied even a loan guarantee program. His War Department went so far as to charge the Red Cross for cleaning the blankets it had lent.

Like Hoover, the *Chicago Journal of Commerce* spoke for the Republican business community: "If the federal government were to set aside funds to be used for disaster relief...the appropriations might climb to appalling heights. If relief of sufferers were to become a government task, the self-respect of the recipients of funds would be decidedly damaged. And the moral injury would have definite effects on the material fortunes of a recipient in after life, causing a rapid sapping of his initiative, and he may spend the rest of his life demanding more aid as his right." It does sound familiar. The Great Engineer laid down his line: "No relief to flood sufferers by action of Congress is desirable, but rather all efforts should be concentrated on formulation and passage of adequate flood control measures."

There it was! "No relief to flood sufferers." That was the line that needed attack, the line that would seduce large numbers of the southern black population away from their traditional Republican voting patterns (Lincoln, of course, was a Republican). That, and Hoover's shameful, hypocritical campaign promise to "do something on behalf of the Negro more significant than anything which has happened since Emancipation," to work toward subdividing land into smaller holdings and build up small farms, with negro ownership. Once he was President, he did absolutely nothing to bring this about. He would not even attend a gathering of philanthropists — his own friends — come together to consider the plan. Blacks had thought that once he was president...

But there would be no land resettlement scheme, and nothing like it. There would be only repeated, ever emptier promises, and a pursuit of a "lily-white" southern strategy to wrest the South away from traditional Democratic control.

Some recent historians would argue that Hoover does not deserve a racist image. He thought, they claim, that if Republicans could field a higher class of white candidates, southern Democrats could no longer play a white supremacist race card; he thought he could encourage a Republican black elite that could work smoothly with the new white leadership. He wanted race out of southern politics, a progressive Republican party forcing troglodytic Democrats to court the blacks, and thus create real political power for them.

But if those were his plans, they were not acted upon. Instead, what everybody black and white could see was the lily-white strategy, period. And if it looked like a duck and walked like a duck... In any case, the 1932 Roosevelt presidential campaign had plenty of ammunition.

"Can you get me details on Hoover's role in dynamiting the levee?" asked Tugwell, as he rose to pay the check.

"Let me pay half," said the blattid.

"No, no — I've just been promoted to full professor. I've got money to burn..."

"Truly? Well then, very much thank you. And I will send you any information I find."

"Here's my card. You can call me at home or at school."

25. Kidnapped Encore

G felt a little like a spy. Twice-weekly, he called his findings[18] into Tugwell, his handler, usually outside of work. His co-workers at Ives

18 Gregor did come up with some interesting tidbits, which delighted his new friend. With regard to the flood, G was able to detail Hoover's massive rehabilitation plan, based on the new concept of "human engineering", first tried out in the refugee camps. The money, of course, was to come not from government, but from "those strong men who with definite purpose exert a greater influence on the situation from the outside than from in." The devastated areas would pull themselves up by their own bootstraps, and demonstrate a general model for economic change. What was not so well know was how all this worked out — or didn't. "You are not called upon to donate," he told the strong men, "but to invest some of your money in the integrity of these people, and I know you will do that."

He knew wrong. There was no trickle down from this flood. Out of 500 banks in Mississippi, only 115 gave anything at all. So according to the *Memphis Commercial-Appeal*, Hoover called a meeting of thirty Memphis bankers and businessmen and simply told them their quota. There was uncomfortable silence. One protested. Then Hoover began to curse, and threaten. About 25,000 black refugees were in camps in Memphis. It was 2PM. He gave the strong men until 5 PM that day to pledge the money. "If not," he warned, "I'll start sending your niggers north, starting tonight." No niggers to do the dirty work? He got his pledges.

He then adopted a strategy made famous 40 years later by Sen. George Aiken. The Vermonter's wry solution to the Vietnam war? "Let's just say we won and go home." Hoover simply declared success: "We rescued Main Street with Main Street," he crowed, and the lapdog press dutifully reported it. But the President's proclamation of success was not the same as success: he had created only credit. And since credit involved risk, the strong men demanded either collateral or a high potential return. But devastated areas are not good risks for high return, and destroyed crops and already-mortgaged land make for little collateral. Neither lender nor borrower could afford the loans.

Hoover's massive financing effort accomplished next to nothing. Would the private

& Myrick were unaware of this aspect of his research. His classic, now famous study, *Fundamentals of Risk Management,* had yet to be published, and was known as a work-in-progress only to Mike Myrick. For the others in the office, he was just the new kid on the block — a role that was getting somewhat old — the new, foreign, employee, the subject of one of Mr. Ives's whackier piano pieces, a member-of-the-team doing different work from everyone else in the office. Yet in late July of 1932 he made a splash big enough to impress the most doubtful of his colleagues.

On March 1st of that year, two-year old Charles Lindbergh Jr. was kidnapped from his parents' home in Hopewell, N.J. On April 8th the $50,000 demanded in the ransom note was delivered in a Bronx cemetery, but on May 12 the child's body was discovered in a marsh near the Lindbergh home. This celebrity child-murder drove the Chino-Japanese war, the Great Depression and every other item of world importance from the front pages and set off the most intense manhunt in American history. Gregor, too, was swept along. After all, he himself had been the object of a kidnapping, self-approved perhaps, but still full of drama, danger, and consequence.

He had been interested in kidnapping for the past five or six years as a phenomenon of prohibition. The first ransom kidnapping in America, as far as he could tell, occurred only in 1874, an earlier time of great economic hardship. And with economic hardship come schemes to survive.

Kidnapping had begun to soar even in the affluent twenties, a natural development co-evolving with the growth of organized crime. It became a game played among criminals, a means of disposing of rivals by "taking them for a ride", murdering them, or just holding them for ransom. The practice flourished because most victims were people "disinclined to confer with the law" — gamblers, speakeasy owners and others on the fringe of society. But it wasn't long before underworld brains saw the potential of kidnapping law-abiding citizens, especially rich and famous ones — for fabulous amounts of ransom. It was the age of "the snatch racket": even Charles Gates Dawes, ex-vice president of the U.S., barely escaped capture.

---

sector play hero? Clearly not. Either Hoover did not get the message, or he chose to ignore it and simply claim victory. Tugwell and his friends were grateful to Gregor for focusing them on this data.

The Great Depression exacerbated everything, and hit gangland especially hard. With booze not paying its usual dividends and bank robbers finding banks hardly worth robbing, top bootleggers and bank men diversified into widespread kidnapping.

"Kidnapping is the feature crime of the present," said the head of the St. Louis Chamber of Commerce. "It offers big rewards and reasonable safeguards, and some of the best criminal brains of the country have abandoned more dangerous, less remunerative pursuits."

The St. Louis Police Chief told a House Judiciary Committee that kidnapping was easy. "On some pretext armed men lure the victim to a lonely place where he has no option except to get into a car. In few moments, blindfolded, bound and helpless, he is whisked into another state, held there in a safe house from ten to twenty hours and moved on to a third state. They have a regular circuit established so that jurisdictional problems will up the kidnappers' safety." In cases of family recalcitrance, torture could be used to loosen up funds.

Between 1929 and 1932, 2,500 ransom kidnapping cases were reported and many times that number went unreported. "IF YOU WANT YOUR HUSBAND BACK UNHARMED DO NOT CONTACT THE POLICE" was a powerful disincentive to reporting. Cooperation with the underworld seemed the most prudent path.

Even Lindbergh resorted to using shady contacts to help. Micky Rosner, a notorious con man, moved into the command center at the Hopewell house, and much to the dismay of the police, the family believed he could use his underworld contacts to find the child. Rosner and two of his cronies took over the living room, filling it with cigar smoke, ordering Mrs. Lindbergh around, and publicly accusing family friends of the crime. Even Al Capone got into the act with an offer to spend $10,000 of his own money to track down the kidnappers — in return for a pardon. The offer did not fly.

In a world turned topsy-turvy, it was crucial for robbers to get the Lindbergh crime solved as quickly as possible — so the cops would call off the dogs. Such a successfully accomplished outrage made it tough on everybody. Sixteen kidnappers were sent up for life during the first three weeks of the Lindbergh search; racketeers were picked up "at every hydrant" all over the country and grilled for all they were worth. Every gangster await-ing trial had reason to curse the kidnappers. Every stool pigeon in America was pushed around and threatened by the police. The entire world of cops and robbers was committed to solving this case.

Gregor, too, took a professional interest in the event. The general uproar sidetracked his other investigations, and he devoted an intense week of July heat to the insurance consequences of the kidnapping corner of the Great Crime Wave. He reasoned thus:

If money were of little import, the human risks associated with ransom would plummet. If Ives & Myrick were to create a kidnapping rider to their theft policies, victim families would be financially protected, and vic-tims themselves be less threatened by desperate gambits based on financial fear. No longer would a son have to ask "How much is mother worth to me?" No longer would a wife suspect her husband of shilly-shallying with someone else while she was held a week in captivity waiting for money to be collected. The fact of a kidnapping would trigger a quick, almost cut and dried, response leading to the return of victims.

But what to charge for kidnapping insurance? — that was Gregor's challenge. In order to quantify the actuarial table, he needed a formula to gauge the probability of a person being kidnapped. After two intense nights of work, when others in his tenement were up on the roof trying to stay cool, he arrived at the following formula, now known in the industry as the Samsa Conjecture:

$$P_k = \frac{0.833nC(cW)(S)^2(J)}{A^{1/2}}$$

where

P_k = the probability of being personally involved in a kidnapping,

and 0.833n represents the fraction 1.25 n/1.5, the probability change due to the number of previous kidnappings, the 1.25 in the numerator rep-resenting the increase in risk as kidnapping momentum increases, and 1.5 in the denominator the decrease in risk as community concern, personal caution and police protection rises. In addition,

C = number of children in the family

c = the celebrity of the family or individual on a subjective scale of 1-3

S = the Index of Suffering, an original contribution of Gregor's, now in standard use among economists.

$$S = \frac{(\text{unemployment rate in percent})\ (\text{inflation in percent})}{1 - (\text{probability of situation continuing another month})}$$

J = the Jahrzeit (Ger. *season*) a Germanism which has traditionally remained in the formula like the Q (=*Quelle*) as the initial of an author of Genesis, and

A = age of the victim in months.

Like Clyde Tombaugh, Gregor spent the next two weeks checking the validity of his formula before mentioning it to Mike Myrick. He went through the entire *N.Y Times Index* ("kidnapping") for the years 1874-1932 (coverage for 1905-10 was for some reason not available), and found that his formula predicted the kidnapping (P_k > 0.75) for 86% of all reported victims. Like Clyde Tombaugh, he calmly went to his supervisor's office, knocked politely, and said "Mr. Myrick, I've found something you may be interested in."

Interested? Myrick was delirious. It was an insurance industry coup, something current and hot, something no other agency had even dreamed of, and he quickly ran it past the actuarial department. Two days later he phoned the *New York Times* and the *Wall Street Journal*, and Gregor was once again a minor celebrity, this time of actuarial fame.

But the topping on the sundae, the whipped cream and the cherry, was the phone call he got on July 29, 1932. Mrs. Verplank, not too subtly, bellowed down the forty foot aisle, "Mr. Samsa, Gov. Roosevelt is on the phone for you." The office gossip knew no bounds.

The next day he was in Albany at the Executive Mansion, meeting with the Governor, Prof. Tugwell, Prof. Moley and Prof. Berle. They wanted him to join the Brains Trust for the final push of the campaign. He was to be in charge of Hoover research, and was more than welcome to join in brainstorming alternatives to current political structures. The group felt his European background would add a fresh perspective to their fears of provincial American thinking.

Both Ives and Myrick were happy to grant him a leave of absence, with pay, until the election, and longer if he needed it. If FDR lost, they would have their star employee back. If Roosevelt won, they would have a voice in Washington, close to the ear of the President. It was a no-lose proposition.

Gregor would not return to Ives & Myrick. He commuted twice weekly to Albany or Hyde Park, and then was kidnapped to Washington. Miss MacPherson, the quiet young woman at the desk across the aisle, was thoughtful and sad.

26. Bonus Now

B ut this is to skip ahead.

Though he was in the middle of his chapter on "Protective Standards", the Governor's phone call was so tantalizing, so exhilarating, so flattering, that he could not concentrate. After thirty minutes of staring at the page in front of him, his mind in six other places, he got up from the desk, made his excuses to the colleagues nearest him, and left the office. At the second floor landing, he checked to see if anyone was in the hall, (the coast was clear), and he slid down the banister, right off the flat, smooth newel post at its bottom, landing only inches before hitting the glass of the lobby door. Out he walked into the thick summer heat.

"Hey, Mistah Gregor," yelled Charlie, "You out early today."

"Oh, yes, Mr. Chollie. I have to make a celebration."

"What y'all celebratin?"

"I...I don't know. I'm just...happy."

"Well you probably de only one on the street, 'ceptin me of course. Whatcha gonna do for celebratin?"

"I don't know. What would you do?"

"What would I do if I was happy, which I am? See that pretty girl walkin over there? I'd up and ask her to the movin pitchers. If I was you, you know. Ain't no white girl goin to the movies with me, iffn you know what I mean?"

Gregor refused the gambit.

"What would you go see?"

"Well, les see here..." He picked up a Herald Tribune from the stand, and thumbed to the entertainment section. You gots Boris Karloff in *The Mummy*. Too scary. You gots *Grand Hotel*. Don know what dat's about. You gots *Scarface* with Paul Muni, what about dat? Hey, you gots the Marx Brothers. *Horsefeathers*. You seed that? Mr. Lionni was tellin me about dat this mornin. They's always funny. You gots *Dr. Jekyll and Mr. Hyde*. Fredric March..."

"Is that the Mr. Hyde from Hyde Park?"

"What's Hyde Park?"

"Where the Governor was born. Where he lives."

"Well, I don know. Maybe. I think it about a man turnin into a monster or sompin. Mr. Schwab was telling me bout it a couple days ago."

"What kind of monster?"

"I don know. I ain't seed it. He jus say a monster. Man changed into a monster."

"Well, thanks, Mr. Chollie. Maybe I go see that one. Does it say what time it plays?"

"Lowe's Seventy Second St. Playin four o'clock, six o'clock, eight o'clock, ten o'clock. You got just enough time to get up there for the first show, iffn you get a cab."

"Thank you so much again. I think I will go see that. And I'll tell you about it tomorrow, ok?"

"Ok, Mistah Gregor. You better get crackin, though. That girl already a block away. She gwine turn the corner and you lose her."

"Mr. Chollie, better I go by myself. Not so much problems that way."

"Hey, ain't no problems. Pretty girls is paradise."

"Yes. But not everybody are allowed in paradise."

"Ain't it de trut, ain't it de trut! Well, you have youself a good time, and you come tell me everything about the monster, you heah?"

Gregor did actually think about trying to catch up with the willowy blond — for about four seconds — and then he walked over to Broadway to see about catching a cab.

Happy and sad. *Zwei Seelen wohnen, ach! in meiner Brust,* he thought, as the cab sped uptown. One aspires to ... upward-, out-embracing. But however, there are certainly many pretty women out there. Look at that one. My goodness. The cabbie apparently felt the same way: he swerved over into the right hand lane, and gave a piercing "wolf whistle". Gregor thought the term was peculiar, since as far as he knew, wolves did not whistle. He was thrown hard against the side door.

"Sorry, buddy. Can't let a doll like that go by without an editorial comment, know what I mean?"

"Yes, that's all right. I was not hurt."

Yet he was hurting. It was times like these, times of inspiration, of hope, times where he could refocus on some notion of mission — these were the times he felt his loneliness most intensely.

"Loew's Seventy Second, 3:52 PM. See, I tol' you I'd getcha there in time. Thirty-five cents."

Gregor gave him an extra dime, and got out under the grand marquee. He loved this theater. A quarter was a lot to pay for admission, but the feeling of sitting under that enormous blue dome — that alone was worth it. The cloudlike images projected by some hidden set of machines, the twinkling of implanted electric stars, the huge space — together, they induced in him a readiness for the largest experiences. They brought back the spacetime flight which left him in America. And the walls, dimly seen. That ring of painted backdrops to the greatest scenes in the history of the theater. The Roman Capitol, the Forest of Arden, the bottom of the Rhine. He felt immersed in the great wash of human history and human potential. Important for a blattid. He leaned back in the plush seat, breathed slowly, deeply, and waited in bliss for the lights to dim.

The blaring newsreel fanfare shocked him out of his reverie. But given his new role as historian and social activist, snapping-to seemed a small price to pay. *En garde!* Watch the newsreel, reflect, report — that was his new job, his step from theory to praxis. The predictable cadence and melody of the announcer's voice, resonant, authoritative, rang out the lead feature: "Bonus Army Dispersed", read the title, with passionate string music under. "It's war!" the deep-voiced announcer cried, as cavalry, horses and tanks sweep down Pennsylvania Avenue, citizens fleeing in front of them.

The greatest concentration of fighting troops in Washington since 1865, the Third Cavalry from Fort Meyer, and the First

Light Tank Regiment, grim and relentless,

(soldiers chasing a woman and child across the street)

the Twelfth Infantry from Ft. Washington, all assembled with a simple purpose: to route the Bonus Army from government property which they have been occupying without permission,

(dismantled shacks and piles of lumber)

property which has to be torn down to make room for new buildings.

(tank across scene)

Mein Gott, Gregor thought, where are we? I have see this before in Vienna...

The Bonus veterans have defied their leaders.

(Crowd of veterans, police on horseback)

The police cannot handle them since the riot this morning which ended in one death and dozens wounded.

(Soldier throwing smoke bomb.)

So they're being forced out of their shacks by smoke bombs and tear gas,

(smoke bomb exploding)

hurled by the troops who have been called out by the President of the United States.

(big fire, troops in gas masks)

Gregor's wound began to tingle. He hadn't noticed it in weeks. He was glad the willowy blond was elsewhere.

Mr. Hoover doesn't blame the veterans entirely. He claims that the disorder and defiance were caused by foreign Reds and a large criminal element in the ranks of the veterans.

(people, their belongings in their arms, fleeing from the fire)

It's a spectacle unparalleled in the history of the country, a
day of bloodshed and riot reminiscent of actual conditions in
France in '17.

(horses herding men in white shirts)

Sullen, disgruntled, the veterans give way unwillingly before
the steady advance of the soldiers.

*(isolated men backing up before phalanx of soldiers; being crowded
into a group on a street corner.)*

The tension is terrific: real drama of the highest rank.

In America they tell you how to think about things. Drama of the highest rank, like Sophocles, yes? Ignorant Americans!

But the orders of the President and Secretary of War must be
obeyed.

Ach so! Even when they are wrong and stupid? This is Hoover goes mad.
He pays for this. We see to that. I call Mr. Tugwell.

(pan of crowd lining the streets watching the action)

Gradually the Bonus Army realizes that they'd better be good,
and a general retreat begins, interrupted here and there by a
stubborn veteran.

*(Cop with hammerlock on white shirted man, pushes him away
into the crowd.)*

In Vienna they club. Hard. They break his head.

*But resistance isn't practical. They soon find out that it doesn't pay
to monkey with a buzz saw.*

What is that – a monkey with a buzz saw? I try to remember that
expression.

And there's an occasional free ride to jail or hospital.

(loading people into a paddy wagon)

And to make sure the men will really stay out, the soldiers
have orders to burn down the unsanitary and illegal camp,
and the roaring flames sound the death knell to the fantastic

Bonus Army.

(Tank emerging from roaring flames)

Mein Gott, it *is* war. A hundred miles from here. The Hoover will stop at nothing. *Alles in Ordnung.* These men have serve their country. Their children are hungry. Look at those children running...

> Many have gone back home, betrayed by unscrupulous lead-
> ers, but some still sincere in the adventure that failed, and that
> ends so disastrously in the shadow of the beautiful dome of
> the Capitol of the United States of America."

(Capitol dome seen through smoke and flames.)

Gregor drifted back fifteen years to the midst of the Great War. He didn't know how long he was gone, then couldn't make out what was happening on the screen. A parade of women with bathing suits in Atlantic City, New Jersey. But they weren't bathing. And there was no Atlantic to be seen. The same authoritative voice, this time pointedly jocular:

> And so another Miss America Pageant ends, but the American
> Beauty Rose seems to be in full flower on every street in
> America!

(pan of beautiful women walking on Fifth Avenue. Wolf whistle over.)

THE END
FOX MOVIETONE NEWS

MDCCCCXXXII

The screen went blank. Gregor sat there, disoriented. He had forgotten what he had come to see.

****

For those readers who may have forgotten their history, let me remind you about the Bonus Army's first march on Washington.

Back in 1925, Congress had re-considered the military wage during the Great War, had "adjusted" veterans' compensation, and authorized certificates, payable in 1945, as an acknowledged, but postponed debt. Given the extreme hardships of the depression, a national veterans' movement began to grow — asking for immediate payment to cover the hard times. Not an outrageous demand.

W. W. Waters, an unemployed veteran from Portland, Oregon, conceived the idea of a march on Washington, an encampment even, until Congress should vote the allocation of funds. Without even an Internet, he spread the idea, and others in his circumstances began to drift eastward — drift, stream, and eventually pour — many "riding the rods", as they headed for the nation's capital. They camped along railroad rights of way and climbed into boxcars of slow-moving trains. Train crews looked the other way: no telling when they themselves might lose their jobs. The newspapers barely noticed it until there was trouble in East St. Louis on May 21, 1932. Local railroad officials became upset, and sent guards to prevent the boarding of east-bound trains. Demonstrators got belligerent: gangs soaped the rails, uncoupled cars, and generally raised hell. The police arrived, and with them, the press. All of a sudden, the issue was national news.

Men, some with families, now with no way to get to the capital, became unwanted tourists in towns along the way. Municipal authorities rounded people up and deported them — elsewhere. The publicity generated public fear and liberal outrage, and more and more marchers headed for Washington to join the movement. Trains could not be adequately watched; every arriving freight dropped dozens of marchers in the D.C. railroad yards. By the end of May, there were a thousand of them, by June two thousand, then five, and by July there were upwards of eleven thousand "Bonus Marchers" camped all over the city. An enormous Hooverville was established on the banks of the Anacostia river, south of the government buildings. There was no water supply, and less than primitive sanitation: the stench reached even into the halls of Congress.

What to do? Many were demanding drastic action. In late June, the House passed a bill authorizing immediate payment of the bonus certificates, but the Senate rejected it in July — and Congress went home. The marchers kept increasing. Their momentum would be hard to stop.

Attendant to concerns about Law and Order, Hoover could think of nothing better than suppression. Rather than meeting and negotiating with the marchers, on the morning of July 28th, 1932, he authorized his army chief-of-staff, Gen. Douglas MacArthur and his aides, Maj. Dwight Eisenhower and Capt. George Patton to unleash the U.S. Army against them. These three personally directed the deployment of cavalry, infantry and tanks Gregor had seen in the newsreel. It was war — conducted by warriors. They swept through the buildings of Pennsylvania Avenue, routing all squatters, then marched up Capitol Hill and on toward Anacostia. There, they fixed bayonets, flung tear gas and seized all who resisted. One veteran was killed, many were wounded, and thousands suffered respiratory distress. The evacuation completed, the soldiers razed and burned the shacks and tents the marchers had used for shelter. It was a frightening scene. The next day's *New York Times* featured a full page of photos. Rex Tugwell reported the effect on FDR:

> *About 7:30, when Roosevelt called from his bedroom and I went in, the page of pictures was open on his bed. They looked, he said, like scenes from a nightmare. He pointed to soldiers stamping through smoking debris, hauling resisters, still weeping from tear gas, through the wreckage to police wagons; women and children, incredibly disheveled and weary, waiting for some sort of rescue. In the lower right hand corner, the victorious general, one of the few in our history who had led armed troops against civilians, stood nonchalantly by a fence, immaculate and smiling among the vagrants, drinking from a paper cup.*

> *Roosevelt, spreading a hand over the picture page, reminded me that we had been going to talk more about Hoover, but so far as he was concerned, there was no need now. (In Search of Roosevelt, p.192)*

Tugwell reminded Roosevelt about Gregor and his Hoover research, and the Governor asked him to set up a call for later in the day.

27. Yet another metamorphosis

The screen flickered again, 8, 7, 6, 5, 4, 3, a two second gray space and then a mountain appeared, piercing the clouds, haloed by stars:

A Paramount Picture,
then
ADOLPH ZUKOR
PRESENTS
Fredric March
Miriam Hopkins and Rose Hobart
in
Dr. Jekyll and Mr. Hyde
A Rouben Mamoulian Production

Ah, yes. A man turns into a monster. G began to re-focus. But some men need no turning, he thought. And some turn regardless.

With an appropriate amount of suspicion, Gregor settled into his chair for Hollywood's latest contribution to the new horror-movie rage. His experience with American cinema did not create much confidence. He remembered someone saying "Hollywood almost made a great picture once, but they caught it in time."

Mamoulian's *Jekyll and Hyde* must have been one that got away.

Bach! The G minor fugue. String transcription, but still...Bach! Ja, ja, get on with the titles, please, I don't know these people. Robert Louis Stevenson...I've heard of him. Ah, organ, hands on organ, that's the real sound. Gregor was sucked in.

It's hard to know how many of you have seen this masterpiece. When MGM decided to film another Jekyll and Hyde with Spencer Tracy, they bought the Mamoulian rights from Paramount, withdrew all distribution and stuck the negative in their vaults. They wanted no competition, especially as Fredric March had received an Academy Award for his performance. When the film finally resurfaced in 1967 for a directors' festival, many excellent scenes had been cut. But that day in 1932 Gregor saw the whole haunting, penetrating, erotic work. Through the entire last half, his tegmina pulsed and his wings tingled.

But most of all his mind swirled. A plan to separate human good from human evil! Yes. If you could only do that, and could somehow corral the evil and defang it, the better half might be free to build a brave new world. "It's the things one can't do that always tempt me," says Jekyll. Beware, Henry Jekyll, beware. I know this story better than you do, G thought. "There are no bounds"? Beware.

Gregor watched, his mouthparts gaping, as the upright, exemplary man of science mixed his beakers. He watched through flame and bubbling liquid. His ommatidia caught the skeleton in the corner of the lab. Truly Mr. Mamoulian was a master. And then, the agony of transformation. Jekyll-March, the hitherto matinee idol, now a dark, fanged monster with wide-set eyes. What are his first words? "Free! Free at last!", words which echo ironically in our own time in the voice of Martin Luther King. "Free at last!"

He looks at himself in the mirror, grins, yes, I have done it, laughs, stretches, dances and gets gleefully dressed. Out into the London rain. Agile as a cat. He takes off his top hat and lets the raindrops cover his face. He opens his mouth for a drink from heaven. Never had such happiness, such boundless joy in the created world been caught on film. It remains, to this day, unique. "Free at last!" The irony, unbearable.

The pregnant plot played out, with G half-attending to the film, and half to his own turbulent thoughts. "You ain't no beauty," the poor girl says. "Under this exterior," he answers, "you'll find the very flower of a man."

Hyde so primitive as to be primordial, the missing link Gregor failed to be for Scopes. Was this the prophesied devolution, the come-down of the up?

When was Stevenson? Nineteenth century? He must have known about thermodynamics, everybody talked about it, the Second Law, the inevitable movement toward decay. And Darwin. Mendel. They knew about the evolution of species. The seeds. The roots. Of science. The deep unconscious, source of monstrous projections. Fractured images of the psyche, multi-layered, intuitive, creative. And also the source of *verboten* requests to a technicized world.: I love you. "Tell me you hate me," he says. Ah, Je-kyll. I kill. Under this exterior I hyde the poisonous flower. It was impurities in the drink that fetched the metamorphosis! What impurities? From where?

"Thou was not born for death. immortal bird", he quotes, a second before disaster. G knew the poem — *"for many a time I have been half in love with easeful Death, Call'd him soft names in many a mused rhyme..."* The black cat springs, tears into the songbird's throat — and Jekyll's hands begin to darken at this hint of Nature's grisly counterpoint.

Hyde — H for Hoover. Hoover is Hyde to FDR's Jekyll, vicious to the underprivileged, call out the army, strike them with your cane. What's inside Roose-velt? A rosy world? Or more darkness? His utopian project, we've seen those. Please to conduct the revolution, Madame Guillotine. "I give you up because I love you so."

Hyde's rough, toothed face against Ivy's white bosom. Flapper-whore! You deserve everything you get. Dark skin, thick lips, broad flat nose on white softness. The Scottsboro boys. The marching of the sheets. They'll lynch him, just you wait and see. He's lost. "A lotion won't do the trick, sir. No, sir. It's more than that, sir."

The horrifying end, the caped fall from crucifixion. The mob gathers round, and stares amazed at the metamorphosis of monster to man, calm and beautiful — in death. Free at last.

Gregor staggered from the theater. He knew now why FDR had called him. About the outcome, he was not so clear.

28. Surrealpolitik

The roach was tireless. He slaved away with an ardor and diligence avail-able only to those with giant neurons and double ganglia. By Election Day, 1932, working full time and more, he had assembled a seven volume dossier on Mr. Hoover: every damning phrase and paragraph from every article in every newspaper and magazine across the land — including the man's own words, so easily used against him. It was not yet our sleazy age of negative campaigning, focusing voter attention on sensational, irrele-vant distractions. No, G's research was solid history, economics, politics and sociology. It spoke truth about power to a population presumed intel-ligent. Tugwell, Moley and Berle spun this material out to the public — again not in the current debased sense of "spin", but carefully, logically, teachers that they were — until the President was definitively snared in his own undoing.

Roosevelt 42 states, Hoover 6. Electoral College: 472 to 59. It is true that almost any Democrat could have beaten Hoover, he of the "Hoovervilles" — so frustrated and irate were the American masses. But the landslide was enough to give one pause. So much faith sits uneasily on any mere human being.

Yet FDR was at ease, apparently confident, during this most uneasy winter. Farmers brandished rifles when the tax men came to foreclose; apple sellers crowded the streets, but how many apples could "the common man" eat? People were hungry, marriage was rare, bank accounts were overdrawn. And on Roosevelt's 51st birthday, January 30, 1933, Adolf Hitler became Chancellor of Germany.

FDR, tanned and relaxed from a twelve day cruise, disembarked at Miami, the day after Valentine's, the day after all Michigan banks had been closed down by order of the governor. On the Ides of February, he rode in an open car to greet a crowd of 20,000 supporters at Bay Front Park. He rode in a light blue Buick convertible, along with Raymond Moley, who had come down to Miami to report on the Cabinet search, and with Gregor Samsa, who had been rewarded for his Herculean labors with a Caribbean cruise on the *Nourmahal*.

Gregor Samsa on Vincent Astor's yacht. Now there's an image to ponder! This child of the Jewish quarter of Prague, this circus freak, this erstwhile elevator boy and dumpster diver, this toiler in the innards of insurance. What a rise was there, my countrymen.

Seated in an open car, driving along a dark street on the way to the park, Moley remarked to his companions how easy an assassination would be. But FDR was fearless. "I remember T.R. telling me me that the only real danger is from a man who does not fear losing his own life. Most of the crazy ones can be spotted first."

In the crowded, well-lit park, shortly after nine, Moley and Gregor hoisted the President-elect[19] up on top of the back seat, where he could be seen. Roosevelt spoke entertainingly for two minutes to much laughter and applause, then lowered himself into the seat of the car to greet Mayor Anton Cermak of Chicago, who was visiting his father in Miami.

Then, a popping in the air. Roosevelt thought it a firecracker, Moley a backfire. Gregor was the first to spot a short, swarthy man, standing on a rickety folding chair twenty feet away pointing a revolver in the direction of the President-to-be. After the first shot, a nearby woman grabbed his arm, and subsequent bullets made their wild ways through the crowd. The gunman was tackled and subdued by bystanders and Park Police while Secret Service men bulled their way toward the center of the violence. "I'm

---

19 The Twentieth Amendment, moving the presidential inauguration back from March 4th to our current January 20th, did not go into effect until October 1933. Its intention was to reduce the amount of time the president may serve as a lame duck by six weeks. FDR's first inauguration was the last to be held on the older date.

all right! I'm all right," Roosevelt yelled. But Mayor Cermak was not all right, nor were four others. The mayor's shirt was covered in red, and blood streamed from from lung to mouth. Secret Service shouted frantically for the car to evacuate, but FDR ordered the driver to stop so the mayor's body could be lifted into his, the first vehicle which would be free of the crowd. He tried to find a pulse as Cermak slumped forward. "I'm afraid he's not going to last," he whispered to G, as the car made for Jackson Memorial Hospital. The man from Hyde Park coached his friend from Chicago: "Tony, keep quiet — don't move. It won't hurt if you don't move." "I'm glad it was me and not you," the mayor gasped. It's true. Gregor was there, and heard it. There is honor even among politicians.

In the ER waiting room, Moley approached Gregor. "I think it would be good for you to visit our would-be assassin. Find out if he acted alone or if there are others. Get back to the railroad car by 11:30."

Armed with a hand-written note from Roosevelt, G took a cab back to the park and made his way to the 21st floor of the Dade County Courthouse, overlooking the scene of the crime. There, surrounded by Secret Service, was an unemployed bricklayer, one Giuseppe Zangara, 33, come to the United States ten years earlier aboard the steamer *Martha Washington*. So much was Gregor told. He went into the cell, and asked to be left alone with the prisoner. Secret Service reluctantly retreated. G could repeat the conversation almost verbatim.

"Hello, Mr. Zangara. I am Gregor Samsa, a friend of Mr. Roosevelt."

"I am friend of nobody."

"Mr. Roosevelt wants you to know he is all right."

"Too bad. I am better kill him. Too crowded. Too much crowds."

"Why do you want to kill him?"

"Because rich people make me suffer and do this to me."

He lifted his shirt to show G a large, keloid scar on his flank and abdomen.

"Rich people make me to go out from school," he continued. "Two months I am in school and my father come and take me out and say 'You don't need no school. You need to work.' Six years old, he take me out of school. Lawyers ought to punish him — that's the trouble — he send me to school and I don't have this trouble. Government!"

"Do you hate the government?"

"Yes," he answered, through clenched teeth. "Because rich people make me suffer and do this stomach pain to me."

"The rich men make you suffer?"

"Yes, since they sent me to work in a big job." He clutched his abdomen and groaned.

"Your belly hurts?"

"Because when I did tile work it hurt me there. It all spoil my machinery, all my insides. Everything inside no good."

Zangara was barely five feet tall. At sixteen, he left home to carry a gun in the army. He had come to the conclusion that the real causes of exploitation — and of his constant stomach pain — were political leaders. He was going to kill King Victor Emmanuel, but he never got the chance. So he came with his uncle to America. He joined a union, and saved his money. In the prosperous twenties, he sometimes made $14 a day. Then his uncle decided to marry, and Giuseppe had to move out of the apartment they shared. From that time on, he lived in complete isolation, an angry hermit who took no part in the Italian community around him. A stranger to wine, women or song, his whole life revolved around his stomach pain.

When the depression struck, he took his savings and traveled from city to city with no clear goal. He wound up in Hackensack, N.J. where he lived in one $10-a-month room and rented the room next door to prevent anyone from living near him. For the winter he moved to Miami.

By February, 1933, he had less than a hundred dollars to his name, and his stomach was pure agony. He decided he was going to get even, and kill Herbert Hoover.

"I kill that no good capitalist," he told Gregor. "He make the depression. He make unemployment and the soup lines. He make burning in my stomach."

"But Mr. Roosevelt works against Herbert Hoover. He is your friend."

"Hoover and Roosevelt — everybody the same. Hoover too far away. Washington too far. I have only $43 dollar."

"So Mr. Roosevelt came right to you, to Miami."

"I read in the paper he is coming, and I don't must go to Washington. I make Roosevelt suffer. I want to get even since my stomach hurt. I get even with capitalists by kill the President. My stomach hurt long time."

Gregor was dealing with a nut case. This man could only act alone. Who would act with him? G probed a possible insanity defense.

"Did you know what you were doing when you shot at Mr. Roosevelt?"

"Sure I know. You think I am crazy? I gonna kill president. I no care. I sick all time. I think maybe cops kill me if I kill President. I take picture of President in my pocket. I no want to shoot Cermak, just Roosevelt. I aim at him, I shoot him. But somebody move my arm. Every American people mistreats me. You give me electric chair. I'm no afraid that chair. You one of capitalists. You is crook man too. Put me in electric chair, I no care."

At the time of the interview, Zangara was charged only with four counts of assault with a deadly weapon. But three weeks later, when Mayor Cermak died, the charge was changed to first degree murder. Only thirty three days after the event, the wiry Italian got his wish. Strapped down in "Ol' Sparky" at the Florida State Penitentiary, he railed at the observers, "Lousy capitalists — go ahead, push the button." They did.

On the train, Gregor reported his interview to a much-relieved Brains Trust. The President-elect was quite moved to hear, "I no hate Mr. Roosevelt personally. I like him, but I hate all presidents, no matter from which country, and I hate all officials and everyone who is rich."

"Do you think this was a political act?" Moley asked the roach.

"He said he thought anarchism, socialism, communism and fascism were stupid. Also religion, God, Jesus, heaven, hell and any thought of soul. When I asked him if he believed anything he read, he said, "I don't believe in nothing. I don't believe in reading books because I don't think and I don't like it. I got everything in my mind.

"Did you get any sense about what he did believe?" Roosevelt asked.

"I asked him that. You know what he said?"

"What?"

"The land, the sky, the moon."

The men and the roach sat in silence. Beyond the ticking telegraph poles, the moon in the sky shown full on the land and the track back to Washington.

324

WASHINGTON, D.C.

29. Dreaming Of Immortality
In A Kitchen Cabinet

The White House was running over with Roosevelts. There were Franklin and Eleanor, of course, and divorced Anna ("Sis") and her two children Anna and Curtis, and later on little John. There was Eliot ("Bunny") , who came with his short-lived first wife, and James ("Jimmy") and Betsey with little Sara and Kate. There was Franklin Jr. ("Brother) with all of his Groton and Harvard friends, and his little brother, John. And they all had friends, and their children had friends.

It's a big house — four floors — with many beds, famous and not-so-famous. But plenty of cots were needed too when the whole Roosevelt kit and kaboodle arrived together, or even in part, and the halls rang with laughter and childish screams, often provoked by the President himself, tickler, wrestler and pillow-fighter extraordinaire. Under the Hoovers, there was silence and constant tension. For Mrs. Hoover the slightest protocol error was an offense. The Roosevelts couldn't care less. To the sometime horror of the servants, Mrs. Roosevelt herself would serve tea, getting in the way and disrupting the order of service. Guests didn't give any priority to the President; they might even leave a gathering before he did. The stately dining room felt more like a crowded cafeteria, with so much hearty noise, the servants could do the dishes in the pantry next door (*verboten* before) without bothering a soul. What was an official building under the Hoovers had become a happy home.

What wasn't so wonderful was the kitchen. To be blunt, it was old and filthy, a facility unworthy of any middle-class household, much less of being America's "First Kitchen." The moldy, dark wood, with eight administrations' worth of grease and dust, was simply unscrubbable. Hinges were like to fall off cabinet doors. The White House kitchen: with Taft's huge, outmoded gas range, corroded sinks with rotting wooden drains, and an ancient, rusty dumbwaiter to hoist the precious china and silver. The refrigerator had a wooden interior, and smelled nothing short of evil. Lit by dangling overhead bulbs, the electric wiring was frayed and dangerous. There were rats.

In fact, the whole basement of the west wing — the service areas on both sides of the vaulted central corridor — was dark and shabby and somewhat surreal, with Dr. McIntyre's clinic neighboring on a pantry full of tin cans. FDR tried to put the best face on it, elegizing "the pleasant smell of groceries, spices and coffee" as he rolled his chair through a makeshift route from the Oval Office to the house, but Eleanor was not so enthusiastic. The idea that one had to raid a medical office to get the silverware was a bit much for her practical mind. Thus, one of the first and most radical innovations of the New Deal was a new kitchen — and an entire new service area — for the President's House.

What chaos! For several months, all cooking was done in the midst of a dozen men with wheelbarrows full of dirt. You couldn't tell if you were in the White House or some mine or quarry. The kitchen was a far worse mess than before, with not infrequent periods sans gas or water. The service area became a maze of tunnels and pipes, as a huge cave was excavated under the driveway of the North Portico. 4,200 square feet of storage and work rooms. No more tomato cans in the medical clinic.

Rewiring circuits from DC to AC led to the discovery that all the White House plumbing was rusted; rotted pipes had to be replaced, more and more flooring and walls were ripped out — and not just in the basement. The heating pipes from the furnace were broken, with plaster dust seeping in, and spreading throughout the rooms. The First Lady's bathroom sewage left not by pipe but by trough, a menace to public health. There was much work to be done.

But finally all was gleaming and new, especially the kitchen, now suitable for public view. And Eleanor in fact invited the forty-nine young Homemakers of Tomorrow (one from each state and the District of Columbia) for the "first, last and only tour of this part of the Executive Mansion," an event later written up in the *Journal of Home Economics*. The contest winners were quite keen on the seven spacious windows, the electric fan to draw off fry fat, the room's rounded, dust-preventing corners, the shiny stainless steel, the state-of-the-art electric ranges with red handles, the eight electric refrigerators and, best of all, the new, electrically-operated dumb-waiter replacing the old wooden one pulled by a rope. Each teenager had to press its red and black buttons, and they delighted in the smooth, purring sounds of the lift.

As you can imagine, Mrs. Roosevelt was as concerned with the people who worked in the kitchen as with the much-photographed electric range. Not only was the cooking and serving equipment inadequate when the new administration arrived, but there were practically no provisions for the servants, no place for them to sit down when they had a few minutes off duty, no suitable place for them to eat if their work kept them past mealtime. "I have always believed," said the First Lady, "that governors' houses and the White House should be examples, that they should set standards, be models of convenience for the people who work there." The places lacking were provided.

As might be expected, the new kitchen was more popular with the theorists and designers than with the help, who continued to use dishrags and towels, and left the dishwasher and dryer to itself. They continued to slice and chop by hand, even after the electric company held an in-service training on the new machines. The potential revolution suffered a serious setback when Mingo the cook's wife almost sliced her finger off in the electric meat cutter.

But there was one effect of the new kitchen that was entirely positive — at least for Gregor. Replacing Taft's giant French gas range with the General Electric Industrial had opened up five and a half feet of wall space, and uncovered a vacant wooden closet, four feet wide, extending back ten feet into an adjoining room. Gregor, always comfortable with laborers, was the first administration figure to hear about this, and reported it immediately to the First Lady, the overseer of all renovation. The two of them, together with Missy LeHand, the President's Private Secretary, tramped down into the workspace to view the discovery.

"What do you think?" G asked the women.

"Well, we won't be really needing the space when the storage chambers are done," offered Missy.

"But it would be a shame for a such lovely room to be unused," said G.

"You think it's lovely?" ER was reflective.

"Whoo," shuddered Missy, "it gives me the creeps. I can feel the ghosts blowing through my bones."

"Do you really like it, Gregor?" the First Lady wanted to know.

"Yes, I do. It's dark and thought-provoking. It's close. It makes me feel protected and..."

"Why don't you take it, then?"

"What?"

"Take it. Move in. Where are you living now?"

"Near Dupont Circle."

"It must take you half an hour to walk," Missy observed.

"Twenty minutes."

"That's not bad," said ER, "but wouldn't you rather live here in the White House — rent free — with us and Missy, and Louis?"

"But where would I live?"

"Here, in this newly discovered room."

"But it's not a room, it's a closet," Gregor objected. "There are no windows. There is no light."

"Gregor, come with me," said Eleanor. "I want to talk to you. Missy, will you excuse us?"

"Certainly."

Eleanor led G eastward down the long vaulted corridor, the two of them dodging wheelbarrows, wires and pipes, until they arrived at the small White House library. After brushing off the dust on his jacket, she invited him to sit down next to her on the Duncan Phyfe couch.

"Gregor, I don't know how to say this, but you know I always speak the truth, and that I have your best interests at heart."

His own heart sprang into his throat.

"What is it?"

"Gregor, you're a wonderful person. We value you greatly. But you are a roach person. There's no way around it. We ignore that, we treat you no differently from anyone else, we don't even have to work at it any more — you're simply our friend, Gregor Samsa, trusted colleague — and roach person."

"I'm not denying…"

"Nothing to deny. But you may be denying *yourself*, denying yourself certain pleasures with your human, forgive me, human imposture. You know you are a roach. We know you are a roach. Why not feel free to act more like a roach? Franklin often speaks of the Four Freedoms. You use only three of them: you have freedom of speech, you worship as you will — I don't know if you do, but you could if you wanted to — you are free from want, at least relatively so compared with many. But you're not free from fear. What did Franklin say at the inaugural?"

"The only thing we have to fear is fear itself."

"Yes, and he believes it with all his heart. But do you?"

"I'm not afraid."

"You are afraid of being who you are. You pass reasonably well as a human, but you're a cockroach, and you don't give yourself the opportunity to act roach-like, to experiences the joys of a roach, to bring the blessings of genuine roachness to the people around you. "

"People don't like roaches."

"People don't like roaches, but that's because they don't know *you*. Why don't you be you? Don't be afraid! You have so much to offer! You'll have even more to offer."

"You want me to move into the closet in the kitchen — and be a roach? A roach in a kitchen cabinet?"

"You make it sound silly. But I know roaches like small, dark spaces. I know they like the close smell of food. And I'm not even a roach."

"That's true. They do."

"Say 'I do.'"

"I do. I like small, dark spaces and the close smell of food."

"Well, there it is — all yours. You can be around more, you can be more helpful to us and to the staff. They all like you. They trust you. You can play with the children at bedtime instead of going home. You'd *be* home. Consider it the Fifth Freedom: the Freedom to Be a Roach."

In retrospect it does sound silly. But there was Eleanor Roosevelt asking Gregor Samsa to come out of the closet (as we would say now) — by moving into one. To become a member of the traditional Kitchen Cabinet — and to take up residence there. So does the world tease us with metaphors, language revenging itself on reality. But the First Lady was never less than persuasive. Gregor gave notice at 1825 T Street, and moved into 1600 Pennsylvania Ave.

****

"Let Gregor be Gregor." The new philosophy paid off all around. The children loved it. They began by just riding on his back, falling off in the carpeted hallways when he (intentionally) jerked around or accelerated quickly, and they laughed and laughed. Booker DuBois, one of the maintenance staff, rigged up a harness to stabilize the ride, and they were able to add "Bucking Blattid" to their hilarious games. But eventually the most fun of all was climbing the walls, and even walking the ceiling. It required much extra strapping, and was looked on with initial concern by the relevant adults. But there was never an accident, and after a few days, the game took on the safe but exhilarating aura of a circus ride.

The East Room was best for "Roach the Roof", as little Anna had named it. It was the largest room in the building, with the most uncluttered wall and ceiling space, and the marvelous view of the concavity of the great chandeliers. While G's mosaic scan was somewhat fuzzy, the children were sharp-eyed as gulls. "Awk, awk!" little Elliot squawked his first time up. "Awk, awk, gawk, gawk, yech, these lights are disgustingly filthy. Gregor almost fell off the ceiling with surprise and laughter. But it was true. The cleaning staff had a monthly routine of cleaning the 22,000 hanging pieces of glass in the East Room chandeliers. Percy would go up on a high ladder, hand piece by piece down to Arvid, mid-way, who would then hand the pieces down to a team of women who washed each one with alcohol, polished it with felt, and handed it back up the chain. It took days, even alternating chandeliers monthly. The glass did sparkle, but the other-

332

than-glass — the interior brass, the porcelain insets, and the electric bulbs themselves were positively grimy. When Gregor brought this to the Percy's attention, he said, "I knows it, boss, but ain't no way to get in there. You'd have to come in from the top, and the chandelier too wide to reach to the center. I figgur it's part of the muzeem — George Washington's grunge."

Come in from the top? Who better than Gregor, perhaps with a small helper strapped into the harness? In the egalitarian spirit of the early New Deal, he volunteered a seasonal cleaning of the chandelier interiors to the applause and admiration of the staff. And he had no more trouble recruiting assistants among the children than Tom Sawyer did finding help whitewashing the fence.

One thing led to another, and persnickety little jobs began to fill in the cracks of G's daily schedule. When his sophistication about music became known, he took over the onerous chore of deciding who was to perform at White House events.

He sorted through fan letters to the President from people who wanted to give him something back for the hope he had given them: Mrs. Martha McGregor, whose husband earned $3.50 per week wanted her little girl to dance for him; Hickey, the "Cowboy Caruso" a young man with infantile paralysis, asked to sing "The Star-Spangled Banner"; Edward G. Alterman felt FDR would be inspired by a demonstration of the "Theramin Wave — a scientific musical mystery"; Georgette Ivers would entertain the President by playing the piano wearing mittens; Mrs. Emma T. White, a black mother, wanted to come, with her family of nine who play by ear, with Rufus, her baby of eighteen months conducting in perfect time; Fred Carlson and his little niece, Suzette wanted to play "My Country 'Tis Of Thee" on their violins for the president — and at "every capital of the 48 states." It required Gregor's European cultural sensibility plus Solomonic wisdom to consider such requests. At least that's what he was told by those who wanted off the hook.

So tactfully did G handle these requests that he became the UCDM, (acronyms were pandemic), the Unofficial in Charge of Difficult Mail. Like the bill from the haberdasher for two dozen ties sent to the President, unrequested, ties so awful they were discarded immediately. Or requests for souvenirs: "Please send me," one man wrote, "a wishbone the President has eaten on." Or this from a woman in Seattle: "Please send me a mousetrap from the White House." (Gregor actually honored both these requests, unofficially, using his own money for postage.)

But mail was easy — compared to people. A guest staying in the Empire Room had asked for help packing while she went to breakfast, and when a chambermaid had trouble closing one bag, she unpacked it, intending to rearrange the clothing — and discovered a fourteen inch silver tray engraved "The White House, 1889". She ran to Gregor to ask what to do. "Maybe Mrs. Roosevelt gave the tray to her," she suggested. "She would never do that," he told her. "It's not hers to give away. It belongs to the American people. Just bring it up to me." "But what if she looks in her bag before she goes?" Gregor laughed. "She'll never ask you about it, and if she ever comes back, she'll be ashamed to look you in the eye." He took the tray back to the pantry.

Tactful, but decisive. It was this kind of performance that endeared Gregor to administration and staff alike. One afternoon, G passed the President scooting down the second floor hallway in his chair. FDR spun around and yelled at Gregor's back.

"Gregor, come see me in the Oval Office at four.

"Oh no," thought G, "what did I do now? Maybe a children got hurt playing Periplaneta. Swinging around by the arms — I knew it was perhaps dangerous. I'll explain to the President. He will understand. I talk to the children, get them to stop."

However, the four o'clock interview was not to admonish, but to reward. When Missy LeHand showed Gregor into the Oval Office, there was the President with Rex Tugwell and a man G did recognize — but vaguely.

"Gregor, good to see you. You know Rex, of course. Have you met Henry Wallace, my new Secretary of Agriculture?"

"And my new boss," Tugwell added, having just been appointed Assistant Secretary.

Henry Wallace! Yes, that was the man from the party. Gregor was thinking back to FDR's birthday at the end of January when he had gotten just the slightest bit tipsy on Dvořák vodka, a large bottle smuggled in the diplomatic pouch by the Czech ambassador — Dvořák vodka, the bottle with the great man's face on the inside. You held it up to the light, peered through a hole in the frosted glass, and there he was, the most sober of composers, staring at you through an alcoholic lens. So perversely charming was that bottle, that Gregor could not turn down a little taste.

And in that attenuate daze, he had met a man — this Henry Wallace, he was sure of it — who spoke of things not spoken of. Perhaps he too was tipsy, but Gregor remembered, as if from a tongue which, having wagged, moved on, he remembered words like "the conjunctions of Saturn and Jupiter...", like "In the long run, karmic justice...", like "...work out the spiritual foundations for a true creative expression for the American people." Henry Wallace, who toward the end of their conversation noted, "Fundamentally I am neither a corn breeder nor an editor but a searcher for ways of bringing the Inner Light to outward manifestation, and outward manifestation to Inner Light."

"Nice to be knowing you."

Washington parties!

And here he was now, what was it? Secretary of Agriculture? Responsible for supporting the farmers and feeding the entire nation in this time of excess, dearth, and starvation?

"For want of a nail, the shoe is lost, for want of a shoe the horse is lost, for want of a horse the rider is lost." George Herbert's "prudent saying" could be extended: For want of the rider, the Kingdom was lost, for want of the Kingdom, Gregor was lost. That insect could not know that eleven years down the road, FDR would cave in to conservative party bosses and Southern Democrats, and dump Vice-President Wallace for the 1944 ticket, replace him with the more acceptable Sen. Harry Truman — Harry S. Truman who half a year later would step into the dead President's shoes, order the bombing of Hiroshima and Nagasaki (the proximal cause of Gregor's suicide), and vigorously pursue the cold war and the national security state from which we — and the world — have yet to recover. How different it might have been if President Wallace, pacifist, visionary, crusader for international cooperation had...

For want of the nail of political courage...

But this, Gregor could not know.

Wallace stood up and offered his hand. "We've met, I believe. At the party."

"Yes," G replied. "It is nice to seeing you again."

The President gestured for them all to sit down.

"Gregor, you've been hanging around in my Kitchen Cabinet long enough. It's time for you to become official. The Secretary, the Assistant Secretary and I have decided to offer you the post of — what was it?"

Tugwell chimed in.

"'Special Assistant to the Assistant Secretary of Agriculture in charge of Entomological Affairs.' In other words, my consultant on bugs."

"Will you accept?" the President asked.

Gregor hesitated. "What is job? What I must do?"

Wallace spoke of working with USDA entomologists to develop a national pest control policy, perhaps working with the latest pesticide discoveries like DDT.

"First job, however, is to get rid of the ants in the kitchen," FDR injected. "They're out of control, I'm told. And there was a huge cockroach yesterday in the elevator — not you. I mean a real cockroach, one about three inches long. Scared the dickens out of one of the chambermaids."

So principled was Gregor Samsa, that he actually hesitated here. To make a somewhat extended, anachronistic comparison, it was a bit like Jewish leaders being asked to coordinate transports from the ghettos. But after a few minutes' conversation, G came to a similar decision: "Better I should do it than them."

And it *was* better. Gregor's was the earliest voice — three decades before Rachel Carson — to speak out (in vain) against widespread use of organic poisons. He accurately predicted some of the uncontrollable secondary effects of pesticide use: the possibility of developing resistant strains, the death of natural predators, the possible explosion of a even more destructive populations. And what about the effects of such poisons in human food? There were no answers — but the problems were already visible to insect eyes. The large chemical companies, of course, were not interested in such speculation. This was a time of emergency, and all strong solutions were deemed necessary. As usual, strength (and money) won out over caution.

But not in the White House kitchen. Gregor quickly got on the ant problem — worst during large culinary affairs. He set the kitchen table legs in shallow plates of kerosene, but the ants soon contrived a path up the wall, over the ceiling, with an aerial drop to the kitchen table. The problem was now worse: the ants were still in the food, but now they were also falling from the skies into workers' hair and faces. And the meat tasted of kerosene.

Back to the drawing board. He lined the walls with salt, or soap flakes, or talcum powder, or baking soda. After weeks of experimentation, largely on himself, he finally hit on boric acid. He found that, while he could avoid ingesting it, still, small amounts were absorbed right through his cuticle, making him ill enough to want to avoid it. Diatomaceous earth also worked, its rough-edged particles becoming embedded in his waxy surface, opening avenues for infection and water loss. But he felt abrasions were too unkind a cut, and he abandoned this line of research. Boric acid, odorless, non-staining: that was the way to go. For that alone, he will be occasionally remembered by millions of New Yorkers.

During the time of his experiments, the New Deal also progressed. The famous first hundred days, so pathetically imitated in our own time by a do-nothing Congress and its fraudulent "Contract With America." The real first hundred days: its immensely larger and more courageous kinds of experiments than his own. Gregor found himself first admiring, then awed by the leader behind them.

And so, by and large, was the nation. By May, 1933, Washington was swarming with people animated with wonder and excitement, adventure, even elation. There had never been so much hope, as the new Administration, young, without political experience — or corruption — settled into gear, trying to put the country to rights. Conferences, hearings, briefcases bursting with plans and reports, men and women reorganizing agriculture, banking, the structures of business and industry. The capital, for the first time, really felt like the center of the country, a forgotten revolutionary center: the government, the President, truly vested with the will of a confused population — help us, save us! Even the business community looked to Washington for solutions.

A midwestern manufacturer, for instance, came to town, along with a dozen colleagues to find out just what a thirty-hour-work-week bill might mean. He was bewildered, willing to "go along", and so were his associates. "Everywhere," he remarked, "small businessmen are the same as at home, not knowing what it's all about, apologizing for asking questions, but whipped in advance, agreeing to a revolution as casually as if it were just the next step forward." Such was the national mood. Open.

At the same time, common people were moved to offer advice to the man whose voice came into their living rooms. Letters piled up in his "bedtime folder", and he read through them every night and morning. America was bringing itself to Washington, urging the immediate actions promised by the President in his inaugural address, and granting him extraordinary powers to bring them about.

In one hundred days he took control of the banking system, took the country off the gold standard and embargoed gold exports; he began a complete reorganization of the Federal Government and the management of all farming. He undertook commodity price-fixing, re-inflation of currency, government refinancing of farm and home mortgages and regulation of securities. The railroad bill and the Tennessee Valley Authority programs signaled the nationalization of public services. A huge public program put unemployed men and women to work building bridges, growing forests, building roads, painting, writing, performing dance and music and theater.

Beer! The beginning of the end of prohibition! And more importantly, the end of Hoover's prohibition of direct Federal aid to the needy. Strong, perhaps dangerous stimulants to recovery these were, but necessary to urge the country from the Slough of Despond. One Hundred Days.

"This great Nation will endure," he had told it, "will revive and will prosper. So, first of all, let me assert my firm belief that the only thing we have to fear is fear itself — nameless, unreasoning, unjustified terror which paralyzes needed efforts to convert retreat into advance." Restoration meant applying "social values more noble than mere monetary profit," he had said, and learning that "our true destiny is not to be ministered unto, but to minister to ourselves and to our fellow men." He would lead them. "I am prepared," he promised, "to recommend the measures that a stricken Nation in the midst of a stricken world may require." And so he did. Gregor, and many others, adored him.

Walking down third floor east one afternoon in May, G heard a voice calling out from the Lincoln bedroom.

"Hey! C'mere."

It was Louis Howe, the President's cherished personal advisor, a wizened, asthmatic gnome of a man who had used his personal pull to commandeer the famous room, and turn it into a sick bay for himself and his oxygen.

"I want to see Franklin. What's he doing?"

"He's in a meeting with the British Ambassador."

"Tell him to come to my room when he's through with that bloke."

Just like that? Order the President around? Make him scoot around in his wheelchair like some crippled servant? Still, Louis had spoken. Gregor waited outside the Diplomatic Reception Room till the interview was over, and conveyed the request.

"Louis wants to see me? Where is he?"

"In his room, sir."

"Get McDuffie. Bring the chair, Mac. I've got to go to Louis's room. He wants to see me."

Amazing, G thought.

That night, as he lay thigmotactically content in his kitchen cabinet, the smell of the next morning's bread wafting under the door, he thought about the Howe-Roosevelt connection. Here was a brilliant, ugly little man who had fastened himself to FDR at a low point of his life, and stayed tightly with him even through 1921, the year of his polio attack, the year that was likely to mark the end of his political career. Howe realized he could gain power and reputation only from behind the scenes, as an aide to a more acceptable and charismatic figure. He applied what he had learned as a seedy freelance reporter, studying politicians and businessmen at state-house and racetrack, had made FDR "his man", his puppet, his attractive front, planning his campaigns, his strategy, his tactics, writing his speeches, advising him on appointments, being teacher, psychiatrist and priest rolled into one. He had made himself indispensable.

Physically, he reminded Gregor of Amadeus, the secretive, moribund, but powerful *éminence grise* of a public operation. Functionally, he operated as a kind of hideous Lindhorst, a mephistophelian sculptor of men, scheming others' ambitions into being, then claiming his due. "It is easier to be forgiven for being wrong than forgiven for being right," he had once remarked, *a propos* of nothing. Too acerbic. Gregor didn't trust him.

Yet, what had he brought to pass that was in itself objectionable? Did not much of the President's extraordinary output originate with Howe? He had even written the "fear itself" line — inserted it at the last minute in the inaugural address. Was he objectionable just because he was manipulative? Was there anything wrong with being manipulative, if the manipulation led to worthy goals? Should he, Gregor, adapt Howe's strategy? Use FDR's power to achieve his quest? His wound began to tingle. FDR and Wallace! Henry would help him. They were on the same mystical path, he sensed that.

Gregor's ambition — not for himself, but for humanity — was great. He would need great shoulders to stand upon, Newton's "shoulders of giants." Even a cockroach standing on a giant's shoulders may see farther than the giant himself. Franklin Delano Roosevelt had giant shoulders, shoulders of a football player with years on crutches, years propelling himself in a chair. His moral shoulders were huge with *noblesse oblige*. His spiritual shoulders? Well, he had Henry Wallace close at hand. And now he had Gregor. It was a system, a plan. Why not? Insert roachwise into the crevices of government, tickle the appropriate ears, earwig to the world, and do it! He was already well-placed. He fell asleep to the sweet smell of steaming sourdough.

30. The Wound And The Bow

He awoke to
    Scent of magnolia, sweet and fresh,
And the southern smell of burning flesh

Maybe he wasn't awake. That song going round and round in his flaccid sensorium, *the southern smell of burning flesh and the southern smell of burning flesh of burning flesh*...the six million six million *strange fruit hangin* the six million down giant nerve fibers six million *burning flesh*... fiber! fiber! fire!

He sprang out of his straw nest, and flung open the door to the early morning kitchen. Henrietta Nesbitt, the head Housekeeper, was standing, unflappable, grim, at the smoking door to the electric oven.

"Good morning, Gregor. You're up early."

"What's burning? I smell something burning."

"I'm burning the feather dusters. Go put something on."

"What?"

"Go put something on I don't talk to strange naked males."

"What? Oh. Oh, I'm so sorry."

G went back in his room and put on his kimono.

"I thought I smelled fire. What do you mean you're burning the feather dusters?"

"Just what I said. I told the staff two months ago I wanted no more feather dusters. They just lift up the dust and throw it around to settle right down again. Vacuum cleaning only. We have new Hoover vacuums. Did they listen? Even after they were warned? So I'm burning the feather dusters."

"Maybe they don't use anything called Hoover. Is it the same Hoover?"

"No. I don't know. In any case, it doesn't matter. It's on-going insubordination."

"It makes a terrible stinking."

"That's why I'm doing it at 4:30 in the morning. The smell should clear by the time the 6:30 shift arrives."

"I thought it was — I don't know what. In my dream. A lynching. Isn't that strange? Then I thought it was six millions of piglets tossed into the fire."

"If I were Mr. Wallace, I could never live with myself. Killing those pigs may be good economics, but what kind of a man..." She shook her head.

It is one of the more tasteless ironies of history that in the year 1933, and for half a dozen years after, the phrase "the slaughter of the six million", the image of naked corpses shoved into ovens, was connected to a most unkosher cohort of piglets which Wallace's Department of Agriculture had ordered killed. He had little choice. Pork prices were so depressed that farmers were failing left and right. The pig population did not stand still as politicians debated policy, and by early April totally disastrous, unsalable surpluses were in pregnant prospect. The fledgling Secretary of Agriculture had been forced into one of the most unpalatable political decisions of his career, one that was to haunt him for the rest of his life in government: he issued orders for six million piglets to be slaughtered — a slaughter in process as Gregor and Mrs. Nesbitt stood in the smoky kitchen. An attempt was being made to distribute the meat to the poor, but logistical problems were proving too great, and only about a tenth was being eaten. The rest went to the ovens.

"I'm sorry if the smell disturbed you," the Housekeeper semi-apologized, "but the kitchen is not a place most people sleep. I forgot you were in there."

"It's all right. I have much to prepare for the children that come."

"Yes, I do too. Fifteen cots on the second floor. Toilet accommodations for seven in wheelchairs. Oxygen for three."

"And I have stage to set up. Including somehow the appearance of a *deus ex machina* — and we have no machines."

"What are they doing?"

"Sophocles' *Philoctetes*."

"I mean what do they need machines for? What kind of machines? We have plenty of machines. The machine shop can…"

"This is a play. They do a play."

"Why does a play need a machine? What sort of play?"

"A Greek play."

"Why don't they do an American play?"

"This is a play about someone who can almost not walk."

"That's hardly appropriate."

"It is famous. A good choice. You come tonight and see. I think the President likes it."

"Let me know if you need any machines."

"Are the feather dusters done? They are not smoking any more."

Gregor spent from 2 to 6 PM with fifteen 7th through 12th graders from Montgomery and Arlington counties, who, under the auspices of the new, FDR-inspired, National Foundation for Infantile Paralysis, soon to be christened "The March of Dimes", had come together to make a company called Leaping Hart Theater (as, I suppose, in Isaiah's "Then shall the lame man leap as an hart").

Fifteen crippled children. A writer friend of mine once remarked, "If you have a terrible story you need to save, put in a crippled child. If it's *really* terrible, make it a blind, crippled child." Well, nobody was blind, but the crippled-child strategy, conscious or unconscious, made this troupe a winner. They could have performed the fiery end of *Götterdämmerung* with no singing and only a cigarette lighter, and still have wrung hearts of stone.

The full range of morbidity was represented. Nine children manifested the popular image of the disease, flaccid paralysis of various muscle groups resulting from destruction of spinal motor neurons with associated atrophy of musculature. Five children had mild to moderate breathing difficulties due to viral attacks on the upper spinal cord. Two of these had to use mechanical ventilators to push air through a tracheostomy into their lungs. In one child the virus had attacked the brainstem and the nerve centers that control swallowing. He drooled constantly and his voice sounded as if it came from the bottom of a swamp. There was a spittoon attached to his belt, and a tube which reached his mouth. The collective wisdom of the group (there seemed to be no director) was such as to cast him in the role of Heracles returning from the dead to order Philoctetes back to war. He was vocally quite convincing.

The staging of the play presented few difficulties. The wily Greeks had perfected a form of drama designed for the great outdoors, with no fancy sets or lighting. The play's one technical problem needed an individual solution in each venue: how to achieve the *deus ex machina* entrance of Heracles at the end. In the fifth century BC they used a crane. We know this from an Aristophanes play in which a character ascends to heaven on a dung beetle and appeals to the scene shifter not to let him fall. But by 1933 there was no room for a crane in the East Room of the White House, and, in any case, Leaping Hart did not own one. Given historic preservation norms, hanging a pulley from the ceiling was definitely taboo. Besides, there was no masking available as there was in Athens. It *was* feasible for an entrance to be made from the top of one of the high windows which backed the platform at the south end of the room, but the Secret Service was firmly opposed to any scaffolding outside the building.

With few options left, Gregor hit on a scheme only he could have conceived. Just before the audience was admitted, little Katie, Jimmy Roosevelt's youngest daughter, approximately 35 pounds, would be "roach-roofed" into the bowl of the southernmost chandelier, the one hanging just beyond the edge of the platform. She would be given a closed container of dry ice (contributed by the NIH), which she would open on Neoptolemus' line "Let the Gods take note: I will not force the man." By the time of Philoctetes' "O comrade, hush! Behold on high a newer divinity…" there should be a considerable volume of smoke streaming down from on high. During Heracles' speech, she was to wave her hands above the dry ice container, and the turbulence would create a numinous, eerie effect, as if the atmosphere were speaking. That, plus Barney Donaldson's unique almost-voice offstage should do the trick. With no other solution in sight, Leaping

344

Hart was game, and willing to try it even without rehearsal, since Katie was nowhere to be found that afternoon — and since only she was light enough to serve.

At 7:45 the guests, having eaten a simple meal in the State Dining Room[20], were admitted to the East Room for the eight o'clock show. Nine Roosevelts with six Roosevelt children were in attendance. The entire cabinet was there, with spouses, along with Louis Howe, Dr. McIntyre, Missy LeHand, Mrs. Nesbitt and her husband Henry, and the British Ambassador and two of his aides. Forty-four chairs were taken by twenty four parents and twenty siblings of the actors. It was a typically variegated audience for the Roosevelts, who had overthrown the Washington social scene with their inclusiveness.

At 8:10, the President rolled his chair to the front of the platform.

"My friends, I want to welcome you here tonight, partly as your official host, but more importantly as an authentic representative of the hundreds of thousands of crippled children in our country. It is only in recent years that we have come to realize the true significance of the problem of our crippled children. There are so many more of them than we had any idea of. In many sections of the country there are thousands who are not only receiving no help but whose very existence has been unknown to doctors and health services.

"Infantile paralysis results in the crippling of more children and grownups than any other cause. Modern medical science has advanced so far that a very large proportion of children who have become crippled can be restored to useful citizenship. What we are about to see tonight is an inspiring example.

"Let us remember that every child and indeed every person who is

---

20 Neither Eleanor nor Franklin seemed to care much about food. Under their regime, meals at the White House ranged, by general agreement of guests and staff, from indifferent to terrible. People remarked on the oddness of "eating such fare with gold knives and forks." Hemingway ate at the White House once, describing his meal as "the worst I've ever eaten. We had rainwater soup followed by rubber squab, a nice wilted salad and a cake some admirer sent in." The Roosevelts offered that in hard times, it would be improper for the White House to be luxuriant in its offerings. Probably rationalization.

restored to useful citizenship is an asset to the country and is enabled 'to pull his own weight in the boat.' In the long run, by supporting such work we are contributing not to charity but to the building up of a sound Nation.

"I am pleased to present to you this project of our new National Foundation for Infantile Paralysis, our very own neighbors, the schoolchildren of the Leaping Hart Theater Company in a performance of ... help me out here..."

"Sophocles' *Philoctetes*," stage-whispered the wheelchaired stage manager.

"Sophocles' *Philoctetes*," echoed the President. "I have to be frank — I don't know the play, and I'm looking forward to experiencing it. Ladies and Gentlemen, The Leaping Hart Theater."

I didn't mean to patronize the performers by citing their disabilities. As one can't ignore a rhino in the bedroom, one must acknowledge such obvious encumbrance. But according to Gregor, these children were extraordinary in more ways than one. They performed this text as if they meant it, almost as if they had written it. Daring directorial decisions had been made — such as placing a budding fifteen year old girl in the role of Odysseus, and a tiny, oxygen-supported seventh-grader as Neoptolemus — which added resonances not normally encountered. It was one of those performances too odd to ever forget.

The stage manager wheeled herself over to the light switches at the south door, and plunged the room in curtained darkness. A short chorus of off-stage breath evoked the sound of wind and sea. Odysseus enters, identifies the scene,

"This is the sea-encircled, sacred isle of Lemnos,"

and describes to young Neoptolemus, Achilles' son, how ten years earlier, the Greeks had abandoned a man on this remote shore. The story is told: how Philoctetes had been bitten on the foot by a sacred serpent, and how his malodorous wound and agonized screaming made him poor company on the warrior voyage to Troy. (G felt dampness under his shirt). On stage, the almost-mature fifteen year old, and her pre-pubescent partner evoked mother-son energies unknown, in this context, to Sophocles. Their skimpy tunics displayed limbs both shapely and shapeless, and several examples of cruel-looking straps and braces.

346

And now the motivating detail: oracles have proclaimed that the Trojan war cannot be won without help from Philoctetes and his invincible bow, gift to him from the God Heracles. Cunning will be needed to achieve this.

> *Odysseus:*
> *To gain the weapons we must have resort*
> *To some deception: we must steal the bow.*
> *Neoptolemus:*
> *I like not that; for theft is not my forte;*
> *We can persuade — or capture him by force.*
> *Odysseus:*
> *Neither. He is a maniac in hate,*
> *And rather would he languish on this isle*
> *Than help his enemies to capture Troy.*

A maniac in hate. Formidable expression. Only several hours earlier, Adolf Hitler had been firing up a crowd of 40,000 in München. Philoctetes, however, had other reasons for his feelings: abandonment by friends makes for resentment-twisted souls. Odysseus reminds Neoptolemus that the old sailor's arrows are inevitably lethal, and that a battle would be futile. Trickery is the only way.

> *Odysseus:*
> *The little shameless thrift we use today*
> *Earns us the life of honor and renown.*
> *We shall be called saviors of the State.*

(Gregor's stain began to spread. I wonder who else in the political audience may have been in early diaphoresis.)

Neoptolemus is persuaded to take part in the deception. Just one little lie today, and afterwards all will be honest. Many a man has footed that muddy slope. Having set loose his plot, Odysseus hides and leaves Neoptolemus alone with the Chorus.

Modern productions of Greek drama are invariably limited by ignorance of how the Chorus was actually used. There was no Labanotation to indicate the dance steps, and the only ancient Greek music extant consists of a dozen or so notated fragments, none directly connected with the drama. Each company must come up with its own response to the remarkable texts. Shunning the stereotyped back-of-hand-to-forehead approach, Leaping Hart had invented a quietly terrifying convention: lines were delivered by changing groups of speakers accompanied by sparse ticking of teaspoons on metal — oxygen tanks, spokes and frames of wheelchairs, support rods of braces. The "steps" consisted of rhythmic, hypnotic pulsations of small cyclical movements: up and down on crutches, back and forth in chairs, in and out of audible, visible breath. The overall effect of this basically improvised activity was devastating — the human condition intensified, the throbbing of life forms in the ever-tightening grip of death.

Itself a species of the wounded, the Chorus bewailed Philoctetes,

deserted, stalled and bedded like a beast,
he suffers hunger, pain with torturing thought
Of food and comfort, while the only soul
To greet the bitter groanings of his grief
Is mocking Echo, faint and far away.

Philoctetes' groans are heard — coming closer, and now the groaner, himself, appears. Again, a daring directorial decision: a strapping, 17-year old young man, with no visible deformity, save for the stain on the left foot of his flesh-colored tights. (His symptoms consisted entirely of debilitating pain (like Philoctetes), and minor weakness against resistance. Though he looked sound, his courage must have been immense!) Imagine the effect of a chorus of obviously crippled children reacting with horror and pity towards a "normal" person — i.e., us! The Chorus jumps back when they see the wounded man, yet Philoctetes is drawn to them, overjoyed to hear his native tongue!

Neoptolemus tells him of the war and wins his confidence by sharing pretended scorn of the Greek leaders. (Gregor's wound began to soak through his jacket, and onto the yellow upholstery of the uncomfortable East Room chair. He slid forward in his seat.) Having been confirmed in his opinion of the Argives, Philoctetes pleads with his new false friend to take him home to Greece "as freight", to store him in the hold where he will least disturb the crew. The young man, moved, but duplicitous, accepts. The trap is laid: Philoctetes and his unerring bow will be aboard

Neoptolemus' ship, where he will be carried to a Trojan battlefront, with or without his knowledge or consent, to win the war for his enemies. A theater of cruelty production.

Just as they are leaving for the ship, the only "stage effect" occurs, and a remarkably well-done one it was. Gregor reported that a small balloon, hidden at the dorsum of Philoctetes' foot, under his tights, was slowly filled with beet juice from a bulb/reservoir affair surreptitiously pumped at the actor's hip. The audience can see an abscess begin to pulse and swell, and Philoctetes drops to the ground:

> Neoptolemus:
> But come, my friend; what terrors take you now?
> Philoctetes:
> Ai! ai! ai!
> Neoptolemus:
> You call the Gods to help?
> Philoctetes:
> Yes, yes, that's it! — a moment's feebleness;
> Perhaps the access of too sudden hope.
> Neoptolemus (aside):
> His age and his abjection torture me.
> Was it the office of Achilles' son
> To cheat the helpless? (to Philoctetes) Come, sir, all is well:
> Give me but leave to help thee: tell me how.
> Philoctetes:
> Alas, my child, the pain again! Ai! ai!
> We're lost — ai! ai! By heaven, it eats me up!
> Hast thou no sword, good youth, to shore it off?
> Lop off my foot at once and spare me not.

And so on. Harrowing. You may be sure that the cracked-voice screams were authentically recalled from the young actor's very own pain. They did not scan in the neat iambs above, but drew themselves out at excruciating length.

The agonized Philoctetes gives Neoptolemus the bow, asking him to care for it until the seizure is over, when a second spasm (the balloon grows), worse than the first, makes him beg for death; let Neoptolemus slay him! He wills his young friend his bow. Neoptolemus assures a pathetic, begging Philoctetes that he will not abandon him, when still another unbearable paroxysm twists the cripple.

He wants to be carried to his cave, but any touch is intolerable, a situation almost impossible to watch. Then, a huge pumping, and the balloon bursts, soaking the actor's foot and lower leg in dark redness. Faint, dripping with sweat, the sick one falls to the ground into sleep.

The chorus urges Neoptolemus to make off with the bow. "No", the young man says:

The oracles demand the Man;
And 'twere a sorry boast to steal his bow
And leave the deed half done.

In ironic juxtaposition, Philoctetes awakens, sees Neoptolemus still with him, and lovingly praises

the undreamed-of goodness in my guest,
Watching beside my bed, enduring all —
My outcries, my malodorous malady —
With ever-tender pity!

And Neoptolemus' eyes go blank as he imagines betraying this suffering victim. Zombie-like, he asks the chorus to help Philoctetes to the ship, but the cripple objects: it would be too awful for the men to deal with him. Only his proven friend should help. Neoptolemus hesitates. Philoctetes thinks him overcome with disgust.

"Everything," Neoptolemus thinks aloud, "Everything becomes disgusting when you are false to your own nature."

He can bear it no longer. He confesses the plot to take Philoctetes and his weapon back to Troy to help win the war.

The maimed-one is twice-betrayed, furious, his love turned to hate of "one so seeming-innocent." He demands the return of his bow. Neoptolemus hesitates again, and Odysseus, who has been hiding, watching the scene, steps out to secure the weapon. Philoctetes sneers at his enemy, "the skulking animal that lurked without".

Here again, I must remind the reader of the surplus visual richness: the handsome youth confronting the beautiful leg-braced maiden, his nemesis, their false "son" in between them.

Neoptolemus has had enough. He rebukes the manipulative Odysseus, suffers his vicious threats, and heroically returns the bow to its true owner. Ever pragmatic, Odysseus considers the arrow cocked at him — and stalks off-stage.

Philoctetes thanks the boy, and again begs the promised transport to Greece. Neoptolemus decides to do it, and take the consequences.

Vapors begin to pour from the sky. *"O comrade, hush!,"* Philoctetes demands.

Behold on high a new divinity
Compels the worship both of heart and knee."

But with the down-rushing down of mist, came the up-rushing up of vomitus. G clamped his tibia against his face, and ran out of the room, his coat dripping brown fluid, and his mouthparts wet with dinner. Dr. McIntyre sprang out of his chair and followed him out the door to the corridor.

"Gregor, wait!" the old man yelled, but the Assistant to the Assistant Secretary of Agriculture ducked into the Men's room, without heeding him. The doctor followed, and found his colleague inside a stall, hunched over the toilet. He waited for the retching to stop.

"Something you ate? Do I have to worry about forty more cases of food poisoning?"

"I don't think so. It was the play. Seeing the play."

"That bad, huh?"

"No. Good."

"Really? Well, we're missing the end."

"I know the end."

"What happens?"

"Heracles orders from the heaven that Philoctetes slaughter the Trojans for religion's sake. I think that is what makes me — you say upczech?"

"Upchuck. What about that stain on your back?"

"It's nothing."

"It's enough for a $200 upholstery repair at taxpayer expense. Why don't we go down to my office and take a look?" He helped the roach down the east spiral staircase to the ground floor clinic near the kitchen.

"Still feeling sick?"

"No. I am better."

"But something is still juicy back there. The stain is growing. Take off your jacket and shirt, and let's see what's going on."

Gregor felt confident caring for his wound, and normally did not seek medical help. Still, McIntyre was so friendly, and so forceful, that G followed his instructions. The doctor removed the dressing.

"Impressive. Six or seven centimeter wound, friable, weeping, raised borders, what's this? Maggots? Je-sus, Gregor, what have you got going here?"

"It's just a few maggots. They don't get any worse."

"Your friends, huh?"

"I feel as if I know them. They tell me of my mortality."

"Very medieval. How'd you get this damn thing? How long have you had it?"

"I have it since 1915 — eighteen years."

"And it's never healed?"

"No. Is a reminder."

"Of what? More mortality?"

"My father. He throw an apple at me. An apple. In my back. I don't like to talk about it. Maybe brown is from the apple. "

"Still?"

"It reminds me."

"This is a useful wound! Better than a secretary. Reminds you of what?"

"It is useful. Apple in *Gan Eden.* The Garden at Eden."

"Sin?"

"Yes."

"Are you sinful?"

"A cage in search of a bird."

"I see. But the wound is not like this all the time. What makes it worse? What makes it weep so?"

"Different things. Various."

"What brought it on tonight? What in the play?"

"When the boy is tricked and made to be not true to himself. And it gets worse when the play is so cruel. It almost make me cry, but my wound cries instead."

"And the vomiting?"

"When the God is going to make him kill people with his bow..."

"Would you rather he never forgave his countrymen for their reaction to his wound? Wasn't it better forget it, to resolve the issue?"

"Not with killing. More killing."

There was silence as the doctor opened a white wall-cabinet.

"What do you think this play is about?" McIntyre asked, pulling sterile gauze pads and tape from the shelf. He swabbed the wound with hydrogen peroxide. "Those little maggots get pretty bubbly. Happy new year!"

"I think it is about ways to betray your humanity."

"I think it's about a person poisoned by narrow, fanatical hatred," the doctor averred. "Isn't that a line in the play? Something about fanatical hatred?"

"A maniac of hate."

"Yes. He can't get rid of the poison, and every now and then it grows to bursting. After he goes to Troy with them, I bet he has no more trouble from his wound."

"The disease is Neoptolemus' selfishness and betraying and Odysseus' manipulationness and the boy's weakness to be tricked... "

"Calm down. All right if I re-dress the wound?"

"Yes, go ahead."

"So the problem is Neopto...what's his name?"

"Neoptolemus."

"This play is not called 'Neoptolemus'. Philoctetes is what it's about, and he was not so nice a guy, correct?"

"They made him that way. His thus-called friends."

"Maybe, but you'll agree he was a bit much. His stinking wound was a metaphor. You believe in metaphors? He was a stinker."

"What is stinker?"

"Someone you don't want to be around."

"All right. Yes. He is a stinker. And so is everyone else."

"But Philoctetes is a *necessary* stinker. They can't just use his bow to win the war — they need the stinker himself. With the stink. A bad character who is also indispensable...This adhesive tape ok? It's all I have."

"Yes, ok."

"A hero with an incurable wound," he went on bandaging, "like yours, my friend, perhaps like yours. His strength was inseparable from his wound — they couldn't have one without the other, could they?"

"If he hadn't been bited in the first place..."

"Ah, but he was. And by a sacred snake, they said, no? Sacred. Not some old rusty nail with *Clostridium* on it. This was no accident. It was a lesson. For you. For us. This horrible stinker, Philoctetes, with his smelly, shit-filled wound, is also the master of a superhuman art. Genius — and disease. Normal people need genius. But they have to take the smell that goes with it. Would you like to live with your great Beethoven? Talk about stinkers..."

"I would not like to live with Beethoven."

"So? Want to put him on an island? Worship him from afar where his howling won't disturb you, won't disturb the music?"

"Some of the music also howls."

"There, you're all clean and neat. Except for your shirt and jacket, which I suggest you launder thoroughly. Want a jonnie to get you to the kitchen?"

"No, it's ten meters. I make it home half-dressed. Mrs. Nesbitt is still upstairs."

"Gregor, I'll tell you how I think things are." The doctor was washing his hands. "I think we live in a world where above fuses with below. You can't have a divine weapon, a sacred tool, without its abominable, human owner vomiting curses and fouling his nest." He dried his hands, and opened the office door. Gregor stepped into the hallway.

"Oh," the doctor recalled, "You told me what made it worse. What makes it better?"

Gregor turned around and faced the old man.

"Forgetting. Makes it better when I forget."

31. Mein Kampf, Dein Kampf

Christmas Eve, 1935.

Gregor had been invited to the President's reading of *A Christmas Carol* — an annual event anticipated with pleasure by the large, and ever-expanding presidential family.

This was not some species of flattering the king, for truly FDR's was a classic performance, complete with stage voices, props, and dramatic business that kept the smaller children on the edge of their seats, squealing with fear and joy. Harry Hopkins, a first-time guest, commented, "The President reads aloud better than anyone I know — he takes infinite pains with each word and phrase — placing the emphasis just right — and withal reading with such obvious pleasure. And you laughed when he said 'humbug' in a loud voice and 'good afternoon' even louder...The president had read this story to his children every Christmas for many years — and the little book is one of his priceless possessions."

And indeed, as in the earliest days of his parenthood, the performance was held in the presidential bedroom, with the smallest children piled on the bed, the larger ones on drawn-up couches and chairs, and the parents and guests sitting and standing against the walls. It was a happening mirrored perhaps in other households around the country, but here achieving a perfection of technique and good feeling that must have been rare.

The Assistant to the Assistant Secretary of Agriculture left his room at 6:25 that Tuesday evening, and climbed the circular stairs to the first floor, where he checked his cubby for late-arriving Christmas mail. Along with a Christmas card from the People's Bank, and a candy-cane wrapped with pipe-cleaner to resemble a thin, red-striped reindeer (cute), he pulled out a small package, brown paper, wrapped with string. There was no return address, and since the hour was getting late, he just stuck the items in his pocket, and made his way upstairs to the west wing.

The Christmas Eve reading was perhaps the only punctual time in the Roosevelt year. This was a long story, and by the end, the smallest audience members were just about gone. Some simply fell asleep, but others would begin to fidget and whine, so 6:30 — and no later — seemed the right time to start. Gregor entered an already crowded room, and found a good place for himself under a couch on the north wall. Under-a-couch brought back mixed emotions, and memories of a confusing time in Prague, but it was the only empty space in an over-packed room.

Eleanor Roosevelt, her usual charming self, called the event to order:

"Friends, and wonderful family, we're so happy you can join us tonight — some for the first time, and welcome! — to hear this marvelous tale, so relevant in this time of hardship, when meanness often rules, and generosity goes begging. Have a cup of tea or milk or juice — there's post-prohibition egg-nog for the grownups — and settle in for what? the 30th? 31st? annual reading of..." and here she cued the audience who all chimed in,

"Charles Dickens' 'A Christmas Carol'!"

She took her seat, and out from the master closet came the President, in striped pajama pants, ascot and dressing gown, his "precious book" clasped, with crutch, in his right hand, doing his best imitation of John Barrymore for the applauding crowd. He sat down on the bed, scooted the littlest ones over, covered his legs with the comforter, and began his tale.

I have endeavoured in this Ghostly little book, to raise the Ghost of an Idea, which shall not put my readers out of humour with themselves, with each other, with the season, or with me. May it haunt their houses pleasantly. Their faithful Friend and Servant, C. D., December, 1843.

Marley's Ghost
Marley was dead: to begin with. There is no doubt whatever about that....

Through the cage of dangling feet, Gregor could watch the children on the bed, and those sitting on the far side of the bed, and the grownups lined up on three walls. He could see the President's left profile and gesturing hand.

Mind! I don't mean to say that I know, of my own knowledge, what there is particularly dead about a door-nail. I might have been inclined, myself, to regard a coffin-nail as the deadest piece of ironmongery in the trade. But the wisdom of our ancestors is in the simile; and my unhallowed hands shall not disturb it, or the Country's done for. You will therefore permit me to repeat, emphatically, that Marley was as dead as a door-nail.

This was good! Gregor was expecting some treacly tripe, served up by Sentimentality, Inc., the thriving, leading corporation in depression America. Relieved, he settled in for a good time. But rolling on his right side, he felt the package in his pocket digging into his tegmen, and after a minute decided he'd better move it, perhaps take it out of his pocket all together.

Scrooge! a squeezing, wrenching, grasping, scraping, clutching, covetous, old sinner! Hard and sharp as flint, from which no steel had ever struck out generous fire; secret, and self-contained, and solitary as an oyster. The cold within him froze his old features, nipped his pointed nose, shrivelled his cheek, stiffened his gait; made his eyes red, his thin lips blue; and spoke out shrewdly in his grating voice. A frosty rime was on his head, and on his eyebrows, and his wiry chin. He carried his own low temperature always about with him; he iced his office in the dogdays; and didn't thaw it one degree at Christmas.

It was hard to extract package from pocket in the tight space under the couch, and as he pulled it round, it made an embarrassing crinkling, causing a child's face to appear upside down from the couch above, wondering what was going on. G gave him a conspiratorial hush sign, and the face disappeared. He continued his move more carefully.

The fog came pouring in at every chink and keyhole, and was so dense without, that although the court was of the narrowest, the houses opposite were mere phantoms. To see the dingy cloud come drooping down, obscuring everything, one might have thought that Nature lived hard by, and was brewing...

There! Free at last! That feels better. Gregor looked for a moment at the rectangular solid, and though there was no return address, he noticed that the address handwriting was decidedly European. The package had been sent to E.P. Dutton, his publisher, and forwarded to Ives & Myrick, probably the last address Dutton had for him. G recognized Mrs. Verplanck's handwriting forwarding it on to the White House. His curiosity was piqued. I can listen to the story and open this quietly, he thought. I'll just see who it's from, then deal with it later.

'Bah!' said Scrooge, 'Humbug!'

All the children began to laugh, just as Hopkins had mentioned, so fierce was the President's line reading. Gregor used the commotion in the room to bite through the string, and slip the contents from the wrapping. A book and a long letter...from? It didn't say, at least not on the first page. Berlin. Who did he know in Berlin? And the book...*Mein Kampf*...ah, yes, *Mein Kampf,* he'd never read it. Heard about it, of course, but.... He shuffled one-clawed through nine sheets of the long communication. Who would have the time to write such a thing?

'What right have you to be merry? What reason have you to be merry? You're poor enough.'

On and on. Last page...Amadeus Ernst Hoffnung! Amadeus! Oh, how wonderful to hear from you. I thought you might be gone by now. Those empty spaces on the mirror...Amadeus!

What else can I be,' returned the uncle, 'when I live in such a world of fools as this? Merry Christmas! Out upon merry Christmas! What's Christmas to you but a time for paying bills without money; a time for finding yourself a year older, but not an hour richer; a time for balancing your books–and having every item in 'em presented dead against you?

What to do? He wanted to listen to the President's story, but Amadeus, Amadeus had written! All those pages. It must be important. And so he did what any of us might have done in such a predicament: he tried to take in both, to be mostly present for the reading, but also to get a preview of the news he would devour later in his closet.

Berlin

21 September 1935

Most Honorable Gregor Samsa,

...a kind, forgiving, charitable, pleasant time: the only time I know of, in the long calendar of the year, when men and women seem by one consent to open their shut-up hearts freely, and to think of people below them as if they really were fellow-passengers to the grave...

I send this letter and Gift (observe the multilingual pun) like a note in a bottle from the Less-Than-Happy Isle of Ditchland. My copy of Wo Sind Sie Jetzt? credits you with the important Principles and Practice of Risk Management, which the library of Humbled University Across The Street lists (without owning) as published by E.P. Dutton and Co., New York, which the New York City Phone Directory lists at 124 Madison Ave. - and the trail leads no farther. Tot. Which I hope and assume you are not. So on this solstice, truly a time in which light turns to darkness, I once again utilize my ever-resourceful father to scheme letter and poison into the U.S. diplomatic pouch, to be trudged to you, via publisher, safely out of this once-great, now grating, country. The Gift is in the turgid original, so as to minimize inspection by your monolingual postal thieves, assuming you have any in the land of dreams. I hope all arrives intact.

...more than usually desirable that we should make some slight provision for the Poor and Destitute, who suffer greatly at the present time. Many thousands are in want of common necessaries; hundreds of thousands are in want of common comforts, sir.' `Are there no prisons?' asked Scrooge...

Yes, Berlin is the manger for this letter, and Humboldt University is across the street from my little apartment, to which I have betaken myself to be closer to the cranky-house of the famous Herr Doktor Professor Siegfried Werner, the very he of Werner's Syndrome, though his interest in it seems merely scientific, even prurient, but not personal: at eighty-six, he's healthy as a dog. And I am not. But enough about me for the moment. Let me get right to the point.

...stooped down at Scrooge's keyhole to regale him with a Christmas carol...

Gregor, this is no joke. I don't know that this letter will even reach you, but if it does, Y O U M U S T D O S O M E T H I N G to alert the American structure of Power to the real situation in Germany.

If he could only know where I'm reading this!

It seems you've become an important author, a theoretician of risk. Surely your word will be listened to. I have been following the coverage of our events in American papers, and I assure you that you have absolutely no realistic informations. Last week, at the annual Nuremberg rally, Hitler announced the "Reich Citizenship Law" and the "Law for the Protection of German Blood and German Honor". So now we know who is "officially Jewish", that is, a member of the living dead, eliminated from any kind of civil or social existence. People who don't exist have a poor prognosis, especially here. The living dead may soon become the dead - period.

Darkness is cheap, and Scrooge liked it. But before he shut his heavy door...

Last Monday, the day after the Party orgy, graffiti denouncing the new laws was found on the Jungfernbrüke, a few blocks from my apartment. The afternoon papers gave it lots of play, and that very evening I heard yelling in the street. Cat-curious, I went down to follow the crowd. Men and women, presumably Jewish - in any case, patronizing Jewish stores - were being rounded up and herded over to the bridge, where they were ordered to scrub off the graffiti using river water and their own clothing. When things got too dull, the SA boys borrowed whips from the cart-drivers gathered for the show, and added choreography to the Gesamtkunstwerk. You ought to see the Jews jump! Nijinsky would be jealous. One young girl lost an eye. The

police kept order - that is, they kept the sightlines clear,
and made sure no one disturbed the performance. In the middle of
the cleansing, a car arrived carrying four old men, apparently
grabbed at some ceremony of their own. They were made to polish
the grimy metal with their prayer shawls - to great cheering
and howling. The sacred garments, now ripped and filthy, were
thrown into the Spree. Then the whole cleaning crew was marched,
drill step, all the way to the Jüdischer Friedhof where, I hear,
they were forced to help with the difficult work of turning over
gravestones. I have to admit I have a limited appetite for such
entertainment. I went home from the bridge to vomit (I do this
often) and to begin this letter to you.

Gregor didn't know if he could go on reading. Perhaps he should just
listen to the story, and read the letter later.

*The chain was long, and wound about him like a tail; and it was made
(for Scrooge observed it closely) of cash-boxes, keys, padlocks, ledgers, deeds, and
heavy purses wrought in steel. His body was transparent; so that...*

The roach couldn't concentrate. His eyes went back to the pages on the
floor in front of him.

Since God alone knows what you know (though you don't know
what God knows), let me backtrack for the benefit of news-de-
prived Americans. Even before the Führer began to führen, there
was "unofficial" boycotting of Jewish businesses, pushed by the
bully-boys in brown shirts, who also punished anyone patronizing
Jews in any way. So "because of Jews" "German citizens" had to
suffer. Even talking to a Jew, having a conversation on the
street, could get you accused of "race pollution" and "civic
disloyalty", and lead to being paraded through town with a sign
around your neck. The unofficial boycotts were peppered with
equally unofficial violence. Naturally, there was the same kind
of police protection.

With such "mandates" from the people, our governments began
to act. A pastiche of wondrously creative local laws almost
obviated the need for "unofficial" populist action. And now,

after three years of this, Jews are no longer allowed in parks,
in theaters, libraries, museums, on beaches, or into any club.
They can't be guests in hotels, or get service at restaurants.
One profession after another has un-licensed them. They can't
open stores, or be allowed into workers' unions or any jobs they
control. They can't be lawyers, they can't be tax consultants,
can't be lifeguards, or actors, or salesmen, or stock brokers.
They can't rent out park chairs, they can't distribute movies,
or deal in art works, or currency. They can't be engineers,
they can't sell guns. What have I forgotten? No Jew can be a
detective, a guard, or an accountant. No Jew can be a guide, a
peddler, an auctioneer, no Jew can manage anything - factory,
house, estate, or land. Needless to say, all the new business
and job opportunities have gone to Aryans, who are ever more
grateful to the regime. You wouldn't like it here.

*A slight disorder of the stomach makes them cheats. You may be an undi-
gested bit of beef, a blot of mustard, a crumb of cheese...*

G felt his stomach gurgle. He hadn't eaten dinner...

In areas where Jews are not yet banned, other ways are found
to shut them down. Tax authorities won't deal with legitimate
Jewish agents, so few property owners are interested in hiring
them. Sugar has been cut off to Jewish bakers and candy-makers,
destroying their businesses. Jewish newsstands can't get newspapers. Jewish businesses can't put ads in directories, in newspapers, on billboards or the radio. You don't read about these
things in your papers. We don't need to read about them in ours.

It's true. I read more than most. The *Times*, the *Tribune*, the *Post*, the
Worker... How come I don't know this? Terrible!
`You will be haunted,' resumed the Ghost, `by Three Spirits.'*

But not everything, dear Gregor, is bleak. Though many jobs
are no longer available, at the same time, to balance things
off, certain jobs have opened up for the children of Abraham

and Isaac: cleaning public toilets, for instance, and sewage plants. Jobs at rag and bone works are considered possibly "suitable" for Jews. But outside of such work, they have to fend for themselves.

Ah, but what if they succeed - in fending? How could success be made less likely? Travel bans and invalidation of passports are obvious. But how about no parking for Jews, with special license plates to identify Jewish cars for special harassment? Ingenious. Original. In a few cities we now have prohibition of drivers licenses, and in München, restriction from public transportation. It might be better to move. But Jews can't rent their homes, sublet, or sell them to come up with any cash. Retirement benefits and pension contracts have been cancelled, and all insurance policies. Two years ago Jewish students were kept from taking finals, so couldn't complete their schooling - and their job prospects were already ... poor. All student loans had to be paid in two weeks, regardless of contract; those in default had engagements with the police, and they wasn't nice.

My God. Those poor...

And the stink! Yes, they smell, those Jews - when Jewish streets aren't cleaned, water is shut off, and no municipal services are available. The police, when present at all, are an occupying army, attacking at will. Many town centers are off-limits to Jews, and the remnants of Jewish culture are under siege: Jewish art and music is censored - "decadent", you know - and even your American jazz is assailed as "a barbarian invasion supported by Jews." Thorough. But not quite thorough enough.

...incoherent sounds of lamentation and regret; wailings inexpressibly sorrowful...

Because they are persona non grata, Hebrews need to be easily identified, and our rush-hour passengers are not about to put up with checking IDs. So in several cities, including my own, pretty yellow stars are required to be worn, with strict punishment for forgetting. I suspect this is the just the tip of a fashion alert. And names. Lots in a name. So Jews can no longer name their children with "Aryan sounding names" which might confuse us. They all have to adopt "Israel"or "Sarah" as middle names, and use them on all identification. Now you can tell all bruchs by their covers.

Gregor was breathing hard.

We German-speakers are of course addicted to Law and Order. So a few weeks after Herr Hitler became Chancellor, Herr Goering drafted 40,000 brown and black shirts into the police forces, with unlimited opportunity to indulge any pent-up sadism. I clipped the following marching orders from the horse's mouth: "Police officers who make use of firearms in the execution of their duties will, without regard to the consequences of such use, benefit by my protection; those who, out of a misplaced regard for the consequences, fail in their duty will be punished in accordance with the regulations." Clear enough?

...found himself face to face with the unearthly visitor...

We now have 53 concentration camps around the country, centers for imprisonment and torture of anyone anyone thinks might oppose the regime. And something new - we have a certain GESTAPO - some post office employee's suggestion for a name - Geheime Staatspolizei - to run them. Since the Night of Long Knives - do you know about this? - guard duty is granted exclusively to Gestapo "Death's Head Units". You can imagine. Under the good old brown shirts, the camps were mainly there to give victims a hell of a beating, then ransom them to relatives or friends for as much as the traffic would bear. Comparative paradise. But now, under the black-shirted Totenkopfverbände - we shall see. I did clip the following for you from the new official camp rules:

Article 11. The following offenders, considered as agitators, will be hanged: Anyone who politicizes, holds inciting speeches and meetings, forms cliques, loiters around with others; who for the purpose of supplying the propaganda of the opposition with atrocity stories, collects true or false information about the concentration camp; receives such information, buries it, talks about it to others, smuggles it out of the camp into the hands of foreign visitors, etc.

Article 12. The following offenders, considered as mutineers, will be shot on the spot or later hanged: anyone attacking physically a guard or SS man, refusing to obey or to work while on detail, or bawling, shouting, inciting or holding speeches while marching or at work.

Caveat emptor.

"I am the Ghost of Christmas Past," the delighted audience chanted together with the reader. Gregor looked out from his cavern, his attention momentarily diverted.

`Long Past?' inquired Scrooge: observant of its dwarfish stature. `No. Your past.'

He drifted back to Amadeus, reluctant, but driven...

Oh, and in order to populate the camps (we want to get our tax dollars worth), there's the new SD, the Sicherheitsdienst. Security, Gregor, security. We now have 100,000 part-time, and 5,000 full-time informers directed to snoop on every citizen in the land and report the slightest suspicious remark or activity. You can imagine how many petty feuds are being settled. No one can say or do anything without wondering how SD microphones or overhearing agents - your son, for instance, or your father, or your wife or best friend, or your boss, or your secretary - might interpret it.

One of the fascinating, if lesser, tasks of the SD is to identify who votes "No" in the Führer's plebiscites, which at this point, garner only 98% approval. Members of the election committee number all ballots, and the SD makes up a voters' list. Since the secret ballots are handed out in numerical order, it's easy to identify the dissidents. There is some debate about whether this would be more effective overt or covert, but at the moment, they seem more interested in identifying nay-sayers.

It's all legal, of course. Law and Order, natürlich. Did your papers report "The Enabling Act" last March? If so, I missed it. It gives Hitler exclusive legislative powers for four years. Exclusive. The German Parliament turns over its constitutional functions, and takes a long vacation. But since this "Law for Taking Away the Distress of People and Reich" required a change in the Constitution, Hitler needed a 2/3 vote. It's hard to get 2/3s of legislators to slit their own throats. What to do? Part of the problem was solved by the "absence" of the 81 Communist deputies: they were all "outlawed" and sent to concentrations camps. Goering felt sure the rest of the problem could easily be dealt with "by refusing admittance to a few Social Democrats," and since Hitler was allowed to arrest as many of the opposition as "necessary", he got his 2/3 majority - though the Nazis had won only 44% of the previous election. Mathematics can be truly...

There goes Friday, running for his life to the little creek. Halloa. Hoop. Hallo.'

The President gave such a whoop, cried out so effectively, both voice and echo, that Gregor looked up sharply, and out through the barricade of legs.

`I wish,' Scrooge muttered, [the President's voice caught up with sobs] putting his hand in his pocket, and looking about him, after drying his eyes with his cuff: `but it's too late now.'

Gregor was truly moved by FDR's performance. His heart went out to Scrooge, trying to break out of his shell. But the metamorphosis was incomplete. And the sheets of paper were burning in his claw.

Mathematics can be truly amazing.

So now we have a perfectly legal dictator, who, with no higher authority to limit him, has taken the country completely into his own mad hands. All other political parties and all trade unions have been abolished. The Reichstag does meet occasionally to be harangued, but its members have been hand-picked by the Party, selected on the basis of how loud they can cheer. Hence, real elections are a thing of the past. But even if we had them, we would never know what we were voting about. I criticize the American press. Oh, mote, oh beam! Our news is handled by Dr. Goebbels, "Minister of Propaganda and Public Enlightenment". Need I say more?

Germany, Eternal Land of Law and Order - if you are German. But Jews can't use the justice system to protect themselves should the government onslaughts get a tiny bit illegal. All our courts are now packed to enforce policy, not judge it. The object of the law is to protect the state, not the citizen. Our Commissioner of Justice opines that the law and the Führer's will are the same. Last week, he advised a group of judges to "say to yourselves at every decision: 'How would the Führer decide in my place?'" If Jews are a menace to the state, then all laws oppressing them are legal - and just. It's logical. Last year Goering complained about defendants still having so many rights that convictions were impeded. So Jewish lawyers were barred, and since Aryan lawyers can't serve Jews, Jews now have to represent themselves against highly trained adversaries. Schlau.

But to be fair, not only Jews suffer this way. We now have "Peoples' Courts" with jurisdiction over all political crimes. Two professional judges and five others chosen from among Party officials, the SS and the Armed Forces. All proceedings are closed, and there is no appeal from decisions or sentences - which usually involve executions. Who would dare testify for the defense of anyone accused of "treason"? After the murder of her husband on the Night of Long Knives, Erich Klausener's widow tried to sue the State for damages. Her lawyers were whisked off to Sachsenhausen concentration camp, until they formally withdrew the action. Dr. Erich Klausener - the leader of Catholic Action!

G had to take a break. He stared blankly out in front of him, then drifted slowly into the here and now, the here and then, of Dickens.

Scrooge was older now; a man in the prime of life. His face had not the harsh and rigid lines of later years; but it had begun to wear the signs of care and avarice. There was an eager, greedy, restless motion in the eye, which showed the passion that had taken root, and where the shadow of the growing tree would fall.

Gregor, too, was older. Chitin does not age as obviously as skin, but from the inside he could feel a subtle cracking, a reticulation of scar tissue at once deadeningly sullen and incisively inscribed. The pattern approximated the look of roots, but where would such roots be nourished? His eyes dropped again to the papers.

`The Night of Long Knives again.`

Yes, the Night of Long Knives. I can't recall...

'I have seen your nobler aspirations fall off one by one, until the master-passion, Gain, engrosses you...'

`Was this reported? Read through Mein Kampf. Begin`
`anywhere — it's all of a piece. You may be tempted to`
`dismiss it as the ravings of a paranoid schizophrenic`
`with barely enough education to make a difference.`
`But last June 30th such dismissals went to unquiet`
`graves — along with several hundred of Hitler's former`
`collaborators.`

"Not like our good children here," Eleanor commented into the middle of the reading. She was referring to the tumult of "every child conducting itself like forty".

`There had been some criticism of the regime, even from the`
`conservative Right. The revolution, some thought, should slow`
`down, the arbitrary arrests stop; the persecution of the Jews,`
`the attacks against churches, and especially the arrogant behav-`

ior of the storm troopers had gone too far. An environment of general terror was not good for business. But Hitler, Goering and Himmler did not take kindly to criticism. They needed to purge any SA moderates - and to liquidate all other opponents, Left or Right. So on that Saturday night, a coordinated series of bald-faced murders took place. In Munich, Ernst Roehm, Minister of the Reich, one of the founders of the Nazi Party, Chief of Staff of the SA, was taken off and shot in the head. Seven out of thirteen commanders of the SA were similarly killed. The SA! Had not these Brown Shirts and their leader helped seize power, and did they not even now control the streets? What daring to take on this group and their leaders!

The immense relief of finding this a false alarm. The joy, and gratitude, and ecstasy...

Simultaneously in Berlin, von Schleicher, former Chancellor of the Reich , General Kurt von Schleicher, was murdered in front of his house. Klausener was killed in his office at the Ministry of Communications. Gregor Strasser was killed in the street. All were murdered without explanation by ruthless gangs, mechanical death robots, killed out in the open, in front of witnesses. To whom would a witness complain? Bodies were left where they fell - in ministerial offices, in alleys, cellars, bedrooms and bars, slumped in cars, or floating in swampwater. After a few hours, police would come and take the corpses away. The Night of Long Knives.

"I am the Ghost of Christmas Present", the audience chimed in again. Gregor realized he was barely taking in the Christmas plot.

Hitler was secure enough to claim responsibility in an out-rageous Reichstag speech: "It was no secret that this time the revolution would have to be bloody; when we spoke of it, we called it The Night of Long Knives". He not only claimed the actions as his own, but laid down his right to repeat them: "I was responsible for the German nation; consequently, it was

I alone who, during those 24 hours, was the Supreme Court of Justice of the German People. In every time and place, rebels have been killed. I ordered the leaders of the guilty shot. I also ordered the abscesses caused by our internal and external poisons cauterized until the living flesh was burned." The Reichstag deputies rose as one and cheered. The next day, they legalized the absolute monopoly of the Nazi Party.

And now these Nuremberg Laws. Gregor, I tell you there is gathering death energy such as has never been seen before, energy without any control. There are no voices left to speak against it - all rational people have fled, and their writings have been banned. Last year, at the Opernplatz just outside my window, Goebbels ordered a ritual burning of "immoral and destructive" documents and books. Your favorite authors, Gregor, and mine, were deemed too left-wing, too Jewish, or just too un-German to continue living and breathing. Up in flames went Thomas Mann, Rainier Rilke, Albert Einstein, Sigmund Freud - a fiery show specifically designed to enlighten the liberals of Humbled University. Heine wrote that those who begin by burning books end by burning people. His works, of course, went into the flames. Old man Spengler, I believed, survived, but I'm sure he's less than pleased with the conflagration.

mince-pies, plum-puddings, barrels of oysters, red-hot chestnuts, cherry-cheeked apples, juicy oranges, luscious pears, immense twelfth-cakes, and seething bowls of punch, that made the chamber dim with their delicious steam. In easy state upon this couch, there sat a jolly Giant, glorious to see, who bore a glowing torch, in shape not unlike...

His stomach began to hurt as never before. Was it an ulcer?

Gregor, I must repeat: there is only one power in the world that can stop this insanity - the United States of America. There will be a war - of this I am sure.

...for Tiny Tim, he bore a little crutch, and had his limbs supported by an iron frame.

"Just like yours, Grandpa, shouted little Katie, she of Heracles' smoke. Everyone, including the President, laughed. Everyone but Gregor.

Only the United States has the economic strength and the untested arrogance to call Hitler's bluff. I don't know how you are to do it, but someone has to alert the American government. Your President Roosevelt may be able to understand the dynamics. You must get to him somehow, make him listen - show him this letter if nothing else. Make him read Mein Kampf. Make him to know that Herr Führer means every word in it. He must understand that. He must understand that, just as in '17, America will have to go to war. You must begin now, building up material and moral force for a quick, overwhelming victory - or all is doomed. Things can't wait until Hitler has overwhelmed all of hollow Europe - which he will. I don't know what to say. It sounds ironic and preposterous, but maybe the continuation of human, humane culture is up to you, poor thing.

He told me, coming home, that he hoped the people saw him in the church, because he was a cripple, and it might be pleasant to them to remember upon Christmas Day, who made lame beggars walk, and blind men see.'

Look around: all the values and institutions of liberal civilization are collapsing. People no longer distrust dictatorship; there's no longer a widespread, clear commitment to constitutional, elected government under the rule of law. Security seems more important to people than rights or liberties, their freedom of speech, freedom of publication, assembly. We're not committed to reason any more, to public debate, to education, science, or even to the improvability of the human condition. If Hitler Germany triumphs - and I assure you only the US can prevent it - Fascism will be the tidal wave of the future, hostile to any progressive politics, encouraging military and police as the only way to subvert subversion. Flag-waving will be the royal road to electoral success. Women will stay at home and bear children for armies, artists will be liquidated as degenerates. A lunatic set of beliefs will ride on the latest technologies....

If these shadows remain unaltered by the Future, the child will die.' `No, no,'said Scrooge. `Oh, no, kind Spirit. say he will be spared.' `If these shadows remain unaltered by the Future, what then? If he be like to die, he had better do it, and decrease the surplus population.' Scrooge hung his head to hear his own words...

The activists will be those veterans for whom the war was a peak of personal achievement - simple inspiration or glory in brutality, men for whom uniform and discipline, sacrifice, blood, arms and power are what make masculine life worth living, men with a sense of savage superiority, not least to women and those who had not fought. These men will oppose all social transformation, all working-class movements, all foreigners, all sub-humans who might contaminate or pollute the world. These will be the men opposing us.

Do you think we can win against the hysterically nationalist and xenophobic, those who idealize war and violence, anti-liberal, anti-democratic, anti-proletarian, anti-socialist and anti-rationalist, those dreaming of blood and soil and a return to the values modernity destroys? Do you think we can win against those who can make the trains run on time?

`A place where Miners live, who labour in the bowels of the earth,' returned the Spirit...

Gregor was not sure he could stand up against such force. He was not sure he could stand up at all, not sure he could make any difference in this deadly, vicious undertow of history. His heart was thumping fiercely.

...he saw the last of the land, a frightful range of rocks; and his ears were deafened by the thundering of water, as it rolled and roared, and raged among the dreadful caverns it had worn, and fiercely tried to undermine the earth.

Built upon a dismal reef of sunken rocks, some league or so from shore, on which the waters chafed and dashed the wild year through, there stood a solitary lighthouse...

And let me return to one final dimension, Mr. Jewish Cockroach. A glance at any page of Mein Kakampf will demonstrate the centrality of antisemitism. You, Mr. Jew, are everywhere, a convenient symbol for everything hateful in an unfair world - not least its commitment to the ideas of the Enlightenment and the French Revolution which emancipated you, and made you so much more visible. You symbolize every conceivable villain: the hated capitalist financier, the revolutionary agitator, the rootless intellectual, every aspect of "the competition". You're too damn smart. You take a disproportionate share of professional jobs. You're a foreigner, a loathsome insect. Besides which, you killed Christ. Do you think you and yours are going to get out of this alive?

...he was thinking of an animal, a live animal, rather a disagreeable animal, a savage animal, an animal that growled and grunted sometimes, and talked sometimes, and lived in London, and walked about the streets, and wasn't made a show of, and wasn't led by anybody, and didn't live in a menagerie, and was never killed in a market, and was not a horse, or an ass, or a cow, or a bull, or a tiger, or a dog, or a pig, or a cat, or a bear. At every fresh question that was put to him, this nephew burst into a fresh roar of laughter; and was so inexpressibly tickled, that he was obliged to get up off the sofa and stamp. At last the plump sister, falling into a similar state, cried out: `I have found it out. I know what it is, Fred. I know what it is.'

Do you think you and yours are going to get out of this alive? Not without help, Gregor, not without big help. I urge you, with this, my dying breath, to somehow get to the President. This ancient pullet does not cry wolf. The sky is falling. Cluck, cluck. Bawk, bawk, bawk, bawk, bawk, bawk, bawk, bawk, bawk! Sssssssss.

I suppose I owe you a few words about my condition. I send

this package without risk: my life is already forfeit. I have
at last played out a "typical" role: the average age of death
in Werner's Syndrome is forty years. I am now exactly forty,
the scene of a grotesque race to the bottom. Which contestant
will have the honor of bringing down the beast? Forty years
old, and ancient as Corruption, a boy within a corpse. My skin
is atrophic and sclerodermatic - that is, I look like a cross
between an elephant, and the drought-cracked lands of your midwest. Continuing the American tour, my nose is dark and bubbled,
somewhat like the black, volcanic rocks of the Moon Craters
Monument. My face is the penultimate version of the picture of
Dorian Gray, except that I am now completely bald, the better
to see the misshapen skull, my dear. General calcification is
turning me into one big bone, though not even the dog seems
interested. Cataracts keep me from seeing clearly except in the
strongest light - such as I am now shining on this paper; I know
what it's like to look fuzzily out of a mosaic eye. Perhaps we
are converging: my leg and foot ulcers remind me of your wound,
also unhealing.

But every cloud has its sulfur lining: I can hardly walk
around for the pain, and this, you see, is good, since last
year I broke my osteoporotic right hip exercising my right to
exercise. Ewing's sarcoma, I have discovered, is a lovely little
cancer of the tissue around my left femur. Dr. Werner, the glad-
hand, tells me it's better to have this than meningioma. Thank
God for little blessings. My scleroderma is lately rejoicing in
the company of sclerotic arteries, though I can't say my heart
is as happy, especially at the insufficient trough of the anterior descending coronary, now almost completely occluded. My
kidneys, not to be left behind, are trying out their new act;
"End-Stage Renal Disease". Catchy title. The good doctor Werner-
San is proposing I become a human guinea pig for a new machine
which will suck out my blood, launder it, and give it back,
presumably cleaner and unharmed. I think I will pass. The good
news is that my central nervous system has been totally spared,

the better to appreciate and reflect on life's gifts. In short, my friend, I am a one-man Museum of Pathology, soon to be closed to the public. How poetic is Justice!

No need to write back. I enclose no address. The dead are not known to be avid readers.

Remember me!

Amadeus Ernst Hoffnung.

Gregor was in tears. Through his own silent moan he heard the distant voice of the most powerful man in the world. He listened as if hypnotized.

...a boy and a girl. Yellow, meagre, ragged, scowling, wolfish; but prostrate, too, in their humility. Where graceful youth should have filled their features out, and touched them with its freshest tints, a stale and shrivelled hand, like that of age, had pinched, and twisted them, and pulled them into shreds. Where angels might have sat enthroned, devils lurked, and glared out menacing. No change, no degradation, no perversion of humanity, in any grade, through all the mysteries of wonderful creation, has monsters half so horrible and dread. Scrooge started back, appalled. He tried to say they were fine children, but the words choked themselves, rather than be parties to a lie of such enormous magnitude. `They are Man's,' said the Spirit, looking down upon them. `This boy is Ignorance. This girl is Want. Beware them both, and all of their degree, but most of all beware this boy, for on his brow I see that written which is Doom, unless the writing be erased...

32. Disorder And Early Sorrow

Agitated though he was, Gregor knew better than to threaten White House celebrations with Amadeus's news, and found himself greeting laconically the most merry wish of "Merry Christmas!" and reflecting on the wisdom of Scrooge's "Bah! Humbug! What reason have I to be merry when I live in such a world as this?" After the reading, he retired to his closet, re-read the letter, and wept himself to sleep.

On Christmas morning, when much of the world was rejoicing in comfort and joy, G was taking a chilly walk alone down Pennsylvania Avenue, along Constitution and up Louisiana as if some unknown force was urging him to leave, just leave, there's Union Station, get on a train. But where to go? Where was the world acceptable? Back to starving proto-fascist Europe? Not likely. Africa, throttled by imperialism? South America, run by plutocracies for personal benefit? Antarctica? Too cold. His legs would stop working. Ridiculous thoughts. Here he was, close to the ear of the most powerful man on earth, a man through whom... Too cold. Better head for home. Bye, Union Station.

Circling around back east, he looked up at the huge Central Post Office, and instinctively clutched Amadeus's letter in his pocket. On a frieze over the great columns he spied two blocks of text. Fuzzy, hard to see, but they were enough to make him stop and try to focus.

MESSENGER OF SYMPATHY AND LOVE
SERVANT OF PARTED FRIENDS

CONSOLER OF THE LONELY
BOND OF THE SCATTERED FAMILY
ENLARGER OF THE COMMON LIFE

He supposed they were talking about the Post Office. *Die Winterreise* came galloping up from his music spring. *"Die Post bringt keinen Brief für dich. Was drängst du denn so wunderlich, Mein Herz?"* The mail brings no letters for you, so why do you throb so strangely, my heart? Ah, but he had a letter! He did have a letter. Bond of a scattered family, a servant of a parted friend. He walked fifty meters back, and stood under the right hand text. It was possible to use his tibias to manually squint.

CARRIER OF NEWS AND KNOWLEDGE

Yes, bad news, bad knowledge, Amadeus, you bastard!

INSTRUMENT OF TRADE AND INDUSTRY

...for one industrious, all-powerful roach...

PROMOTER OF MUTUAL ACQUAINTANCE
OF PEACE AND GOODWILL
AMONG MEN AND NATIONS.

Certainly. Now I make a such a difference. Franklin and I. Franklin and I and the U.S. Army, Navy, Air Force and Marine bombs promote Peace and Goodwill! *Jawohl!* His claw pierced the paper in his pocket. Very poetic, these buildings.

As G walked northeast along Massachusetts Avenue, the gay despair of the Schubert song drove him along like a two-horsed rig without a sled behind, Hobbes and Rousseau, Gregor$_1$ (Hopeful) and Gregor$_2$ (Hopeless), Henry Jekyll and Fredrick Hyde, galloping, galloping, *Liebeslied* and *Liebestod*. Before he knew it, he came smack onto the corner of Mt. Vernon Square. Ahead, on the left, a noisy crowd of black families were milling under the marquee of the Park Theater.

Charles Laughton
Clark Gable
in
Mutiny On The Bounty

Christmas matinee at noon, thought Gregor, Family Time. And his throbbing heart clenched up in his back with the contrast of his solo act. Best, perhaps, not to beat at all, my heart, oh my heart.

377

But it continued beating, and his legs led him into the thick of the crowd, partially out of a need for closeness and warmth, and partially out of curiosity, for the scene no longer seemed a simple waiting-for-the-doors-to-open. It felt more like a demonstration, or even the beginning of a riot.

"We all comin in whether you like it or not!"

"You pays your quarter apiece, and a dime for each kid — an you can come in just fine. But not before." The short, stumpy man guarded the door to the lobby, a pathetic white cork holding somehow against the black sea. The frightened attendant in the ticket booth did her best to pretend none of this was happening.

"We don't got no quarters..."

"Hey, we don't got no *dimes*!"

"And we don't got no Christmas dinner like youse goin home to."

"We want a movie where it's warm. Like here. Free! Spirit of Christmas!"

"Mo-vie! Mo-vie! Mo-vie! Mo-vie!" chanted a quickly escalating chorus, the effect thickened contrapuntally by a smaller second chorus of "Free, free, free, free".

The cork signaled to the ticket booth. The ticket booth picked up the telephone. Gregor was not in any mood to witness the aftermath. Even as he reached the end of the block, he heard the sirens approaching.

New York Avenue down to Pennsylvania, homeward bound, there. But was this a journey home? Was this home, this beautiful white house, classical, symmetrical, standing behind an iron fence in a well-trimmed park — in the midst of general misery? The President and his wife were certainly aware of, and even felt guilty about, the contrast; they had affronted Washington high society by trying to live more humbly than their predecessors. But home. Home it would be if the President would read Amadeus's letter, if he would take it seriously, do something about it — whatever he could. Maybe this is home. Maybe this will be home. Gregor stiffened his resolve, clutched the letter once more, marched past the guard with only a nod, in through the North Portico, and down to his room. Plop. Onto the straw. Overcoat still on. To stare into the darkness and wait.

****

Three days he waited, and on the third day he arose and went to Missy for an appointment. Though he wanted to honor the President's need for Christmas, he knew, as did everyone else in Washington, that on January 3rd, FDR was to address a joint session of Congress, the first such gathering since Woodrow Wilson's call for war, nineteen years before. If any statement about Germany were to be made, it would have to be discussed now. So on December 28, 1935, at 3:58 in the afternoon, Gregor made his way up to the Oval Office, Amadeus's letter in hand, Scotch-taped as needed.

The President was looking well after his brief Christmas respite. His family and friends had been worried about his sallowness and sagging energy. But this afternoon he was nothing short of perky.

"Mr. Herr Doktor Samsa!" With some difficulty, FDR stood up to greet him. "So you survived my Christmas reading?"

"Not survived. It was excellent. *Primo.* Everyone loves it."

"They're just flattering me."

"I have seen the great actors, in the great theaters of Europe, and ..."

"And you decided it would be more interesting to read your letter. I saw you there under the couch."

"No, I..." Gregor felt suddenly defensive. FDR's teasing had missed its self-deprecatory point.

"I'm sorry, I didn't mean to accuse you. I'm sure the letter was important — more important than the hundred thousandth reading of sentimentalia, well-written as it may be."

"Actually, the letter is interesting. And important. It is why I come to see you now."

"Oh?"

"I have a friend from Vienna, Amadeus Ernst Hoffnung, the owner of the circus I escape to from Prague. "

"With a name like that, he *should* be interesting. God-loving, serious hope. That's what we need."

"He is not your average circus-owner charlatan — you say charlatan? — type of person. Very, very smart he is, well-reading, interesting in many things. Also he is dead-sick. He may even be dead now. The letter took some months to get to me. I do not heard from him in thirteen years."

"I can see why it would be hard to concentrate on Dickens. What did Amadeus Ernst Hoffnung have to say?"

"I am hoping you can have time to read the letter."

"Well, let's give it a look."

Gregor handed over the sheets.

"It came with a book, *Mein Kampf*."

"Ah, yes. I've heard of it."

"You must read this book. I give it to you when I am finished."

"Looks like this letter has been through the wars."

"You mean the holes? I was clutching it with my not soft fingers."

"Here." FDR picked up some papers from the desk. "You read this, while I read yours. These are notes for my speech to Congress next Friday."

They both settled into chairs. Gregor could not believe what he was reading. For several years, he had been aware of all the carping from the left: FDR was trying to save capitalism; he was legitimating banks and big business, asking for their help; the New Deal was just the Old Deal in sheep's clothing. But this speech, the opening salvo of next year's campaign, this speech was ... revolutionary:

> *I've given big business its chance with the NRA and the RFC, and it has resisted all my pleas, has denounced every measure to help the desperate and the hungry as socialistic or some kind of effort to "Sovietize" the US. Now big business must be clearly identified as the enemy, as a discredited special interest.*
>
> *We have invited battle, and we have earned the hatred of entrenched greed.*
>
> *The enemies of progress are clear: business and financial monopoly, speculation, reckless banking, class antagonism, sectionalism and war profiteering rule America.*
>
> *Never before in all our history have these forces been so united against any one candidate as they stand today. They are unanimous in their hatred of me — and I welcome their hatred. I would like to*

have it said that in my first Administration the forces of selfishness and lust for power met their match. For my second administration I want it said that those forces will have met their master. I throw down the gauntlet.

Gregor felt the tingling in his husk that passes for sweating in blattids.

Every item of reform has had to be fought for inch by inch, and now the fight grows harder as recovery proceeds and renewed business profits can be poured into lobbies, control of mass communication, resistance to change of any sort.

G looked over to the man in the chair, the "Leader of the Free World", his crutches at his side, his braces showing below his cuffs. As if conscious of being stared at, FDR looked up from his reading.

"Gregor, this isn't the first time I've heard things like this. I've had two letters this year from Bill Dodd, our ambassador in Berlin, which talked about similar things. Not so focused on Jews. More on the general spirit of aggression. Is Hoffnung Jewish?"

"No. I don't think so. I never actually ask to him. But he knows much about Jewish thinking and Jewish history."

"He writes well. This is a very sad letter."

"You finished?"

"No. What I've read so far."

"It's saddest at the end. Saddest about him."

"I'll keep reading."

Gregor could not concentrate further on the President's notes. He skimmed them through to see if there were any references to Germany or Jews. None that he could find. Oh, there was this:

A point has been reached where the people of the Americas must take cognizance of growing ill-will, of marked trends toward aggression, of increasing armaments, of shortening tempers — a situation which has in it many of the elements that lead to the tragedy of a general war.

We need a two-fold neutrality that would bar the sale of military supplies to aggressor nations. Our help to other nations threatened by

aggression must be confined to moral help. They can't expect us to get
tangled up with their troubles in days to come.

That certainly would not satisfy Amadeus, nor speak to his predictions. G and the President would talk about it. That is why he was here.

"Terrible. Just ghastly." The President put the sheets down on the end table. "It makes me feel lucky to simply be paralyzed. I hope the poor man will be able to rest soon, God bless him." He had tears in his eyes.

"Mr. President, what can we do about it?

"Do? About Hitler? Not much. Germany is a sovereign nation; it does what it likes. Right now there are Germans wondering what they can do about the way we treat our Colored. Want them to intervene?"

"But we don't kill our Colored."

"Same as they do. An occasional lynching. The Scottsboro boys still in jail waiting for the chair. But mostly we starve them, break up their families, keep them from voting, from having any say..."

"But making concentration camps..."

"Concentration camps? So do we! Remember last year Gene Talmadge in Georgia, rounding up labor organizers, keeping them for months behind barbed wire outside Atlanta? Gregor, we've got to deal with our own issues before we can go messing with others'. Here, look at this."

He handed G the letter he had been reading.

"Read it out loud. Just start right there in the middle..." Gregor wondered why the President was making him perform.

"About that time they were rushing the stairway...we put a table against the door."

"He's describing an attack last week on textile workers' headquarters in Montgomery, Alabama. Read louder. Give it more expression."

" A portion of the glass door was exposed above the table, and bricks began to come through the glass...(a newspaper phoned at this point.) I said, 'They're tearing the building down. They're tearing the offices apart and beating our men up...if it is possible for you, I don't know how much longer I will be able to talk, send in some state police, if you can, because, I said, I can't talk to you any longer.'

"Good reading!" the President exclaimed. Have you had experience with these things? Here, try this one." He reached into his "bedtime folder" — the collection of citizen letters he usually read late at night, but which he often studied during the day. Gregor took a postcard minutely written in a woman's hand.

"That one's from North Carolina, I believe," said the President.

"The mayor led a mob of 200 people to the house of a union organizer. On the lawn outside, the town alderman said, 'if anyone in the bunch will go with me, I'll stick a match to the house and burn them up like rats, kids and all.'

This is from North Carolina, USA?"

"It's not from North Carolina, Bavaria. We've got our work cut out for us right here, Gregor. Oh, here's a good one. You up for one more? Michigan. Up on the peninsula.

"One of the leafleters was attacked by four or five men who kicked him in his stomach finally forced him to the cement and there a separate individual grabbed him by each foot and each hand, and his legs were spread apart and other men proceeded to kick him in the crotch and groin and left kidneys and around the head and also to gore him with their heels in the abdomen. After they left I stayed there until practically all the literature had been gathered from the ground and it became very quiet around there and relatively still."

"But doesn't the Wagner Act make this things illegal?"

"My friend, there's the Law of the Land and the Law of the Jungle. People are angry out there. This past year alone we've had two thousand strikes involving more than a million workers, and police and company thugs have left a hundred dead and six times that many wounded — all because some folks need a bit more bread for their meager tables, and Gregor — that bread might eat into the profits. Greed! It sickens me. That's what we've got to concentrate on. Give the common man some power against rich employers. That's why the NLRA is crucial. We've got to get that really working."

"So there will be no more killing..."

"So there'll be a Wagner Act at all — with teeth."

Time out! this historian cries.

****

383

Wagner Act. NLRA. NRA, WPA, CCC, RFC, AAA, the whole alphabet soup of the New Deal. Perhaps a little reminder would be welcomed by those for whom, three score and three years later, the story is somewhat hazy.

The Wagner Act, officially the National Labor Relations Act of 1935, the single most important piece of labor legislation this century, was instituted to eliminate employer interference with workers' ability to organize. Through a National Labor Relations Board appointed by the President, it established Washington as the final arbiter of labor disputes. The act defined "unfair labor practices" such as setting up a company union or firing workers for organizing or joining unions. Under the Act, the NLRB, when petitioned, could order elections for workers to choose a union and make it mandatory for employers to bargain with any union so chosen. You can see why it might raise a few hackles among the ruling class.

The NLRB was the Great Satan of capitalist discontent. Any employee or labor organization could go to a regional office and file a charge of unfair labor practice. A field examiner would then investigate the case by talking to employer and employees. If the investigator and regional director found evidence to support employee claims, they again suggested settlement without legal action. But if the employer refused to comply with the Board's requests, the regional director could issue a complaint citing the unfair practices in detail. If the employer still refused to make accommodation, he could answer the complaint at a hearing before a trial examiner. Only 5% of cases ever reached this stage. At the hearing the employer could call his witnesses and cross-examine witnesses for the Board. Any labor unions interested in the controversy could comment. The trial examiner would then file an "intermediate report," and anyone concerned had time to file objections. The report — with objections — was reviewed first by the Board's own review section in Washington, and finally by the Board itself. If the NLRB found the employer guilty as charged, he was again urged to bring himself within the law without further litigation. If he refused, the Board would petition a circuit Court of Appeals to direct the employer to conform with the findings. Even then, the employer had the right to a Court review. It was only when the Circuit Court of Appeals upheld the Board's order that the employer came under legal compulsion to obey the law. And even then, he might still appeal to the Supreme Court.

I go to this level of detail to give the reader a feeling for the cautious and gradualist approach to solving problems that were commonly health- and even life-threatening for the worker. A polite and plodding response to urgent cries for help. Nevertheless, employers, used to the government easing their way, reacted with the rage of scorned lovers.

"We'll have to be giving our examiners hazardous-duty pay," said Roosevelt, only half joking. "Here, look at this." He handed the roach a file marked "NLRB". Gregor scanned a clipping from a newspaper in North Carolina:

> *When the NLRB examiner moved into town he found a situation as tense and unpredictable as a Saturday night saloon thirty seconds before the first bottle smashes the mirror behind the bar. "The s.o.b. thinks he owns the town," commented a shop owner on Garfield Street. "Let me an' him go downstairs in the cellar an' see who comes up."*
>
> *The Wallace, Idaho Gazette: NO MEALS FOR GODDAM COMMUNISTS*
>
> *Times-Ledger, Florenceville, Indiana: SECOND POISONING OF NLRB ATTORNEY*
>
> *Steubenville, Ohio Post-Examiner: TRIAL EXAMINER HANGED IN EFFIGY*
>
> *Newton, Iowa Clarion: At a hastily called press conference today, Gov. Nelson G. Karschel declared, "You can tell the cockeyed world that there will be no Labor Board hearings in the military district of Iowa."*
>
> *"Look at the editorial, there, on that pink page," the President suggested.*
>
> *WAGNER ACT DENOUNCED: Dictator Roosevelt's latest excrescence is the National Labor Relations Act, passed last week by a close margin of both houses. While claiming to "smooth out obstructions*

to the free flow of commerce", it has already succeeded in making an intolerable situation infinitely worse. The Act is patently one-sided — exclusively a labor law. It prejudges the employer to be a scoundrel without rights in equity. It penalizes him for even a mild expression of personal opinion, but it provides no penalties for fraud, coercion, or violence on the part of any hotheaded labor minority. It sets up a Board that is simultaneously judge, jury, and prosecutor, and provides no real opportunity for an impartial court review of the Board's decisions. It violates the right of free speech, the rights of property, the inviolability of a contract. It promotes lawlessness, destroys discipline, and encourages strikes against society. It represents a vicious and subversive political philosophy, a dangerous intrusion of radical bureaucracy into private enterprise, and a threat to the entire industrial structure of the U.S.

"Unadulterated twaddle," the President declared, "based on ninety percent ignorance!"

"Yes, certainly," said Gregor. "But can we get back to helping the Jews in..."

"Helping the Jews? We're already called "the Jew Deal". We've got Rosenman and Lehman, and Morgenthau, and Brandeis and Cohen. And Frankfurter, with all his brilliant "hot dogs" inserting themselves in every roll of government. We've got 82% of American Jews behind us. How much more can we help?"

"And don't forget the niggers!" Louis Howe poked his head in at the door, at which he must have been listening through FDR's last tirade. He, too, was now in a wheelchair, dragging two green tanks along with it, with oxygen mask at one hand, and a pack of Sweet Caporals at the other. A great stench of incense and stale tobacco came with him through the door. Eyes sunken, more wizened, smaller, more simian than ever, Howe spat out crazy lines between coughs, wheezing, pulling in enough breath to continue, his voice coming as if from the far side of the grave — where in four months the rest of him would abide.

"The niggers your wife sleeps with. The nigger commies she sodomizes." FDR began his roaring laugh, privy to some private joke, perhaps remembering more newspaper madness they had shared.

"Ah — listen, Gregor Samsa, listen to his insane laugh. This is not the laugh of a simple paralytic. No, this is the laugh of a crazed syphlitic..."

"These are all quotes, Gregor, genuine, recorded opinions..."

"...so poisoned with mercury treatments as to be a mercurial play-boy, a cynical fomenter of class hatred, a power-mad dictator, agent of Soviet Russia, a very traitor to his class, the most destructive man in all of American history! Marx without a beard. Lenin without a mustache. A slick old thimble-rigger building a huge political machine in Washington paid for with waste and extravagance, and your tax dollars, a hog-joweled, weasel-eyed, sponge-columned, jelly-spined, pussy-footing, four-flushing, charlotte-russed Commonist! What can you expect from such a man?"

FDR was convulsed with laughter — which made this misshapen homunculus, this eccentric, guiding genius cough even more, trying to contain his own. The President calmed down, sighing, and brought his mentor up to date.

"Gregor wants me to do something about Hitler, about his treatment of the Jews."

"Mr. Samsa, a man like this (he indicated the President) cannot carry your banner. A man like this...why even, did you see, the American Jewish Committee opposes any suggestion of Frankfurter going on the court? They already have Brandeis, their liberal Jew. They don't want to 'fan the fires of antisemitism', as they say. Have you heard Coughlin lately? Enough already with the Jews!." He broke into an uncontrollable coughing spasm.

Gregor picked up Amadeus's letter, and waited for him to stop.

"My friend in Berlin assures me we will have to go to war with Herr Hitler. We must prepare. He send me copy of *Mein Kampf.* You have read it?"

"Read it? I read it on the toilet, and wipe my ass with it shit by shit. We know it well, my ass and me."

"Could we make our references to Germany stronger?" the President asked.

"Franklin, what's in there is enough. The speech will cover aggression, increasing militarization, the threat of war. But we're not going to war, remember? Congress won't buy it. The voters won't stand for it. They won't stand for you if you stand for it. Did you see the petition that came in yesterday?"

"No. What petition?"

Howe shut down his oxygen, waited one two three four five seconds, and lit up a cigarette.

"A hundred and fifty-four thousand students from all over the country: "I refuse to bear arms in any war the United States Government may conduct." Signed. Name and address. That's the tip of a very big, very cold iceberg, Franklin. You think the Great War vets will step in and take the place of their kids? Besides, supposing you could get the country behind you, and you could recruit an army, and you did go to war with Hitler. Or Franco. Or whoever. You know who would be president? All your friends who control steel, oil, shipping, munitions, and mines. When the war is over your government will be in their hands."

"What do you think of that, Gregor?" the President asked.

"I don't know what I think. But I think I have to go. My appointment time is finish. The smoke is making me hard to breathe and think." He didn't mention the wound weeping in his back.

"Labor, Gregor," the president said. "Let's choose our battles. For the moment, labor versus capital. If we win this, we'll have seventy-five million more voters behind us, and next term, we'll be able to do what needs doing. Keep me informed about Germany. Whatever you find out."

"I will." He felt dizzy and confused, and left the two men behind the closed brown door, to plot the speech, and the second presidential campaign.

33. Days Of The Locust

As March sunlight gilded their breakfast tables, Washingtonians read in the morning papers that in two weeks the Japanese cherry trees around the Tidal Basin would be in full bloom. The same day Kansans breakfasted by lamp light and read in their morning papers that one of the worst dust storms in the history of their State was sweeping darkly overhead. Damp sheets hung over the windows, but table cloths were grimy. Urchins wrote their names on the dusty china. Food had a gritty taste. Dirt drifted around doorways like snow. People who ventured outside coughed and choked as the fields of Kansas, Colorado, Wyoming, Nebraska and Oklahoma rose and took flight through the windy air. (Time Magazine, April 1, 1935)

Dust unto dust. Rapes of wrath. Who can forget the haunted faces in dust-bowl photography, or the eerie dust-beginning of Steinbeck's great dust-bowl novel? Dust storms were Nature's cloud over the New Deal, upping all antes, downing much hope. The drought that had plagued agriculture in the early 1930s returned with a vengeance in 1934, and by the following spring, mid-Westerners were watching their farmland blow away.

And after the dust clouds came the locusts. The sky would darken inter-

mittently, this time with hungry living creatures, their habitats parched —
living, swarming creatures, leaving no flora behind them — a secondary
plague perhaps, not as well remembered as the dust, but for those whose
lives and livelihoods were decimated, the straw that broke the dying camel's back. In 1936, various species of "devastating hoppers" were reported
to have destroyed U. S. crops valued at over $100 million. South and
Central America were in locust-crisis: northward swarming from Mexico,
and westward swarming from the mountain states threatened the agricultural fields of California and the forests of Oregon. The U.S. Department
of Agriculture took a serious view of the situation and set about to avert
the worst. In the depth of the depression, vast crop and income losses were
not propitious for recovery — or for re-election. Among others, Gregor
was tapped to serve.

> "Know then thyself, presume not God to scan;
> The proper study of mankind is man — says Man."

Thurber's witty comment on Pope notwithstanding, there is some
wisdom in species self-study. As it took women to unpack the culturally
hidden dimensions of womanhood in the 60s and 70s, men to look into
the interstices of maleness in the 80s, and organizational self-study to fuel
the Quality Improvement movements of the 90s, so there is unique value
in insects researching *Insectiva*. It takes one to know one.

Gregor, you recall, once Political Analyst for Hoover Affairs, had been
rebaptized "Entomological Consultant", assistant to the Assistant Secretary
of Agriculture, his handler, Rex Tugwell. In this new role, he had successfully solved the ant problem in the White House kitchen with his brave
discovery of boric acid as a non-toxic insecticide.[21] Meeting with both
Tugwell and Wallace, G was asked for help in keeping locust swarms out of
California and Oregon. Here was the problem:

On the one hand we have the charming green and yellow grasshopper, of Grasshopper and Ant fame, the gracehoper, "always jigging ajog,

---

21 The days of heroic experimentation-on-self seem to be over, as the current scientific community comes down *en masse* against a proposal by researchers to self-inject
with an experimental HIV vaccine. Science marches on no longer; timid shuffling
seems the order of the day.

hoppy on akkant of his joyicity." He is the pride of every child over three who is taught to delight in, not scream, at the prickly creature landing on wrist or cheek. (The younger set seem aware of the secret threat, universally terrified at the attack.) On the other hand we have the swarming locust — not a different species, but the same species transformed like a mutant teenager in Halloween black and orange, with shorter legs and longer wings, ripe for swarming. What makes our green, chirping Jekylls transform into death-dealing Hydes? That is the question.

Food shortage clearly has something to do with it, as post-drought swarming would attest. But swarming also occurs out of excellent conditions, when population expansion leads to crowding. Was crowding itself the key, drought forcing large numbers into small habitable areas? And if crowding were the stimulus, critical mass, as it were, how might the response be aborted; how might individuals be preventively dispersed? Entomological researchers, Gregor among them, stood at this crossroads.

There are several ways to think about the problem. Modern science would council a rational approach: controlled experimentation on isolated elements of the puzzle. The ancients, however, took an entirely different tack. The Hebrew Bible describes the beasts — swarms of devourers, multipliers, gallopers, whizzers, shearers, concealers, finishers — such are the Bible's Hebrew words for "locust". What did the Hebrews do? They ate them! The Rabbis decided that locusts were to be included among the "clean edible animals" in dietary law; come the plague, no more plants, yum!, locusts instead. The heads, legs and wings were stripped off; they were toasted and ground into meal. Some enthusiasts, like John the Baptist, ate them raw. With honey. Leave it to the Jews!

By the time of the writing of Revelations (ca. 69 AD), we are into a more modern sensibility, at least with respect to locusts.

> *And the sun and the air were darkened by reason of the smoke of the pit. And there came out of the smoke locusts upon the earth: and unto them was given power, as the scorpions of the earth have power. And it was commanded them that they should not hurt the grass of the earth, neither any green thing, neither any tree; but only those*

men which have not the seal of God in their foreheads. And to them it was given that they should not kill them, but that they should be tormented five months: and their torment was as the torment of a scorpion, when he striketh a man. And in those days shall men seek death, and shall not find it: and shall desire to die, and death shall flee from them. And the shapes of the locusts were like unto horses prepared unto battle: and on their heads were as it were crowns like gold, and their faces were as the faces of men. And they had hair as the hair of women, and their teeth were as the teeth of lions; and the sound of their wings was as the sound of chariots of many horses running to battle. And they had tails like unto scorpions, and there were stings in their tails; and their power was to hurt men five months. And they had a king over them, which is the angel of the bottomless pit. (Rev. 9:3-11)

I use the word "modern" in that the image on John's screen is so intensely psychological: the devourers turned inside, gnawing inescapably at the heart, inside the skull of "those men which have not the seal of God in their foreheads." Gregor spoke a lot about this passage when he explained his locust work to me. He was intrigued by its flat contrast with Proverbs 30:27: "The locusts have no king, yet go they forth all of them by bands." Normally, the Greek Testament transforms and builds upon its Hebrew predecessor. Yet "king" is not "no king".

Gregor's radical move was the equation, *king = no king*, that is, the lack of a guiding principal was the bottomless pit. The better part of him wanted to work with locusts entirely as a psychic metaphor — much as Jung later did with UFOs, except that G imagined being able to control them psycho-politically, using majoritarian thought-forms. But this was too arcane for even Henry Wallace, who advised him to stick to Cartesian duality and get out the Bunsen burner. He even provided a budget to convert a small White House pantry, empty since the move to the underground north storage space, into a basic laboratory in which Gregor might perform repeatable, reportable experiments. Keep must be earned. So G was forced by social, cultural, and political pressure to perform the famous — if merely "scientific" — experiments which bear his name.

His classical experiments for the USDA were directed at two areas:

1. finding the factors that produced gregarious, swarming behavior in populations of what were once solitary individuals, and

2. exploring techniques to prevent such metamorphosis, and such behavior.

The work on the first group was typical of the simplicity of ground-breaking science. Experimenting with immature, wingless hoppers supplied to him by the Ag Department, he noticed a tendency for them to gather thigmotactically in the corners of their cages, and therefore introduced circular containers to eliminate clumping. He divided the floor into thirty-six sections, put in hoppers eighteen at a time and recorded their positions after they had settled down. Non-swarming hoppers, including migratory locusts reared in isolation, ended up two or more to a section 35% of the time. But hoppers "reared crowded" ended up two or more to a section 50-70% of the time. Conclusion: hoppers used to crowding choose crowds. After four days of solitary confinement, they would unlearn, and revert to 35%.

Was the learning visual? Gregor placed individual hoppers in small celluloid cages set down in crowds of other hoppers. When freed, they did not then tend to aggregate. But when they were place directly in amongst the crowd, they did learn to aggregate. Blinded hoppers (Gregor made little hoods), also became gregarious. Touch seemed to make the difference.

While humans, for instance, might be moved by the touch of a loving hand, they are often repulsed by similar stroking from a claw. Gregor knew this well. Did touch for locusts have to be from another locust, or would other kinds of touch do? G found that a cage full of roly-bugs — terrestrial crustaceans, not even insects — could turn locusts gregarious. What else might do so? In a fit of inspiration, after having witnesses a riotous tickling scene with the Roosevelt kids, he invented his celebrated "Locust Tickling Machine" (Fig. 1),a jar with many fine wires and threads rotated by a wind vane. The kitchen staff found it most amusing to see a large electric fan blowing down on a field of children's pinwheels, tickling 64 grasshoppers, each in their individual 64oz. mayonnaise jars. The result? Wire-tickled hoppers became gregarious. He was homing in on an answer.

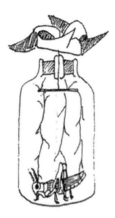

Fig. 1 Heuschreckekitzelapparat (Locust Tickling Machine)

It was the "vision vs. touch" series which led Gregor to his most important work, the discovery of what he called smeltrons, what we today would call pheromones. How could he be other than the first? How could humans, with the nasal sensitivity of a fireplug, possibly notice such a factor? His crucial experiment was as follows:

In the tunnel leading to the Executive Office Building, G set up two parallel runs of glass tubing, 10 meters in length, with setups as in Fig 2.

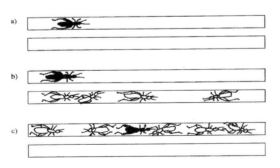

(Fig. 2). Gregor's discovery of smelltrons

The test locust in (a) marched 30% of the time, in (b), with visual stimulus, 34% of the time (statistically insignificant difference), and in (c), with visual and tactile stimulus, 84% of the time. Predictable. The surprise came when G repeated the experiment, replacing the glass partitions with wire. This time, (a) produced 31% marching, and (c) 82%, as before, but (b) produced 55% marching, a significant increase. Some new stimulus, not visual, not tactile, seemed to be at play. The numbers were similar no matter what kind of wire was used, though in (b), marching decreased very slightly as the gauge of the mesh decreased. Evidently, something small was being carried in the air between compartments.

Unlike his human colleagues at the Ag Department lab on Constitution Ave, G could smell something going on. In fact, for him, the odor of a gregarious colony was quite different from that of an equal population of individual hoppers, and became more intense as the colony prepared to swarm. It was the difference between a sunny, placid F major, (as, he said, in the opening of the *Pastoral Symphony*) and a slightly acrid, antsy C# minor (as in the opening of the Mahler Fifth). The change from individual to swarming colony was for G an olfactory modulation as sweeping as anything in Wagner. Almost every member of the White House staff — including upper-level administration — was asked to smell the two extremes: no one could tell the difference. "Just smells like bugs to me" was the typical response. (G delighted in diagnosing "human anosmia" (Greek, ιιοι + *osme*, smell) because it sounded like people with their noses cut off, a favorite image from Gogol.)

He postulated the existence of "smeltrons", a species of volatile chemicals secreted in minute amounts which might be responsible for anatomical, physiological or behavioral change. Perhaps the name was unfortunate; it was replaced in the 50s by the now common "pheromone" (from the Greek *pherein*, to transfer, and *hormon*, to excite.)

His assumption of intra-specific chemical communication was not without precedent. About ten years earlier, Karl von Frisch (subsequently of "dance of the bees" fame) had demonstrated a similar phenomenon. Having marked a minnow with an incision near its tail, he was surprised to see its schoolmates fleeing when he reintroduced the wounded fish among them. Philoctetes, of course, comes to mind. Frisch assumed that some "alarm substance" was being emitted, warning the school away from a potential threat.

There was also the early work on sexual attraction in the silk-worm moth *(Bombyx mori)*, underway at about the same time, but it is unclear if G was aware of it. Though he denied it, it was definitely in the air in the biological community of the mid- thirties. Male moths were attracted miles away to empty cages which had once held a female. When their antennae were coated with lacquer, they could no longer orient to even the most attractive, neighboring female. Evidence was strong for some air-borne molecular process.

I don't mean to accuse G of plagiarism. Darwin and Wallace did come up simultaneously with Evolution, and there is no reason Gregor might not have hit independently upon the idea of smell-communication. What is clear is that, with his invention of the electroantennograph (Fig. 3), he contributed immeasurably to the investigation.

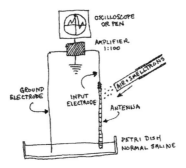

Fig. 3. Electroantennograph. Filtered air containing test samples is blown over the antenna, which responds electrically to bio-active materials at picogram amounts $(1 \times 10^{-12}$ — one trillionth of a gram) undetectable by the human nose.

Why not, thought Gregor, why not use the smell organ itself as a bio-logical conductor, and measure quantitatively the activity of potential smeltrons? With the invaluable help of James Johnson, a White House electrician and ham radio enthusiast, Gregor was able to set locust antennae into a circuit which, suitably amplified, would write its enthusiasm, or lack thereof, on a cathode ray screen, or moving piece of paper. He of course used only one antenna per hopper, and honored his experimental subjects as crippled war-heroes in the battle of Science vs. Darkness.

The electroantennograph enabled him, and other later investigators to test thousands of compounds, organic and inorganic, even complex, difficult to analyze mixtures such as vacuum cleaner air or used alcohol from chandelier scrubs. After a year of painstaking work, three compounds stood out as being especially provocative — in a class by themselves:

1. An ethanol extraction of the bark of the Guatemalan trey bush, (*Porplexyia ornamentata*), sent to Henry Wallace from one of Nicholas Roerich's biological/spiritual expeditions — which were to bring the Secretary of Agriculture such grief [22]. Depending on concentration, it could either attract or disperse. The material was too rare and too politically hard to come by to be of much practical use.

2. An acetone extraction of thorax chitin from young, dead male swarmers. A disperser, related perhaps to von Frisch's "alarm substance". On the surface, this might seem an excellent source, but Gregor was against the kind of large, frontally aggressive activities that would be necessary to acquire sufficient quantities. (The Manhattan Project's quest for U^{235} and plutonium pre-figured.)

3. Human female axillary sweat. A attractant. This seemed to have the most promise, especially in warm regions where the locust problem was greatest. Just a simple absorbent pad taped under each armpit between the months of June and early September — from White House staff alone — might contain enough smeltronic activity to protect all of Montgomery County.

How protect?

A. An attracting smeltron, while possibly bringing large groups together,

---

22 In 1934, Wallace had sent his admired Nicholas Roerich — a Russsian painter, writer, archaeologist, philosopher, occultist, and public figure — to Central Asia to collect drought-resistant grasses. But once in Asia, Roerich focused his researches on trying to find the legendary Shambala. Britain and Japan thought him a Russian spy, and Wallace recalled him and his expedition. During the 1940 elections, Republicans seized on the diplomatic scandal and what they saw as Wallace's bizarre religious tendencies. During the 1948 campaign, several journalists, Westbrook Pegler and H.L. Mencken among them, accused Wallace of being "messianic" and mentally "off-center", helping to destroy his Progressive Party run against Truman for president. And so, with Wallace again displaced, we suffered the cold war and its hotter sequelae.

disrupts mating by fatiguing olfactory sense and masking normal olfactory plumes. The end result is a population unlikely to reach swarming density.

B. A dispersing smeltron, like any anti-deodorant, keeps individuals far enough apart to preclude the touching necessary for swarm metamorphosis. A dispersing smeltron acceptable to Gregor had yet to be found.

Two other potential strategies, longer term, seemed to others to be worth thinking about.

C. Attractive smeltrons might be used to lure the insects into traps. Tractor-drawn trappers — the Simpson Locust- Crusher, the Adams Locust-Pan, and the King Suction Machine — were hopelessly inadequate in decimating large swarms. But if they could actually pull locusts in? Some members of the White House Security Staff, especially the Park Police, were passionate about this strategy. Gregor, as mentioned, was not enthusiastic about genocidal approaches. Moreover, he argued that no one knew what proportion of a wild population would need to be killed to make a difference. If only smeltron-sensitive males were trapped, it might require 85-90% capture — a difficult goal to achieve. Then, what to do with the trappees? Burning them might set off incalculable smeltronic effects. There was little commercial promise as a foodstuff in a predominantly Christian population. Trap deployment and maintenance would be expensive. Gregor was against it.

D. A longer range strategy of greater interest to Gregor might have involved attractive smeltrons as bait in sampling traps. If population and density trends could be accurately read, insecticides could be more sparingly applied, only as needed, and increasing trap hits might have provided early warning to farmers and USDA agents urging preventive or protective action.

I say "might have", because there was no big locust outbreak in 1937. Nor in 1938. And with the recession of '37-'38 came slackening enthusiasm for WHIRL (White House Institute for Research on Locusts), and a drying up of meager funds. It was not until April 1939, fully eight months after Gregor had dismantled the mayonnaise jars, and given 64 pinwheels to a group of visiting Alaskan children, that an unusual infestation of grasshoppers appeared in the Big Smokey Valley of Nevada. But by that time, Hitler had invaded Czechoslovakia.

34. Aghast From The Past

. . . Bput by that time, Hitler had invaded Czechoslovakia. Thus does an era pass with the drop of an independent clause. Yet that was how it felt. It could be argued that the era ended on the night of November 9th, 1938, when *Kristallnacht* laid down its fiery shards. Ninety-one Jews dead, hundreds seriously injured, thousands more humiliated and terrorized, eight thousand Jewish businesses gutted and 177 synagogues burned to the ground. Not bad for a night's work. And who paid for the damages? The Jews, of course, as 30,000 of the richest were arrested, and released only on surrender of all their wealth. Within a week, Goering ordered an indemnity of one billion marks to be paid by the impoverished Jewish community. And if Jews thought their insurance policies might cover their damages, they found out that the rules had changed — insurance payments to Jews were prohibited. For Gregor, as for many international observers, the new order had definitively arrived.

One might also argue that, domestically, the era had ended with the end of the New Deal. Over five years, it had strode, then skittishly stepped, and finally inched against the limits of the possible in changing the dynamics of American life. Dams, parkways, and public buildings had been built. One could drive majestically across the Golden Gate Bridge. The Jefferson Memorial proclaimed FDR's idol, the man whose words "I TREMBLE FOR MY COUNTRY WHEN I REFLECT THAT GOD IS JUST" now stand in foot-high letters overlooking the Tidal Basin. In cities throughout the country, there were housing projects for the poor and the black, there were more hospitals, firehouses, schools and airports, and the blind now had talking books. Inner-city youths were roaming the forests with the CCC, planting trees, and not suspicion. Writers were paid to write, painters to paint, actors to act.

Yet after five years of activist government, unemployment was essentially the same, the large-business community was still ferociously opposed, plotting its revenge, and again the seeds of political reaction were sprouting as Martin Dies and HUAC began to flex their adolescent, red-baiting muscle. And finally, there was resistance from the New Deal's very *raison d'etre,* the common man. A white farmer in Tennessee told one of those WPA writer types,

"I hold to the good old ways; that's the best ways, when all is said and done... Take this TV and A, this electricity stuff, they talk about these days. It would come through here if we'd vote it in. Everybody studied it over. But you take this electricity, them wires — why they's power in them wires. Power to kill a body. Wires will come down, then it's mourning for somebody. Yes, we're afraid of that stuff. They's things the good Lord never meant mankind to fuddle with. So we turned the TV and A down."

(I have to say this reminds me of recent fulminations against the Cassini Probe. "They's plutonium in that can. Power to kill a body. That can comes down, it's mourning for somebody." Are we to say the latter is enlightened and the former benighted?) In any case, the New Deal had reached its asymptote, and the era was over... waiting for something. That something seemed to have a German accent.

With locust funding drying up and public apathy setting in, Gregor was spending much time over at the Museum of Natural History, his second attempt, this time as biologist, to compass the scope of animal, vegetable and mineral. It was not yet the era of "interactive" museums. Many exhibits seemed right out of Fischer von Waldheim's *Zoognosia: tabulis synopticis illustrata, in usum praelectionum Academiae Imperialis Medico-Chiurgicae Mosquensis,* that huge leather volume, with tables and illustrations of every known species of animal — his first reading jag *chez* Amadeus.

Yet it was one particular beast which had initiated his visits, a creature far from *Insectiva*, a party at the large-size end of *Animalia* which called to him. It was Ickes, he recalled, who had first spoken to him of *Moby Dick*, — this in regard to G's study of English. The head of the Public Works Administration thought he might be ready for this torrent of high and mighty speech. And lo, the very day of that encounter, Gregor felt a copy calling to him from the library shelves at the end of his hall, the Rockwell Kent edition it was, one of the proud productions of the WPA. *"Call me Ishmael,"* he read, and then, *"Whenever I find myself growing grim about the mouth,"* (he did feel tension in his mouthparts), *"whenever it is a damp, drizzly November in my soul,"* (it was precisely damp and drizzly, in a strangely chitin-chilling April), *"whenever I feel myself involuntarily pausing before coffin warehouses* (or the U.S. Army Museum of Pathology), *and bringing up the rear of every funeral* (or bad-news session) *I meet; and especially whenever my hypos get such an upper hand of me, that it requires a strong moral principle to prevent me from deliberately stepping into the street, and methodically knocking people's hats off* (not an unamusing prospect, he thought) — *then, I account it high time to get to sea as soon as I can. This is my substitute for pistol and ball."*

Standing in the middle of the small, cream-colored library, with its green rug and its chandelier once owned by James Fenimore Cooper, Gregor knew he would spend his next year with this book.

I have in front of me G's own Modern Library copy of *Moby Dick,* full of underlinings, word definitions, marginal starrings, question marks and comments. What a rich gloss on what was absorbing him from June 1938 (the date of acquisition is on the inside front cover) until August, 14, 1939 (written with an exclamation point, under "Finis" on the last page). It's hard for me to imagine that Gregor, a non-native speaker of English, could fully penetrate what Lewis Mumford so well characterized as a Symphony: "Every resource of language and thought, fantasy, description, philosophy, natural history, drama, broken rhythms, blank verse, imagery, symbol, is utilized to sustain and expand the great theme." Even in the 40's when I knew him, Gregor's spoken English was not perfect; he was constantly asking me for connotations and elucidations of even common expressions. Still, the annotation is dense, and bespeaks a deep involvement.

He reads

Men may seem detestable as joint stock-companies and nations; knaves,
fools, and murderers they may be; men may have mean and meagre faces;
but man, in the ideal, is so noble and so sparkling, such a grand and glowing
creature, that over any ignominious blemish in him all his fellow should run
to throw their costliest robes. ...This august dignity I treat of, is not the dignity
of kings and robes, but that abounding dignity which has no robed investi-
ture. Thou shalt see it shining in the arm that wields a pick or drives a spike;
that democratic dignity which, on all hands, radiates without end from God;
Himself! The center and circumference of all democracy! His omnipresence, our
divine equality!"

and adds as doubly underlined *"Richtig!"* in the margin, as if Melville
had captured and expressed his profound love of Equality and Fraternity. At
the same time (such is the unbearable tension of the book), he marks *"Ego*
non baptizo te in nomine patris, sed in nomine diaboli", Ahab's anti-baptism
of the harpoon dedicated to the destruction of the White Whale, with a
marginal note which continues on the next page:

AMERICAN MALICE, THE ROOT. "I AM DARKNESS LEAPING OUT OF
LIGHT." I TOO. NO FAUST. AHAB DYES, ACCEPT DAMNATION RESIGNED
TO FATE. NO LOVE FOR FELLOW WRETCHES (LEAR), BUT UNCOVERS
WHOLE HATE, TURNS HARPOON, MADE FOR UNHUMAN WHALE ON
HUMAN CREW!

Marking his similarity with Ahab, he underlines Ahab's strange scar:

Threading its way out from among his gray hairs, and continuing right
down his tawny scorched face and neck, till it disappeared in his clothing, you
saw a slender rod-like mark, lividly whitish. It resembled that perpendicular
seam sometimes made in the straight lofty trunk of a great tree, when the upper
lightning tearingly darts down it, and without wrenching a single twig, peels
and grooves out the bark from top to bottom, ere running off into the soil,
leaving the tree still greenly alive, but branded. Whether that mark was born
with him, or whether it was the scar left by some desperate wound, no one could
certainly say.

and notes in the margin, "MINE IS TREE OF KNOWLEDGE GOOD/EVIL", referring, obviously to his apple-induced, unhealing wound, and "THE INFINITE OBSCURE OF HIS BACKGROUND", referring both to the mad Captain and himself.

Given his decision six years later for ritual suicide, I find his starring of Queequeg's un-suicide exceptionally interesting:

Now that he had apparently made every preparation for death; now that his coffin was proved a good fit, Queequeg suddenly rallied; soon there seemed no need of the carpenter's box: and thereupon, when some expressed their delighted surprise, he, in substance, said that the cause of his sudden convalescence was this; — at a critical moment, he had just recalled a little duty ashore, which he was leaving undone; and therefore had changed his mind about dying: he could not die yet, he averred. They asked him, then, whether to live or die was a matter of his own sovereign will and pleasure. He answered, certainly. In a word, it was Queequeg's conceit, that if a man made up his mind to live, mere sickness could not kill him: nothing but a whale, or a gale, or some violent, ungovernable, unintelligent destroyer of that sort.

To this his comment was "GREAT MAN, NOT A 'COMMON MAN'", alluding to the rhetoric of the New Deal, about which he was conflicted.

It is probable that he identified too, with Ahab's remarkable prey. The short comment next to *"He piled upon the whale's white hump the sum of all the general rage and hate felt by his whole race from Adam down,"* was "JEWS/ME", and his subsequent visits to the museum, as much to worship as to study, bespoke a wonder akin to self-recognition.

The back cover and the thick binding page before it gave him room for a few general notes which I reproduce. They comment on themselves:

AHAB "MORE DEMON THAN MAN": ENERGY, PURPOSE, SPEED, DIRECTION, COST. AMERICA

ALL OTHER BOOKS ARE EVASION OF WHITE WHALE. HAPPY END — HA!

BATTLING AGAINST EVIL — POWER NOT LOVE. BETTER BECOME MORE HUMAN.

MAYBE AHAB CHASE "FUTILE"— WRECK BOAT, NO OIL AND CAUSES MATERIALS LOSS AND KILLS MANY HUMAN LIVES; BUT ALSO NOT FUTILE AT ALL — MOST IMPORTANT IS THRUST OF HUMAN SPIRIT. "NO IN THUNDER".

THIS BOOK A FEROCIOUS ACT AGAINST WESTERN MAN, AS VIOLENT
AS WAR AND CATASTROPHE — AS REVENGE-FULL AS A'S PURSUIT OF M.D.

It was the Cetology chapter, he told me, that took him to the museum for the first time. No sperm whale there, but a model of the biggest of whales, the Blue, the principal kill of the present day. Blue reaches its full size, 100 feet, at 11 years, lives 20 to 25 years, and weighs 150 tons — four times the estimated weight of the biggest prehistoric monster. G would sit in the huge, balconied room from whose ceiling the whale was suspended, looking up. When what neck he had began to hurt, he would view from the balcony — but he preferred the lack of distance from below, the sense that any moment he could be crushed — like a bug. His early visits were done, Melvillian Baedecker in hand, for purposes of study. But after study — what? — prayer?

****

Gregor was on his way from White House to Museum one drizzly late August day, walking slowly, already in a meditative space, when he felt something whop down on his head, and found himself looking out of a net. Standing at the other end of a five foot handle was a man in a gray municipal uniform, accompanied by a burly, armed member of the Park Police.

"All right, just take it easy and nobody'll get hurt," said the gray one. "Department of Animal Control."

Taking something of a chance, he let go of the net handle with one hand and reached around to his back pocket for his wallet. Shiny silver-badge-with-blue-center G couldn't read.

"Just come with me. Truck's over there." White bakery-type van with appropriate municipal markings.

"What's going on?? Get this thing off me!" Gregor was screeching unsympathetically. The cop drew his pistol just in case. Handcuffs too large.

"We've had a complaint, several complaints. We've been watching you."

"I work at the White House. I live at the White House. I'm an Assistant to..."

"Tell it to the Judge!"

"Tell it to the Judge!" the blue one echoed, more profoundly. In these days, things were tense around Washington.

Gregor knew resistance would be catastrophic, so followed his captors to the getaway van where he was de-netted and strapped onto a wheeled gurney borrowed from the morgue. Much of the trip was spent with the cop in the back of the van trying to keep the gurney from crashing into the walls at each deceleration and turn.

The van headed south to Anacostia, once site of the Bonus Encampment, now also home to the main animal impoundment center, euphemistically known as a "Shelter". Gregor was off-loaded by dog-catcher and cop, wheeled into the front office, briefly questioned, name rank and serial number, then into the back, a great room full of wheeled cages, (the better to roll you to the gas, my dear) as immortalized in Vittorio De Sica's "*Umberto D.*"

"Wait a minute," G shrilled, "Don't I supposed to get a phone call to my lawyer?"

Such a request had never been made before. Catcher, cop and clerk conferred, and wheeled G back to the office.

"What's the number?" asked the clerk.

"I can dial it myself," the insect averred.

"Not unless we unstrap your things there," the cop observed, "which we ain't about to do."

"TE4-2200."

"F-E-4-2-2-0-0." The clerk had to say the numbers out loud in order to get them right. Hand over the mouthpiece: "She says it's the Department of Agriculture."

"Hey," growled the cop, "I thought you worked in the White House..."

Gregor left a message with Rex Tugwell's secretary, and was wheeled back into the local Bedlam. The barking and yowling were that of an unplumbed circle of Dante's hell.

What would you do if you were hypersensitive to noise, and found yourself caged in the midst of 97 decibels of sound? Gregor wrapped his Burberry (a Tugwell hand-me-down) around his poor knees, which brought the input down from that of "a plane at takeoff" to only that of "raucous music; the subway" — somewhat more bearable. But distraction, distraction, what to do? what to read? Partly exposed in coat pocket by dint of unusual wrap-around, two envelopes, the forgotten stash of Thursday's post. Gregor, an inveterate reader of even junk mail and cereal boxes, grabbed for succor. A bill from Fischer Scientific — the centrifuge, no doubt — and a letter from KMM at Ives & Myrick, 46 Cedar St., New York City, N.Y. But who was KMM? G tore into the envelopes, first the bill — business before pleasure — then the thicker packet from... he shuffled the pages through to the end... "Yours forever, Katherine (MacPherson)."

Katherine MacPherson. Katherine MacPherson. It must be Miss MacPherson. Miss MacPherson who sat at the desk across the aisle. I never knew her first name. What could she have to say?

April 5, 1939
That was three weeks ago. Is the post kaput?

Dear Mr. Samsa,

It has taken me four years to write you, I've been in such agony, unsure whether to take the chance. But Gregor (may I call you Gregor?) I shall never be able to forget you or master my love for you.

What?? (G had yet to discover that life was truly stranger than fiction.)

I have your picture (the one from the jacket of your book) in my desk drawer, and every day I sneak many glances at it, pretending to be looking for envelopes or something.

I know what you must be thinking: who is this woman? - I never even noticed her. And it's true. I sat next to you for years, too bashful to even glance across the aisle except in secret, too frightened to speak to you who knows so much about so many things.

When you left I thought I would recover. "Out of sight, out of mind," we say in America. But we also say "Absence makes the heart grow fonder," and almost every day I found my mind wandering, thinking resentful thoughts about Mr. Mullen, who sits unworthily at your desk, less and less able to do my work. Last week I found myself pacing the office, thinking only of throwing myself on your neck and smothering you with kisses. I knew then it was time to write.

Perhaps you think I am too forward. What right have I to make such assumptions that you would be interested in me? Let me assure you that I am a respectable and honest woman in all senses of the word. Our first kiss would be my first kiss - and to no one else in the world, for after you, I no longer wish even to look at anyone else.

Mr. Samsa, Gregor, I am not a frivolous or gullible girl. I have done much thinking about intermarriage and its dangers. I know that those of the Jewish religion do not like to marry out- side their race. So for the past two years, I have been study- ing Judaism, and I can tell you it is a moving and impressive religion. I was brought up to think of the Old Testament as "old", replaced by the "New" Testament, interesting as history, but no longer really important. But now I have read the "Old" Testament two times all the way through, and I can truly say that it contains a lot of wisdom. If we were to be married - even before, if I even knew you were interested - I would be willing to convert to your beautiful religion. I think Katherine Mary MacPherson would be a funny name for them to see in their class. (Ha ha.) But I would be a good, kosher wife, and no longer just a "shiksa". (You see, I have been learning Yiddish, too, out of a book of common expressions.)

My mother and my father (especially my father) I know would object to me marrying a Jew. But they were both killed two and a half years ago in an automobile accident in Illinois, where they lived, so there is nothing to worry about that they would make trouble at a wedding or anything else. Their death was also something that freed my mind and heart to think more seriously about you, I mean about you and me.

I know how you love the German poet R. M. Rilke as you once quoted some lines of his about a panther in a cage when you saw

Mrs. Verplank pacing up and down outside Mr. Ives's door waiting for him to get off the telephone. So I read some of his poems (in English translation, of course), and I found this (you probably know it) which so expresses how I felt when we first saw each other long years ago. It's about Mary (my middle name is Mary) when the angel comes to make his annunciation.

...his gaze and that
with which she looked up struck together,
as though outside it were suddenly all empty
and what millions saw, did, bore,
were crowded into them: just she and he;
seeing and what is seen, eye and eye's delight
nowhere else save at this spot -: lo,
this is startling. And they were startled both.

I'm not assuming you necessarily had the same reaction I did, but I did feel like I was looking into the whole world when I first looked at you. Maybe I'm just "meshugga" (I'm joking), but I really believe in Love. I believe that when your heart tells you something so strongly, even if your head laughs, that some larger truth is speaking, and you must at least listen and consider very carefully. And Gregor, even if you don't hear the same voice, the truth may be speaking for you too, for it is a judgment on the possibility of Katherine and Gregor - both of us together.

"Mr. Samsa", I am dying of longing to see you once more, to sit and quietly talk - though as usual, I would probably be struck dumb. But this I know with all my heart - I cannot live any longer without you. Farewell, my dear one. If you knew how I suffer...

Please write me what you think. I anxiously await your answer.
Yours forever,
Katherine (MacPherson)

Gregor checked the postmark on the envelope. April 20. She must have hesitated to post it, he thought. And then he thought, *"Gott in Himmel!*

What I am to do now? She will kill herself, with me to blame." He re-read the letter several times amidst the awful din.

Tugwell arrived late in the day, worked something out in the front room, and took G back to the White House in a taxi. He studied the letter all the way up 14th Street, and handed it back to his despairing colleague. "ER," he said, "This is a problem for ER. She's the queen of thank-you notes."

And indeed Eleanor Roosevelt was concerned and helpful. She assured Gregor that this was not a suicide note — it was far too full of hope. She instructed him in the use of phrases such as "Thank you so much for your kind letter," and "Unfortunately, I am not available for a serious relationship," the "unfortunately" added to save Miss MacPherson's self-esteem, the "presently" (G's suggestion), subtracted to indicate closure. Gregor was advised to take time to describe his current activities (supportive of her worth and right to know), while emphasizing that he was much too busy to undertake a serious writing relationship.

The finished letter was a masterpiece of tact, checked and rechecked before being sent. But it was good, kind work in vain: his letter was returned eight days after being sent, with a red stamp on the envelope — "NO LONGER AT THIS ADDRESS."

35. Wars Of The Worlds I:
The Spirit Of St. Louis

The Library of Congress is housed in two massive buildings east of the Capitol. It contains phone books from every city, town and municipality in the country. There were six Katherine MacPhersons listed in Manhattan, seven K. MacPhersons, six and eight in Queens, four and four in the Bronx, three and four in Brooklyn, and three K's in Staten Island. Gregor spent the next week making phone calls: several K/Katherines were unreachable, and none of the others was right. Quite a few sounded suspicious of the caller. Unpleasant. Given her letter, he imagined she wouldn't be listed under a husband's name, or a parent's.

Failing in New York, he repeated the process for Boston, Chicago, San Francisco, Los Angeles, and then, fearing she may have moved to the Washington area to try to find him, for the District of Columbia, and nearby cities in Maryland and Virginia. Nothing. He didn't know which might be worse: finding her, or not finding her. About to go on to second order cities — it was an overwrought education in American geography if nothing else — he realized the new phone books were not yet out, so any recent listing would not be there.! The search was doomed. Had he killed someone? He might never know. Not salutary for one inclined to guilt.

The silver lining in the cloud was that he became a habitual user of the the Library of Congress. The cloud inside the silver lining was that the Library of Congress subscribed to every newspaper published on earth, and

Gregor became acutely aware — in all details, in several languages — of the dismaying events unfolding off the coast of Cuba, and now Florida.

On May 13th, the Hamburg-American Line's luxurious cruise ship, the *St. Louis,* had set sail for Cuba, carrying 930 Jewish refugees, among the last allowed to leave Germany. Goering thought it a good way to export some rich swine — after confiscating all their goods and property. Goebbels found it good propaganda to create a liberal Nazi image, and the Hamburg-American Line saw it as a way to bolster their declining earnings. Each passenger had paid a steep ticket price (especially steep after having been relieved of all their wealth) and a large fee for an official landing certificate (fraudulent, as it turned out) signed by Colonel Manuel Benitez, Cuba's Director-General of Immigration. Only a few days earlier, they had been anxious victims of ever-increasing Nazi terror. But on board — surreal! — they were treated as human beings, cruise passengers entitled to the luxury that normally accompanies such bookings. None were aware that a few days before departure, Cuba's President, Fredrico Bru, victim of of domestic pressure from antisemitic groups, and furious at not being given a cut of Benitez's scam, had announced his intention to invalidate their papers. Ersatz "landing certificates" would not be considered valid: they would need regulation visas approved by three separate Cuban Departments.

Conversation, deck games, dances, chamber music and elegant meals were a heady experience for these lucky members of a recently-despised race. Then, on May 23 Captain Schroeder received a telegram from Hamburg-American: MAJORITY YOUR PASSENGERS IN CONTRAVENTION OF NEW CUBAN LAW 937 AND MAY NOT BE GIVEN PERMISSION DISEMBARK. Fears returned with clutching intensity. On the 27th the *St. Louis,* now a floating prison, docked at Havana. Only twenty-eight passengers were allowed to leave the ship — twenty-two who had hired high-priced lawyers in Europe to obtain regulation visas, a Cuban couple, and six visiting Spaniards. Nine hundred and eight passengers remained on board. Their distress became a front page story in newspapers throughout the world. Would they be sent back to Germany to die in ghettos or camps? There were many details to the dickerings.

On June 1st, President Bru ordered the ship to leave Cuban waters, harumphing that Hamburg-American was degrading governmental dignity by pressuring about its passengers. The St. Louis headed northwest toward Florida. Cables to the U.S. State Department were rebuffed: no landings would be permitted in New York or any other American port. A U.S. Coast Guard cutter shadowed the ship to prevent the foolhardy from swimming ashore.

Gregor copied down a letter from Bishop James Cannon, Jr. he found in the Richmond, Virginia *Times-Dispatch:*

> "....The ship came close enough to Miami for the refugees to see the lights of the city. And while this horrible tragedy is being enacted right at our doors, the government makes no effort to relieve the desperate situation of these people but rather gives orders that they be kept out of the country. Why don't the President, the Secretary of State, the Secretary of the Treasury, the Secretary of Labor confer together and arrange for the landing of these refugees who have been caught in this maelstrom through no fault of their own? The failure to take any stops to assist these distressed, persecuted Jews in their hour of extremity is one of the most disgraceful things which has happened in American history and leaves a stain and brand of shame upon the record of our nation."

At five PM on June 2nd, the roach was in the President's office, a copy of Bishop Cannon's letter in hand. Roosevelt read it thoughtfully.

"What would you like me to do?"

"Whatever you can think of. What about temporary visas until the end of hostilities? Or a Presidential directive — finding? — concerning this special case? Or at least to register a protest! If we can't come to their physical aid, we can certainly come to their moral aid."

"And when 'President Rosenfeld' is destroyed by the anti-Jewish lobby, who will stand up to Hitler? Neville Chamberlain? Who will protect your people from American antisemites? Have you heard Father Coughlin lately, his fireside chats? Thirty million listen — every week."

"And a hundred million don't."

"Furthermore, my friend, there are legitimate security concerns. Do we know who all these people really are? Three or four spies, some saboteurs among the nine hundred? Nazis threatening to kill their families back home unless they do their dirty work?"

It may be apt here to provide some insight from someone who should know — the usually silent ex-President, Calvin Coolidge:

"The political mind is a strange mixture of vanity and timidity, of an obsequious attitude at one time and a delusion of grandeur at another time, of the most selfish preferment combined with the most sacrificing patriotism. The political mind is the product of men in public life who have been twice spoiled. They have been spoiled with praise and they have been spoiled with abuse. With them nothing is natural, everything is artificial."

Gregor had independently come to similar conclusions. He was beginning to understand a political mind so different from his own. He flattered and cajoled; he appealed to the President's patriotism by citing the triumphalism in the German press: ROOSEVELT CONFIRMS HITLER POLICY; REFUSES TO ADMIT CRUISE SHIP JEWS! Loath to have an extended confrontation, the President suggested Gregor take the matter up with the Secretary of State, Cordell Hull. Gregor called the next morning. The State Department transcript reads as follows:

G: Hello, Mr. Secretary, Gregor Samsa here.
H Yes.
G: I'm at the White House, working for
H: I know who you are.
G: How are you?
H: Fine.
G: Mr. Secretary, the President asked me to contact you about this terrible tragedy with those 900 refugees.
H: Yes.
G: And there have been so many things back and forth.
H: Yes.
C;: Guaranteeing money and so forth.
H: Yes.

G: You see?

H: Yes. Well, I talked with the President about twenty minutes ago.

G: Yes?

H: And I talked to Carson down in Havana.

G: Yes?

H: He brought up the question they might go out to the — the islands — our islands down there. What the devil are they?

G: Virgin Islands?

H: Yes. I took that up at once and found we couldn't unless they had a definite home where they were coming from, and a situation to return to.

G: I see.

H: I think the Jewish organizations will work it out if the financing will be made certain... They've got a real chance of doing it, that's what I'm trying to say.

G: I see. But...

H: We'll do what we can, you understand, but they need a man there who knows how to dicker with them on the financing.

G: I see.

H: This is a matter primarily between the Cuban government and these people.

G: I see.

H: And not this government.

G: I see. Well, would you mind if I call you again tomorrow?

H: Yes, sir. I'm keeping up with it the best I can.

C,: And I can call you again?

H: Yes, sir. Anytime.

G: Thank you.

H: Yes.

G: Thank you.

He did call again, the next day. With similar results.

G: Mr. Secretary?

H: Yes, sir.

C: How are you?

H: Good.

G: *I'm calling you about this St. Louis, the German boat.*

H: *Yes.*

G: *It seems the Cubans are demanding more money than can be raised by the Jewish organizations.*

H: *The situation, you see, is that the — the folks in New York don't want any money to get in the hands of the Cubans and the Cubans do.*

G: *Yes?*

H: *My men are working down there with the — the man who represents the New York people .*

G: *That's right.*

H: *I forget his name.*

G: *Well— there's nothing that 1 could do, or that they should do?*

H: *Nothing I see right now. If I find out anything I'll let you know.*

G; *Thank you so much.*

H: *Yes.*

G; *Thank you.*

H: *Yes.*

G: *Goodbye.*

On June 6, at 11:40 PM, under orders from Hamburg-American, and with no resolution in sight, Captain Schroeder turned his ship to the northeast, and set course for Europe. A committee of passengers addressed a telegram to Franklin D. Roosevelt: WE ASK IN GREAT DESPAIR YOUR ASSISTANCE FOR DISEMBARKATION AT SOUTHAMPTON OR ASYLUM IN BENEVOLENT NOBLE FRANCE. Perhaps the President read an invidious comparison into the double adjective. For whatever reason, there was no response. Captain Schroeder, followed several days later; REGARD THESE PASSENGERS AS DOOMED ONCE THEY REACH GERMAN SOLL STOP WANT TO BE ASSURED NO SINGLE POSSIBILITY OF ESCAPE SHOULD FAIL TO BE GIVEN UTMOST CONSIDERATION STOP TIME IS OF ESSENCE BOAT HAS COMPLETED MORE THAN HALF OF TRIP Roosevelt silence. It was left to the "New York people" to cable the Captain: ANY IMMIGRATION THIS SIDE OF WATER OUT OF QUESTION STOP THIS NOT COMMUNICATED TO PASSENGERS BUT WISH YOU TO KNOW.

Gregor also knew. For the entire week he had been on the phone with

Department Secretaries and underlings, with negotiators still working in Cuba and with the Joint Distribution Committee handling things in New York. On June 12, as the French Minister of the Interior was accepting 250 refugees, and the British were about to match that number, Gregor, somewhat relieved, but more than slightly bitter, composed the following to the President of the United States:

FROM: G. SAMSA
TO: FDR
RE: ANTISEMITISM
Dear Mr. President,
The apparent resolution of difficulties for some passengers of the St. Louis is good news for them, and for the European democracies, but reflects little credit on the actions of the United States government. Based on our behavior, already the Völkischer Beobachter is claiming acceptance and confirmation of Nazi Jewish policy (see enclosed).

I know you are sympathetic to the victims and you are reluctance to act publicly based on true fears of reaction. You would prefer to labeled anti-Nazi than pro-Jew. And I can understand this reasoning. However I must ask you to consider: being only anti-Nazi or anti-Hitler is also a way to not to consider the larger meaning of what is happening. Thought and debate become limited by normal language of politics.

But something much beyond normal politics is happening, something which leads the entire world to a condition where people and people, people and State are set at terrifying odds, where no person can trust any other person. Then aggressive "self-defense" at all costs will become the primary and permanent operating principle of people and nations. This is not a world you or I want to live in. It is not, I think, a world that even can survive.

I would like to talk you out of my Jewish experience, both here and in Europe of my youth. I do not pretend to he a pious Jew to grant myself permission to speak or claiming any authority. Still, I have of necessarily done some thinking about this, and would share my thinking with you.

Who are the Jews?

The Jews are a nation, of course, a dispersed nation. Some would argue through inbreeding and culture, a race. Therefore, an attack on Jews, per se, is genocide, one of the few international taboos. I'm sure you understand this.

I would thus like to go on to a deeper answer, a generality which understands more than these particular people. "The Jews" (I will using quotes here to indicate my extended metaphor) represent everything not digestible to status quo in society, everything otherness, everything "getting in the way", everything resisting domestic or integrated or converted, everything that will not be expelled,- like poor people, "orientals", Negroes - like cockroaches. "The Jews", just by their existence, always reopen the wound of all-that-has-not-yet-been-accomplished-by-society. "The Jews" therefore are fit for only one thing: extermination.

At the moment, Herr Hitler calls only for Jewish expulsion from German-controlled Europe. If he extend his control, there will be more and more refugees to expulse. But I predict his actions will grow to a demand for extermination. I need no crystal ball here, or especially smart. Anyone who reads Mein Kampf would come to the same judgment. Once that limit is breeched, there will be no hope: First the Jews, and then "The Jews". The slaughter machines will gear and no one will be safe anywhere. Society will be controlled by the strongest members, demented, moronic, selfish. There will be no "Jews" left to question things, to confront the community, to bless it with creative discords rather than just legitimize and propagate. There will be no more art except art which glorifies the State. The world will collapse into an ice age of Fascism. The Jews will be dead, "The Jews" will be dead, and humanity as a whole will be dying. There will be no more past to haunt the present, and no more future. There will just be Power.

417

The Jews are not "Over There".

Four years ago, Sinclair Lewis wrote It Can't Happen Here, and your own Federal Theater produced adaptation all across the USA. We mustn't let the exaggerations of the work blind to the fact that it already is happening here, both to Jews and to "Jews". I have followed this closely. There is real, everyday, antisemitism growing stronger in this country. Your reference to Father Coughlin the other day was correct. But before last year he had never mentioned Jews. Now he harps with them constantly. And he is not the only one blaming Jews for the depression and the possibility of going to war. Last week Gallup poll: "Who do you suspect of having too much power?" - Jews, 60%. It would be to laugh at where it not so sinister.

I see the ads: hotels and clubs, whole professions simply closed to Jews - just as in Germany. Almost every private university I have checked, and many public ones do admissions to curb the number of Jewish students. Harvard and Yale use tricks of seeking "geographic diversity", but we know what they mean: keep out more New York Jews I read the application forms: such questions - religious affiliation?, have your parents ever used another name? I look at Help Wanted ads, even in our Washington Post. In today's paper I find 13 ads containing "Christians" or "Protestants only need apply." These are from a utility company, three banks' a publishing house, an engineering and an industrial company, a hospital and three law firms. Is this even legal? Can Jews be blamed for changing their names?

Prejudice has moved past private bigots and semiprivate social discrimination. It now affects our careers, lessens our earnings and limits our moving around - including where we can live. I see apartment buildings in Bethesda and Alexandria with signs that "Jews and Negroes Need Not Apply", and Mr. Morganthau tells me that residential communities make new home buyers to sign "covenants" barring sale to unwanted groups.

Is it just Jews? No, this already concerns "Jews". Two months ago I found an issue of the Harvard Crimson - a paper I read at the LOC to keep track of upper class thinking. There was inside a report of a talk to students at the Law School by a partner at Kilpatrick, Stockton and Finch on what it looks for in hiring:

"Brilliant intellectual powers are not essential. Too much imagination, too much wit, too great cleverness, too facile fluency, if not leavened by a sound sense of proportion, are quite as likely to impede success as to promote it. The best clients are apt to be afraid of those qualities. They want as their counsel a man who is primarily honest, safe, sound and steady.

Jews and "Jews" - not essential. And if not essential -then what?

What is antisemitism?

It seems to me that antisemitism is deeply imprinted social act, something (apparent in the pogroms) like ritual murder - the community must be cleansed of "Jewish" filth. Power without power must he made powerless. Many aspects of American history make us open to fascism excess: the religious foundation of our "City on a Hill", our multinational people, our relatively political and economic independence from the rest of the world, all the subtle but everywhere carryover of force and violence from the pioneering days - all this makes for potentially explosive.

I have read in Walter Benjamin: "The world is simplified when tested for its worthiness of destruction." We like simple in America.

Please excuse my ramblings and my bad English. The one opinion I want to say is that if you feel the political need to not talk about Jews, you must decide how not to talk about them in a better way.

Respectfully, your friend,
Gregor Samsa

****

Charles A. Lindbergh said;

419

"The Jews are among the major influences pushing this country toward war."

Lindbergh, the Lone Eagle, said:

"Though I sympathize with the Jews, let me add a word of warning. No person of honesty and vision can look on their pro-war policy here today without seeing the dangers involved in such a policy, both for us — and for them. Instead of agitating for war, the Jewish groups in this country should be opposing it in every possible way, for they will be among the first to feel its consequences."

He said:

"Their greatest danger to this country lies in their large ownership and influence in our motion pictures, our press, our radio, and our Government.... We cannot blame them for looking out for what they believe to be their own interests, but we also must look out for ours. We cannot allow the natural passions and prejudices of other peoples to lead our country to destruction."

Lindy, the American Hero, said:

"This speech may well be my last. If free speech ends in this country, it means we are no longer a free people. It means we are about to enter a dictatorship and probably a foreign war. The Roosevelt Administration has been treating our Congress more and more as the German Reichstag has been treated under the Nazi regime. Congress, like the Reichstag, is not consulted. As a nation we've been led along like children with sugared promises and candied pills."

And then he said:

"The President is moving toward cancellation of the congressional elections."

The man who crossed the Atlantic alone in *The Spirit of St. Louis* said:

"There is really only one danger in the world — and that is the yellow danger. China and Japan are really bound together against the white race. There can be only one efficient weapon against that alliance...Germany itself could be that weapon. The ideal set-up

would be to have Germany take over Poland and Russia, in collab-
oration with the British, as a bloc against the yellow people and the
Bolsheviks. But instead, the British government, and the fools in
Washington have to interfere. The British envy the Germans and
want to rule the world forever. Britain is the cause of all the trouble
in the world today."

****

Having led a Crusade against the Muslims at 34, the French King Louis IX, at 56, became obsessed by a memory of the Holy Land. In 1270 he returned again, returned knowingly to a land smitten by the plague. He died in Carthage, black with buboes, and his body was brought back to France. All along the way, through Italy, the Alps, Lyon, and Cluny, crowds knelt as the procession passed. It reached Paris on the eve of Pentecost in 1271, and funeral rites were solemnly performed at Notre-Dame. Without awaiting the judgment of the Church. his people considered him a saint, and prayed at his tomb. Twenty-six years later Louis became Saint Louis.

****

Charles Lindbergh's flight was sponsored by a group of St. Louis boosters, in a bid for world publicity and more local business.

36. Wars Of The Worlds II: Neutrons And Neutrality

The neutron. Now there's an entity our contemporary politicians can love. Electrically neutral, bipartisan as it were, generally shoulder-to-shoulder with the gang, but heavy enough to throw its weight around at the behest of others. A well-placed tool in the pantheon of power.

And the perfect tool it was to sidle past the electric fence of the nucleus: where a cyclotron might hurl a positively charged particle past electrostatic repulsion using tens of millions of electron volts, a neutron can simply amble in at ten thousand, there to nuzzle or destabilize to its heart's content.

In late 1931, when G was at Ives & Myrick developing risk management, there *were* no neutrons. Twentieth century atomic theory, in a typically dichotomous way, held that there were only two basic building blocks: heavy, positively charged protons in the nucleus, and light, negatively charged electrons spinning round, planets in the nuclear solar system. Particle weights were clear, charges had been determined. That the nucleus was, with the exception of hydrogen, heavier than its charge would suggest, must be the result of "nuclear electrons", a fifth column within, offsetting part of the proton positivity.

But after January 1932, thanks to James Chadwick, there were neutrons, heavy as protons but without a charge, neutrons out there in public consciousness, and neurtrons swirling in the head of one Leo Szilard, Hungarian physicist, at that time skulking around London. In mid-September '33, he had a vision at a traffic light, a green-means-go vision that drove him through the next six years, and drove human history into a potential abyss:

As the light changed to green and I crossed the street, it suddenly occurred to me that if we could find an element which is split by neutrons and which would emit two neutrons when it absorbed one neutron, such an element, if assembled in sufficiently large mass, could sustain a nuclear chain reaction. I didn't see at the moment just how one would go about finding such an element or what experiments would be needed, but the idea never left me.

Here was a fateful intersection of concepts: both "nuclear chain reaction" and the "critical mass" needed to set off and sustain it, for only with many atoms close together could the particles attain an ejaculatory cascade. And what would come from a furiously expanding neutron burst? More neutrons, radiation, heat — and energy — explosive or controlled. The splitting of atoms.

Why would anyone want to split atoms? Well, as Fred Allen once said, someone might need half an atom. Gregor had other ideas about the freeing up of energy contained in the nucleus. He remembered his Einstein studies back in 1917. Using $E=mc^2$, he once calculated that one kilogram of coal, if converted entirely into energy, would yield 25 billion kilowatt hours of electricity, or as much as all the power plants in Germany and Austria could generate in five months. If the neutron could unlock the door to such a storehouse...

He remembered something else too, something Szilard also recalled. Gregor and Szilard were brother H. G. Wells fans, especially fond of his 1913 novel, *The World Set Free*. Each had been electrified by the visionary lecture of Wells's Professor Rufus, commenting on Mme. Curie's discovery:

And so we see that this Radium which seemed at first a fantastic exception, a mad inversion of all that was most established and fundamental in the constitution of matter, is really at one with the rest of the elements. It does noticeably and forcibly what probably all the other elements are doing with an imperceptible slowness. It is like the single voice crying aloud that betrays the silent breathing multitude in the darkness. Radium is an element that is breaking up and flying to pieces. But perhaps all elements are doing that at less perceptible rates. Uranium certainly is; thorium — the stuff of this incandescent gas mantle— certainly is; actinium. I feel that we are but beginning the list. And we know now that the atom, that once we thought hard and impenetrable, and indivisible and final and — lifeless — lifeless, is really a reservoir of immense energy. That is the most wonderful thing about all this work. A little while ago we thought of the atoms as we thought of bricks, as solid building material, as substantial matter, as unit masses of lifeless stuff, and behold these bricks are boxes, treasure boxes, boxes full of the intensest force. This little bottle contains about a pint of uranium oxide; that is to say about fourteen ounces of the element uranium. It is worth about a pound. And in this bottle, ladies and gentlemen, in the atoms in this bottle there slumbers at least as much energy as we could get by burning a hundred and sixty tons of coal. If at a word in one instant I could suddenly release that energy here and now, it would blow us and everything about us to fragments; if I could turn it into the machinery that lights this city, it could keep Edinburgh brightly lit for a week. But at present no man knows, no man has an inkling of how this little lump of stuff can be made to hasten the release of its store. It does release it, as a burn trickles. Slowly the uranium changes into radium, the radium changes into a gas called the radium emanation, and that again to what we call radium A, and so the process goes on, giving out energy at every stage, until at last we reach the last stage of all, which is, so far as we can tell at present, lead. But we cannot hasten it....

Why is the change gradual? Why does only a minute fraction of the radium disintegrate in any particular second? Why does it dole itself out so slowly and so exactly? Why does not all the uranium change to radium and all the radium change to the next lowest thing at once ? Why this decay by driblets;

why not a decay en masse? Suppose presently we find it is possible to quicken that decay? Given that knowledge, mark what we should be able to do! We should not only be able to use this uranium and thorium. Not only should we have a source of power so potent that a man might carry in his hand the energy to light a city for a year, fight a fleet of battleships or drive one of our giant liners across the Atlantic; but we should also have a clue that would enable us at last to quicken the process of disintegration in all the other elements, where decay is still so slow as to escape our finest measurements. Every scrap of solid matter in the world would become an available reservoir of concentrated force. Do you realize, ladies and gentlemen, what these things would mean for us? It would mean a change in human conditions that I can only compare to the discovery of fire, that first discovery that lifted man above the brute.

In 1933, while Gregor dreamed of neutrons unlocking energy, Szilard, his secret partner, was pondering how to bring that about. Though Wells had spoken of uranium, Szilard spent six unfruitful years wooing skeptical investors for trials with beryllium, indium and thorium. So when in January '39 Niels Bohr announced Hahn and Strassmann's neutron splitting of uranium in Berlin at the Carnegie Institution in Washington, Szilard slapped his forehead, and jumped on a train to get a first hand report from his countryman Edward Teller.

****

Early in the afternoon of a cold, sunny Sunday, the day after the "Fifth Washington Meeting on Theoretical Physics" had ended, Gregor was lying on his back, taking in the sun on the Institution's spacious grounds, unconcerned with the turmoil released on Saturday. He had given himself the day off to celebrate — two days late — Mozart's 183rd birthday. As he lay on a rock, absorbing the healing rays, playing the painful Masonic Funeral Music in his head and speculating on the mysteries of life in death, he heard voices coming closer, speaking — what was it? — Hungarian! He had spoken a smattering of that mysterious tongue in his European days, and sounds with meaning began to penetrate the Mozart and the brain-rust.

425

Szilard and Teller were walking the path along the edge of Rock Creek. Teller:

"He was mumbling and going on as usual — one got only the general drift. But then Fermi took over and gave his usual elegant presentation, with all the implications, including developing Meitner's idea that the uranium had split."

"Did Bohr agree?" Szilard asked.

"*Azt hiszem, igen*" said Gregor, in Hungarian, as he sat up on his rock.

The physicists jumped, and the insect was embarrassed at surprising them.

"I'm sorry. It was in the *Star* last night. A report on the conference. It said Bohr and Fermi agree."

"Who are you?" Teller asked in English, tactfully moving the language away from Gregor's attempt at Hungarian.

"Oh, I am sorry again." Gregor jumped down off the rock to offer his claw. "Samsa. Gregor Samsa. I am pleased to meet you. And you."

"Leo Szilard."

"Edward Teller."

"Are you in physics?" Szilard wanted to know.

"No, I am researcher working at the White House." This, Gregor had decided, was the term that best described his sundry duties. Szilard's ears pricked up.

"The White House of President Roosevelt?"

"Exactly so."

"What do you research?"

"Slightly this, slightly that. Momentary I am working on whales."

"Ah, a biologist."

"Whales in the White House?" Teller wanted to know.

"In the Natural History Museum."

Teller inspected Gregor, bushy brows over black eyes, and decided to change the subject.

"What else did the newspaper say?" he asked.

"It said the new discovery has no practical significance for power source — at least not now."

The two physicists looked at one another.

426

"Good!" exclaimed Szilard.

The reader will not understand this remark without knowing that Szilard's first pronouncement upon hearing Teller's report on Bohr on Hahn was this: "There is very little doubt in my mind that the world is headed for grief." For at least three years, the image of Hitler/bomb had been haunting him. He longed for a conspiracy of silence among atomic researchers — self-censorship, no publication. He had been unsuccessful in selling this idea to the physics community.

To evade Gregor's inevitable "Why good?" Teller thought it best to talk of something else.

"Why are you here, Mr. Samsa, at the Carnegie Institution?"

"It's one of my favorite spots. I like this rock very well. I come here for special things."

"And today's special thing is?" asked Szilard.

"I am ashamed today's special thing is not today. I pretend this is January 27."

They both looked at him quizzically.

"Mozart's birthday. I always celebrate."

Teller flew into an unexpected, slightly ridiculous rage.

"I cannot understand, simply can not understand why otherwise sane adults — presumably sane adults — and excuse me, I have no reason to suspect you are not sane — or not sane — why these people — so many people! — why sane people worship this man and his trivial music, count him among the great treasures of the human race!"

"You don't like Mozart," Gregor summarized.

"I like running my fingers up and down the scales, the arpeggios, the stupid spelled-out chordal basses. The actual process of playing them is very enjoyable."

"He is a first class pianist," Szilard commented.

"But you don't like chordal basses."

"Oom-pah-pah-pah, oom-pah-pah-pah predictable boring. What he could have done with left-hand counterpoint with a little imagination. A genius, perhaps, but no talent, absolutely no talent."

Gregor was stupefied.

"There is of course the twelve tone row in the G minor Symphony

427

where he reaches his hand out across the centuries to Webern. But that's the only really interesting thing in 110 volumes. People say he died too early. You would say that, wouldn't you? Leo, here, would say that. As far as I am concerned, he died too late. I mistrust all pretensions to self-sufficiency."

"He is a Beethoven pianist," Szilard explained.

"You prefer Beethoven." Gregor was still catching up.

"Imponderable, Beethoven..." Teller commented. And he began to drift away in a strange decrescendo of ever-stronger, but ever-sparser, adjectives.

"Blunt...determined......tense.............combative............... belligerent............."

In the pauses one could hear the creek, and the occasional *cheer-up, cheerily, cheer-up, cheerily* of some early robin.

"Doom-foretelling................... no concessions........................... not a concession..................... explosive.............................." Pianissimo now. "Explosive................." Gregor thought he had gone into some kind of semi-trance. Szilard ignored the whole event, used to Teller's fanaticism, enveloped in his own thoughts.

"Grand, central fury..............................."

The three had begun walking southward without ever deciding to do so, strolling along the rambling banks of Rock Creek, peripatetically present at a madman's monologue. Teller's eyes were focused into psychic space, as if detoured into some difficult problem in quantum mechanics.

"Low predictability quotient.........0.1 perhaps..................."

Was he still on Beethoven?

The three walked together in silence, the beginning of a four mile stroll towards the Potomac in Georgetown. Teller came to and continued the interrupted conversation as if nothing had happened.

"So you are friends with the President? You get to talk with him?"

"How did you get this job?" Szilard inquired.

Over the next several hours, Gregor spun out his story to the intently curious scientists. And in exchange, parking themselves on a bench at the Tidal Basin, the Hungarians related a layman's version of "The Story of Nuclear Physics". Beginning with Becquerel's 1896 papers on radioactivity, and on through Curie's discovery of radium, Lawrence's cyclotron, Cockcroft's splitting of the atom, Chadwick's discovery of the neutron, and

428

his own conceptions of chain reaction and critical mass, Szilard, with Teller accompanying, played out the findings and errors that had led humanity to its fateful crossroads. The conversation paused at this pause in the world, and the three watched in silence as the steam-driven crane hoisted the last marble block of the day, pink with sunset, up high on the almost finished Jefferson Memorial. After a minute, Teller announced abruptly, "I'm cold. I have to go home." And to Szilard, "You are coming?"

The two men got up.

"Nice to meet you, Mr.... Samza, is it?"

"Thank you. It was nice to meet you, too."

Teller hailed a cab to take them to his Garfield St. home. Gregor sat for another hour till the sun went down, and street lamps came on in the approaching darkness. Then he walked across the Mall and through the Ellipse back to the White House.

****

As spring of '39 put out its feelers, and warmed toward the glory of April's cherry blossoms, Gregor noted with interest that the public was being bombarded with mixed messages about uranium fission, touted as "the greatest scientific discovery since radium". Science Service, a respected news agency, played down the risks:

> *Physicists are anxious that there be no public alarm over the possibility of the world being blown to bits by their experiments. Writers and dramatists have overemphasized this idea. While they are proceeding with their experiments with proper caution, they feel that there is no real danger except perhaps in their own laboratories.*

Also dismissed or minimized were "forecasts of the near possibility of running giant ocean liners across the Atlantic on the energy contained within the atoms of a glass of water", or of replacing steam engines with "atom-motors"; or suggestions that "the atomic energy may be used as some super-explosive, or as a military weapon." It was as if the greatest scientific discovery since radium had little or no import.

But Gregor had taken on Szilard's concerns: news from Europe —

the March occupation of Czechoslovakia, for example, Czechoslovakia, the largest European uranium source — indicated that German military expansion might soon overrun Belgium, whose colony in the Congo was the principal uranium source of the entire world.

Szilard's campaign for secrecy had few American targets: in the U.S., almost no fission work was going on, and no research at all of the possibility of a nuclear chain reaction. University researchers were unaccustomed to seeking federal support, while government scientists, though interested, thought the whole thing too far-fetched for any military import. Yet the Hungarian's fears were well-founded: French disclosures did prompt German action. Once Joliot's "Number of Neutrons Liberated in the Nuclear Fission of Uranium" appeared in the April issue of *Nature*, the president of the German Bureau of Standards urged buying all uranium in Germany, banning exports, and negotiating contracts with Czech mines. In Hamburg, physical chemists alerted the War Office in Berlin to "the newest development in nuclear physics, which will likely make it possible to produce an explosive many orders of magnitude more powerful than conventional ones." Germany became the first country to study nuclear fission as possibly applied to weapons. In September 1939 her greatest remaining physicist, Werner Heisenberg, was exploring how the metal might be made to explode. There was definitely something to worry about.

At Columbia, Szilard begged and borrowed what equipment he could to do rudimentary experiments in radiation physics. Among other experiments, he irradiated frankfurters and salami — I am not kidding — and left them for months in a lab refrigerator, checking now and then to test their appearance and taste. While salami is a far cry from weapons, he was again years ahead of his time, inventing a controversial technology with which we struggle today.

****

On Tuesday, July 11, 1939, Gregor's phone rang at 7:30 in the morning.
"Samsa here."
"Szilard. How are you? Ready for a little trip?"
"Szilard! Where are you?"

"On Nier's phone at the cyclotron lab. At Columbia."

"What kind of a trip?"

"We go hunting."

"I don't do hunting. I don't kill things, any kind of animals."

"That's good, Samsa, but this is man-hunting, and I guarantee you'll enjoy it. Pack a bag for a couple of days, and be out on Pennsylvania Avenue at two o'clock. Teller will pick you up. You'll be driving up to Princeton and stay overnight at Wigner's. He's a great mathematician. You'll like him."

"What man do we hunt?"

"Tomorrow morning you and Wigner and Teller will pick me up at my place, and we'll drive out to Long Island..."

"Yes?"

"...to visit an old friend of yours, the Professor."

"I don't know professors on Long Island."

"I didn't say you knew him, I just said he was your friend. Trust me, Samsa. I'll see you tomorrow morning early."

And he hung up. A typical Szilard move, the kind that made him an outcast in polite society.

At precisely two PM, the precise Edward Teller pulled over to the curb in front of the White House gate. Gregor threw his small cardboard suitcase in the back seat, and climbed in. They headed north on Fifteenth Street.

"Where are we going?" the passenger asked.

"Wigner's."

"I mean where are we going tomorrow?"

"To meet with Einstein."

"Albert Einstein?"

"You know any other Einsteins?"

"In fact, yes. Izzy Einstein."

"We're not going to visit Izzy Einstein. We're going to visit Albert Einstein."

Gregor could barely contain his excitement. His early admiration for the scientist and thinker had grown into worship for the philosopher and humanitarian, the socially committed, self-sacrificing, generous and idealistic *Mensch*.

"Why... are we going? Why to Long Island? I thought he was at Princeton."

"Wigner called his secretary, and wheedled his vacation hideout. The old man needs better protection."

"Why am I going? Who am I to...?"

"You're going because you know the President. You're our in-White-house expert."

"Expert on what? I'm not an expert on anything."

"Expert on what the President is like, what he listens to, what kind of thing will get his attention."

"Why do we need his attention? Is this another idea of Leo's?"

"We are going to trump Hitler on the bomb."

"What is trump?"

"You don't play bridge."

"Is it a card game?"

"Yes."

"No."

"That's because you're not a physicist."

"What is trump?"

"Trump is when you get the better of someone. Surprise them."

"We are going to surprise Hitler?"

"And ourselves. You'll see. Be patient."

Teller switched on the radio as they drove north through Chevy Chase and Bethesda. They heard the tail end of the Beethoven First Symphony. When it was over Gregor ventured,

"I thought you didn't like scales. Too predictable."

"Don't be stupid. Was that predictable?"

"No."

"Don't insult Beethoven."

Gregor sulked. Though he had no high regard for his own intelligence, he was not used to being called stupid. *Eine Kleine Nachtmusik* came on.

"Now that's stupid," Teller remarked as he switched off the radio.

"It may not be ultimate profound, but how you can call it stupid? What is stupid?"

"Not the music. It's stupid to play *Nachtmusik* at three o'clock in the afternoon. Do they think Mozart didn't know what time it was?"

432

Gregor vowed never to engage Teller on music again.

Baltimore. Wilmington. Philadelphia. Trenton. G was fascinated by the signs, the changing landscape, the surging traffic. Turning off Route 1, they swung east through dark, lush woodland and pulled into Princeton Junction. Teller called Wigner from a pay phone and got directions to his house. The exhausted travelers were trundled, with little ceremony, into guest room beds. They had to be up early.

Five AM. Change cars. Through the Jersey woods and flats in Wigner's light blue Chevy. Over the George Washington Bridge to the upper west side and Leo Szilard's hotel near Columbia. It was a sparkling morning, already hot, as three Hungarians and a Czech drove across the new Triborough Bridge and past the New York World's Fair with its 700 foot high trylon representing "the finite" counterposed against a 200 foot perisphere, representing "the infinite". As the others made no lascivious comments, Gregor, too, was silent.

Szilard went into a hilarious monologue concerning his visit to the Fair on opening day in April. "Building the World of Tomorrow". What a theme! Would Szilard miss such an event? Never, he said, was American inanity so succinctly displayed. A brave new world of corporations. A display of air conditioning by the Carrier Corporation in — what else? — a 100 meter diameter pseudo-igloo. Many missed the point of Dupont's "Wonders of Chemistry" displayed in nylon on the shapely legs of half-naked models. Pickle pin souvenirs at the Heinz Pavilion, and "Mickey's Surprise Party", a cartoon about a mouse with gloves shown by the National Biscuit Company, followed by mouse crackers, of course. There was the Life Savers parachute tower, a triple mixed metaphor, and a pavilion where you could place long-distance calls for free, except no one knew anyone else's long-distance number. There was a Westinghouse robot which swept a floor, pushing the dirt around and around, and twenty-one model homes, none of which would last more than five years, nor would you want to live in any of them. And most depressing and moronic of all, "Futurama", a depiction by General Motors of the world as it will be in 1960, if people will be able to breathe that long, given all the cars. Szilard had come away with a souvenir pin that said "I have seen the future." The funny thing was — he had.

Three Hungarians and a Czech. Both driver and navigator had IQs one and a half times higher than their weights, so naturally, once out on the Island, they became hopelessly lost. Driver and navigator confused the Indian names in their directions and drove to Patchogue on the south shore, instead of to Cutchogue, on the north, a detour that took two hot, sweaty hours. Finally in Peconic, their secret destination, they drove around asking vacationers in bathing suits the way to "a Dr. Moore's cottage." Strangely enough, no one seemed to know.

"Let's give it up and go home," Szilard whined from the back seat, a far cry from yesterday morning's mischievous enthusiasm. "This is fate. It might be a terrible mistake obtaining Einstein's help to apply to the government. Once the government sets its claws on something..."

Gregor felt indicted. He knew Szilard didn't mean to be invidious, but still, he could have been more sensitive.

Wigner insisted they go on with their quest. "This is ridiculous," he said. "Every child knows Einstein." Szilard, perhaps cynical, perhaps consulting the child within, had a bright idea: "So why don't we ask a child? There's one over there. Pull over." A sunburned boy of seven was standing at a drug store corner intent on tying a float on his fishing rod. Szilard leaned out of the window:

"Sonny!" The boy looked up. "Do you know where Einstein lives?"

"Of course." He looked at them with scorn for the generic stupidity of adults, and pointed the way around the next corner.

The strange musketeers drove up to a two story white cottage at the terminus of a dead end lane and saw Einstein out in back, wearing a torn undershirt and rolled up pants, pulling a small dinghy onto the backyard shore. Friendly hails in German. Gregor was introduced, his heart beating madly in his back, like that of any teen-age girl, breathless with adoration. "I am honored to meet you," the great man said. G gave a bashful smile.

The Professor invited his visitors to a cool screened porch overlooking the Sound, and brought iced tea for all.

"So, gentlemen, what can I do for you?"

Szilard, Teller and Wigner presented a short seminar on the latest advances in nuclear research to a wild-haired, undershirted elderly man who had not been *au courant* for years, a man whose attention was directed solely at the mathematics of his unified field theory. They told him how neutrons were behaving these days, how uranium bombarded by neutrons had been made to split or "fission", and how this might create nuclear chain reactions and nuclear bombs. $E=mc^2$. His reaction was classic Einstein:

"Daran habe ich gar nicht gedacht," "I haven't thought of that at all."

The Professor had believed that atomic energy would not be released in his lifetime, that it was only "theoretically possible." He puffed on his pipe.

His next utterance was philosophical: "If this works, it would be the first source of energy that does not depend on the sun." The others nodded dutifully.

The talk became political. Hitler was both lubricant and catalyst. Within half an hour, pacifist Einstein had reluctantly agreed to sound some kind of alarm about atomic bombs to beat Nazi Germany to this frightful weapon. "You cannot create peace by preparing for war," he warned. But Szilard was convincing: "If we make the bomb, and Hitler knows we have done that, he will be afraid to use his, and we will not have to use ours."

"What shall we do? I could warn the Queen about the Congo mines."

"Good, but not enough," Szilard urged. "You must write to President Roosevelt to warn him. We have to begin large research. Industrial size. Only the government has enough money."

"This will be expensive," Einstein offered.

"More expensive than pencils and paper." Teller's bitter jibe at theoreticians.

"What am I to write?"

Szilard picked up his briefcase. "I brought along some drafts, in case you were willing. I have a short letter and a long letter — just to give you an idea." They held their breaths. The old man was not offended.

"Let me see."

He carefully read both, while his visitors discreetly followed his expressions.

"Will it be better to send a short letter or a long one?"

Here Gregor was able to offer some expertise. "My suggestion is you write something to catch the President's attention, short, and if he is interested, you can make a full presenting with all facts. That is how he likes to work."

It sounded good to all of them.

"What about others, other physicists?" Einstein asked.

"Everyone is afraid to make a fool of himself, to initiate any kind of action. You are not."

"That is because everyone knows already I am a fool."

"So," Wigner observed, "your position is unique."

They all laughed.

Einstein agreed to write something and submit it to the group next week for approval, and the crusaders left with elevated heart rates. Three Hungarians and a Czech. On the way home Wigner was changing lanes and pushing the speed limit. How unlike him!

Back in Princeton, Einstein requested another meeting the following week. Teller and Gregor came up; Szilard came down. Over the next month drafts were sent back and forth to develop a compromise document, shorter than long, but longer than short. Physicists have a deep need for data. At least experimental physicists. The final, famous document read as follows:

```
Albert Einstein
Old Grove Rd. Nassau Point
Peconic, Long Island
August 2nd, 1939
F. D. Roosevelt,
President of the United States,
White House
Washington, D.C.
Sir,
Some recent work by E. Fermi and L. Szilard, which
has been communicated to me in manuscript, leads me to
expect that the element uranium may be turned into a new
and important source of energy in the immediate future.
Certain aspects of the situation which has arisen seem
to call for watchfulness and, if necessary, quick action
on the part of the Administration. I believe therefore
that it is my duty to bring to your attention the fol-
lowing facts and recommendations:
```

In the course of the last four months it has been made probable- through the work of Joliot in France as well as Fermi and Szilard in America-that it may become possible to set up a nuclear chain reaction in a large mass of uranium, by which vast amounts of power and large quantities of new radium-like elements would be generated. Now it appears almost certain that this could be achieved in the immediate future.

This new phenomenon would also lead to the construction of bombs, and it is conceivable-though much less certain-that extremely powerful bombs of a new type may thus be constructed. A single bomb of this type, carried by boat and exploded in a port, might very well destroy the whole port together with some of the surrounding territory. However, such bombs might very well prove to be too heavy for transportation by air.

The United States has only very poor ores of uranium in moderate quantities. There is some good ore in Canada and the former Czechoslovakia, while the most important source of uranium is the Belgian Congo.

In view of this situation you may think it desirable to have some permanent contact maintained between the Administration and the group of physicists working on chain reactions in America. One possible way of achieving this might be for you to entrust with this task a person who has your confidence and who could perhaps serve in an unofficial capacity. His task might comprise the following:

a) to approach Government Departments, keep them informed of the further development, and put forward recommendations for Government action, giving particular attention to the problem of securing a supply of uranium ore for the United States;

b) to speed up the experimental work, which is at present being carried on within the limits of the bud-

gets of University laboratories, by providing funds, if
such funds be required, through his contacts with private persons who are willing to make contributions for
this cause, and perhaps also by obtaining the co-opera-
tion of industrial laboratories which have the necessary
equipment.

    I understand that Germany has actually stopped the
sale of uranium from the Czechoslovakian mines which she
has taken over. That she should have taken such early
action might perhaps be understood on the ground that
the son of the German Under Secretary of State, von
Weizsäcker, is attached to the Kaiser Wilhelm-lnstitut
in Berlin where some of the American work on uranium is
now being repeated.

    Yours very truly,

    Albert Einstein

The next step was to find a carrier, since Gregor warned that mail
often got lost in the huge, but over-stuffed, inbox. Who would be best to
hand-deliver it? Only Einstein + Hungarians could come up with the idea
of Charles A. Lindbergh. He was famous. He was a hero. The President
would not overlook a message from him. So Szilard wrote Lindbergh a
letter: They had "once met at lunch about seven years ago at the Rockefeller
Institute," he reminded the flier, "but I assume that you do not remember
me, and I am therefore enclosing an introduction from Prof. Einstein."
Intriguing beginning. Einstein's note asked Lindbergh "to receive my friend
Dr. Szilard and to consider carefully what he has to tell you. The subject
may seem fantastic to a man not involved with science, but deserves attention in the public interest." Szilard's letter finished by inviting Lindbergh
to meet with him to consider how "large quantities of energy would be liberated by a nuclear chain reaction, and to discuss how to make an attempt
to inform the administration." Why they thought this letter would not also
be lost in an inbox was unclear.

    Lindbergh, of course, was not interested in making one with his enemy,
FDR. The crusaders waited impatiently for an answer. Five weeks. Like

most Americans, Szilard tuned into Lindbergh's first major radio address, hoping to glean some hint of his intentions. Carried by all three networks, Mutual, National Broadcasting and Columbia Broadcasting, this analysis of the international crisis was heard by the largest audience ever for any single speech — and in it, Lindbergh denounced Roosevelt as a war-monger for his efforts amend the Neutrality Act to sell arms to the beleaguered nations abroad. After listening, Szilard called Einstein with his rueful conclusion: "I am afraid he is not our man."

Who else? Compton at MIT? No. Too proper. He would be put off by Szilard. Who then? After more wrangling about academic politics, they came up with a compromise dark horse: Gregor. After all, he lived in the White House, he was on a first name basis with the President, he could stay on top of the matter to see that it was not ignored. Some have greatness thrust upon them. G argued that he was just a lower-level functionary with nowhere near the clout of any of the other candidates, and that he was already in trouble with the President over their differences about the Jewish refugees. He thought he was possibly "on the outs" — his most recently learned idiom. No matter. There were few other choices. He accepted his assignment.

That it took Gregor a full three weeks to get an appointment was a reflection of the chaotic goings-on at the White House. The world was exploding. At dawn on September 1st, Hitler's tanks had rolled across the Polish frontier — seven German divisions, supported by the Luftwaffe. On the 3rd, Britain and France had declared war on the Reich, and on the 8th, Roosevelt had proclaimed a National Emergency, and escalated his public and private lobbying, trying to get Congress to repeal the embargo on shipping arms abroad. His Fireside Chat that first week of September was a deft, if disingenuous, plea to prepare the nation for a struggle it did not want:

This nation will remain a neutral nation, but I cannot ask that every American remain neutral in thought as well. Even a neutral has a right to take account of facts. Even a neutral cannot be asked to close his mind or his conscience.

I have said not once but many times that I have seen war and that I hate war. I say that again and again.

I hope that the United States will keep out of this war. I believe that it will, and I give you assurance and reassurance that every effort of your Government will be directed toward that end. As long as it remains within my power to prevent, there will be no black-out of peace in the United States.

On September 21, he called a special session of Congress to ask that they amend the Neutrality Act so as to permit the United States to provide France and Great Britain with war matériel. Lindbergh said "I told you so."

It was October 11th by the time Gregor made his way up to the outer vestibule of the Oval Office for his 5:45 appointment with the President. Fifteen minutes, just before dinner. He had better talk quickly. But instead of ushering him immediately in, FDR's aide, Gen. Edwin ("Pa") Watson, asked to see the materials Gregor had lugged along. Time was wasting as Pa squinted through a few of them. Then he got on the phone and summoned two ordnance experts, Army Col. Keith Adamson and Navy Commander Gilbert Hoover to join them in the vestibule. The military men looked over the documents, and then all three were ushered into the Oval Office. It was already 6:10. There was no time left for the meeting. Good thing the Roosevelts were always late for dinner.

"Gregor what are you up to?" the President asked, looking at the folders cradled in Gregor's four arms. G had never seen FDR so tired; he was alarmed by the greyness. He imagined the exhausting struggle of moving from bed to wheelchair. Dozens of times a day this huge man had to heave his aging, crippled body around in the unending burdens of office: a constant stream of people to be seen, decisions to be made, correspondence to be read and answered, newspapermen to persuade, all this in the ever-present context of prolonged depression, and global problems of unprecedented scale. The President looked tired unto death.

"What bright idea have you got now, my friend?"

With his chin, Gregor pushed Einstein's letter off the top of the top pile of folders, dropping it unceremoniously on FDR's desk.

"Sorry, that was awkward. I didn't mean to be rude."

"Believe me, I know what it's like to have my hands full."

One could see in this response why the President was so well liked —
unless he was hated. Gregor handed the upper pile to Col. Anderson, and
the lower to Commander Hoover, who each began perusing them as FDR
read Einstein's message. When the President finished, he looked up at G.
In his role as a staff scientist, Gregor launched into a well-rehearsed, but
poorly delivered sermon on nuclear fission. After several minutes, Roosevelt
interrupted him:

"Gregor, what you are after is to see that the Nazis don't blow us up."

"Precisely."

The President got on the intercom and asked his secretary to bring some
brandy all around. When the General had served the four and poured a
snifter for himself, Roosevelt, indicating the letter on his desk, said tersely,

"Pa, this requires action. Call Briggs at Standards get a Committee
together to study this uranium business."

The Uranium Committee — Lyman C. Briggs, director of the Bureau
of Standards, the nation's physics lab, Roberts from Carnegie, Adamson
and Hoover from the military, Gregor, Szilard, Wigner and Teller — produced a report for the President on November 1st. While emphasizing
chain reactions as a potential power source for submarines, it did note
in addition that "if the reaction turns out to be explosive in character, it
would provide a possible source of bombs with a destructiveness vastly
greater than anything now know," and recommended "adequate support
for a thorough investigation."

It was November 17th before Briggs heard from Pa Watson. The
President had read the report carefully, and would put it on file. And on
file it remained, until well into 1940. Roosevelt had other things on his
mind, political matters — like the November presidential election. It had
been a huge decision whether to run for an unprecedented third term. And
for the first time in his career, he was in serious political trouble. America
did not want to go to war; while Roosevelt — perhaps in part because of
Amadeus' letter — privately thought it inevitable. This dynamic did not
escape his opponents.

Herbert Hoover:

Here and now America must summon reason to control emotion. The first policy of calm realism is not to exaggerate our immediate dangers. Every whale that spouts is not a German sub. The 3,000 miles of ocean is still a protection. The air forces, tanks and armies of Europe are useless to attack us unless they establish bases in the Western Hemisphere. To do that they must first pass our Navy. It can stop anything in sight now.

It is nonsense that we cannot defend freedom here even if the Old World fails. Our ancestors, with sparse population and resources for the first fifty years of this Republic, sustained liberty here when most of the world was ruled by despots. We can do it again if we have to. The hope of mankind and the hope of civilization is that democracy survive on this continent. Those who advocate war should never forget one thing: the first necessity of any great war is to set up dictatorship. We should be sacrificing the last sanctuary of liberty in the world in the belief that we are defending liberty.

He hoped Roosevelt was listening.

He was.

37. Wars Of The Worlds III: Of This World And The Next

Elections bring out the worst in people — the duplicity of dignitaries, the gullibility of the electorate. While in 1940, neither Franklin Roosevelt, nor Wendell Willkie could be characterized as duplicitous — they were both extraordinary men — still, when chips were down and each thought he might come up short, cigar smoke vied with mirrors, and tactics became devious all around.

FDR chose to run against Hitler (with Willkie a poor third), and as President-During-International-Crisis, he defined the territory. Willkie, though equally committed to defeating Nazism, ran as a "peace candidate", accusing FDR of sneaking the country into war, while the President, knowing war was coming, promised to keep the peace. At one point, the Roosevelt staff considered exposing Willkie's affair with Irita Van Doren to counter the Willkie staff's threat to publish Henry Wallace's letters to Roerich, his guru. ("The price of corn," the Republicans said, "was determined by the spirits.") But a deal was struck: no Wallace letters; no exposure of Willkie's private life.

The spin-meisters were whirling like dervishes, and Gregor was disgusted. The radical thrust of the New Deal had been forgotten as the powerful flexed their muscle, and a gullible, suspicious public fed and bloated on confusion.

By the week before election, Gregor needed out. October 27th was the closing day of the World's Fair, and ever since hearing Szilard, the roach had been curious about "The World of Tomorrow" — official version. On that closing Sunday, he took the 6 A.M. train to New York and got to the Fair Grounds shortly after one. It was a cold, wet, gray day, but still the most crowded day of the entire fair.

Crowded, but melancholy. The Fair had opened in brightest hope, and was now closing amidst crisis and fear of war. It had been a financial failure, too, with much money owed, and as Brecht often pointed out, in America, this is the greatest crime. For all the razzmatazz, later attendees felt guilty in a guilty land.

On this closing day, lines were impossibly long for all the major exhibits: it would be hours before Gregor could get into Futurama; he had to leave at five to catch the last train back at seven. So he stood for a long time, just taking in the scene, thinking thoughts with the grayness of the day. He was facing the courtyard of the Westinghouse building, a huge affair, an omega lying on its side, the last letter of the Greek alphabet opening its legs to a penetrating central tower. It was as if the entire fair had been designed by freshmen of the School of Freud.

Omega, why omega? Ah! The symbol for electrical resistance, the ohm. Westinghouse. Electrical. But resistance. Why resistance? Why not voltage, amperage, flow? Ohm. What did Gregor know about Ohm? Georg Simon wasn't it?, a high school teacher forced to leave his job for the crime of "experimenting", living hand to mouth in disappointment and bitterness, yet able to prove eternal laws of electricity. But perhaps the building wasn't referencing Ohm after all. Perhaps it was just what it was, an omega, the last letter, the end. "I am Alpha and Omega, the beginning and ending, saith the Lord." Is this really the end? It's the last day of the fair, but it was not always the last day. It was once the first day. Still, even then, on the first day, the building lay there warning, accusing. In the beginning is the end. Prepare.

G shook his head and pressed his sides with his middle arms to force a spiracular sigh. "This is silliness thinking. It's only a courtyard-making shape." And with the shaking off, he noticed the crowds of people peering at something on the ground. What was it?

The roach wandered over, and sifted through to center. The "something" was a hole, just a hole, somewhat under a foot in diameter, a dark hole into the earth. Ah! The Time Capsule! He had read about this. Several articles. The Time Capsule. He pulled back to the outside of the circle and looked around for some explanatory words. And there they were, surrounding a diagram and cutaway reproduction in a plexiglass tube.

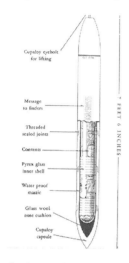

Gregor studied the text. In September of 1938, this metal cylinder had been installed in its "Immortal Well", there to rest for 5,000 years, until 6939. 6939! The fingers twitch at writing such a date, and so did Gregor twitch and shudder, casting his thoughts in that direction. So much trivial was lodged therein, just as Szilard had said. A Mickey Mouse cup, a rhinestone clip from the Five and Dime. What was this all about? Was a mouse clothed and shod the symbol of our civilization, a central artifact for future anthropologists? Gregor bought a copy of the beautifully printed instructions for finding and interpreting the capsule. On its title page:

THE BOOK OF RECORD OF
THE
TIME CAPSULE
OF CUPALOY
DEEMED CAPABLE OF RESISTING
THE EFFECTS OF TIME FOR FIVE
THOUSAND YEARS. PRESERVING
AN ACCOUNT OF UNIVERSAL
ACHIEVEMENTS. EMBEDDED IN
THE GROUNDS OF THE
NEW YORK WORLD'S FAIR
1939
SEPTEMBER 23, 1938

So much for the World of Tomorrow. This moment was about the freezing of the Cherished Now. Gregor sat down on a bench, and leafed through his purchase, increasingly amazed. A little girl tugged on her mother's arm: "Mommy, look at the big bug reading a book!" Mommy shushed her, and pushed her on into the courtyard.

The Book of Record began with a quote from Job, in small italics centered on the page: "All the days of my appointed time will I wait, till my change come. Thou shalt call, and I will answer thee." Gregor stared, almost shattered. His mouthparts dropped. Why this? Why this quote? Is this a copy meant only for me, as Dr. Kafka's Door to the Law? What has this to do with that little girl? With "The World of Tomorrow?" This book is aimed at me. Clearly. Me. He carefully turned the next page. On the left, a drawing of the omega, with an outsized capsule pictured deep under the ground between its feet. On the right, a red, gorgeous, illuminated, initial "W":

WHEN WE SURVEY THE PAST and note how perishable are all human things, we are moved to attempt the preservation of some of the world's present material & intellectual symbols, that knowledge of them may not disappear from the earth.

For there is no way to read the future of the world: peoples, nations, and cultures move onward into inscrutable time. In our day it is difficult to conceive of a future less happy, less civilized than our own. Yet history teaches us that every culture passes through definite cycles of development, climax, and decay. And so, we must recognize, ultimately may ours.

Who wrote this? Spengler's ghost? Surely this book was not a corporate message of — what did Szilard call it? American inanity in a Brave New World?

Gregor spent the next three hours in talmudic study of this thin volume — as if it were holy writ, a kaballistic coding of mysteries. He read of the

PREPARATION OF THE CAPSULE

of the consultations with *"archaeologists, historians, metallurgists, engi-*

neers, chemists, geo-physicists, and other technical men of our time." He marveled that Cupaloy had been created, non-ferrous and extremely hard, an amalgam which *"in electrolytic reactions with ferrous metals in the soil, becomes the anode and therefore will receive deposits, rather than suffer corrosion."* Science! This marvelous metal had been cast in seven segments (the mystic seven!) seven feet in total length, seven segments containing a Pyrex glass envelope to enclose its artifacts in an atmosphere of nitrogen. *"The materials inside the crypt have been selected for permanence and have been treated, so far as possible, to give them resistance to time. Material which would ordinarily be published in books has been photographed on acetate microfilm; a method that not only promises permanence but also makes possible the concentration of much information in small space. Metal parts which might be subject to attack by moisture have been coated with a thin layer of wax. No acids or corrosive substances are included in the crypt's contents or in the materials with which the Time Capsule is sealed, nor are any materials included which are known to decay or dissociate into corrosive liquids or vapors."*

There it was — the secret of human striving, the quest for immortality, live burial with not only hope, but instruction for resurrection. *Ewig...ewig.* Down in the deep, dark hole. "Pluto, I come from Pluto!" rising again in consciousness. Uprising through descent, light from darkness, knowledge from ignorance. And next,

RECOVERY OF THE CAPSULE

Speech across the millennia to those who will read no English— if they read at all. My God, what presumption, what chutzpah to suppose that someone in the appointed year — *"the 6,939 year since the birth of Christ, year 10,699 of the Jewish calendar, the 36th year of the 160th Chinese cycle, the 6,469th year since the birth of Mohammed the Prophet, the 7,502nd birthday of the Buddha, the 7,599th anniversary of the first Shinto emperor, Jimmu Tenno"* — what magnificent gall to order that world (should there still be a world) around.

When to dig, you ask? You future beings. Why, when the heliocentric longitudes of the planets on January 1st match the listed table, a combi-

447

nation of astronomical events unlikely to recur for many thousand years.

Where? Where to dig, should you care to dig? Latitude 40 degrees, 44 minutes, 34.089 seconds north of the Equator; longitude 73 degrees, 50 minutes, 43.842 seconds west of Greenwich, coordinates *"accurate enough to locate an object one-tenth of a foot or less in diameter at a particular position of the surface of the earth."*

"When it has been brought up out of the ground, let the finders beware, lest in their eagerness they spoil the contents by ill-considered moves." Ill-considered. Will there still be such a notion?

"Let the Capsule be transported with the utmost care, at once, to a warm, dry place. Cleanse the outside of mud, slime, or corrosion. Then cut off the top carefully at the deeply scored groove which has been left to guide the saw. Should gas rush out when the saw penetrates the crypt, let there be no alarm, for this is a harmless gas enclosed as a preservative." The hortative-subjunctive. This is how we address our saviour-heirs.

The tension was building, page by beautifully printed page. What, thought Gregor, what other than Mickey the Mouse will represent us to our accommodating friends? Ah,

THE CONTENTS OF THE CAPSULE

I have Gregor's copy in hand. This is the only section which he chose to underline, sentence by sentence, as if hypnotically underscoring a Now at the edge of darkness:

WITHIN the limitations imposed by space, the problems of preservation, and the difficulty of choosing the truly significant to represent all the enormous variety and vigor of our life, we have sought to deposit in the Time Capsule materials and information touching upon all the principal categories of our thought, activity and accomplishment; sparing nothing, neither our wisdom nor our foolishness, our supreme achievements, nor our recognized weaknesses.

We have included books and pictures that show where and how we live: some in apartments like dwellers in cliffs, but comfortably;

others in detached houses; still others moving about the country in homes mounted on wheels.

We have set forth the story of our architecture, by which we have reared soaring pinnacles into the sky.

We have described the offices and factories where we work, the machines that write, compute, tabulate, reproduce manuscript a thousandfold, sort out, and file; the machines that stamp and fashion metals; the machines and methods with which metals are knit together by electricity and cut apart by gas; the complex techniques of mass production, with which articles that consist of scores of different materials, requiring hundreds of operations to assemble, can nevertheless be sold among us for a few cents.

We have described in text and picture the arts and entertainment of our day; the games we play; the history & development & present attainments of painting, sculpture, music, the theater, motion pictures, and radio.

We have included copies of representative newspapers & magazines of this day, containing news, articles, fiction, and advertisements broadly characteristic of our period. We have also included a novel, the most widely read of our time. For good measure we have added specimens of our cartoons and "comics," such as daily and weekly delight millions in our newspapers and in our moving picture theaters.

Ours is a day of many faiths. We have provided descriptions of the world's religions, numbered their followers, and enclosed the Holy Bible, a book which is the basis of the Christian faith. We have provided outlines of the world's principal philosophies. We have discussed the all-pervading and effective educational systems of our time, and told in text and pictures the story of the training of our young.

We have included a copy of our Constitution, and something about our government, under which we live as free men, ruled by our own

449

elected representatives chosen at regular intervals by the votes of all, both men and women. We have included, also, a history of our country and a chronological history of the world.

Our scientists have measured the speed of light and compared the distances of the planets, stars, and nebulae; they have charted the slow evolution of primal protoplasm into man, fathomed the ultimate composition of matter and its relation to energy, transmuted tho elements, measured the earth and explored it, harnessed earthquake, electricity, and magnetism to probe what lies beneath our feet; they have shifted the atoms in their lattices and created dyes, materials, stuffs that Nature herself forgot to make. The stories of these achievements have been set forth in the Time Capsule.

Our engineers & inventors have harnessed the forces of the earth and skies and the mysteries of nature to make our lives pleasant, swift, safe, and fascinating beyond any previous age. We fly faster, higher, and farther than the birds. On steel rails we rush safely, behind giant horses of metal and fire. Ships large as palaces thrum across our seas. Our roads are alive with self-propelling conveyances so complex the most powerful prince could not have owned one a generation ago; yet in our day there is hardly a man so poor he cannot afford this form of personal mobility.

Over wires pour cataracts of invisible electric power, tamed and harnessed to light our homes, cook our food, cool and clean our air, operate the machines of our homes & factories, lighten the burdens of our daily labor, reach out and capture the voices and music of the air, & work a major part of all the complex magic of our day.

We have made metals our slaves, and learned to change their characteristics to our needs. We speak to one another along a network of wires and radiations that enmesh the globe, and hear one another thousands of miles away as clearly as though the distance were only a few feet. We have learned to arrest the processes of decay; our foods are preserved in metal or frost and by these means we may have veg-

etables and fruits in any season, delicacies from foreign lands, and adequate diet anywhere.

All these things, and the secrets of them, and something about the men of genius of our time and earlier days who helped bring them about, will be found in the Time Capsule.

How our physicians have healed the sick, controlled pain, and conquered many diseases, has been recounted there; how we have suppressed epidemics through the enormous undertakings of our system of public health; how our drugs end biologicals are compounded, and the enormous and varied list of them.

There are included samples and specimens of the new materials of our time, created in the laboratories of our engineers and chemists, on the looms of our mills, and in the forges, furnaces, and vats of our factories.

There are also samples of the products of our farms, where machinery has turned scarcity into abundance; where research has produced plants never seen in nature; where science now is able to produce plants even without soil.

There are also many small articles that we wear or use; that contribute to the pleasure, comfort, safety, convenience, or healthfulness of our lives, articles with which we write, play, groom ourselves, correct our vision, remove our beards, illuminate our homes and workplaces, tell time, make pictures, calculate sums, exchange values, protect property, train our children, prepare our food.

Believing, as have the people of each age, that our women are the most beautiful, most intelligent, and best groomed of all the ages, we have enclosed in the Time Capsule specimens of modern cosmetics, and one of the singular clothing creations of our time, a woman's hat.

That the pronunciation of our English tongue may not be lost, a "Key to English" has been prepared and printed in this book. That our vocabulary may not be forgotten, we have included in the Capsule a

451

dictionary, defining wore than 140,000 common words and phrases. That our idiom may be preserved, we have provided also a dictionary of slang and colloquial expressions. Finally, that our method of writing may be recovered, should all other record of it disappear, we have included a book in which the Lord's Prayer is translated into three hundred different tongues; also the fable "The Story of the North Wind & the Sun" translated into twenty-five languages. These may serve, as did the trilingual Rosetta stone, to help in the translation of our words.

In the Capsule there are only two actual books of our time, in the size and form to which we are accustomed. These are this book and the Holy Bible. All the rest have been photographed page by page on microfilm, which by the small space it requires has permitted us to include on four small reels the contents or equivalent of more than seventy ordinary books—enough in their usual form to fill the Capsule's crypt several times over. A magnifying instrument is included, with which the microfilm may be read.

Should those who recover the Capsule wish to know our appearance, and how we dress, act, and talk, there have been provided two reels of significant and typical scenes of our time, in pictures that move and speak, imprisoned on ribbons of cellulose coated with silver. If knowledge of machines for projecting these pictures and voices has disappeared, the machines may nevertheless be recreated, after recovery of the Capsule, from photographs and descriptions.

Each age considers itself the pinnacle & final triumph above all eras that have gone before. In our time many believe that the human race has reached the ultimate in material and social development; others, that humanity shall march onward to achievements splendid beyond the imagination of this day, to new worlds of human wealth, power, life, and happiness. We choose, with the latter, to believe that men will solve the problems of the world, that the human race will triumph over its limitations and its adversities, that the future will be glorious.

TO THE PEOPLE OF THAT FUTURE
WE LEAVE THIS LEGACY

Verweile doch, du bist so schön. Gregor found himself weeping. "Stay a while, you are so fair" — the one thought forbidden Faust, the thought that would trigger his eternal night.

For Gregor, too, it was an outlawed fantasy — that this world, with its petty vagaries, its conniving souls, all teeth at throat, that this vale of tears was worthy of love; that human life — solitary, poor, nasty, brutish and short — was to be honored and obeyed. Why bother? For Mickey Mouse? And yet he wept. He wept for the sewer of uncertainty and terror which was his life and the lives of those around him and of those across the seas; he wept for an ungrateful biped resistant to transformation; he wept for the metamorphoses which might never come about — not so much for their absence, as for their potential to sweep all this away — the wires and the comic books, the Bible and the cars, the "many small articles that we wear and use..."

Vanity, all is vanity, and yet not so. He looked around at the sad, yet wondering crowd, and he found them lovable, all lovable in their sadness, and lovable in their awe. (Nine years later, George Orwell would publish *1984*: "If you want a picture of the future, imagine a boot stomping on a human face — forever.")

On the subway to Penn Station, he looked at the other passengers, and leafed listlessly through the little book which had brought him so high and so low. At the end, a section called MESSAGES FOR THE FUTURE FROM NOTED MEN OF OUR TIME. There were only three short statements: Robert Millikan thought that *"if the rational, scientific, progressive principles win out in the struggle against despotism, there is the possibility of a warless, golden age ahead for mankind."* More science, less war: Gregor was doubtful. Albert Einstein was something less than cheery: *"Present production and distribution of commodities is entirely unorganized so that everybody must live in fear of being eliminated from the economic cycle. Furthermore, people living in different countries kill each other at irregular time intervals, so that also for this reason anyone who thinks about the future must live in fear and terror."* It was Thomas Mann who spoke evocatively of a strange continuity with the citizens of the future, people who *"will actually resemble us very much as we resemble those who lived a thousand, or five thousand, years ago. Among you too the spirit will fare badly — it should never fare too well on this earth, otherwise men would need it no longer."* Something glimmered in G's ganglia, but he was too exhausted to fan the flame. His trip home was indolent and slack, a mini-hibernation against the chill.

****

The next day, October 28, at Madison Square Garden, Roosevelt, self-styled Man of Peace, took full credit for the neutrality legislation of the 1930's, laws he had fought ferociously to block in Congress. "Those were measures to keep us at peace," FDR boasted, "And through all the years since 1935, there has been no entanglement and there will be no entanglement." The crowd loved it.

In Boston, two days later, he said, "And while I am talking to you mothers and fathers, I give you one more assurance. I have said this before, but I shall say it again and again and again: Your boys are not going to be sent into any foreign wars." "That hypocritical son of a bitch!" Willkie exclaimed. "This is going to beat me!"

On Monday before the election, Henry Wallace, with Roosevelt's approval, made the following remarks: "Every sign of opposition to the President leads to rejoicing in Berlin. I do not wish to imply that the Republican leaders are willfully or consciously giving aid and comfort to Hitler, but I do want to emphasize that replacement of Roosevelt, even if it were by the most patriotic leadership that could be found, would cause Hitler to rejoice. I do not believe that the American people will turn their backs on the man that Hitler wants to see defeated. I'll say too that every Republican is not an appeaser. But you can be sure that every Nazi, every Hitlerite, and every appeaser is a Republican."

That night, it was Willkie's turn at a Garden full of screams and flags. Muriel Rukeyser: "Women throwing hats, the searchlights pouring heat, the cheers, the circular portrait of Willkie, the banner as tall as a brownstone house, NO THIRD TERM. Room for 23,000 in Madison Square Garden — number of tickets passed out: 145,000.

House Minority Leader JOE MARTIN: Shall we take the first step toward dictatorship?

THE CROWD: No!

JOE MARTIN: Shall we take the first step toward war?

THE CROWD: No!

JOE MARTIN: Is the presidency a personal dictatorship?

VOICE OF SPEAKER: This is the method of Roosevelt.

THE CROWD: But it is not the method of Democracy."

As Mark Twain said, "There is no distinctly native American criminal class except politicians." *Sicut erat in principio, et nunc, et semper, et in saecula seculorum.*

38. Wars Of The Worlds IV: Orientalia

Votes: for Roosevelt, 27,243,466; for Willkie, 22,304,755.

States: for Roosevelt, 38; for Willkie, 10.

The Hungarians were delirious: success behind him, FDR could fully concentrate on their atomic concerns. The day after the election, they gathered at Teller's to plot. To plot and to party — for that night, the God of Gratuitous Gifts had scheduled a Bartok night at the National Ballet. Gregor's phone rang at six.

"Hello, Szilard here."

"Dr. Szilard, hello. It's Samsa."

"Of course it's Samsa. I called your number."

As usual, Gregor was a tad behind in repartee.

"Samsa, get on your tuxedo. We're going to a dancing."

"I don't have a tuxedo, and I don't like to dance."

"You're not dancing. It's music by Bartok. Kindler is conducting at Constitution Hall, a friend of Teller's. Left him four tickets, and Frau Teller is indisposed. That means you."

"Who is dancing?" Gregor asked, needing to be sure he wouldn't be embarrassed as in the days of the Gregor craze.

"Who is dancing? Who is dancing? I don't know. Dancers. From the National Ballet. I don't know names."

"Is it all right if I wear a brown suit? It's my best clothing."

"You'll stick out."

Gregor was used to this.

"You won't mind being seen with me?"

"We'll pretend we don't know you. Constitution Hall at 7:30. Goodbye."

A typical Szilard phone call.

"What are they dancing...?"

But he had hung up.

It must be admitted that brown-suited Gregor was out of place at the white-tie event. It was the first time the National Ballet and the National Symphony had collaborated in a production requiring large orchestral forces, and Democratic culture-vultures were still cocky-drunk with victory. But in the lobby, Szilard pulled a black beret out of his pocket, set it jauntily tipped over Gregor's right epicranium, Wigner wrapped a gay, red scarf around his cephalothoracic juncture, and the three Hungarians stepped back and looked at their creation.

"*Artiste*," Teller declared.

"Nothing to be ashamed of," Wigner added.

"Ja, ja, Szilard commented, "let's not make it goes to his head."

In they went, eighth row center, orchestra.

"What do we see?" Gregor asked.

"I don't know what we are seeing, but we are hearing Bartok. *The Miraculous Mandarin.*" For Teller, it was always the music, first and foremost. Dancing was a superfluous footnote.

"I don't know this," said the roach.

All had to admit that they had never seen or heard the piece: it had been banned in Europe since its composition just after the Great War. The audience would soon see why.

"Why a Mandarin? Why oriental?" Gregor asked.

They looked in the program.

"Mysterious character," Wigner quoted. "Alien world."

"Like you, Samsa," Szilard noted.

Little did he know how right he was. What a setup. A lonely, sex-starved alien watching a show about a lonely, sex-starved alien.

The lights dimmed, and the audience quieted down, expectant. But instead of the *mysterioso* beginning suggested by the title, the orchestra plunged right into a fortissimo, honking evocation of a modern city, alienated from nature and everything natural, sounds of raucous inhumanity. Audience members were already squirming in their seats. Gregor protected his knees.

The curtain rose on a shabby room in a derelict apartment, an expressionist fantasy of squalor. The wallpaper is peeling, the furniture is comically crippled, and in the corners, piles of shabby, odd things. G was particularly struck by the filthy stuffed eagle perched next to the horn of an old phonograph. His master's voice? Ives would have loved it.

It was quickly apparent that this was the hideout of three criminals, used as a storeroom for their stolen goods. One is lying on the bare mattress, staring at the ceiling; a second is rummaging through every drawer, hoping to find — what? Money? Jewels? The third is arguing violently with a beautiful young girl, whom they have apparently kidnapped, and are holding for their occasional pleasure. He turns his pockets inside out, then pulls her violently around to rub her face with the extruded cloth. "What can I do," she cries out, "It's not my fault..." (Gregor had never seen a ballet with words). The first thief jumps off the bed, and runs at the girl. "What can you do? You can catch us some men!" And he forces her to the window and tears off her blouse, displaying her, half naked, to the street below.

Gregor was bowled over. At first attracted by the despair in her huge eyes, he was now drawn by a rush of longing for her thin — almost emaciated — dancer's body. He could see every rib, every costochondral juncture of her exo-endoskeleton. Her nipples stood out like chitinous protrusions from her bony frame. Her arms — the bones — strung together by ligaments and sinews — just like his own. She was his longed-for human counterpart, a non-fatty sister he could finally claim in soul — and body! Wait! This is a ballet, a show. She is a dancer, part of a company, not a maiden to be rescued by a brown knight in a White House. Still, he found himself breathing quickly, his tegmen rising uncomfortably against the back of the chair, and even his wound beginning to perceptibly moisten, though from the sweetest kind of pain. Off in a far corner of his mind, he wondered how he might inveigle a meeting...

The girl stands at the window, pressing her nipples against the glass; the men hide and await their prey. The music become intensely serpentine, the first of three increasingly luminous seduction themes. She waves her hands at the passersby in the street. The first thief sticks his head out of the closet. "Got anyone?" "Yes," she nods. "Good." They hide again. Footsteps come up the stairs, and she positions herself in the middle of the room.

Now he could take her, now, before she demeans herself. He could just run up on stage, grab her in his arms, and disappear with her into the District of Columbia night. Teller, with one slight cough and phlegm-trapping snort, brought him back to irreality.

The door opens and frames an old roué with wrinkled face and waxed mustache, his top hat shabby as his shiny coat, his collar dirty sporting a cheap, gaudy tie, the flower in his buttonhole speaking of ancient sexuality, long past its prime. Gregor was as repelled as was the girl.

The old man looks her up and down, repugnantly self-assured. The music fairly cakewalks. He is delighted, and amused by her putting her blouse back on. He takes off his hat; his hair is slicked and pasted over his skull. As he begins to peel off his dirty gloves, the girl, by rubbing index finger and thumb together, tries to set the terms of engagement. "Money," he says, "What's money? It's love that counts." The three thieves spring from their hiding places. Gregor was overjoyed to see them. They toss the old man among them and finally out the door, down the stairs, as the music comes to comic climax, perhaps imaging an off-stage contact, stair to pudendal nerve. The second thief imitates the old man's wooing and warns the girl to do better next time. He rips off her blouse again and lifts her over to the window. Gregor found himself pressing his private parts against the back of the chair.

The second seduction theme winds its way into the air, and the scene is repeated, this time with a handsome student. Again, Gregor was despairing, though now more from jealousy than disgust. The young man blushes deeply and casts his eyes down, just as G would have done, had he not been hidden by darkness. Oh no! She likes him. She loves him! She looks at him with delight. The third thief signals from behind the student's back, thumb and index finger, thumb and index finger. "Do you have any money?" she asks. He shakes his head sadly, and turns to go. "No, no," she cries and holds him from behind, as the two begin to sway in a melancholy, ever more sexual waltz. The thieves have had enough of this, and once again come to the rescue of a heavily-breathing Gregor. Down the stairs with him! Outside, in the courtyard, we hear him sobbing faintly.

"You want love?" the second thief screams at her. "I'll give you love..." and he begins to take down his pants. The third thief draws his knife. "Don't waste her time, or I'll cut it off." A quick up-buttoning. Back to the window for the third time, that famously third repetition celebrated by fables east and west. Gregor wondered whether the three roomers in Prague had ever accosted his sister: he had never thought of it before.

He focused on her scapulae as the bones caressed her chest wall. Would that he could nuzzle up between them. The exotic transformation of the seduction music turned her vertebral column into a slowly waving sine, spine, sign, and then, hup, she was frozen in horror, dactyls clawed on windowpane. What was it? What could be next? The third repetition. Gregor remembered the title: The Miraculous Mandarin, it must be the Miraculous Mandarin. The girl retreats from the window, tries to hide. The second thief pulls her out from under the bed — and the door opens.

Was Gregor hallucinating? With his right eye he saw what presumably all others saw: a black-pigtailed Chinaman of broad, yellow face, with exaggeratedly slanting eyes, unblinking, stare fixed, like that of a fish. But with his left eye, he saw a huge insect, antennae braided, hanging from under a skull cap, orangey-yellow, icteric and sick. With his beret, he covered his eyes alternatively: Mandarin, monster, Mandarin, monster, then binocularly, he allowed the images to fuse. Both Mandarin and monster were identically dressed in a richly embroidered silk garment studded with lucent jewels. Of money there was no doubt.

The girl is frightened, repulsed, yet bound by his implacable, serious stare. Would she be appalled by *me*?, G wondered. She backs away, but the thieves push her forward. The Mandarin stands still in the doorway, staring,. The third thief tickles the girl's back with his knife. She motions the Mandarin to sit. And so he does, slowly, his set face never registering the slightest emotion, always staring at her, staring.

The girl begins her show, the seduction dance of all times, slow, but relentlessly building. She locks the door and dances on, less and less inhibited, finally spinning herself face up against the Mandarin. Seeing his unblinking stare, she bursts into laughter and plops onto his lap. *My* lap, thought G, I'll be kinder to you than he. It's me you want. And he covered his right eye.

From now on, Gregor watched himself on stage. Others in the audience may have thought he was a painter imaging a two-dimensional transformation.

With the laughing, half-naked young woman wriggling in his lap, the Mandarin insect begins a measured metamorphosis, eyelids flickering, breaking his fixed stare, his chest beginning to heave, his hands to twitch, his fingers reaching toward her face. He begins to shake, and frightens the girl, who jumps from his lap and backs away. Her laughter has stopped.

Mandarin insect rises and follows her around the room, his face distorted and imploring. The girl backs behind the table, behind the chairs, but he presses on, and finally dives to grab her ankle. She tears herself free, and he leaps at her again, alarmingly nimble and grotesque, tearing off her skirt, leaving her entirely nude. Now it is he who begins to dance provocatively, with fantastic gestures and acrobatic twists. Strange sounds come from his throat as he jingles his money at her and clutches his heart, his thighs. Tears stream from his eyes, Gregor's eyes. He is completely out of control, spinning, jumping, whirling, crashing, breaking windowpanes and glasses, spilling beer. It is impossible to escape: he grabs the girl and sinks with her to the floor. Gregor was wet at head and abdomen. Only his thorax was dry.

Did he yell out "Thieves!" before or after they jumped? A few people in the audience seemed to be looking at him. He pulled his beret off his right eye, and watched in stereoptic horror as the thieves pommeled the Mandarin, and released the girl. They hold him upside down and shake him. Gold coins roll around the stage. They pull the jeweled chain from his neck and pluck the rings from his fingers. "Let's kill him," the first thief offers, and the three erupt in horrendous laughter, throwing him on the bed and heaping blankets and pillows and rags on his face. Gregor knows he will not suffocate. His spiracles will save him. "Finished", the second thief announces when the Mandarin has stopped thrashing. Gregor wants to take a blanket to the shivering girl. The thieves each eye their naked accomplice.

But so does the Mandarin. His head emerges from under the pillows, his glassy eyes again fixed on his love. "Oh no," thought Gregor, now seeing only Chinaman, "Get him, get him!" And the thieves seemed to respond, pulling the Mandarin from the bed. As soon as his feet touch the floor, the inscrutable oriental bounces up, almost six feet in the air, and again hurls himself at the girl — only to be tackled by the third, knife-happy thief. "No you don't," orders the first, smacks the knife from his colleague's hand, and pins the Mandarin's arms. Gurgling in his throat, he continues to stare at the girl with fiery, goggling eyes. The third thief grabs his knife, and to the surprise of all, runs it into the Oriental's abdomen. (Gregor twitched violently.) The body slackens, the knife is extracted — and the Mandarin, jumps up again, right for the girl. From the corner, the first thief grabs a rifle — BANG! — the audience jumps — and a huge hole appears in the middle of the Mandarin's forehead. He staggers and totters — and is once again at the girl, chasing her with grotesque jumps. "Give him peace," Gregor prayed. He rarely prayed.

"Kill him," the girl cried, "you've got to kill him!" But how? The thieves grab the yellow man, wind his pigtail around his neck, and standing on chairs, string him up to the chandelier. G could imagine this scene in the more affluent East Room. Lindbergh, perhaps.

The chair is kicked from under the Mandarin's feet. The light goes out under his weight. Darkness. Silence. Holding of breath. A dim and green-ly-eerie light begins to emanate from the executed victim, especially from his eyes, still scanning the room for his beloved. Cautiously, slowly, the thieves cut him down; he drops to the floor — and again he rises and rushes at the naked girl — who catches him in her arms, wraps her warm body around him, and gives him a deep, long kiss.

It is *Liebestod* again, the love in death in love, which allows him to rest. The wound in his belly begins to bleed. The hole in his head begins to ooze gray slime. His hug slackens, his arms drop, his legs give way beneath him. His stare is fixed — in bliss. Slowly the girl lowers the body to the floor. The music swells, the curtain falls. The Mandarin is — miraculously — dead.

Gregor was dripping. Teller was involved in string harmonics and harp glissandos, ponticellos and quarter-tone slides. Szilard remained concentrated on the cello subject of the Mandarin's suffering. His only comment was "Too skinny. That girl was too skinny." What mathematician Wigner made of the whole thing nobody knew: he was silent for the rest of the evening.

****

Did I mention that on the closing day of the Fair, while Gregor was meditating on the Time Capsule, representatives from the United Church of God held a ceremony at the Japanese Pavilion to implore there be no war between America and Japan? Perhaps they should have held it at the American Pavilion. Or both.

In the face of dominating pressure and a history of exploitation by the West, now allied with China, Japan had, in the last decade, been agitating for a "Greater East Asia Co-Prosperity Sphere", an assertion of power posing a dilemma for Washington. Stimson and Morgenthau believed an embargo on oil and scrap iron would cripple the Japanese war machine, but Hull feared provoking Japan into seizing Southeast Asia. In late July before the election, after lengthy debate, Congress banned all export of scrap iron and aviation fuel to Japan, and the war took a startling new turn when, on September 27th, the Japanese signed a Tripartite Pact with Hitler and Mussolini, in which each pledged to aid the other "should any be attacked by a power not at present involved in the Pacific War."

The reference to America was clear, and with this "act of defiance" — threatening a possible two-ocean war — tempers shot up nationwide. In November, post-election, Roosevelt approved a loan of $100 million to the Chinese for their struggle against Japan, and in January all forms of iron, copper and brass were added to the embargo.

Thus provoked, starving for resources, in July of '41 Japan invaded Indochina. Roosevelt issued a stern warning to the Japanese ambassador: if his nation persisted in trying to seize the oil resources of Southeast Asian countries, "an exceedingly serious situation will immediately result." He then froze $131 million of Japanese assets in the U.S. and cut off trade with Japan that brought in 80% of the island nation's oil.

Japan was left with three alternatives — 1) abandon all imperialist offensive and defensive pursuits on the continent of Asia, withdraw from

Indochina and China and make a deal with America in order to ensure resumption of oil imports, 2) accept slow strangulation, or 3) fight.

On the morning of December 7th, 1941, in ancient samurai tradition, Japanese war planes bombed American forces at Pearl Harbor. It was the most brilliantly conceived and executed surprise attack in the history of warfare, killing over 2,400 American sailors, sailors, marines and civilians, wounding 1,178 more, destroying 149 planes, sinking the battleships *Arizona, Tennessee, West Virginia,* and *California,* capsizing the *Oklahoma,* and running the *Nevada* aground — all at the cost of 30 Japanese lives.

The next day, following an address by the President, ("Yesterday, December 7, 1941 — a date which will live in infamy..."), it took only thirty-four minutes of debate for Congress to declare war on Japan. Three days later Germany and Italy, honoring their pact, declared war against the United States, and Congress reciprocated. As a result of the attack on Pearl Harbor, a previously divided nation entered into the global struggle with virtual unanimity.

The following weeks were truly frightening for Americans. The day after Pearl Harbor, Japanese forces attacked Guam and Wake Island, strategic U.S. protectorates, and within a week, all resistance had been defeated. On December 10th, British carriers were sunk, and on Christmas Day, Hong Kong surrendered to the Japanese military. Two days later, Manila was occupied, and U.S. troops were forced to flee to the fortress of Corregidor on Bataan. The "little yellow-bellied Japs" were a force to be reckoned with.

Panic reigned. A Japanese invasion of the West Coast seemed immanent; there were nightly rumors and alarms. Cities and towns from San Diego to Seattle were blacked out; anti-aircraft guns fired sporadically. In the five days following Pearl Harbor, the FBI rounded up some 16,000 "subversives" on the West Coast, mostly Japanese, and some 1,200 German and Italian seamen. Japanese-Americans were as panicked as their compatriots, destroying "all things Japanese" in their homes for fear of being suspected and attacked.

Gregor was most upset.

FROM: G. SAMSA
TO: FDR
RE: CIVIL RIGHTS OF ALIENS
DECEMBER 12, 1941

War threatens all civil rights, and although we have fought wars before with our personal freedoms largely survived, still there have been times of large abuse, when hysteria and hate and fear are running high, and when minorities are unlawfully abused.

Everyone who cares of freedom, about a government of Law, must fight for it also for the other with who he disagrees, for the right of the minority, for the underprivileged with the same passion of insistence as he claims his own. If we care about democracy, we must care it as a reality for Japanese, for Germans and Italians, for those who are against us as well for those who are with us. The Bill of Rights, I understand, is for all on our American soils, not only citizens, all here are alike before the Law. If we really love justice, and really hate the bayonet and the whip and the whole Gestapo method of handling human beings.

It is one thing to protect against sabotage, but much another thing to throw out of work honest and loyal people who are of another accident of birth.

In fighting fascism, we must not let fascism happen here. We must not forget what we are defending: Liberty, Decency, Justice. I am hoping you will keep all this in mind in the next weeks and months.

Sincerely,
Your friend,
Gregor Samsa

The President agreed, Attorney General Biddle agreed, but Lieutenant General John Lesesne DeWitt, Commanding General of the Western Defense Command, embracing California, Washington, Oregon, Arizona, Nevada, Idaho, Montana, and Utah did *not* agree. The mucky-mucks were in Washington, three thousand miles away. What did they know? Just the other day there was a report from a Federal Intelligence Agent that some twenty thousand Japanese in the San Francisco area were "ready for organized action." The city would not even cooperate in an organized blackout. "You people," he told a Bay Area gathering, "You people do not seem to realize we are at war. So get this: Last night there were planes over this community. They were enemy planes. I mean Japanese planes. And they were tracked out to sea. You think it was a hoax? It is a damned nonsense for sensible people to think that the Army and Navy would practice such a hoax on San Francisco."

He denounced the citizens for "criminal, shameful apathy" in failing to black out the city. "Remember that we're fighting the Japanese, who don't respect the laws of war. They're gangsters, and they must be treated as such. If the planes had dropped a bomb or two, it might have awakened some of the fools in this community who refuse to realize that this is a war." "If Los Angeles," he shouted, "If Los Angeles, which knows Japanese far better than you do, if they can be scrupulous with their blackouts, why not you? Have you noticed that — whether by design or accident — virtually always the Japanese communities are adjacent to very vital shore installations, war plants, and electrical stations? Such a distribution of the Japanese population would appear to be something more than simple coincidence."

DeWitt wanted Japanese evacuated from the Western Defense Command Area of which he was in charge. He also wanted Germans and Italians — all enemy aliens — to go. This did not go over well with political leaders of large German- and Italian-American constituencies. Never mind that Laguardia was Mayor of New York, and Rossi Mayor of San Francisco. The most unthinkable problem would be to evacuate Joe DiMaggio's father, a resident of Oakland, offending America's greatest hero since Charles Lindbergh and Babe Ruth. But DeWitt would tolerate no exception. "If you make a single exception, you're lost."

Continuing allied losses in the Pacific fed national paranoia; fears of a Japanese invasion increased. The press, as usual, fed all fires:

Damon Runyon:

"It would be extremely foolish to doubt the continued existence of

enemy agents among the large alien Japanese population. Only recently, city health inspectors looking over a Japanese rooming house came upon a powerful transmitter, and it is reasonable to assume that menace of a similar character must be constantly guarded against throughout the war."

Westbrook Pegler:

"The Japanese in California should be under guard to the last man and woman right now and to hell with habeas corpus until the danger is over."

Henry McLemore:

"Let us have no patience with the enemy or anyone whose veins carry his blood. Personally, I hate the Japanese. And that goes for all of them. Everywhere the Japanese have attacked to date, the Japanese population has risen to aid the attackers. What is there to make the Government believe the same wouldn't be true in California? I am for the immediate removal of every Japanese on the West Coast to a point deep in the interior. Herd 'em up, pack 'em off and give 'em the inside room in the Badlands. Let 'em be pinched, hurt, hungry and dead up against it."

Lest the reader think this was all right wing hydrophobia, let me cite the influential liberal, Walter Lippmann, who, in a column titled "The Fifth Column on the Coast" warned of the "imminent danger of an attack from within and without, supported by organized sabotage." He thought the whole coast should be treated as a war zone, to be handled under special rules.

The *Los Angeles Times* editorialized as follows:

"THE QUESTION OF JAPANESE-AMERICANS

A viper is nonetheless a viper wherever the egg is hatched. A leopard's spots are the same and its disposition is the same wherever it is whelped. So a Japanese-American, born of Japanese parents, nurtured upon Japanese traditions, living in a transplanted Japanese atmosphere and thoroughly inoculated with Japanese thoughts,

Japanese ideas and Japanese ideals, notwithstanding his nominal brand of accidental citizenship, almost inevitably grows up to be a Japanese, not an American in his thoughts, in his ideas, and in his ideals, and himself is a potential and menacing, if not an actual, danger to our country unless properly supervised, controlled and, as it were hamstrung."

Needless to say, such media opinions took their toll. There were many reports of attacks on Japanese men, women and children. Law enforcement was reluctant to take up their cause, or even protect them — sheriffs had to run for office next election. City councils, too, had to answer to the electorate. State and local government urged the federal Administration to take action, to avoid substantial vigilante activity. Southern congressmen pressed for forced evacuation.

Mississippi Senator John Rankin:

"This is a race war. The white man's civilization has come into conflict with Japanese barbarism. I say it is of vital importance that we get rid of every Japanese, whether in Hawaii or on the mainland. Damn them, let's get rid of them now."

Tennessee Senator Tom Stewart seconded him:

"The Japanese, as a people, are cowardly and immoral. They are different from Americans in every conceivable way, and no Japanese should ever have the right to claim American citizenship. A Jap is a Jap anywhere you find him, and his taking the oath of allegiance to this country would not help, even if he should be permitted to do so."

Attorney General Biddle continued to object, and together with General Mark Clark and Admiral Harold Stark, Chief of Naval Operations, ridiculed the idea that the Japanese could mount any kind of serious attack on the West Coast. Congressman Leland Ford from Los Angeles reported that he had called the Attorney General's office "and told them to stop fucking around. I gave them twenty-four hours notice that unless they would issue a mass evacuation notice I would drag the whole matter out on the floor of the House and of the Senate and give the bastards everything we could with both barrels. I told them they had given us the runaround long enough, and that if they would not take immediate action, we would clean the goddam office out in one sweep. I cussed the Attorney General himself and his staff just like I'm cussing you now and he knew damn well I meant business." His constituents liked tough talk.

With the loudest voices of the country in chorus behind him, General DeWitt issued a memorandum to the Secretary of War summarizing his demands. Stimson brought it to a meeting of FDR, ER, Biddle, Hoover, Hull, Morganthau, Hopkins, Perkins, Ickes, Gregor (invited by ER because of his December 12th memo), Wallace and Frankfurter in the form of four questions:

"1) Is the President willing to authorize the War Department to move Japanese citizens as well as aliens from restricted areas?

2) Should we undertake withdrawal from the entire strip DeWitt originally recommended, which involves over 100,000 people, if we include both aliens and Japanese citizens?

3) Should we undertake the immediate step involving, say, 70,000, which includes large communities such as Los Angeles, San Diego, and Seattle?

4) Should we take any lesser steps such as the establishment of restricted areas around airplane plants and critical installations even though General DeWitt states that this would be wasteful, involve difficult administrative problems, and might be a source of more trouble than 100% withdrawal from the area?"

Over the fierce and passionate pleading of Biddle, Wallace and Gregor, FDR said he would approve whatever Stimson thought best. The result was the famous — infamous — Executive Order 9066, issued on February 19th in which the President authorized *"the Secretary of War, and the Military Commanders whom he may designate [read DeWitt], to prescribe military areas in such places as he or the appropriate Military Commander may determine, from which any or all persons may be excluded."* In other words, all Japanese out wherever DeWitt wanted them out. In addition, *"The Secretary of War is hereby authorized to provide for the residents of any such area who are excluded therefrom, such transportation, food, shelter, and other accommodations as may be necessary in the judgment of the Secretary of War, or the said Military Commander."*

In other words, all Japanese in the western half of all coastal states, would be "provided" with relocation and internment centers for the duration.

Gregor was horrified. It was yet another version of the St. Louis story, paranoia and selfishness run rampant. In a handwritten note to the President on February 20th, he wrote,

I am heartbroken over your decision concerning the Japanese Americans. It is two days until George Washington's anniversary. What would he say about this?

Discouraged,

your friend,

Gregor Samsa

The very next day, there was an answer in his mailbox:

THE WHITE HOUSE

WASHINGTON, D.C.

Dear Samsa,

I am sorry you are so disturbed by the Executive Order, but I am a practical man. What must be done to defend the country must be done. This is a decision for the Secretary of War, not for the Attorney General, not for Mr. Hoover, not for any of the others at the meeting, including myself - or you. The military may be wrong, but it is they who are fighting the war, and must be respected. In addition, public opinion seems to be on their side, so there is no question of any substantial opposition which might tend to disunity. We are all doing the best we can.

FDR

****

For the next days, Gregor vented his angry despair to the monuments of the Mall. On Friday, he visited the whale again at Natural History, on Saturday, the Greco paintings at the National Gallery, and on Sunday, Washington's Birthday, the Monument. Gazing southeast from the windows at the top, he scanned the buildings along Independence Avenue:

Agriculture, the Smithsonian Castle, the Freer... The Freer! Why hadn't he thought of it before? He skittered like lightening down the stairs, beating the elevator by fifty feet, and walked briskly down the Mall towards the Capitol. He crossed 12th Street, and climbed the steps of the unimposing granite building.

The Freer Gallery in the '30s and '40s held the premier collection of oriental art in the United States, perhaps in all the west, works collected by Charles Freer, freight car magnate, who donated it to the Government in '23. Gregor needed to drink some wisdom from the east, an apt balm for his current weeping of wound and soul.

He made his way through the arcaded corridor to the western galleries (east meets west!), turned into the room marked JAPAN, and was immediately dazzled by the gold leaf and pigments of Yeitoku's mystical screens. In front of "Pines on Wintry Mountains", he heard in his inner ear the pregnant opening of *"Der Abschied"*, last and greatest song in his favorite of favorites, *Das Lied von der Erde*. Afflicted with a soon-to-be-fatal heart disease, having written his great Eighth Symphony, haunted by the "lastness" of ninth symphonies, Mahler had written these songs to forestall his fate, and poured into them his threshold vision of life in transit to death. *Der Abschied* was the goodbye, the one-way journey up the mountain, the transition to eternity, and always sent shivers through G's heart. "Pines on Wintry Mountains"... he could hear the *"ewig"*-singing clouds. He stood there for forty-five minutes, coming to balance, coming to understanding.

Enough. He turned to go. At the doorway of the screen room his eye caught sight of — what? a monk? a Buddhist monk? — anyway, someone in a saffron robe meditating on something in a small corner cabinet in the room across the hall. Drawn by the monk's gaze, he ambled over to see the object. The robed figure was so close to the cabinet, Gregor had to delicately peer over his shoulder while trying not to interrupt his communion. Fortunately, the monk was shorter than he.

Beautifully mounted on green silk was a piece of parchment about four inches wide and eighteen inches long.

Six fiercely painted characters — Chinese or Japanese — Gregor didn't know — ran from top to bottom, bold, assertive, each ideogram calling out its selfness while still evoking the chain of which it was a part. Gregor peeked around the meditator's waist to check the brass plate on the floor of the display:

"CALLIGRAPHY ATTRIBUTED TO FU SHAN (1607-1684)"

Not too helpful. Sounds Chinese. Is this the Chinese room? Is this a Chinese monk?

Having a large cockroach peer in around one's waist might be enough to break concentration of the deepest meditator, and the man moved aside with a gesture signifying "Your turn."

"Oh. Oh, thank you," said Gregor. "I didn't mean to interrupt."

"You can't interrupt. It's all of a piece."

472

Gregor felt he was being offered the edge of some great wisdom — but it was awkward to bite in this random setting.

"I'm sorry. I pushed you aside."

"Perhaps you need to see this."

"Maybe I do, but — I can't read it. Do you know what it says? I recognize that character, 'heart' — it looks like a heart, but I don't know the others. Are they Chinese or Japanese?"

"They're Chinese, classical, seventeenth century, but most are quite similar in Japanese. No problem reading them. Especially after three years, Chinese Studies major at UCLA."

"You? What is 'UCLA'? A temple?"

"Hell no, it's a big university. University of California — Los Angeles. You're not from here?"

"I...I'm living here now fifteen years or such, but I have not been to California or Los Angeles. And since we are talking so much, maybe I should introduce myself. Gregor Samsa."

Gregor held out his claw. The yellow monk student placed palms together and bowed deeply. Gregor wasn't sure if he was serious or making fun.

"Yoshio Miyaguchi. You can call me Josh. Novice at Nipponzan Nyohoji Temple, on 16th Street. 4900 block. Way up. Where are you from?"

"Here. In Washington. I live on Pennsylvania Avenue."

"Where on Pennsylvania?"

"1600 block."

"1600 block? There's nothing there but the White House."

"That's were I live. In the basement. In the kitchen."

"Are you a cook?"

"No. I just live there. I help out, I do what is needed."

"A handyman?"

"What is that?"

"Someone who does whatever job comes up."

"Yes. That's what I do. I'm a handyman. Sometimes the President doesn't like my work."

"You know the President?"

"Of course I know the President. We live in the same house."

"I mean, he talks to you?"

"It would be uncomfortable if he didn't."

"Could you give him a message from me?"

"I suppose. He gets many messages."

"He may listen to this one."

"What is it?"

"I'll tell you in a minute. First let me tell you what this poem says."

Gregor had almost forgotten the calligraphy.

"Oh. Oh, yes. What does it say?"

"The six characters are (he pointed to each one) NATURE, PEACE, MEET, HEART, NATURALLY, and FAR."

"What does that mean?"

"It means something like: if one's inner nature is at peace, heartmind — that 'hsin' there is a combination you don't have in English — if one's inner nature is at peace, heartmind naturally meets — or blends with — the universe in its farthest reaches."

"And it seems you find this very interesting."

"I do."

"You want your inner nature to be at peace."

"I do. I'm working on it."

"That's why you were studying this calligraphy."

"That's part of why."

"What's the other part?"

"To give myself courage."

"For what?"

"My father just committed suicide."

"Oh. I'm sorry."

"It's not your fault. Stop apologizing, please."

"I'm sorry. Oh. I'm sorry. I mean, whose fault it is?"

"It's your boss's fault. Or your landlord's. Or whoever he is."

"Who?"

"The man in the white House."

"Roosevelt?"

"Not Willkie."

"Why is it his fault? Does he know your father?"

"Not at all. That's what makes it worse, Samsa-san."

"I don't understand."

"Nor do I. Have you heard of Terminal Island?"

"No."

"It's just off Los Angeles. Off San Pedro. It's got two shipyards, and Reeves Airfield. It also has a colony of Japanese fishermen. They all thought they'd better sign loyalty oaths, and they did, but there's some general named DeWitt…"

"I know of him."

"Dewitt wants them off the island. All of them."

"I know this."

"My father owned a pharmacy — the Ishi Pharmacy. Regular medicines and Japanese medicines. It took him and my mom seventeen years to build up the business. There were four kids. He sent two of us to UCLA. My little sisters are in high school. They want to go to college. And now — BOOM! Evacuation. Just like that. Give everything up. Everyone. Not just my parents. Everyone."

"I was in a meeting about this. There was nothing I could do."

"We had six days to move. The junk men came around like vultures. They offered my mother $5 for a $500 set of china. You know what she did? She broke the plates, one by one, right in front of their eyes. My father had no time to clear the shelves or make any contacts for selling stock. The junkmen told everyone the government was going to seize all their household belongings."

"That's not true."

"So I found out. But they said it was true. They were buying up refrigerators, radios, stoves, furniture for two or three dollars, loading up their trucks and driving away. We were left with nothing, not our homes, not our gardens, not our cars, not our ships, not our nets. What good were nets where they were taking us?"

"What happened to your father?"

"He left a note, then swallowed a whole jar of morphine. Might as well use it as abandon it. Want to know what it said in his note?"

"No."

"Thank you."

"Why?"

"For being discreet."

"You are brave to face all that. I hope the calligraphy helps."

"I don't need to be brave to face all that. I need to be brave for something else."

Silence.

"I am going to commit *seppuku*. In protest of what the man in the White House is doing to my people."

"With a sword? With a friend chopping off your head?" Gregor was alarmed.

"No, Samsa-san. This is 1942. I am going to be modern. Gasoline. Texaco. I will follow the great path of self-immolation."

It took Gregor a while to respond. Was he joking? He seemed like a regular college kid, Josh, Josh in a yellow costume. Granted, he was oriental. Perhaps inscrutable, as everyone said. G probed gently.

"How will you do this?"

"On the first of March, I will go to the Capitol Steps..."

"Why the first of March?"

"It's my birthday. It will give me time to prepare."

"Why not the White House?"

"It's not just the President I hold responsible. I read the papers. I go to the Senate to hear the speeches. It makes me ashamed to be American. I want to be at the Capitol, the symbol of this country. I want to look at the Library across the parking lot, the Library of Congress. I want to think how much nobility and wisdom is there, how much there is to respect in the world, how much is being ignored."

"You are not afraid how much it will hurt?"

"I'll show you how I'm working on this. You may need to know. I want you to stand right there and stare at those characters. Remember: NATURE, PEACE, MEET, HEART, NATURALLY, and FAR. Just keep looking at them and listen to me. This is what I tell myself as I look at them."

Josh positioned Gregor directly in front of the calligraphy, and moved around behind him to whisper in what he thought was his ears. G was used to this mistake. He moved his right knee out to the side, and allowed Josh to speak.

"Death is not the end of life, just a brief transition to another state before rebirth. You agree?"

Gregor tentatively nodded.

"So I understand my suicide is not an escape, but simply an act of compassion. Compassion for my father, and compassion for the senselessness of the world."

"I thought you said it was protest."

"Quiet. Listen. I'll get to that. My task in the next week is to become truly selfless, desireless, and enlightened enough to prepare for the moment of passing. Those I leave behind — my mother, my brother, my sisters, even the world at large — will respect what I am doing. I tell myself that. They won't resent it, they won't reject it, they may not be ready for such an act themselves, but Samsa-san, you will see, they will not grieve — but praise They will understand that choosing one's own time and place and manner of death with peace of mind is the most important thing, more important than length of life. They will know my father's clarity as well as my own. They will compare their own clarity, and if they find it lacking, they'll be stimulated to think more clearly, to be more mindful. If General DeWitt becomes more mindful, if the man in the White House becomes more mindful, the world will be spared much agony. To this degree, my immolation will be an act of protest, hopefully not in anger, but as a goad towards greater clarity."

"But burning alive is so... destructive."

"Samsa-san, are you dense? I told you — and you agreed — there is no creation and no destruction. Conservation of mass-energy-intention. Read Einstein. Why then fear death? Personal extinction is irrelevant. We are absorbed into a collective consciousness, a Great Totality. You will be too, someday. You will be a no-longer-mere-entity, you will be aware of every other entity in the universe, free from the constraints of time and space, without beginning and without end."

"I would be afraid to burn myself."

"You'll get used to it. And to help you, your new friend Josh is going to make a very special request. Will you do it for me?"

"What? Do what?"

"You have to agree first. Then I'll tell you."

Gregor continued to stare at the six characters. Then,

"Yes. I agree."

"Good. I knew you would. I want you to be my *kaishaku*."

"The helper who cuts off the head? I can't. I..."

"No cutting off of heads. This is 1942, remember? When the samurai speaks to the *kaishaku* before or during *seppuku*, the standard response is *go anshin*. Say it. Say it.'

"Go anshin. What does it mean?"

"Say it again."

"Go anshin."

"Good pronunciation. It means 'set your mind at peace.'"

"Go anshin."

"Excellent pronunciation. You're a natural. Next Sunday, when we go up the Capitol steps..."

"We??"

"Of course. The *kaishaku* accompanies the celebrant — always. When we go up the Capitol steps, I want you to watch me very carefully, sensitize your antennae, and if you feel me getting unclear you must say...?"

"Go anshin."

"Precisely. And then I can do it. Aren't you glad we met?"

"No."

"You will be. It's my gift to you, and the gift of the Gods. Goodbye, Samsa-san. I will see you at seven P.M., a week from today, east side of the Capitol, in time to illumine the twilight. Wish me well."

Gregor was speechless.

"All right then, don't wish me well."

He turned to go.

"Wait," cried G. "What is the message for the President?"

"I thought you'd never ask. Tell him to set his mind at peace."

He took G by the shoulders and gently turned him back to the glass case.

Yoshio Miyaguchi walked out of the Freer Gallery, leaving Gregor to stare at Fu Shan's characters, NATURE, PEACE, MEET, HEART, NATURALLY, and FAR.

39. Wars Of The Worlds V: Of Fire And Ice

"Perform what? Sepukoo? Does he need any help from us?"

Roosevelt was in a genial mood, propped up in bed, the phone tucked under his chin as he ate his English muffins.

"What? To death? At the Capitol? Why?"

(Long pause.)

"Well I don't see how that accomplishes anything. Have him come see me. Four tomorrow. Well, find him, goddam it. Check his monkerie or what have you. Look, Samsa, we can't have the press on this. You're the point man. Whatever resources you need, you've got them. Call the FBI, call the Capitol Police, call the Fire Department if necessary. You stop this maniac, or you're out of here! I mean it!"

The President was not as genial as he had been three minutes ago.

Temple Nipponzan Nyohoji had not seen Yoshio Miyaguchi since the weekend. He had not returned to his apartment. The FBI and the District Police were on his case — nothing all week.

On Sunday, March 1st, from 6:30 in the warmish, early spring evening, Gregor waited in the parking lot at the east façade of the Capitol. No yellow-robed monks. At 6:55 he was approached by a short, pot-bellied, new-bearded, somewhat seedy-looking oriental man wearing a blue New York Yankees jacket and cap.

"Got a match, bud?"

"Uh, no — no, I don't smoke. Sorry."

"That's ok, I have a lighter. Follow me in five minutes. Not before."

Gregor had been fooled.

"Go anshin," he whispered.

"My mind is at peace."

"Good luck."

The Yankee fan joined the tourists scattered on the steps, forbiddingly shadowed in late-evening light. He walked all the way up under the portico to inspect the head of Washington, flanked on the left by an angel with a pen, on the right by an angel with a trumpet. Pen and trumpet. So be it. He stood for a moment at the Columbus doors — those Ghiberti-like portals, here transformed from Gates of Paradise to Gates of Hell — for the Red Man. The tourist in the blue New York Yankees jacket with its white insignia turned and took in the dome of the Library of Congress, green oxidized copper, the red light streaming over the shoulder of the Capitol finding its hidden glow. He stood for a minute, breathing deeply through his mouth, then walked slowly down eighteen broad steps to the second landing. Standing there a moment, looking directly at Gregor below, he gave him a tiny, dismissive wave with his right hand, as if to say, "It's OK. Stay down there. I don't need you." Gregor's eyes sought out his face. Yoshio Miyaguchi gave him a wink.

Then, with a well-practiced, lightning gesture, he popped open his jacket, turned the gas can over onto his chest, flicked his lighter, shot up in flames, and sank to his knees in *seiza* posture, perfectly centered, perfectly framed. Gregor's first thought was "How beautiful he looks!"

But then he panicked, and looked wildly around for the Police, the FBI, all the agents he assumed would be prowling. And indeed, they were coming, running from north, south and east, fooled, as he had been, by a simple, unexpected costume — too late. The puffing crowd of law enforcement stopped at the first landing, eighteen steps below the flames.

Miyaguchi's roommate, Ken, the real *kaishaku*, caught the scene with his Leica — the photo which became the famous Life Magazine cover of March 6, 1942. Gregor ran up the steps to the group and shook the first blue jacket he contacted.

"Help him. Can't you try to help him?"

Miyaguchi's charred body fell forward, as was proper in *seppuku*.

"Cool it, buddy. The guy's a crisp. Besides, the only good Jap is a dead Jap."

40. To High Siberia

But love grows old,
And love grows cold...

It has been shown that Blattid giant neurons acquire a slow, rhythmic pulse when stimulated consistently two, four or eight times a second. The output frequency is approximately three per second, a metrical march irrationally related to the input, and still a mystery to insect physiologists. But such a phenomenon might account for the habitual creative revery Gregor (like Charles Ives) experienced when riding the railroad. Was it the rhythmic flashing of telephone poles or ties, or perhaps the clicking of iron wheels over intermittent temperature gaps? Experiments have yet to be done.

It was Saturday, June 12, 1943. Gregor was seated mid-coach, left side, staring out the window at the verdant Maryland morning. Normally myopic, he was slipping into fuzzier territory yet as the alpha rhythm began to prevail. It had already been the strangest of days, leaving the White House at six AM, the first family asleep, exiting unheralded like some hotel guest with an early check-out. Not even check-out. Walk-out. The White House had been his home for more than a decade. He had seen its babies born, its children grow up and leave for college. He had witnessed the ever-increasing distance of Eleanor and Franklin, as she became more empowered and liberated, and he weaker and more enslaved.

The last four years had been the worst: the war had brought the President and his blattid guest to loggerheads, and what was once a blossoming friendship had now become — what? — a toleration at best, a loss of interest on the one hand, and a loss of respect on the other. The President did not need moral superiors to criticize him with their silence, to mutely berate him on behalf of Jews or Japanese. He didn't need "friends" who lectured him through stilted, moralizing memos. Gregor, on the other hand, didn't need heroes with moral feet of clay. What was once a falling-in-love had metamorphosed into deep disappointment and occasional despair. Cynicism lurked around the corner, and in the face of such a threat, the best thing for him to do was to turn away and leave.

Still, who can easily exit such a setting? A free home at the seat of power. A fly's eye view of the people behind the roles. An embarrassed Roosevelt, for instance, wheeling impulsively in on a — surprise! — naked, dripping Churchill emerging, cigar in mouth, from his bath. "The Prime Minister of Great Britain has nothing to hide from the President of the United States," intoned the Englishman. Priceless. Unreported in the New York Times. Only Gregor had witnessed it, passing by chance along the third floor hallway. It was something to tell his grandchildren. So he stayed. Perhaps longer than he should have.

The last two years — maybe more, maybe since the *St. Louis* affair — had felt like a marriage gone stale, with neither party wanting to admit the change, each holding on to the formal daily round to avoid facing up to acid emptiness. Gregor felt the point of no return had been his failure to stop Yoshio Miyaguchi from committing *seppuku*. For all the controversy surrounding the New Deal, that single, almost irrelevant event had been the Administration's hugest scandal, the FDR version of Hoover's attack on the Bonus Army. In the weeks following, Gregor expected at each moment to be called on the carpet, to be punished according to the enormity of the crime, to be strapped onto a table, perhaps, and to have the suicide note burned into his back by a moving acetylene torch. But — nothing. The waiting was grievous. He re-read and obsessed on that passage in *The Idiot* about the unutterable agony of certain impending death — but there was no priest to hold a cross to his lips as he mounted the imagined scaffold.

At the same time, just as Dostoevsky described, he became aware of the immense value of each moment of life, the infinite importance filling every conscious crack and surface of his existence. He waited in this heightened state through the entire month of March and into April, but no remonstrance seemed forthcoming, the acetylene torch failed to materialize, and as spring faded into summer the St. Louis and its doomed passengers seemed swept into the dustbin of history, present at first only in its absence, as a bright light will leave a hole in visual space, then fading to a vaguely dissonant coming and going, nothing mentioned, nothing gained.

For his part, the President had suffered what was to be suffered, and had let the blaming largely go: he was big enough to forgive, and small enough to forget. Gregor imagined Eleanor playing some role here, counseling her husband, as Heracles did Philoctetes, to turn his attention to the real war. Then too, the world was about to witness in his cowardly, duplicitous dumping of Wallace. FDR was selectively averse to confrontation. Why contend when you can avoid?

Gregor had lived through a numbing '42 and '43, watching the world, like Benjamin's Angel of History, crumble around him.

A Klee painting named "Angelus Novus" shows an angel looking as though he is about to move away from something he is fixedly contemplating. His eyes are staring, his mouth is open, his wings are spread. This is how one pictures the angel of history. His face is turned toward the past. Where we perceive a chain of events, he sees one single catastrophe which keeps piling wreckage upon wreckage and hurls it in front of his feet. The angel would like to stay, awaken the dead, and make whole what has been smashed. But a storm is blowing from Paradise; it has got caught in his wings with such violence that the angel can no longer close them. This storm irresistibly propels him into the future to which his back is turned, while the pile of debris before him grows skyward. This storm is what we call progress.

Old Dr. New Deal had metamorphosed into Dr. Win-the-War, a man who wanted to be introduced as "Commander in Chief", rather than as

"President", a man whose political and national security concerns were so blinding as to wed him to Breckinridge Long, major donor to the Democratic Party, and Assistant Secretary of State for, among other things, Refugee Affairs and Visas, the two together singing the Great Fear Duet about flooding the nation with Communist and Nazi spies disguised as refugees. This, from the man who intoned so inspiringly, "The only thing we have to fear is Fear itself."

Visa requirements became tighter, and shut down almost entirely as the Nazis escalated their quest for a Jew-free Europe. Such fugitives were "not of the desirable elements," Long said, and Eleanor called Long a fascist, and FDR said "Never call him that again," and Eleanor, mother hen to all refugees, said, "I won't call him a fascist, but that won't change what he is." For the President, the political risk over Jews was not worth running.

Roosevelt, the crippled-boy-playing-soldier, building a "Map Room" in the White House for military briefings — because Churchill had one. Roosevelt the conductor-of-smallest-affairs, sending a memo to his naval aide (delivered by Gregor): "Will you tell the Navy Band that I don't like the way they play the Star Spangled Banner — It should not have a lot of frills in it. F.D.R." (Gregor didn't like it either.) Roosevelt-the-Cheerleader, insinuating his way into people's living rooms in the face of Japan's victories in the Philippines, Hong Kong, Burma, Thailand, Malaya, and the Dutch East Indies, in the face of their threats to Australia and India, in the face of their foothold in the Aleutians, in the face of the closing of the Burma Road and the isolation of China, In the face of Hitler's attacks on Moscow and Leningrad and his U-boats winning the battle of the Atlantic — that radio voice, confident, optimistic, making certain that the American people never wavered in their determination to fight to victory. "No matter what our enemies in their desperation may attempt to do to us — we will say, as the people of London have said, 'We can take it. And what's more, we can give it back — with compound interest.'" Roosevelt-the-banker.

And yet, in spite of domestic internments, in spite of dark defeats in the Pacific, Roosevelt-the-leader, who insisted the war against Germany have highest priority, the Roosevelt who saw Hitler as the most dangerous enemy, urging his naked friend Churchill to side with Stalin in pressing for immediate invasion of Western Europe. Churchill resisted, seeing a landing in France as risky at best, and the President backed down, while Stalin concluded that Russia and Germany might be slaughtering one another so that capitalists could dominate the world.

And Roosevelt the miracle worker: rehabilitating the economy, converting from peacetime to wartime production, building new plants and establishing priorities of manpower and matériel, all requiring centralized control and planning on a level unique in American history. The '42 State of the Union speech: goal — 60,000 planes, 25,000 tanks, 20,000 anti-aircraft guns, 6 million tons of shipping. The '43 State of the Union: goal — 125,000 planes, 75,000 tanks, 35,000 guns, 10 million tons of shipping. The creation of a military-industrial complex. This storm is what we call progress.

700,000 planes, 200,000 tanks, 80,000 guns...The train rolled on through Harper's Ferry, and Gregor was becoming dizzy, dizzy in ganglia, dizzy in heart. He tipped his hat down over his eyes and let the planes, tanks and guns grind their way off the stage, transubstantiated beyond ploughshares into the thinnest of air.

Slowly, as if from a great distance, a drone added its voice to the monotonous clicking of the train, a droning melody, the most trivial, the barest of tunes,

That little hiccup, how perverse! But I could hide in that crack, tighten my wings on it, keep from falling through. I could hide there and listen. The newspaper boy from this morning. It's his tune. The ancient-looking newspaper boy in the park — under the willow-oak, weeping. Barefoot. Grinding away, his little crank, ceaseless turning.... Should I not go west? Leiermann, should I stay with you? Will you play my song? Did he smile? I remember the gap in his teeth. Why was there no one else around? On a sunny Sabbath day, no tourists? And ice, why was there ice? Did I dream it? No. I bought a New York Times, *a real* New York Times *for a real ten cents. Here, I have it here.*

Gregor whipped his hat off his eyes, and pounced down upon the *Times* lying on the seat next to him. The eight column headline battered his eyes:

PANETELLERIA YIELDS, CONQUERED BY AIR MIGHT

The Italian 'Gibraltar' is Knocked Out by Record Avalanche of Bombs. Troops Take Over in 22 Minutes as New Design in Warfare Emerges

There, it's real, you see? He tore open the paper as if to test its materiality. On page four was a summary of the week's events in Los Angeles:
ZOOT SUIT RIOTS CONTINUE
No photo. Gregor did not know what a zoot suit was, but thought he'd get it from context:

> Now in their tenth day, disturbances between sailors and Mexican youths continue to make life in the City of Angels more interesting. This week, civilians joined servicemen in chasing, stripping, and occasionally beating zoot-suiters or non-zoot-suit-wearing Mexican Americans and blacks. On Monday evening, June 7th, thousands of Angelenos, in response to twelve hours' notice in the press, turned out for a mass lynching. Taxi drivers offered free transportation to the riot areas.

> Police preferred to watch, rather than intervene. Concerning the hands-off policy, one officer commented, "We're paid by the public to represent public opinion." A young sailor, iron pipe in his hand, observed that "These zoot-suit foreigners are a smack in our face. We're going to straighten them out."

> Military officers were momentarily powerless to control the disorderly bands of approximately 75 servicemen. One MP had this to say: "If we were to exercise decisive and immediate authority, we'd have to incarcerate and court-martial thousands of our men for disorderly conduct, disobeying direct orders, inciting to riot, going AWOL — even mutiny. Can you imagine the enormous propaganda victory for the Axis with that?

> On June 9th, local government became involved when the Los Angeles City Council passed the following resolution: "NOW THEREFORE BE IT RESOLVED, that the City Council by Resolution find that the wearing of Zoot Suits constitutes a public nuisance and does hereby instruct the City Attorney to prepare an

487

ordinance declaring same a nuisance and prohibit the wearing of Zoot Suits within the city limits of Los Angeles."

Gregor still wasn't sure what a zoot suit was. But it didn't sound good. He did know what a sailor suit was — and that didn't sound good either. At least here. He recalled sheets and hoods parading down Pennsylvania Avenue. He thought again of Alice, the lovely antenna-like hair of Alice Paul. All these years together in Washington...where did their friendship go? Did her White House arrests separate them forever? Was she even still alive? *Où sont les neiges d'antan?*

For all the President's reluctance to confront, it was FDR who had finally broken the impasse, and shattered the ongoing vacuum of politeness. At the '42 Christmas party, the President took Gregor aside, and asked him if he were up for a special assignment and a little adventure. He could give few details, but he could assure G it would make maximum use of his many skills, would probably change the world, and would be of great benefit to humanity — Gregor would just have to trust him. Trust, of course, was the principal victim of the last five years, and G was leery, even suspicious. The icons "benefit to humanity" and "change the world" were still moving, but their resonance had been muffled by the disappointing realities of the last years, and evoked in G's thorax only muted strings, *pianissimo, da lontano.* But the embers flared when the President whispered, "Without you and Einstein, this might never have come to pass." Putting two and two together was easy compared to putting Gregor and Einstein together. "Myself and Einstein," he thought — "in the same motion, in the same sentence!" The letter he had delivered. The lecture he had given — bad as it was. Perhaps something had come of them after all. Samsa and Einstein — benefactors of the world.

"This has something to do with a science project?" he asked.

"If you take the assignment, you'll be instructed further. I can't tell you more just now."

"Like a sacred mystery."

"I suppose you might say that." The President was weak on sacred mysteries. Gregor would have done better to interrogate the Vice-President about such things — but the Vice-President would have been entirely ignorant.

"Let me think about it and I'll let you know." In his heart, he already knew.

****

Had he had any doubts about taking the assignment, they would have been settled by a remarkable coincidence. Seeking counsel, he phoned up Leo Szilard. Three times he called, only to be greeted by busy signals. Giving up, he got ready for bed; the phone in his cabinet rang as he was slipping into straw. It was New Year's Eve. Who could be calling? A late date?

"Hello, Samsa here." (He had never lost this European habit.)

"Samsa, Szilard."

"Leo! I was just calling you. Three times. Your line was busy for the last hour."

"That's because I was calling you. Three times. Your line was busy for the last hour."

"How peculiar! What do they say? Great minds think alike?"

"Only mediocre minds think. Great minds don't think at all."

"Um...yes. Well, mediocre minds think alike, then."

"Speak for yourself."

"Leo, does your great mind know what I was calling about?"

"Of course."

"What?"

"The same thing I was calling you about."

"What is that?"

"Going to Site Y."

"What's Site Y?"

"You mean the President hasn't asked you to go?"

"Well, he did ask me to go on an assignment — an adventure — but he didn't say what or where."

"I want you to go. Wigner and Teller agree. Teller is going himself. Wigner will consult."

489

"Go where?"

"Site Y."

"Where is that?"

"I can't tell you."

"Do you know?"

"Of course. But I can't tell you."

"Well, what is site Y?"

"About that, I can tell you even less."

"Less than nothing?"

"You've never heard of negative numbers? We want you to go."

"Why?"

"You'll see."

"Does this have something to do with…what we went to Peconic about?"

"What's Peconic?"

"Einstein."

"Oh, yes. The Peconic State Parkway. We got lost. It has little to do with Einstein."

"Would he go? Einstein?"

"No. And they wouldn't want him."

"Leo?"

"Yes?"

"I think I should go."

"Great minds think alike. Let me know how things develop."

Click. As usual, Gregor was left staring into the phone.

On Saturday, January 2nd, 1943, Gregor sent a note to the President agreeing to take the assignment. The following Wednesday, at a chance encounter in the West Wing, FDR, whizzing past at 10 ft/sec., waved briefly from his wheelchair, and yelled out between cigarette-holder-clenching teeth, "Got your message." Gregor heard nothing further for several months. The subject never came up. There was a note in mid-April from Szilard:

```
Samsa,

Be warned about Site Y. No one will be able to
think straight. Everybody who goes there will go
crazy. Stay sane. That's why we need you. LS
```

A month later, two railroad tickets arrived in his box via interoffice mail: for June 12th, The Capitol Limited to Chicago, and the Super Chief from Chicago to Lamy, New Mexico, coach, no sleeping cars Was this a trusting gift, or an easy-out invitation to leave? By May, Gregor was excited enough to think of it as gift, to put out of his mind the impish fact that "Gift" in his mother tongue meant "poison". He had three weeks to settle his affairs and prepare to go off "for the duration", a phrase he took to mean "the duration of the war." It turned out to be for quite a bit longer. Probably eternity. But of this, he was not aware.

That evening, pulling out of Cleveland, Gregor's daze — or was it doze? — was rudely interrupted.

"Did that New York Times pay full fare?"

"Huh? What?" Gregor pulled his cap off his eyes.

"So, Mr. Bug-eyes, did that paper pay full fare, it should take my seat?" The speaker was a short man of about sixty, in a rumpled, shiny blue gabardine suit with a hideous "modern" purple tie, coke-bottle glasses sitting awry on an enormous nose, and a feathered fedora perpendicularly adorning his bald head. He removed his hat, but not out of politeness.

"Oh. Oh, I'm sorry. I didn't know this was reserved."

"It vasn't. But now it is." The man plunked his hat down on the newspaper-vacated seat, took off his suit jacket, folded it less than neatly, and shoved it in the small rack above. He began to lower his lumbago carefully into the seat next to Gregor.

"Your hat!" the roach yelled.

"Just testing. To see if you vas a Lendsmann. A goy vould let me sit on it."

"Well – I'm Jewish — but *anyone* would..."

"You know someting?"

"What?"

"You don't look Jewish."

There was a pause. Gregor was savvy enough to know it was a joke — but was he suppose to laugh? He *didn't* look Jewish. His seatmate stared at him. Maybe this was a serious comment.

"You know someting else?"

"What?"

"It's a good ting you don't look Jewish. It's Jews that got us into this war..."

"That's not true..."

The man began to stage-sob effusively.

"My poor husband... dying of kencer, my only son about to be killed in Nort Efrica..." Other passengers were staring. "Oi, veh iz mir!", he called to the ventilator in the ceiling.

"Your husband?"

"That's vhat dey say. It's the Jews. You like my ecting?"

This is the seatmate Gregor had been waiting for? All the way to Chicago with this guy? He's probably going to Lamy, New Mexico.

"You don't believe me? Here, come vit me." He pulled Gregor up by the sleeve out into the aisle, and pushed him along to the end of the car.

"In dere..."

"That's the restroom."

"Go in dere."

"With you?"

"Vhat you tink, I'm some kind of a funny? I vant you should see someting."

Gregor entered with great reluctance.

"Look!" He pointed to the urinal. Though there was some kind of wetness on the floor, the urinal itself was reasonably clean. "Vhat you see in dere?"

"Pee?" asked Gregor, doubtfully.

"No! What are you talking? Dere's no pee — it's clean. You need glesses? Vhat do you see?"

Gregor was panicking. He was always nervous at exams.

"'American Standard?'" The brand name was glazed in blue at the bottom of the urinal wall.

"You're getting varmer. Vhat else do you see? Vhat's at the bottom, dummkopf?"

"Drain holes for the water."

"And de pee."

"Drain holes for the water and the pee."

"And?"

Gregor stared at the drain holes. He had never looked at them before. He usually stared at the wall. They were arranged in the shape — of a Star of David! Two intersecting triangles of holes forming a Jewish Star.

"Aha. De light is dawning."

"Well, I can't believe they did that on purpose..."

"Vhat, you tink the Mogen David fell in dere by accident? Vhat color is pee? You hoid of the yellow star? You hoid of Hitler? Vat is the message of this urinal?"

"Urinals don't have messages."

"Against stupidity," the analyst exclaimed, smacking himself on the forehead, "Gott himself is helpless. The message of dis urinal is 'Piss on Jewish.', 'Piss on de Jews'. Am I right? I'm right. And vhat is the next message?"

Gregor stared at this odd man, his heartmind spinning.

"'Flush dem down the toilet.' Det's the message of the urinal. OK? Cless trip dismissed. Back to de seats!"

Gregor fairly staggered back down the aisle, nudged along by his would-be mentor. It was not the first time he had encountered cultural antisemitism, but, specious or not, this example was uncommonly striking. The two sunk back into their seats.

"So vhat are you, bashful, Mr. Bug-eyes, you don't introduce yourself?"

Though G thought it might have been up to the *newcomer* to introduce himself, he reflexively apologized.

"Oh, excuse me. You just took me by surprise. I was dozing. I was... Gregor Samsa, here." He was still agitated enough to introduce himself as if on the telephone. Actually, he was thinking that Einstein would say that he could *also* be considered the newcomer in his own inertial frame, and that it was *his* responsibility to introduce himself, and he remembered Einstein was not wanted wherever he was going...

"Schwartz C. Leon. The 'C' is for 'Comma'. You can call me 'Mr. Schwartz.' In America ve use first names. Eqvality. Fraternity. Vhere you are headed?"

"New Mexico."

"Vy not Old Mexico? Don't they have big cockroaches down there?" He burst out singing. *"La cucaracha, la cucaracha..."* Again, the other passengers turned and stared. They had never heard the song with a Yiddish 'r'. "How does it go after that? Ve didn't speak Spanish in Varsava. Or am I not supposed to talk cockroaches?"

"You are from Warsaw? I am from Prague. But I have been many times in Warsaw. In fact, I left my appendis in Warsaw with a Dr. Bong. Do you know him?"

"A terrible man, a terrible man. I don't know him, but vhat else vith such a name? I didn't know you people had appendises."

"It was before, when I was nineteen. What's wrong with his name?"

"A Bong by any other name vould smell like feet. Before vhat?"

Gregor realized he was unpracticed in the arts of avoidance. What would he do if Mr. Leon asked about his destination?

"Before the war." He thought he'd better change the subject. "You got on in Cleveland?" he asked.

"My daughter had another baby. Five breeding daughters I have. I ken't keep treck of the grandchildren boithdays. But you're again changing the subject."

"No, I... what's the subject?"

"The subject is the moider of the Jews. You know vhat's happening in Chicago? You ever been in Chicago?"

"I haven't. What is happening?"

"Very suspicious, someting very suspicious."

"What?"

"Vhat a nosy you are! In de Univoisity...I live near de Univoisity, 57th and Voodlawn...in the Univoisity dere's a football stadium, Stegg Field, right around de corner from me."

"I don't know much about American football."

"*Machts nichts.* Neither does Mr. Hutchins. Dey stopped doing football years ago. Too much brawns, not enough brains."

"So?"

"So vaht do you tink they are using dis football stadium for?"

"I don't know. Baseball? Graduation ceremonials? Isn't June when is graduation?"

"Graduation ceremonials vit barbed vire and guards vit guns?"

"What do you mean?"

"Since lest October I am vatching de trucks, de men vit coats and ties going in and out. I wrote down names. Stoiling Lumber Company from de city, Goodyear Rubber Company — all de vay from Ohio on de license plate. A big truck from Neshional Carbon Company, in and out, in and out, a closed truck, I couldn't see vhat is in dere, but it vas lots of it, I'm telling you. Listen, the Mallinckrodt Chemical Voiks all the vay from St. Louis, in Missouri. In and out. In and out. About thoity-four gengsters, Beck-of-the-Yard Boys ve call 'em, probably from behind de stockyards, they look like. Every morning in, every night out. You vouldn't vant to meet dem in a dark elley. Crowbars some had, and helmets.

A car, big, bleck, Dupont 4 on de plate, vit fency people in it. Tvice in and out two veeks apart. And the barbed vire. Oily on, barbed vire. And de guards — outside at the barbed vire, foist dey are building fires in oil drums to keep varm, den they are getting portable fireplaces hooked up to ges. Den fur coats dey get, raccoon fur coats for all de guards. You know eny guards vit fur coats? You know vhat costs a raccoon coat? Dis is big bucks, let me tell you. Raccoon fur coats and tommy guns. You tink I'm telling a story?"

"No, I believe you."

"You tink I could make such monkey-business up?"

"You have a sharp eye."

"Vat de eye doesn't see, de heart doesn't feel. So Mr. Bug-eyes, vhat do you see, vhat do you make on it?"

"They must be building something there in the stadium."

"Brilliant. But vhat? In the vest stands, under them. Vhat you think?"

"Wood, rubber, carbon, chemicals ..."

"*I* tink they are going to round up the Jews and kill them. They are building some kind of det camp in there."

"That's impossible. Who? The University? The government? They don't do things like that."

"You remember December, oily December, the government said two million of our people vere moidered in Europe?"

"The State Department Report, yes. And five million more were in danger..."

495

"Mr. Bug-eyes reads the newspaper."

"I work in Washington."

"So?"

"What do you mean, 'so'?"

"So vhat do you know, Joe? Vhat do you know about vhat ve're doing about it?

"Nothing."

"Ve're not *doing* nothing, or you don't *know* nothing?"

"Roosevelt has decided not to do anything about it."

"And vhat vill the Jewish community do about *det*?"

"I don't know. Demonstrating? Striking? Voting for someone else?"

"Not if they're in prison — or dead. Vhat happened vit the Jeps? You tink ve don't round people up if dey're a threat?"

"You think the government is going to round up Jews and kill them?"

"You tink they aren't?"

Gregor reviewed everything he knew about Breckinridge Long and the antisemites at State, about FDR's sometime cowardice and vulnerability to political pressure, about the militarization of his thought, and the general mood of the white-sheeted, zoot suit hating, Coughlin-cheering electorate — and though he would like to have answered "No!", he wasn't so sure.

"I need to go to the bathroom," he said. "Please excuse me." He squeezed past Mr. Leon, walked back up the aisle, and after a wait for a little boy and his father, was able to lock himself in and think. After some minutes alone. he felt able to face his tormenter, prepared to rationally discuss what he knew and what he thought.

When he returned to the seat he found a note scrawled over a Barney's ad on page 7 of the *Times*: *"May you have a happy next Passover with the Angel of Death passing over you. But check behind your neck for unexpected markings. Next year in Jerusalem. Selah. SCL."*

****

Chicago, Union Station. Filthy arching glass roof, high up, far away. Corinthian columns. Dark wooden benches the color of my tegmen. Shiny. Smooth. Oh, to rub against them. Find the Santa Fe Chief to Lamy,

New Mexico, wherever that is. Thirty-six hours — if all goes well, no floods or fire.

Track 22. Gregor could barely see the engine, many cars ahead, a new, state-of-the-art diesel, yellow and red. Up into the coach car. Half-way down the aisle. Suitcase up on the rack. He thought how comfortable that rack might be for a long and drawn-out night. Instead of propping himself upright, being careful of his seatmate, he could just climb up stretch out in the baggage rack if there were room. Even if there weren't room, he could squeeze in flat between suitcases and roof, the cool cream-colored metal pressing down on him, his legs tucked up or under. He thought of Kafka's trapeze artist, curled up in the luggage rack — but then, that was a compartment in a European train, just the artist and his manager, with no others to look on and gawk. American luggage racks offered no privacy — a symptom of democracy, he supposed. Still, he lay his suitcase flat, next to another similarly disposed, and thought he might use that expanse as a bed should the need arise. These preparations made, he plopped down into a velveteen seat, next to an ancient negro who nodded minimally and resumed his snooze, his cracked, pill-rolling fingers dancing an endless round, silently cranking.

The train was pulling out as he returned from restroom and confirmation-of-the-yellow-star, to find the safe space above being plundered by a family in the forward row, mother and father directly in front, an eight-year old son, and eleven-year old daughter across the aisle where Gregor could watch their antics. Father was a burly one, using all his strength to squeeze their belongings on top of Gregor's and the neighboring suitcase. The canary cage went in last, safely wedged. The bird did not sing.

Mother was attending to the bickering brother and sister, via variations on the theme of "If you don't stop that, you're going to get it." What "it" was, was unclear, but whatever it was, it was enough to inhibit the mutual sadism for several seconds at a time.

Already the flash-by was sending Herr Samsa into singular space, reflective, expansive, making uncommon connections. A fateful omen. The mutual meanness of the children. The institution. "That to secure these rights," he had memorized, "governments are instituted among men." What rights? Life and Liberty, he recalled. Was that all? Why, I asked him once, could he not remember happiness — "the Pursuit of Happiness"? "Because I never wanted to pursue it," he answered, simply, "People who pursue happiness abandon contentment." A thoughtful response. But was Gregor content?

His heartmind gathered energy. Those children. The war of all against all, he had read that in Hobbes. But was it really "all"? *He* would not make war, for example. But then, he was not a man. He had met selfish people, many of them ready to make war. But he had met selfless ones — Eleanor, Einstein, Szilard, Alice, Amadeus, Ives.... but the selfless ones, are they wise? They're good, virtuous, but are they...accurate? For surely, selfishness prevails, ego-driven solipsism driving the chariot of self-interest. Can they deal with lack of moral scruple? No. America does not believe in irony.

(In relating G's thoughts here, I am reminded of a story Alan Ginsberg told at Princeton, several years ago. He and his friends were attending the deathbed of William Carlos Williams, the great, world-affirming doc-tor-poet of Paterson. At the end of a life of service and love, the old man rose up on his elbow, and motioned his students and friends to come closer. They closed in, all attentive, to hear a saint's final words. In a croaking whisper, he made them aware of the summary thought of his eighty-year life. "There are a lot of bastards out there," he rasped. And he died.)

Flashing past Princeton, Illinois, Gregor experienced a similar reflec-tion. The selfless ones don't admit, he thought, don't even understand the power of self-will. They go by a higher law than self — and are vastly disadvantaged. The reigning powers are tooth and claw. Every page of history tells the same story, and he turned the pages in his mind. No ideal without some corruption of self-love, no human achievement not undermined from within. Approaching Fort Madison, Iowa, he decided that one can't simply sweep the contradictions under the rug saying that humans would be good if only political institutions would not poison them, if only faulty economic institutions could be improved, if only ignorance could be replaced by education — baloney (his new word)! If humans are basically good, how is it they have created exploitive institutions and fanatical religions? Democracy — what chance does it have against the guile and malice of self-interest — with its sentimental schemes for a benevolent community?

"Rochelle, you cut that out!" The cry rang out in the somnolent darkness.

"White folks' burden, those kids," muttered Gregor's seat partner, the first words G had been aware of. Clacking of the wheels. Dimness and quiet settled in once more. But not in Gregor.

What had he already lived through, seen with his own eyes? An accelerating slide toward barbarism. And democracy itself supplying the grease! His father had told tales of professional armies, ignorant perhaps, clashing by night, but clashing among themselves, and may the best soldier win. No more. Now we have democracies at war — with the active participation — and victimization — of entire populations. The poison gas of the Great War, the bombing in this one. He felt for his newspaper in the dark. Democracies need demons, not soldiers, to fight, subhumans — Japs and Jews. And Krauts. Barbarity? Unimportant — compared to really weighty matters like making money. Why *should* a nation acknowledge any law beyond its own strength? The will to live truthfully always bows to the will to power.

He fell into disturbing dreams, dreams of insect-like men, indifferent to life, men more thing than living-thing, streaming in and out of churches, worshiping yet more things, different things — steam irons, steak knives, a box of matches. In the darkened nave of a large cathedral, a girl-child was selected, a human girl-child — — selected to be queen. Insect-men carried her to an altar in the choir, and held her down while streams of cohorts emerged from side aisles and chapels, carrying a mass of items from "The World of Tomorrow" — cameras, portable radios, electric percolators, vacuum cleaners, plastic dishes — and burying the child under their weight. As the pile grew, it was circled by dancers and musicians, croaking and scraping their legs, whistling through spiracles, ticking polyrhythmically. "To Death," they sang, "To Death," "Oh Death, where is thy sting?"

"La Plata, Missouri," the conductor called out, as early-morning-gently as the roaring of Bottom's suckling dove. It woke Gregor, saved him from the final hoarding of the objects, and the revelation of the crushed corpse beneath them. "Long live death!" the insects had cried, and the sound still echoed in Gregor's shell.

499

Newton defined force as the product of mass and acceleration. Simone Weil defined force as the ability to transform a man into a corpse. And at Kansas City, Missouri, Gregor sensed the ultimate polarity: not day and night, not male and female, but the polarity between those that have the desire, and thus the power, to kill and those who do not. The killers were things and the lovers of things, entranced with all that is thing-like and mechanical like themselves, ever ready to transmute organic to inorganic. Men of having, not of being, men who must possess or die. Men of abstraction, quantification, bureaucratization and technique. Men not afraid of total destruction. Where would such men lead us? He sat up starkly in his seat, and watched the dawn grow slowly in the Kansas sky.

Kansas. Toto, I think we're in Kansas. FDR's favorite film, shown repeatedly in the West Wing screening room. Gregor saw a bedraggled sextet skipping wearily hand in hand, silhouetted on the horizon, the end of *The Seventh Seal* prematurely born. Dorothy was there, leading Scarecrow, Scarecrow leading Tin Man, Tin Man leading the Cowardly Lion, with Toto running circles around them; innocence, intelligence, feeling and courage exhaustedly cavorting at the outskirts of Newton, Kansas. This was no dream. They were real. Escaped. Home. Home in the heartland.

But who was that in front, leading them? Not Oz. Not Death. The train was pulling quickly past them — hard to make him out. He seemed to be a white-bearded hassid, in black caftan and fur hat, dancing in religious ecstasy, the only non-weary member of the crew, skipping backwards so as to keep his bleary-eyed charges in sight. Gregor's wound began to wet; he moved forward, away from the seat. Was it Benjamin's Angel of History, the past in front of him, backing into the unknown future? Were those wings, or merely perturbations in the wheat? *Ein jeder Engel ist schreck-lich,* terrible, dreadful, frightening. He knew his Rilke. Who can we use then — not angels, not men... We don't feel at home, in this, our world of meanings. His back toward what's ahead, how could the bearded one not miss the road, not lead his pilgrims astray? Sin. In the bible, called *chatah* — to miss the road, to go astray. Was he leading them into sin — or through *chatah*, to *tshuvah*, return, Self, to the right way, back to God? The Master of Return and his hopeful, errant flock, disappearing behind the wheatfields of Kansas.

The Talmud says of the Master of Return, the lost sinner skilled in finding the way home — repentance — it says of him that he stands even above those who have never sinned. But who among us has never sinned? In this twilight world of incendiary bombs and torture, of ritual, reciprocal, irrational loathing, even the newborn is old enough to die. Do I need to read the paper? Each day shrinks the number of ways to say "hope". Brown juice down back.

There *are* those who have never sinned. In Prague, at Altneu, Rabbi Tsanck, Gregor remembered, all the children gathering for stories of the *Lamed-Vovniks,* the thirty-six Just Men, indistinguishable from the rest of us, the thirty-six for the sake of whom God lets the world continue. His pill-rolling seat mate, gone with nod and grunt at Dodge City — he could be one, a Lamed-Vovnik. They are often unknown, sometimes unknown even to themselves, and for these "unknowns", the spectacle of the world is an unspeakable hell. "When an unknown Just Man rises to Heaven, the rabbi said, "he is so frozen that God must warm him for a thousand years between His fingers before his soul can open to Paradise."

But if just one *Lamed-Vovnik* were lacking, the sufferings of mankind would poison the souls of even infants, and humanity would asphyxiate, clawing at each other in agony. The *Lamed-Vov* are the hearts of the world, sink and drain for all collected grief. One legend the rabbi told — that one of the thirty-six is the Messiah. If the age were worthy of it, He would unveil himself. G's seatmate? The Messiah? Yet to be revealed? Let us worship. Let us pray.

In the seventh century, Adalusian Jews prayed to a teardrop-shaped rock they thought was the soul of an unknown *Lamed-Vovnik,* petrified by suffering. Other *Lamed-Vovnikim* were said to have been transformed into dogs, even insects. Be on the lookout. Worship! The Messiah who will come only when He is no longer needed. Xenophanes noted that "were cattle to postulate a god, it would have horns and hooves." The satanic fury of Hobbes: "Men, Women, a Bird, a Crocodile, a Calf, a Snake, an Onion, a Leeke, Deified!" The Messiah.

Such were the thoughts skittering through the ganglia of a Czech Jewish blattid as he rode the Santa Fe Chief through Kansas and Colorado, and on into New Mexico, *en route* to the unknown. Was this trip yet one more flight from an implacable, gruesome "benediction"? Or was the western desert to be his scene of grail transcendence?

Leaving Las Vegas, New Mexico, forty minutes from Lamy, Gregor put into operation the plan which FDR, master of intrigue, had scribbled for him on a White House napkin. Carrying his suitcase, he walked forward through the train to the baggage car, entered it using an FBI skeleton key, and located the wooden crate he had sent to the station ahead of him. Opening the padlock, he, with suitcase, climbed in, closed the lid, fastened it from the inside, and waited, cozy and thigmotactic after his disturbing, exhausting journey. At Lamy, he was loaded, gently ("FRAGILE SCIENTIFIC INSTRUMENTS. HANDLE WITH CARE. THIS SIDE UP"), onto a cart, and left standing under the station portico in the evocative, early evening light.

LOS ALAMOS, NEW MEXICO

41. How To Make An Atomic Bomb. In Fact, Two.

I have to admit to being a few minutes late to pick up Gregor at Lamy. The truck was unexpectedly low on gas, I had no ration coupons with me, and had to go back to Administration to fetch some — which left Gregor lying in his crate, peering out the air holes at Galisteo Valley for what I imagined to be an anxious quarter hour. It turned out otherwise. But more of that later.

Before I begin my report on the last phase of his life, the time we shared together on the mesa, I want to present an overview of the Manhattan Project, the grand scheme, as it were, the event terrain in which Gregor's trajectory occurred. Like all grand schemes, it began with an insight, and an insight about that insight.

The light — which grew to be "brighter than a thousand suns" — first dawned in Leo Szilard's brain at that street crossing in London. If there were an element, he reasoned, which would fission when struck by a neutron, and which, in fissioning, would release more neutrons — then a "chain reaction" was possible.

Imagining such a chain, I always think back to the story (clearly apocryphal) my father told me when he was teaching me chess. The putative king of some foreign country was so pleased by his subject, the putative inventor of chess, that he offered him any reward he pleased. The wily strategist played humble, and said, "I have few desires. But if you would put a grain of wheat on the first square, and two on the second, and four on the third, and so on, I would much appreciate it." "Nothing easier," said the innumerate king, and ordered his steward to attend to it. Point implicitly made, the story deteriorates rapidly, as the computation of 2^{64} is indicated, and the immoderacy of the consequences ensue: "more wheat than exists on earth," "more wheat than stars in the sky", and so forth — an accumulation even William Gates might turn down.

But in a chain reaction situation, rapid multiplication of neutrons is a fact, two producing four, four eight, until, in a rather small space, in microseconds of time, unthinkable neutron densities can occur. And when each of these neutrons is capable of splitting some special, neutron-sensitive atomic nuclei, much brouhaha may ensue.

It turns out that when these extraordinary elements split, the masses of their products do not add up to the original mass, but come out slightly smaller. Enter Einstein, thirty-five years earlier. 1905, the famous $E = mc^2$. Here is another profligacy of number, the speed of light being so great, and the squaring of that speed so extravagant. Numbers aside, Einstein's equation says, simply, "even a very small amount of mass can be turned into a colossal amount of energy." The trick is to do it.

In 1938 Hahn and Strassman demonstrated that uranium had split into lighter atoms under neutron bombardment — the event Bohr communicated to that wild meeting at the Carnegie Institution in Rock Creek Park. Physicists ran back to their labs and began bombarding uranium with everything they could throw at it, and in 1939 Lise Meitner and Otto Frisch formulated an explanation of the process, which they named "nuclear fission". It seemed uranium might provide a real-world demo for Einstein's equation. In 1940, Glenn Seaborg detected something strange while bombarding uranium in his Berkeley cyclotron. The unexpected guest was not a lighter fission product, but a heavier new element, never before seen on earth, plutonium, the result of neutron capture — without fission — by uranium. It turned out that plutonium, too, was able to fission under neutron bombardment.

Two heavy elements, both capable of splitting under neutron bombardment, and releasing excess neutrons and Einsteinian energy. One might think uranium the preferable beast, since it was relatively plentiful. But it turned out that the actually performing uranium was U^{235} — a "contaminant", 0.7% of the U^{238} metal from the mines. Because they were isotopes of the same element, the two could not be separated chemically. Because they were so similar in weight, it was only with great difficulty that they could be separated physically. And without separation, the mix was pretty bland, explosion-wise. But the path was clear: if U^{235} could be isolated and stockpiled, or if enough Pu^{239} could be produced, either of them might be used to tickle the Einstein equation to climax.

As I mentioned before, Szilard had one other key insight, (one wonders if there is something in Hungarian water) — the notion of critical mass. The reason all the uranium on the planet does not set itself off and explode is that it is too dilute: should a stray neutron split a uranium atom the secondary neutrons produced would fizzle out before they could enter and split another atom: no chain reaction would occur. Same with plutonium, had there been any on earth. But — what if those atoms were concentrated — brought together in a small space? Then, secondary neutrons might penetrate their close neighbors, and tertiary neutrons theirs, and the chain would begin to rattle. Szilard called this "critical mass". How much uranium, how much plutonium would you have to pack into how much space for critical mass? That was unknown.

Enrico Fermi decided to find out. In 1942, there was only unseparated uranium to play with, and that is what he did. Where do you play? In a stadium. In a squash court under the west stands at Stagg Field at the University of Chicago, right around the corner from Mr. Schwartz C. Leon's apartment on Woodlawn Ave. Schwartz was right to be concerned with the guards and the comings and goings — right, but for the wrong reason. On December 2, 1942 at three in the afternoon, the consequences of piling up enough uranium in one place became clear: embedded in 771,000 pounds of graphite (from the National Carbon Company), piled brick by brick, 80,590 pounds of uranium oxide and 12,400 pounds of uranium metal (from Mallinckrodt) "went critical", and began to produce a potentially enormous flux of neutrons — till Fermi dropped the neutron-absorbing control rods into the pile. The wily Italian, using Szilard's original notions, had invented a nuclear reactor. The afternoon did more than demonstrate the truth of theory: one of the byproducts of the pile reaction was plutonium. Fermi had also invented a "breeder". On December 2, 1942, right around the corner from Schwartz's apartment, the nuclear age had begun. Today, a Henry Moore sculpture sits commemoratively on the site. Could Fermi have blown up the entire city of Chicago? Possible, but unlikely — according to his 6" slide rule. Since word was that "Fermi never makes a mistake,[23]" breath-holding physicists hung out on the balcony and watched. And Chicago didn't know anything about it.

Neutron sources, nuclear fission, uranium, plutonium, the idea of critical mass. Everything material and intellectual was in place to make a bomb. Still needed was the catalyst of will.

It is no accident that European scientists were the first to imagine that Germany had already begun developing a bomb. I thought about this often as I partook of the concerts and learned discussions of the *émigrés* at Los Alamos. German thought, German art, German philosophy, German science monopolized peak after peak in their cultural heritage. Consider: the atomic bomb is the ironic legacy of Beethoven. And Goethe, Kant, Schopenhauer, Einstein and Mann. If German *Geist* could consistently produce such giants of the mind, then surely Germany — even Nazi Germany — must be well on her way to exploiting original discoveries made by German scientists on German soil. That America must play catch-up to an already advanced German bomb project was the universal, powerful assumption, practically a certainty, the catalyst for the gargantuan striving of the Manhattan Project. No matter that many top Jewish scientists had been exiled. Planck was there. Von Laue was there, Hahn was there, Weiszäcker was there — Heisenberg was there. All you needed was one Heisenberg.

The Europeans were motivated, but Roosevelt had been sitting on Uranium Committee reports for almost a year. The British, however, their senses sharpened by a rain of German bombs, were not so nonchalant. In July of '41, a group of British scientists visited the States to try to stir up more urgent activity. Important research had been done for a year, both on the design of a weapon, and on the separation of uranium isotopes. But with bombs falling, and the country stretched to its limits, Britain could simply not move on to the massive manufacturing necessary to bring about

23 For which infallibility, Fermi was nicknamed "The Pope".

a weapon before the end of the war. Persuaded by some high-level scientific politicking, on October 9, 1941, FDR agreed to put all possible resources into the expeditious development of a nuclear bomb. The Manhattan Project was born.

This was a double race, both with Germany, and between the two known fissionable metals. Which would be ready faster — a uranium bomb or a plutonium one? There was no telling, so both would be simultaneously pursued. Two huge secret cities were created, employing tens of thousands of workers, none of whom had any idea what they were working on. Oak Ridge, Tennessee was charged with separating out U^{235}, and Hanford, Washington with the creation of plutonium. These astonishing industrial operations were to feed their products into the brain of the operation — Site Y at Los Alamos. There, on the New Mexican mesa, mathematicians, physicists, chemists, metallurgists and ordnance experts worked together to design and produce a weapon that could be carried in an aircraft, and, when dropped, might actually explode.

Once the theoreticians had determined the likely critical masses involved, the initial design plans were fairly straightforward. A large gun would be built inside a bomb case. Using well-understood engineering, a sub-critical bullet of uranium or plutonium would be fired into a sub-critical target of same, and the two, coming quickly together, would form a critical mass, a neutron flood, a consequent explosion. The only problem was that, for almost a year, there was not enough U^{235} to work with, and almost no plutonium at all. Oak Ridge's progress was slow — uranium would probably work well, but not enough separated U^{235} could be produced out to make more than one weapon during the likely duration of the war. Hanford began at essentially zero — by the fall of '43, there were only milligram quantities of Pu available: all the plutonium on earth could be placed on the head of a pin. Still, as the reactor technology pioneered by Fermi matured, it looked as if quantity production of plutonium would be less problematical in the long run than uranium separation. The health risks were larger, as we will see, but plutonium seemed the more likely basis for a substantial nuclear arsenal.

All great enterprises have their crises. In July of '44, there were finally gram quantities of plutonium to work with, and it was discovered by Emilio Segrè that the metal available from the reactors was actually a mixture of isotopes. One of them, Pu240, was an alpha emitter, and source of "background" neutrons, creating a million and a half spontaneous fissions each hour. With such pollution, the gun design would simply fail: that thin hail of unwanted neutrons would condemn any plutonium gun to fizzling pre-detonation. Separating plutonium isotopes would be even more difficult — and much more dangerous — than separating uranium. That tack was out of the question. The race seemed lost, the project hopeless.

Oppenheimer was devastated, and considered resigning as Lab Director. But as we will see, Gregor and Seth Neddermeyer came to the rescue, and were able to salvage the plutonium bomb with a new design. The "implosion bomb" replaced the gun model: only implosion could develop critical mass quickly enough to avoid pre-detonation. It was Gregor's implosion idea that was tested at Trinity in July of '45. It was Gregor's implosion idea that destroyed Nagasaki in August. It was Gregor's implosion idea that took his life.

Implosion design was far trickier than the familiar ballistics of cannons. A ball of sub-critical plutonium had to be compressed in microseconds, absolutely symmetrically, in order not to fizzle. (Fizzling, by the way, meant exploding with the force of five or six tons of TNT, rather than fifty or a hundred.) Achieving this almost instantaneous spherical compression provided the drama of the last phase of the work. Explosive lenses had to be developed, shaped charges of various materials which would focus the otherwise unpredictable shock waves. A container was needed to reflect escaping neutrons back into the fission. A timing circuit and detonating system had to be invented which could trigger the jacket of lenses with fantastic accuracy so that pressure waves from all directions would converge in step towards their target. An internal initiator was needed at the center of the plutonium core to provide an exquisitely timed burst of neutrons to initiate the process. And finally, diagnostics had to be developed, ways of measuring all these processes — wave profiles, neutron flux, materials stress: super-high speed cameras, new x-ray devices, magnetic sensors, radiation detectors — all this without being able to test the crucial materials in full-scale assembly.

There was much doubt that such an intricate scheme could succeed; there was far more confidence in the uranium gun design. Since not enough U235 existed for both test and bomb, the uranium bomb was not tested until Hiroshima. It worked — as expected. Not so with with implosion bomb. After much debate, it was decided to gamble more than half of the world's existing plutonium to run a test of the real implosion device. In May of '44, site selection began, and in August the Trinity site was chosen. Gregor arrived at Trinity a year later, two years and a month after his advent in New Mexico.

42. Applied Thigmotaxis

Those two years began in a crate, on a dolly, under the portal of the ATSF station at Lamy.

Now, you or I would not like to lie there in such a coffin — even with air holes: being buried alive is a common and terrifying nightmare. But blattids have other ideas about tight, dark spaces. I have spoken several times about thigmotaxis: those fifteen thigmotactic minutes I inadvertently bestowed on Gregor turned out to be world-changing, so forgive me if I focus on them with the dark light they deserve.

Blattids, we know, have a predilection for pressure, a strong need to be touched on all sides at once. In the wild they find joy in the crannies of peeling tree bark, the moist cracks in limestone caves, or the wet layers of leaf litter on the rainforest floor. For the more civilized, there are the interstices of kitchen cabinets, gaps between bathroom tiles, all sorts of chinks in baseboards, window frames and trim, and the inscrutable architecture of water heaters, refrigerators and stoves.[24]

What, though, for outsized Gregor? The crate was a rare chance for him to indulge an appetite rooted at his core, and to encounter the insights of

---

24 Research by Koehler, et al. on 1,700 German cockroaches, has shown that individuals of various types prefer different size spaces. Roaches were given the choice of eight new plexiglass homes, each with a different size interior. One and two-week old nymphs preferred the ceiling 1/16” from the floor. Adult males, as might have been predicted, chose the largest arena, a spacious 1/2” between ceiling and floor. Gravid adult females opted for 3/16”.

this ecstatic state. Climbing the switchbacks to the site, we shared the front seat of the truck, and I apologized profusely to him for making him wait. I found his reply remarkable.

He had lain there in the box, he related, sensible of the darkness, yet for that very reason, all the more aware of the crepuscular light pouring in through three breathing holes at his head focused directly on the mosaic of his eyes. As the light poured in, he felt himself pouring out, sucked into the vast, arid nakedness of the Galisteo valley. I quoted Leconte de Lisle: "Nature is empty and the sun devours; be endlessly absorbed in its relentless flame, bathe in the divine Void." But no, he said, that wasn't it at all. It was — on the contrary — concentrating, *reculer pour mieux sauter*, the power of the yang dot in the midst of the yin teardrop. I brought up the Müller-Lyer Illusion with him as a possible example. He had never heard of or seen it. It was difficult to draw it in the bouncing truck, but I scrawled an approximation on the back of my pickup instructions:

He was, in fact, amazed, noting how the outward arrows make the line appear shorter, while the inward-pressing ones seem paradoxically to extend it.

"That's it," he said. "The expansive power of extreme compression." He spoke of Charles Ives, a composer I did not then know, and his explosive quarter-tone harmonies. I noted the expansive conciseness of Sanskrit or Japanese words, with which a single expression or character might translate into an entire English paragraph.

This was a remarkable discussion for two strangers. Perhaps we were both avoiding the obvious questions: Who are you, Where are we going, and Why? Still, I learned much about the sensibilities of this new arrival, and it was surely this conversation, in the midst of our hair-raising climb, which created the space for our ensuing friendship.

It also set, Gregor assured me shortly before he went down to Trinity, it also set him thinking about the themes of light-from-dark, centrifugal-from-centripetal, life-from-death, and death-from-life which so transformed site Y and the world. Light breaks where no sun shines. How? Crush the limited three-dimensional, and arrive at the infinite symbolic? Dying flesh, birthing spirit?

I found Gregor's last written communication to me in my box the day of his departure south. It was a thank you note for my accidental "gift of time and darkness", those pregnant fifteen minutes in the crate. His early mesa experiences were deeply suffused with the light of things seen in that darkness, visionary intimations of an unearthly gleam. As Jung maintained, "The sole purpose of human existence is to kindle a light in the darkness of mere being." That light seeped in — and out — out in strange and fateful ways.

It is likely that the first scientist Gregor met was Seth Neddermeyer, a young physicist from Cal Tech, recently arrived, whose slouched demeanor would make a drill sergeant tremble (and there were several drill sergeants on site). G was attracted to his tall, stooped figure, his narrow, insect-like shoulders supporting an enormous head, his thick, black-rimmed glasses and unkempt beard. He had probably been "Mr. Weird" all his life, and even here, among the oddball geniuses[25], he was an outsider — the perfect friend for Gregor. On the evening of July 2, about three weeks after G's arrival, the two of them were walking among the Sundt apartments, pale green (as was every building) two story, four family dwellings. Into the darkening sky there drifted the lush strains of a lovely piano melody.

"Do you know that piece?" asked Gregor.

"No," replied Neddermeyer, "I don't know music. 'Don't Sit Under the Apple Tree', I know that. 'I'll Be Seeing You.'"

"You leave a girl behind?"

"Girls don't like physicists."

Gregor felt he was prying, and changed the subject.

"That's a Brahms Intermezzo, A major, my favorite." They stopped to

---

25 "At great expense, we have gathered on this mesa the largest collection of crackpots ever seen," General Leslie R. Groves told his assembled officers, myself among them. "And it's your job to keep them happy."

listen for a moment. "Must be Teller. Or Frisch? Whose place is that? I can't tell one Sundt from another."

"That's Teller's. I was at a party there the week before you came."

"That A major is one of those jewels — art works — tiny, gleaming art works, which contain absolutely everything the great masters load into their largest works. This little piece is all of Brahms in a nutshell, an extreme compression of his glorious energy."

The combination of the evening light and the idea of "extreme compression" evoked a rush of Gregor's Lamy epiphany (as he called it), never far from his consciousness, but now intensified by Brahms, and perhaps heightened by the uncomprehending consciousness off which it reflected. Neddermeyer was very bright, but not in this way. Gregor began to describe his experience, explained thigmotaxis, and the sense of power coming at him, into him, out of him. He described himself as a hollow vessel, a being in a shell, compressed and concentrated by the celestial light focused on his core.

Neddermeyer lit up. Gregor had planted a seed. The implosion bomb idea was born.

The next day was spent gathering materials for the "experiment" they cooked up. Some TNT "borrowed" from the crew blasting out the basement for the cyclotron, several lengths of 2" cast iron sewer pipe from the "free" bin at the salvage yard, and a number of stove-pipe sections from Eric Jette's porch (with his permission), a relic of the despised Black Beauty stove the Jettes had replaced with a hot plate. Fifty yards of primacord fusing, two tuna fish sandwiches, two apples, and two bottles of Ballantine completed the picnic preparations.

The next morning, on the Fourth of July, 1943, Gregor and Neddermeyer set out on a trek down the steep side of the mesa, into the Los Alamos Canyon, and wound up nestled among the caves and rocks of the mesa wall four hundred feet below, a mile and a half north of the main laboratory area. The fencing had not yet been completed, the MPs were not yet patrolling the perimeter, and man and bug were free to play to their hearts' desire while the world above them was being patriotic, celebrating the Land of the Free and the Home of the Brave in the midst of a war. Gregor and Neddermeyer, too, were being patriotic — more profoundly than they could have known. An observer might have mistaken them for large little boys having fun, playing with matches and firecrackers on Independence Day. And indeed that was part of it, science and a little insanity. By the time they had chosen a safe-looking spot, shielded by overhang to minimize the noise, it was 11 AM, and already 93 degrees. They downed the sandwiches and most of the Ballantine, and saved the apples for after the test, code-named "Gregor at Lamy".

Neddermeyer placed the 2" pipe inside the stove pipe, and the two of them packed the cylinder with TNT, symmetrical around the inner pipe. Gregor then strung the detonator wire 75 feet away to behind a large rock, which they would use for protection; Neddermeyer saw to the connections, one at either end of the cylinder, 180 degrees apart. After checking the system, he joined Gregor and detonator behind the boulder.

The physicist uncapped his beer. Gregor followed suit.

"Here's to extreme compression."

"Extreme compression," echoed the roach. The clinking brown bottles sounded sharp in the dryness of the rocks.

"Would you like to press the lever?" asked G.

"No, no. The inspiration was yours. I would say you get to press the lever."

"You are sure?" Gregor was nothing if not considerate. "This might be a great moment in history."

Neddermeyer made a sweeping comic gesture for G to go ahead, and they both crouched down behind the barrier. Gregor plunged the lever.

BOOM! Then BOOm, BOom,Boom, boom, as the sound echoed in the canyon. When the dust cleared, pipe and stovepipe were nowhere to be seen.

"Damn!" said Neddermeyer. "How can we do this experiment if we can't find the results?"

"Let's try it again," said Gregor, "over there, in that angle. I think the walls will hold."

They repacked another length of stovepipe with pipe and TNT. Again G ran the wire while Neddermeyer made the connections.

This time the explosion was better behaved. The plumbing pipe flew out above the cloud, bounced off an overhang a hundred feet above, and clattered down the side of the cliff calling obvious attention to itself and its landing. The stove pipe had again dispersed into the unknown. Neddermeyer ran out to claim the prize.

"Yow!" he yelled, burning his hand on hot metal. Gregor joined him. They visually inspected the twisted, bent, now-solid rod lying on the ground.

"I would say we did it. Extreme compression. Hollow no longer."

"*Reculer pour mieux pauser*," punned the roach. Neddermeyer did not speak French.

"What?"

"Pull back, the better to pause."

"What does that mean?"

"We should stop and think about this."

"Hell, no. We should take this right to Colloquium Tuesday. I think we've got the gun design beat. You can't possibly fire a missile down a gun as fast as you can collapse a hollow vessel from all sides at once. What did you call yourself? A shell? Shell we dance?" asked the gawky physicist, unwontedly joyous and frolicsome.

He grabbed Gregor by the upper legs, and swung his light body around in a circle amidst the debris of the explosion.

"Stop! Stop! I get dizzy," screamed the Blattid. He didn't mention his legs might come out.

As if in a demonstration of angular momentum, Gregor's body angled toward the ground, and within two decelerating turns, his bottom legs scraped the dusty tuff.

"Sorry," said Neddermeyer. "I was happy."

On July 6th, Seth Neddermeyer brought his twisted rod to the weekly meeting at which scientists from all divisions — much to General Groves' discomfort — shared their work and thoughts. Loose lips sink ships, and all that. The colloquium was Oppenheimer's great victory over Groves' military fetish for compartmentalization and secrecy. Without it, the "long-hairs", as the General called them, would not have felt they were doing "science" — exchanging ideas in open community — and might have quit. Groves was pragmatic enough to see that.

Neddermeyer took his turn towards the end of the meeting, the last of three speakers from O-division (O for Ordnance). He presented his plan in terms of a hollow sphere of sub-critical material, to be compressed to criticality by a jacket of explosives. The pipe was a first effort, involving simpler geometry. Gregor sat at the back of the gymnasium which doubled as Theater Number One — the one with cushions on its benches. The metaphysical origins of the crushed pipe were never mentioned, nor was Gregor's role as lab assistant and drinking partner. That was all right with him: he felt that being too closely identified with any particular operation might compromise his "neutrality" as Risk-Management Consultant.

But he was not prepared for the scorn and derision voiced by this community of scholars and scientists, everyone supposedly colleagues and friends. Admittedly, this was a proposal "from left field", as he had learned to say. Nobody else was thinking about implosion. The gun method was the method. Period. There was, to put it mildly, overwhelming skepticism.

Captain Deak Parsons, the Director of O-division, thought it was a joke. "With everyone grinding away in such dead earnest here, we need a touch of relief. But I question Dr. Neddermeyer's seriousness. To my mind he is gradually working up to what I shall refer to as the Beer-Can Experiment. As soon as he gets his explosives properly organized, we will see this done. The point to watch for is whether he can collapse a beer can without splattering the beer." In short, military contemptuousness toward an unkempt civilian. Parsons pronounced it "clearly unreliable", and a potential diversion from the more urgent program of designing and testing the gun-assembly.

Others joined in the denunciation, though more politely. How will you keep the tamper and core from squirting out like water squeezed between cupped hands? If the explosive does not produce an entirely even shock wave around the central hollow sphere then wouldn't it be destroyed before it went critical? Just a tiny imbalance would tear the sphere apart. How will you make a spherically symmetrical shock wave? Richard Feynman summed up the group's opinion of Gregor and Neddermeyer's scheme: "It stinks" — an opinion he would subsequently be too ashamed to mention.

Though originally one of the skeptics, it took Oppenheimer only the final fifteen minutes of the meeting to open up to the idea. He had been wrong before: best not foreclose any possibilities. He took Neddermeyer aside, along with Gregor, who was consoling him, and said, "We'll have to look further into this." A crucial change of heart for good or ill: had Neddermeyer's work been stopped, we would have had no atomic arsenal — at least till long after the war.

(On July 16, the Nazis rounded up 30,000 Parisian Jews, and transported them to concentration camps. Twenty survived.)

The implosion work puttered along, the slouching outcast working in his pariah cabin on South Mesa, far from the main Tech Area, with little budget and no staff. Progress was slow until the fall when John von Neumann, the revered Princeton mathematician, came to consult. "A non-trivial visitor," one of the theoreticians commented. In going over Project history to date, Teller informed him of the implosion thrust. Von Neumann's intuitive excitement over the idea led the two of them to work out more detailed calculations than had previously been done. Results? A correctly designed compression could reach such enormous energy as to obviate the need for tricky hollow spheres: a simple, sub-critical mass could serve as a bomb core. Develop implosion, they said, and there will be reliable bombs far more quickly.

With Von Neumann and Teller behind it, Neddermeyer's work began to make slow progress. He added a few men to his group, and worked methodically with the simple Fourth of July model: metal cylinders wrapped in a jacket of high explosives. He varied the spacing of the detonators and the thickness of the explosives, hoping to find some configuration that would produce smooth, symmetrical closure. He worked with army photographers to develop a camera that would record the implosions. With those photographs the disastrous jets were discovered which might sound the death-knell for the plan.

Oppie thought he needed help, and brought in George Kistiakowsky, from the National Defense Research Committee to lead the explosives division. It was becoming clear that a charge detonated simultaneously from several points would lead to high velocity jets and complete wave chaos. So Kisty engaged Jim Tuck, one of the British delegation, to work on the problem. A tall, rumpled physicist from Oxford, he had been working in England on shaped charges for armor-piercing shells, high explosives hollowed out like an ice cream cone with the pointed end forward. Instead of a normally divergent, bubble-shaped shock wave, a shaped charge converges into a ferocious, high-speed jet with entirely different, more controllable geometry. Rather than try to smooth out divergent, colliding shock waves, Tuck proposed an arrangement of shaped explosives that would produce a converging wave to begin with. No one wanted to tackle anything so complex so late in the war, but it seemed that complex explosive lenses might be the only way to make implosion – and the preferred use of plutonium — succeed. It was a far cry from that Fourth of July firecracker in the canyon. Neddermeyer was disconsolate about the kidnapping of his implosion brainchild. Nevertheless, science marched on, to the tune of a different drummer.

But Gregor knew what he knew: that without his vision at Lamy, there would never have been an implosion bomb. In his ever-discerning heart-mind, neutrons of guilt began a slow chain reaction.

43. Among The Ancients

In September, the aspens, *los alamos,* turn color, a quivering vibrato of golden-yellow leaves, gorgeous in its collective effect, a living mountain-side, calling.

There are two legends told about the aspen. One holds that the Saviour's cross was made from aspen, and that when the tree realized the purpose for which it was being used, its leaves began to tremble with horror and have never ceased. The other legend, diametrically opposed, is that when Christ died on the Cross, all the trees bowed in sorrow except the aspen. Because of its pride and sinful arrogance, its leaves were doomed to continual trembling.

Gregor, the Prague-schooled Jew, preferred the first. Because of his ability to see in the ultraviolet, he was acutely aware of what new agers would call "aura": for all of the aspen's visual aggressiveness, its etheric impression was far from arrogant. Rather it was much like himself — sensitive, making up for shyness with apparent éclat, caressing in a bashful, tentative way. He felt a brotherhood there. About the Cross, who was he to say? The aspen has a long, straight trunk. So what? In America, it's "innocent until proven guilty".

But aspen-guilt or not, crucifixion was inescapable on the mesa. The blood-red sunsets on the Sangre de Christo Mountains, rising 13,000 feet, 30 miles across clear desert, were unspeakably evocative, and not of any old *sangre* — blood, say, of soldiers at Ypres or Guadalcanal, blood of

Bluebeard's wives, or Pharaoh's waters. For splitting the front of Truchas peak was an immense natural cross — cleft down the mountain face, with two horizontal fissures, slightly disjunctive. Throughout late spring and early summer, the only remaining snow would be packed into those enormous crevices, appearing white against granite during the day, and turning albedo pink, then preternaturally red at sunset, a 10,000 foot, blood-red crucifix. Something to think about.

And between the Sangres and Gregor's mesa, the canyon, filled with emptiness, an intimate nudity of landscape with only shadows to cover its private parts. A landscape bathed in luminous air, as if on the bright edge of the world, an atmosphere which Willa Cather felt as "something soft and wild and free, something that whispered to the ear on the pillow, lightened the heart, softly, softly picked the lock, slid the bolts, and released the prisoned spirit of man into the wind, into the blue and gold, into the morning, into the morning." That, and the crucifixion.

In the canyon there were no newspaper headlines, no books of opinion, no blaring radios with their undercurrent of panic. There were only the great sky, the air, the ancient rocks. with tiny wildflowers blooming, and rarely, the sound of a rill, whispering seductively to its opposite, the sand. Time seemed on hold, and war seemed far away.

But above the canyon, on the mesa between the mountains, the clock was ticking, the minute hand drawing ever nearer the presumed midnight when Hitler would call the world to attention with nuclear weapons. Experimental blasts (Ordnance Division) from the side canyons gave notice to the old timelessness that a new and threatening age had come.

Those blasts were heard in the pueblos along the Rio Grande. As were other blasts, like the whistle-blast calling pueblo men and women away from homes and traditional roles to the buses that would carry them up the hill to be ditch-diggers, and maids for scientists' wives; like the blast of cash on a barter economy, the blast of well-meaning tourism on an older way of life — turning pot making, for example, from practical use and gift exchange into mass production to satisfy the Hill's artistic tastes, and its acquisitive demands.

Little did the Pueblo-dwellers know that one man, with his love of their earth, would so change their lives. In the summer of 1928, while Gregor was still smarting from Sacco and Vanzetti, and learning the insurance business from Charles Ives, a rich, young polymath named Julius Robert Oppenheimer moved out to New Mexico to hasten a cure from TB. He rented, then bought, a cabin in the foothills of the Sangres, a rough-hewn log cabin, two rooms downstairs, two up, with a staggering view of rolling. pine-clad slopes, flower-covered fields in summer and snow-capped peaks in winter. He called it (mysteriously) *"Perro Caliente"*, the hot dog, referred to it as his "ranch", and spent every summer there for the next forty years, riding and exploring in the mountains.

TB + hot dog = destiny. When, fourteen years later, he was chosen to head the Project, he prevailed upon the Manhattan District to choose the area he knew so well for its most crucial site. Remote, yet accessible, the setting was also prodigiously beautiful, a crucial factor, he thought, in attracting and retaining the personnel he would be seeking.

Much the same reasoning determined his need to buck security by encouraging senior scientists to have an occasional meal off-base, at Edith Warner's "teahouse", down the hill at Otowi Bridge. One summer day in 1937, Oppenheimer had horsebacked by in cowboy boots and jeans, and stopped for refreshment. He stayed all afternoon, and visited many times thereafter. A decade later he could attest to the power of "Miss Warner's" to nourish the heart, break the tension of work, and keep uprooted people human, a high priority for Oppie, one invisible to Groves.

Edith Warner, another health-seeking immigrant to New Mexico, had found at Otowi the inner peace she had been seeking. From 1928, when her tearoom was opened, she welcomed tourists with home cooking and vegetables and fruit grown in her garden. The meals she cooked on her old wood stove were always simple: stews flavored with herbs on big terra-cotta Mexican plates; posole, an Indian dish of parched corn; lettuce in a black pottery bowl from San Ildefonso; fresh baked bread; a bowl of raspberries, or her renowned chocolate cake for dessert. The house had no electricity; the only light in the two small dining rooms came from the fireplace, and from the candles on each table. The fragrance of burning piñon mingled with the smell of baking bread, a feast for the nose to garnish the feast for eyes and tongue. The food and atmosphere made her a treasure for Hill residents, and she was soon besieged with requests for reservations, weeks ahead. In mid-1943, for security reasons, Oppenheimer asked Edith to serve only Los Alamites, closing her small restaurant to outsiders. He could not tell her why, except to say that their work was very important to the war and very secret. She asked no questions and prepared dinner every day for ten people.

Gregor was a guest on the evening of September 14th. Edith was not only cooking, but also serving that night.

"Where's Tilano?" he asked the Bethes, his table companions.

"I think he's dancing today," Rose Bethe responded, "It's Turtle Dance time. We went last year."

"Why turtles?" asked Gregor, his intraspecific curiosity tweaked.

"They have turtle shells tied around their knees keeping time, and gourd rattles to sound against them. It's a rain dance."

Hans drew a vectored sketch on an envelope: "All the movement is vertical, like this, reaching up high to the sky and deep down to the earth..."

"Where the turtles live," G observed.

"*Ja. Genau.*"

Rose slapped her husband's hand. Groves had banned the speaking of German among the scientists.

"Each of these vertical lines pass through a dancing man, the link that ties earth and sky together. See?"

Rose was less diagrammatic. "You really should see one of the dances. It's like going over into another world. Have you been to the ruins?"

"No," admitted Gregor. "I've been thinking to go. Also to a dance."

The front door eased opened, and Tilano trudged in, wearily waved two dead rabbits at the guests, and disappeared into the kitchen. He had played hookey from Edith's to participate in the dance, and had stopped at the rabbit traps before coming in.

Gregor was fantasizing doing a Roach Dance for the Indians as his ticket of admission, a "real Gregor", no teams, only one dancer — the real one. How astounded they would be...

"I never forget a dance we see at Taos Pueblo last spring," Rose continued. "The gray branches along the fields, the willows beside the stream, the silent vegetation, the guardian mountain..."

"It was as if modern man and all his works were not yet dreamed," added Hans. "Tell him about the dance."

Rose: "When we got there, nothing was happening. Then all of a sudden fifteen, maybe twenty men run out into the plaza from behind the church…"

"With drums and notched sticks to rub like this " Hans gestured with his knife and fork.

"Like locusts," the ex-Ag department entomologist added. The Bethes couldn't quite make the connection.

"Once the music started, groups of girls and young men came from three directions, each singing its own song, completely unconcerned with fitting in with the other."

"Ives's marching bands!"

"No bands. (Again, the Bethes were innocent of the reference.) "No instruments. Just singing. Not even connected to the men with the sticks and drums. The girls circled them and did something like this, like they were smoothing out something, the earth maybe, over and over smoothing, mysterious — but also gay. And the men walked around them in the opposite direction, not even dancing, just shuffling along. Then all of a sudden everyone let out a huge cheer and everything stopped — and then began all over again, exactly the same way, though the music varied a little."

"There might have been different words," Hans thought.

"Then around five, the circle suddenly broke and everyone went off toward the kivas, laughing, at ease, gay like children after some kind of long game. I thought, no wonder we white people watch these ceremonials with such envy. If we could only dance out our dreams like that…"

"No wonder, also," added Hans, "that Miss Warner, in spite of her closeness to Pueblo people — or even because of the gap she can't jump — she seems often so lonely."

But Edith Warner was not lonely. Edith was an adopted daughter of the Pueblos. Her spiritual devotion to the land, her life of poverty and gentle ways made her a welcome departure from most Anglos. And with such an image, she was not long at Otowi before an Indian of indeterminate age — fifty, sixty, seventy? — long black braids swinging down his back, arrived to help her run her tiny place, rented from the Pueblo. It was Tilano, "Uncle Tilano", Atilano Montoya, he of the waving rabbits, come to build, come to visit, come to stay, an extraordinary man, gentle and deep, but always jovial, his face reflecting kindness, humor, and a network of wrinkles that seemed more a product of laughter than of age.

Edith and Tilano became companions, and shortly, housemates. He built her a fireplace, helped with the garden, did much of the heavy work, set the traps, and tended the cow and the chickens. He spoke a language of seasons and rocks, of bones and shells, of deer and eagle, of thunder and streams. He saw things Anglos don't see. He was grateful for everything, forgave everyone any trespass, and was humble before the life he had been given.

And that life was no ordinary one, bound by the invisible walls of the Pueblo. Tilano had crossed the Atlantic, seen the great cities of Europe — London, Paris, Berlin, Rome. Edith was fascinated. A group of Indians from San Ildefonso had gone to Coney Island— Coney Island! — in the summer of '27 to dance for the sweating New Yorkers. There one Bostok, an animal trainer, had seen them, and asked these human animals to go with him on tour. "Paris was the best place," Tilano told her. "We stayed there a long time — a month or more. The people clapped lots when we came out on stage. In the street they crowded around us and always asked, 'Are you *really* American Indians?' Soon we learned some words of their language and could answer them."

"What did you perform?" she asked him.

"The Eagle dance. But not like in the Pueblo. In Europe, we didn't paint our bodies, and we used any old kinds of feathers to make eagle wings and tail, but the French loved it, oo-la-la. To paint our bodies, to use real eagle feathers would make it too real, too sacred. Not in a music hall or a stadium."

"I'm sure the French were impressed," Edith said.

She had seen the Eagle Dance, its beaked head-dresses giving the men the piercing look of birds. Their feathered arms truly became wings, and the balance of their movements, the soaring of their voices, turned the earth into air.

"What could they possibly feel watching you — without knowing this land, its heights, its colors, the mesas, the rising clouds, without having seen the enormous rainbows?"

Tilano shrugged. That was the moment Edith knew she would live with him.

****

On September 14, as Gregor was sitting down to table, Tilano was washing off body paint before coming home from the dance. It was an exhausted old man who waved the rabbits at the guests. It was an exhausted old man who insisted on serving dessert and coffee. Impersonating the animal-gods, exchanging quotidian reality for a time-world as old as the zodiac, suspending human thought so that a surge of divinity might come streaming through him — and then, at day's end to become Tilano Montoya again, a five foot, four inch man, heavy with years — this was exhausting. His hand trembled as he poured Gregor's coffee and set down his cake.

"I heard you were dancing today," said the roach.

Tilano shrugged, that same shrug that had won Edith Warner's heart.

"You've seen the dancing?" asked the dancer.

"No."

"Hot stuff. I take you next time."

"I want to study up my anthropology before I come." Gregor, ever the scholar. Tilano guffawed, interrupting the quiet conversations in the room.

"You scientists!"

"I'm not a scientist. I'm a risk assessor."

"What kind of risk?"

Gregor was caught. Nothing to do but be honest.

"I can't tell you."

"I know what you're up to. It's no secret. It's all over Santa Fe."

"What?"

"You're planning a submarine base in that pond up there where the ducks swim, and those blasts — you're building a secret passage to connect it with the Rio Grande, and then out to sea."

From the next table, Dick Feynman, yelled out: "He's caught us! He knows about the ducks!"

The whole room burst out laughing: in July, Feynman had convulsed a community meeting with an impromptu lecture on the thermodynamic-military potential of the ducks in Ashley Pond.

Tilano whispered to Gregor, "You come with me tomorrow. I'll show you some of *our* secrets. More powerful than white man's medicine."

"What kind of secrets?"

"If I told you, it wouldn't be secret, would it? I'll pick you up at the east gate tomorrow at two. Are you free?"

"I'll make time."

"Good. I want to show you something special."

Edith came up behind Tilano, and took him by the ear.

"That's enough, now. Off with you, before you spill hot coffee all over our guests. Sufficient unto the day..."

"...is the goodness thereof, " returned Tilano, as he shuffled off with an exaggerated pout.

Edith sometimes played Stern Mama to Tilano's Bad Little Boy, a Mama who could be quite effective at times: Tilano had given up serious drinking since moving in. She knew that though she often idealized him, finding in his ancient culture all that seemed lacking in her own, Tilano was just a human being like herself, with strengths and weaknesses. She felt she had something she could offer him, another form of knowledge complementing his, another pattern of living, a second shore to contain the river of life.

Edith Warner was a soft-spoken woman, naturally reticent, a woman whose silence had increased with the secrecy of the war years. When she occasionally joined her guests after dinner she would listen, as if to the wise men of the Pueblo, saying nothing unless she were asked a direct question. Then she would give an answer as down to earth and simple as the meals she served. But in her secret heart, she was the quintessential transplanted romantic. Driven west by ill-health — a lingering, unstable, depression — she found her healing in this desert country, in her little house by the Rio Grande, gradually becoming a fixture of the region, and finally going native — in her own way, hoping "to bridge the gulf of racial heritage" and have the Pueblos call her "one of us," hoping to absorb a landscape where mesas were "ancient beings who have seen much," feeling "very small and of little worth in the presence of great spaces and deep silence, but not afraid". Such were her fantasies, come to life.

Siren call of the spirit: the Los Alamos mesa that rose above her home had already been occupied by another redemptive fantasyland: Ashley Pond's "Los Alamos Ranch School For Boys". A delicate, sickly child like Edith, Pond had fled his domineering family by coming west to build his health, and to found a school where "city boys from wealthy families . . . could regain their heritage of outdoor wisdom at the same time that they were being prepared for college and the responsibilities which their position in life demanded." His boys wore shorts and slept outdoors even in the harsh winters; they rode horses, grew gardens, and shared studies. On camping trips, they were sometimes ordered to ride, work and sleep naked. One wonders exactly what was going on.

More curious still was the mechanical Taylorism they were being trained in, the school's deep commitment not only to Thoreauvian skills, but to industrial management practices. Every activity was broken down into units, to be performed with maximum efficiency under the searching eyes of faculty and peer supervisors, a training in "the spirit of competitiveness", which included not only the work, but the boy himself. A rigorous program of monthly testing measured every part of his body, with posted results. Ranch School boys would be able to go forth to run their fathers' urban factories and banks. As one school brochure put it, "the speed of modern life in and near the large centers of population depletes the nervous energy of youth— that energy on which, in the next generation, they and their country must depend." Ranch School graduates would re-emerge into the urban world to lead their depleted, effete contemporaries.

For good or evil, all this came to an abrupt end when yet a third redemptive fantasy alighted on top of the mesa-which-had-seen-much, and was to see much more. On December 1st, 1942, the Los Alamos Ranch School received notification that it was to be closed, and its lands and buildings taken over by a secret army facility. A second letter from Secretary of War Stimson insisted that the school simply walk away, and "refrain from making the reasons for the closing of the school known to the public at large." The government was deadly serious. Oppenheimer and Groves were expecting to move into its fifty-two buildings, with its working farm and self-contained water and power, as soon as the students moved out. By mid-December, the road up to the school was being transformed, as hundreds of bulldozers, ditch-diggers, and earth-moving machines broadcast their deafening noises to the mesa above and the valley below. School residents watched precious stands of trees, lovely meadows and groomed playing fields "improved" out of existence by the Army Corps of Engineers, while Pueblo dwellers saw sacred burial grounds upturned, and hunting areas emptied of game. Wages for laborers, and later, for other help covered the surface of discontent, but the people of the Pueblos had their stoicism sorely tested.

Anglophile Tilano was seen by some as turncoat. But redemptive fantasies, especially of large mass, have large momentum.

****

Gregor was waiting at the East Gate at two P.M. , as instructed, under a cloudless, blindingly bright September sky. Two-fifteen. Two-thirty. Had he heard wrong? Had Tilano only been joking? Was this an example of the famous "Indian time" he had heard about? He was sorry he hadn't brought something to read. The agonized putt of a weary engine climbing became perceptible, came closer, and then in the distance, on the relatively level road to the gate, G glimpsed Tilano's notorious sky-blue '34 Ford pick-up chugging toward him. When it pulled over, G opened the door.

"Why don't you ride in back?" Tilano suggested. "It'll be more fun. It's only a few miles down the hill."

How like Tilano to make that suggestion. Gregor had never ridden in the back of a pickup, except inside a crate. Now he sat on a pile of old tires. The wind blowing through his antennae created a veritable symphony of sunshine, sensation and scent.

Ten minutes later, they pulled off the road at a little gate. "TSANKAWI CLIFF DWELLINGS AND RUINS," the sign said, "0.2 mi." Gregor jumped out of the back and looked around. Nothing spectacular apparent. Tilano opened the gate, and the two of them hiked down a little hill, then started to climb.

"So tell me about this," said G., "Be my guide."

Tilano didn't answer, but kept trudging ahead.

"When did the Indians live here?"

"Five hundred years ago. My people. The Anasazi." He was a little out of breath after the short climb. "Maybe that's why he's not talking. Getting old," thought G.

"Left because the rain stopped. Moved down to the valley and built the Pueblos."

They climbed up a narrow trail worn half a foot into the rock and emerged on a plateau with a breath-taking view of the Jemez and the Sangres, the Pajarito plateau between them, with its lowlands of piñon-juniper, and occasional Ponderosa clutching at the sparse damp of arroyos. They stood together at the edge of the cliff, and breathed in the view.

A little over a million years earlier, 300 million years after the Carboniferous appearance of cockroaches, huge eruptions of the Jemez volcano covered the area as far as the eye could see with thick volcanic ash, called tuff. The Pajarito plateau was sculpted by streams, leaving the thrilling geography of mesas and canyons staring back at them.

"Is this the way it was then? The climate? The vegetation?"

"It was always dry. But not too dry to live. Then it was too dry to live. We came down from the mesa."

"Why would you want to live on top of the mesa? Where did you farm? Where did you get your water?"

"Down below. Climbing up and down carrying water six times a day is good for you. And you could see invaders coming. Not like us, in the valley. We didn't see you coming. But you can see all this from up at the lab, right? There's something else I want to show you. The secret."

They tracked back from the edge of the cliff, and returned to the deep-worn trails leading upward. At one point they had to walk sideways to traverse a path worn shoulder-high between two rocks.

"How would you carry water through this?" Gregor asked.

"Strong arms. You couldn't do it. Arms too skinny."

By the time Gregor decided not to be insulted, they had reached the top of the mesa. Again, a heart-wrenching view. After walking a while, Tilano pointed out the ruins of a 300 room apartment complex surrounding a huge courtyard. "*Sic transit gloria.*" was all he had to say. Where did he learn Latin? his companion wondered. At the edge of the mesa, Tilano sat down and stared in the direction of San Ildefonso, his Pueblo, eight miles to the northeast. He was often inclined to carve out a "moment" for himself, to call a halt to his activities in order to sit and ponder on the great, unanswerable yet utterly necessary questions.

"Why are we stopping? Is this the secret?"

Tilano just sat there, staring, not responding. Gregor, feeling ever the foreigner, resigned himself to the idiosyncrasies of his guide, and lay down on his back in the late-afternoon sun. After half and hour, Tilano said,

"Edith is not playful enough. She doesn't like it when I pinch her behind. But it's good for her."

An unanswerable opinion.

"Laughter is from the gods."

Gregor could only nod his head, unobserved.

"Why don't you two have a phone?" he asked, feeling non-sequitur was the order of the present. "We always have to send someone down to set up dinner schedules. Can't you afford one?"

"It's not only the money; if we were rich we still wouldn't have a phone. I have been in homes and heard those phones ring. The church bells are more to my liking. They call you to prayer, but they are polite and not in such a hurry. The phone is like a knife; it lunges at you, then it lunges again: no mercy, no consideration, only determined to make you bow to its wishes. Edith agrees. No phone."

"Is Edith your first wife?"

"What makes you think we're married?"

"Oh, I'm sorry, I just..."

"Everybody suspects us of hanky-panky. We have our separate beds, you know."

"I didn't mean..."

"My wife died in childbirth. I raised Domingo all by myself till he left home."

"Your son."

"Yes. Then I got lonely."

That was all for the next quarter hour. Then Tilano sprang up, and said, "It's almost time for the secret."

He led G along the side of the mesa to a long ladder, and clambered down, signaling to the roach to follow. They wound their way along a narrow path, and were greeted with a Park Service sign: SHARP DROPOFFS, PLEASE KEEP CHILDREN CLOSE TO YOU.

"I no longer have a child to take care of," Tilano said joylessly. When Domingo was young, I would have to teach him how to behave: a father must hand down the laws. Of course, there is always disobedience, and I didn't want to crush my son. He would never learn if he didn't have a chance to go wrong. But there is a line one must draw, and beyond this point — well, there has to be punishment. I would not hit; I would just call him to me, and hold both his hands and look at him. He would lower his eyes. Then I would tell him what he had to do."

Now it was G's turn to stop, as a paralyzing memory came across him. He looked out from the side of the cliff onto a landscape as different from Prague as could be imagined. Prague, magic, golden city, flowing with Vlatava's liquid energy. Here, instead, was yucca, sand and saltbush. Yet floating over this alien environment was the figure of his father, with his loud voice and his belt, ever ready to be stripped off — that whooshing sound! — to wound and punish. Tilano was forty feet ahead before he sensed Gregor standing, staring.

"What's the matter? Were you thinking of *your* children?"

"I don't have children. I had a father. Sometimes I imagine the map of the world spread out with him stretched diagonally across it. And I feel as if I can live in only those regions he does not cover, or can't reach. He's very big, my father, so there are not many regions, and not very comforting ones — marriage and children is not among them."

"It could be worse," Tilano said sadly. "You could have children that think differently than you. And who am I to speak with any authority? I can scarcely read or write. I'm just a working man who at this age has to be careful not to work too hard. Now I think I am lazy — and a lazy man ought not to impose his views on anyone else. But my stories are memories I have accumulated, memories of a long life, and now I have a use for them. I say to myself: through me younger people can learn about what it was like in the past, they can find out about their family. If there are people who don't care about the past, they are lost."

"What does your son do? Domingo."

"He works at your lab. Maintenance. He looks after all you scientists.

You leave your laboratories in a mess, he says, and someone has to pick up after you or everything would stop cold."

"That's probably true."

"Perhaps I did not worry enough in the past about the issues Domingo thinks about. Perhaps I ignore what is right in front of me — so much injustice, so much exploitation — in order to go my own way from day to day."

"Maybe ignoring is what makes you so healthy."

"I always wanted to be helpful to others. In this country people are not encouraged to work for one another — to share and live as brothers and sisters, the way God would wish. My grandfather told me, 'Everyone for himself in America!'"

"It's a strong community up on the hill. Different."

"But the Anglos are always fighting: dog eat dog. They like to lord it over others — us, the Indians, anyone who gets in their way, that's what Domingo says. They treat us like children. I only wish they *would* treat us like children. Then they would be nice to us, and let us grow up and have our own lives. That's what Domingo says. It feels good to help Edith. It makes me feel I belong somewhere. She needs a man to help her."

There was a long pause, barrenly pregnant, then Tilano slapped Gregor on the back.

"Come on. The light is right. You have to see the secret."

They walked another quarter mile on a trail along the cliff side, and stopped in front of a tall rockface inscribed with a six-foot standing figure, a man with a head, two arms and two legs. Tilano gestured at it.

"That's it."

"What about it?"

"It's a petroglyph carved five hundred years ago just for you."

"Why do you say that? It's nice, but..."

Tilano glanced at his watch. "It's twenty to five. You're going to sit here, quietly, for the next two hours, and watch that man up there. Don't argue."

Gregor knew objections would be useless, so leaned back against a boulder to begin his assigned vigil. It was a while before he could really focus on his task. In the beginning, he was most aware of Tilano's silence. He was not silent, G thought, because he has nothing to say. He is silent because

534

he understands the world, and he knows that words and more words won't do much to make the world any better.

That being settled in his mind, Gregor began to focus in on his assignment.

Petroglyphs are far from frozen in their rocky settings. They were probably the first experiments in kinetic art. Some lines are cut deeply, some are shallow. The former can be seen in full, straight-on light; the latter can be seen only when the sun angles across them. The most shallow lines can be seen only at the extremes of dawn and dusk. And so a petroglyph transforms throughout the day.

At about 5:30, the figure on the stone began to grow — antennae! Gregor was doubtful at first, but as the sun sank lower and lower, there was no doubt: there were two lightly feathered antennae, materializing from the previously unadorned head. Next, lo and behold!, a third pair of limbs, growing high out of the thorax, reaching in praise for the sky! The final touch — at 6:35 — little hooks appeared at the ends of all limbs, and a set of cercae emerged at the bottom of the abdomen. 6:45 — the metamorphosis was complete: a man had turned into an insect!

"Well?" Tilano inquired. "Ready to go?"

Gregor was speechless.

"Not ready to go?"

"Is it...my ancestor?"

"It's not mine."

"My ancestor in the New World..."

"Seems more like the Old World to me. Very, very old."

G pushed himself away from the boulder, and swayed, not quite able to balance. Then he did something he rarely did in public: he dropped on all sixes, and scuttled on ahead of his guide. Tilano simply watched without judgment or surprise. As the trail snaked around to the beginning of the loop, Gregor, his face only a foot off the ground, came to an abrupt halt. Half buried in the earth, there glistened a piece of carved obsidian, red light reflecting off deepest black. G stopped and dug the object out. Such non-crystalline symmetry could only have been fashioned by the hand of a man.

535

"G turned back to Tilano. "Arrowhead?"

"It's a spearhead," said the Indian.

"From?"

"From your ancestor. It's a gift."

G held the object in his claw, and saw two of his hooks through the black volcanic glass. For the first time since his change twenty-eight years ago, he felt he was not alone.

A lizard jostled a bush on the valley floor, six feet below the path. The spell of recognition was broken, and it came to Gregor that he was holding a token of war. He was not the only one on this land involved in creating death and suffering. Yet the ancient spear-maker had invoked his gods in beauty, called them forth with soaring voice, dancing body and solemn prayer.

And now there was a new group of warriors in the very same world, intent on invoking forces deep within ubiquitous dust, calling forth with new voice the powers of the universe.

"If our hearts are right the rain will come," the first group sang. "If we can beat the Germans we can win the war," chanted the second, "heart" having dropped out of the equation. G knew that his was the group of the ancients, and not that of his colleagues. And yet, the energy in the atom — was it really different from that which lurked in the dormant seed, which sprang out from the crashing wave or the ardent fire? Long ago men had learned to call forth such energy by making themselves one with the need of earth for sun or rain. These transformations were Gregor's birthright.

That night, under full moon and clouds, it snowed on the mesa. And as the snow fell quietly to the waiting earth it seemed to Gregor like a transfer of soft white down from eagle's breast to earth's breast, sent by the gods to those who remembered how to ask, as well as to those who had forgotten.

44. Tricksters Appealing And Appalling

After stealing the sun and the moon from the Village of Light, Coyote came back over the mountain to his own Village of Darkness. He went right to the Chief's home with a crowd of people following him, and lay the two bags down on the ground. The chief poked at them with his feet and said, "I don't trust anything coming from over there on the other side of the mountain."

Coyote didn't say a word, but opened the sun bag and let it out to speak for itself. Everything turned bright. The Chief shielded his eyes. "Too bright. It could make us blind. Take it away." But the people paid no attention: they were happy to have light.

Then Coyote took the Moon out of its bag. "And this will shine in the night." The people went "Oooooh!" But the chief grumbled. "This is not as bright, but is even more dangerous. People will go out at night instead of sleeping. They'll make love all the time, and be too tired to hunt or gather food."

But the people loved the stolen sun and the stolen moon, and they made Coyote their new chief.

I have before me a 1986 photograph of Richard Feynman shaking hands with Ronald Reagan, a bizarre juxtaposition of one of the deepest public minds of our century with one of the most shallow. Like the image of Gregor's handshake with FDR at Town Hall, the photo captures a moment of poised trajectory: Feynman would leave the White House that day to go home to die of Waldenström's macroglobulinemia, the second rare cancer to afflict him. Eight years earlier, a six-pound tumor was removed from his abdomen, but his current bone marrow ailment could not be cut out. The thickening of his blood would clog his damaged kidneys, and eventually choke off his brain — a brain anatomists would save from the crematory to search for what made it tick. Oppenheimer had died of cancer, Fermi had died of cancer, a host of other Los Alamos men were to die of cancer. But Feynman would never admit that the cause of his strange illnesses might lie forty years in the past in the newly radioactive sands of New Mexico. He would just die, as he lived, seeking intellectual adventure, unsatisfied to the end: he didn't want machines "and all that stuff" keeping him alive — he thought it was "sort of dumb". That was the word he used: "dumb". After several days in coma, he opened his eyes and briefly whispered his last words: "This dying is boring."

The doddering Reagan, himself well on his way to Alzheimer land, had had the photo inscribed by the White House calligrapher — "To Richard Feynman, Thanks for a job well done" — and had signed it underneath. The sad fact, the fact that sums over all Feynman's deficiencies, is that the job was not at all well done, and that the one person on the investigatory Commission with an independent mind failed to bring much fire to his work, or much revelatory light to the findings.

At 11:38 AM, Eastern Standard Time, Tuesday, Jan 28, 1986, the world stood open-mouthed as seven astronauts plunged to their deaths amidst the gorgeous, but improper, fireworks of the Challenger Space Shuttle. At one minute into the flight, a flickering light appeared where it did not belong — at a joint in the side of a huge booster rocket. At 73 seconds, the fuel tank burst open, releasing an explosive spray of liquid hydrogen, and the vessel blew apart in a cloud of flame and smoke. The crew cabin separated from the orbiter, plunged 65,000 feet, and slammed into water at 207 miles per hour. No one survived.

What went wrong? The President appointed an "independent" investigatory commission to find out, "an outside group of experts," he promised, "distinguished Americans who have no ax to grind". Independent. Seven out of the thirteen members had direct ties to NASA, and the Chair, William Rogers, ex-Attorney General, and Secretary of State under Nixon, was a lawyer for the firm representing Lockheed, the corporation responsible for launch operations. Neil Armstrong, one of the appointed commissioners, wondered why an independent commission was necessary at all. And Chairman Rogers alerted the world that "We are not going to conduct this investigation in a manner which would be unfairly critical of NASA, because we think — I certainly think — NASA has done an excellent job, and I think the American people do."

The fact is that NASA had been in serious downhill spin since the high days of the moon-landing, suffering from politicking and boondoggling and attendant cover-ups. A little investigation revealed the inescapable:

— that O-ring seals had failed in 10 out of 23 flights. To prevent an interruption in flight schedule, waivers had been signed which allowed the flights to continue despite the safety threats.

— that the decision to launch was made in the face of many adverse conditions:

— that Morton-Thiokol, the developer of the booster rockets, had warned many times — even the night before the launch— about the shrinking and hardening of the O-rings in low temperatures. They had never been used at less than 53 degrees. The temperature that morning was 28.

— that ice on the launch pad was at hazardous levels that day — including "internal ice" coating the piping around the main engines and changing the frequency of vibration to one which could cascade and shake the machine to pieces.

that high seas that day would have prevented recovery of the re-usable solid rocket booster — a $26 million hit to an already tipsy budget.

Feynman was instrumental in directing national attention at the problem of the O-rings with his theatrical demonstration at the televised hearings. He had a glass of ice water brought, pulled out a pair of pliers, pulled a piece of O-ring out of Exhibit A, dipped it in the 32 degree water, and demonstrated to millions of viewers the subsequent stiffness. Those rings had to be pliable to fill the contracting and expanding spaces between booster segments. At launch temperature that day, they were bound to fail. QED.

A national sigh of relief was heard. The problem was "solved" by a genius scientist, and dramatically taught by a brilliant teacher. But even the

New York Times questioned the Rogers Commission's exculpatory report. In an editorial on February 25th, it wondered why the Commission could not explain NASA's demand that liftoff proceed. The *Times* was perplexed by the Commission's bafflement concerning NASA's "changed philosophy" of launch safety, and puzzled by its sudden decision to put engineers "in the position of proving it was unsafe to launch, instead of the other way around." Other critics noted further that

— the Commission didn't hold NASA's top officials responsible for not acting on flight safety when they knew about the long history of O-ring problems.

— the Commission never determined who was responsible for the decision to override Morton-Thiokol's objections to launch.

— most importantly, the Commission failed to answer — or even to ask — the question of why NASA officials behaved so differently with respect to that particular flight. What possible pressures were acting on them to make them send up a space shuttle they knew could explode?

These failures might be expected from the "disinterested" members of the panel, but are more blamefully related to the one truly independent member, Dr. Richard P. Feynman, the man who signed himself, in a letter to Chairman Rogers, "Commissioner Feynman, Nobel Prize, Einstein Award, Oersted Medal and utter ignoramus about politics." As the O-rings might have been expected to fail, so might Feynman, in any social or political thinking. Not only did he fail, but his contribution was crucial in having the problem examined from the bottom up, and not from the top down.

Why the "go", then? What went unmentioned in the *Times* story of official bafflement was a fact known to all — that on the night of the ill-fated launch, President Reagan was to deliver his State of the Union address, a paean to "America moving ahead", including a live conversation with Challenger astronaut-teacher Christa McAuliffe, designed to promote NASA and the "Teacher-in-Space" program. What rule of objectivity required the *Times* to leave this "coincidence" unmentioned? What blindfold or mouth gag kept the Rogers Commission from exploring it — especially in the face of persistent rumors that "a White House official" — presumably Donald Regan — had ordered NASA, "Tell them to get that thing up!" no matter what, so the President might make his PR pitch to America. Not one person from the White House was interviewed — only NASA officials were asked if there had been any pressure. The new director of NASA, himself a suspiciously politicized appointee, had cancelled — without explanation — an earlier, good weather time, a few days previous, and had been frantically taking Democrats off the guest list for the launch. Could it be that this mission, at just this time and no other, was to serve a political purpose?

Feynman was incapable of engaging such a question. So much did he value his special vocation that, unlike many of his colleagues, he shaped his image to exclude any but scientific issues. "I don't like to speculate about things I don't know very much about. I don't see that it's useful," he told one interviewer. "I don't have a very good understanding of international relations and human characteristics," he told another. Human characteristics? Had he so marked himself off from ordinary beings as to be a stranger to things human?

****

Dick Feynman was always fascinating. I knew him when he was a grad student at Princeton, at the time he was recruited by Bob Wilson into the Manhattan Project. His initial refusal was typical: he was too busy on his thesis doing "real physics". The project sounded like "engineering" to him, a pedestrian activity he disdained. Though he finally joined because of some inarticulate notion of "patriotic duty", over the years he developed his selfishness into a full-blown "Principle of Active Irresponsibility". He said "no" to all academic committee assignments — one of the few professors that could get away with it. In spite of his being a famous teacher — on the lecture platform where he could show off — he took on very few graduate students, and even fewer theses to supervise. "You need concentration," he said. "You need solid time to think. If you've got a job administering anything, say, then you don't have the solid time. So I have invented another myth for myself — that I am irresponsible. 'I am actively irresponsible,' I tell everybody. 'I don't do anything.' If anybody asks me to be on a committee... 'No! I'm irresponsible. I don't give a damn about the students!'

Of course I give a damn about the students, but I know that somebody else'll do it! So I take the view 'Let George do it,' a view which you're not supposed to take. But I do, because I like to do physics. I'm selfish, okay? I want to do my physics. I have to disregard everybody else, then I can do my own work."

"Why 'active' irresponsibility?" the interviewer asks.

"I got the idea of "active irresponsibility" in Los Alamos. We often went on walks, and one day I was with the great mathematician von Neumann and a few other people. I think Bethe and von Neumann were discussing some social problem that Bethe was very worried about. Von Neumann said, "I don't feel any responsibility for all these social problems. Why should I? I was born into the world, I didn't make it." Something like that. I thought it was kind of brave to be actively irresponsible. 'Active' because, like democracy, it takes eternal vigilance to maintain it — in a university you have to perpetually watch out, and be careful that you don't do anything to help anybody." He accepted the President's invitation to join the Rogers Commission, he said, only because his wife, Gwyneth, insisted. Ever of service to the ladies.

He concentrated on his science, and on enjoying life in topless bars, drumming on the beach, telling jokes — usually at other peoples' expense. He thought, "if I am very good at understanding something and developing a new kind of knowledge for the world, then that's what I should do. There are plenty of other people who are better at ethics."

That was certainly true. Feynman had the moral development of a charming four-year old, seducing bar girls, undergraduates, colleagues' wives, refusing to sign a *New York Times* ad against the Vietnam war. "I have not been following things closely enough," he responded.

One day, while wandering in the desert, Coyote heard a bulb on a bush say, "If you eat me, you will shit." "Want to bet?" he said, swallowed the bulb, and continued on his way. "Stupid bulb," he thought. "I'll shit when I want, and no sooner." Just then, he gave out a little fart. "Oh, this is what the bulb meant. But I'm great even if I fart a little." Then it happened again, really strongly, and again, even more strongly, and incredibly loud. "Well," thought Coyote, "that bulb may give me the farts, but it will never make me shit." The next fart lifted his hindquarters up into the air, and blew him ten feet ahead onto the ground. "Oh, you old bulb! I dare you to do that again!" — and with an earth-shaking blast, he flew twenty-five feet into the air. Coyote began to take this matter seriously. He grabbed onto a log, but both he and the log were blown high into the stinky air, and the log came down on top of him, and nearly broke his back. He grabbed on to a poplar tree, but the next fart tore its roots out of the ground and sent both of them flying.

Coyote ran to the nearest village, and got the people to pile logs and boulders on top of him, but his explosion scattered the debris in all directions, destroying some houses, and the people shouted angrily at one another, and the dogs howled. Coyote laughed till his insides were sore.

Then he began to shit, at first only a little, but then more and more, so much that he had to begin climbing a tree to keep above the pile. He climbed higher and higher till he reached the small branches at the top, and when one of them broke, he lost his footing and fell right through the shit pile, right down to the bottom. He stuck his head out, and opened his eyes, but he couldn't see very well because his eyes were coated with shit.

"I have invented another myth for myself," Dick said. It never ceases to amaze me how of all the notable scientists who passed through Gregor's life — Einstein excepted — it has been Feynman who has achieved most public affection. Vulgar of speech, mandarin, abrupt, capable of the most vicious disparagement in the spirit of self-aggrandizing play, a would-be con man as morally shallow as he was intellectually deep, Feynman succeeded in cultivating an entranced following throughout his life and even after his death, consciously generating amusing anecdotes and "Feynman stories" on tape, and in best-sellers like *Surely, You're Joking, Mr. Feynman*, and *What Do You Care What Other People Think?*. After his death in 1988, he was lionized in several high-profile biographies, and his fame increases even today, with beautiful book/tape packages of his lectures sold at chain stores. He was the most competitive person I've ever met. He had to be the best in the world at whatever he chose to do. Aggressive and loud as a New York cab driver, he needed to debunk anything he thought was "hokey-pokey".

I don't mean to sound so cranky; I often liked him too. He was an attractive character — if you weren't one of his targets — and I, myself, would love to add to the heap one story about the aging Feynman which captures, I think, his delightful — if self-entranced — Paul Bunyan swagger. In 1982 I bumped into Dick in Geneva, and we decided to go over to see what was happening at CERN, the European particle accelerator. Because he was there, they took us on a VIP tour. We were led into a huge underground cave with most impressive hi-tech equipment. Very James Bond. A giant machine the size of a two story building was going to be rolled into the line of the accelerator. Tracks, control panels, scaffolding, men climbing all over it. Dick asked "What experiment is this?" The director said, "This is your theory of charge-change, Dr. Feynman. This is an experiment to demonstrate, if we can, your 1967 theory." Feynman gestured at the huge machine. "How much does this cost?" he asked the director. "Thirty-seven million dollars." Feynman looked at me, then back to the director. "You don't trust me?" he asked. There was laughter all around, but I knew it was a serious question.

What is it about Dick Feynman that seems so seductive to our turn of the millennium culture? Is it Authority laughing at Authority? Hedonism as Final Trump? The Mystery of "Genius"? Our collective Lust to Feel Inferior? Good PR? It's worth contemplating.

Like myself and almost everyone else, Gregor too was attracted to the Pied Piper's call. As classically cultured and morally discriminating as he was, still he found Feynman amusing, stimulating, and after a few months on site months found himself slipping into the role of his playmate and partner-in-crime.

The main issue that provoked them both was a hyper-inflated, self-important, and probably irrational security apparatus. It had began, reasonably enough, with the general secrecy of the project: railroad tickets to an unknown destination, no allowed talk about the nature of the work, etc. It already had some silliness attached, given the guarded isolation up on the mesa: fake names for the more famous people — Enrico Fermi became Henry Farmer (though Mr. Farmer would never respond to paging); Niels Bohr was Nicholas Baker, and so forth. School-age children were registered by first name only, and were warned not to tell anyone who they were.

Everyone's address was "Box 1663, Santa Fe, New Mexico" — children were even born in that box — place of birth on their birth certificates: Box 1663.

But in the fall of '43, the whole security thrust escalated to heights that seemed offensive and ridiculous to the international circle of scientists long used to open communication. Military mind was off in high gear. A memo in November initiated a new level of chaos with a wholesale clampdown on language:

Since employees must necessarily talk with one another concerning problems related to the work in the performance of their duties, it is advisable to invent fictitious terms or code names, which are not descriptive, for reference to secret or confidential matters which it is necessary to discuss. The invention of such language is left to the individual organization so that the terms used will not be uniform throughout all phases of the general project.

So atoms became *tops*. Bombs became *boats*. An atomic bomb was a *topic boat*. Uranium fission was *urchin fashion*. Uranium, however, was also called T, from its code name, *tube-alloy*. U_{235} was T_{235}, or sometimes *tenure* (2+3+5=10; uranium = ure. Clever?).

Can you imagine the resulting Babel? Can you imagine Feynman's hilarious parodies?

Driven by Gen. Groves' penchant for military secrecy, a "Loose Talk" campaign was begun with ubiquitous signs, posters, literature, even inserts into the dials of rotary telephones, warning residents to "HEW to the line", attempting to inculcate a general paranoia in which even family should be viewed with suspicion. "MUZZLE UP! There are at least three occasions when the mouth should be kept shut — when swimming, when angry, and WHEN OUR COUNTRY IS AT WAR!!" "Loose Thinking" was imagining you had the right to speak freely, or trust others, or even be neighborly. "Security Education Officers" spread out on the mesa to promote the campaign, each instructed to be "tactful" and yet to "sell himself and his work to all concerned."

Groves' new goal was not just to bottle up military secrets, but to make Los Alamos completely invisible to the outside world. And so in October, the Daily Bulletin crammed by GIs into kitchen doors contained the following.

```
It is deemed necessary in the interests of security to
institute censorship over all personal communications
to or from any personnel at Site Y. Censorship will
accordingly be instituted, effective immediately, over
all such communications under provisions of paragraph
3D of War Department Training Circular No. 15 dated 16
February 1943, which provides as follows:
```

This, for the flavor of the language. Because traditional military means of censorship — punched letters, censorship stamps, envelopes with flaps resealed — would call attention to the Project, residents were henceforth required to censor themselves. All letters were to be sent unsealed, then read, sealed, and sent on by the censor. If contents did not meet with censor approval, a letter would be returned to the writer with comments and instructions. Booklets were issued with rules about what could be said — and what could not. Twelve-year old Nella Fermi had a letter returned in which she had written a friend about studying fissioning amoebas in her biology class. The word "fission" was *verboten*.

Naturally, Feynman had a good deal of trouble with this. Knowing his delight in solving puzzles, his wife Arline, afflicted with terminal TB, began a letter exchange in code from her Albuquerque hospital bed. Feynman, and shortly his father, gladly joined in. These letters were one of the first targets of the new Censorship Office, which notified Feynman of Regulation 4(e): "Codes, ciphers or any form of secret writing will not be used. Crosses, Xs, or other markings of a similar nature are equally objectionable." So much for kisses. Feynman refused to comply, citing his sick wife's mental health. They asked for a key to the code. He said he didn't have a key — it would spoil his fun. Treading lightly, the new censors said that if Arline would enclose a key for their benefit, they would remove it before the letter reached Feynman. Good enough.

But Arline's sense of mischief had been piqued. Informed (somehow) of Regulation 8(l), requiring censorship "of any information concerning these censorship regulations or any discourse on the subject of censorship", she began sending letters with sentences such as "It's very difficult writing because I feel that the [deleted in black] is looking over my shoulder." Dick would respond with scholarly red herrings such as "It is interesting how

the decimal expansion of 1/243 repeats itself: .004 115 226 337 448..."
and the baffled censors would go scurrying over the numbers as possible
cipher for important scientific secrets. They never cracked the code — as
there was none.

While Dick and his family were thus having fun, Gregor, to his surprise, found *himself* a target of expanded security. In early December, he
received a letter from Col. Peer De Silva, the Chief Intelligence Officer at
Los Alamos, informing him that secure naming had been expanded to a
second level of Site Y personnel, and that from henceforth, he would refer
to himself as George Samson. Being by nature far more law-abiding than
Feynman, he went into existential angst. Samson. Why Samson? Did he
want to be identified with a biblical hero who slayed thousands? Or was
it because of his fatal attraction to...what? Would that there had *been* a
Delilah in his life! But no. He was as celibate as the Pope — and I don't
mean Fermi. Gregor meant the real Pope — Pius XII — the one who chose
to be "neutral" in the face of Nazi persecutions.

Delilah. Who or what was his Delilah? Delilah from *lilah*, "night" in
Hebrew. What was the night Gregor loved, the night that would cut off
his strength and undo him? That very afternoon he betook himself to the
small collection of books up on the balcony of Fuller Lodge which must
have been the remains of the Ranch School library, and there found a nineteenth century Bible, dusty and un-used in this world of Science. Where
is Samson? Somewhere in the middle of the Old Testament. Samuel?
Kings? No. He was a Judge for twenty years, the last of the Judges of Israel.
Judges. There he was. Judges, xiii-xvi. Gregor read through the story of
this Superman figure, a loner, not the leader of a Hebrew army like other
Judges, but a one-man scourge of the hated oppressor Philistines. Samson's
life was miraculous from the start: an angel announced his coming to his
mother, and forbade her to cut his hair, "for the child shall be a Nazarite
unto God." A Nazarite, that is "one who is separate", one marked off from
ordinary human beings and devoted to the spiritual life. Surely that fit,
though the Biblical Samson was more like the Feynman of wine-wom-
en-and-song, than like Gregor. But God's process of divine selection had
always been murky. Perhaps Gregor was to be the true Samson, the one to
fulfill God's will at last. But what was God's will?

What a silly story, he thought. Why does Samson give Delilah four teasing chances to ambush him? Why doesn't he learn what she is after? Why does he get "tired to death" of her asking how to bind him, and confess his secret? I wouldn't do that. There must be some hidden message.

The reader may be amused at thin-limbed Gregor considering himself a Samson surrogate. For anyone raised with images of Victor Mature and Hedy Lamarr, it is a surprise to find that there is no indication at all that Samson was a brawny type. DeMille might have been more theologically correct in having him played by the young Woody Allen, oddly empowered by the Spirit of the Lord coming upon him.

Why do men need Delilahs? Gregor wondered. Why do they need bombs? Because they are glamorous and exciting? Because men yearn to be swept away by some passion beyond reason? Because they want to be present at the Fall? Because anger is aphrodisiac? To be naughty? Because they would know Death? Why do I need Delilahs? Why do I need bombs?

And the blinded Samson said, Let me die with the Philistines, and he leaned on the pillars with all his might, and the temple fell on the lords and on all the people. "So the dead which he slew at his death were more than those he had slain in his life." And afterwards? Then "there was no king in Israel: every man did that which was right in his own eyes."

Was this a good death, a suicide redeeming a mis-spent life? It was not how Gregor would choose to go. Still, he took this thought-exercise seriously enough to begin melding with George Samson: he began calling himself "G".

Standing on a mountain, Coyote looked off into the distance and saw a light. It was fire, and Coyote decided to get some for mankind. He gathered a team of good runners — Fox, Wolf, Antelope — and after traveling a great way, they reached the house of the Fire People, who held a dance in honor of their visitors.

The Fire People were the first to dance, and Coyote complained that he and his friends could not see, so the Fire People made the flames higher. Then Coyote's team complained that they were too hot, and went outside to secretly take their positions for running.

Coyote had made himself a head-dress of pitchy pine shavings with long fringes of cedar bark. He danced around the blaze, and made sure his head-dress caught fire, then yelled for the Fire People to put it out. In the midst of the excitement, he ran out into the night. Pursued by the Fire People, Coyote passed the fire to Fox, who ran and passed it to Wolf, who ran and passed it to Antelope.

But the Fire People were faster still, and they caught and killed the fire-thieves — all but Coyote, who gave his fiery head-dress to Tree, and ran off into the darkness. And since then, men have been able to draw fire from the wood of trees.

With quivering claw, G returned the Bible to the shelf. As he gave a time-dividing, spiracular sigh, his ommatidia registered the thickness of the book to its right, an timeworn grey-green volume with an faded, indistinct title. It took left and right claws to draw it from its space, and open to the title page:

Theodor Benfey
A Sanskrit-English Dictionary,
with references to the best editions of Sanskrit authors and etymologies and comparisons of cognate words chiefly in Greek, Latin, Gothic, and Anglo-Saxon.
London, Longmans, Green, and Co., 1866.

Perhaps his excursion with Samson had fired up his ancient history; perhaps his sharing another's story had stroked his understanding of *Atman* as *Brahman*. In any case, quasi-exhausted from his tryst with multiple Delilahs, he decided then and there to learn Sanskrit. If Oppenheimer could do it, so could he. Confident from the dust layer that no one else would miss it, he tucked the book under his arm, and went for a walk in the early December snow.

****

Dick and Arline had been having fun with their codes until the censors, completely infuriated, had tossed in the trash her cotton sack containing a love letter written on the back of a disassembled 500 piece picture puzzle of St. Basil's Cathedral in Moscow. She had been reading *Anna Karenina*, and exposed to such passion, had fallen head-over-heels in love again with her handsome, funny, attentive young husband. She had procured this puzzle, express mail, from a catalogue, spent four days assembling it, had carefully turned it over (with the help of a nurse) between two chest films, and had spent another two days pouring her heart out on the gray cardboard back. The censors, recognizing the onion domes, were brought to the end of their rope by the presumed Commie plot. They would later be censored for their unilateral destruction of property, but still, the puzzle was gone, and Arline's message with it. She was devastated — and Dick was incited to riot. What could he pull that would really shake the system? He left his office in the Tech Area, and went for a plotting walk in the early December whiteness. He bumped into Gregor at the northern edge of Ashley Pond between the Tech Area and Fuller Lodge. Feynman noticed the fat book under G's arm.

"Whatcha got there, Samsa?"

"Samson. Do you mean Mr. Samson?"

"Oh yeah. New names."

"What's yours?"

"Mrs. Delilah. Wanna dance?"

He grabbed G by the collar, and threw him roughly onto the snow.

"What's the name of that dance?" asked the white-faced scholar, as he gathered up his Sanskrit dictionary, and wiped it carefully on a dry section of his overcoat.

"It's called The I'm Gonna Get Those Fucks Waltz" You like it?

"No. What 'fucks'?"

"The goddam censors. Know what they did?" He launched into the story in vituperous detail.

"So what can you do about it?"

"I'll sue the bastards. I'll lean an open bottle of piss on their door and ring the bell and run away. Or maybe I won't run away." He took a swig from a lab bottle of ethanol in his coat pocket. "I'm gonna raise some hell. I just haven't figured out how yet. What's that book?"

Gregor handed it over.

"Been over to Oppie's?"

"No. I got it from the Lodge."

"Why?" He took another swig.

"I don't know. It called to me."

"You need medical attention? You hear voices often? Tell me about your mother."

"I'm not joking. It's time for me to know some Sanskrit. I don't know why."

"I know why."

"Why?"

"Because me and you are gonna play a good trick on the boss."

"Why do you want to do that?"

"Just to get him for setting up this censorship bullshit."

"He didn't do it. Groves did."

"Groves doesn't know Sanskrit. It'll have to be Oppie." He took another swig of ethanol. I'm unna go for a walk and scheme this thing out. I'll meetcha at your place at seven." And he was off, kicking up snow, and shaking it off the trees at the side of the pond.

Gregor went back home. Home was a chicken coop in a field near Deke Parson's house on the north end of Bathtub row. How had G had come by such a fashionable address? Not through rank, certainly, but just by being a nice person. He had been scheduled to occupy a bachelor apartment in the already over-crowded men's dorm, right across the hall from Feynman. So at the housing office, he offered to take any existing sub-standard housing instead, and the housing officer jumped at the chance to save a room. A short walk around the site revealed the perfect place. It was his. The Corps of Engineers even got it insulated it before cold weather set in: while insulation is not crucial for a blattid, it does make for a more productive day.

Seven o'clock came and went. So did eight. No Feynman. At a quarter to nine, Gregor heard out-of-tune singing and rhythmic bashing of flower pot on frying pan. It could have been "Don't Fence Me In", but he wasn't sure. When G answered the complex, extended knocking, he found Feynman sitting on the ground in front of his door.

"I gotta give up this alcohol. It's ruining my drumming."

"Do you want to come in, or would you rather sit in the snow?"

"Um unna give up alcohol. And cigarettes. Yup. And cigars and coffee... No good for drumming...

Gregor helped him up, marched him in, and sat him down on a bale of hay.

"You think if I give up all that stuff I'll get moraller and moraller? Thas no good..."

In less than a minute, he was asleep, draped over the bale, like a wet, pathetic rag doll. The smartest rag doll on earth.

The next morning Feynman was up at six, the crack of a late dawn.

"Hey, Samson, ass outta the sac. Let's work out our plan."

The plan involved safe-cracking, lock-picking, and breaking and entering. For Feynman's infamous techniques, I refer the reader to *Surely You're Joking*. This job, however, had a new, ingenious twist. The physicist pulled a folded piece of paper from his coat pocket, ink all running from the last night's snow.

"I woulda done this myself, except some damn bastard stole the Sanskrit dictionary from the library."

On the paper — a blank back-of-page from the Daily Bulletin — he had scrawled a verse in his arrested adolescent handwriting:

Roses are red,
Violets are blue,
The Sanskrit Mole
Is You-Know-Who.

"I want a translation by four thirty. Into Sanskrit. Think you can do it? Sure you can do it. I have complete confidence in you. Then, you know what we're gonna do? Tonight we're gonna plant this message in Groves's safe, in Parson's file cabinet, in Bethe's, in Serber's, in Teller's, in every goddam group leader's most secure lockup. And guess who's going to get blamed?"

"You."

"Nah. I don't know Sanskrit. Who knows Sanskrit around here? Who gets intellectual points for knowing Sanskrit?"

"Oppie."

"You betcha."

"So what's the point?"

"Why does there have to be a point? Oppie gets blamed, that's all. The place gets shaken up about a mole. You know what that is? A spy. Maybe our leader, Dr. Director, is a spy. It's funny. Laugh."

Gregor actually did laugh at the intricate silliness. And it seemed innocent enough. Clearly no one would blame Oppie: he would never pull such a prank. Besides, it might be fun to jump right into Sanskrit on a poem that could hardly be ruined. And to spend the night sneaking around with Feynman — it could be interesting.

"Put it there, pod'ner," he said, imitating a phrase he had heard on the radio last night. He held out his claw.

"You Raven, kimosabe, me Coyote, ugh," said Feynman, who saluted, Indian-fashion. Gregor bowed back, Sanskrit style.

"Why Raven and Coyote, kimosabe?"

"Raven and Coyote heap big tricksters, blockhead furriner. Get 'em to tell you Coyote stories next time you're down at the Pueblo. I'll be back at four thirty to check your work. I warn you, I'm an expert on Sanskrit, so it better be good."

****

The main character of the paleolithic story-world has always been the Trickster. Among Plains and Pueblo Indians, Trickster took the form of Coyote, the archetypal hero, bringer of great boons – fire, chief among them — and teacher of humankind. He was creator god, innocent fool, evil destroyer and childlike prankster — all rolled into one.

Western culture has been less prone to honor Tricksters; from the establishment point of view, they bring chaos and topsy-turvy strife; they shatter boundaries and break taboos. But even a cursory search among Western heroes will find them — from Hermes and Prometheus to Brer Rabbit. Satan is a grand trickster figure, along with his carnival brothers, Pulchinello, Punch, Kasper, clowns, jesters and buffoons, all anathema to the Masters of Decorum.

In general, Trickster is powerful but vulnerable: he often comes off worse for wear, punished for his arrogance. We think of Satan. We think of Prometheus, opening his wife Pandora's box, or alternatively chained to a rock, an eagle eating the seat of his soul — his liver. Yet in most cultures Trickster is neither condemned for his defiance of the powers that be, nor mocked as a fool for defying them. Rather, he is praised for illustrating the tragic pattern of man in his would-be self-reliance, facing the much larger powers of the universe.

Trickster and Prankster — is there a difference? Which was Feynman? Pranks are usually thought of as simply mischievous jokes, perpetrated by less-than-adult mentalities. Whoopie cushions, fake vomit, exploding cigars, harassment by banter, ridicule or criticism. Such pranking is mostly unoriginal, conventionalized cruelty, pointless humiliation which does nothing to raise consciousness or alter power. But the best pranks can involve imagination, poetic imagery, unexpected. deep levels of irony or social criticism. And truly great pranks can create synaesthetic, metaphoric, poetic experiences which are unmistakably exciting and original. I think of Alfred Jarry writing *Ubu Roi*, André Breton being taken to the cemetery in a moving van, or Gerard de Nerval taking a lobster on a leash on a walk through the Tuileries? "It does not bark," he said, 'and it knows the secrets of the deep."

There is a continuum between Prankster and Trickster. We, in this culture, are not likely to be sensitive to the staging. A society whose exchange value might consist in poetic images or humor rather than dollars — unimaginable for us. But judge him as you will, Feynman came from such an inconceivable, utopian world. The name "Prometheus" means "forethinker"

****

Gregor spent all day on Feynman's verse — on company time. The problem was that Benfey's *Sanskrit-English Dictionary* was just that: Sanskrit to English, and not vice versa. It took a great deal of insect patience to turn through six hundred odd pages of nonsense script hoping to find each of the ten or so words in the poem. In addition, he could never find the word "violets". Maybe he just missed it. Maybe there are no violets in Sanskritia.

So he substituted "lilacs" — without telling Feynman. Close enough for government work. Though a native speaker might guffaw, the written poem, in broken Sanskrit, looked quite beautiful:

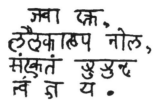

Feynman came at four thirty as promised, and was overjoyed at the work, hot off the Sanskrit press. They hand-drafted eight more copies for distribution, and headed for the dining hall (it was steak-night) and then to their nefarious business. It was the first time they had spent any extended time together.

Dick was quite nonchalant about breaking and entering. "You look so worried," he said. "People do it all the time," he assured Gregor. "Get stuff out of other people's offices. It's okay. We're not even taking anything. We're just putting."

Using paper clips and a small screw driver, Feynman could get into any room within two minutes. The locked file drawers took somewhat longer, and the safes somewhat longer than that. But Feynman was often able to check a notebook he carried, and then concentrate on finding only one out of the three numbers needed for a combination. Sometimes he didn't need any.

"Where did you get the combination?" Gregor asked after Feynman went right up to Cyril Smith's safe and opened it.

"I've been in Smith's safe before. He's a physical constant man. I tried *pi*, 31-41-59, that wasn't it. I tried *e*, 27-18-28, and that wasn't it. But Planck's constant worked like a charm on the safe. 66-26-07. And his secretary has the file combination on the lip of her desk drawer. See? A lot of them do."

"I thought you sandpapered your fingers, and listened very carefully for inner clicks."

"Yeah, that's what everybody thinks. They get it from the movies. But they don't read the safe-cracking books Arline sends me. It's all psycho-logical. Or they use drills and nitro — which we don't wanna do here. It wouldn't be no fun."

Gregor was feeling more relaxed as lock after lock opened, and the Sanskrit lyric was distributed. After a while, he simply tried to make con-versation, as Feynman tried various combinations.

"What did you think of Cairo?"

"Ain't been there."

"I mean the Cairo Conference last month."

"Don't know nothin about it. Should I?"

Feynman didn't listen to the radio, didn't read newspapers or even novels. History didn't really exist for him. Very American. It was also the secret of his seeing everything with fresh eyes. The virtue of ignorance.

"FDR, Churchill and Chang Kai-shek decided to wipe out the Japanese Empire, and accept nothing but total, unconditional surrender. No mercy."

"Yeah, well it serves those buck-toothed, yellow-bellies right. Bright, though. They're bright. Gotta say that." Gregor dropped the subject.

Grove's office was last on Feynman's list.

"I've got a special little present for his royal Fatness. Arline suggested this."

He handed G a letter pulled from his jacket pocket.

Dear Sgt. Groves,

For twelve years I have been working with cockroaches at my lab at Columbia University in Bogota. Because I am fearful that we are destroying the planet with irreversible pollution and nuclear radiation. In order to survive, I believe the cockroach, which has been around for many years, about 350 million years, has the answer. I have now proved it, and I would like to make my discovery available to you and the soldiers under your command.

I have developed a race of super cockroaches by feeding chemical pollutants and radioactive toxins to them for three years, and my roaches developed immunities to the pollutants and toxins. I then extracted their hormones and made a cock-roach vitamin pill which cures acne (for your troops), menstrual cramps (for the WACs in your charge), arthritis (for you), and makes everyone invulnerable to nuclear radiation. I have been taking cockroach vitamin pills for over a year now, and my colds and coughs have almost all disappeared.

Sgt. Groves, you and I both know that mankind is destroying the planet, and it is important that you and your men be spared. Metamorphosis is the answer. Roaches are a race above.

Please call me at PU9-4244, Santa Fe at your convenience to set up a meeting.

Sincerely,

Dr. Joseph Stark, PhD.

"It's funny, but..."

"Funny? It's a goddam riot, and it'll send him up the wall. Sgt. Groves? He'll have a fit. Arthritis? Only someone on the inside would know that. And all the radioactivity stuff...plutonium 94, atomic weight 244? He'll go apeshit."

"But won't he think it's me?"

"You? Why you?"

"Well..."

"Does he think you're so stupid enough to incriminate yourself? No. You've got to gauge your enemy's intelligence, Samsa. He'd never suspect you."

Gregor, in spite of his leeriness, found himself getting into the game.

"I think the name ought to be more Latin American."

"Like what?"

"How about Simon Bolivar?"

"That don't sound Latin American. It's gotta end in a vowel."

"Are you kidding? Simon Bolivar *was* Latin America. The Liberator. The George Washington of Columbia, Venezuela, Ecuador, Peru."

"You mean he's a real person? We'll get sued."

"He died a hundred years ago."

"But it already says Joseph Stark."

"Who's that?"

"He owned a hardware store on Central Avenue. Stark's. When I lived in Far Rockaway when I was a kid."

"Simon Bolivar is funnier."

"What if he doesn't get it?"

"He'll get it. They teach military history at West Point."

"And he'll think it's some kind of a military attack."

"Maybe."

"But it already says Stark. I'm gonna have to type it over."

"So?"

"But we're here now. In his office."

"So come back tomorrow. He's not even on site. He's in Washington this week."

"Believe me, he'll hear about it as soon as the first of these Sanskrit things gets discovered."

"Even better. He'll think it's just those damn civilians who don't know how to maintain security. Then when he gets back, he'll find something in his own safe."

"A-plus for Samsa! I mean Samson, or whatever your name is. I'll do it. Simon Bolivar it is. B-o-l-i-v-a-r?"

"You got it."

Rabbit was carrying a large pack on his back. "What's in the pack? asked Coyote. "Nothing you would want," Rabbit answered. "OK, then let's see that nothing," Coyote demanded. "No," said rabbit, "You won't like it. You'll be angry." "I'm already angry," Coyote yelled, and he tore the pack off Rabbit's back and ripped it open. Out jumped a cloud of fleas, right onto Coyote's back. He ran off scratching and howling. "I told you you wouldn't like it," Rabbit called after him.

These are the stories Gregor was told at the Pueblo.

45. And With His Stripes We Are Healed

Outside, across the great waters, there was the great war. But inside, behind the barbed wire, there were the little wars.

Like the war between Teller and Bethe over who should *really* be head of the Theoretical Division. Or the war between Neddermeyer and Parsons over how implosion work should proceed. Kistiakowsky once told me that when he reads books on Los Alamos "everything looks so simple, so easy, and everybody was friends with everybody," but that certainly didn't jibe with his recollections. Nor mine. When you put a lot of original, outstanding, competitive people together you can count on friction increasing proportionately.

Internecine strife among the elite was not the worst of it. As any sociologist could easily have predicted there was frank alienation, and subtle class war, between the "men" of the military, and the civilian "eggheads" — the scientists and their families.

Enlisted and drafted GIs, men who had hoped to "fight Nazis" or "kill Japs", found themselves cutting wood, collecting garbage, fixing plumbing, selling soda, cigs and stamps, checking groceries and cashing checks for civilians who seemed to be "slumming it," enjoying life at a rustic camp at taxpayer expense, people who whenever they wanted to, could return to their ivy-covered universities. Who knew who they were or what they were up to? "Slackers", they were called in private, "phonies", "tech-area jerks", "longhairs". Men, women and children! Many of these GIs had had to leave families and loved ones behind, and now suffered without visits, without phone calls, with censored mail. Worst of all, the incendiary rumor prevailed that the Army was not about to "waste good men on this project", men who "could be out there winning the war." Consequently, the MPs guarding the gates and checking passes were often less than friendly; the scientists didn't know if they were being protected or imprisoned. As a recent government publication laconically put it, "Considerable hostility developed between the Tech Area civilian workers and the military workers in the Post Administration...and a considerable portion of the business was done at arm's length."

Things grew even worse with the arrival of the SEDs. In addition to the regular Corps of Engineers who ran the Post, a "Special Engineering Detachment" was sent up to work in the Tech Area, a unit of drafted physics and engineering students — some of them with PhDs. Although the Army had failed to get the senior scientists into uniform, it did try to militarize the SEDs. But these boys were quite different from regular Post soldiers. In spite of their uniforms, they looked — and acted — more like baby professors than combat troops.

I remember a hilarious incident — at least some of us thought it was hilarious — shortly after the SEDs came up the Hill: a formal military review had been scheduled in the field between the Lodge and the Big House — the single men's dormitory. For us, it was just a festive Sunday afternoon parade, but for Groves it was important enough to invite high brass from Washington to come inspect. The whole scientific community came with dogs and children to see the show. The MPs, the Post soldiers, the WACs, and even the military doctors looked smart as they marched across the field, but the SED boys were awful. Their lines were crooked, they couldn't keep in step, they grinned, waved and shouted at friends on the sidelines. And the situation was not helped by the fact that they received the loudest applause from the bleachers. Our soldierly visitors were not very pleased; one general even called it a disgrace to the army. Nevertheless, these young scientist/scoffers had all been classified as non-commissioned officers. Many were completely without basic training. And yet they outranked the hard-working GIs, ordering them around, and playfully expecting salutes. Worse yet, civilian scientists trying "to counteract the military regime", became invested and pushy about SED promotions, an infringement on military prerogative which was not too gracefully accepted. Civilians vs. military was one level of struggle. Civilians, military and SEDs upped the ante to a three-body problem which was too complex to be solved without divine intervention.

Enter Jesus Christ, potential Redeemer! The military and civilian directors, aware of growing tension, came up with a scheme to harness the Christmas energy of Peace-on-Earth-Goodwill-towards-Men in order to solve, or at least ameliorate, the problem. Little did Groves or Oppie know what forces would be released.

The Mesa Chorus, led by Donald (Moll) Flanders, would present its first annual performance of Handel's *Messiah* at 7PM, Saturday, December 18th, at Fuller Lodge. Because the GIs, by and large, preferred to spend their Saturday nights in the more alcoholic setting of the PX, attendance would be required, but the odium of enforcement would be diluted by a free, fancy meal at the Lodge beforehand, and free drinks and dancing afterward. Only the middle portion of the choral work would be given, a section semi-flirting with interesting soldierly gore, and hopefully short enough to hold the attention of any whose musical stamina was shaped by the three minute surges of the top ten. Moreover, one of their own, Rudi Schildknapp, lead trumpet of the Schildknapp Six, would be employed at a critical moment to blast out a crackling downscale of heavenly trumpets. As Rudi improvised exclusively, half the audience was hoping he would get it right and not embarrass them, while the other half was rooting for him to take off and show the longhairs what one of them could really do.

The plan, of course, was to get the soldiers there, even if coerced, to have them mix with the scientist civilians over a good meal, to have them all enjoy, or at least tolerate a piece of music which had proven ever-popular, at least among the choral music set, and then to top off the new bonds of friendship and experience with easy-going, hopefully incident-less physical contact of social dancing — with Groves playing the familiar role of cultural despot and censor in the less familiar guise of DJ. Could anything but greater harmony result?

How long was the concert? Groves wanted to know. Oh, about forty minutes, Moll assured him. Fine, said the General. Then there'll be time for a little Christmas-y talk afterwards, just so they'll get the picture, and not go out drunk after civilian' wives. And the Nobel Prizewinners might also be moved to a little charity for their inferior fellow humans. I'll ask the chaplain to say a few words, will that be all right? Sure, said Moll.

****

Gregor was excited. He loved *Messiah*. It was nothing a Jewish boy in Prague had been expected to love, but it was nothing any boy in Prague could miss. As a child, it had seemed to him that each April, every church in *Staré Město* had entered some frenzied *Messiah* competition. Until he was fifteen, he had steered clear of this goyish mania. But one day, a lovely young girl with long, dark hair handed him a leaflet for a performance at four PM, in five minutes, right there, right at St. Mikulás, right around the corner from his house. She looked very Jewish, this one. Maybe she sang in the chorus. It must be all right for a Jew to go into a church, if it's only for a concert. His parents would not be home until six. They'd never know.

Gregor was ravished by the experience. He used the word in every possible meaning: he was seized and violently done to; he was overcome by horror, joy and delight; he was pre-sexually bewitched, for the long-haired one was in fact singing soprano in the front row, and never had such an angelic voice issued from such sensuous purity. This concert, too, was of the Easter portion of the work, and from "Behold the Lamb of God" to the last "Hallelujah", he was transfixed with wonder. Jews didn't make this kind of sound in their churches. Synagogues were filled with the discordant rumble of davvening, each worshiper finding his individual prayer voice and rhythm, chanting, whispering, singing, crying, repeating phrases over and over, lost in the brumming of the crowd. Sometimes a cantor sang. But this — this! Could it be his Jewish faith was shaken? Unspeakable. It is music, music that hath ravished me! He got home before the rest of his family, and never mentioned his experience, even to his sister Grete, a budding violinist.

He had tried to hear *Messiah* every year since then, but with all the changes that had occurred along the way, he had managed to bat only

562

about .300. So what a boon — right here, in his own community, an annual *Messiah*! The sad part was that he could no longer sing it, as he had in his late teens and early twenties, in the face of his father's rage. Not that his father was an observant Jew — it was strictly High Holidays with him, and whatever social practice was necessary to maximize profits. But for some reason, the idea of his very own son singing — singing! — about Christ, advertising a false messiah — the faintest whiff of this image sent him into catastrophic fury. In fact, one of these seizures, the most terrifying one in Gregor's memory, had been on the very night before Gregor's change. He hadn't made the connection. But still, not to be able to sing this, to be kept from pouring his heart into the clean and glorious lines... Metamorphosis had many boons, but being unable to sing *Messiah* was not one of them. His voice was too scratchy.

Gregor came early, picked up a program, and sat down in the front row. Fuller Lodge's tables had been pushed back, and the room was filled with dinner and folding chairs, even on the balcony. As he read through the program, people slowly filtered into the room, some in suits and dresses, many more in uniform. The growing rumble reminded him of davvening.

"Behold the Lamb of God", ok. Hey, where is "He Was Despised" and "He Gave His Back?"...must not have an alto soloist. (For the first time in ages, Gregor grew aware of his own back, and the smiting by his father.) "Surely He Hath Born Our Griefs..." "And With His Stripes..." "All We Like Sheep", good, good. What? Genia Peierls is the tenor soloist? She sings "All They That See Him?" Easy, G, take it easy. "He Trusted In God", ok, and at least we get "Thy Rebuke", even if it is with Genia... "Lift Up Your Heads"?? What? Where's the death? Where's "He Was Cut Off Out Of The Land Of The Living?" How can they skip that, skip Death??

Gregor thought he had better give up reading the program, so he could listen with a receptive heart. They would do what they would do. This wasn't Carnegie Hall.

Choosing to do the Easter portion of *Messiah* for Christmas had been a trans-Atlantic compromise. Though written as an Easter piece, and traditionally performed in Europe during Easter time, in coming to America the *Messiah* had shifted seasons, and along with them, content. Though the Puritans had banned the celebration of Christmas, post-Puritan America has embraced it with a vengeance, currently exhorting all to worship at the mall of one's choice. Perhaps in the land of the Easter Bunny and the electric chair, crucifixion is seen as barbaric, but Christmas, not Easter, is where most American celebration is concentrated, and with it, most concertizing. *Messiah* has become a Christmas piece, and most American performances restrict themselves to its first section concerning Advent and the birth of Christ. For reasons completely incomprehensible to Europeans, the meat of the oratorio is left out, and the introductory portion is capped with the Hallelujah chorus — a masterwork written to praise Christ's ascent to his heavenly throne. "A premature ejaculation at best," commented Hans Staub, concerning this practice.

But if this was their country, and if Americans were determined to put on part of *Messiah* at Christmas, the new influx of Europeans were going to be damn sure it was the Easter portion that was performed.

The piano in Fuller Lodge was, appropriately, a living example of both the Heisenberg Uncertainty Principle, and Neils Bohr's — excuse me, Nicholas Baker's — Principle of Complementarity. You were never quite certain what the pitches were because you could not have accurate tuning of two or three of the multiple strings at the same time. If one was in, the others were surely out. Then too, the instrument existed in some duple state averaged between Hammerklavier and Harpsdischord, as Joyce was pleased to call it, a soft touch bringing out the clinging, plucking quality of frayed felt, while a strong attack manifested the sound of bare wood core on metal. You could never elicit the two at the same time, and a complete description of the instrument would have to include aspects of both. Otto Frisch, an excellent Mozart pianist, was quite the sport to agree to play on it. But no one was about to move Teller's Steinway grand over through snow and frozen mud for a forty minute performance at the Lodge. Besides, such accompanying cacophony took the burden off the chorus to sing in tune. No one would think of blaming Frisch, and no one could really indict the singers.

At 7:20 the chorus entered a restless hall to great applause, and the full-bearded Moll Flanders, computation leader in the Theoretical division and thus Dick Feynman's boss, dressed in unwonted, too large tailcoat and white tie made his way to the front. Even the GIs whistled and stomped. Moll had permanently endeared himself to the whole community with a show he had put on in the early fall: "The Moll Flanders Ballet Workshop [the poster said] presents the premier of an original ballet — 'Sacre du Mesa' — to the futuristic music of George Gershwin." Everyone in his company had had ballet training except him. But he pointed out with impeccable logic, that in order to dance General Groves, [Groves was in Washington], he didn't need ballet training, since the General himself had had none. QED. Tonight he would surpass that feat.

The "house lights" went down, and in the first of only two wrong decisions that evening, he broke the suspense with two mere announcements: The concert was beginning at 7:20 because, as the contemporary world has amply demonstrated, the Messiah always comes late. The audience simply took this in, confounded. Also the chorus "All we like sheep" had to be scrapped at the last minute because too many had gone astray and the shepherd was still out looking for them. Chuckles from the cognoscenti. He signaled to Otto, and the Overture began, *grave*, perhaps more striking than usual for being in an indeterminate key. Then, a truly extraordinary event occurred. When the moment came for the *Allegro moderato* to begin, Moll walked over to stand at the side of the upright piano, placed his elbow on top, and performed that three-part fugue all by himself. He whistled the soprano voice out of the right side of his mouth, the alto out of the left, and vocalized the bass part with accurate, wordless humming. You don't believe me. I was there. I am not a gullible man. I heard it with my own ears. He must have been practicing this in the shower for the last twenty years in preparation for that night.

Messiah is one of the grandest works of western culture. It is simply not appropriate for a serious conductor to whistle the overture in public performance. But the effect, rather than being ridiculous, was to create a lodge-full of gaping at the wonder that is man. No problem was too great for one who set his mind to it, no achievement too difficult. The Fuller Lodge was riddled with people who had dedicated themselves to excellence: none could gainsay Moll Flanders' accomplishment.

The music jumped from E minor to G minor, an artifactual glitch of abridgment, noticeable to few in the audience since "Behold the lamb of God" had caught them up, every last one of them it seemed, in its net of falling lines. Were there some there who had never heard *Messiah* before?

What were they expecting? Something churchy? That is not what they got. Rather they were bathed in an ominous summoning to pain and passion, set in a post-whistling context which included even them, the sinful of the world. Those who knew recognized the voice of John, the same voice that cried in the wilderness, "Comfort ye, my people." The Lamb was about to be chosen, the Passover Lamb, the sacrifice upon whom all sins would be heaped and slaughtered into renewal, the Lamb whose blood would be smeared on door jambs to frighten Death away, the Lamb that would conquer the wolves, the conquering Lamb.

What about this Lamb? Handel took great pains to describe its scorn-filled whipping. "*He gave his back to the smiters, and his cheeks to them that pluckèd off the hair.*" Blood and hair clotting together on the prison floor. Here is perhaps the only major artwork which celebrates saliva as such: "He hid not his face from shame and spitting," spit in the face, a cadence, ach-ptoo! But without an alto soloist, the audience was cheated of secretions. Instead they were assured, in no uncertain terms, that the Lamb was burdened with their very own doings: *Surely he hath born our griefs, and carried our sorrows.* The fierce F-minor cries, the painful, discordant suspensions: *He was wounded for our transgressions; he was bruised for our iniquities*, a catharsis of pity and terror.

Even the Jewish and Italian mothers of many in the audience would not have been able to evoke such a sense of guilt. The thoughtful were carried emotionally along, while at the same time wondering about the phenomenon of the Messiah. Is this suffering biped the Saviour of the world? How odd. The Messiah's function is to be victorious. Christians thought of Christ. Jews thought through their own lens of the "true" reference, the continued oppression and persecution of Israel throughout the Christian and pre-Christian centuries. The current Nazi attacks, the pogroms of the nineteenth century which had brought their parents to the New World, the persecutions of the eighteenth century, the seventeenth, and on back to the Exile, where the image of the Lamb converges with that of scattered Israel.

"*And with His stripes we are healed.*" What is that about? Why should one's agony be inversely proportional to another's? Conservation of Wound? Conservation of Tears? Conservation of Pain? Beckett has told us: "The tears of the world are a constant quantity. For each one who begins to weep somewhere else another stops. The same is true of the laugh."

Handel lingers over the word "healed" as if to lay soothing balm upon Christ's — and our — wounds. Yet at this very moment, G's wound began to weep. As he searched his soul for cause, he heard someone in the soprano section, he couldn't tell who, articulating the melismatic syllables of "healed" as "hee-hee-hee-hee-heeled", in effect a subtle but demonic, underlying cackling, as if to say that no matter what the unction, the wound is too great to be cured — you'll see. Hee-hee-hee.

And now, skipping over the strayed "All We Like Sheep", Genia Peierls stepped out in front of her row to sing "*All they that see him, laugh him to scorn. They shoot out their lips and shake their heads, saying*": Enter the scornful.

Genia, the Russian wife of the *émigré* German theoretician, Rudolf Peierls, and mother of the brilliant, beautiful, precocious Gabrielle, age 12 going on 40, had recently arrived with the British mission, and was already the most talked-about character on the mesa. No matter what the issue or activity, Genia was there, in the front row, taking things energetically in hand, running everything with ringing voice and Russian disregard of the definite article. The less generous, or more easily intimidated, spoke of her as a terror — always telling other people what to do. In this instance, she had insisted in singing the tenor recitative preceding "He trusted in God", because, as she forcefully observed, "How will audience know who speaks?!" And although she was right — it was important to identify the excerpted voice of the chorus — the transition did little to soften the brutal choral metamorphosis from a confessing people of God to an unruly crowd in obscene play at a public execution. So does Jekyll turn unexpectedly to Hyde.

He trusted in God that He would deliver him: let Him deliver him, if he delight in him. Such assertive contemptuousness! The trivializing, de-le-gitimizing of God, putting his capitalized pronoun on a syncopated weak beat, now ironically, self-flatteringly strong. What pristine nastiness, abundantly clear. Genia stepped forward again to sing Handel's comment, justified only by her own: "Is very important!" *Thy rebuke hath broken His heart. He is full of heaviness. He look'd for some to have pity on him. But there was no man, neither found he any, to comfort him.*

And surely she was right to do so. Not only was this Gregor's favorite moment of *Messiah*, with the single most touching note in music slipping into place in the piano's middle voice, a pensive entwinement of suffering and beauty. In the pause after *pity on him*, a luminous E rises half step to a questioning, consoling F, as if at least one human heart might go out to Jesus from the frigid emptiness answering his gaze. But it was also the theological key to the work: Here was the heart of it. As every culture has known and proclaimed, something is wrong with the human race. Things are not as they should be. There have been many intellectual explanations — mythological, religious, philosophical. But here is the psalmist's prophetic assessment: the primal fault is that we disdain God. *We have turnèd everyone in his own way.* The biblical word for this is "sin."

Gregor felt connected to Genia Peierls for the first time. Perhaps he sensed for a moment why she was the way she was. At the same time, he, in that moment of E to F, felt terribly, agonizingly lonely. And his wound, not so much stripe as crater, bled its brown tears.

The listeners had to interpolate the moment of death. But G found this not as egregious as he had expected. The whole textual strategy of *Messiah* is one of brilliant, evocative avoidance. Charles Jennens, an otherwise unremarkable British gentleman, had provided his friend George Fredrick with a libretto of theological genius, portraying every shade of devotion from piety, resignation and repentance to hope, faith and exultation. And all this without resorting to narrative, as in the Passions of Bach, the misery composed directly into the music. *Messiah* commands attention because of what it does not show, for the most part indicating, rather than depicting events. And therefore the death of Jesus, that epoch-making moment, really could exist as a lacuna between his unrewarded search for comfort and the triumphant "Lift Up Your Heads" which followed. Praise be to Moll and Genia for demonstrating this.

"Lift Up Your Heads"; "The Lord Gave The Word"; "Their Sound Is Gone Out". And so, for the Jews, the Ark takes its place in the Temple, for the Christians, the Son takes his place in Heaven, and the preachers tell the world — but some do not hear. *Why do the nations so furiously rage together?* Jim Tuck, the gawky six foot comedian of the newly-arrived Brits, he of explosive lens research, stepped out to sing, less than accurately but with conviction, to sing of the kings of the earth, of the rulers that counsel together against the Lord. Again, the demonic chorus: Let us break any bonds with the Anointed, and cast away their yokes from us. And what will happen? This time Willy Higinbotham, a "real" tenor, stepped forward to describe the smashing and breaking that will ensue, an image which reminded Gregor of the piled up debris confronting Benjamin's Angel of History.

And then, the great moment, the moment incoherently misplaced in American versions, the great Hallelujah Chorus. The piling up of debris? *Hallelujah! For the Lord God Omnipotent reigneth* — which at first blush is not a very encouraging vision of the future. But what if it were to become the case — that *the kingdom of this world is become the kingdom of our Lord,* and that over such a peaceable kingdom *He shall reign forever and ever ?* It did give one pause, in the midst of the battle of Stalingrad, the submarine warfare, and the maiden flight of the V2.

Two hundred two and a half years earlier, King George had stood in his excitement, dragging the court to its surprised feet around him, and now the European aficionados led the audience in Fuller Lodge in this traditional ninth inning stretch, though many of the GIs, worshipers in someone else's church, didn't quite know what was happening, and rose with quizzical expressions under their crew cuts. Fiercely cued by Moll, Rudi Schildknapp's five trumpet notes came in right at measure 57, and though several of his cohorts applauded defiantly right then and there, they were shortly cut off by the impregnable momentum of the music.

For all the radiance of that performance, at that time, in that place, there was one moment that stood out above all others. Willie Higinbotham, with his strong tenor voice, came in too soon after the breathtaking pause just before the final cadence, shattering the dramatic silence in the Lodge. After the concert, Otto Frisch consoled him with congratulations. "I've heard *Messiah* perhaps thirty times in my life," he said, "and I've always wanted someone to come in too soon. It was very satisfying to me." The story even followed him to Washington where he went to lobby for civilian control of atomic energy late in '45. I heard it there several times in scientific and diplomatic circles.

In spite of George Bernard Shaw's opinion alleging "the impossibility of obtaining justice for that work in a Christian country," the night's *Messiah* excerpt had been an exhausting forty-three minutes for Gregor. He leaned back against brown wetness — to decompress. But before the audience could conclude the event was over, Chaplain Capt. Jonathan Maple walked onstage, making his way through the departing chorus members, who were taking places at the back of the hall. Chaplain Maple was a gaunt thirty-five, with a high forehead under short black hair accentuating his skull-like visage, his somber eyes magnified by thick, round glasses. He had recently arrived on the mesa, a permanent replacement for the guest ministers, rabbis and priests whose coming-and-going Groves felt might compromise security. He had an office in the Big House, and was available by appointment for consultation. This, however, was his first general public appearance, and even those who might otherwise have fled stayed around to assess this new member of the community. I had mentioned Moll Flanders' two mistakes of the evening. This was the second.

Chaplain Maple began innocuously enough:

"I want to thank Dr. Flanders, Dr. Frisch, and the thirty-four members of the Mesa Chorus for their gift to us tonight."

Audience applause for those at the back.

"But I also want to acknowledge the appearance of someone invisible — more than someone — three, four, perhaps a dozen invisibles whose voices have been haunting the evening. Can you think who they are?"

No answer from the room of thinkers and doers.

"I am referring, of course, to the psalmists and prophets who supplied Mr. Handel with his texts, and us with our spiritual itinerary."

Some mumbling among the crowd. The one comment I clearly caught was, "Now we have to sit through a sermon?" Others seemed intrigued.

"Have ye not known? have ye not heard?
Hath it not been told you from the beginning?
Have ye not understood from the foundations of the earth?
It is he that sitteth upon the circle of the earth
And the inhabitants thereof are as grasshoppers..."

The quotation came out of the blue, entirely unprepared by the previous remarks. Furthermore, the Chaplain's voice had taken on a new quality

— or was it the Chaplain's voice at all? The closest approximation was the disembodied voice heard at all hours of the day and night over the Project PA system, but here shorn of its electronic quality. Perhaps it was a practiced ventriloquy used in his denomination. In any case, it seemed to come from the three sides of the balcony rather than from the speaker in front. Gregor, at first joining the audience in the search for the source, was drawn to attention by the characterization of "grasshoppers". After a pause for the exotic voice to dissipate, Chaplain Maple continued.

"Those were the words of First Isaiah, the author of much of Handel's text *Hear, O heavens, and give ear, O earth: I have nourished and brought up children and they have rebelled against me.* Thus begins the first and greatest of the books of prophets: a testimony with visionary authority, proud genealogy, cosmic scope — and an indictment of the rebellious children of the Lord."

A few soldiers stood up to leave, but were signaled back down by imperative sergeants.

"I say 'First Isaiah'. Do all of you know that the 'Isaiah' of the Old Testament is not one, but at least three different people, writing scores of years apart? [Silence.] I hope I am not shocking anyone. These are the words of the First Isaiah, who began to preach in the reign of King Uzziah, in the eighth century BC. First Isaiah was a visionary moralist, calling upon a country in the summit of its power. Uzziah had built the economic resources of Judah as well as its military strength. In Jerusalem there were engines, invented by skillful men, on each of the towers, capable of shooting arrows long distances, and heaving great stones.

But Uzziah's strength had become his weakness. He grew proud, and angry at meddling priests, and as his anger mounted, leprosy broke out on his forehead. *And King Uzziah was a leper to the day of his death, and being a leper, he dwelt in a separate house, for he was excluded from the house of the Lord.*

In the year that King Uzziah died, First Isaiah had a vision: he saw the Lord sitting upon a throne, high and lifted up. Above the throne stood the seraphim, and each one had six wings; and with twain they covered God's face, with twain they covered His feet, and with twain they did fly. Insect-like angels, shielding men from the radiation of God."

Scientists and military brass took wary note. Radiation? The radiation of God? Did the Chaplain know something he shouldn't? Gregor, tachycardic, again noted the insects.

"Those were years of power struggles and shifting strategic alliance. The huge kingdoms of Egypt and Mesopotamia, Babylon and Assyria, alternately triumphed, while tiny Judah played its cards as cleverly as it could, seeking protection without humiliation. First Isaiah lived through the reign of four Judaic kings, and he counseled each to rely not on military protection, but on God. History, he proclaimed, was a stage for God's will and God's work; the rising and falling of willful nations was mere detail.

The West Pointers in the audience struggled to recall their Military History courses.

The louder First Isaiah spoke, the farther he was pushed from centers of power. So he let it be known that politics itself, with its arrogance and disregard of justice, was the problem — not the solution. And why, Ladies and Gentlemen, and Children of all ages, why is that?

A grand pause. When no answer came the chaplain continued.

Because politics is based on the power of the sword. You know First Isaiah's words: some of you have laughed at them. He announced the day when nations '*shall beat their swords into plowshares and their spears into pruning hooks.*' Are you still listening? First Isaiah proclaimed the day when '*nation shall not lift up sword against nation, neither shall they learn war any more.*'

It had become clear that this was to be no short, simple thank-you speech from the religion Division. Some in the audience became restless, some transfixed. The GIs knew they could not leave, and the civilians felt they could not abandon them.

"What were First Isaiah's flight instructions from the Lord?" continued Maple. "Now hear this, friends:

'*Go and say to this people* (this people is you):
Go and say to this people
Hear and hear, but do not understand;
see and see, but do not perceive.
Make the heart of this people fat,

and their ears heavy,
and shut their eyes;
lest they see with their eyes
and hear with their ears,
and turn and be healed.'

What?? What could these instructions mean? Isaiah checked them twice. Prophets are normally charged with making people see and understand; they aim to mobilize their hearts, not put them to sleep. 'How long?' Isaiah asked, appalled. 'How long this tactic?' God's plan was uncomfortably clear:

'Until the cities be wasted without inhabitant and the houses without man, and the land be utterly desolate.'

Maple paused to let the thought sink in.

"It is hard to be a prophet," he added. And again that voice from nowhere and from everywhere:

"Why is my pain unceasing,
My wound incurable,
Refusing to be healed?'

Gregor could not believe his ears.

"I cry by day, but you do not answer:
and by night, but find no rest.
I am a worm, and not human;
scorned by others and despised by the people.'

Why, Isaiah, why? Could it be, my poor Isaiah, that only an outsider, only an exile, can claim the humanity society denies?

Gregor was breathing quickly.

"God's plan was decimation; First Isaiah was assigned to cover the news. Reduce Israel to a remnant, and let things begin again. And the Jews were scattered, and their Temple destroyed.

Pause. Silence. Many Europeans' thoughts shifted course toward Europe.

But in the Exile, a prophet arose who lifted the meaning of the events from mere political history to a cosmic drama of world redemption. This was Second Isaiah, the poet responsible for chapters 40 through 55, for much of the *Messiah* text, a lyrical visionary of the heart. For Christians, Second Isaiah spoke the words that most clearly presage the coming of Christ. The historical, human order is to be overcome by the suffering servant, in Christian thought, the crucified Saviour.

It is not just a few thousand Jewish exiles to whom this prophet speaks, as they sit weeping by the waters of Babylon. Second Isaiah addresses every exile all over the world, every human at a loss to find God, every blind man trying passionately to penetrate the darkness of the future. That, Ladies and Gentlemen, is you.

The root of the problem, indeed the root of all evil, is your false sense of sovereignty, and stemming from it, your pride, your arrogance, your presumption.

'They worship the work of their own hands,' the Prophet says, *'that which their own fingers have made. They have chosen their own ways, and their soul delighteth in their abominations.'*

But the Lord is weary of such offerings. Where is contrition? Where is regret?

'Bring no more vain oblations; your incense is an abomination unto Me.
When you spread forth your hands,
I will hide My eyes from you;
Even though you make many prayers,
I will not listen.
Your hands are full of blood.'"

Things were becoming truly uncomfortable. This might have gone over in some small southern Baptist church, but this was the Fuller Lodge at Site Y. Chaplain Maple seemed to sense this, and pulled back.

"Let me say a few words about history. This is what the prophets discovered: History is a nightmare. We generally assume that politics, economics and warfare are the substance of history. To the prophets, it is God's judgment of man which is the main issue. They look at history from the point of view of Justice, judging its course not in terms of wealth and success, victory and defeat, but in terms of corruption and righteousness, violence and compassion.

574

We should not expect the darkness of our history to be dispersed soon by any clever technical or political strategy. We will not receive answers concerning the future because we ask questions of those who cannot know, the vain gods of the nations.

The only solution of the historical problem today lies in the prophetic concept. Second Isaiah speaks to the exiled remnant of our time, to those in prisons and concentration camps, to those separated from husbands or wives, from children or parents, to those toiling in despair in foreign lands, to those in the hell of modern war. He speaks to every one of us in this room.

How should we respond to his words? Ironically? Dismissively? Angry at their seeming pretentiousness, at the immense gap between the proffered solution and the catastrophic reality in which we live?

Two and a half centuries ago, we opted for *means* to control nature and society. It was a right decision, and we have brought about something new and great in history. But we excluded *ends*. And now the means claim to *be* the ends; our tools have become our masters, and the most powerful of them have become a threat to our very existence.

A century and a half ago, we opted for freedom. It was a right decision; it created something new and great in history. But in that decision we excluded the security without which man cannot live and grow. And now the quest for security splits the whole world with demonic power.

What is the world you are making? Wars, victories, more wars. So many tears. So little regret. And who can sit in judgment when victims' horror turns to hate? What saved Second Isaiah from despair was his messianic vision of man's capacity for repentance.

A Lieutenant Colonel unknown to me walked out. Perhaps he had to relieve himself, but of what was unclear.

Only one thing stands in the way. Do you know what that is? What stands in the way of repentance is the worship of power. Why are human beings so obsequious, so ready to kill and ready to die at the call of kings and chieftains, presidents and generals? It is because we worship might, we venerate those who command might, we are convinced that it is by might that man prevails."

This was heresy to the more uniformed in the crowd.

"The most striking feature of all prophetic polemic is the distrust and denunciation of power in all its forms. You who work here know what I am talking about. The hunger for power knows no end; the appetite grows on what it feeds."

Maple's between-the-lines was growing ominous.

"Now as then, the sword is the pride of man; arsenals, forts, chariots and bombs lend supremacy to nations. War is the climax of human ingenuity, the object of supreme efforts; men slaughtering each other, cities blown to ruins. What is left behind? Agony and desolation. And you think very highly of yourselves, don't you? You *are wise in your own hearts and clever in your own sight.* But into your world, drunk with power, bloated with arrogance, comes Isaiah's word that the swords will be undone, that nations will search, not for gold, power or harlotries, but for God's word.

It seems inconceivable, doesn't it? But to Isaiah it was a certainty: War will be abolished. You shall not learn war any more because you shall seek other knowledge. Your hearts of stone will melt, and hearts of flesh will grow instead. Are you ready for the metamorphosis?"

Richard Feynman got up to leave.

"But wait!" the Chaplain called after him to no avail. "We have forgotten an Isaiah, the Third and last Isaiah, the strangest and most mysterious of the three. In transit from the second, he begins with gentle, female imagery:

'*Rejoice ye with Jerusalem, and be glad with her, all ye that love her: rejoice for joy with her, all ye that mourn for her.*
That ye may suck, and be satisfied with the breasts of her consolations;

[A titter from the young girls in the audience. Feynman paused at the door.]

As one whom his mother comforteth, so will I comfort you, and ye shall be comforted in Jerusalem.'

Happy ending. Nice and tidy. The American Way. But the Bible is not born of shallowness. [Feynman completed his exit.] I skip to the end of the book and read you the comments of Third Isaiah. After all Flesh has come to worship the Lord, God schedules a little field trip:

'*They shall go forth, and look upon the carcasses of the men that have trans-gressed against Me: for their worm shall not die, neither shall their fire be quenched; and they shall be an abhorring unto all flesh.*'

The unending destruction of flesh. The eerie excursion of the chosen to look upon the World's Fair, the abhorrent, endless process of corruption.

'*Through the wrath of the Lord is the land darkened, and the people shall be as the fuel of the fire: no man shall spare his brother.*
And they shall snatch on the right hand, and be hungry, and they shall eat on the left hand, and they shall not be satisfied: they shall eat every man the flesh of his own arm.
Therefore hath the curse devoured the earth, and they that dwell therein are desolate: therefore the inhabitants of the earth are burned, and few men left.'
So that the Lord '*may do his work, his strange work, and bring to pass his act, his strange act.*'"

Little Paul Teller started to cry. Mici carried him out.

"Well may you cry, my young friend. It's a grisly scandal of a text. The reality of Third Isaiah's judgment is indeed grim, but it is dishonest to pretend that reality is otherwise. Where do you in this room fit in this reality?" With a wave of his arm, he indicated the entire room. "What's wrong with this picture?"

The tension exceeded the punctured silence before the final Hallelujah. But there was no Hallelujah — only the disembodied voice again:

"'*Woe to those who call evil good and good evil,*
Who put darkness for light and light for darkness!'
'*The stone will cry out from the wall,*
Woe to him who builds a town with blood,
And founds a city on iniquity.'

Chaplin Maple strode quickly from the silenced room. He was not seen again on site. The dance that followed had a forced and frantic quality. Gregor left early to go home to bed. I remained to assay the effects.

46. Ritual And Vision

As short and strained as the post-Messiah party was, the lab directors' socio-cultural experiment did have some significant results: Gregor was drawn into Otto Frisch's work on the critical mass of U^{235}, and also met someone he might have missed, Pvt. Rudi Schildknapp, the climax-providing trumpet player in the Hallelujah Chorus.

Frisch, of course, was more than just the Project's best Mozart pianist and accompanist. In late '38, he and his aunt, Lise Meitner, had puzzled out the meaning of Otto Hahn's letter describing unexpected "isotopes that have the properties of barium" found in neutron-bombarded uranium. "Fission", Frisch had named it, suggested by the amoeboid shapes he sketched on an envelope to imagine the process. At Birmingham in '39, working with Rudi Peierls, he had toyed with numbers which showed that only a small amount of that heavy metal could make a bomb that would change the world. His results catalyzed the British MAUD Committee report, and FDR's decision to go ahead with the Manhattan Project. Though that night, he and Gregor discussed only the virtues and vices of Mozart's arrangement of Handel, and the nature of such risky musical experiments, Frisch was not just another rehearsal pianist.

Behind his gentle, cultured exterior was a man bitten by the bug, a scientist driven to quiet lunacy by the question of critical mass. Exactly how much uranium would it take to explode? He had almost pinned it down on paper. Would the material world confirm his calculations? At the following Tuesday night colloquium, perhaps stimulated by his discussion with Gregor about hazardous experiments, he rose to make a confession to the congregation.

"You know I've been playing with my blocks out at Omega Nursery School," he said in his Austrian accent, "and soon Papa will be able buy us enough blocks for a real test."

He was referring to the small cubes of uranium hydride he had been stacking in a tiny pile to measure neutron production. The hydrogen acted to slow down fast neutrons so that the uranium became more sensitive — responsive to both fast and slow. Purification of U^{235} was increasing now, and Oak Ridge was starting to ship workable quantities.

"Last Wednesday, so attracted was I by Lady Godiva [his name for the naked uranium assembly] that I leaned over her to see better her intimacies. Ah, the vulnerable naiveté of men. She was sub-critical, of course, but as I was peering into her cracks, out of the corner of my eye I saw the little red lamps on the monitors — they had stopped flickering, they seemed to be just glowing. I thought maybe the flicker had speeded up so much it could no longer be perceived so I reached out and swept four hydride blocks on to the workbench, and the lamps went back to flickering. Question for the group: what happened?"

The audience yelled out without raising hands, like the gang of smart kids they were.

"You were acting as a tamper."

"You were tampering with a naked woman."

"You reflected neutrons back into the pile."

"With your molecular hydrogen, you watery beast."

In the pause after the storm, Gregor the Risk Consultant raised a troubled voice.

"How long were you exposed?"

"I don't know. Maybe two seconds."

"Can anyone calculate the approximate dose?"

Four and twenty slide rules sprang into operation. Feynman (no slide rule) yelled out.

"Only one full day's permissible load. You'll need twice as much to be killed".

The slide rules seemed to agree. I must say that wartime standards were more radiation-generous than they would be today.

"So I must still be alive," Frisch continued, "and therefore I want to propose an experiment. When enough tenure arrives, I want to make a real explosive device, full-size by my calculations, but leaving a big hole with the center missing so enough neutrons can escape before a chain reaction will develop. But — we make the center, too, and we drop it fast through the hole so for a split second we have real conditions for atomic explosion. And we see what happens."

There was silence in the room.

"We see if experiment fits theory," Frisch explained.

Feynman broke out in loud laughter. "That sure would be ticklin' the tail of the dragon."

That was what the experiment was called ever after: "The Dragon Experiment." Oppie was for it, so G's continuing reservations carried little weight. It would take a year for enough fissionable material to arrive from Oak Ridge to work in full-scale, but work it did. At Omega, a remote laboratory site on another mesa far from the main labs, Frisch's group built a ten foot iron frame, "the guillotine" they called it, which supported vertical aluminum guides into, through, and beyond a hole in a table of uranium hydride. The uranium hydride slug, 2" X 6", would be raised to the top of the guillotine, and dropped through the hole, momentarily forming a life-size critical mass. True, the hydride form would react more slowly than would the pure metal used in the Hiroshima bomb, but the Dragon would stir, and dangerously. Enough to confirm Frisch's calculations. Twenty million watts of energy were produced, with a temperature rise of 2 degrees per millisecond and a release of 1015 neutrons. The experiment was done on April 12th, 1945. So was the life of Franklin Delano Roosevelt.

But I am getting ahead of myself. 1944 was an eventful-enough year, the last complete cycle in Gregor's life. After meeting and talking with Rudi Schildknapp at the party, G attended a rehearsal of the Schildknapp Six, a snappy GI jazz combo, Rudi on trumpet, Matt Dvorsky on alto sax, Eddie ("Bennie Goodman") Bingham on clarinet, Ken Woodward on piano, Elliot Stringer on bass and Max Loach on drums. When G, expected, walked into the afternoon-dark Theater No. 1, the band, obviously prepped, broke into its own version of the current Xavier Cugat hit, *"La Cucaracha,"* with Woodward switching over to concertina and Loach to maracas.

La Cucaracha, la cucaracha,
Ya no puede caminar;
Porque no tiene, porque le falta
Marijuana pa' fumar.

"Hey, man, you know this song?" Rudi yelled out, as the band continued behind him.

"I don't speak Spanish well," G answered. "I'm just starting to study."

"*Cucaracha* — that's you, man," Rudi pointed out. "It's pertinent. Listen up. Dig it."

Un panadero fue a misa,
No encontrando que rezar,
Le pidio a la Virgen pura,
Marijuana pa' fumar.

"*La cucaracha, la cucaracha,*" the others continued, while Rudi came down off the stage into the dark house.

"Nice to see you, man. These are the real words. Guiterrez taught 'em to us. No Xavier Cugat bullshit. Marijuana to smoke, that's the scam. You ever smoke?"

"No...it's hard for me..." Gregor indicated with a sweep of forearm the contents of his thorax.

"Oh, yeah. Right. Well, we can maybe do something about that. Me and the guys will work on it. Hey, stick around awhile. All right, boys, that's it for *Cucaracha...*"

"Very nice," commented Gregor, with little comprehension, as the remaining five took a cigarette break. After the rehearsal, Rudi invited G to the party at the San Ildefenso pueblo the following Sunday, after the festival. Gregor did want to see the dances, so he said yes, and spent the night with his beginning Spanish book, *El Camino Real. "Qué es el burro?"* it asked on page one. *"El burro es un animal. El burro es un animal importante. El hombre pobre usa el burro. El hombre rico no usa el burro. El hombre rico usa el automóvil."*

****

Sunday, January 23rd, was the Saint's feast day, the high point of the year for the San Ildefonso Pueblo. It would be a typical crisp winter day of dazzlingly blue sky, the snow-capped Jemez range to the west, the Truchas to the east, and the mysterious black mesa to the north, all looming beyond the roofs of the immaculate square. But for Gregor and me, it began in the dark, before sunrise, (much as his last day would begin, eighteen months later, two hundred miles to the south.)

Late Saturday, the dancers had gone up into the hills behind the pueblo to metamorphose into animal gods. All during the night, the sound of chanting voices could be heard up high, and the faint sound of drums from deep in the village kivas. When Gregor arrived at five AM, the stars were singeing the icy wind with their brightness.

The pueblo itself seemed deserted, not a footprint to be seen in the bare-swept plaza, as the great cottonwood kept watch over the sleeping houses. Towards five thirty, small groups of Indians began walking along the road that borders the Pueblo on the east. A small woman came up behind Gregor.

"Soon they come from over there," she said, pointing to the arroyo in the cleft of the hills. "All kind of animal, deer, buffalo, other kind, I know not how you call him. You watch, You stay there. Soon they come." And she continued on her way.

Suddenly the sound of a deep-throated Indian drum began pulsing in the semi-darkness. Gregor could barely make out the group of four old men gathering at the entrance to the pueblo. They seemed not to be in any costume; they looked like uncles or grandfathers from anywhere except for their braided hair and headbands. They began to sing — and the world became transformed. It was *Messiah* once again, but this time not via one German Anglophile's brain. Rather, it seemed the messiah of the ages, the ur-earth spirit, rising up with the power of life in the trusting voices of these four men. Gregor's four days of Spanish study did him little good with their Tewa song. But somehow it was clear: they were invoking man's kinship with the gods, and with the spirit of all living things.

Behind the chorus, women and children gathered quietly, looking toward the east, toward the morning hill. The sky behind grew lighter and lighter, the light began contracting around one particular point, calling the singing and drumming toward it, upwards. A tall, dark Indian appeared at Gregor's side. He was dressed in regular western clothes, and was apparently a visitor from another Pueblo, another tribe.

"Indian sing for *all* men," he said, deeply earnest. "He sing for good things for this pueblo, for Indian, for all people everywhere. He sing for rain to come so summer fields grow. He sing for *everybody, everywhere.*" Over and over he kept repeating this as though he thought it something Gregor might not believe.

"Indian singing for *everybody, everywhere.* That what the song say. He telling them animals bring good things, not just for this pueblo; good things for everybody, for you, for me, for this people, for all people in the whole world."

Suddenly, with blinding intensity, the first small segment of sun broke over the top of the hill, and a plume of dark smoke began to rise from the head of the arroyo high between the hills. The landscape seemed to give birth. Small figures could be made out, moving along the dark dots of juniper. On the crest of the hill two Deer/men lifted antlered heads in a great nodding Yes, then made their way toward the square, dancing a zigzag trail down the slope of the hill. The Buffalo men hunched slowly down the arroyo, naked to the waist in the coldest part of winter, their bodies painted with symbols, their magnificent head-dresses built ingeniously from green twigs and horn. Antelope children pranced carefully behind them. Together, they sang and gestured an ancient ritual, renouncing hatred and enmity toward all creatures, promising to take life only for the sake of need. The Animals approaching were prayed to as gods, and asked to lay down their lives for the sake of all the living.

Once inside the square, the Sacred Animals wove their way through the groups of onlookers. As the divine animal/men passed nearby, the waiting Indians threw sacred corn meal on them. Corn, the grain that grows only via humans. What Gregor was understanding in these magic minutes was that animal-men could emerge from the sunrise, with Godhead shining on their shoulders, in an atmosphere of enjoyment, even relief, as though some ancient, vital magic had been worked once more.

The sun was now up in full splendor, and the dancers disappeared into the ceremonial house on the South Plaza. They would come out to dance many times during the day, as the plaza filled with visitors and a myriad of booths for the display and sale of the Pueblo's famous pottery.

Not every member of the Los Alamos community who wanted to attend was ready to brave the cold of the pre-dawn opening . I cast no aspersions here: cold is harder for mammals than for blattids. But by nine AM, the square had already begun to mill with spectators in carnival mood. Gregor's mind went back to Vienna, the circus, Amadeus, Tomzak, Violetta, George Keiffer, Katerina Eckhardt... He could almost smell the popcorn and beer. But his heart was still coming down the arroyo with the animal/human gods. What a temptation to think of himself as one of them. Ridiculous. But who more than he knew of that intersection, that interface, that haunting doppelganging? Why, he could probably pull rank if he wanted to. Ach, too much of soldier thinking," he said. Still, he admitted having the strangest urge to embrace himself, half from shyly valuing his own split being, half from fearfully trying to hold it together.

The tourists, many, but by no means all, from the Hill, seemed smitten by both reverence and condescension. Hill residents especially went in for the pageantry but, university denizens all, couldn't just enjoy it; they had read up beforehand; they had to figure out the rhythmic sequences or the symbolism.

And of course, Heisenberg *mutatis mutandis,* the observers affected the observed. Though the crowd was filled with good intentions, the Law of Unintended Consequences prevailed, and the Pueblo suffered increasing incursion of Anglo ideas, Anglo aesthetics, and Anglo economics. The famous traditional pottery metamorphosed from red, black and tan to a plain black less likely to clash with the Wedgewood back home. Performances were scheduled — like Plains Indian war dances — which had no tradition behind them, and little relevance to the feast at hand — because the tourists liked them. Those who made their way into Indian households were shocked to find refrigerators and other appliances, Grand Rapids Furniture, brass bedsteads, linoleum floors, soda pop, and ordinary dishes. While they set their own tables with Maria's Martinez's famous black plates, Maria herself set her table with oilcloth and plastic dishes. What did they expect when it was men from our very own mesa that had wired San Ildefonso for electricity? What we Anglos were observing was ourselves forcing inexorable change, turning an indigenous subsistence culture into a tourist trap. Such is progress.

Tilano was very stern on feast days. He gruffly forbade all tourists from taking photos while slyly encouraging them to do so, and afterwards, he took great interest in the results. Perhaps this was his double-soul, as confused as Gregor's. G munched on a round loaf of bread from the beehive ovens, and watched him, spied on him, with a good-humored sense of recognition.

Artificial as it may have been, the Comanche war dance in middle of the day was thrilling. The men looked proud and glorious in paint and war feathers, those men who in "real life" were our furnace stokers, our caretakers and technicians, our janitors, firemen, and cooks. It was not hard to feel that the aggression being danced was directed at us, who so demeaned the dancers with steady work and seductive salaries. In the high afternoon, the bright sun melted the snow and thawed the ground, turning it all into all-too-familiar mud. The dancers slipped and slid, a visual metaphor for their tottering world. One of them — the sardonic social critic? — had painted a Ford V-8 symbol in blue on his chest. Then there was little Tony Martinez, who lived on site at the mesa and went to our nursery school, dancing with his father Popovi Da, both dressed in feathers — quite a change from their daily denim on the hill. It looked to me like they were playing Indian.

What a rotten thought.

From the point of view of most of us on the hill, our interest in things Indian was virtuous, and consistent with the high ideals of motley community we were living out behind barbed wire. We were the only group of Anglos who were not just "interested in their welfare" or "curious about their cultural patterns." They were part of our lives on the mesa, and we, therefore, were part of theirs. Quite a number of Indians now lived in apartments on the hill. They wore western-style clothes to our square dances. Many of us felt they were tired of being pressured to stay traditional for the benefit of tourists.

A cynic might point out that, as construction and maintenance staff, they were allotted the poorest housing of all — corrugated metal quonset huts, with minimal room separation and no insulation from heat or cold. He or she might notice the silence in which many of them worked, especially the women, the maids, a silence enforced by their limited grasp of English, and our near-complete ignorance of Spanish and Tewa. But what could we do about any of that?

The old people of the Pueblo objected to the young ones busing up to the hill. They lamented the lost ways of a once-stable agricultural economy, where men tilled the soil and women cared for the family. But the young people seemed to want a different life, a better life for their children. So up the hill they came. Thus, too close to be threatening, they became our exotic "friends", a romantic alternative to our ambivalent pursuit of a technology for violence.

Gregor, his antennae permanently tuned to duality, was fascinated by what he could gather of Pueblo religion. Good Catholics, they seemed, but with other gods and ceremonies. Here were Corn Dancers bringing a statue of San Ildefonso from the church and setting it up in a shrine so it could better observe ancient dances with no relation to Christianity. Gregor remembered a joke the Orthodox Jews in Prague used to tell about a Reform rabbi who would be happy to say a *brucha* (blessing) over a Christmas tree, if the petitioner would tell him what a *brucha* was. Pueblo Indians — the reform Jews of native America. The party that night was a perfect example of wringing out the old ways, and ringing in the new.

The event was scheduled in the largest hall in the village, a long, chilly, adobe building whose walls were hung with evergreen boughs, and whose broken windows were artistically covered with beautiful Navaho blankets and rugs. Clusters of crepe-paper streamers — red, white and blue — had been tied to the rafters. Kerosene lamps on the walls gave out a soft light, and a fire glowed in the huge black stove. The walls were lined with benches which soon filled up with shy Pueblo families dressed in fiesta clothes, looking like postcards of "Indians of the Southwest". As each woman entered, she headed for the table with a large tray of edibles balanced on arm or head. Then to the benches, these women, solid under their fringed blankets, with their men standing near, and a tapering line of excited, but obedient, children sitting by their sides. The table piled up with simple offerings, but a decided change from the mess halls on the mesa: stewed meat and pinto beans hot with chile, salads with pineapple, cabbage, apples and raisins, Jell-O molds, one in the shape of Tunyo, the Black mesa to the north, canned peaches, spiced bread pudding, and several baskets of warm round-loaf bread, with plenty of butter and jam. The long tables were set with plates, silverware, and coffee cups without saucers on the flowered oilcloth covering.

Then came the Yankee invasion. Crammed in among Indian offerings: hot dogs, hamburgers and buns brought by wives in fur coats over slacks and jeans, their leather-jacketed men lugging ice chests and cases of Coca-Cola. The Europeans, especially the British, were more elegant than their American cohorts, in their overcoats, suits and ties, and more dressy dresses. The Jim Tucks even showed up in tux and ball gown. Perhaps it was their family pun.

Because there was no electricity in the hall, an electronics team from the hill set up a special generator and connected the record player from Fuller Lodge, all to the great interest of the village children. For all the PhDs involved, they could never get it to work right, and the evening's music would consist of Indian drums and chanting, and offerings from the Schildknapp Six. About 7:30, Po made a welcome speech, first in English, then in Tewa, and the motley group settled down to a pleasant, friendly, and in today's lingo, "multicultural" meal and evening.

The Indians opened the post-food festivities with a Comanche war dance accompanied by drums and a chanting men's chorus led by Tony Montoya, our janitor from the Big House. We countered with the Schildknapp Six doing their own versions of several pop numbers of the day: "Would You Like To Swing On A Star?", "Mairzy Doats" "Is You Is Or Is You Ain't My Baby?". At one point during a fast break in "Paper Doll", Dave and Kay Anderson broke into a jitterbug to the wild applause of the Americans. The band fed off the energy, some other couples joined (it was a young crowd up on the hill), and the Indians watched with smiles and giggles to see white thighs flashing under swinging skirts. The

Indians answered our shenanigans with an elegant Dance of the Braided Belts, with its intricate movement from the men, and graceful, acquiescing answers from the women.

After a break for coffee and Coke, our band went inappropriately risqué with a slow-dance version of "Besame Mucho". No Spanish-speaking Indians went cheek-to-cheek, and since there was no alcohol, neither did the scientists, thus setting the tune as an oddly-awkward concert piece. But now the band was high in Latin transformation, and on came "Brazil" and "That Old Black Magic", with maracas and sticks. Suddenly, Rudi cut the band off, and picked up the PA system mike.

"Ladies and gentlemen," he began, "please join with us in wishing a happy fortieth birthday to our favorite health and safety advisor, the great jitterbug himself, Mr. George Samson."

While the Indians responded with light applause, it took a few seconds for the Los Alamites to remember the codes, and figure out just who was being congratulated. But when the band broke into a spirited version of "La Cucaracha", there was no more doubt: the spotlight was on a most-surprised Gregor. It was not his fortieth birthday. It was not his birthday at all, as far as he knew, either his original birthday, July 3rd, or his born-again day, some time in the summer, he didn't know just when, he only knew it was hot.

The crowd — at least the Americans, and some Spanish-speaking Indians — followed the band into the familiar chorus, though the Indians were bewildered and amused by the change of text from *fumar* to *bailar* — smoking to dancing. Each group had its own variety of puritanism.

Gregor, filled with the animal-god energy of the day, was halfway ready to accede to the request implied by all the little shoves and murmurs, to take center stage and do or say something. It was not the first time he had thought of performing a Cockroach Dance, the Gregor behind "The Gregor" — which dance-craze this crowd was probably too young to remember. In a state of relative undress he could even spin and fly, and skitter all over the ceiling. Wouldn't the children love that? But something held him back. Perhaps simple bashfulness, perhaps the instinct of a proper guest to not upstage his host. Perhaps it was caution called up by "That Old Black Magic", wariness of a too-shocking exhibition which might bring out the latent but strong hatred/fear of witches Tilano had mentioned, witches — who could transform themselves into animals for evil purpose. So G simply waved modestly, and withdrew into the crowd and himself until the moment had passed.

Though the Indians were prepared to go all night, as was their custom, the denizens of the hill had to be at work by eight. So at exactly eleven (musicians' union hours?) the band shut down and packed up, and a general white-skinned exodus began. Gregor approached Rudi.

"It's not my birthday. And I'd hate to tell you how much older I am than you said."

"Really? You don't look a day over forty, so we made you forty. We just wanted an excuse to play "La Cucaracha" since we rehearsed it. And also, just between the two of us, the *marijuana que fumar* is here." He patted his jacket pocket. "*No le falta.* It's our birthday gift to you — even if it ain't your birthday."

"But — I told you I can't smoke."

"But I told *you* we were going to work on it. Matt — the alto player — works with Barnett in the hospital, and he's borrowed a certain piece of new equipment."

"What?"

"Nosy bugger, aren't you?" He gave G an affectionate jab in the snout. "Have faith. It ain't a needle. Just be patient a few minutes."

The band finished loading the van, and the other five, with waves and winks, hitched rides home with other cars going up the hill.

"C'mon, get in," Rudi said to G, "It's just you and me. And the reefer."

Gregor got in the passenger seat of the '36 Dodge. Rudi gunned the engine, and cranked up the heat.

"We're gonna need to stay warm. But there's an almost full tank of gas. Your tax dollars at work."

They drove off — north into the night.

"Where are we headed?" asked the neophyte.

"Oh, I thought we'd head up towards the holy mountain for our spiritual journey."

"The Black Mesa?"

"Yeah. Why not? No one will be up there now. We can park, stay warm, and play with the little smoke."

"I don't know if I really want to do this."

"What are you, an American? With that accent?"

"Why do you ask that? What's wrong with being American?"

"Hey, I'm proud to be American. It's just that, you know — we're violent, and booze makes it worse. Reefer would be good for us, more mellow. We all got a God-given right to get high. But no, it's too — I don't know — weird or something for Americans. But George Washington smoked reefer. It's a certified fact."

"Well, I'm just not sure I'm emotion ready. It's been an over-rich day."

"It's already tomorrow, man. Twelve oh six. Rich day, rich night, how can you complain?"

Gregor was silent, taking in the starry sky, and the huge shape looming up in front of him.

The Black Mesa, which the Indians call Tunyo, is a 2.7 million year old geological formation, sacred to the Pueblos, a stark, isolated volcanic butte rising abruptly from the desert, strange, dark and huge, and even more evocative on a fierce moonlit night. In daylight, its color contrasts sharply with the buff, red and gold rocks of the area; in the dark, the imagination can go wild.

"You know the story of that thing?" Gregor asked.

"No. Do you?" Rudi asked in response.

"Do you know Tilano, Edith Warner's friend?"

"Who's Edith Warner?"

"You've never been down to her little tea-room?"

"No."

Gregor was conscious for the first time of the class difference enforced by the project.

"Tilano is an Indian from the Pueblo who lives with her now."

"Hubba hubba..."

"I think they're just friends. I can't imagine them, you know..."

"You can't imagine a lot of things."

Rudi pulled the van over off the side of the road and nestled it, front out, in a depression in the rising wall of Tunyo's foothills.

"Let's get out and take a look," said Gregor.

"Hey, it's freezing out there."

"I don't get cold."

"Well, I'll get cold, then. I've been heating up the van so we could be comfortable for a while."

"Tilano told me about Tunyo," Gregor said. There used to be a huge giant who lived on top who ate little children in the Pueblo. Name of Tsabiyo."

"Don't tell me that, man. You'll scare the shit out of me."

"It's ok. He's dead now," the roach reassured his friend. "After years of lost children, the cacique made medicine for protection, and some Twin War Gods killed Tsabiyo by getting eaten and then cutting their way out of his stomach."

"That's disgusting, man." Gregor was enjoying upsetting him.

"When he died, the mountains in the four corners of the earth exploded, and smoke and flame and his blood flowed out like streaming lava."

"So there's no more giant."

"Well, I don't know. Maybe his son is still around. When the Pueblo kids are bad, the mothers say, 'If you don't do what I tell you, I'll feed you to the giant for supper.' It works — so there must be something to it."

"So someone could still be up there?"

"I've never been up on top, but Tilano says there's a ceremonial stone circle, and right in the middle there's a huge boulder in the exact shape of a skull."

"The giant's skull?"

"I can't say."

"Man, cut it out. Let's just smoke some reefer in peace."

"Every autumn someone dressed as Tsabiyo comes to the village with a whip in his hand to punish bad people and children."

"Gonna find out who's naughty and nice, huh?"

Rudi took the paper bag from his jacket pocket, pulled a packet of rolling papers from his shirt, expertly rolled a cigarette with one hand, and then three more. Gregor watched with the fascination he always had for someone doing things superbly.

"So how am I going to smoke those?"

"Just a minute, I ain't finished yet."

Rudi took a small dropper bottle from his pants pocket, and ran a thin stream of greenish liquid along the seam of each cigarette.

"Is that to keep them rolled?" asked an ingenuous Gregor.

"Nah. Spit'll do that. This is some high-powered medicine from our GI medicine-man-witch-doctor lab. You'll like it. OK, Kilroy, follow me."

"I thought we were staying in the van."

"We are, but we're going in back."

Rudi and G each got out.

"Around the back, roach."

He held the left back door open.

"Inside."

Gregor crawled in, and found the dark closeness quite pleasant. The band instruments and PA system had been packed and tied-in tightly along the right side of the van, leaving a long narrow space of free floor on the left.

"On your back, kook. Oh, wait. I guess you can just crouch down there if it's more comfortable."

"What are you going to do?"

"Speaking of George Washington, you are of course familiar with the famous George Washington Crile, and his contributions to the study of surgical shock?"

"I can't say..."

"That's all right. I never heard of him either. Barnett gave Matt a report he wrote called "'The Resuscitation of the Apparently Dead.'"

"Now wait a minute..."

"Don't get upset, it's just about his G-pants, which, in case you're interested ain't no relation to G-strings, (Gregor didn't know what G-strings were). The G-pants — G is for gravity — were his dying gift to the Air Force last year. Or so I'm told. The G-pants (he pulled them out of a wooden Red-Cross box in the van) go tight around your legs and abdomen, in your case, we'll just snuggie them around up to these middle legs, like so, and we'll tighten up the strap up here, like so, and we'll tighten these around your ankles or whatever you call them, and then we attach this pump to the old valve. Comfy?"

"Yes. I think I see what you're doing."

"Elementary, my dear Samson."

"You know I breathe through the holes in my sides..."

"Hey, what do you think I am, a dummy? I suffocated plenty of insects in my time. Now, I light up one of these little stickies..."

Rudi pulled out his Zippo, lit up one of the reefers, and blew the smoke into the intake hole at the bottom of the pump.

"Wait," he said, "This way is gonna just close up the air space. I got a better idea."

He detached the pump from the valve at the waist, and inserted the end into one of the ankle seals.

"Now it'll hold the smoke and still give you some space to breathe."

He worked rhythmically for a few minutes.

"Feeling anything yet?"

"Just a little dizzy."

"OK, I'm gonna push on your back between pumps, all right?"

It looked like an exotic version of CPR, perhaps something you might see in a field hospital.

"Oh, that's much better, much deeper," the patient said.

The doctor himself was not exactly unaffected by being smoke-mediator to the pump. His boisterous laughter got Gregor going too, and a duet, at times giggly, at times uproarious, echoed faintly in the cold desert night.

"It is tonight," Gregor announced, "that we must die laughing." And at this pronouncement they both almost did.

(Gregor's report of his experience astonishes me, a John Aschenfeld who has never had the pleasure of such intoxication. Alcohol has made me a little gay and foolish, and sometimes confused, but the kind of aesthetic and synthetic couplings G experienced — including the heightened sexuality — well, my *vino* has never yielded such *veritas*.)

The chocolate Rudi later shared was for G almost unbearably intense. The human bodily envelope, with its awe-inspiring endurance for pain, has surprisingly little capacity for pleasure at too high a pressure. Imagine, then, the levels which could be built up inside a hard, chitinous shell! And it wasn't just chocolate sensitivity. Even in the echoing confines of a metal

593

van ringing with laughter, G reported being able to hear the slightest rustlings outside: the scurry of a lizard, the whistle of wind, the howl of a coyote ten miles away. The tympanic membranes at his knees were in a state of high alert; his whole nervous system seemed hugely enhanced, his giant neurons pulsing rivers, his inward eye enlarged. His thoughts themselves became stimulants, not product. The simplest words, the most trivial ideas, assumed new and strange guises; the word "egg" for instance, had him initially in stitches, until he stumbled into the profundities of eggness, and was astonished at ever having found it so simple.

At one point, Rudi got out his trumpet, put in the mute, and began to evoke a quiet, snaky path — or so it seemed to Gregor — an arteriole knotting together the earth and spirit worlds. G observed in amazement how the musical notes turned into numbers and imaginary numbers, how the melody, still sensuous, metamorphosed into a huge arithmetical process in which numbers begot numbers in a net that enveloped the universe. His silly euphoria was gone now, replaced by a state close to anxiety, but somehow numbed and non-threatening.

Rudi put down his trumpet.

"You know what's funny?"

"What?"

"Next week is the birthday of my brother's graduation. Yeah, he was a January graduate."

"From where?"

"From life. Commencement into the other world."

"What do you mean?"

"You know those dead bodies in Life Magazine? They all look like people. I mean they're dead, but they're all ... intact, sprawled out maybe, but they look like people, you know? Wanna hear about my brother?"

"If you want to tell me." Gregor was too humane to refuse.

"You'd think that soldiers on the front line — like the Marines at Guadalcanal, right? — you'd think they'd be hit by bullets and shrapnel and all that, you'd expect it, right? But you know what split open my brother's skull?"

"What?"

"His buddy Frank's detached head."

594

Gregor didn't know if he was prepared to hear the rest of the story.

"It's true," Rudi continued. "Artie Giannini came over to tell us about Karl — that's my bro. He got hurt by the same guy. Frank's legs kicked Artie in the neck and crushed his windpipe. Got him a discharge, though. And a purple heart. Got Karl graduated, good old Frank. Wanna know what happened to Frank?"

"Not really."

"OK, I'll tell you. They were cleaning up the Japs, right?, going on a sweep, and all of a sudden there was this blinding flash a few yards in front of them, and this head comes flying back and whacks into my brother's face, and these legs go another way and kick Artie in the throat. See, Frank was up front with a mine strapped to his belt, and he picked up some friendly fire from behind. It hit the mine, and blew him into three pieces."

"Oh."

"I don't know what happened to his chest."

Rudi began to laugh. Gregor saw laughing fangs and animal spittle, and nausea came on him, distantly. He tried to get up, but found he could barely summon the will to move. It was as if the bonds of matter and spirit had been severed.

"Frank's guts were all over the hillside. Karl wound up wrapped up in 'em. I don't know how. Sort of like a blankie. That's what Artie said."

G had raised his body enough to grab the handle, and open the rear doors out to the starlit night. As he inched his way out of the van, Rudi waxed philosophical:

"Some guys complain about being up here with this ridiculous project whatever it is, but that's because they don't know what's really going on over there. I'll take the domestic bugle corps anytime." He shut the doors which Gregor had left open. "Gotta conserve heat..." he yelled after his friend.

Gregor could no longer feel his body; he moved by sheer willpower in an unresisting medium. In spite of the Ruditalk behind him, he now felt a flaccid, dumb benevolence, a total softening of the nerves. Things seemed to glow around the edges, their contours standing out sharply against whatever background. Everywhere he focused his gaze seemed real and clear, but everything on the periphery seemed infinitely far away.

595

Perhaps it was the piercing quality of the high desert air, but he could swear he felt rhythmic pulses of cold in his gullet, the way a human might on inhalation. A sharp gust of wind whipped his antennae from back to front, and as G tried to smooth them back in place he felt them detach from his headpiece. He reached out, panicked at the thought of their blowing away into the dark desert, but he found that his middle pair of legs would simply not move: he was hemiplegic, a biped. What Dr. Lindhorst had warned him about. He dropped to all fours. There! A quadruped. Better than nothing.

An unwonted tingling in his front claws made him pull them off the ground, and sit back up against a boulder, and stare at them intensely. He held up his right claw the better to focus on it, and found that in making the arc around to eye level, two of his hooks seemed to turn flittingly into — fingers? He couldn't believe his eyes. He played with the phenomenon. He seemed to be surrounded by some invisible, egg-shaped membrane. When he thrust his arm past the border, the distal part metamorphosed into tingling fingers, tingling fingers on a tingling hand, a hand with a wrist, a hand with a wrist and forearm. As he pulled his arm back through, it would turn again into familiar, comfortable chitin. He tried his left arm: same amazing transformation. Same with both, simultaneously. He thought of a 16th century woodcut he knew, a man poking his head out of the sub-lunar, terrestrial sphere into the unlimited, star-streaked cosmos. He was afraid to try poking through with his head, but even now he could feel unaccustomed tastes in his mouth, and unaccustomed thoughts of power: reefer seemed a secret weapon to confuse the enemy and render him helpless. A Bureau of Dispensation. A Bureau of Disinformation.

"Help!" he screamed — and screamed and screamed, until he heard the van door open, and the staggering steps of Rudi Schildknapp, approaching.

"What's up, buddy? Oh, you got it bad."

Rudi reached right through the barrier, grabbed a tibia, pulled Gregor up to unsteady hind legs, and walked him to the cab of the truck.

On the way back up the hill, G was unfazed by his barely-present driver, zonked out of reason and reaction-time, offering up their lives to hair-pin turns. He was focused on the offer that might have been made to him: to step back into the human world, to go back to the way things were so long before, to bid goodbye to exile and loneliness, to re-embrace the ordinary. "I wipe my face," he thought, "and chitin drips off, melting. I can turn into whatever I want. *Verwandlung*. Beyond body. Beyond thought." Rudi, leaned over to yell in the side of his head:

"Hey, George. Hey, Bugger!"

Gregor just stared out at the winding road coming up fast in front of him.

"Hey, anybody home? I got a question for ya."

With no answer, and probably none forthcoming, Rudi continued.

"Which came first, the reefer or the roach? I mean why do they call this little thingy here a roach? Were there roaches when reefer was invented? I used to go the the museum, and look at the dinosaur exhibits, you know, behind glass and they paint the background and you can't tell where the real stuff ends and the fake stuff begins, and I swear, I remember it really clear, there were huge marijuana plants growing all over. I mean they were probably stuffed, but it looked like some significant shit!"

"No," said Gregor. Said or thought. " It's a gift, a poisonous gift." By which he meant that he was more valuable in his present form.

"What kinda gift?"

"From the insect god. A gift from the insect god. The holy insect ghost."

Rudi thought about that for a while, and then said,

"George, you sure are one fubar'd cat."

That's army for Fucked Up Beyond All Recognition.

47. Pluto Redux

Today I was reading about Marie Curie.
She must have known she suffered from radiation sickness
her body bombarded for years by the element
she had purified.
It seems she denied to the end
the source of the cataracts on her eyes
the cracked and suppurating skin of her
finger ends
till she could no longer hold a test tube or a
pencil
She died a famous woman denying her wounds
denying her wounds came from the same source
as her power

          Adrienne Rich

Plutonium, like Gregor, was something new on planet Earth: the crossing of their world lines was probably inevitable. Once neutrons had been harnessed, once atom smashers were conceived, once the labile nature of heavy metal nuclei had been demonstrated, it was only a matter of time. It fell to Glenn Seaborg, a tall, lanky, Michigan Swede to stick in his thumb and pull out — Element 94.

On August 20, 1942 Seaborg's group successfully precipitated a microscopic particle of plutonium, less than 1 μgm, from a large mass of neutron-bombarded uranium in an experimental Oak Ridge pile. One microgram is very little. One U.S. dime weighs 2.5 grams — 2,500,000 micrograms. But good — and bad — things come in very small packages, and the step from zero to 1 μgm was a huge one: a theoretical beast had been born into the material world, and snared in Seaborg's elaborate net.

Conservative Swede that he was, he named element 94 after the planet Pluto, discovered, as you know, twelve years earlier. In this, he was echoing Martin Kaproth's logic when, in the fateful year of 1789, he named the newly discovered "uranium" after the newly discovered Uranus. Droll Swede that he was, Seaborg chose Pu, rather than Pl, as the chemical symbol for the new element. He thought the metal would be rambunctious and stinky to deal with, and he thought "P.U." would best capture its unpleasantness. It was a thoughtful gesture: Pu^{239} was one of the nastiest characters ever to materialize on the world stage. But who cared then, in summer '42, with only a microgram on earth?

Transmuting U^{238} to plutonium in a chain-reacting pile was one thing, but extracting the baby from the mother quite another. The new element was present at a concentration of 250 parts per million — a tiny amount, uniformly dispersed through two tons of uranium mixed with highly active fission products. It was like looking for a needle in a haystack, except the needle was dispersed in tiny pieces, and the hay was lethally radioactive.

Seaborg's separation tricks were ingenious, and too complex to go into. Suffice it to say that, in spite of his success at this micro-level, he knew he'd have to work in industrial-scale concentrations to find out anything useful. In peacetime he might have waited for a pile to be built, de-bugged, and operating large enough to provide gram quantities of plutonium. But that was a luxury the bomb program could not afford: he needed a way to make more plutonium without a pile. It was wartime — he commandeered the 45-inch cyclotron at Washington University, and arranged to have 330-pound batches of uranium bombarded with neutrons for months at a time. Such long and intense treatment yielded several hundred millionths of a gram, an amount hardly visible to the naked eye. He then had to devise techniques for teasing out and provoking his tiny ward.

The discipline of ultramicrochemistry was young, but already there;

Seaborg took a crash course. He learned to manage manipulations on the mechanical stage of a binocular microscope, using fine glass capillaries as beakers, and small syringes mounted on micromanipulators to inject and removed reagents. Tiny centrifuges separated precipitated solids from their mother liquids. His first balance consisted of an almost invisible platinum pan attached a single quartz fiber fixed at one end. He would micro-load the micro-pan and observe how far the fiber bent. It looked, he said, "like invisible material being weighed on an invisible balance."

Oh for Lilliputian chemists here. Seaborg was 6'3" and one of his graduate students, Lou Werner, was 6'7". It was a comical sight. But techniques improved, reactors and cyclotrons churned tortoise-like away, and a year and a half later, in February 1944, the first plutonium delivery was made to Los Alamos, a small, experimental quantity, less than 1 mg. A three-hundredth of a dime. For the experimental physicists who had been marking time watching the theoreticians' song and dance, it was as if the Holy Ghost had arrived, descending from the skies like the messiah. From Gregor's point of view, however, the clouds of glory contained more than a whiff of sulfur.

You will perhaps recall his swoon at the Jemez Hot Springs, his uncanny sensitivity to a vaporous Pluto-sulfur amalgam, the vulture and the star. And now, with the arrival of that to-him invisible metallic speck, those words from Celan, over and over in his head, *Es sind noch Lieder zu singen jenseits der Menschen:* there are still songs to sing on the other side of Mankind. It was ominous and confusing. But one thing was clear: the arrival of macroscopic plutonium significantly upped community risk.

The issue had been somewhat foreseen: back in the spring of '43, design and construction began of a building to house the CM Division (Chemistry and Metallurgy) — post-plutonium. "D-Building" was completed and occupied in December, the host awaiting the guest, the bridegroom awaiting the bride. It was a facility as nearly dust-free as the air-conditioning of the time would permit. Typically, it was designed more to protect the plutonium than its handlers.

Environmental safety had few precedents in military culture — military reservations were typically egregious neighbors, immune from the most basic state and local laws. From a civilian point of view, the Project should have thoroughly investigated the dangers of radioactive waste, and determined preventive and protective strategies. Any activity should have awaited investigatory results. If recommendations had called for changes in the program, those should have been made. If research revealed insoluble problems, or did not yield clear-cut guidelines, the plutonium program should have been terminated. Either that or the Project should accept moral and legal responsibility for damages in the name of war.

But this was the Army, not the real world. Without military precedent, all safety and environmental details were up to General Leslie Groves, a bull of a man who prided himself on getting things done ahead of schedule and under budget.

In 1962, the General published his particular history of the Manhattan Project, a self-promoting book dramatically entitled *Now It Can Be Told*. "All design," he wrote, "was governed by three rules: 1, safety first against both known and unknown hazards; 2, certainty of operation — every possible chance of failure was guarded against; and 3, the utmost saving of time in achieving full production." He represented Project safety as a glowing utopian program of universal health care for all who lived and labored behind the fences — a health plan including prevention, family care, and hospitalization so complete that he had to defend it against charges of "socialized medicine".

But the reality was far from the claim. The indisputable first priority was speedy production; the second, prevention of information leakage, liability or bad publicity; and absolutely last, the health and safety of workers and unsuspecting neighbors. This put Groves and Gregor on a collision course, in a most unequal battle. And David does not always slay Goliath.

Gregor began his job naively by applying the systems of risk analysis he had invented for Ives, and which by now were considered standard, even classical. His projected program included worker training, safe design, vigilant quality control, and effective regulation. To begin, he would need accurate estimates of every risk, its probability and potential destructiveness. But this was a new world of dangers.

He knew what had happened to the pioneers of radioactivity: many of them had not lived long. And here his charges were now, likely to work with materials millions of times more active than those of the early experimenters. What is it they could expect?

He personally remembered the New Jersey scandal in the twenties: all the workers at United States Radium, young women licking their brushes to a fine point while painting luminous watch dials, suffering a wide variety of bizarre illnesses — rotting jaw bones and bone marrow, acute long-term anemias, weakness, infections, cancers of all sorts. He of course did not know the Adrienne Rich poem I put at the head of this chapter, but if he's still out there, I'm sure he is reading it with approval.

Gregor, naturally, was not the only one aware of radioactive issues. The National Bureau of Standards had published a secret 1941 handbook detailing the dangers of radiation exposure: handling of radioactive materials; bombardment by proximity; breathing of radioactive dusts and gases: intake of elements by mouth or skin contact. It even raised the question of cancers emerging years after exposure. With such authoritative history and material, G was sure he could forge ahead with his Herculean task. It turned out to be more a story of Samson than of Hercules.

Safety depended on the pre-war, and somewhat questionable, concept of tolerance, the amount of radiation living systems can absorb without permanent damage. How valid were the standards? Were all the risks, toxicological and radiological, fully perceived? Would these new and strange substances pose unknown safety problems — such as container failure under constant particle bombardment? Were there better ways to detect radiation? Could radiation damage be treated if not prevented? These were Gregor's questions for a wide-ranging program of research.

Without clearing it first with Groves or Oppenheimer, he put out a memo to the community describing his dual mission: "Protection of the health of the workers on the Project," and "Protection of the public from any hazards arising from the operation of the Project." He spoke of trying "to establish tolerance doses, to predict more accurately future health problems, to devise means of detecting ill effects to personnel, and to discover methods of treating any person who might be injured."

The Project, he wrote, had a "moral obligation to the personnel and the community", and this moral obligation was "to make certain that the weapons being developed would be a force for good, and that that workers and citizens would not end up unwitting victims of the State, even in wartime." (You might have thought that after living in the White House for eleven years, he would have understood "going through channels." But channels were soft in the FDR Administration.)

The day after his memo, he was escorted by military police to Gen. Groves' office. It was not a pleasant scene.

"Sit down, Mr. Samson."

"Thank you, Sir."

"Samson, just who gave you permission to put out that memo?"

"No, one, Sir. I thought it would be helpful to clarify our responsibility."

"Samson, look, we've all got to get used to working together, the military and the crackpots. I'm on one side. Which side are you on?"

Gregor recognized this as an old Leninist phrase, but doubted the General meant it that way.

"I suppose I'm part of the not-military side. But it's in everyone's interest to..."

"It's in everyone's interest," the General roared unexpectedly, "for us to drop our bomb on Hitler before he drops his on us." Then, more calmly: "And that will require certain priorities in our work. *I* am the one who sets those priorities. Who is the one that sets those priorities? Say it."

"You are the one to set the priorities." Gregor was not liking this discussion.

"Now I understand, Mr. Samson, that you are not a soldier, and therefore do not have to simply take orders from me. Therefore I will explain certain things to you — for the first and last time, I may add — so that we will both agree on our plan. Are you ready to listen?"

Gregor thought of his father.

"Yes."

"Would you like to take notes, since I hear you're a literary type?"

"No." Literary type? At the moment, he was more like a sullen child.

"I will take up the points as they appear in your memo." He took a copy from his desk. "The line between safe and dangerous radiation dosages defines everything — millions of dollars in construction, many months' difference in production time. There are already accepted industrial standards for safe dosages. Perhaps you are unfamiliar with them. We will not be wasting time or money re-inventing the wheel."

"There are absolutely no agreed-on standards in the medical community," Gregor responded. "The 'tolerance dosages' we have now are based on little or no evidence. Moreover, we don't know much about fast neutrons, and we know almost nothing about slow neutrons, and nothing at all, I believe, about alpha or beta emission. These radiations are all here now, and will get worse when plutonium really arrives. We don't even know how thick the gloves should be."

"It doesn't matter how thick the gloves are if people won't wear them because they can't do their jobs wearing them. And they won't wear them. The machinist won't wear them. They say it's impossible to run a machine tool wearing gloves."

"But of course they're forbidden to know why they need to wear gloves," Gregor injected.

"You think everyone is as concerned as you?"

"If they're not, they should be — or the District will be paying out lawsuits until the end of the century."

"Ah, lawsuits. There will be no lawsuits, Mr. Samson, if we define our health and safety responsibilities accurately, and with appropriate limitations. May I remind you that this is war, war with a totalitarian maniac. War is not about health and safety: it's about survival. Our boys in Italy and the Pacific have no right to stop work because of safety considerations. What makes you different? Do you want every worker here at the Site worried about everything we don't know, spreading panic, calling for production boycotts until we are 100% sure of the last jot and tittle? You health people better keep things in perspective. You let your humanitarian concerns get in the way of duty, and you may wind up sacrificing humanity."

"The least we can do is rotate workers through heavy radiation jobs."

"Oh, yeah? You don't think rotation will invite suspicion and have people wondering about their work? And have you asked the men about rotation? They get good pay for risky work. You take a civilian off a high-paying job, and he'll quit, leave the Project. And what if he comes down with something, and goes for medical attention? You think we won't get asked what's going on here? Are you prepared to tell the national medical community what we're doing? That's where the suits will come from. And the scandals. We've got to keep our people happy — and keep them here. We've got to inspire confidence among the troops, even if it means fudging. You egg-heads with your damn principles! You think we need some kind of ethical debate over means and ends? We need the right kind of health people here who can see the larger picture, and not worry the community about petty issues. And you're not going to stand in my way, understand? Dismissed."

Gregor had dismissed himself long before. There was one point Goliath had made with which he agreed: research did seem something of a luxury when he could not even keep informed of, much less regularly inspect, all the technical operations at Site Y. He would begin hazard studies immediately. He would be everywhere. He would get Feynman to borrow records, exposure logs, accident reports, from locked files. He didn't need much sleep. He would work quietly: no more memos. He was getting the picture of how to work on health and safety issues here at Site Y.

So was Gen. Groves. The very next day, he appointed Dr. Stafford Warren as head of the Medical Section of the Manhattan Engineering District, commissioned him colonel, and designated him as his official medical advisor. Warren had the kind of credentials Groves was interested in: he had worked extensively as a consultant for the Eastman Company in Rochester, was supportive of the ethos of industrial production, and he had the endorsement of Eastman's corporate policymakers. But his outstanding quality was that he was absolutely loyal to General Leslie R. Groves. He became Groves' confidante and personal physician — even though he was only a radiologist — and thereby took on the role of Gregor's nemesis.

Dr. Warren's first act was to put out his own memo to contravene G's. Rather than investigating possible hazards, and determining limits to be set for their possible elimination, the Medical Section's mission would be henceforth to determine "what protective measures should be taken to eliminate or protect against any *specific* health hazard of a *serious* nature." [italics mine]. The word "specific" gutted G's interest in low-level radiation: "a fishing expedition," Warren called it. And the statement obviated the need to study long-term effects, since it required the problems to already be "serious". The very health hazards most characteristic of radiation and atomic injury were neatly avoided. In addition, all site inspections would be "advisory only", with no power of enforcement or authority to halt dangerous practices or order changes in procedure. This power would rest exclusively with Groves.

When Gregor confronted Warren about his refusal to do low-level emission and long-term effect studies, he was informed that all research would be directed at producing "clear, usable information on 'acute' illness." Warren wanted minimal expense, immediate results, and a workable cost-benefit analysis — which he saw as practical wisdom necessary to get the job done. G saw it as purposeful ignorance.

Groves promoted Warren to lieutenant-colonel. The saddest part was that over the next months, mesa health culture drifted in the official direction: "If this is all we need to know, we don't want the legal responsibility of knowing more." People worked rapidly, began to see Gregor's scientific concerns as impediments, and continually made health decisions based on incomplete knowledge and unclear definitions.

For all my philosopher's distaste for the General, I have to admit that he was consistent. The issue for him — pure, unadulterated Groves — was control. That is how he had built the Pentagon; that is how he would build the atomic bomb. Militarize health care, and you have the means to prevent information from leaking. Doctors under military control can be forbidden to report hazards to either patients or the broader medical community. They can be ordered to tell patients they can best be treated by on-site medical experts. They can be ordered to tell patients that their injuries are not job-related. His press release after the Trinity explosion that ended G's life was typical. Ostensibly coming from the commanding officer of the Alamogordo Air Base, it read:

```
    Several inquiries have been received concerning a heavy
explosion which occurred on the Alamogordo Air Base reservation
this morning.
    A remotely located ammunition magazine containing a con-
siderable amount of high explosives and pyrotechnics exploded.
[Nice touch, that "pyrotechnics".]
    There was no loss of life or injury to anyone, and the
```

property damage outside of the explosives magazine itself was
negligible.

Weather conditions affecting the content of gas shells
exploded by the blast may make it desirable for the Army to
evacuate temporarily a few civilians from their homes.

Groves, concerned with limitation of liability, made no mention of
radioactive contamination. The District and its three major sites became
a vast, unofficial medical experiment with radiation exposure, plutonium
and uranium inhalation and ingestion, phosgene gas poisoning, and beryllium overexposure. There were no controls, no scientific supervision, and
no access to details which might aid treatment. There were consequential
accidents and real injuries. There were corresponding calls for loyalty in
a climate of secrecy, censorship, dissimulation, and threat. The priorities
were clear, and delay was unthinkable. Groves did his best to prevent massive fish kills from heat and radiation at Hanford — to appease the influential salmon lobby and avoid bad PR. But no human danger could be
allowed to slow the production and employment of plutonium.[26]

Gregor did what little he could. He worked with electrical engineers
to develop a portable counter for alpha emissions. He brainstormed with
mechanical engineers on safe design for plutonium-handling equipment.
He tried to promote his "unofficial" rules for working with radioactive
substances.

---

26 It's sad to say, but in cast-in-concrete military tradition, Groves' approach has
lasted to this very day. When the AEC detected startling levels of radiation after
major atmospheric tests in Nevada during the 50s, it changed its report and lowered its readings in the interest of "national defense." The Government suppressed
studies showing a relationship between nuclear testing and leukemia in southwestern
Utah, along with studies showing wide-scale I^{131} contamination in milk. (Last year,
the National Cancer Institute predicted that 75,000 Americans have developed or will
develop thyroid tumors as a result.) When farmers brought suit against the AEC for
the deaths of thousands of sheep following atmospheric testing, the AEC persuaded
the court that the sheep died from natural causes. In 1953, President Eisenhower
recruited a specialist in psychological warfare to try to counteract the rising concern about nuclear weapons, nuclear testing and fallout. The consultant suggested
the government donate a quantity of fissionable material for "peaceful uses". Thus the
catastrophic nuclear power program was begun specifically for propaganda purposes.
And of course it worked, generating a blizzard of "Atoms for Peace" media around the
globe. The dissimulation continues.

In August, the inevitable happened: a vial of plutonium exploded in the face of Spencer Lusk, an SED chemist, who spontaneously gasped and swallowed, taking the material into his stomach and lungs. Gregor, one of the first on the scene, was confronted by the obvious and unanswerable questions: How to determine how much had he taken in? What were his risks, what were his chances for recovery? What to do to save him? The arrival of quantities of plutonium from Hanford lay only four months away: Policy or not, answers had to be found.

Plutonium decays very slowly — it's half-life is 24,400 years. It emits mainly alpha particles, heavy, charged helium atoms, which do not penetrate flesh, and so cannot be easily scanned. Once inside the body though, it sits there, being deadly. How, then can plutonium in urine and feces be measured? A bone-seeker, it tends to stay put, yielding up, for example, less than a trillionth of a gram per liter of urine. What was the relationship between excreted and retained plutonium? And most important, since dust contamination was most likely, how could plutonium in the lungs be measured?

On the last question, G came up with a rough method, but one which for many years provided the only approximation for inhaled Pu. The workers called it the "Hot Snot" test, in which the inside of each nostril was swabbed with one square inch of filter paper. Readings higher than 100 counts per minute were arbitrarily seen as problematical, but all Dr. Warren would allow was a warning to improve technique. Better than nothing.

By June of '44, batches containing gram quantities of plutonium began arriving at Los Alamos, and were quickly used and reused in extensive chemical and metallurgical experiments — more than two thousand separate experiments were logged by the end of the summer. Gregor needed all six legs.

In July, came the plutonium crisis (see Chapter 39), and G's demoted star went into a kind of complex retrograde. Disband the plutonium project? Gregor was associated with such opinion. Focus the work uniquely on plutonium implosion? Gregor's thigmotactic hijinks with Neddermeyer were well known. July of '44 was Gregor's month for being whispered about, consulted, praised and damned. Even Dr. Warren tried to mend some fences. When District Engineer K.D. Nichols recommended that maximum permissible dosages be increased, Warren invited G into his office to put the following question:

"What dose of gamma radiation do you feel a superintendent can order one of his men to be exposed to with reasonable assurance that the chance of permanent damage would be slight?"

Gregor, honest as ever, confirmed Warren's attitude toward him. "I would say a superintendent should never order anyone to expose himself to more than low tolerance. Before you ask someone to be overexposed, there should be an accurate determination of the dangers by a senior radiologist."

"Don't you think wartime demands greater risk?" asked the senior radiologist of the risk assessor.

"Only as long as the men are fully informed about the danger, and only if they volunteer. This is a democracy at war, I believe, not a fascist state, even at Los Alamos. That means open discussion and voluntary action."

"I see. Well, If any cases of acute or chronic exposure come to our attention, we will notify you." Needless to say, Gregor was never notified.

Metamorphosis of being, transmutation of elements, now transvaluation of values! It was all a bit much for the company doctor with the brown nose. He would never ask George Samson his opinion again. Such are the forms of rationality in human affairs. Ultimately, the issue between the two was not risk but power, the power to impose risks on the many at the behest of the few. Groves and Warren's primary concern was not with the risk of plutonium, but with the risk of regulation, and all through history, shamans, priests, court advisors, astrologers, lawyers have served rulers and the rich, legitimating risk and reassuring the victims. This Gregor would not do.

His Gregor-month ended in a blue, Sisyphean funk, with a sense of tenuous connection between his being and his world. In spite of all the recent attention, he felt more symbol than substance, ripe for evaporation, ripe, as Camus might note, for suicide, a common response to the absurd. I worried about him enough to insist, perhaps inanely, that he accompany me to the evening of Disney films scheduled for August 1st. I was surprised to hear that he already intended to go, and was looking forward to seeing Walt Disney's *Fantasia*, about which he had heard much, but never seen.

It was the first time the film was to be shown on the mesa, and Theater Number One was packed with couples, children and dogs in spite of the fact that it was a Tuesday night with crisis-hectic work next morning. It was a hot stuffy spell for August, and Gregor hung his jacket on a peg at the door as we entered. After the usual false starts on the part of the projectionist, the audience was pacified with a plate of *hors d'oeuvres* — three short cartoons from the Disney studios, either randomly affixed to the main offering, or in subtle, even diabolical, commentary.

The evening began with an Academy Award winner — best cartoon of the previous year — *Der Führer's Face*, in which Donald Duck, Chaplin-like, dreams he is working at a munitions plant in Nazi Germany, surrounded by images of Hitler, and constantly forced to salute. He awakens from his nightmare to see a shadow with a raised arm. He starts to "Heil!", but notices the shadow is that of a small Statue of Liberty on his window-sill. He jumps up in his red, white and blue pajamas, and kisses the statue, exclaiming, "Oh Boy! Am I glad to be a citizen of the United States of America!" The film ends with a ripe tomato hitting a caricature of Hitler in the face, obliterating him. "The End".

Most, if not all, adults in the audience must have seen this as a typical "patriotic" offering from a studio newly committed, like themselves, to war work. Perhaps some of the Europeans with a deeper understanding of fascism, and a more shallow understanding of America, may have joined Gregor in wondering about the fascist projection of the Statue of Liberty, and the meaning of Leslie Groves as *Führer* in their own lives. Nevertheless, they, too, were all glad to be citizens of the United States of America.

The next tiny offering was *Private Pluto*, a 1943 creation which most certainly did not win an Academy Award, a silly little story whose tenuous military theme consisted solely of the fact that Pluto had been assigned to guard a pillbox against possible saboteurs. Two chipmunks, however, (the ones with sped-up voices, eventually to become Chip'n Dale), have turned the bunker into a storage area for nuts [Groves' "crackpots"?], which occasions poor Pluto's unsuccessful attempt to oust them. The applause was tepid, even from the children. For Gregor, however, the film brought up perplexing memories of the anonymous and questionable "Giant Mole-Person" in Amadeus's circus, a digger down into the underworld, a denizen of tunnels and darkness. For G, it was no accident that the title was *Private Pluto*, a multi-layered pun suggesting some snickering comment on the war. Pluto! There he was again. Third appearance. Pluto the planet. Pluto the new, deathy element. And now Pluto, this apparently ridiculous cartoon dog, guarding the underground like Cerberus. Marx had suggested that all great facts and personages appear twice, first as tragedy, second as farce. But what about third appearances? Before G could speculate on the answer, he was greeted by an even more provocative comment on the comment, a 1935 offering, forward-looking, forward-condemning, *Pluto's Judgment Day*.

The poor mutt chases a young kitten into Mickey's house, and is severely reprimanded: "You'll have plenty to answer for on your judgment day," Mickey intones. "You lie down and behave yourself!" Poor Pluto lies in front of the fireplace and resentfully watches his master pet his victim. He sleeps. He dreams. Another dream. Another nightmare. A trial at the mercy of a ruthless tomcat, and judgment before a feline jury.

Pluto is sworn in on a phone book which transforms into a large mouse-trap, snapping his paw. Three cute little kittens sing

He drank our milk
He ate our fish
He even stole our liver.
And then he chased poor uncle Tom
And pushed him in the river.

Uncle Tom? Uncle Tom? thought Gregor.

One very round cat says, "That great bully picked on me because I was so fat. He chased me under a steam-roller," and walks off the witness stand, his surprise profile flat as a pancake. (The children laughed and laughed.) The courtroom mills with signs: DOWN WITH PLUTO, GET PLUTO, as the jury files in and out the deliberation room through a revolving door. It looks like the fires of hell are not far away. A spark from the fireplace wakes the dog, and brings him back to reality.

The kids, ever-innocent sadists, loved this one, and yay-ed enthusiastically. Gregor's wound was already sweating, and the main feature hadn't even begun. I had to reach over and put my hand on his knee to stop it from quivering during the change of reels.

I suppose most, if not all of you, have seen *Fantasia*, that 1940 masterpiece of Faustian overreach. In the years between my viewings, I have usually remembered it via its creator's idiotic assertion concerning the Pastorale sequence, "This will make Beethoven!" Nevertheless, overall, it is an impressive animation achievement, and a rare flower in the jungle of mechanically reproduced art. Had I had children, I would have taken them to see it. And seeing photos of Stravinsky and Disney pouring over the score to *Rite of Spring* makes one critically humble.

Gregor, strangely and not so strangely, seemed to focus in on one of the lesser musical events, Paul Dukas' symphonic scherzo, *The Sorcerer's Apprentice*. Surely there were echoes of his Spengler studies in the teens and twenties, and the theme of man losing control of his tools was ever present on the mesa. He told me afterwards that he had had to memorize the original Goethe poem, *Der Zauberlehrling*, in grade school in Prague:

Stehe! Stehe!
Denn wir haben
Deiner Gaben
Vollgemessen! —
Ach, ich merk es! Wehe! Wehe!
Hab ich doch das Wort vergessen!

[Stop! Enough!
For we've had
Our fill of your gifts.
Now I realize to my sorrow! Awful! Awful!
I've forgotten the magic word!]

he recited, along with the gestures that went with it. Remarkable, what we remember! Still, the multiplication of uncontrollable brooms, and the subsequent flooding was not what most moved him. He was struck most by the short dream sequence in which Micky stands on a rock conducting the planets and the comets and the sea, the surprisingly benign aspiration of a little man given complete control of the earth and its elements, a diminutive Everyman sharing Tom and Huck's dream of "having a spectacular lot of fun without being malicious." Why could the scientists not understand this? So much fun they were having!

The other thing he mentioned to me was one of the least-appreciated sight gags in the film: Mickey is awash in a whirlpool, hanging onto, and frantically searching, a book of magic for the missing words, trying to find the formula to make the water stop — and he licks his finger to turn the page. G found this both hilarious and profound.

But the hilarity, even the profundity, vanished quickly, when, on exiting the theater, Gregor put on his jacket in the newly chilly night. Thrusting his arms into into its pockets, he came up with a folded piece of paper. We stopped at a street lamp outside Fuller Lodge to read it. It had been pasted up, letter by letter cut from Life Magazines (I won't try to reproduce its mangy heterogeneity), and it read:

MISTER INSPECTOR
YOU THINK YOUR SO SMART
YOU THINK THAT THEN US
YOU KNOW MORE.
WELL I'M HERE TO TELL YOU
YOU OLD FUCKING FART
YOU WON'T KEEP US
FROM WINNING THE WAR.
ABOUT OTHERS YOU WORRY
THAT THEY WILL GET SICK
BUT ITS "U.S." THAT
YOUR MAKING FLOUNDER
WELL GO SNIFF AT YOURSELF THEN
YOU COWARDLY PRICK
STICK YOURSELF IN THE OLD
GEIGER COUNTER.

"Feynman?" he asked me.

"Doesn't sound like Feynman. He's not that patriotic."

"And he wouldn't rhyme "flounder" with "counter". Think I should find a Geiger counter?"

"Sure, why not?"

We headed for the tech area, Building Q, headquarters for the Health Group. No one was working, and G let us in with his key. He grabbed a counter from the lab office: Nothing.

"Must be just a joke."

"A pretty awful joke," he muttered. "Let me try one more thing."

He returned from Hempelmann's office with one of the new alpha counters and turned it on. We both jumped at the burst of clicking. A quick sweep located the source at his head: his beret and his antennae were both hot.

"You think it's plutonium?" he asked.

"What other alpha-emitters are we working with?"

"None I know."

"Let's check your head more carefully."

The beret was hottest at its center, and must have been the depository for the poison. Because of the way G's antennae were curled up, the chemoreceptors at the base were uncontaminated, though when he focused attention on them, he was aware of slight tingling. Only the distal thirds of each antenna was active, and G almost nonchalantly broke them off.

"Don't worry, they'll grow back. My version of a crew cut. I just won't be as attractive to females." I didn't know if he meant human females or blattids.

G recorded the incident in detail, delivered the note to security, and the beret and antenna-ends to the Decontamination Unit the following day. After being carefully examined, he received operational radiological clearance.

The culprit was never identified. Gregor was strangely calm.

614

48. Brief Über Den Vater

Apparenly I was not the only one to be worried about Gregor's mental and spiritual health. Oppie, with his all-observing, eagle eye noticed it too, and invited G in for a talk at T-Building. I think it was genuine care here, and not just security concerns.

"Gregor, have a seat. "

"George."

"I won't tell. How are things going? Still healthy? That incident was — still is — very worrisome."

"I'm feeling fine," G assured him. "It's well known who'll inherit the earth."

"Insects.

"Naturally."

"Sounds like a line from a Nazi marching song. Today Germany, tomorrow the world. "

"It does. Sorry. I was joking."

Oppie puffed on his pipe.

"Smoke bother you?"

"It actually does. I'm sorry."

"No, no, it's fine." He put out his pipe in an ash tray. "Don't apologize so much."

"Yes. I'm good with radiation, but terrible with tobacco smoke."

"Well, we can avoid at least one of them." He dumped the ash tray into the trash.

"I just wanted to see how you were — and I have a little job for you, if you want it, something you may enjoy."

"What's that?"

"I hear that the rumors about us down in Santa Fe are getting a bit close for comfort. It was one thing for folks to be talking about a home for pregnant WACs, or the ducks, but now folks are talking about the explosions..."

"I thought they would."

"Yep. And we need to put something out that seems reasonable — and will cut off any more speculation."

"Disinformation?"

"Does that bother you?"

"That's what Dr. Warren is doing with health and safety hazards."

"I know. There's nothing I can do. I'm overruled by Groves. But this is not going to hurt anyone. I'd appreciate it if you could help us."

"With what?"

"We need to spread a story that will account for all the civilian scientists, for the secrecy, and for the explosions. Any ideas?"

"How about an electric rocket? We're making an electric rocket."

"I like it. Let's do it. An electric rocket. Very good. We can call it the G2."

"Like the V2."

"Exactly. Now, I was thinking that you and the Serbers could get whatever story around better than the gumshoes themselves. Bob and Charlotte are up for it. I'd like you all to head on down to La Fonda and talk it up. Talk loudly, talk too much. Talk as if you've had a tequila too many. Get people to eavesdrop. Say things about us, like the how place is growing, and somehow slip in the electric rocket business. No one will know about this except the four of us. You'll be spied on, of course. You'll be reported by other Los Alamos folks. We'll protect you if you get into trouble. Sound like fun?"

"Why me? Why the Serbers?"

"The Serbers? Can you think of anyone more unassuming-looking than Bob Serber? Or anyone fiercer and more believable than Charlotte? A drunk Charlotte? And you? You just have that *je ne sais quoi*. I think you'd make a good team. That's my administrative specialty, remember? Teams. Will you do it?"

Gregor had not expected such Feynman-like mischief from the celebrated leader of Site Y. Was Oppie scheming revenge for the Sanskrit mole? Did he know G had been involved? But every person ever thus accosted has testified to Oppie's charming persuasiveness. Gregor was no exception.

"All right. I'll do it."

"Good. Good. It may help cheer you up, too."

"You don't think I'm cheery?"

"Well, if someone had tried to shampoo me with plutonium, I'd be ... a little glum."

"That's because you're not going to inherit the earth."

"Like you."

"*Jawohl, mein Herr Direktor.*"

They both laughed.

On Wednesday, August 30th, in the year of our Lord 1944, the trio — as odd as the Marx Brothers or the Three Stooges — checked out through the East Gate, driving the Serber car down the hill at sundown, heading for La Fonda, the adobe inn at the end of the Santa Fe Trail, a large, high-class establishment where a century ago, travelers could seek refreshment, dancing, gambling, and sex, and where now a less ferocious crowd of local businessmen, artists and tourists held sway. It seemed a good night — no transient weekend crowd, more crowded than other weekday nights, no other major events going on, and a spell of cool weather that would make it tolerable indoors.

The trip was splendorous, with red light glowing on mesas, rocks and sand, the vegetation turning to iridescence. But the crew was less intent on observation than on conversation. It was the first time the Serbers had had a chance to quiz Gregor on his insider's knowledge of last month's choice of Sen. Harry Truman as FDR's running mate.

"I'm not surprised," he surprised them by saying. They had been most surprised. "The President has his strong points, but loyalty is not one of them, especially around election time. He liked Wallace, they were good friends, but even if he hadn't been already out, that convention speech demanding equal rights and equal wages for blacks and women, getting rid of the poll tax — he would have been ousted then and there."

"But there was a ten-minute ovation," Bob protested.

"But delegates follow orders from party bosses. They can cheer all they want."

"And the bosses had already picked Truman?" asked Charlotte. "How do you know?"

"I had a letter from Eleanor."

"So?" asked Bob?"

"So Hannegan got to FDR...Robert Hannegan, the Party Chairman. *You* liked Wallace, I liked Wallace, but big business, the bosses, southern conservatives ...Hannegan estimated a loss of three million votes if "that leftist radical" was put up again."

"Why Truman?"

"Another Missourian. A friend in a high place. No big enemies. The President wrote Hannegan that he himself would vote for Wallace, but he didn't want to dictate anyone to the Convention. So Hannegan pushed Truman right on through."

"If he wanted Wallace, why didn't he put up a fight?"

"I don't know. He's tired. Didn't want to split the party. Many reasons."

"But I hear he may not make it through the term. So we get Truman for President?"

"It's a disaster. Truman surely doesn't even know about what we're doing out here — the President wouldn't have told him. Who do we want determining post-war atomic policy — one-world Henry or crime-fighting Harry? Whose finger do we want on the trigger? Not Truman's, I say Ominous. Ominous."

For the rest of the trip they debated world dynamics under a possible President Truman. It was not an enjoyable start to a supposedly enjoyable evening.

They arrived at La Fonda about nine, anxious and self-conscious, in spite of having rehearsed a dozen scenarios through, from sappiness to expertise, during the week. Gregor scanned the newsstand on the way in, and snatched up the latest issue of the *Partisan Review;* Charlotte bought a *New York Times* and folded it up into her straw bag.

Taking a table in the middle of the room, they ordered drinks and tried to coax the conversation as naturally as possible toward electric rockets. They mentioned the forbidden name "Los Alamos" very loudly, several times, but no one turned around; the groups at other tables seemed oblivious. "…the electric rocket plant at Los Alamos…" They might as well have been talking about adding machines — or, as Bob Serber suggested, nuclear physics. Snobs and intellectuals, all the customers, a total loss.

Somewhat daunted, the terrible trio decided to change sociology, and took off for El Sueño Loco, a decidedly greasy dance bar catering to a less elegant crowd — mostly construction workers, including some who worked on the hill. Surely, they would be hungry to learn the longhairs' secrets. To the accompaniment of a blaring jukebox, the three of them rushed for a red, plastic booth at the side of the dance floor. The boys reminded Charlotte of Role #7, Mata Hari, and urged her up to solo at one end of the bar. Bob, 5' 4", made for the other end, swaggering in jeans and boots, fingers in belt with turquoise and silver buckle. Ol' Roberto Serbo in Role #4: the Mysterious Dude Rancher from Down Mexico Way ordered himself a drink. Gregor, left behind, did what he had been wanting to do for the last hour and pulled out his *Partisan Review*. Wallflower Intellectual was not one of the rehearsed numbers. It reflected his uneasiness at the assignment, his native shyness, and his intense interest in an article whose title had caught his eye on the newsstand: "Franz Kafka, a Re-evaluation on the Occasion of the Twentieth Anniversary of his Death," by Hannah Arendt. He had heard that name before. He didn't know her work, but he sensed she might have something crucial to say to him.

Twenty years ago, in the summer of 1924, Franz Kafka died at the age of forty. His reputation grew steadily in Austria and Germany during the twenties and in France, England, and America during the thirties. His admirers in these countries, though strongly disagreeing about the inherent meaning of his work, agree, oddly enough, on one essential point: All of them are struck by something new in his art of storytelling, a quality of modernity which appears nowhere else with the same intensity and unequivocalness.

The light was not very good to read by but, his appetite whetted, he pressed on, focusing ambient light onto the page with a glass of water. Ten minutes later, a dejected Mata Hari plopped heavily into the booth.

"So? What happened?" Gregor asked. " I saw you dancing with *Señor Muy Hermoso*."

"Quick on the draw, but dull as a dead toad. Good dancer, though."

"Did you tell him about electric rockets?"

"He'd worked on the hill for a while, so I thought I had him. I told him we were up there now — but all he could talk about was wanting to get a job on a ranch. I said, 'It's quite a place, up there, don't you think? So mysterious and secret, and it seems to be growing by leaps and bounds. Notice all the different license plates around town?' He just kept telling me how he wants to run a ranch someday. No more beating around the bush: I went for the jugular: 'But what do you suppose they're doing at Los Alamos?'"

"What did he say?"

"He said, 'I dunno. You sure dance fine. I hated working at that place. Just want to get me a ranch and own some horses. You come to town often? You sure dance fine.' That's what he said."

"I see."

"But Old Mata Hari was not going to take that for an answer. She went in for the follow-up: 'We come to town as often as we can, but they don't like to let us out much. What's your guess about what cooks up there?' 'Beats me,' he says. 'Can I have another dance later?'"

"Didn't get to electric rockets, huh?"

"Hey, don't give me a hard time. You don't look like you got to electric rockets either. Take your snout out of that magazine and go do your Peter Lorre European Spy-in-Reverse. What are you reading?"

"It's an article on Kafka."

"833.72," said the librarian. "That's the Kafka section. I can't make a more brilliant comment, because I haven't read him."

"You're not missing anything," Gregor offered. "Or rather, you are, but nothing you'd want to take in."

"Why's that? He's famous."

Saved by the bell. The clock chimed eleven, and Bob came sidling back to the booth, a cat-and-canary smile on his face.

"Hey, you guys are supposed to be out spreading the word."

Charlotte gave him a withering glance.

"I can't function," G said. "The music's too loud."

"Was it too loud for you to catch my big scene?"

"Guess so," said Charlotte. "What happened?"

"Well, I go up to this big guy, see (switching to Cagney), and out of the blue I grab him by the lapels, see, and I sez to him 'You know why they're making all those explosions up there, don't you? They're tests. They're testing electric rockets! That's what they're doing at Los Alamos."

"And?"

"And he grunted and ordered another drink."

"Do you get congratulations or condolences?" Gregor inquired.

"Which one of you got to say 'electric rockets' to a listening person?" Silence. "Then congratulations, 'cause I win."

"My hero," said Charlotte, sarcastically. "Let's get out of here. We're total failures and we have to get up early. This is a job for Intelligence, no matter what Oppie thinks. Let them work on the electric rockets, and we'll stick to atomic bombs."

Both Gregor and Robert, wheeled around accusingly at her at her extreme breach of security.

"My dear scientists and rational human beings," she countered. "Have we not demonstrated empirically that we can say whatever the hell we like without consequence? Ease up."

But they did all look around for the gumshoes. Even they were not apparent.

Charlotte drove on the way back. As they were heading out of town, Gregor commented, "Did you know that Dick Feynman pasted a photo of Hitler on his ID card last year, and he was six months flashing it at every gate before anyone picked up on it?"

"Does Groves know that?" asked Bob.

"These are Dick's private experiments," Gregor answered.

As is often the case, the most talkative car-ride out in daylight is often followed by a silent ride back in darkness, the centripetal night taking its toll, with fatigue added in. The three rode the rest of the way involved in their own thoughts. Robert may have fallen asleep until the road began to climb and curve.

Gregor, though, was not sleepy. He was anxious to get back home, back to his article, back to the possibility of a crucial communication. But what he read so infuriated him, he pulled out his typewriter to write a response.

P.O. Box 1663
Santa Fe, New Mexico
30 August 1944
Dear Doktor Arendt,

You may find this amusing or vile, but two months ago, I bought a new copy of The Trial and set it to fire. Or I tried to set it to fire. I stuffed a bucket with paper and kindling, got a nice blaze, perfect for an auto-da-fe, and dropped the book into the flames. It quickly snuffed them out, my room filled with smoke, the fire department arrived, and I had a hard time to explain my actions.

To you, however, I will explain. I have just read your "Re-evaluation" in the Partisan Review, and I feel that while you make certain points against the grain of most opinion, you surely join the mob of critics to worshipp an idol who walks the world with poison steps.

For you, Herr Kafka is a Jewish outsider using his only weapon - thought - against a "misconstructed world". You see his characters as "facing society with an attitude of constructively defiant, outspoken aggression," as ready to act against a such world "for the sake of human values." You cast Herr Kafka as a man of the Enlightenment, an emancipating moralist, writing his utopian, romantic belief in Reason.

But surely this is false. This writer's heroes are far from fighters. His is an atmosfere of fascist terror, and his characters are products of such gruesome world. What kind of models are they for the general reader? They react to the most horrifying events as if they were perfect normal; they carry out their duties, without to understand them, in blind, slave obedience, where following rules is more important than the rules themselves, more important than the morality of the rulers. There is no emancipation here, because in Kafka's world, there is no real self to be emancipated. There is no real personality, no real love. Human beings regress, even biologically, back to apes, dogs, moles, mice - even insects - their struggle is only of unresolved interpretive furies, full of nothing but unproductive hypothesis. This is a world of unfreedom, not emancipation, and any transformation Herr Kafka offers does not go toward liberation or clarification but to damnation.

I agree with you that Herr Kafka rings an alarm bell, and describes the world the way it is, and should not be. But is it making emancipation to depict the world's insanity? Rather Kafka evokes a destructive, unconsolable picture of the way things simply ARE. He offers no political or social vision, no encouragement for human beings as members of human community, only a nihilism that makes alienation and dehumanization. His characters are so powerless in their fear and chaos that they seem victims of inexplicable forces; they are not capable of reflecting on their submission. They can only sit "outside the Law", remain silent and obey.

Herr Kafka's stories may help intellectuals with their feelings of helplessness and self-contempt, but finally they justify the ways of a banal, bureaucratic and incomprehensible fascist system. Readers become Herr Kafka's victims, unfit for life, allied with death, tangled in the endless labyrinth of his obcessions and konfusions. His work suggests no solutions to the problems he explores, and will never, ever, in Kleist's lovely words, "help humanity to cultivate a field, to plant a tree, to beget a child." His crazed cosmos, impenetrable, eccentric, offers no human dignity to a race in need of such. Do we have to read it simply to call everything into question, the whole intellectual tradition of the West?

Surely you and I share the same goal: the liberation of the human spirit from the dictator institutions and machinelike admnistration of the modern world. But the unrestricted pessimism of this Prague insurance agent convinced of the impossibility of all guarantees - this does not serve our needs. In short, Herr Kafka is bad for the world. I hope you will come to agree and,

against the current of current opinion, truly "re-evaluate" this
overvalued writer .

Sincerely yours,
George Samson
Box 1663
Santa Fe, New Mexico

It took him four drafts — retyping each. The final version (above —
from my carbon) is half the length of its predecessors. It was one exhausted
blattid who, at the 7:30 morning whistle, turned out the lights, and nestled
in among the straw. But the whistle was punctuated by a rat-tat-tatting
on his door. It was Bob Serber, early riser, mouse-like and concerned, last
night's *New York Times* in hand.

"Have you seen this? Do you know about it?"

"What?"

"Here. This." He pointed to two column inches on page one: NAZI
MASS KILLING LAID BARE IN CAMP. "Some place named Maidanek,
near Lublin. Mass graves, death chambers with some kind of asphyxiation
system — carbon monoxide and Prussic acid, furnaces for burning bodies,
warehouses crammed with clothing and shoes from the dead — they estimate 100,000 killed. Look at this. Jars of ashes for selling to relatives,
bodies stamped on their chests before burning — all gold teeth extracted.
Do you believe this? The Russians found it end of July." He looked at
Gregor, the paper shaking in his hand.

"I've got to go to sleep," G said, and crawled back deep into the straw.
Serber stood there for a minute, then left, closing the door gently behind
him. Something strange was up with Gregor, and something stranger with
the world.

49. The Old World Dis-Covered

On hearing the news of the first concentration camp found and freed, Gregor went to sleep. But then he had been up all night. The world also went to sleep — with less excuse.

Although the Soviets gave it lots of play, the few stories and pictures published in the States had little impact on public opinion. People remained skeptical — except for those who already knew. The one British report on the camp was widely seen as "a Russian propaganda stunt." Hitler dismissed the news as an Allied attempt to defame Germany.

In that same summer of '44 the Russians overran three other eastern camps: Belzec, Sobibor, and Treblinka. In doing so they actually freed few prisoners since the retreating Germans, fearful of being discovered, were evacuating and destroying the camps as best they could. Perhaps low numbers explain low interest. Also, almost none of the prisoners left behind were Jewish: most Jews had long since been disposed of. These early Russian liberations were mostly of common criminals, communists, gypsies, homosexuals, Seventh-Day Adventists, and political prisoners — not groups to evoke widespread cries of protest from a war-weary West, and perhaps another reason for small response.

But in my view, the primary reason behind the lethargy was Western reluctance to give the Soviets credit for an accomplishment the Allies had evaded. The camps' existence had been known in upper circles for almost two years — there had been no lack of reports. Liberating them, bombing the rail lines which fed them, was not considered militarily important. It was not until the end of the war, while running down an already-defeated Germany, that the Americans and British began to liberate camps. And then the media began to crank. A large current publication of our National Holocaust Museum is called *1945, The Year of Liberation*. That the Soviets had already been at it for half a year is almost unmentioned. Maidanek, the first of the camps to be photographed, is not in the table of contents. The cold war was well underway in the middle of the hot one.

Although Americans were reluctant to believe in Nazi death camps, they were quite unskeptical about a Nazi bomb. Hitler and Goebbels kept hinting about a "secret weapon" soon to be completed which would quickly decide the war.

It seemed a brashness of despair. The Germans were on the run. The allies had re-taken Paris at the end of August; Verdun, Dieppe, Artois, Rouen, Abbeville, Antwerp and Brussels in the first week of September . These last were especially important to Project scientists because, unlike the general population, they knew Belgium was a major repository for uranium ores mined from the Belgian Congo — those very ores about which Einstein wrote the Queen. The Alsos Project[27] was busy tracking down the ores known to have been captured by the Germans.

There was a comical scare (in hindsight) concerning large amounts of thorium, a possible alternative to uranium, which had been moved to Germany. Did this mean the Nazis were developing a thorium bomb, or using thorium to potentiate uranium? After much tense investigation, it was discovered that the shipment was part of a plot — to corner the postwar market on a toothpaste additive. Brush your teeth with Thoriia — the scientific toothpaste!

Real evidence concerning the reputed Nazi bomb project was maddeningly elusive. It looked as if "no large military programme is underway for the

---

27 The scientific intelligence team, authorized by Groves in late '43 that followed the Allies advance, seeking information about the state of the German bomb project. Given the crucial nature of the question concerning the pace of the American project, it is curious that such a unit was not initiated sooner. Here we can see the limits of Groves' obsession with security: in order to know what to look for, agents would have to be briefed on the state of Site Y research, and might well be able to give American secrets away.

employment of T.A. products[28] in the near future"[29], but Groves wanted every last lead nailed down before drawing conclusions — every ounce of uranium ore recovered, every German lab searched for hints about nuclear piles and possible plutonium production. Epistemological snafu: negative findings were no findings: it was always possible something was missed.

Early in September, the OSS gave Sam Goudsmit, the scientific director of Alsos, a copy of the 1944 course catalogue of the University of Strasbourg, a demonstration school the Nazis had set-up in the occupied city just over the French border. Three nuclear scientists were listed on the faculty, including Carl Friedrich von Weizsäcker, the one potentially dangerous scientist mentioned by Einstein in his letter to Roosevelt. Groves was alerted. When the French captured Strasbourg on November 24th, Alsos was not far behind, now with one more member on the team: George Samson.

Gregor had been flown to Paris on the 23rd, when the capture of Strasbourg looked imminent, in preparation for the investigation. Groves, too, had an assignment for him, though unlike Oppie's it wasn't expected to be fun, nor was it out of concern for G's health: rather it was to get him out of Groves' graying hair, at least for a while, another Siberia tour, as was Los Alamos itself. G was a native speaker, he reasoned, and thus could pass more easily among suspicious Germans. He was also not a physicist, so that if he were captured, he could provide no technical information to German scientific intelligence. Gregor knew it was a self-serving ploy, but he was ready for a break, and the thought of re-visiting Europe at Army expense was an attractive one.

At a dinner in Paris on the 25th Goudsmit told Gregor and Vannevar Bush[30] of the disappointing cable from Lt. Col. Boris Pash, the FBI-trained security officer in charge of the mission.[31] It seems all the targeted scien-

28 Tube Alloy, that is, uranium.
29 Conclusion of a joint British and American Intelligence Committee, October 1944.
30 FDR's director of the Office of Scientific Research and Development, in Paris to promote a revolutionary new type of shell fuse.
31 Pash, a fanatical anti-Communist, in the previous year, had questioned and secretly recorded Oppenheimer about his left-wing affiliations, and had concluded Oppie was a Party member gone underground, and possibly a spy. Groves' choice of him to head the Alsos project had complex political ramifications within the Manhattan District.

tists had evacuated in advance of the French. But the next day, following a faint lead, Pash led his men to the Strasbourg hospital where seven nuclear physicists, disguised as medical personnel, were unmasked and captured. A second cable asked the Paris team to come investigate.

It took Gregor and Goudsmit almost a week to make the normally five hour drive from Paris to Strasbourg, given the many icy detours to avoid pockets of fire and sporadic German resistance: the Dutchman swore he'd never ride in a jeep again. The Czech didn't much like it either. They arrived, exhausted, on December 3rd, to comb through the boxes of documents Pash had seized over several days. That very evening, in the apartment of an absconded physicist, Gregor and Goudsmit, munching K-rations by candlelight (not romantic — there was no electricity), read through files captured from houses and laboratories. These were not secret scientific documents but simply informal communications between scientists, mixing news about work with family tidings. Gregor found a copy of a letter to *"Lieber Werner"* — must be Heisenberg — about the problem of finding the "special metal" — must be uranium — in slabs rather than powdered form, slabs which could be used in "the large furnace" — must be something like a reactor. But these recent considerations were so basic, so far behind all problems long ago encountered and solved by the Manhattan District. An urgent request to the government for money for "two slide rules" had the physicist and risk manager in stitches.

The details gleaned from these papers led to a clear but astounding conclusion: the Germans had no bomb project! Their elementary work had been entirely focused on the possibility of a reactor, perhaps at some point to power ships, a project to simply achieve "the production of energy from uranium."

Sufficient unto the day was the joy thereof. At 6 AM, Gregor and Goudsmit collapsed, fully clothed, into twin beds in the dark bedroom recently occupied by the children of the house.

"Sam, said Gregor, as sleep descended, "isn't it wonderful they have no bomb? Now we can stop with ours."

Sam was already fast asleep, but Gregor imagined how happy he must be. He scanned the murky room and was surprised by a wave of sudden sadness as he focused on the toys. Somewhere there were two children, forced from their home, fleeing an avenging army. He and Sam had stolen their beds, these comfortable beds they must be missing at this very moment. In the faint light, he could make out an electric train, a movie projector, a toy microscope, an aquarium. Had the fish been fed? He got up and looked for a box of food, but could find none. His foot struck the leg of a card table, jostling it, sending a clattering to the floor. Sam stirred and snorted. G felt around in the dark to find a scattering of what felt like medals, cloth and metal constructions with small figures, perhaps playing sports. Little athletes with their rewards. Then one with — was it? — it was. A swastika. He held it up against the the dim light of the window, a disheartening silhouette. His sympathy for the children began to wane. And then, how mean, he thought. How many children at Los Alamos have American flags and pictures of Roosevelt in their rooms. What do they know? Gregor was too tired to clean up. "I'll do it in the morning," he said out loud to no one, and, under a framed picture of Hitler too dark to make out, he drifted off to insensible sleep.

****

Not everyone was as convinced as Gregor, Goudsmit and Pash that the Strasbourg papers guaranteed no German bomb. What if they'd been planted? Now that the general whereabouts of Heisenberg and several other physicists were known, shouldn't they be tracked down and captured or killed to keep them from falling into the hands of the Soviet Union, our "ally"? That was the thinking.

Werner Heisenberg was the chief prize, "target number one". Plans were afoot for a joint Alsos-OSS venture into Switzerland for the rumored occasion of a Zurich lecture by Heisenberg; the object: "to deny the enemy his brain." Allen Dulles, chief of the OSS office in Bern, was reluctant to upset the diplomatic apple cart, but Groves had been pressing to get Heisenberg since the beginning of the year, and Oppenheimer had asserted he was the one physicist sure to be at the center of any German bomb project. Philip Morrison and several other scientists discussed the kidnapping plan, and while they thought it "operationally interesting", they considered it ill-advised. That is, if the German bomb was in an advanced stage of development, the theoretician Heisenberg should no longer be crucially important. On the other hand, if he *was* still crucially important at this stage, the bomb was not a serious threat. But Washington was not interested in such astute reasoning.

Groves was enthusiastic about a man he called "a very reliable and able OSS agent, Moe Berg, a former catcher for the Washington Senators and the Boston Red Sox, and a master of seven foreign languages." You may recall Charles Ives' comment about Berg on that June day of 1923 when Gregor took Alice Paul to the Princeton-Yale game at Yankee Stadium: "Moe Berg is too slow for a shortstop. He should learn to catch."

Moe Berg did learn to catch — and one of the challenges thrown at him was an offer to use his Princeton education, and his seven languages, by becoming a spy. In 1943 he was recruited by the OSS (Office of Strategic Services, the predecessor of the CIA)[32]. His assignment now was to catch the heavy-hitter of German nuclear physics and take him out, if necessary. He was to attend the Zurich lecture. If Heisenberg said anything indicating the Germans were close to a bomb, he was to shoot him there, on the spot. But he needed help, for while his German was passable, he was far from the "master" Groves believed, with the fluency necessary to make such a portentous and irrevocable decision. Goudsmit and Pash, in consultation with Allen Dulles in Bern, decided Gregor would be the perfect partner to listen between the lines. On December 17, G was taken by jeep from Strasbourg to Basel, and then by civilian car from Basel to Bern for a final briefing with Dulles. He was outfitted in appropriate Swiss clothing, and given his "L" pill — the lethal tablet he was to chew if necessary. Since cyanide works by inhibiting cellular oxidation, OSS doctors were convinced it would work, even in Gregor's case. It was heartening — in a way — to know they had given him such thought.

Thematic, too. His rendezvous point in Basel had been the main arcade of the Kunstmuseum. Since he had been dropped an hour early, he had decided to briefly inspect its collection. The painting grabbed his eye immediately with its strange shape, the painting Dostoevsky had obsessed

---

32 For an excellent life of this complex and somewhat mysterious man, see Nicholas Dawidoff, *The Catcher Was A Spy,* Pantheon, 1994.

about in *The Idiot* — Holbein the Younger's *Body of the Dead Christ in the Tomb*.

There could be no question what it was, even before he was close enough to focus. What other free-standing painting is five feet wide and ten inches high? Gregor turned into the room, and stood before it, appalled. I suggest that any of you who don't know this work inspect a copy: no mere description can do it justice.

It shows the Saviour, dead in a box, freshly dead: the blood not yet pooled, and the thin skin of the face barely suggesting that hypoxic blueness that will shortly engulf the corpse. Rigor mortis and gangrene have yet to set in. One can almost feel the warmth departing. There is no hint of beauty, of transcendence, no spirituality, no supernatural aura, as was commonly represented by painters of the time. This was simply the remnant of a man who had undergone unbearable torment, had been wounded, beaten, tortured, carried his cross and suffered the agony of crucifixion. It had been modeled, according to tradition, after a Jewish corpse fished out of the Rhine. The blank, fishy eyes are rolled up into the head, the mouth hangs limply open, and one fingernail catches in the soiled and rumpled sheet, bunched up at its ends, too large a size for the already cracking coffin.

With the extremity of this work, Holbein was surely illustrating the depth of his faith: that from this unspeakable condition, Christ could rise in glory. But for Dostoevsky, the painting was the ultimate challenge to belief: how could any one seeing such a corpse possibly believe in the central mystery of Christianity — the Resurrection? There are no onlookers, plunged in sorrow. The holy meat is inconsolably alone. Death is horrible, implacable, and corruption in nature regnant. How could the laws of the world be overcome if even Christ could not conquer them? Here is Dostoevsky's summary:

*Looking at that picture, you get the impression of nature as some
immense, merciless, and dumb beast, or to put it more correctly,
much more correctly, though it may seem strange, as some huge
machine of the most modern construction which, dull and insensible, has clutched, crushed and swallowed up a great, priceless Being
worth all nature and its laws, worth the whole earth, which was
perhaps created solely for the coming of that Being! The picture sees to
give expression to the idea of a dark, insolent, and senselessly eternal
power, to which everything is subordinated, and this idea is suggested
to you unconsciously. The people surrounding the dead man...must
have been overwhelmed by a feeling of terrible anguish and dismay
on that evening which had shattered all their hopes and almost all
their beliefs at one fell blow. They must have parted in a state of the
most dreadful terror, though each of them carried away within him
a mighty thought which could never be wrested from him. And if,
on the eve of the crucifixion, the Master could have seen what He
would look like when taken from the cross, would he have mounted
the cross and died as he did? This question too, you can't help asking
yourself as you look at the picture.*

Gregor had surely been struck by something similar, for in his copy
of *The Idiot* this passage is double-lined in the margin with his comment
"urgent call for metamorphosis".

As he walked from Dulles' office, the L-pill clicking against its container in his trench coat pocket, the Dead Christ floated in front of him.
"Cyanotic means blue," he thought. "Better to leave no body behind."

****

Moe Berg met the train at the Zurich Hauptbahnhof. The signal (each
carrying a green book — Gregor: *Die Welt als Wille und Vorstellung*; Berg:
Ernie Pyle's *Here Is Your War.*) was transmitted and received, and the
men walked off together into the station for beer and wurst. Their cautious checking-out period was short, since the food reminded Gregor of

the first time he had seen Moe Berg at Yale-Princeton time, and Berg was impressed and touched by G's elephantine memory of the game — one of his best. Gregor modestly explained his vivid recall: it was his first and only ball game, and his senses were heightened by being on a first date. Berg was sorry the relationship didn't work out, and thought Gregor's suggestions about batters running to either first or third would make interesting hyper-baseball worth further study. In short, they hit it off quite well. They stayed together that night in Berg's room at the Engelhof, and didn't get to sleep till three, though the next day might very well have been their last. But there was much to talk about.

On the morning of the 18th, the two settled on their personae. Berg, with his dark, surly looks, prided himself on being able to fit in anywhere — Berlin or Tokyo or Morocco.

"I was once walking down the street in Rome," he told his partner, "when two American soldiers pulled up in a jeep. One guy says, 'Let's ask this guinea where the hotel is,' and I tell him, 'It's three blocks up with a green awning. You can't miss it.' 'Where'd that guinea learn to speak such good English?' he says to the other guy. I said 'Princeton, class of '23,' and walked away."

Today Berg decided he would be Ahmad al-Jabiri, an Arab businessman. Gregor settled on Gunther Stoßmann, a Swiss post-doctoral student in biology. For some reason he was set on keeping his initials, perhaps as a memory aid.

Ahmad and Gunther arrived at the Eidgenössische Techniche Hochschule (ETH) small lecture hall on Rämistrasse at ten minutes to four, hung their hats and coats in the anteroom (Gunther traded fedora for beret), and took seats in the second row. Ahmad checked the gun in his right jacket pocket. Gunther checked his L-pill. The room was close to full with twenty or so faculty and graduate students who had come to hear the world's greatest physicist discuss his recent work on S-matrix theory. Ahmad would have had trouble following such a talk in English, much less German, so he concentrated on identifying the people in the audience, of whom he knew only one from a photograph: Carl Friedrich von Weizsäcker, recently missing from the University of Strasbourg.

Heisenberg, with two other faculty members, entered the room at 4:10.

There was no security of any kind. After struggling to crank up the board, he began to speak from typewritten sheets of paper. Ahmad, always the good student, took copious notes. He was thrilled by actually seeing his target, the man he had been studying for six weeks. "Frail, 5'6", 110 pounds, reddish-brown hair with a bald spot" he jotted down. "Dark, three-piece suit; wedding ring." Then, perhaps unnecessary, "artistic hands, heavy eyebrows emphasize bony structure over eyes." He made a quick sketch with an arrow pointing at the eyes. "Sinister," he labeled them. Heisenberg seemed to notice his interest. "H. LIKES MY INTEREST IN HIS LECTURE," Ahmad wrote on his pad, and showed it to Gunther, who nodded. "If he only knew what we were doing here." Gunther nodded, and thought the same thing.

Warming to his work, Heisenberg began pacing back and forth while he spoke, his left hand in his pocket. "Continuous seeming quizzical smile," Ahmad wrote. Fifteen more minutes. He was approaching the fateful decision point in his assignment. If anyone could build an atomic bomb to drop on his mother, brothers and sister, it was this man here. But there had been no hint, he thought, no mention of a *Wunderwaffe*, nothing about explosions or a bomb. Another note to Gunther: "AS I LISTEN, I AM UNCERTAIN WHAT TO DO." Gunther: "HE'S DISCUSSING MATH." Ahmad: "I KNOW HE'S DISCUSSING MATH. BUT WHAT IS THE MATH ABOUT??" "APPARENTLY ABOUT ELEMENTARY PARTICLE COLLISIONS — WHAT GOES IN AND WHAT COMES OUT." " I HAVEN'T HEARD ANYTHING ABOUT T OR PRODUCT." "I DON'T THINK IT HAS ANYTHING TO DO WITH T OR PRODUCT." "WHAT IS HE — DISCUSSING MATH WHILE ROME BURNS?" Gunther nodded.

I won't bother you with the equations Heisenberg was scribbling on the board. But there are a few things about S-matrix theory which will help you hear the ironic echo of recursive metaphor. Heisenberg's major creative work during the war was not on a bomb, but on a new, basic theory of such elementary particles as might be produced when a high-energy cosmic ray strikes the earth's atmosphere or some more solid piece of matter. He was working on the radical notion that these events could be understood only by assuming a universal minimum length, a new fundamental constant in the universe, to limit the possible changes in momentum and energy of colliding particles. Events on this side of the fundamental length could be observed and measured; events on the other side could not. Not ever. Collision, and the transformations themselves, are unobservable events. What goes in and what comes out of the unobservable region he represented by a Scattering Matrix, a table of transformation possibilities, obeying relativity, conservation and symmetry constraints which restricted its array. From his equations, he was able to calculate simple examples of scattering cross-sections and cosmic-ray showers without recourse to the forbidden area of knowledge. He was hoping to replace a possibly futile search for a complete quantum field theory with a likely more productive quest for thorough matrix representation.

Without really being able to follow the formal manipulations, Gregor (not Gunther) felt immediately that he himself was a macro-metaphor of the micro-world under discussion. For surely there was an unknown and unknowable event of transformation, now playing out in sets of possibilities. He tried to construct his own matrix: wound and not-wound, quest and not-quest, bomb and not-bomb, death and not-death. What were the symmetries? What, besides tears and laughter, was conserved? Of one thing he was certain: Heisenberg should not be killed.

"SCRATCH THE PLAN?" he wrote his partner. "WHAT DO YOU THINK?" came back. "I THINK SCRATCH THE PLAN. DEFINITELY." "YOU'RE PROBABLY RIGHT." It's not clear what Moe Berg would have concluded were he alone. Perhaps the same thing, perhaps not. But it is surely true that Gregor was largely responsible for Heisenberg's survival — and their own. It was not fear or survival instinct that shaped his conclusion. His considered opinion, reinforced by further research, was that Heisenberg was a loyal German, but an anti-Nazi who, by remaining passive during the war, kept Hitler from thinking a bomb could be built. What six thousand scientists and staff on the mesa were working for, this one man had accomplished by default — at considerably less cost. As they gathered their hats and coats, Ahmad whispered to Gunther. "Can you get Bohr to invite him to Los Alamos?" Gunther said he'd ask when he got back.

They followed the post-lecture group to a dinner at the Kronenhalle, and took a table as close as they could to that of Heisenberg and his friends. The room was noisy, and they couldn't hear much without attracting attention.

They did catch two crucial turns of conversation, marked by the silences which followed: Heisenberg was extremely upset by the news that Erwin Planck, Max Plank's son, had been arrested and condemned to death for some connection to the July attempt on Hitler's life . There seemed to be few details. The second was a sentence of Heisenberg's which was subsequently given much play in Paris, Los Alamos, and Washington. The din in the room had momentarily quieted, and both Ahmad and Gunther wrote down what they heard: one of the professors at Heisenberg's table had challenged the master: "Well, now you have to admit that the war is lost." "Yes," he conceded, "but it would have been so good if we had won." More room noise excluded the rest.

"It would have been so good if we had won." What could he have been thinking of? Who was the "we"? Surely not Hitler, or Heisenberg would have taken a different wartime tack, or been more enthusiastic about punishment for the plotters. Perhaps it was fear of the Russians. Whatever it was, that remark, reported back by Berg and Gregor, was for decades profoundly damaging to Heisenberg's relationship to the post-war international physics community.

Yet its implication was clear: there surely was no German bomb. For would a man with such a weapon make such a remark? That was the message Berg and Gregor took back to their de-briefings: no bomb, a message which had Groves gushing with praise for the mission. "Without B and G's report," he told me later, "I would have probably worked our scientists to death in a race to be first." As if he had ever stopped working them to death.

****

Death. Death was much on Gregor's mind as he waited at the Zurich airport for a flight to Paris and back to the States. Several hours earlier, he had debated whether or not to return the L-pill. The decision was made when Dulles took it from him at the de-briefing. What would he have used it for, he wondered. Some gaunt bearded man waiting at his departure gate reminded him of the Holbein Christ. Yet how dignified he was. Death and dignity. Perhaps there was some sphere of interaction there, with dignity emerging from the unobservable region as a byproduct of annihilation. But how is it possible for God to die? For Jews, never. God is the microstructure of the world. But Christ? Christly sacrifice? "Take, eat, this is my body." Providing food so that others might live. That death is neither murder nor disappearance but some life-giving discontinuity, a break in the curve closer to nutrition than destruction. The only rite Christ left to his disciples was the Eucharist, an acceptable and accepted gift. And if we had killed Heisenberg and then ourselves? Who would have been the victim? Or would it have been a saving, mediating "offering"?

A fundamentally necessary, beneficent discontinuity in the curve — a man-god appears on earth for the first time, or an insect-man — there must be discontinuity, or we arrive where we are headed. A discontinuity, the old making way for the new, a life-giving severance, a slight flaw, like that crack in the Holbein coffin, opening out into escape. Yet a coffin *was* a place to hide after all the work and suffering which had preceded, after all the work and suffering that was to follow. We all need a vacation — away from prying eyes.

And what would Kafka say? Probably something like "From a certain point onward there is no longer any turning back. That is the point that must be reached."

As he waited for the plane, Gregor felt he was in an old, old country in an old, old world.

50. In The Blackest Of Forests

In the air, on the less-than-comfortable B-29, he composed a long letter to Leo Szilard detailing his recent adventures, findings and thoughts, and mailed it from La Guardia — while still outside the censors' reach. Then another long plane ride to Chicago, and on to Alamogordo Army Air Field, for the bus ride 160 miles north to Santa Fe and Los Alamos. It was the first time he had been in Alamogordo, but it would not be his last. His last would be his last.

****

It may be worth briefly reviewing the Project Gregor had returned to, an enterprise much modified by reorganization around plutonium and implosion design. In July, Segrè had established that a gun design for plutonium would not work, and the lab went into crisis. The only alternative would be to solve the immensely complex implosion problem suggested by Gregor and Neddermeyer's early experiments in the canyon. Enrico Fermi and his family had arrived in August, and "The Pope" was appointed associate Lab director, and head of F-division, a catch-all gang of trouble shooters for interdisciplinary problems. The changes had lifted Lab spirits, though there was only dim light at the end of the tunnel. If there *was* an end of the tunnel. Bob Bacher took on a newly-created "Gadget-Division" focusing on bomb design, Kistiakowski continued to lead the X (explosives)-division, investigating explosive lenses, Luis Alvarez was developing micro-second detonation systems, and Robert Brode led the development of arming devices which could not trigger while the bomb was still in the airplane. Edward Teller and his stupendous ego continued to be a thorn in almost everyone's side, but Oppie valued him too highly to let him go. He was appointed leader of a small "Super and General Theory Group" to work on problems not directly related to immediate production.

"Super" was the name for his hydrogen bomb idea — a fusion weapon with many times the explosive power of anything possible via uranium or plutonium fission. Teller's beloved brainchild, it was a bomb within a bomb, requiring an atomic blast to achieve the temperatures needed to crush hydrogen. Gregor found it appalling. The weapon currently being developed on-site was projected to explode with the force of 10 kilotons (10,000 tons) of TNT over an area of 10 square miles, a figure horrible enough. Teller's calculations for the Super predicted a similar effect over 1,000 square miles: it would require only one superbomb to entirely destroy New York City. Teller and his group did some targeting calculations: serious earthquake-level damage would occur if the bomb were detonated underground or underwater near a continental shelf. Even more exhilarating was the calculation that if a superbomb burned a 10 meter cube of liquid deuterium 300 miles above the atmosphere, the blast could lay waste a million square miles. Boys will be boys.

Teller, however, was not the only physicist whose thoughts tended toward the inhuman. In April of '43, Fermi, in Chicago, had proposed the possibility of using fiercely radioactive isotopes bred in an atomic pile to poison the German food supply, a preemptive strike against a similar possible German attack. Such might be an alternative in case a fission bomb proved impossible. Oppie swore Fermi to secrecy — a secrecy within the overall secrecy of the Manhattan Project — and the Italian went quietly to work. Oppie discussed Fermi's idea with Teller, and the two agreed that Strontium 90 might be the best agent, not hard to separate from other radioactive products and, a calcium replacement, depositing itself quickly and permanently in bone. Oppenheimer, the man dedicated to *ahimsa* — doing no harm — wrote to Fermi, "I think that we should not attempt a plan unless we can poison food sufficient to kill a half a million men, since there is no doubt that the actual number affected will, because of non-uniform distribution, be much smaller than this."

The reader will recall Wittgenstein's fourth-grade class debating what might define a human being.

Gregor had returned to an enterprise where both the best and worst of men had been caught up in the whirlwind of technical challenge, and been unpredictably brutalized by their struggle. The new pace was frenetic, the energy high, the collegiality blinding and inspiring. The Germans were losing the war, and though there was still some fear of a desperate *Wunderwaffe*, it was the Japanese who seemed destined to be the Gadget's target.

****

On his second day back, Gregor checked his mailbox. In it, he found a surprise. He had almost forgotten he had written.

365 W. 95th St.

New York 25, N.Y.

20 December 1944

Dear Mr. Samson,

Thank you for your provocative letter. I hope you will have patience with the extended answer I believe such a letter demands.

I must admit I found your auto-da-fe amusing, though not for its slapstick quality. Rather it demonstrates an unfortunately typical misdirection of goodwill: destroying the messenger does not invalidate bad tidings.

We agree, I think, on the message Kafka brings to a miscon-structed world: the ancient admonition to "Know Thyself." The truth of our time must be disclosed or uncovered from within its all-pervasive and seductive trappings. It requires a scalpel as sharp as Kafka's to do such deep surgery. Modern man stands amidst the confusion of the time seeking guidance, and Kafka provides not only guidance, but the intellectual momentum for constructive escape.

Let us look together at two of Kafka's little parables, in some ways contrasting, even contradictory, and in some ways additive. Here is the first:

"He is a free and secure citizen of the world, for he is fettered to a chain which is long enough to give him the freedom of all earthly space, and yet only so long that nothing can drag him past the frontiers of the world. But simultaneously he is a free and secure citizen of Heaven as well, for he is also fettered by a similarly designed heavenly chain. So that if he heads, say, for the earth, his heavenly collar throttles him, and if he heads for Heaven, his earthly one does the same. And yet all the possibilities are his, and he feels it; more, he actually refuses to account for the deadlock by an error in the original fettering."

Even so is the world, a place where freedom and security are protected by chains which, while not seriously limiting earthly activity, keep one from falling off. But Kafka tells us that earthly freedom - that granted by "the world" - is not enough. For there is a dimension of other-than-earthly activity which also belongs to any citizen of the world: he is bound also to this transcendent realm, and gives up his citizenship at his peril. That is Kafka's first great message: not one of limitation, but one of transcendent connection, a connection which also protects from too great immersion in the ordinary. True, there is conflict, tension, even paralysis in this situation, and you, Mr. Samson, may see the protagonist as defeated by his sadistic author. But the protagonist is not defeated. He is actually aware of the possibility that there is no error in the structure, that if deeply perceived and adroitly handled he may be able to bountifully operate within these strictures, as a poet does within the limitations of sonnet form. It is not stubbornness or stupidity behind his analysis. It is the smell of real freedom.

The second story is this:

"He has two antagonists: the first presses him from behind, from the origin. The second blocks the road ahead. He gives battle to both. To be sure, the first supports him in his fight with the second, for he wants to push him forward, and in the same way the second supports him in his fight with the first, since he drives him back. But it is only theoretically so. For it is not only the two antagonists who are there, but he himself as well, and who really knows his intentions? His dream, though, is that some time in an unguarded moment - and this would require a night darker than any night has ever yet been - he will jump out of the fighting line and be promoted, on account of his experience in fighting, to the position of umpire over his antagonists in their fight with each other."

The most obvious level of this tale concerns man embattled between the forces of the past and the imperatives of the given future. It pictures a crushing, suffocating thought-world miraculously evaded. However you choose to interpret the story, Mr. Samson, it again urges corrective action. True, the night will have to be at its darkest - to provoke, to inspire and to hide - but such a condition is already a regular occurrence in our dark times. And the man who can dream such a jump, such a discontinuity, such a transformation, that man is more than halfway toward its realization. Let Kafka whisper in your ear, and things may evolve which have never appeared before.

Forgive my presumption in suggesting that you concentrate not on the fetters, or the darkness of the night, but rather on the taut potential for situational metamorphosis. Kafka discloses what our blinded eyes have ceased to see, and such revelation has the power to trigger the springs of action.

As it has not yet appeared in English, and would be difficult for a non-native speaker to penetrate, I imagine you have not read BEING AND TIME, the important work of my friend and teacher, Martin Heidegger. It is impossible to summarize this complex work, but let me alert you to its existence, and hope you will spend some time with it when and if it is translated. To whet your appetite, let me simply mention that a key node in the work concerns the experience of "Angst", a word with no English equivalent, approximately rendered by "uneasiness" or "malaise," a feeling of non-normality occasionally experienced by reflective and serious people, perhaps you yourself. Common things may seem uncanny, odd or unfamiliar, as if from some other planet. Heidegger argues that Angst is a crucial experience in pushing beyond the "they-world", a blinding, deafening, stultifying continuum of idle talk and stereotyped expectations. One who is transformed by Angst is given the space to escape such a world - by seeing how strangulating it really is. Kafka's heroes are characterized by nothing so much as Angst, and are therefore given an opportunity to transcend denied to most people. Inasmuch as the reader identifies with these characters, they too, are asked to see the world as unheimlich - uncanny, but also etymologically "not-at-home", and themselves as no longer unquestioning members of the "they". Kafka's animals are the supreme metaphors of potentially redemptive self-alienation. The animal metamorphoses you mention - into "apes, dogs, moles, mice - even insects" are not simply "regressions" - these characters are adventurers out of the "they-world" into the the possibility of other experience and deeper understanding. There may be many "unresolved interpretive furies" and "unproductive hypotheses", but Kafka's writing would not be "true" were it otherwise.

You may be interested in Heidegger's understanding of the fruits of Angst, painful as they may be. Angst draws out, e-ducates, the authentic self, which then interacts with an authenticated world via Sorge, or care, both caring-about and caring-for.

Again, again at the risk of being presumptuous, let me say that you seem to be a caring person, perhaps just by nature, or perhaps after having experienced some kind of transformative Angst. My counter-suggestion to you is that you be the one

to re-evaluate this extraordinary prophet and teacher, and to
engage him not as an enemy, but as a friend. "An enemy," as the
Russian proverb says, "will give in, but a friend will argue."
Kafka never does give in, does he?

I remain yours sincerely,

Hannah Arendt

What a nice, thoughtful letter! Gregor was not half so interested in
re-evaluating Kafka as he was in seeing what this Heidegger was about.
He realized Professor Arendt had been unaware of his native tongue,
and had assumed he could not read the text. But surely he could —
if only he could find one. Like Kafka, Gregor had trouble giving up,
giving in.

Book emergency! Realizing he had little chance of finding the German
original in Santa Fe, or, for that matter, anywhere in German-hating
America, G brought an announcement over to the Daily Bulletin Office
that very afternoon:

WANTED: A BOOK OF A PHILOSOPHER MARTIN HEIDEGGER CALLED
APPROXIMATELY "BEING AND TIME" ("SEIN UND ZEIT"?) IF ANYONE OWNS
SUCH BOOK, I WOULD APPRECIATE TO BORROW IT FOR A SMALL WHILE.
THANK YOU. GEORGE SAMSON.

Next evening, returning from work, he found a note in his mailbox:

I HAVE A COPY OF SEIN UND ZEIT. IT WILL BE MY AMBIVALENT
PLEASURE TO PRESENT IT TO YOU AS A GIFT - IN THE GERMAN SENSE.
VICTOR WEISSKOPF.

A curious note, but there it was. Whatever one may say about the Los
Alamos community, it did not lack high European culture.

Vicky Weisskopf was an Austrian theoretician, a longtime resident of
Germany, who, fleeing the Nazis and the war, had emigrated through
Copenhagen (with Bohr), Zurich (with Pauli), and had finally taken up
citizenship in the United States, teaching at Rochester and Stanford. In
1943 he was recruited for Site Y by his old friend from Göttingen days, J.
Robert Oppenheimer. When Gregor came knocking, he and Ellen invited
him in for the book — and a glass of wine.

"So, my friend, you've got the urge for mystical Teutonic death-deviltry?"

"No — I just got an interesting letter from a woman who recommended the book."

"Who is that?" asked Ellen.

"Professor Hannah Arendt. Do you know her?"

"Of course we know her," Weisskopf said. May I see the letter?"

"I have it at home. It was an exchange about Franz Kafka. But she mentioned *Sein und Zeit*, and I though I would look at it."

"Well don't look too hard. What did Nietzsche say? — "When you look too long into an abyss, the abyss also looks into you."

"Yes. 'Whoever fights monsters should see to it that in the process he does not become a monster.' And then that line about the abyss. But what has this to do with Heidegger? Professor Arendt thinks he holds the key to Kafka and to life."

"To her life, perhaps. Hannah Arendt was his lover."

"How do you know that?"

"It is, as they say, well-known in German university circles.

"She didn't mention that."

"I'm sure."

Ellen, a Dane without her husband's immersion in academic politics, took off for the kitchen to prepare a snack. Weisskopf got up to fetch the book.

"Well, there you go. It's yours. You may keep it on the condition that you never bring it back." He handed the black book over.

"Thank you. What did you mean in your note about it being a gift in the German sense?"

"Gift. Das Gift. Giftig."

"You mean poison? Poisonous? I thought *Kafka* was poison."

"Like unto like."

"How so?"

"It is not for me to tell you how to understand it. But I can give you some facts. Do you know anything about Herr Doktor Professor Martin Heidegger?"

"No. I've been away from Europe since 1920."

"And it's true these things don't seem to concern the American press. I understand. That book came out in '27, I believe. George Placzek brought it to my attention, gave it to me."

Gregor examined the volume in his hand: *Jahrbuch für Philosopie und phänomenologische Forschung, Band VIII.*

"I tried to read it several times at the end of the twenties," Weisskopf continued, "but it was hard, and there wasn't enough time to really study it. I knew only a little about Heidegger then, but I soon found out more than enough: The man is an absolute Nazi."

"Why, what...?"

"I was living in Berlin in '32 and early '33. The bands of brown-shirted students were roaming the streets, beating up Jewish students — or anybody that looked Jewish. My office looked out on the university courtyard — a front row seat. The police didn't interfere, of course, and more than once I had to pull a Jewish student into my office so he could escape through the back door. Heidegger was put up for University Rector, but the faculty resisted. The students took them on — these same violent Nazi students, clamoring for their man, Heidegger. I'm not sure how many of them knew exactly his politics, but he was a young, radical professor, extremely popular with all those students fed up with academic conservatism. They wanted to ask the big questions, to overthrow traditional thought. Heidegger's lecture notes were being circulated in mimeograph — they seemed truly revolutionary. The more the faculty was threatened, the more the students were for him. And he was for them, demanding active participation at all times — active participation from all militant philosophy students! Discipline. Service. He replaced Husserl at Freiburg, and as Hitler rose, so did he. In May of '33 he was appointed Rektor of the University. His inauguration address was so important it was printed in the *Berliner Tageblatt* — and we knew where things stood."

"What did he say?"

"I can't quote you chapter and verse, but it became the bible of Nazi university reform. It was about self-determination of German universities, and need to develop leaders to bring Germany to its spiritual destiny — the German radical students who were already marching. So-called academic freedom had to be expelled because it was, he thought — I remember this phrase — 'no more than taking it easy, being arbitrary in one's inclinations, and taking license in everything.' This is academic freedom?? The most extremist students had to lead the faculty to discover its real destiny in service to the state. He ended by quoting Plato: 'All greatness stands firm in the storm...' The language was Nazi language — stupid and obsequious, heroic nationalism, the general, empty ravings of a party hack in power. This, from the genius author of *Sein und Zeit!*"

"What did he do as rector?"

"What did he do? He expelled all the Jews on the teaching staff, he made every faculty member fill out a questionnaire on his racial origins and take an oath about his racial purity, he made the Nazi salute obligatory before and after class, he organized a University Department of Racial Matters directed by the SS, he took all financial subsidy away from Jewish students and gave it to SA and SS militants, he set up mandatory classes on racial theory, on military science, on German culture... Let's see...What else?"

"Thank you. That's enough."

Ellen brought in a plate of crackers and cream cheese, but G was too upset to eat them, and took his leave as soon as was polite, his "gift" trembling in his claw. The mid-January sky showered him with Heisenbergian cosmic rays as he made his short way home from Weisskopf's, placed the questionable book down on the table, and lay down in the straw to think.

****

For all of Weisskopf's vehemence, Gregor was still curious. More than curious: he could swear he felt a definite force, pulling him toward the black object on his table. How could he reconcile the two opinions of Weisskopf and Arendt? Vicky was one of the most widely educated Europeans on site, a gentle man of culture, an excellent pianist. She was a major thinker — he had heard of her. Maybe she was his lover back in her student days, when, in the twenties? But why would she be still so enthusiastic now, after his Rectorship, in light of his Nazism? He had to at least look between the covers. He opened the book at random: "*67. Der Grundbestand der existentialen Verfassung des Daseins und die Vorzeichnung ihrer zeitlichen*

Interpretation.""67. The Basic Content of Dasein's Existential Constitution, and a Preliminary Sketch of the Temporal Interpretation of it." Better start at the beginning.

Like Vicky, he found the reading hard, even as a native speaker. It was not just that he had been away from the language for many years, and was superficially rusty. Heidegger's strategy seemed to involve destroying or digging under, around and through the everyday language which formed a concealing crust over the problem he was pursuing. Gregor decided that on first reading he would skip the parts that were too complex to easily follow. Still, and in spite of the noisy party going on at Fuller Lodge, he was able to make a first beachhead in the difficult terrain. Surprisingly, it was for him the most intense of page-turners.

He read of Heidegger's fascination with *Dasein* as an object of investigation which might reveal the nature of Being itself — not the collection of qualities that different beings manifest, not the grammatical convention, the empty copula of "The ball is blue", but "is-ness" itself — what "is" is — behind all manifestation. "Reveal' — in the way that Arendt had used it — creating a clearing in the world's "hiddenness" so that pure Being might be experienced. *Dasein* seemed for Heidegger a specifically human characteristic, humans — the beings that inquire into *Dasein* — but he knew it was broader than that, for it seemed to relate even to him. *Dasein, da-sein,* there-being. But where is "there"? In some abstract, German philosophical space? No! There is here, in the world. *Dasein* was all the possibilities G was in all his relationships with people, objects, events in his everyday world. This seemed potentially rich, perhaps even rewarding. Thank you, Doktor Arendt.

The language was strange, twisted, violently hyphenated as only German can be. There were new, made-up words existing in neither German or English — like *nichten*, "to nothing". He learned that not only he, but everyone, had been "thrown" into the world, so that *Dasein* was a *Geworfenheit*, a "thrownness", into the infinite facets of "thingness" and "factness", and that because of our deep association with things, and others-as-things, we come not-to-be-ourselves. Gregor's flesh tingled under his carapace. He read Heidegger's intense portrayal of *Dasein's* self-estrangement in "publicness" in which every kind of spiritual priority is suppressed in a leveling down of sentiment and expression, in which "every secret loses its force" as "something that has long been well-known." The passivity and even barbarism of the "they", were just extensions of their everydayness, bearing no moral responsibility and no ethical guilt.

Gregor needed to take a breather from such searing intensity. He took a five minute stroll under the cool sky. The party at the Lodge seemed to be winding down. He thought of the *Daseins* inside, enveloped in their small-talk, in the prefabricated flux of conventional sentiment and mindless curiosity, indulging in what Heidegger was now characterizing as "inauthentic life", an inevitable and distinctive component of "being-in-the-world". He felt distant from them, and in this distance was aware of his *Angst* — a repudiation of his *Dasein's* "theyness". Did he need further alienation from his fellow creatures? Nevertheless, the book called to him, and he returned to its perusal, refreshed.

"Inauthenticity" — bad? No, necessary, Heidegger explained, as if preternaturally commenting on Gregor's recent thoughts about the Fuller partiers. Alienation was positive because *Dasein*, when made aware of its loss of self, was motivated to strive to return to authentic being. "Fallenness" into "facticity" was a absolutely necessary precondition for the struggle toward true *Dasein*, toward repossession of self. It reminded him of the *felix culpa* of the Christians, Adam's "happy fall" which set up the ongoing drama of human redemption by God. But here, there was no "God", only a call to authenticity.

And then — there it was — the term he had been looking for, the condition he had been wanting to know about since reading the letter: *Sorge*, care. Care seemed to be the relationship between the inauthenticity of being-in-the-world and the striving for *Dasein*. How tantalizing this was. It seemed it might answer questions that had flitted, ghostly, through his heartmind, never standing long enough to be posed. We feel *unheimlich*, Heidegger says, "homeless", "unhoused" in *Angst*, and *Dasein* reacts by anchoring into a *Dasein*-for, *Sorge*, "care-for", "concern-for and -with", a concern for others something like solicitude — all in moving towards a larger *Sorge*, a caring-for, an answerability-to Being itself, a Being that transfigures beings. Desire and hope are the reaching out of Care, a reaching out toward freedom. Gregor felt inundated in a newly-discovered reality of his own essence: I care, therefore I am. Care, says Heidegger, is the primordial state of *Dasein's* being as it strives towards authenticity.

Years of unadmitted pain seemed to melt away as Gregor reconceived his own story in the bright light of this black-covered volume. This was respite larger than another walk under Orion's sword, and he plowed on, ecstatic, to Part II, the section on Time, with its central image, the punchline as it were — the section on "Being-towards-Death." His joy-ride came to a screeching halt.

Sein-zum-Tode. Being-towards-Death. According to Heidegger, *Dasein* can achieve wholeness only when it faces its "no-longer-being-there", its *nicht-mehr-da-sein.* There is nothing with more potential for authenticity than one's own death. No power of "theyness" can take away this fundamental truth — that all authentic being is a being-toward-its-own-end. Heidegger quotes a medieval homily which Gregor had often heard in Prague: "As soon as man is born, he is old enough to die." Death is perhaps the identifying phenomenon of life: *Dasein* cannot "be" without its end.

The they-world is not unaware of this phenomenon, and has created many evasions of authentic death: euphemisms, social taboos, medical optimism and death-talk. Gregor thought of his friends working in the "Gadget Division", creating a death machine without equal in the history of the world, yet never — never! —mentioning the word. No Dead Christ realism here! A true being-toward-the-end, says Heidegger, is one which continually tries to keep in focus its own finitude "in an impassioned FREEDOM TOWARD DEATH — a freedom which has been released from the illusions of the 'they'" Freedom. Freedom. Gregor had never felt so strongly the chitinous fetters which bound him. Being-towards-death was the absolute condition of freedom.

And here Victor Weisskopf's voice came to him, in an I-told-you-so aria on Teutonic death-obsession, images of Dr. Lindhorst, the operating room table, Hans Holbein, the *Leiermann*, the *Liebestod*. But even within this morbid miasma he still felt the inalienability of his personal death as a profoundly bracing, even liberating, awareness, and in the uncertain glimmer of the end of night, he read about *Dasein's* authenticity manifesting in conscience, summons and resoluteness. In resolutely projecting itself forward toward its own free death, *Dasein* attains its personal and social destiny. The 7:25 AM siren reoriented him to everyday space and time in all its fallenness. "Oppie has whistled," as Fermi was wont to say.

****

At the 5:30 go-home-for-supper siren, Gregor trudged out of D-Building, the center of plutonium work, bleary-eyed from lack of sleep. Since West Mess was serving steak that night, he thought he'd eat at North Mess, as it would be a lot less crowded — and head home to hit the sack. He was just raising potatoed fork to mouthparts when the fire siren shrieked and the loudspeaker cried, "FIRE IN THE TECH AREA! FIRE IN THE TECH AREA!"

The North Mess crowd went ashen. It was everyone's greatest nightmare, an event so potentially catastrophic that all except Gregor — whose job it was — had relegated it, like *Dasein*, to the remotest parts of their minds. There was a rush to the coat racks; people bundled up and ran towards C-Shop where the flames were raging, just inside the Tech Area fence. Frantic MPs were struggling to keep the area clear, while children ran under their linked arms. The Administration Building with all its records was right next to the fire. Would it catch? The fire-fighters seemed to be making little headway. Had there been a wind, the whole town might have gone up in flames. The roof of C-Shop collapsed.

Gregor found himself huddling next to Genia and Gaby Peierls.

"Thank God there's no wind tonight," he said.

"All that water doesn't do bit of good. Perhaps sabotage, you think? *Bozhe moy*, thank God is not D-Building."

Though his relationship to the *Bozhe*-Deity was unclear, Gregor found himself in silent, but fervent Amen.

"Where are the SEDs when we need them?" Gregor wondered aloud.

"Stuck in barracks for goddam infraction of some goddam rule," Genia answered. "SEDs would be good! Look at wasting of all that water."

After more than two hours, the flames flickered and died, and the freezing populace, reeking of smoke, went back to their homes, a few insiders chastened by the thought of what might have happened had the nearby plutonium burned, melted and scattered itself on ashes to be breathed.

When Gregor got home, he found a Western Union envelope tacked to his door.

It was good the censors had already gotten to it, as he might have been too tired to open the envelope. The telegram read WARNER CHOCOLATE CAKE RECOMMENDED STOP LEO. He fell asleep with his overcoat on, pondering its meaning.

51. No Piece Of Cake

He half-awoke to the smell of smoke. In the vagueness of alpha-state he confused his spacetime with that of the White House kitchen cabinet, the southern smell of burning flesh, Mrs. Nesbitt burning feather dusters...and then, no, the world was his chicken coop, his own chicken coop in Los Alamos, and, located with scanning antennas, his own overcoat setting off his neural smoke alarm. The 7:25 siren again framed up his still slightly ragged reality, and he noticed the telegram, yellow against the creosote floor.

WARNER CHOCOLATE CAKE RECOMMENDED STOP LEO. Well, that was easy, even this early in the morning. Go down to Edith Warner's for some of her chocolate cake. But too straightforward, Leo. Not good cryptography. Now why go for chocolate cake? Was this just another Szilard ha-ha? There was only one way to find out.

At noon he asked if he could borrow my car, and took an extended lunch break from his task of checking C-shop cleanup for hazards. Edith and Tilano had no phone, so a short trip down the mountain was necessary to arrange a place for dinner. When he arrived, Edith had his chocolate cake all ready. How did she know he wanted it? In fact, he hadn't come for cake, only to make a reservation. Gentle, but firm as usual, she asked him to wait in the small bed- and sitting room that faced out to the east, the room she saved for talks with friends. Gregor was honored to be thus ushered into her personal life. Like most of her guests, he was mildly intimidated by her quiet strength, her efficiency, her determined neatness. He sat on the bed and tried to understand this woman through her environment.

Low ceiling with hand-hewn *vigas*, whitewashed adobe walls. Tables under each window and, on the north wall, a desk between two book-shelves. Except for the Bible and the few art books, Gregor recognized none of the titles. On the top shelves, Indian pottery, a Navaho doll, a pair of candlesticks. On the desk, a tiny white stone carving. Gregor got up to examine it more closely. It seemed like an insect, a scarab, a beetle — per-haps even a blattid. Was this their secret bond? A call to attention? Did this intensely quiet woman have secrets to reveal?

Gregor sat back down again, feeling furtive, embarrassed by this glimpse of what he took to be a private, mysterious icon, almost as if he had come across her brassiere or a pair of underpants. He waited quietly, sitting on the bed, staring out the long, sliding windows toward the Sangre de Cristos, studying the play of light and shadow on their snowy walls.

Edith returned with a cup of tea garnished with a thin lemon slice and a spicy clove — and a plate with the largest slice of her chocolate loaf cake G had ever seen served up. Like a true modern Puritan, she usually denied herself, while indulging others — but in moderation: her cake was usually served in half-inch slices. This portion was fully three inches thick.

"This is an awfully large piece," Gregor observed, as politely as he could, not wanting to reject her kindness.

"You look hungry. Your coat smells of smoke. Did something happen?"

Gregor began to describe last night's fire.

"Better drink your tea while it's hot," Miss Warner suggested.

The visitor sipped his tea, and after a while found himself describing another fire he had witnessed as a child in Prague, a synagogue burning in Josefov, the Jewish ghetto, perhaps by dint of arson.

Miss Warner listened quietly, asking occasional questions. When Gregor put his tea-cup down and picked up his fork for the cake, she said she had to help Tilano, and left the room.

What a strange woman, Gregor thought. So polite and friendly, yet so hidden. He sucked on the luscious cake, cold from its storage in the snow, let it fill his mouth space, then sipped the hot tea to melt and dissolve it, and wash it deliciously down his gullet. As you probably know, roaches do love chocolate cake. The third time his fork cut the surface, it was stopped by some hard object inside. Was it a nut, a large, unbroken piece of chocolate? G felt around its periphery, then exhumed a film can from its cakely vehicle. Leo! You nut! Even more surprising was the obvious inference that Edith Warner, Edith Warner of the trim shirtwaist dresses and upswept gray hair, the quiet, unflappable, a-po-litical Edith Warner was in cahoots with Leo Szilard on this — what? — trick? — communication tactic? — espionage? He didn't know what to call it because he had no idea what was in the can. It sounded packed when ticked by claw.

Gregor wiped off the container, stuck it in his pocket, and finished the tea and cake. Not a balanced lunch, but it would surely do for today. When Edith did not reappear, he assumed she was being discreet, and decided to repay her in kind. He walked out into the dining room, and peered into the kitchen, where she and Tilano were arranging canning jars on a pantry shelf. "Thank you for the cake," he called in. "You're very welcome," she said. "Thank you for the news and the story. 'You're welcome.' "I pay you for the cake..." "No, thank you, it's already paid for". "I hope to see you soon," he said, and walked out to the car.

G was conflicted about whether to report right back to C-shop, or to stop at his room to inspect the contents of the can. High curiosity won out over responsibility: he drove right to my house, entered his shed in back, and locked the door behind him.

The film can was densely packed with three onion-skin sheets of sin-gle-spaced typing, extractable only with the help of a cuticle scissors, which left some puncture wounds in the thin sheets. He unfolded them, smoothed them out, and settled down to read. Before revealing the con-tents of this communication — which was, yes, from Leo Szilard — some context might be helpful.

Leo Szilard was the man Gen. Leslie R. Groves was born to hate, "the kind of man," he once said, "any employer would have fired as a trouble-maker." [As if Szilard had not dreamed up the concept on which Groves' whole operation was based!] For his part, one of Szilard's deepest instincts was to question authority — and "stupid" military authority in particular. The conjunction of these two had all the makings of *opera bouffa*: The Unstoppable Force meets The Unmovable Object.

One way an unstoppable force defeats an unmovable object is to go around it — and Szilard continually went over, under, and to the side of Groves' head — several times, via Einstein, to the President. Generals do not like this. In a 1946 interview, Groves commented that "Only a man of Szilard's brass would have pushed through to the President. Take Wigner or Fermi — they're not Jewish — they're quiet, shy, modest, just interested in learning. Of course most of Szilard's ideas are bad, but he has so many. And I'm not prejudiced. I don't like certain Jews and I don't like certain well-known characteristics of theirs, but I'm not prejudiced."[33]

Prejudiced or not, Groves kept a wary eye on his nemesis, at one point drafting a letter labeling Szilard an "enemy alien", and proposing that he "be interned for the duration of the war." That this was not done was probably due to the questionable clarity of files such as this from Army counter-intelligence:

> The surveillance reports indicate that Subject is of Jewish extraction, has a fondness for delicacies and frequently makes purchases in delicatessen stores, usually eats his breakfast in drug stores and other meals in restaurants, walks a great deal when he cannot secure a taxi, usually is shaved in a barber shop, speaks occasionally in a foreign tongue, and associates mostly with people of Jewish extraction. He is inclined to be rather absent-minded and eccentric, and will start out a door, turn around and come back, go out on the street without his coat or hat and frequently looks up and down the street as if he were watching for someone or did not know for sure where he wanted to go.

It would be hard — even for Groves — to find a jury to convict. The general had several times tried to get Szilard to sign a document promising "not to give any information of any kind relating to the project to any

33 transcript of Groves interview, March 8, 1946, Szilard Papers

unauthorized person," but even though Szilard had initiated a campaign for self-censorship and secrecy among nuclear scientists, he refused as a matter of principle to sign such a statement — of course because Groves had asked.

Thus Gregor was about to get involved in a dynamic which was larger, of longer standing, and of more moment than a single blattid, sitting alone at his table, might have realized.

The cake-papers read as follows:

27 January 1945

Dear Samsa,

Your letter of 20 December received through Trude and much appreciated. Alsos evidence sounds compelling, and Heisenberg's remark definitive. One might have expected the housepainter to harness German Wissenschaft more aggressively, but I also imagine him saying Nein! to any project that might take longer than the ever-receding "two more weeks" he thinks it will take to win the war. Self-limiting megalomania.

With your news in hand, I have drafted a petition to Roosevelt to be signed by scientists here in Chicago, and chez vous at Site Y. I will gather signatures at the former, if you will take care of the latter. Einstein has agreed to provide me with a letter of introduction to the President so that I can personally present the petition, and the point of view of those most capable of considering the implications of our new weapons.

However small the chance might be that our petition may influence the course of events, I personally feel it would be a matter of importance if a large number of scientists who have worked in this field went clearly and unmistakably on record as to their opposition on moral grounds to the use of these bombs. Of course you will find only a few people at Y who will be willing to sign. We will have more here, since we are revving down, and have some perspective, while you are revving up, and have less. Scientists tend to be confused about "moral issues."

Please read carefully, and return a copy with comments via

the same channels. I will then send a final draft. I hope you are doing well at 2,400 meters. How are your red cells? Do you have red cells?

Best,

LS/MFT

The petition followed:

A PETITION TO THE PRESIDENT
OF THE UNITED STATES

Discoveries of which Americans are not aware may greatly affect the welfare of this nation in the near future. The liberation of atomic power places in your hands, as Commander-in-Chief, the fateful decision whether or not to sanction the use of atomic bombs in the present phase of the war against Germany or Japan.

We the undersigned scientists have been working in the field of atomic power. Until recently we have had to fear that the United States might be attacked by atomic bombs and that our only defense might lie in a counterattack by the same means. Today, with the immanent defeat of Germany, and the apparent non-existence of any German or Japanese bomb program, this danger is averted and we feel impelled to say what follows:

The war must be brought speedily to a successful conclusion and attacks by atomic bombs may very well be an effective method of warfare. We feel, however, that such attacks on Japan could not be justified, and ought not to be made at any time without seriously considering the moral responsibilities involved.

The development of atomic power will provide

the nations with new means of destruction. The atomic bombs at our disposal represent only the first step in this direction, and there is almost no limit to the destructive power which will become available in the future. Thus a nation which sets the precedent of using these newly liberated forces of nature for destruction may have to bear the responsibility of opening the door to an era of devastation on an unimaginable scale.

If after the war a situation is allowed to develop in the world which permits rival powers to be in uncontrolled possession of these new bombs, the cities of the United States as well as the cities of other nations will be in continuous danger of sudden annihilation. All the resources of the United States, moral and material, may have to be mobilized to prevent the advent of such a situation. Its prevention is at present the solemn responsibility of the United States—singled out by virtue of her lead in the field of atomic power.

In view of the foregoing, we, the undersigned, respectfully petition: first, that you exercise your power as Commander-in-Chief to rule that the United States shall not resort to the use of atomic bombs in this war unless the terms imposed upon Japan have been made public in detail and Japan, knowing these terms, has refused to surrender; second, that in such an event the question whether or not to use atomic bombs be decided by you in the light of the considerations presented in this petition as well as all other moral responsibilities which are involved.

Gregor was impressed by this effort. He checked the clock, then placed the sheets under his bedstraw and returned for the afternoon to inspect the nooks and crannies of what was once C-shop for radioactive contamination. But as the clean-up crew seemed protectively dressed, as per his morning's instructions, and the meter readings were quite low, as hoped, his mind began to drift back to the task Leo had assigned him: how to get the signatures. It seemed the fastest and most powerful route might be to go from top to bottom. Oppie's signature on the first line would do more to induce others than hours of his own begging one-to-one. True, he had only a draft version, but it seemed fine to him as is, and perhaps Oppie might have some suggestions he could forward to Leo. From all he knew of Oppenheimer — his ascetic yet caring life, his depth of thought, his wide-ranging culture, his fundamentally religious and poetic worldview — Gregor was certain of a sympathetic response.

Which only goes to show that blattids, even the most perspicacious and sensitive ones, may have a simplified view of human *Dasein*: Oppie was outraged.

"How dare you pressure the President?" he said after perusing the draft. "Do you think he doesn't know all this — plus far more about the military and political dynamics than you do? What makes you think scientists have any right to influence political decisions? Do we have special, relevant knowledge here? No protesting or fiddling with politics is going to save our consciences or our souls." He knocked his pipe out into an ashtray, and took his feet down from the desk. "Want to know something? I personally think it would be best to drop the damn thing as soon as possible to give the public a real picture of what they're dealing with — assuming it works."

Gregor had never seen — or even heard of — Oppie dressing someone down à la Groves. A questionable honor. He felt like a bug under the great man's wrath, and left the office with his papers and an ambiguous, perhaps servile, nodding of the head.

He thought of all the things he might have said. He thought of quitting the Project. He thought of becoming a spy, of giving information to the international community, or at least to the allies; he thought of a direct appeal to the American people. Yet on reflection, he realized that Oppie had not, even in his fury, prohibited circulating the petition. What a strange, driven man! Groves would have torn up the paper and warned him about spilling one word of it. He could hear his voice: "I'll have you executed for treason!" But not Oppie. A more nuanced relationship to power.

In his mailbox on the way home, Gregor found the following note:

```
Samsa, I'm sorry I blew my stack at you today, but I
still believe I'm right with regard to policy. I saw in
the Bulletin you're looking to read Heidegger. I would
suggest you do the Bhagavad Gita as a chaser, esp. XI:12
. JRO, the Sanskrit Mole.
```

Gregor, of course, had read the *Gita*, but was not so schooled in chapter and verse as to recognize offhand the reference. He and I never spoke of any further *Gita* research. I assume from knowing him that he had somehow procured a copy and studied what needed studying. It is only these many years later that, in quoting the above note from his files, I felt compelled to check. Instructing the reluctant warrior, Arjuna, the god Krishna counsels renunciation of desire and relinquishment of any fruit of action. Then, and only then, will authentic death emerge — a part of XI:12's cosmic effulgence:

If the radiance of a thousand suns
were to burst into the sky,
it would be like the light of the Great Spirit
in the true majesty of his form.

52. Rite Of Spring

We called it "the Little Green Schoolhouse." Some with finer color sense called it "the Bilious Green Schoolhouse." But the institutional color was a trivial flaw in a beautiful state-of-the-art building built, unlike our housing, for the centuries. The school had been conceived by a university of Minnesota education professor who had fantasized a radical high school for brilliant children of brilliant scientists, and if a school building alone could be *summa cum laude*, this would be it. Anchored in cement poured into rock (a Corps of Engineering tragicomic spectacle of by-the-book construction), it housed well-lit, well-equipped classrooms and laboratory space looking out on mountains and athletic fields fairly screaming *mens sana in corpore sano* — a worthy, updated successor to Ashley Pond's "Los Alamos Ranch School For Boys". But a school is not a school building. It is an interaction between students and teachers, and in the real world of Site Y, the former were too young, and the latter were too few.

It may be hard for a culture saturated with white-haired scientific icons to conceive that the average age of the Los Alamos sage was twenty-seven. To be a parent of a high-school age child, the typical Los Alamos family would have had to begin breeding at age eleven. Only the most senior scientists had junior-high aged children, and these were few. Much to General Groves' despair, most couples used the high mountain air and the free medical care to begin their families. This situation was captured in a celebrated piece of arrhythmic Los Alamos verse:

The General's in a stew
He trusted you and you
He thought you'd be scientific
Instead of just prolific
And what is he to do?

Well, two things he had to do were to hire an obstetrician, and to build more day-care facilities. Another was to adapt the school building to an elementary school population, with a small amount of space reserved for older "brilliant children of brilliant scientists". And even this upper division failed its utopian plan since the great majority of high schoolers came from laborers' homes with little or no academic tradition. Some of the kids boasted of being expelled from previous schools, many snuck out windows as soon as attendance was taken, almost all raised projectile-hell when left unattended, and achieved the scholarly success one might expect.

The maladroit thinking with regard to students was matched only by the paucity of thought concerning faculty. Yes, there were major academics from all over the world on campus — but they were far too busy to become elementary or high school teachers. Their educated, academic wives were an obvious pool, but in Groves' mania to minimize housing and maximize security, any wife who could work was recruited for the urgently needed pool of secretaries and human calculators. In short, there were only three full-time teachers involved in Central School — and not one physicist. But, as I have said, it was a beautiful building.

Nella Fermi and her friends Jane Flanders and Gaby Peierls were the stars of the small but savvy pre-adolescent crowd. They were not used to being with children of non-academic parents, and so had formed a tight, defensive circle which outsiders condemned as snobbish. The outsiders were right. Nella was the thirteen year old daughter of Nobel Prizewinner Enrico Fermi; Jane, one of the daughters of mathematician Moll Flanders, of *Messiah* fame; and Gaby, the twelve year old intellectually precocious daughter of Rudolf — but more significantly of Genia Peierls, the terrifying-to-some Russian whirlwind. There were no boys their age socially or intellectually acceptable, so they spent their romantic time flirting and occasionally necking with GIs and junior scientists they could not bring home. A proto-dangerous crew.

Gregor was shocked and flattered to find in his mailbox one early spring day, a calligraphied letter of invitation:

The Mademoiselles Fermi, Flanders and Peierls
cordially request the presence
of
Mr. George Samson,
also known as
Herr Gregor Samsa,
to their presentation of
"Images of Change in a Fable of La Fontaine"
at the
Alliance Française
Central School Classroom Eight
Monday, March 19, 1945, at 16:45
RSVP

Gregor wrote back immediately to all three, gratefully accepting. Although he spoke adequate French, his acquaintance with classical French literature was filled with holes, and La Fontaine was one of them.

The "Alliance Française" was a group of precisely three students — Nella, Jane and Gaby — that met irregularly after school with Peg Bainbridge, who had taught French at Radcliffe, and Françoise Ulam, a native speaker, both of whom were too busy to teach. Besides, they reasoned, if any language should be learned by Los Alamos children, it should be Spanish. Nevertheless, the three girls assigned themselves topics and presentations in French, and assigned Peg and Françoise to supervise them. Gregor was the only other adult in the room, and he was eager to learn.

The three girls entered from the hallway at precisely 4:45, as if for a performance of "Three Little Maids From School", pert as schoolgirls well could be, and filled to the brim with girlish glee. They began with a choral reading of the La Fontaine poem *La Chatte Métamorphosée en Femme*, "The Cat Metamorphosed into a Woman", with vocal solos, duets and trios charmingly arranged throughout the text. Gregor could follow well the sense, though their French pronunciation ranged from Northern Italian, to German London, to Amherst, Massachusetts.

It seems a man had fallen madly in love with his cat. His affection was so deep and his prayers so fervent that Fate – *le Destin* — granted him his dearest wish, that she metamorphose into a woman and become his bride. (Shades of Pigmalion!) And a loving bride she was: never was man so completely adored. The enchanted groom looked forward to the wedding night with his beloved wife, the cat-no-longer. In the midst of marital bliss, a group of mice began gnawing away at a mat in their bedroom, and the good wife sprang out of bed and pounced upon them. What must the poor husband have thought?

La Fontaine's moral: once things have set in their natural forms, Nature scoffs at any attempt to change them. Neither sticks nor stones will force a change in natural inclination. *Jamais vous n'en serez les maîtres./Qu'on lui ferme la porte au nez,/ Il reviendra par les fenêtres.* You'll never be Nature's master. If you push it out the door, it will climb back through the windows. A delightful image, and probably true. Gregor resolved to read all of La Fontaine.

But now the scenario abruptly changed as the maidens called "Exhibit A, Mr. George Samson, aka, Herr Gregor Samsa to the stand!" Nella set out a stool for him at the front of the room, next to the teacher's desk. The adults looked at one another, surprised and wary. The three girls pulled classroom chairs up to surround him.

NELLA

Mr. Samson, *comment vous appelez vous?*

GREGOR

My friends call me "G". You may call me G. My French is not so good. Can we speak English? Or German?

GABY

We can speak German.

JANE

I can't speak German. We all speak English. We should speak English. Mme. Ulam, Mme. Bainbridge, will it be all right to speak English for the questioning?

NELLA

Seminar, not questioning.

JANE

For the seminar?

FRANÇOISE ULAM

But does Mr. Samson want to be questioned?

NELLA

Oh, yes, he was invited. He said he wanted to come.

JANE

And look, here he is.

PEG BAINBRIDGE

For?

GABY

For a seminar on *La Chatte*.

GREGOR

It's all right, Peg and Françoise. I don't know much about *La Chatte*, but maybe I can help.

NELLA

Ah, but you *do* know much about *les insects, n'est-ce pas?* And metamorphoses?

There was a moment of embarrassed silence. Where was this going? Even in the tight, smart community of Los Alamos, Gregor's class affiliations (*Insectiva*) were rarely openly discussed. Still, he felt, there was really

666

nothing to be embarrassed about. He belonged here. He even had a white pass and could enter the Tech Area.

FRANÇOISE

Gregor, are you sure you want to...

GREGOR

I'm fine. Yes, Nella, I have certain insights into insects and metamorphoses.

GABY

Do you think it is really possible for a human to fall in love with an animal? Not love an animal the way I love Shard...

JANE (helpful)

Her poodle.

GREGOR

Yes, I know Shard.

GABY

...but "in love" — moony, swoony, luney, smooch, smooch, smooch...?
The girls giggled. Gaby had fallen in latest love last week with one of the GIs, a mounted MP guarding the Tech Area perimeter. Peg and Françoise settled back for some pre-teenage silliness.

JANE

We want to know if you think that love and sex between species is possible, and whether you would approve of such an affair, even if they were consenting adults and were married. I mean how would he...you know, it's too big.
More giggling, even from the faculty.

NELLA(ever serious)

And would the one who was metamorphosed be able to love the metamorphoser? Wouldn't she hate him?

Gregor felt a wash of sweet, piercing back pain as his heart melted in a flood of Alice, the ball game, the park, their rueful night together, the years of difficult silence since. It was too much to speak of to children. Besides, it was probably not generalizable. He chose to skirt the issue:

GREGOR

The woman in the story seemed to be in completely human form.

NELLA

Maybe only her *mari* thought so. I know some people in love who think their heart's desire is beautiful even if he is ugly as a toad. (A wink at Gaby. Jane blushes.)

GREGOR

No. The poem says the mice didn't fear her anymore because she had changed.

NELLA

But how did she change? Did *le Destin* change her? How would he do it? All at once? Little by little?

GREGOR

She might just wake up one morning changed. Isn't that what your father does — change things? — pouf! — from one thing to another?

NELLA

I don't know what my father does. Did she just pounce on the mice, or did she eat them?

GREGOR

I don't know. La Fontaine doesn't say.

GABY

What would you do?

GREGOR

I don't eat mice. Just like you.

JANE

Why would *le Destin* want to change her?

GREGOR

Je ne sais pas. Fate is strange. Don't you think it's strange you are up here in the middle of the desert?

GABY

Well, if animals can turn into people, can people turn into animals?

NELLA

We already know that.

GABY (asserting her acknowledged higher IQ scores)

We don't. There may be more to Exhibit A than appears. For example, if La Fontaine is correct that inner nature will always assert itself... Mr. Samsa, how long have you...you know... (hand gestures) been this way?

GREGOR(after a quick calculation)

Almost thirty years now.

GABY

That's a long time. How old were you before?

GREGOR

Twenty-four.

NELLA(catching on)

So you have been this way longer than you were that way.

GREGOR

Yes, I suppose so.

JANE (mathemetician's daughter)

Do you think it's possible then that this is your real self, your real inner self?

GABY

And that the other way, the first way, was only a temporary metamorphosis from this?

NELLA

And that once again, as in La Fontaine, we have a beast temporarily changing into a human being, and not the other way round? You see we — I think I can speak for the other members of the Alliance — we're concerned about the opposite — humans possibly turning into beasts, and we thought you...

GABY

But if you are actually the other way, that *this* is the real person...

Gregor now understood what was going on. Here were three beautiful pre-adolescents, each with budding breasts (ummm, they thought) and budding acne (eeeww, they thought), very smart and sensitive, completely naive, and oh so vulnerable to a community of fenced-in young and not-so-young men whom they spent much time "being in love with". No wonder the fable had moved them. Suppose they were to take some GIs, some junior scientists, under their young wings, allow them into their civilizing plumage? Would beasts climb in the windows? Behind the girls' bravado: defenselessness. Gregor turned emptily avuncular.

GREGOR

We all grow and change...

Peg and Françoise, sensing the impropriety of possible girl-talk in such a setting, decided to bring the seminar to a close. *"Allons-y, allons-y, mesdemoiselles. Il fait tard. On peut continuer la discussion. Merci beaucoup, Gregor.* Thank you, Gregor. *Il faut souper. On va s'inquiéter. A presto, Nella; wiedersehen, Gaby,* we continue next Monday, just the Alliance." Gregor off the hook.

The grownups, of course, were wrong — or only partially right. Yes, the girls were worried about the consequences of their flowering sexuality, but more than that they were bewildered and scared about the world. They did know what their fathers were doing. Not the details of course, but they understood that the explosions in the canyons were not lovingly meant. Nella knew the reality of Mussolini and the Black Shirts. Gaby knew the terrors of an evacuated child, separated at seven from her parents. They had seen posters about Hun and Jap beasts. They were savvy enough to know there must be similar posters about Americans.

The global dimension of their questioning came crashing down on Gregor two days later when, on March 21st, Genia Peierls, Gaby's mother, presented and DJ'd her first community dance to the music of her fellow countryman, Igor Stravinsky's *Rite of Spring*. There was, as noted, much artistic talent on the mesa, and even among non-performers, great enthusiasm for concerts, shows, cabarets, reviews, satires and general letting-down-of-the-laboratory-and-military-hair. Thus there had been excellent attendance at Genia's rehearsals over the last three weeks, and on Wednesday night, the first night of Gregor's last spring, performers of all ages far outnumbered the audience. G had known about the rehearsals of course, but because of his dislike or even dread of Stravinsky's masterwork, had chosen not to participate. Perhaps he only feared what the piece might do to him should he become trapped in its powerful jaws. Once devolved, twice shy.

I, myself, love the work, for me a vicarious, defanged invitation to the world below my neck — I who prefer the foxtrot, or when feeling daring and risqué, the waltz, I who have never been in a physical fight, or intentionally hurt anyone or anything. Except for one thing. Since I feel in a confessional mode, it would be less than honest of me not to share it. It is not without thematic connection to the larger tale.

****

Tenth-grade high school biology is not a likely setting for a horror story, but as I look back on it now, it is, besides my tertiary participation in the birth of the atomic age, the activity I most regret. Frogs were the designated victims, *Ranas pipiens*, amphibians that made the girls go yuk and

671

the boys want to show their killer manliness. I was one such fifteen-year old, smart enough to go to the Twin Cities High School of Science, and manly enough to bat third in the lineup. Is it too obvious to observe that such combination of intelligence and bat, science and testosterone, is an ominous one?

They called it "pithing". You picked up a petted, relaxed, trusting frog in your left hand, its smooth white belly facing you, its legs hanging limply down, its eyes wondering what was wanted. With your left index finger you bent its head forward so the back of its neck was exposed. With your right hand, you took a long dissecting needle, placed its tip at the craniovertebral junction, then thrust the needle down into the spinal canal. The victim's legs would stiffen, its bladder discharge, and its eyes go quickly blank. Then you would twist the needle, reaming out the spinal canal much as Joseph K's assassins twisted the knife in his heart. Like a frog, like a dog. The once-frog then became a "preparation" to demonstrate some trivial biological trick — like a still-beating heart — and then to be tossed unceremoniously into the trash. But the girls were "squeamish". They needed the smart, fearless boys to do it for them. And there I was, pithing-king of tenth-grade biology, hero of the damsels, hunter of the condemned, executioner of the innocent. I can't believe now it was me. Where was the "real" John Aschenfeld? Who was the impostor-double, performing — without a conscience — these unspeakable acts? What was my reward? I didn't "get the girl" — I wasn't yet interested. I already had straight "A"s, so my grade was not in question. Surely *Rana pipiens* was the victim — but so was I for succumbing to brutality, so were the girls, for accepting and valuing it, so was the teacher for requiring and rewarding such assistants. How were all these good, even innocent people sucked into such barbarism? Presumably in service to the tenth-grade god of "Science". As I have said before, and repeat at risk of being over-obvious, this story is not irrelevant.

****

I was speaking of the *Rite of Spring*, a ballet and score universally considered a "seminal work" in twentieth century culture, though not always with awareness of the full metaphorical content of this usage. The *Rite* was born in 1913 (the same year as Gregor$_2$ was conceived), and though it was part of a generalized artistic reaction against effete bourgeois culture, it seemed to call forth, with its abrupt, harsh rhythms and remarkable instrumental sounds, it seemed to evoke more than any other work the threat of barbarity lurking just under the surface of civilization. It hit the public like a hurricane: its opening night sparked a riot at the *Théâtre Champs Elysées*. Audiences had never heard anything like this music which could evoke — or admit — an aggressive, chaotic, innate human savagery of uncontrolled primeval force. The work was banned in Stalin's Russia *and* in Hitler's Germany, where it would not do to acknowledge such barbarism already in practice.

The ballet's plot plays out a pagan ritual of pre-Christian Russia, a ceremony to put winter behind and call forth spring: a virgin is sacrificed by stern elders and a primitive, uncivilized mob, a community which propitiates its gods with orgiastic liturgies of cruelty and murder — so that the cycle of birth, growth and death may proceed.

If such distant, prehistoric activity seemed menacing in a civilized European theater, how much closer it might appear here, in the environment of Pueblo culture, where humans and beasts were dependent on the nourishing earth, here where the civilized society on the hill was preparing to embrace gods of such power as had yet to be experienced.

Genia Peirels was well aware of the correspondences. An outsider among scientist wives, she was positioned socially, and by temperament, to see the larger themes of Project activity. Her choreography hid behind the tradition of satirical events at the dance halls, but her goal was seditious — perhaps a call to rebirth, but also a withering comment from an unheeded Casssandra. She and Stravinsky pulled the wool over most people's eyes — certainly over the eyes of most of the performers. But for some few in the audience, Gregor for one, and for myself, cast as "Scribe", dressed in academic robes, and perched over the event on a high judge's seat borrowed from the tennis court, the message was clear enough — and devastating.

The dance was held in Theater No. 2, the larger of the two recreation halls, the one used for school phys ed, Tuesday night colloquia, and pickup basketball. Tonight, the backboards had been covered with camouflage cloth. It is possible that this was history's first presentation in full-surround sound, for although the recordings were monophonic 78 RPMs, Genia had borrowed twelve speakers from various homes and offices, set them up four, four, two and two along the walls, and had the electronics boys wire them up to Rad Lab's biggest amplifier and Moll Flanders' best-on-campus Victrola with mechanical changer. A stickler for details, she had even installed a new needle.

At the 7:30 starting time, there were few in the audience, a cause for some tsk-tsk-tsking by those of us who had arrived promptly. But it turned out that the small audience was the population remnant from the enormous cast milling about the doors, waiting for their entrances. A small audience was a good thing, too, since most of the benches had been commandeered for alternate use by the imperious producer-designer-director.

The house lights went out, and the room was plunged into the darkness of the first evening of spring. Genia, her shadow, projected by the amplifier's tiny red light, seemed accidentally but appropriately monstrous on the south wall. She flicked the lever, the first record dropped, and the eerie sound of a bassoon playing high above its natural register snaked its way into the room, sounding something like music must have sounded before the beginning of time. Here, my notes, as I wrote them by the light of a spelunker's headlamp:

The first of many flashlights come on, its operator dark behind it, and began to slowly explore the room. As more instruments join, erupting arpeggios from the womb of darkness, more flashlights are added, playing out their spidery criss-crossing of sounds and beams and clearings, building to a short riot of calls in unstable light, tune fragments from the depths of centuries, all of which stop short, the lights coming abruptly together at the centerline. Behind them we sense humanity, invisible, embedded in nature, pre-dating the creation of a personal God. The solo bassoon begins its song again, and the pool of light splits in two and slowly edges its two halves upward to reveal the now-bare faces mounted on the backboards: to the east — Oppie; to the west — Groves.

This scenic revelation occasioned the audience's first and last laugh, which I punctuated with the scratching of my scribal pen. What I was noting down, they didn't know. I wrote on like some manic, unstoppable soloist, accompanied by the gears of the record changer.

Although I was merely a "mysterious" scenic prop, I had taken it upon myself as historian to record my own feelings, and those audience reactions I could fathom, as well as the inadvertent behavior of the cast as they went through their appointed rounds. While the military and worker contingent were previously unfamiliar with the work, most of the scientists, and all of the the Europeans, had heard it before, though none were old enough to have seen the ballet which quit the boards in the twenties after two production failures: audiences would simply not accept what they had been asked to witness. Still, the piece had claimed its own in concert version, and became a great favorite of avant-garde conductors anxious to assault the standard repertoire. Gregor had heard it often enough to dislike it thoroughly — but he, like others, had never really imagined it as a stage work, with human bodies as flotsam and infusoria to the sound. What would Genia come up with as a guiding image? At the opening of the second dance, "The Augurs of Spring", her plan began to reveal itself.

Enter Enrico Fermi in chinos and black leather jacket who, with a snap of his fingers, causes a spot of light to fall directly downward in the center of the floor from the one mid-court bulb Genia had left screwed in. The orchestra begins to pulse with accented string chords, mechanical in obsessive meter, but wildly unpredictable in accent, and the first of the *raboti* enters, carrying one of the missing benches. As the worker leaves, another appears with another bench, and another with another, and so on, until it becomes clear that, under Fermi's direction, they are erecting a structure built from benches, a structure similar to the pile he had conceived and created at Stagg Field. A group of eight children, gloved in yellow, enter from the south door, and proceeded to blow up green balloons and insert them into the matrix of benches, just as Fermi's uranium spheres had been cradled among its graphite bricks. This activity goes on through this and the following six dances, utilizing the set-aside benches of Theater No. 2, all the benches of Theater No. 1, a few from North Mess, and a large load of lumber from various construction sites — so that by the end of the first half, "Adoration of the Earth", a ziggurat reaching halfway to the ceiling has been created by the mechanical work of robot-like participants.

While the levels are rising, we meet two major groups of protagonists. Revealed by exposed bulbs of the south door exit light, we see a group of young men in GI uniforms, on hands and knees, being taught by a masked old hag with gray face, huge nose, gaped-toothed mouth, and hair of shredded cloth. From the chicken feet she holds in both hands, one can gather that this is the Baba Yaga of Genia's youth, the nightmare witch of every Russian child. The group moves jerkily to the orchestral pulse, as the wise woman instructs them in divinations. The class intensifies, the jerking grows wilder — and is brought to a halt by a sudden percussion crash. Three young girls — Gaby, Nella and Jane — appear in street clothes at the north door with lit candles flickering, and with their entrance, we hear the first extended melody, an old calendrical Slavic song, as they move lyrically towards the center, the boys' beat still pulsing quietly behind them. The GIs take leave of their cackling teacher and slowly approach the girls, a Russian chorale tune sounding on four trumpets behind them. At the sight of the boys, the girls place their candles in the middle of the rising structure, and staying well separated from them, begin a reactive dance to the male approach. The music self-stimulates and grows to Bacchanalian frenzy, as the boys mock-threaten the three, lunging at them, and pulling them out of their small group into their own larger one. Perhaps these were the very gestures that had frightened *les jeunes filles,* and led them to quizzing Gregor. Here, the first appearance of the male impulsive principle, a succession of string chords and syncopated drum beats. The boys' unclear intentions induces a sexual panic of vociferous brass and twittering woodwind, frenetic horn calls, short staccato ejaculations interrupted each time by heavy single punches which take over the music's texture. The young men grasp the girls — then freeze, as the Victrola arm retracted and side three dropped, a classical Brechtian alienation effect reminding the audience that no matter how involved they get, this is only a show that invites reflection.

With an extended four-flute trill calling up a primeval melody on clarinets, the "Round Dances of Spring" begin, slow and grave incantations which connect the dancers to the huge earth beneath them. A dragging rhythmic figure is repeated over and over as the young men and girls form separate circles of contrasting motion, the males angular, the women more lyrical. The songs become threatening as the male group adds performers with lab coats and flashlights, and splits into two: scientists and soldiers. Three circles spin around themselves while revolving, planet-like, around the rising ziggurat. At a frightening moment, the orchestral pressure triples, and the three groups leap up on the first three tiers of the structure, women above, military next, and scientists on the lowest level, like electrons quantum-kicked to their alloted energy orbits. The slow dance continues, and the men return to earth as the orchestra quiets, while the three girls watch them from above.

Gregor remarked to me that the massive rootedness of this section reminded him of trying to pick up a small cube of uranium for the first time, a shockingly heavy mass that resisted attempts to free it from the earth. Above the girls, the *raboti* kept slowly building as the next record dropped.

Military vs. Science while the workers continue their work: Genia had caught the essential dynamic of the Project. And now there ensued, to urgent rhythmic beating, "The Ritual of the Two Rival Tribes" — competitive dances, rough skirmishes and flashlight-beam duels of blue and white light. The tymps have loosed the rhythm, and eight horns cry out war. As the men stop to breathe, the girls and the yellow-gloved balloon children plead for peace, but there is no stopping the barbaric tubas and loosed testosterone until, in the "Procession of the Oldest and Wisest One", Niels Bohr is pushed in on a high, rolling stepladder used to service the cyclotron. As the orchestra holds a quiet, long chord, and the others tremble, the great Dane descends, spreadeagles out at center court, and kisses the floor. The earth responds with a long, harmonic, triple piano "yes".

With this kiss comes "The Dancing Out of the Earth", an immense energy of life force, in frenzied celebration, drunk with spring, finally freed from its wintry bondage. There is a wild pulse of drumming in three vs. four, with orchestral outbursts and detached off-beat chords. The whirlpool becomes a boiling cauldron as, to syncopated shrieks on brass and woodwind, the dancers in separate, asymmetrical, electrified clumps leap and fall convulsively out the exit doors as the breathless scene ends.

Several things of note: In this last earth-orgy, there were no more soldiers, no more girls, there were no more scientists or workers. All individual being had regressed from personal sensibility to a liberated collective Unconscious. The musical strategy was exactly that of a cyclotron or cloud chamber: dissonant, brief, irregularly formed musical 'objects' were fired off at one another in a high energy field, collided and released their latent energy. The collision of simple rhythmic and melodic cells, set up fantasmagoric interference patterns — waves and particles at once — while the fierce rhythm encased a basic melody in ways that could scarcely be imagined.

The room is dark and silent, the basketball court empty except for the ever-watching eyes of Oppie and Groves, which now in darkness, with no other distractions, glow clearly from their luminescent sclera. The house lights come abruptly on, and Genia walks on stage dressed as a cigarette girl, hawking "Stravinsky popcorn", "Diaghilev yablaki" and "Nijinsky limonad." The audience laughed, and was left to gather in customary groups to discuss the show.

Still in character, I tried to drift stenographically among the conversations. Klaus Fuchs, a German *émigré* and, as it turned out, Soviet spy, was shocked at the dancers' undisguised joy at "the vulgar splendor of war", and felt the music to be a "virtuoso accompaniment to regression". Much as he admired the Russian people he felt "alienated and shocked by the absence of taste so important in the tradition of German music since Beethoven." An American technician's wife asserted she "had never felt so physical," and went around making people feel her carotid pulse. A psychiatrist-turned-physicist felt the work was "dream-aversive" while his conversation partner, a man I did not know, felt that on the contrary, it was quite frightening precisely because it set up "a regressive dream-collective as a positive accomplishment." One thirteen year old boy thought it was "a lot of laughs."

I found Gregor outside, pacing. He seemed anxious, skittish and depressed, but didn't feel he could leave. "Something is coming," he told me, "something frightening and unknown, some coming giant, of elemental force." He would not say more. Surely he was not referring simply to the bomb here, though that too was soon expected. Was he referring to Yeats' rough beast, its hour come at last, slouching toward Bethlehem to be born? Usually transparent, he could become annoyingly cryptic when distressed.

The lights flickered and the audience took its seats again while I mounted my judge's stand for "The Great Sacrifice", the dreaded second half. After initial darkness and a repeat of Genia's unintended monster show in red, the room was illuminated in the murky light of the single bulb directly above the now twelve foot, balloon-stuffed ziggurat. The record dropped like a pellet of potassium cyanide into sulfuric acid. I resume my scribing:

In the dim light, in tensely watchful silence, the youths mill around, melancholy, desolate, to the strange color of muted trumpets and horn calls. An old Russian tune suggests a human world, but clearly we are in the realm of the subconscious, an area of feeling where the palpable and tangible disappear, and where humans, in a gloomy, shadowed world devoid of objects — except for the sinister ziggurat — move timidly, with the caution of uncertainty and fear. The gloomy coloration seems less an expression of mourning for the upcoming ritual murder, than some mood of the unfree — a quiet bleakness of imprisoned creaturehood. And now the three girls enter, trembling, to dance their circle in the mystery and panic of world night as felt by adolescent maidens: it is precisely through them that the strain of nature's growth can be most clearly sensed. They move around the ziggurat, which now seems a sacrificial pyre in the garish light. They move to a languid legato melody on six solo violas, against a background of pizzicato cellos, they rise and fall from tiptoe, dropping their right hands and jerking their heads. Then — eleven huge chords, one of the most threatening moments in music, and they leap up to the first level of the pile. It is time for "The Naming and Honoring of the Chosen One". To ecstatic shrieks on the wind Gaby, Nella and Jane leap convulsively up and down the sides of the ziggurat to chugging, fragmented rhythms. In the chaotic changing of levels, Gaby seems left above, almost randomly chosen. Gaby, daughter of Genia. What was this mother saying? Gaby would be the sacrifice. She looks down at her friends on the levels below, and the hysterical outburst on upper winds and brass express her fearful dismay. But the elders enter, and soldiers, scientists, workers and children gather round the pyre to praise and glorify her.

And now come the priests to evoke the ancestors, a group of eight masked figures, who emerge from tunnels in the ziggurat to surround the scene. Who they are is unclear. One looks, perhaps, like Einstein, one like

Beethoven, one something like Hitler. With a series of declamatory fanfares, the tribe recalls their ancestors in a slow, reflective march. The music pulses quietly, irregularly goosefleshed by shivers on flute and English horn. Moll Flanders climbs the ziggurat steps to kiss Gaby, and in returning to ground, carries an exhausted Jane to safety. Enrico Fermi likewise claims his Nella, and carries her down to safety. The priests march ceremoniously through the crowd to a striding, pounding rhythm, setting up shifting patterns within the mob. The pulsing and shivering returns, bass clarinet dipping down into and back from the underworld, as all face the pyre and focus their gaze on the platform twelve feet above.

Gaby seems to be in a trance, seated alone, eyes closed, on an 8 X 8 platform, a light directly above her head throwing grotesque facial shadows. "The Sacrificial Dance of the Chosen One" calls her with its opening staccato chords in wild, chaotic rhythm, calls her out of a universe of time to a world so rhythmically shattered as to be beyond any countable measure. Her eyes open slowly, and as she tilts her head sidewards, we see her dawning sense of mystery, then horror, then panic in the face of the unknown just ahead of her. Her first odd act is to reach out to the community below, not for help, but to focus their attention — look here and here — to assist them in the celebration of her death. The orchestra begins to bubble with blood-curdling ejaculations — threats and laughter from the erupting forces of nature over which she fatally presides. She is galvanized into twitches and leaps of increasing frenzy, her attention withdrawn from the group below, and ejected out beyond self to the cosmos. Hysterical turns on the violins and piccolos ascend in a nightmarish way, and she begins to spin, to spin more and more dizzily on the unrailed platform — where is her mother, where is her father to catch her? — as time becomes ever more complex and unbalanced, in a mounting, centrifugal confluence of exaltation, ecstasy, sexual climax, sacrifice and death. It is a mad dance, non-dancerly, naive, the dance of an insect or a factory blowing up. At last she falls, exhausted, her *Dasein* dispersed like windblown seed. She tries to rise, but in vain. Her last breath, a tiny gurgle, a little upward run on the flutes. There is a short silence, and then a final convulsive chord, sharp as the blade of a guillotine. The ritual is accomplished.

No one dared applaud. In the stunned silence the Godfaces were raised off the backboards, floated to the center of the room, and tented quietly over the dead young girl, Oppie and Groves in unwonted necrophiliac caress.

That was it. On a budget of less than ten dollars, Genia Peierls had exposed the tragedy of modern being, exposed the barbarism of human life, of our life, the violence of the soul, exposed the cruelty of nature, the community as a hovering sword, the instinctive savagery of a tribe wedded to Eros and Death, and fate — *le Destin* —, powerful, primordial, random, as the ruler of a godless universe, exposed a sacrifice anti-humanistic to the core, a sacrifice entirely without tragedy, the final stage of a power-struggle between nature and humanity.

The lights came on. The huge cast assembled to embarrassed applause, with slight increase as Gaby got up and descended the platform. Moll Flanders presented the three girls with bouquets of spring flowers sent up from Santa Fe. As if rehearsed, the three of them walked over to Gregor, and presented their flowers to him. He was overcome. What did it all mean? Outside, the equinoctial moon shone brightly.

53. April Is The Cruelest Month

On Good Friday, March 30, 1945, a shrunken Franklin Roosevelt limped zombie-like toward his Warm Springs Georgia spa, too exhausted to acknowledge greetings from fellow patients and friends. Three weeks earlier, he had been propped up on the world stage at Yalta, a sagging husk, victim to Stalin's fierce, portentous depredations and Churchill's wry, observing eye:

> *I am sorry to say that I was quite shocked at the President at Yalta.*
> *He did not look well and was rather shaky. I know he's never a*
> *master of detail, but I got the impression that most of the time he*
> *really didn't know what it was all about. And whenever he was*
> *called upon to preside over any meeting he failed to make any*
> *attempt to grip it or guide it, and sat generally speechless, or, if he*
> *made any intervention it was generally completely irrelevant. It*
> *really was rather disturbing.* (Churchill Diaries)

Three weeks earlier, at his fourth inauguration, as he was summoned to take the oath, he had leaned over to Labor Secretary Perkins and whispered, "Frances, I can't." To which she replied, "Mr. President, you must." He took the oath and began his fourth term.

On April first, no fool, he did noticed the white, pink and yellow azaleas praising Easter near the Little White House, his retreat in Warm Springs, Georgia, and the peach trees under Pine Mountain already heavy with budding, pagan fruit. But in church, he dropped his glasses, then his prayer book, and never smiled.

During the first week of April he seemed to somewhat recover his appearance, appetite, humor, and sense of well-being. He began to work on his Jefferson Day speech, look over new stamps, and play with his little scottie, Fala. News from the fronts was good: British and American troops had crossed the Rhine, the Russians were fighting in Berlin, and in the Pacific, American forces had landed on Okinawa, closest yet to the Japanese mainland. He could push war worries to the rear and concentrate on the founding UN Conference scheduled in San Francisco later in the month — his largest legacy to the world. And he looked forward, too, to Lucy's arrival on the ninth, Lucy Rutherfurd, his mistress and love of the last twenty years, the woman for whom he had given up his marriage bed.

On Thursday, April 12th, Lucy's friend, Elizabeth Shoumatoff, was painting a portrait of the president. It was she who reported FDR's last words at a quarter to one: "We've got just fifteen minutes more." HURRY UP PLEASE IT'S TIME. Cerebral arteriosclerosis does not get better. At one, he slumped in his chair, never to regain consciousness. He had been scheduled to attend a minstrel show that afternoon.

Children were the first to hear the news, the flash breaking into their radio programs, the shortest news flash in history: FDR DEAD. Mommies and daddies were next to learn, and the nation quickly gathered in a net of intensity. People remembered where they were when they heard the news.

In Berlin, just past midnight, Goebbels ordered the best champagne from Chancellery cellars and telephoned Hitler, sixty feet deep in the Bunker. "My Führer, I congratulate you! Roosevelt is dead! It is written in the stars that the second half of April will be the turning point for us. This is Friday, April the thirteenth. It is the turning point!" Even in his drugged stupor, the Führer was in ecstasy. His enemy was dead — Roosevelt the "sick, crippled, criminal Jew". Surely this was a sign that the Almighty would rescue the Third Reich at the eleventh hour. There was joy in a joyless place. Goebbel's secretary wrote, "This was the Angel of History! We felt its wings flutter through the room. Was that not the turn of fortune we awaited so anxiously?" It was "a divine judgment, a gift from God."

In this lunatic atmosphere, national leaders grasped at the stars and, amidst the flames of Valhalla, rejoiced in the death of the American President.

It was Eleanor who broke the news to Truman. For a moment a stunned vice-president could not bring himself to speak; then, "Is there anything I can do for you?" he asked. "Is there anything *we* can do for *you*?" ER countered, "you are the one in trouble now." She left for Warm Springs, breaking an appointment for later that afternoon, an appointment long awaited by Leo Szilard. He had something for her — a memo for her to personally bring to her husband's attention, a long memo on avoiding a nuclear-arms race with Russia.

When the news reached Los Alamos, Oppie came out onto the steps of the administration building to be with the men and women who had gathered. Unanimously pro-Roosevelt, they were devastated at the loss. In addition, they were concerned about the Project of which Truman, apparently, knew almost nothing. Would it continue? Oppie scheduled a Sunday morning memorial service for the entire community.

Another death so soon after Good Friday. Another Saturday of groping thoughts and emotions. Another Sunday, with no resurrection. The mesa was deep in snow, blue shadows in soft whiteness, silent, cold, but consoling. In Theater No. 2, Oppie spoke quietly for three minutes to the whole community:

When, three days ago, the world had word of the death of President Roosevelt, many wept who are unaccustomed to tears, many men and women, little enough accustomed to prayer, prayed to God. Many of us looked with deep trouble to the future; many of us were reminded of how precious a thing human greatness is.

We have been living through years of great evil, and of great terror. Roosevelt has been our President, our Commander-in-Chief and, in an old, unperverted sense, our leader. All over the world men have looked to him for guidance, and have seen symbolized in him their hope that the evils of this time would not be repeated; that the terrible sacrifices which have been made, and those that are still to be made, would lead to a world more fit for human habitation. It is in such times of evil that men recognize their helplessness and their profound dependence. One is reminded of medieval days, when the death of a good and wise and just king plunged his country into despair and mourning.

In the Hindu scripture, in the Bhagavad-Gita, it says, "Man is a creature whose substance is faith. What his faith is, he is." The faith of Roosevelt is one that is shared by millions of men and women in every country of the world. For this reason it is possible to maintain the hope, for this reason it is right that we should dedicate ourselves to the hope, that his good works will not have ended with his death.

That sacrifices still to be made — in American souls and Japanese flesh — would lead to a world more fit for human habitation. Such was Oppenheimer's faith which defined and sustained him through the terrible days ahead.

The community was somber; people spoke of their experiences in FDR's America. The Europeans spoke of contrasting experiences in Europe. Laura Fermi told a cryptic story of answering Mussolini's call for all Italian women to contribute their wedding bands to Italy, of the communal emotion of the women in the room as they exchanged gold for government-issued steel.

Gregor had trouble concentrating. The room seemed to spin; he leaned hard against the standing-room wall and gripped the door jamb. Was it emotion over his lost friend? Friend-enemy? Friend-enemy-father? What had he told the Serbers about the President? How he had betrayed his Samsa father in thought and deed! My son the roach — a boast not made by a Jewish merchant. A failure. He was a failure. He had betrayed his other father, Mr. Ives, and seen hog-mind risk run rampant. Had he betrayed his father the Sanskrit mole, now in trouble with security? He couldn't remember. His legs felt twitchy; his arms all trembled; his antenna were flexing wildly under his cap. And suddenly G became aware of a long-standing pain, becoming ever more acute, in the indurated rim of the wound pressed hotly, oozingly, against the wall. He fell forward, grazing the shoulders of two GIs standing in front of him, then flat, prostrate, onto the wooden floor, tock, like some thin board come thwacking down.

****

He awoke strapped onto a bed, if "awake" can describe his swirling semi-consciousness billowing through the infirmary isolation room. Lt. Jim

Nolan, pediatrician, gynecologist, and surgeon, and Capt. Henry Barnett, pediatrician, were at his bedside. For medical and security reasons they had decided against sending him to Bruns Hospital, 50 miles of rough roads from the site — in Santa Fe. For other, less clear, reasons, they had decided to treat him themselves, and not turn the case over to Lt. Thomsett, the head veterinarian.

Intermittent spiking fever, with wide diurnal variation. Increased muscular twitching. Chills. Purpuric sub-chitinous blisters. Arrhythmia suggesting pericardial infection, perhaps endocarditis, general abdominal tenderness (exquisite) suggesting peritonitis, inflammation of the large joints. Diastolic pressure falling, potential for shock. Hemocytopenia, cellular debris in the hemolymph, coagulaocytosis, increased uric acid in the anal Malpighian tubules. Pustular infection and abscess (probably staphylococcal) in preexisting cuticular wound. The diagnosis was clear: septicemia — generalized infection in the circulating hemolymph, probably metastasized from back wound, threatening all organs, potentially grave, requiring vigorous therapy.

Dr. Nolan had drilled an IV route through Gregor's thoracic cuticle, and inserted two central lines in the softer abdominal area. IV penicillin was delivered at 20 million units/day, supplemented with both parenteral and topical streptomycin. In those early days of antibiotics, one could usually get by with such a combination. In Gregor's interior, intoxicating, grape-like clusters of staphylococci sported their last in the hemolymphatic Bunker. The doctors had incised the abscess, drained and cleaned the wound, cauterized it as best they could, dressed it, and hoped for the best.

Gregor's room had "a view of the lake" — actually just Ashley Pond, but one of the few bodies of water in that part of New Mexico. At the steps to the door just outside his window lay Timoshenko, the huge Great Dane-Russian Wolfhound mix whom Gregor confused with Aage Bohr-Genia Peierls, and when standing on hind legs reaching over the top of the window casing, with Cerberus, barker for the Great Tent of Hell, intent on G's attendance.

"...unhealing wound of Amfortas, king over the Waste Land." It was Barnett, going on while changing the dressing.

April is the cruelest month, breeding

Lilacs out of the dead land, mixing
Memory and desire, stirring
Dull roots with spring rain.
The doctor spouted mixed and questionable balm.
"Cruel for the dead," murmured the patient.
"Cruel for the living. Month of highest suicide rates."
Breeding, mixing, stirring; the patient shivered, sipping on slurry.
a little life with dried tubers
He looked out toward the unfocused Blood of Christs.
In the mountains, there you feel free.
Disturbing dreams
HURRY UP PLEASE IT'S TIME
Who is the third who walks always beside you?
Oppie. So elegant. So intelligent.
...the honey of the lightening...that powerful, immortal...flashing splendor — it is that which is the soul; this is the immortal one, this the Brahman, this the universe.

...a land cursed with drought and sterility. Its Fisher King lies helpless, wounded by the Dolorous Stroke.
"The unhealing wound."
What are the roots that clutch, what branches grow
Out of this stony rubbish?
"Worms."
"Larvae, looks like."
I had not though death had undone so many.
Timoshenko's breath clouds the glass, his vast tongue drools spittle down the pane. The monstrous paw beats rat-a-tat thump against the rafters.

A smell of pipe-smoke fills the room. Or is it sulfur? C-shop is burning! I can't move.

A Quester comes to succor the kingdom...
Disturbing dreams
The blunderings of an innocent fool who has it in his power to release the agony.
And the dead tree gives no shelter, the cricket no relief,
And the dry stone no sound of water.

687

"Sitio."
I will show you fear in a handful of dust.
"3 ccs of adrenalin, here."
Burning burning burning burning
O Lord Thou pluckest me out
HURRY UP PLEASE IT'S TIME
The Brahman is the lightning on account of its untying, on account of destroying darkness, untying or freeing one from darkness; the lightening releases one from evil — releases him who has this knowledge that the lightening is the Brahman; because the Brahman is the lightning.

Porkpie hat on the bedstand. He is everywhere, emaciated, knows everybody, everything. He is ferried to the Grail Castle, where he finds the wounded king bearing Grail and Lance. What does it all mean? Funny you should ask. Or shouldn't ask.

"Oxygen. High-flow."

Find his tongue. Now cut it out. The little mermaid so rudely forced. Metamorphosed.

"Goonight."

The snow grows red at Truchas; the cross stretches its arms, ready to go out for the evening
Into the world of gigantic horror
Into the breakdown of civilization
Into the collapse of values
History has many cunning passages, contrived corridors
And issues, deceives with whispering ambitions,
Guides us by vanities.
"Yes, Doctor."
Neither fear nor courage saves us. Unnatural vices
Are fathered by our heroism. Virtues
Are forced upon us by our impudent crimes.
DEPARTED, LEFT NO ADDRESS
Into the desert of the world without God
Into the absence of Christ
Here is no water but only rock

Rock and no water and the sandy road
The road winding above among the mountains
Which are mountains of rock without water
I AM THE ROACH OF GOD CARBONIFEROUS, A LIVING RUMOR
OF ETERNITY.

After such knowledge, what forgiveness?

"A little prick."

He who was living is now dead

HURRY UP PLEASE IT'S TIME

We think of the key, each in his prison

The thunder is speaking,

Datta. Dayadhvam. Damyata.

Thinking of the key, each confirms a prison

The two physicians sit talking in the dark, while Gregor sleeps. Barnett explains to Nolan the nature of the plot:

"Parsifal's spear is a true pharmakon, at the same time poison and cure."

"Only the weapon which made the wound can cure it, eh?"

Gregor hears them far away:

"Only the bomb."

Into deep darkness fall those who follow action. Into deeper darkness fall those who follow knowledge. Thus we have heard from the ancient sages who explained this truth to us.

Sanskrit has ninety-six words for love.

In the deep night, Alice comes to kiss the wound, and make him whole again..

****

By April, Berlin was defended only by an army of motley volunteers — the Hitler Youth, boys from twelve to sixteen, and the Home Guard — men who were divided into two categories: those with and those without weapons. Morale was low to non-existent. Party members and police cadets set up roadblocks to prevent people fleeing, and scoured cellars for deserters. Lampposts were festooned with corpses labeled "I hang here because I am a defeatist", or "I hang here because I criticized the Führer", or more plaintively, "I am a deserter and thus will not see the change in destiny."

Hitler, as everyone knows, was in his Bunker. But this Bunker was not the secure space capsule of common myth. It was a small air-raid shelter, built quickly to hold an emergency few from the Chancellery, a completely deficient communications center, its few phone lines running through the central Berlin exchange, a claustrophobic den with inadequate water, sewerage, ventilation or power, badly planned, badly built, a ridiculous place to choose as a command center, its only virtue being, as a sarcastic Soviet colonel was later to remark, that it was "near to the shops."

No spiffy SS center this, with shiny boots crisply clicking down hallways. It housed — or rather hid — a commander-in-chief who in person could have commanded neither the respect nor the obedience of his troops. Hitler had been stricken by some rapidly progressive, debilitating, Parkinsonian-like disease, whose symptoms were consistently described in the diaries of those closest to him. Prematurely aged, grossly weakened, stooped, partially paralyzed and uncontrollably shaking, he had become a food-stained, urine-soiled caricature, incapable of writing his own signature, barely capable of reading a wall map even with his glasses. A man often melancholic, an impotent insomniac, sometimes barely able to mutter his wishes, he was still capable of vindictive ragings. He was allowed to lie in torpor for days, like some mud-caked hippo or crocodile, isolated from outside circumstances, cynically manipulated by opportunistic sycophants who, on the one hand, consolidated their power, and on the other, remained slaves to their slavering master. Here were the cream of the German military indulging a corporal from another era, listening to his irrelevant rants and obvious inaccuracies, all against a backdrop of impending disaster. They knew Hitler was incapable of carrying out the simplest of military operations; they held him in utmost contempt. Yet out of habitual subservience and a sense of patriotic duty, they continued to help him destroy their fatherland, carrying out his orders, putting into practice ideas that all acknowledged to be military madness, from an atmosphere of general filth and squalor.

By choosing to remain in the Bunker, Hitler had deliberately abdicated responsibility for the conduct of the war. Overwhelmingly afraid of retribution from his own people, fearful of a revolt, or of being handed over to the Soviets humiliatingly alive, on April 30th, the landscape painter Adolf Hitler either took his life, or was murdered by his Bunker associates. Evidence and testimony is conflicting as to details. His new bride, Eva Braun, and his large Alsatian, Blondi, shared his fate.

Roosevelt and Hitler, the arch-enemies of the century, both stricken, both dead.

54. The World As Will And Won't

Though gaining strength, and outwardly involved in his on-going, continually frustrated, safety work, it was clear to me that by June at the latest, Gregor had made his decision. He seemed simultaneously pregnant and more opaque, as if he were growing, inside the chrysalis of self, another organism, with other goals, which would moult and hatch in the final metamorphosis he had planned.

Our friendship afforded me no special privileges: we spoke often, as always, but there was a veil between us, a withdrawal of candor on his part which would brook no inquiry. "Are you all right?" "Yes, of course." "Is there anything bothering you?" "No, nothing." And he may have been disclosing a subjective truth: from his point of view, pregnant with death, he was all right; nothing was bothering him."

Yet how to explain his June project of "Trials", as he inscrutably called them. Were these trials as in "trials and tribulations"? Or was he putting a host of soldiers and scientists on trial? My own suspicion, based on his spiral notebook, is that he was doing something else — testing the icy waters of death with trial suicides, using a slow but enlightening method.

The "Trials" project began shortly after his second major Oppie encounter. On the morning after an intense, late-night session with Teller, Gregor found a note in his mailbox from which the discussion contents may be inferred:

Samsa,

First of all let me say that I have no hope of clearing my conscience. The things we are working on are so terrible that no amount of protesting or fiddling with politics will save our souls. But I am not really convinced of your objections. I do not feel that there is any chance to outlaw any one weapon. If we have a slim chance of survival, it lies in the possibility to get rid of wars. The more decisive the weapon is, the more surely it will be used in any real conflicts and no arguments will help. Our only hope is in getting the facts of our results before the people. This might help convince everybody that the next war would be fatal. For this purpose actual combat-use might even be the best thing. I feel I should do the wrong thing if I tried to say how to tie the little toe of the ghost to the bottle from which we have helped it to escape. ET

Unfortunately, the Hungarian, for whatever reason — perhaps to win some sort of security points — had sent a copy of this out-of-context communication to the boss, who summoned Gregor to his office that same day.

"How's your meeting?" asked the boss.

"Which meeting?"

"'The Impact of the Gadget on Civilization' meeting. The one you've been postering for."

"Oh, that hasn't happened yet. It's this Friday." Oppie — who knew every detail of every activity on site — was playing dumb. "Will you be able to come?"

"Samsa, I think there's something you don't understand. I'll explain it to you in five words. Want to write them down? The atomic bomb is shit. You understand? The atomic bomb is shit. This is a weapon which has absolutely no military significance. It will make a big bang — a very big bang — but it's not a weapon which is useful in war."

"You mean it's too terrible? Won't be accepted — like poison gas?"

"Too terrible. Too difficult to make. Too expensive."

"So why go ahead now?"

"The politicians want it. They don't spend two billion dollars every day. Your colleagues want it — in case you haven't found out. You don't put in seven days a week of pregnancy, eighteen hours a day for two years without wanting to see your baby born. And you know what? A great discovery is a thing of beauty, don't you agree? Our quiet, binding faith here is that knowledge is good — good in itself. And it's an instrument for our successors, who'll use it to probe elsewhere, more deeply. It's an instrument for technology, for human affairs...."

He put out his pipe. "Sorry for the smoke." Gregor could see him metamorphosing from Hyde to Jekyll before his very eyes, and was waiting for a quote from the Gita — in Sanskrit, of course.

But the quote never came. After a long silence, Oppie simply dismissed him, and went off "to a meeting". He had been in many meetings in the last month — mostly in Washington, along with Fermi, Lawrence and Compton, as part of the Interim Committee — the group designated by Secretary of War Stimson to determine whether, how, and where to use the bomb. Pushed by Oppenheimer, over Fermi's too-taciturn objections, decisions had been made: withholding the bomb was never seriously discussed; a "demonstration blast" was dismissed as being too iffy — it should be dropped without warning on a real military/civilian target — and as soon as possible, before the Soviets became involved in the Pacific. As Secretary of State designate Jimmy Burns had instructed the new President, "the bomb might well put us in a position to dictate our own terms at the end of the war." Gregor knew nothing of these meetings — perhaps a good thing.

It was shortly after this most recent encounter with Oppie that Gregor began his little flip note-pad. He labeled it, matching the printing on the paper cover so that it read "DEATH BY A THOUSAND CUTS SPIRAL NOTEBOOK". It contained what I imagine were quotes from people he had asked to sign Szilard's petition, or had engaged in wider discussion of the ethical questions around the bomb. I have it here.

DEATH BY A THOUSAND CUTS
SPIRAL NOTEBOOK

1 June. A demonstration is not worth serious analysis. Why give away the element

694

of surprise? It would be empty fireworks. Only the destruction of a town would be incontrovertible. IIR (Theoretical)

1 June. If God hadn't loved bombs, He wouldn't have created Japanese. PT (Theoretical)

1 June. It doesn't keep me awake at night. JRR (Gadget)

Carousel was the musical hit of the 1945: "If I Loved You" had made the top ten, and when the calender came round, made a two week excursion into the charts. At Los Alamos, it is true there were gorgeous desert flowers. But the burst that brought joy to all educated hearts was — finally! — a large, and ongoing shipment of explosive lenses, the lack of which had delayed testing dangerously close to deadline. Plutonium was arriving in good supply now, Alvarez seemed to have solved the detonator problem, the initiator design looked good in Bethe's calculations, and only adequate firing circuits remained a problem — one that seemed lightweight compared to those already solved. The Faustian spirit was high.

2 June. Who would evaluate a demonstration? The Emperor? He would never understand that new principles of physics had been mobilized. RF (Theoretical)

2 June. Extra people might die as a result of the delay in making arrangements for a demonstration — even if it was only two weeks. You don't want to have extra people die to make yourself feel good, do you? NFR (Delivery)

3 June. Why are people so scared of atomic weapons? I'm making an important contribution to national and international security. I want to make the weapons safe. I don't trust others to do it. Mostly what I work on is making things safe. AG (Ordnance)

4 June. You want a warning? You're not flying the airplane! SSR (Delivery)

Laboring away at the most deadly work of the Project, at Omega site deep in Pajarito Canyon, as far as possible from labs and town, Louis Slotin was manipulating deadly materials with a screwdriver, playing with assemblies — how much material, in what shape, would go critical. He had used uranium all year, designing constructs named Jezebel, Godiva, Honeycomb, Scripts, Little Eva, Pot and Topsy. Now he was working with plutonium.

8 June. I'm interested in the physics. This is the ultimate toy shop. And I love being a Peeping Tom on Mother Nature. BM (Research)

9 June. My ethics is my own business. It's just between me and my God. If I didn't do it, someone else would. JF (SED)

11 June. Hey, we're the good guys. The United States is the good guy. This is a demonstrable fact. We are good guys. It's self-evidently appropriate to do this work. JJG (SED)

A year later Slotin would be dead, the Project's second nuclear accident victim. But on June 12, just in time for that week's colloquium, he tested two full-scale plutonium hemispheres for the first time, and nailed down their optimal configuration.

12 June. I'm not responsible for the decisions about what to do with this. Is the automobile manufacturer responsible for people killed by drunk drivers? CL (Exterior Ballistics)

12 June. Why is it worse to drop an atom bomb than to firebomb Tokyo or Dresden? AAB (Theoretical)

12 June. It's a matter of posturing. Peace is maintained by being too tough to tackle. It's ok to be an idealist, but you also have to be a realist. There's no such thing as an ideal world. RTL (Fermi Group)

With Slotin's hemisphere announcement, Gregor knew his time at Los Alamos was over, and the moment had come to travel south to the Trinity test site, Ken Bainbridge's project, 160 miles down under.

13 June. When I can't look in the mirror when I shave in the morning, I'll quit. RW (Explosives)

Trinity! What a name! Name upon name! An Oppenheimer product, of course, though there are two different stories as to its origin. The most quoted story is that when queried about a code name for site and test, his mind flashed back to a John Donne poem he had been reading the previous night:

Batter my heart, three-personed God; for, you

As yet but knock, breathe, shine, and seek to mend;
That I may rise, and stand, o'erthrow me, and bend
Your force, to break, blow, burn, and make me new.

Plausible, though hardly what ensued, as the three-personed God o'er-threw him a bit too hard. I prefer another explanation, more related to his fierce interest in Hinduism: for Oppie, Trinity recalled the three forms of Vishnu, the sun god — Brahma, the creator of life on earth; Vishnu, the preserver of life on earth, and Shiva, the destroyer of life on earth. It was, I believe, no accident that his famous comment on the Trinity explosion was "Now I am become Death, the Shatterer of Worlds". It was the meta-morphosis from Vishnu to Shiva to which he was referring. In any case, "Trinity"

.

14 June. I like working on problems that are more than truth and beauty, on problems that have an impact on society and its future. For the first time ever I worry about whether my answers are right or wrong. IF (SED)

14 June. If you say "Get rid of atomic bombs," you say "Let's make the world safe for conventional war." PT (SED)

Name upon name. In August, 1944, Groves had approved a test site in the *Jornada del Muerto* (the Journey of Death) Valley, so named for its lack of water — which left early travelers' skeletons bleaching in the unfor-giving sun. Part of the Air Force's Alamogordo Bombing Range, it had the best attributes of any site inspected: Isolated, yet within commuting distance to the Hill, flat for ease of sighting and instrumentation, walled by mountain ranges east and west, thus shielding larger towns from blast effects, and so uninhabitable that evacuation of indigenous population, if necessary, would be minimal.

June 15. I make a bomb. The fact that I make a bomb doesn't mean it's going to be used. I make a bomb, and it has the potential for evil as well as the potential for good. There is sin in the world. A human being can't touch anything without the potential for sinfulness to be attached to it. MN (Gadget)

15 June. So what kind of a weapon would you like? LLR (Water Boiler Group)

697

Gregor had watched the mesa population dwindle as electronics experts were shunted down to wire up the testing devices, and all available SEDs were pulled off the hill to do the early grunt-work. With risk-protocols as safe as they would ever get under General Groves, and with lab inspections up to date, Gregor received permission to temporarily relocate to Trinity as part of the radiation assessment team.

16 June. It's the President and the Congress who's responsible. And the people that elect them. It makes me uncomfortable, but I have to assume that our national leaders know their business and will act in the public interest. ZR (Teller Group)

16 June. If you want to engage in self-flagellation, you can concoct a scenario where what you're doing is pivotal and humanity goes down the drain and all that. TF (Gadget)

16 June. Some day the Russians will build bombs, so we better have them now and stay ahead. DE (Ordnance)

It was already somewhat late. On May 7, the day the Germans surrendered, the group already in the waste land had carried out a trial explosion using 100 tons of TNT, backbreakingly stacked on a platform, the largest intentional explosion in history. For verisimilitude they had buried a slug of Hanford plutonium in the midst of the pile, like a poor wife doomed to *suttee* on her husband's pyre. The blast sent smoke and debris up to 12,000 feet, and was contained there under an inversion layer.

17 June. I don't experience any moral dimension. I just do what I know how to do. If you try to think rationally about this stuff, you can go crazy. EEH (Research)

Scientists found measurable radioactivity only within a radius of thirty feet from the platform. But they noticed that the cloud was carried right over the towns of Carrizozo and Roswell by a 30-mph wind. Gregor was most upset by this and by the unpredictable conditions for the vastly larger real test in July. He felt that if the bomb went off, the physicists might rejoice — but then leave the consequences to the physicians. On arrival Gregor continued his notebook, and plunged predictably into many experiments with Ground Zero sand, putting it under pressure, incinerating tit with a blow torch, dropping it from various heights under different conditions created by fans.

18 June. I'm a bombhead. It's the thrill of the chase. KK (Gadget)

The setups were primitive, but the results disturbing. If the cloud were to rise only 12,000 feet, and radioactive particles were to condense at the same ratio as the 100-ton shot, a large and dangerous amount of radioactive debris might sediment onto nearby towns.

19 June. As long as sinful men control this earth, there will be need to take up the sword. We're just helping to fulfill prophecy. REY (Water Delivery)

19 June. I was in Tokyo. I seen that laid flat, I mean with other conventional-type bombs, fire bombs, stuff like that. War is not pretty, anyway you look at it. BH (Administration)

20 June. Hey. We all die. We're not permanent fixtures here. GJL (SED)

20 June. Let's quit killing each other. Let's find the utopia. But until Christ runs out of patience and comes back, we'll never find it. AR (Ordnance)

Gregor made enough of a stink to have several instruments added to the array buried directly under the bomb tower — enough to study blast, earth shock, and neutron and gamma radiation which might be dispersed in a wind-borne cloud, instruments sensitive and fast enough to relay their information in the instant before they were incinerated. Imagine his complex, partitioned consciousness here! Alarmed and active for the safety of others, he was at the same time sizing up the dimensions of the under-tower pit which would be his micro-second long coffin.

22 June. If you don't work on these weapons, think of all the people you may be endangering by leaving them undefended. HHL (Research)

Armies of construction men were moving into the Trinity site to erect the hundred-foot tower for the Gadget, the jungle of wires to measure its effects, the communication lines and roadways necessary for construction and transport vehicles.

23 June. I was a career military man. I would have pursued the military with or without atomic weapons. It doesn't make any difference to me — atomic weapons or not. TU (Theoretical)

24 June. Anyone who pays taxes is buying this stuff. Am I more involved just because I use my expertise to build atom bombs? LKN (Theoretical)

All personnel rose at five to take advantage of the cooler part of the day. They broke for lunch at noon, for some crude air-conditioning in the cafeteria, or a swim in the MacDonald ranch house cistern.

25 June. We need even-tempered people handling this. Better me than some nut. VH (Gadget)

Temperatures were over 100 degrees in the afternoon; Gregor was not as affected as some. He felt, in fact, more energetic. But like his colleagues, he was tortured by the alkali grit which covered his exposed parts and ate into his chitin. It was inescapable: the cold showers laved him in water so hard as to leave a thorough crust of magnesium oxide only incompletely removable with a towel.

26 June. I don't ever lose any sleep, and I don't want to dwell on this stuff. BB (Water Boiler Group)

26 June. I'm only a small cog in a complex machine, but I try to do my job competently and earn my pay. EEW (Gadget)

26 June. Safe scientists drink in silence. WL (Theoretical)

There were dangers a-plenty. Gregor had placed himself on the crew excavating and laying instrumentation for the Ground Zero pit. In one day, the workers had to deal with two tarantula bites, one scorpion sting, and a rattler who had taken underground refuge during lunch break. The next day, a march of furious fire-ants whose tunnels had been disturbed, a poisonous black and orange Gila Monster, come to see what all the fuss was about, and of course, ubiquitous and venomous centipedes. Gregor thought it interesting to be cast among the anti-*Insectiva* crowd. He found himself swept along by human group-think, a kind of species-chauvinism that, *mutatis mutandis*, could lead to war. His evening showers were as much to cleanse his soul as his body. And equally futile.

27 June. I'm a human being and I don't like weapons any more than anyone else, but this is the closest you get to playing God. SSH (Explosives)

28 June. I don't feel there's any conflict at all. Because one is concept, and one is practicality. KL (Ordnance)

Nightlife was wretched at Trinity. Poker was the big sport. Some GIs figured out that by driving off-road with lights out, they could escape the ever-more restrictive security regs and have a night on the town in Carrizozo or Soccorro — not exactly the big time, but still enough to use their condoms and beer-money. The only problem was that, driving back blind and blind-drunk in the darkest hours of the morning, they would invariably slice through carefully laid electrical connections or low-slung telephone wires — which then had to be (hopefully) discovered and repaired the following day. A special detachment was assigned to make such daily rounds. "Antelopes" were blamed.

29 June. To some extent I believe in the inherent goodness of our country. RY (SED)

29 June. I'm doing what I can to make waging unlimited war dangerous and expensive. It's like holding up a caution flag to humanity and demanding we make peace. BVC (SED)

If he hadn't before, Gregor came to mistrust the military, which did not always protect and serve. Not once, but twice, "dummy" bombs carrying five pounds of high explosives had landed on base camp at night, dropped by crews from the Air Base on their training runs. Lights in the desert at night? Get those varmints! The first time, the carpentry shop went up in flames, the next time, the stables. One could stay in at night (at least until the end), but even daytime was unsafe. One afternoon a B-29 flew lazily over the test site, its tail gunner hunting antelope with a .50 caliber machine gun. A dozen scientists and technicians in his blind spot directly under the plane were almost ripped to shreds. The fruits of secrecy.

30 June. Mother Nature is a mean bastard. She always collects. The only question is who pays and when. She always collects. HD (Theoretical)

The Waste Land. What better place to read Schopenhauer? Forgive me — I am almost embarrassed to report this — but it was almost inevitable. Life does imitate art, especially among the cultured. Yes, Gregor had read *Buddenbrooks* as a youth, perhaps had even re-read it in Vienna during the First War. And yes, he recalled old Senator Buddenbrooks' epiphany reading Schopenhauer's great chapter, "On Death and Its Relation to the Indestructibility of our Inner Nature" — we had once referred to it during a discussion of animal consciousness. Perhaps he was drawn to the book because of the exigencies of Trinity — but he did think to pack it with him before he arrived.

As his known closest acquaintance, I was asked to dispose of his few possessions after the test site broke up. Chief among them, and heaviest, was a large volume, poorly printed on cheap paper, a war-time edition of *Die Welt als Wille und Vorstellung, The World As Will And Idea*. I don't know where he got it. Émigrés? He had not mentioned plans to read Schopenhauer before he left. I stuck it next to my own translated edition thinking some day to try sections of it in the original. It is only recently that, having begun work on his story, I was reminded of its existence (my Schopenhauer project having succumbed to more pressing affairs), and took it out of dusty storage. And there I found a treasure-trove of Gregor's last thoughts, written in the narrow margins, interlinearly, and on small sheets of paper tucked away in its musty care. There were also underlinings of passages he found particularly important or provocative. For my reader's sake, I will try to boil these down to those that seem most important while filling in some blanks for the Schopenhauer-innocent. For surely, if any, this was a philosophy to die by, and dying correctly was Gregor's larger task, not just for himself, but for helping heal the world.

But what *was* the world? Not an unimportant question. For as one can't purify the heart with lens cleaner, one had best know the patient to cure the disease. The world, says S., is a manifestation of the Will — as cloud is manifestation of atmospheric moisture, and lightning of stripped electrons. Whose will? Category error. *The* will. Not like "I want a hamburger", or even "I want sex". Simply Want, without subject or object. The will to existence. The ultimate, irreducible, primeval principle of being, the source of all phenomena. A little hard to accept, but grant the man this premise, and you are swept along for a thousand pages of heady, thrilling, most persuasive prose.

The Will, however, is blind, and needs eyes and intelligence to see. Outside time, space or causality, it needs objectification to satisfy its motion. The world as we know it, is the product of, and the expression of the Will, the objectification of the Will in space and time, the Will operating via the *principium individuationis,* the principle of individuation, creating things in its wake, you, me, nations, atomic bombs, bringing forth intellect to achieve its goals. Intellect — even Oppenheimer's or Fermi's — serves the Will, and not vice versa.

Because the Will is a fundamental unhappiness, an unrest, a dissatisfaction, a striving for a never-achieved goal, it spews forth want, craving, demand, greediness and suffering. The reader takes great pleasure in Schopenhauer's indictment of the state of things, the struggle of all against all, the turbulent division of Will against itself, *homo homini lupus* bringing forth jealousy, envy, hatred, fear, ambition, avarice, and so on without end, the utter misery of the world. The pages bring forth a strange satisfaction, that mere letters on paper could so express deep human indignation, spiritual rebellion against what is, a sense of triumph in the revenge of the heroic Word.

Gregor's enthusiastic agreement with Schopenhauer's pessimist assessment was marked by an unusual density of underlinings and marginal explanation points. I think of him reading these lines in the midst of filth, heat and scorpions, while trying to mitigate a project burgeoning with cruelty and distress.

But his marginal notes concentrate predictably on something else: intellect's seditious denial of the Will, wily intellect, deploring the schemes and weaknesses of its father, finally capable of opting out, a rebel angel refusing to serve an errant master. "Frighteningly austere," he labels it, "but altogether healthful." "I understand Wotan," he writes, referring to Wagner's god longing for his own annihilation. "I have found only one sedative," he writes in quotes (I think from Wagner), "which finally helps me to sleep during my restless nights: it is a sincere and profound longing for death, the total lack of sensation, complete non-existence, the disappearance of all dreams — the only ultimate salvation!" "Love. Death. Tristan. Amfortas."

But unlike Thomas Buddenbrooks, Gregor did not settle for such peace as death had to offer, liberation from the bonds of exhausted individuality, freedom from the impossible role he had been dealt at the beginning of the First Great War. No. Rather, his remarks indicate a rebellious carrying through, a heroic redemption of the mindless whole by the self-knowledgeable part. "REDEMPTION, NOT FREEDOM IS THE GOAL!" he writes, in the largest of capital letters, and on a sheet of graph paper, he sketches the following diagram.

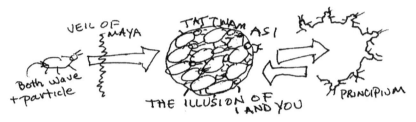

Under the diagram, he writes, "Death is only the setting right of a mistake, a confusion, the disappearance of an imaginary partition, the better to hear you with my dear, carbon to silicon."

Perhaps that was it: carbon to silicon, a carbon-based life form handing over an age to another basic element, silicon, the next analogue down in the Periodic Table, a chemically similar rudiment that would so understand its crystalline interconnections as to thwart entirely the Will and its misguided *principium individuationis*. I am astounded when I imagine Gregor, two full years before the discovery of semiconductors, thirty years before the first practical experiments in artificial intelligence, choosing to symbolically unite himself with the sands of the southwest desert, priest and sacrifice at once.

Perhaps I am over-interpreting.

55. Batter My Heart

On the evening of July 6th, I found a note from Gregor in my box, delivered anonymously by some commuter from the south. It was marked "INDEPENDENCE DAY!", the dateline ostentatiously decorated with crude American Flags and red, white and blue Jolly Rogers, a type of humor I associated more with Feynman than with G. Just another piece of "the new Gregor", I thought.

> Dear John, next time down, please bring the Teller's victrola and their album of Also sprach Zarathustra. Already have permission from Edward and Mici. We're planning a science party down here. You are invited. G

Well. *Très gai.* My impression was that they were already having a science party down there.

I arrived at Trinity site "for the duration" on the 10th, having driven down with Fermi and Sam Allison in Sam's old jalopy. Sam had been chosen to do the countdown for the test, so we stopped in Santa Fe to try to get his old Bulova fixed on the spot, like having a heel repaired. The jeweler couldn't do it immediately, and Sam, frustrated by not being able to pull either rank or historical inevitability, threw an embarrassing tantrum which only trapped him into having to buy a new watch. Fermi played

Chico Marx to Sam's Groucho, while I filled Harpo's silent role — without his talent. Being the last out the door, however, I did hear the owner complain to his wife in the back room, "Goddam longhairs!", and reported this to my companions. "Guess we aren't as incognito as we think," Sam remarked.

A trip with Fermi-Unleashed is a memorable experience. Normally taciturn, perhaps even shy, except when making invariably correct pronouncements on physics, that day he was positively manic. But his hilarity had a sardonic edge, one that would become sharper and more destructive over the next few days. He made crack after crack about radioactive fallout, and about the bomb being far more powerful than anyone had imagined. After experiencing a huge pot-hole-without-springs just south of Socorro, he remarked to Sam, "I guess if we make it down okay in this heap, we'll come out of Trinity alive." He was silent for the rest of the trip.

His jokes were unnerving because, as I have mentioned, "The Pope" was rarely wrong — in fact, never — in my previous experience. Over the past two years, within the physics community, legitimate questions had arisen from legitimate fears, especially concerning the inadvertent ignition of atmospheric nitrogen. The worst-case scenario: the the entire atmosphere going up in flames, destroying all life on earth. Though the explosive magnitude of fission bombs seems child's play today, at the time no one really knew what would happen. The possibility of catastrophe was taken quite seriously — by serious people.

Even in the hazy pre-dawn, early workers were leery of potentially disastrous energies. Back in 1902, Ernest Rutherford, "the father of nuclear physics", wrote, "Could a proper detonator be found, it was just conceivable that a wave of atomic disintegration might be started through matter, which would indeed make this old world vanish in smoke." In the '20s, Arthur Eddington suggested that the source of the sun's energy might be the fusion of hydrogen into helium, and it soon became clear, via $E=mc^2$, that should it ever be triggered, fusion, not fission, would be the more apocalyptic force.

In July of '42, in the pre-Manhattan Project Berkeley days, Teller was already on the trail of a fusion bomb, while his colleagues were discussing more practical fission in Oppie's LeConte Hall office. The Hungarian had been calculating how fission of heavy elements might be used to set off fusion of light ones. He concluded that indeed a uranium explosion could cause fusion in deuterium, but that the generated heat would be sufficient to cause deuterium to react with nitrogen. Nitrogen makes up 80% of the earth's atmosphere: the entire earth might go up in smoke.

On hearing the report, Oppie cut off the LeConte discussions and met with his immediate supervisor, Arthur Compton, head of the the Met Lab in Chicago, to share with him the appalling possibility of total atmospheric or oceanic ignition. Compton urged Oppie's group to continue its calculations, and if the chances for ignition were "greater than three in a million", to call the project to a halt. "Better to accept the slavery of the Nazis than to run a chance of drawing the final curtain on mankind!"

Upon careful re-examination, Teller's figures were shown to be too high. He had neglected to include the heat loss from radiation at the site of the explosion, a student-level mistake! Still, it took several years of laborious calculation to arrive at a real figure, and the project went ahead, with initial re-estimates sliding in at just under the three-in-a-million mark. In short, at the time of Trinity, with all the best minds — Oppie, Szilard, Bethe, Teller, Wigner, Compton and others — working on it. no one was really sure. So Fermi's jokes opened wounds still unhealed.

****

As we approached the Trinity site, we found ourselves following the practice path of the B-29 that would parachute measuring instruments in the final minute of countdown, then photograph the blast from the air, and try to get away. It was truly a heroic (some would say insane) assignment, since no one knew how large the explosion would be, how quickly it would expand, or to what dimensions. All this information was necessary for the safety of the future real-drop plane, but what about the survival of this one? We watched the pilot approach what we assumed was the tower, bank sharply, then attempt to get high and far as fast as possible. By the time we arrived at the gate, we had admired three different versions of this feat. Fermi remarked dryly that Alvarez and Parsons would be on that plane to register the speed and pressure of the fireball, operating and monitoring radio receivers, oscilloscopes, cameras, geiger counters, microphones and transmitters. I had not known that. Funny how one's feelings change when one's own family is involved.

Keeping size speculations going, and fertile ground for Fermi's scare tactics, was a scientists' betting pool, both on the mesa and at the site. You entered for a buck, and the pot would go to the person who most closely guessed the measured yield in tons of TNT equivalent. Teller, ever the enthusiast, had made the most expansive bet: 45 thousand tons. Level-headed Hans Bethe had guessed eight thousand, and cynical Kistiakowsky, the explosives czar, fourteen hundred. He felt he was being optimistic. Norman Ramsey, a Harvard physicist, had made what he thought to be the cleverest bet in the pool: zero.

But it was Oppie's bet — three hundred tons — that was most disturbing. That the project leader, the commander determined to encourage the troops, the man with every detail of the entire project in his head, should guess so low was a slap at all the calculations, all the work, all the hopes that had fueled so many hearts for the last two years. Three hundred tons? At ten million dollars per ton? Why bother? It was discouraging. People didn't talk about it.

Except for General Groves. His spies relayed the betting news, Groves consulted with staff psychiatrists, and with his hard-headed practicality, immediately worked out an alternative chain-of-command, should Oppie break down completely. To minimize the chance, he flew Oppie's old friend I.I. Rabi out from the east coast, though he had no role but "companion" to play at the test. Rabi's arrival in the sweltering desert in a dark suit, homburg, galoshes, and carrying an umbrella was comically reassuring that there was still another world out there.

Gregor scheduled his "science party" off the cuff, for the very night we arrived. There were no competing attractions. Klaus Fuchs, Edward Teller, Otto Frisch and I were invited to appear at 11:45 PM (sharp!) at the little blockhouse 50 yards from the W. 10,000 shelter, a building housing one of the three searchlights which were to illuminate the test and its aftermath. A quarter-moon lit the sign on the door: COME IN, SET

UP VICTROLA WITH STRAUSS SIDE 3, TAKE YOUR SEATS, TURN ON MUSIC. THANK YOU. Had he gone off his rocker? A happening? A performance piece? In 1945?

I opened the door cautiously, and the four of us filed into the small room. At the eastern end was the big searchlight, staring blankly through a bullet-proof window out into the darkness towards the bomb tower. At the western end was a light brown, regulation army desk, and on it a dark brown Gregor, lying naked on his back, lit only, á la Rite of Spring, by a flashlight hanging from the ceiling, three feet above his abdomen. Between the dark light and the light dark were four folding chairs.

There was something acutely embarrassing about this. I'm sure we all felt it, but I, no doubt, the most, knowing Gregor best. We are not normally embarrassed looking at a "naked" animal. In fact, we rarely think of them as naked. It's not just the hair. Is a butterfly naked? An elephant? One would think Gregor's thick, dark, chitinous cuticle would serve admirably for dress. Not so. There were no exposed genitals or private orifices. Nevertheless. Perhaps it was just his position: supine, legs undulating slightly in the air above him, as it was in the beginning — so ultimately vulnerable. We took our seats, and just sat there waiting for something, not knowing whether we had come to the right place. But what other place was there?

Eventually, I remembered the box on my lap. I got up, searched in the dark for an electrical outlet, found one on the north wall, and plugged in the Victrola. Edward took the record out of its album and handed it over to me after making sure Side Three was topside. I put the record on the turntable, and said, partly to Gregor, and partly to the attendant God of Oddness, "Do you want the music now?" It sounded so peculiar, a simple human question, subject, verb, object, so out of place in this dark cubicle, out in the midst of this martian, colonized waste land, with that odd object lying on the table. There was no answer; the legs simply kept waving. What could I do but put the arm on the platter?

The room filled with hiss as the needle traversed the empty grooves around the rim. There followed then a sound that seemed as native to the odd occasion as my voice had sounded foreign, a barely perceptible rumble that seemed to come from the rocks under the sand, from the slow magma under the rocks, a long vibration whispering guttural resonance — perhaps a hymn to the bomb soon to be assembled.

Side 3 of *Also sprach Zarathustra* consists of two sections, *Von der Wissenschaft (sehr langsam),* and *Der Genesende (energisch).* "On Science" (very slow) and "The Convalescent" (energetic). Science. This was a "Science Party". Science here was a slowly growing fugue, the most "intellectual" of musical constructs, the epitome of Learning, a fugue arising, pianissimo, from the depths of the orchestra, reaching out in a long arch towards ever greater, ear-shattering, triple forte wildness. "Science" here was an all-inclusive structure, a fugue subject containing every chromatic pitch in the octave, in common time, triplets and triplet augmentation — all in four grave measures. It lumbered from the simple C major of Nature, to the gnarled B major of Man, a half-tone below, like some underground creature afraid to breathe pure air, a grim Alberich, slit-eyed and clench-jawed, forswearing love and plotting revenge. Science.

I remembered well the Nietzsche passage Strauss was addressing, a struggle I found urgently compelling in my undergraduate years. A "conscientious man" asserts that fear is the original and basic feeling-state of mankind, the source of all its virtues, the fount of Science. Fear of wild animals, including the wild animal in oneself, the "inner beast". Such old fear — refined, spiritualized — is Science.

Nonsense! cries Zarathustra. Fear is the exception. Courage and adventure, and pleasure in the uncertain — *that* is mankind's gift. Stealing the virtues of the wildest, most courageous animals: *that* — refined, spiritualized — is Science.

As Zarathustra's energy overcomes that of the conscientious man, the music quickens. Gregor, beginning in the same supination he must have awakened to on that horrifying morning during the First War, Gregor, here towards the end of the Second, began to wave his legs in startling, unpredicted patterns, almost as if he were spelling mysterious messages in semaphore, finally generating such torque as to flip him off the desk and on to the floor. So Nietzsche's Convalescent:

One morning Zarathustra jumped up from his resting place like a madman, roared in a terrible voice, and acted as if somebody

else were still lying on his resting place who refused to get up. Up,
abysmal thought, out of my depth! I am your cock and dawn, sleepy
worm. Up! Up! My voice shall yet crow you awake!

German-speaking roosters do not say "Cock-a-doodle-doo". Through some strange linguistic contortion, they tend to cry out "Riki-riki-riki". And that is exactly what Gregor did, screeching and bounding nervously around the room, climbing over the walls and ceiling, over the large searchlight, a hair-raising display. The music leapt into completely unexpected flights of fancy, a fantastic dance high in the upper winds, rushing and trilling, while the "Disgust motif" began its feverish appearance until the music, and Zarathustra, and Gregor, all fall down as if dead. After a long pause, seven days in the poem, seven seconds in the score, a rebirth begins which will bring full understanding of their mission on earth — accompanied by one of the most remarkable passages in the orchestral repertoire, astoundingly light, humorous, Till Eulenspiegel once more, and not Death.

Swish-click, swish-click, swish-click. The automatic changer tried to drop the next side, but none was there; Side 3 was all G had requested. He lay, supine again, diagonally disposed on the floor behind us. I took the needle off the record. We sat there in the grotesque light of a hanging, gently swinging flashlight and waited, again unsure what to do. After a pause of perhaps half a minute Gregor, from the floor, recited *"O Mensch, gib Acht!"*, the tremendous eleven line poem which occurs next in Nietzsche, though not in Strauss:

(stroke one)
Oh, man, take care!
(stroke two)
What does deep midnight declare?
(stroke three)
"I was asleep —
(stroke four)
"From a deep dream I woke and swear:
(stroke five)
"The world is deep,
(stroke six)

"Deeper than day had been aware.
(stroke seven)
"Deep is its woe;
(stroke eight)
Joy — deeper yet than agony:
(stroke nine)
"Woe implores: Go!
(stroke ten)
"But all joy wants eternity —
(stroke eleven)
"Wants deep, wants deep eternity."
(stroke twelve)

For the twelve strokes of midnight, Gregor had worked with his right lower leg a contraption previously unnoticed, a hammer hanging upside-down from a cord slipped over a ceiling beam and fastened high on the handle. The reader may easily imagine how by pulling with his toe claws on the latter, the hammer head was caused to strike the metal casing — which emitted not the expected clack, but a surprisingly full, bell-like tone. In this desert where no clocks chimed, it rang out the apotheosis of midnight.

The final bell having struck, G paused a moment, then jumped up, came around to the front of the chairs, leaned back on the desk like an at-ease lecturer, and addressed us directly:

If we shadows have offended,
Think but this, and all is mended,
That you have but slumbered here
While these visions did appear.
And this weak and idle theme,
No more yielding than a dream:
Man is a bridge, and not a goal,
A rope stretched over the abyss
Betwixt beast and Übermensch.
Goodnight, goodnight,
Parting is such sweet sorrow
That I shall say goodnight till it be morrow.

And he reached up behind him and switched off the flashlight, leaving us all in darkness. After several minutes of sitting in silence, Teller decided G was serious about having said goodnight, and got up to leave. The rest of us followed. As I was about to close the door behind me, Gregor said in a low voice, as if to me alone, "Report me and my cause aright to the unsatisfied." Such was the seed which grew into this telling.

Some science party! The partiers drove back to Base Camp stunned and silent after only twenty minutes. Though G must have been quite pleased, his audience dispersed with bare goodnights to its own disturbing dreams. I have to admit I was angry with my friend. Rather than seeing the event as the classic call for help it could have been, I saw it as a self-indulgent celebration of some putative arrival — at the expense of the culture and traditions of the rest of us. Who did he think he was? Nietzsche? The Übermensch? Shakespeare?

We four witnesses, usually united by our musical tastes, seemed to avoid one another over the next few days, as if we had been common witness to some shameful event which would not stand acknowledgment or discussion. I found myself, too, avoiding Gregor in these, his last days. In fact, we never did speak substantively again. He seemed just too distant, too strange. Besides, he was spending much time off-campus with Jim Nolan and Louis Hempelmann, working on fallout issues, consulting discreetly with the Governor's office, and with the mayors of Socorro, Carrizozo and Roswell concerning possible evacuation.

****

Oppenheimer arrived at the site on Wednesday, the 11th, having said goodbye to Kitty and arranged a code message for a successful test. Like many other Los Alamos leave-takings that week, there was an unspoken whiff of "I may never see you again." Embraces were poignant.

That night, in Omega Canyon, at the foot of the mesa, the plutonium ingots were checked and arranged in the vault, and were loaded next day into Bob Bacher's sedan for their destined trip south. Philip Morrison sat in the back seat with two suitcases full of sub-critical pieces, arms draped over each to "protect" them in case of an accident. With a security car in front and trailed by the nuclear assembly team, the portentous load began its five hour trip to Trinity.

Phil and his wife, Phylis, have a regular column in *Scientific American.* I always think of his plutonium trip when I look at their picture each month. Her face is age-appropriate, that of a lovely, deep, elderly woman — which she is. His face, however, scares me no end. The camera does not lie. Phil's is the face of someone brushed by the demonic. Over the years he has been a crucial voice in the the anti-nuclear movement, a prophet demanding social responsibility in the scientific community. But clearly he has been scarred. It's hard to believe that those five hours were innocent.

About eight in the evening, the motorcade turned off a dirt road a mile east of the tower, and pulled up in front of the McDonald ranch house. Its 16X18 living room had been converted by the Army into an assembly site, vacuumed thoroughly of dust, its windows covered with plastic and sealed with tape. Morrison placed the suitcases on a table covered with brown wrapping paper, and removed two hemispheres of plutonium, warm to the touch. Taped to each box were the following instructions:

PICK UP GENTLY WITH HOOK.

PLUG HOLE IS COVERED WITH A CLEAN CLOTH.

PLACE HYPODERMIC NEEDLE IN RIGHT PLACE. CHECK THIS CAREFULLY.

[This, to monitor the neutron count.]

BE SURE SHOEHORN IS ON HAND.

SPHERE WILL BE LEFT OVERNIGHT, CAP UP, IN A SMALL DISH PAN.

****

At one minute past midnight, back at Los Alamos, a second caravan began to move south for a far more dangerous journey. To be "whimsical", George Kistiakowsky, head of X-Division, had wanted to transport the high explosive lens assembly on Friday the Thirteenth. Although not "atomic", this cargo could do far more damage to its carriers should any accident — or even untoward jolt — occur. The men drew straws to see who would ride with it. "Death Wish Movers", they called their operation. Subtitle: "We Move Anything." The cargo was one of two identical assemblies, both zealously supervised by Kisty, who had personally drilled out all the minute cast holes with dental equipment, filled them in with molten explosive slurry, and passed on every one of hundreds of x-ray images. An implosion dress rehearsal was to be carried out on one by Ed Creutz at Los Alamos, and the results called down to Trinity for any last minute adjustments on its identical twin.

The truck with its huge, steel suspension crate crept carefully down the hairpin turns, off the mesa, heading towards Santa Fe. With it were Kisty in a lead car, three jeeps of armed MPs, two sedans of security agents, and a second truck loaded with spare parts: an impressive — and lethal — caravan. Though this was to be a quiet and secret transport, lights flashed and sirens screamed as it drove carefully through any town in the wee hours of the morning, hoping to scare off drunken drivers weaving home late. While there were no accidents en route, the transport did turn out a lot of puzzled sleepers staring out bedroom windows at the supposedly secret mission. By noon on the thirteenth, it had reached the tower after a grueling, twelve-hour, *Wages of Fear* ordeal.

By then, the final plutonium assembly at the ranch house had been underway for three hours. An eight man team in white surgical coats hovered over the hemispheres, searching for holes that might leak neutrons, smoothing down blisters, and rubbing gold foil into any remaining depressions. Four jeeps stood parked, facing away from the ranch house, engines running, getaway cars against the possibility of a slight slip, a moment's criticality. Oppie paced the room until he was asked to leave.

At 3:18 PM, Kisty called from the tower; the explosive sphere was ready for the insertion of the core. The size of a small orange, the 80 pound ball, a whisker away from criticality, was lifted on a litter, and carried to Bacher's waiting sedan. In a cool, green tent hung from the base of the tower, the the core was attached to a manual hoist, lifted above the explosive assembly, and carefully lowered in towards the center. Wind flapped the tent as background to the breath-holding silence. Never before had so much nuclear material been handled, so close to criticality. One jar, one knock, could start a chain reaction. A violent thunderstorm was seen approaching; there was fear a lightning strike might somehow detonate the bomb.

Suddenly, crisis. The core was stuck, unable to reach the center. Someone said "Shit!", and Oppenheimer froze to attention. Bacher quickly figured out the problem: the tube, being cooler than the core, was slightly too narrow. They were left in contact to come to equilibrium, and the whole assembly slid precisely into place, as planned. Bacher had earned his K-rations for the day. After the nuclear crew left, Kisty and his men moved in to replace the charges over the core, occasionally using duck tape to snug up the fit. The re-assembly went off smoothly, the bomb was put to bed at ten, and the exhausted crew went back to camp to sleep or drink off the day.

At eight the next morning, Saturday, the 14th, the assembled bomb began its trip to the top the tower, one hundred feet above the desert floor. The crew didn't want to think about the cable snapping, but a few self-styled "realists" imposed "Operation Mattress," looting three dozen GI bunks, and building a criss-crossed, twelve foot mattress pile under the bomb. Most observers found it amusing. I found it pathetic and frightening. A motor-driven hoist slowly wound the five-ton sphere up the final ninety feet at a foot a minute, several engineers climbing the tower ahead of it, removing platforms so the cargo could pass through. Who knows what would have happened were the wind to have whipped up and knocked the assembly against the sides of the tower?

At the very top, Leo Jercinovic lifted the trap that opened into the three sided shed which would house the bomb, steadied it on through the hole, rebuilt the flooring, and strapped the baby in its cage, a mighty infant, laughably contained. There was no celebration for a job completed: a team of weathermen under Col. Jack Hubbard were now predicting thunderstorms throughout the area for the next two days.

But that was not the worst. The next morning, Sunday the fifteenth, Oppie received a call from Creutz at Los Alamos. The tests on the explosive shell had failed miserably. A nuclear explosion of its Trinity twin was highly unlikely. Oppie got visibly ill; he called an emergency meeting on whether to go ahead with the test the next day. He and Bacher were furious with Kistiakowsky for shoddy work on the explosive assembly, but Kisty was imperturbable. "Have Bethe check Creutz's results," he said. "I'm right. The test results are wrong. I'll bet you my month's salary against ten bucks that it will work." Oppie looked despairing as he shook on the bet.

By late afternoon the final work on the bomb had been done in an electrical storm so violent that Oppie debated lowering the assembly again to the ground. The Gadget was now crawling with wires and switches and cables and looked for all the world like a Gorgon head poised to turn a victim to stone.

A phone call Sunday afternoon filled Oppie's gauntness with energy. It was Bethe from Los Alamos: the Creutz experiments were incorrectly done. There was no reason the explosion should not go off according to Kisty's calculations. Hallelujah! Did Oppie give a little jump?

It was the Sabbath, but there was no rest for the weary. The overcast morning was dedicated to checking the hundreds of instruments focused on Ground Zero: seismographs, geophones, ionization chambers — boxes, meters, dials, transmitters, wires, cameras, microphones, sprinkled all over the desert, many with names out of Winnie the Pooh. Electricians checked Eeyore; physicists, Tigger; radiochemists, Kanga; engineers, Roo — while Death waited above.

Stafford Warren assembled his minuscule fallout team — including Gregor and the weather men — for a noontime briefing. Their main concern was that a radioactive cloud might be caught up in a thunderhead, and pour out swift and widespread consequences. But at this point what could one do other than monitor, and be prepared to evacuate with inadequate forces. All Trinity workers received gas masks, coveralls and booties.

At four o'clock, Oppie climbed the swaying tower in a high wind to be alone with his creation. Did he pronounce it good? Thunder rumbled in the distance as he went over every connection and switch.

Groves, Conant and Bush arrived at five, and Groves immediately began to pester the weather men for accurate predictions. The rain's potential for radioactive fallout did not bother him so much as its capacity to short-out firing circuits.[34]

The weather was deteriorating rapidly. The test was only eleven hours away, and needed to be done in darkness — to be best photographed, and to be out of sight and earshot of sleeping New Mexicans. Teletypes clicked away in Meteorology, planes flew with weather balloons, smoke pots were lit and photographed. Fermi circulated with his own betting pool on whether the explosion would wipe out the world or merely destroy the New Mexico. It was odd behavior, and destructive. Was he trying to cheer people up? What was he thinking?

At dusk, Don Hornig was dispatched to arm the bomb. Alone in the tower, he replaced all the connections from the dummy firing unit with wires from the real one. Leaving the tower, he made sure that the firing switch was open, and its covering box locked. A counterpart switch at the S. 10,000 control center was similarly checked. The Gadget hung over the desert, awaiting its command.

The wind was building; the rain was coming. But a postponement would be calamitous. All energy had been aimed at 4 AM on the morrow. People had been days without sleep, preparing, people who would need to be razor sharp. Still, because of weather, Oppie and Bainbridge were

---

34 In testimony to a Senate Special Committee on Atomic Energy in November 1945, Groves was asked if there were an antidote to excessive radiation. "Senator," he replied, "I am not a doctor, but I will answer it anyway. The radioactive casualty can be of several classes. He can have enough so that he will be killed instantly. he can have a smaller amount which will cause him to die rather soon, and as I understand it from the doctors, without undue suffering. In fact, they say it is a very pleasant way to die. Then, we get down below that to the man who is injured slightly, and he may take some time to be healed, but he can be healed."

besieged with requests to postpone. Groves alone was driven by politics: Truman was waiting at Potsdam for word of results. His comportment vis-a-vis Stalin, perhaps the whole future of post-war relations hung in the balance. For Groves, this test must go, and go tomorrow, as close to schedule as possible. He and Oppie agreed to meet at midnight to review the situation. "Get some rest," the fat man advised the skinny one, and Groves trundled off to a sound few hours' sleep.

Oppie was not the sleeping type. With frayed nerves fueled by caffeine, he sat alone in his room trying to concentrate on the *Gita*. It was close to ten when Gregor knocked quietly at his door.

****

Dear reader, based on discussions with Oppenheimer, I can relay only the gist of what went on in that room at Base Camp. I was not there. But the story falls well into place, and is in nowise contradicted by subsequent evidence or events.

Oppie was as lonely as he had ever been. He received his guest warmly, if with exhaustion. He asked permission to smoke. Gregor nodded. Referring to the book already in Oppie's hand, he was ready, he said, to dissolve the Veil of Maya, to encompass the All in his one small Part, to move in person from Atman to Brahman. Oppie smoked, and nodded. Such metaphysics needed no background. Gregor quoted Schopenhauer, another Oppenheimer familiar, on the inconsequence of individual life or death. "Death," G said, "is the great opportunity to no longer be I." He expatiated on what he called "the wound of I" and for the first time showed the lab director his injury. "How did you get that?" he asked. "My father. An apple." Oppie nodded, construing the words — incorrectly — as part of the myth of the Fall. Gregor spoke of the insect in a cocoon, a being who must cease being what he is in order to be born into his true nature. Oppie rolled another cigarette. Gregor noted the calm with which such an insect dies, giving birth to new life, new ideas, new spectacle. Oppie was had been previously unaware of that calm. "So what can I do for you?" he asked.

Gregor reminded him of their previous discussion concerning Krishna and Arjuna, how he, G, had played the part of the death-aversive prince, and Oppie the part of the Shatterer of Worlds. Now Gregor was asking for the roles to be somewhat reversed, for Oppenheimer to accept Gregor's embrace of death, and to aid him in his goal. "Go on," said the Thin Man. There was a long pause. "I want you," Gregor said, "to smuggle me onto Ground Zero, right now. I have prepared a space under the tower where I can lie among the instruments. I want to greet your child and embrace her."

Outside the silent room the rain could be heard, pelting the tin roof of the mess-hall. Oppie searched Gregor's eyes with his. Never had human gaze so deeply penetrated the mosaic eye. The director felt his own eyes moist over, and Gregor turned, embarrassed, away from too-great intimacy.

"Let's go," Oppie said, got up briskly, grabbed his hat and slicker, led Gregor to his white jeep, and drove out towards Ground Zero in the torrential rain. The MPs waved the familiar figure through the two-mile checkpoint, and in another five minutes they pulled up at the base of the tower. Above, the beast slept quietly while lightning cracked and thunder roared, a cross between King Lear and The Bride of Frankenstein.

Gregor appeared calm as they made their way through the canvas wrap around the tower base. In two interviews, Oppie was unable to characterize his own emotions. "Too complex. Beyond language," was the best he could do. But as usual, he wanted to be cognizant of every detail. Where exactly would Gregor lie in the instrument pit? In what position? Would he be comfortable while waiting? Was there any danger of his drowning if the storm were to continue? Would his presence interrupt any of the instruments or affect the measurements? These last questions were offered not in the spirit of officious administration, but as balm to Gregor — so G would know his plan could be carried out without harming others.

When Gregor was comfortably situated in among the boxes and wires, Oppie wished him well, and said goodbye. "The joy of the worm?" Gregor asked. "The joy of the worm. I don't know what else to say." He reached down and touched Gregor's claw, then closed the trapdoor. He stood leaning on the leg of the tower for several minutes, the rain leaking down his too-large collar, then drove back to Camp. The MPs waved him deferentially through again, without asking where his passenger had gone.

At punctual midnight, Groves pounded on Oppie's door, ready to consult — or rather to be consulted. He had decided, en route to the meeting, that the tower was inadequately defended against last-minute sabotage, and had just dispatched an armed party out into the rain. Two jeeps and a sedan were riding off to the tower — carrying Bainbridge, McKibben, Hubbard, Lt. Howard Bush, head of the MP detachment in the jeeps, and fiercest of all George Kistiakowsky, with machine gun, muttering about Groves' paranoid stupidity. Gregor heard them settle in for the vigil.

Throughout the camp, in the long night, anxious soldiers drank beer, played quiet poker, wrote letters to their sweethearts and wives. A few scientists were compulsively checking their instruments, should the shot be a go. In the blockhouse at W. 10,000, Pvt. John Fuqua checked his searchlight, and was puzzled by the Victrola, and the hammer hanging from the beam. Victrola spelled party, not spies, and since all was well with the light, he decided not to report an incident. He shone his beam over the crisscross of tower girders and the whipping snakes of wires hanging from monster to ground; those guarding the base covered their eyes with their forearms.

Groves complained to Oppie about the doltish weather men who had predicted clearing in time for the test. Since the men were so upset by the failure of their long- and even medium-range predictions, it would be wisest for him to make his own predictions — though weather forecasting was a field in which he had no special competence. Still, someone had to make decisions. Oppie sensed a hidden agenda. Why was the chief meteorologist out there guarding the tower?

****

Let's talk about the weather. I find it necessary to inject a historian's word. Chief Meteorologist Jack Hubbard, in consultation with every group leader, had early on drawn up a list of the best and worst conditions for the test:

```
Best conditions for the operation.
A. Visibility greater than 45 miles.
B. Humidity below 85% at all altitudes.
C. Clear skies.
```

D. Temperature lapse rate aloft slightly stable to prevent dropping of the cloud.

E. Little or no inversion between 5,000 and 25,000 feet to allow cloud to reach maximum altitude.

F. A thick surface inversion or none at all to prevent internal reflections and mirage effects.

G. Winds aloft fairly light, preferred direction from between 6 degrees south of west and 25 degrees south of west. Steady movement desirable to anticipate track of cloud. Horizontal and vertical wind shears desirable for maximum dissipation of the cloud, although such a condition increased the tracking problem.

H. Low-level winds light and preferred drift away from Base Camp and shelters.

I. No precipitation in the area within twelve hours of the operation.

J. Predawn operation desired by the photographic group, although 0930 operation considered best for thermals dissipating the lower levels of the cloud.

Conditions least favorable to the operation.

A. Haze, dust, mirage effects, precipitation, restrictions of visibility below 45 miles.

B. Humidity greater than 85% at the surface or aloft, which might result in condensation by the shock wave.

C. Thunderstorms within 35 miles at the time of operation or for 12 hours following.

D. Rain at the location within 12 hours of the operation.

E. Surface winds greater than 15 mph during and after the operation.

F. Winds aloft blowing toward Base Camp or any population center within 90 miles of the site.

But instead of tailoring the operation around desired weather, Hubbard was faced with a *fait accompli* — Truman was in Potsdam, and weather be damned. July 16th was it. "Right in the middle of a period of thunderstorms," he wrote, "What son-of-a-bitch could have done this?" Everything unwanted was present: rain, high humidity, inversion layer, and unstable wind. None of the optimum requirements had been met. Rain could scrub the clouds and bring down high levels of radioactivity in a small area. Unstable conditions and high humidity increased the chances that the blast itself could induce a thunderstorm. Still, Truman was in Potsdam, and Groves had become the weather man. Such is the pecking order of politics, war and science.

****

At 2:15 Hubbard's men were projecting a lull in the storm, a small possible window between five AM, and dawn at six. Groves seized on the news to announce a definite go for 5:30. The decision made, however faulty, eased the tension, and Oppie seemed to relax with his coffee and cigarettes — until Fermi rushed screaming into the mess hall, fearful of the Camp's vulnerability to radioactive rain, and pleading for a postponement. Evacuation routes were inadequate for the population, he said, and were in any case unusable in the downpour. The Italian Navigator, the Pope, warned of a catastrophe. Groves, sensing Oppie's agitation, sent Fermi away, and suggested that the director accompany him from the madhouse of Base Camp to the relative sanity of the Control Center at S. 10,000. In the face of opposition from those who opposed the possible cremation of their leader, Oppie followed Groves to his car.

At 2:30 AM the storm hit the tower directly, shorting out the search-light, and plunging it into darkness. The photographer Julian Mack sent out a frantic call for soonest possible repair so he could set and focus his cameras. Kistiakowsky grabbed the most powerful flashlight he could find, and in the midst of torrential rain, climbed the slippery, lightning-attrac-tive metal ladder to mid-tower, where he hung on for the next two hours beaming his light toward Mack's cameras. This, from an acrophobe.

At 4 AM, the rain stopped, and the tower guards ended their fright-ful vigil. Joe McKibben had fallen asleep at the foot of the north pier. Bainbridge leaned over him, shook him gently by the shoulder. "Come on, Joe, it's time now." At 4:45, Bainbridge received news of shortly breaking weather. Within fifty minutes, the overcast would be scattered, and wind conditions would hold for the next two hours. He called John Williams at S. 10,000. "Prepare to fire at 5:30."

The final arming sequence began. Bainbridge, McKibben and Kisty would now close all the switches that connected the bomb to firing and timing circuits at central control. The three drove out to a pit 900 yards from the tower, lifted the lid of a half-buried box, and, as Kisty read off the sequence in his thick Russian accent, McKibben engaged the switches that would send automatic timing signals to all experiments. At 4:55 they returned to the tower, where Bainbridge lit the aiming lights for the B-29 pass. Then, both McKibben and Kisty carefully checked Bainbridge as he unlocked the box Don Hornig had checked, and closed the switch, connecting the bomb end of the firing circuit. Not twenty feet away, Gregor listened with fascination to the read-off of instructions.

There was one last step: at the S. 10,000 Control Center, Bainbridge visited the sister box, and threw the switch. Both ends were connected. The Gadget was fully armed, ready for detonation.

****

5:10 AM, July 16, 1945. "It is now zero minus twenty minutes." Sam Allison's voice rang out from loudspeakers strung out across the waste land. No sooner had he spoken than the second phrase of the Star-Spangled Banner, "By the dawn's early light..." blared out, unbidden and unexpected. KCBA, from Delano, California had crossed wavelengths with the Trinity frequency, and was opening its morning Voice of America broadcast. Before "the bombs bursting in air..." the anthem had faded, and was making its way to other etheric realms. The only sound that could be heard was the croaking of toads, and, if one listened ever so carefully, the beating of hearts. One soldier went round back of a trench at Base Camp, and returned muttering, "Too damn scared to piss."

The five minute siren sounded, the five minute flare started up, and fizzled. Many had the same thought: an omen? At zero minus two minutes, Oppie turned to Gen. Farrell, said, "Lord, these affairs are hard on the heart" and gripped a post to steady himself. On Compania Hill, twenty miles away, hundreds of scientists lay on the ground, facing north, away from the site, equipped with blue welder's goggles for protection. Teller wore heavy gloves and an extra pair of dark glasses under his goggles. Bethe was sharing his sunburn oil. Feynman, ever disobedient, was watching directly through the window of a truck, sure that the windshield would protect his eyes from any UV rays. He would be struck temporarily blind.

Base Camp seemed an isle of the dead, with motionless bodies scattered in shallow graves, listening to the hypnotic "Minus 55 seconds...minus 50 seconds... At minus 45 seconds, McKibben closed the switch initiating the automatic timing sequence. At 25 seconds, the music returned — unbelievable! — the "Dance of the Sugar-Plum Fairy" from the *Nutcracker Suite*. Was there ever stranger accompaniment — the delicate chromaticism of a celeste as usher to the nuclear age, surely a pestilent nut being cracked? At 10 seconds a gong sounded — in just the right key. Ken Greisen turned to I.I. Rabi and whispered, "I'm excited now." At 5 seconds, cameras began shooting from the north, south and west, and Sam Allison, distinguished physicist, was seized by fear that the explosion might somehow feed back into the microphone he held in his hand. He dropped it on the desk and screamed as loud as he could, Now!"

****

Desert sand melts at 2,700 Fahrenheit degrees. The temperature at the center of the blast was four times that at the center of the sun, and more than ten times that at its surface. The pressure on the ground below the tower was more than 100 billion atmospheres.

As the fireball prodigiously grew, Gen. Farrell drew in his breath and said, half to his neighbor, half to himself, "Oh, my God! The longhairs have let it get away from them!"

Kisty, blown down by the subsequent shock wave, scrambled to his feet, and, covered with mud, grabbed Oppie from behind. "Oppie, Oppie," he screamed, jumping with joy, "I won the bet, I won the bet! You owe me ten smackers!" Oppie, with a blank stare, reached mechanically for his wallet with shaky hand. "I haven't got it, George. You'll have to wait." The two men embraced.

Epilogue:
Some Considerations Of
The Final Metamorphosis

Gregor's was the most expensive assisted suicide in history. Expensive, and also rich in strands, in complexity, in resonance. After forty years I am still far from a clear gestalt. But while I cannot tie all the threads into a tight weave, I can perceive a loose pattern, an orderliness which may help clarify its meaning.

Defending his role in the August bombings, Oppie once remarked that "the decision was implicit in the project." Looking at the long line of Gregor's path, one might conclude the same thing. For as all life bears death within it, G's unique existence brought forth an extraordinary consummation.

Our culture does not support the art of dying. At one time we understood "the good death" and "the bad death", the possibility of dying authentically, on intimate terms with Death, and the alternate possibility of dying badly, almost inadvertently, a death inessential and false. "Formerly," wrote Rilke, "one knew — or maybe one guessed — that one had one's death within one, as the fruit its core. Children had a little one, adults a big one. Women carried it in their womb, men in their breast. They truly had their death, a death which good work had profoundly formed...and that awareness gave dignity, a quiet pride." And so the poet prayed for faithful dying:

O lord, give each his own death,
a dying which matches the life
in which he met love, thought and misery.

Nietzsche, too, wished to die his own death: not a "detestable, grimacing death, which advances on its belly like a thief", but a death self-chosen: "He dies his death, victorious, who accomplishes it himself."

On the one hand it would seem that Gregor had captured the uttermost prize, a self-chosen, truly-owned, passionate, infinite death, with clear mind, and almost sound body untouched by madness or leukemia. Like Rilke's nun, he would appear to have "plunged into God like a stone into the sea."

On the other hand, his death was deeply problematic. Can there really be an art of dying, a "good death" in this century, in the context of tens of millions of lives intentionally extinguished, and the gaping possibility of planetary annihilation? Can there really be a good death via a weapon of mass destruction? The authenticity paradigm seems desperately inadequate here.

But then one might ask more subtly: just when *did* Gregor die? Was his not a death in parts, expertly accomplished along the way, the bomb being only the final, dramatic, punctuation? An intimate courtship was here, an elegant, graceful dance, with Death disrobing, becoming transparent, and Gregor finally assenting to Death's only word: "Yes". Yes he said yes I will Yes. This was not mass-death, extermination, annihilation, but an I-Thou pact of the most intense kind. No inattention or betrayal here, only an expert leading a willing partner. Fred and Ginger. Death and maiden Gregor.

Perhaps his assent had been tempted by experience, by Double Death. After all, had he not died once before? The first was already a beautiful, clean death, immaculate extinction: the fabric salesman who left no remnant. But then, what did Gregor remember of this, what did he understand? Writing of himself in the third person, G's favorite poet, Rilke, wrote, "If something prevented his dying, perhaps it was only this: that he had overlooked it once, somewhere, and that he didn't have, like others, to go on ahead in order to reach it, but on the contrary, to go back the other way." Perchance, like Rilke, Gregor needed to turn turn back, to revisit his singular moment in an equally singular way.

If the true painter spends his life seeking Painting, and the true poet, Poetry, creating their own goals, means, and even obstacles, then surely — even in the age of mass death — Gregor could be seen as an artist of Life and Death, a journeyman who never betrayed these high powers, his masters.

GREGOR'S SEVEN-SIDED SUICIDE

Faulkner's Quentin Compson was one who "loved death above all, who loved only death, loved and lived in an almost perverted anticipation of death as a lover loves and deliberately refrains from the willing friendly tender incredible body of his beloved, until he can no longer bear not the refraining but the restraint and so flings himself, relinquishing, drowning." Gregor Samsa was not Quentin Compson.

At some point — it's hard to say exactly when — perhaps after the *St. Louis* affair, perhaps after Yoshio Miyaguchi's self-immolation — G began to hear the ticking of his own death's clock, and experience a sense of solitude closing in around him. It was then that his path took on its final trajectory, step by step, trustingly, towards that great invisible border. It was not a surrender, not a simple succumbing to fate, but a conscious act of submission, taken in hand, and made his own. Carl Jung claimed that "the sole purpose of human existence is to kindle a light in the darkness of mere being." Gregor had lit a light that shone even through the immense candlepower of the bomb. While most suicides tend to make death superficial, an act like any other, something to do, G's relationship to death was more exact, a Musil-like combination of "precision and soul", empowering the absence of power — as if in ruptured nothingness there might emerge some luminous power of affirmation.

It seems to me that Gregor's act had seven distinct strands.

1. Despair. All suicide has some component of despair. It may be common personal despondency — a failed love affair, the death of a loved one, the shrinking of one's prospects to zero — or it may be higher level despair — the samurai's noble *seppuku*, the saint's martyrdom *in remissionem peccatorum*. Gregor's was the latter. Jew and alien both, he was

hypersensitive to any mistreatment of "The Other". While his own life might be deemed "successful", the life of a professional operating in the highest circles of power, he remained acutely aware of the plight of the afflicted: the racism — hooded and bareheaded both — of his adoptive homeland; the depredations of the rich upon the poor; the incarceration of innocent Japanese; and most critically the German treatment of Jews, gypsies and "deviants" during the war, and the utter insensitivity of his own Administration in addressing it. If man is wolf to man, it was always "the Other" that was the preferred food. The final blow, of course, was his colleagues' lust to continue working — though the bomb's *raison d'etre* was no more, and the decision to drop it, without warning, on unarmed civilians seemed both arbitrary and cynical. I'm glad he did not live to see the results.

2. Guilt. As sensitive, self-critical, even self-doubting as G was, there was also, as is common, a component of guilt. He knew it was "silly". He sometimes called it "stupid". But he also knew that without his thigmotactic suggestions, Neddermeyer might never have hit upon the implosion strategy, and the whole project might have foundered — completely, or at least long enough for the war to have been less violently ended, and history to have turned out less malevolent. His guilt may have been irrational, but irrationality is part of being human.

3. Buddhist Thinking. My suspicion is that the letter from the dying Amadeus was a short course in Buddhism for Gregor, the analogue to young Prince Siddhartha's encounter with old age, sickness and death. Not that he hadn't understood these issues intellectually before: he was not a student of Spengler for nothing. But Amadeus' communication from Berlin, read under FDR's bedroom couch — an evocative venue — contrasted so ironically with the *Christmas Carol* being sung that it burrowed its way into a deeper level of G's being, prompted a step back from his engagement with the world, and a concomitant semi-withdrawal from ego, per se. His subsequent encounter with Miyaguchi, and the flames of that hero's departure, seared the pattern into his flesh, as it were, and may have served as a model, or at least a spur to his greenhorn Buddhist thinking.

4. Heidegger. A clear turning point, the entrance onto the Interstate, destination Zero, was his reading of Heidegger, and his sympathetic assent

to "Being-toward-Death" as a step toward *Dasein's* authenticity. Though well-warned by Weisskopf, the whole question of Heidegger's nazism did not really come up for Gregor, so struck was he by the truth-force of the work. He of course was not around for the "revelations" which so tarred the philosopher — and justly tarred he was. I'm not sure what G would have made of them. My guess is that he would still have embraced the transcendent center, and discarded the sinful all-too-human husk.

5. Oppie/Schopenhauer/Hinduism was another clear strand, an Ariadne thread out of the maze. That individual death was a mere manifestation of the Veil of Maya; that he, even in his chitinous shell, was Brahman, the universe; that extinction yielded the gift of The Whole — surely this made easier a course which others might have feared to tread. Fool and angel both, Gregor walked it lightly on six legs.

6. Related to that strand is the two-pronged dimension of love — Agape and Eros. For some, the latter must diminish the former. Yet Gregor was innocent enough of erotic bounty to largely escape its toll. Alice was his one love, his one experience of human physical affection, and their one night together was a medium-size slice of the pie of his guilt. But unlike implosion-guilt, it was a slice he would not have done without. Its bittersweet softness coated many rougher elements of his life with a velvety, nostalgic glaze: he was glad he had met and loved, however sad the outcome. And as one cannot love others without loving oneself, so too one cannot love self — enough to renounce it — without having loved others. The Alice affair was Eros' contribution. Of Agape there was no lack. It was "implicit in the project".

7. The Seventh Strand is for me the most problematic. Here G and I simply did not agree. For Gregor, there was a distinct messianic dimension to his mission: "to help save humanity from being bestial," he once put it. He didn't see himself as being *the* Messiah, of course, but simply as aiding in *tikkun*, the healing, repair, and transformation of the world, the redemption of God's creation on earth — the goal of any nice Jewish boy. But being a German-speaking, depth-seeking European, he was also alive to Aryan myths: Parsifal, Amfortas, the Grail, the Waste Land, the meaning of the Unhealing Wound. And he did feel that the unfortunate hole in his back —(I may add in tissue insufficiently vascularized for full repair!) —

was symbolic, was more than symbolic, that it was a sign, a setting-apart, and even a source of power. What could the wound do? It could somehow — illogically — "heal the Waste Land and make it bloom again," and in this thought he found his pride — and I found what little there was of his arrogance.

To me the whole idea was patently ridiculous. The transpersonal dimension of his self-sacrifice was humble, but still megalomaniacal. What possible healing connection could there be between the admittedly magnificent symbol of his death, and its dreadful real-world context? A transpersonal dimension to suicide is vanity no matter where or when or how, a self-imposed, self-deluded struggle one is bound to lose. Gregor's embrace of such primitive thinking led him to imagine that the force of life can only be maintained by the suppression of life — *Rite of Spring* revisited. Nonsense. The idea also led him to the only act of dissimulation I am aware of his committing: his presentation to Oppenheimer that last night was far from honest, I thought, and even baldly manipulative.

Seizing on Oppie's interest in the *Gita*, Gregor made it seem as if he were applying for discipleship to that work, an early initiate, yearning to take a large step along the path of Enlightenment. Actually, he simply wanted his boss to get him past the guards. Can you imagine Oppie's reaction had Gregor said, "I want to commit suicide under the tower in order to help save the world"? The brig — that's what it would have been. The psychiatric service, then the brig — for the duration.

There is a Jewish/Platonic level at which I can understand, and even approve of, G's transpersonal goal: he once spoke to me of what he called "the mission of Noah", his desire to become an "intimate and pure ark of all things, a refuge in which they might take shelter, and where they are not content to be as they are — narrow, shopworn, trapped in life — but where they might be transformed, preserved from themselves, intact." Sounds like Franz Rosenzwieg to me. But he believed it could be. So? So what difference did it make to General Groves, or Richard Nixon, or Ronald Reagan or William Jefferson Clinton? Or to the kids in South Central or the dead babies in Iraq? Et cetera. I won't go into it. As the good Doctor Williams Carlos Williams whispered on his deathbed, his last words of wisdom, "There are a lotta bastards out there." And what, moreover, had

G to offer in this task of salvation? Only his aptitude for termination, his fragility, his exhaustion, his gift for death.

Enough. This too-long, too-emotional critique of Strand Seven threatens to overwhelm reality: the truth was that I found his act enthralling and admirable. Gregor had answered a call to die more profoundly, dreaming perhaps of continuing — inside death — the movement of metamorphosis.

THE HOURS IN THE TRENCH

What must it have been like to lie there between 11 and 5:30, nuzzled among wires and instruments, five hours of listening to the rain, followed by an hour and a half of listening to — nothing? Here I can only conjecture, based on my friendship, my feeling for Gregor's thought and emotion, and some extrapolation of posthumous documents and interviews. At least three themes suggest themselves:

1. Dust unto dust. Gregor used this expression often in the last months of his life, slipped it into discussions that were at first glance inappropriate, but on further reflection provided odd resonance. It was not God into which he plunged. Given his messianic ambitions, Gregor's inward movement was preparation for some manifestation in the *world*, faithful to the fullness of earthly existence. Gregor, Mr. Thigmotaxis himself, was most sensitive to the loving embrace of his environment. And what was the main feature of this high desert? Dust. In spite of the torrential rains of his last night, his pit must have been dry. There was too much sensitive equipment in there for its roof to have been fashioned otherwise. For all the downpour, he had entrusted himself to dust, dry dust, the hot summer dust of the Valley of the Dry Bones. A talmudic voyager, he knew well Ezekiel 37: "there was a noise and behold a shaking, and the bones came together bone to his bone." I am certain that along with his vision of coming-apart, there was a strong expectation of putting-together, of rebirth, atomic matter still conserved, dust to greater dust, *Dasein* to be found again at the pure center of the excessive. After all, this suicide was not a typical act of night, but a patient act of morning.

2. Chrysalis. It can hardly escape the reader that Gregor's descent into

732

the pit before his ultimate transformation smells of insect metamorphosis. Though the word is somewhat ragged by now, a thought which rarely occurs is that the change so well described by Kafka was only the first of a series of polymorphic changes, growing instars evolving toward some radiant end.

I say "toward". But as with all life cycles, there is really no beginning or end. Who is to say that the butterfly is not the egg's way of making another egg? Perhaps the fabric salesman was only butterfly's way of making a more profound butterfly. Or vice versa. Remember Chuang-Tsu's question: "Am I a man dreaming I am a butterfly, or a butterfly dreaming I am a man?"

Most insects have stretch receptors that fire neurohormones when the exoskeleton is pushed beyond capacity. Did G have moral or spiritual stretch receptors which prompted some eccentric molt? What went on physiognomically in those six and a half hours? If beauty is directly proportional to truth, perhaps on that last night he developed splendorous wings, wings like those of a giant Atlas moth. We will never know. "It is the mark and nature of significant truth to stay hidden," Heidegger observes, "though radiant in and through this occlusion." The darkness of night is surer than the light of day.

3. The Animal and the Open. Of this theme I am most certain. It is not the night, it is what *haunts* the night that frightens — and humans are haunted by many things. But here we must recall that Gregor was not entirely human. Why was he so attracted by Rilke's Eighth *Duino Elegy*? Why did he make it the mainstay of his 1918 circus presentations? I refer the reader back to Chapter Five, and G's performance of "*With all its eyes the creature-world beholds the open.*"

Dr. Johnson once quipped that "He who makes a beast of himself gets rid of the pain of being a man." He did not advertise the compensations. Rilke felt that the animal's consciousness put it at great ontological advantage, permitting it to enter into reality without having to be its center. He intuited the consequent sense of inner space — not the inside dimension of any individual being, but the *Weltinnenraum*, the world's inner space, easily perceived by animals, and only with great difficult by humans.

Through all beings spreads the one space:
the world's inner space. Silently fly the birds
all through us.

Why is it so hard for us? Why is the human so cut off from the interiority of the exterior, that extension within, where "the infinite penetrates so intimately that it is as though the shining stars rested lightly in his breast"?

What is outside, we know from the animal's face
alone; for while a child's quite small we take it
and turn it round and force it to look backwards
at conformation and not into that Open,
so profound in the animal's face...

Just as dog can smell what we cannot, and eagle see more sharply, so was G superior to us in his perception of the Open, the vast space of the *Weltinnenraum*. Not only could he see farther and more deeply, even with myopic vision, but his eyes, like our ears, were always open. Without eyelids, he could not leave anything out of himself, withhold himself from any being, or reject any thought — a further dimension of the Open. G's was a life of infinite relations, in a place unbarred to newness — the experience of the Open.

But even an animal "whose Being is infinite for it, inconceivable, unreflective," even an animal which, "where we see the future, sees everything, and sees itself in everything and safe forever" — sometimes that animal too bears "the weight and the care of a great sadness,"

For that which often overwhelms us clings
to him as well, — a kind of memory
that what we're pressing after now was once
nearer and truer and attached to us
with infinite tenderness.

I have heard G quote these lines many times, harking back to his Vienna days, or surfing the sorrows from then to now. Yet there, in the desert night, in the darkness of the gash, waiting for the infinite blow, I am certain he embraced the Open, and was embraced in return, happy at last. This I know, even in the dryness of my bones.

THE LOGIC OF GREGOR'S PATH

I think back on my own life: from high school to college to gradu ate school to post-doctoral work to assistant, associate, and full professorship, a predictable, linear train of academic events, interesting in its way, but compared to Gregor's, profoundly boring. His path looks more like Brownian motion, poor particle G buffeted by random events, punched, kicked and shoved this way and that by a world fraught with explosions. Yet in retrospect, how fiercely determined it seems, as if guided by an inner logic more flowery, yet more iron-clad than my own, toward an inevitable destination: Ground Zero. "For want of a nail the shoe is lost, for want of a shoe the horse is lost, for want of a horse the rider is lost": similar was the vector addition of Gregor's life — yet quite different too, for in his case there was not loss, but gain.

I think of his Vienna encounter with Robert Musil, that bitter, brilliant writer/engineer, combining in himself the strengths and perils of spirit and science, seizing on Gregor as an embodiment of the "Other Condition", secretly attending his talks, and finally articulating for him his role as *Möglichkeitsmensch* — possibilitarian. Could G have done this himself? Would he not have simply dissolved into the stew of Otherness simmering in Amadeus' Wonderkitchen? Musil demanded he find a doorway to the world beyond limited existence; and the raven croaked "Evermore". How fitting that interview ended with a telegram announcing the coming of Roëntgen-of-the-skeletal-hand.

And Wittgenstein. What impertinent author-God would cast the greatest mind in twentieth century philosophy as a fourth-grade schoolteacher in a dung-covered village north of Vienna? Yet there he was, in time to raise the question "What does it mean to be human?". And there G was for him, planting the seed of his last and greatest work, his investigations of the limits of rational thought. And there, too, was Punch the Jude — already and again.

If Alice had no other function in his life (and of course she had many), her poignant encounter with Gregor brought him briefly into the gravitational field of Dr. Max Lindhorst, with his exposition of Eros and Thanatos,

735

and the consequences of Faustian hubris. Forewarned, and four-armed, Gregor left his session with this practitioner with more resolve, direction, and self-understanding.

A chance meeting at Yankee Stadium, a job on 43rd Street, right near Town Hall, free tickets to the first performance of Ives' Fourth Symphony: it seemed clearly destined that Gregor would meet up with his guru, his tutor for the New World, that crusty New England maniac-genius of music and insurance, Charles Ives. Was G to remain an elevator boy all his life? How else could he have come to explore risk — to the point where he was fearless in its face? And he was there for Charlie Ives — calling a strong and beautiful insect out of the table.

The composer was also Gregor's introduction to the concept of Hogmind, and the rage and struggle it could conjure. Yet far from counseling revenge and scorn, *The Insect Sonata*, Ives' grateful gift to Gregor, urged the place of Love in "man's right constitution":

Always preceding power,
And with much power, always, always much more love.

Gregor took this priority with him into battle.

I have spoken at length of the sequence of G's disillusionments: the refugees, the Japanese, the completion and deployment of the bomb. But along with these major events, there were minor details which debrided his surface, as it were, and enabled such traumas to penetrate more deeply. The betrayal of Philoctetes, for instance, and the suppurating wound it left. His tears at the Time Capsule. The six-character calligraphy. The strange appearance of the *Leiermann* in Lafayette Park.

Leo Szilard — he of LS/MFT — once remarked to me that Gregor was the most stimulating person he had ever known, and the only one of his many friends and enemies he would have liked to emulate. I was taken aback. I had never thought of Gregor as stimulating. Inspiring, surely, in his low-key way, but — until the end — gentle to a fault. As for emulating him, well, let's just say he was unique. By the way, having recently stopped smoking[35], it was during this conversation that I inquired about his sig-

---

35   "L.S./M.F.T., L.S./M.F.T." fomed the basis of a slogan in radio ads of the 1940s, and at the bottom of every cigarette pack: "Lucky Strike Means Fine Tobacco."

nature on the cover letter to his petition. "LS/MFT? Leo Szilard Means Fenominal Trouble," he said. I couldn't tell if this was sardonic humor or just Hungarian spelling. His eyes might sparkle in either case.

Tilano was another huge guard rail on Gregor's path. His gift of a petro glyph New World ancestor preserved in volcanic tuff was one of the few experiences Gregor thought of as "mystical". He was my teacher as well. I interviewed him on his 85th birthday in 1955, just before his death, ten years after the bomb. This was what he told me. I imagine he must have shared similar thoughts with Gregor:

Anglos want that which in the nature of things is impossible. They believe that there must be a man who is more manly than a good man can be, and that there is a beautiful woman who is more beautiful than all the other beautiful women. They really think that everything and every people, except us, can be whatever they would like it to be....They are never contented because they are always looking for a happiness which is greater than happiness. They want to find love where they have sown only hate and selfishness. They want to run and never tire, to satisfy all their thirsts and hungers and not be full. They cannot see that the sickness which they all suffer comes from greed, a kind of childish believing that when they close down their minds, the world is not what it always was and always what it will be.

Transcribing this from my old tape recorder, I cried.

Gregor as Jewish

In assessing his life, I have spoken of the need to recall that Gregor was an animal. Though I approach the subject with some hesitation, one cannot avoid acknowledging, too, that Gregor was a Jew. What is a Jew? Herein lies my concern: I hesitate to characterize a group that has so often and so recently been characterized — to death.

Judaism and its children, Christianity and Islam, have long stood against much of the world with respect to the atom. The Hindus were atomists, the Arabs were atomists, affirming the eternity of matter and the recurrence of creation. And in the later Mediterranean, when most westerners believed the world to be ruled by a pantheon of gods with extraordinary powers but strangely human weaknesses, a handful of Hellenic thinkers called for a rational view involving only natural causes and effects, without invoking transcendent powers. God was set aside.

Not so! cried Jews, Christians, and Muslims. The world was created once, in its perfection, *ex nihilo*. Biblical doctrine remains at odds with all theory: for Hebrew anti-atomists, "God created…" was enough, truth was frozen, origins explained; there was no further need to question. Judaism is the only great religion to have produced not a single defender of atomism, at least until modern times.

Now this is a questionable achievement on a resumé for Los Alamos. Not that it wasn't shared by many of the crew. But they were scientists. Or soldiers. They had other things to think about, large problems that could distract them from larger issues. It would be safe to say that Gregor was the only non-scientist, non-military, philosophical possibilitarian on the mesa. Similar to his animal sense of the Open, his free-playing Judaism endowed him with extra sensibility with which to judge the goings-on.

Gregor once invoked his Jewish privilege, and gave me *his* personal definition of a Jew. It was the only time I ever heard him "tell a joke". This was his joke:

It is May, 1940, at a refugee center in Paris, just before the Nazi occupation. The nice woman at the desk is trying to sort out transport requests. She asks a Belgian refugee where she and her children would like to go. "London. I have family." She is marked for London. Next she asks a French communist. "Sweden would be best," he says, "we can organize from there." Finally she asks an old Jew in black gabardine. "New Zealand," he mutters. "New Zealand?" she asks, "Why so far?" The Jew looks at her and says, "Far from what?"

Not exactly a side-splitter. But it will do.

JEWISH OPPENHEIMER AND HINDU SCIENCE

Oppie was similarly schizophrenic — if not worse. For he was not only a Jew, but a Hindu Jew. This was the man who was both father and midwife to the bomb, the man who rode his team through every difficulty and objection. This was the man who named his horse "Crisis". Yet this was the man who also said, "If atomic bombs were to be added as new weapons to the armaments of a warring world, then the time will come when mankind will curse the name of Los Alamos."

Such a statement was a great surprise to the men who, under him, and with his encouragement, were striving to create just such weapons. Yet to a student of the Vaisheshika Sutra, this thought would not seem strange. The atomic theory of Vaisheshika conforms with tenets of Brahminical doctrine — a cyclical cosmos, a multiplicity of worlds, and the retributive consequences of human action. The theory proposes that in the course of cosmic process, atoms unite and separate continually. At the conclusion of a cosmic period, atoms isolate themselves from one another and rest — until they are again set in motion and re-coagulate, allowing souls that failed to reach salvation in the previous cosmic period to receive the fruits of their actions. Oppie might even have had a thought about Gregor's origin, based on the accompanying doctrine of the transmigration of souls.

He probably did not "believe" this. But he did distinguish between "short half-life knowledge" and "long half-life knowledge". Scientific papers came and went. The Vedas and the Upanishads did not. One of his flippant remarks suggests a tantalizing third explanation for the designation Trinity: "At Trinity," he said, "Gregor, the bomb, and the world were all being tested."

Oppie was barely understood by others. For Oppenheimer's "second thoughts", Truman called him a "crybaby" and refused to have anything more to do with him. But for all his moral and intellectual depth, he remained, first and foremost, a scientist. It is sad, but appropriate, that his famous comment on the explosion cited not a moral vision of cosmic apocalypse, but a purely cosmological cataclysmic show, Lord Krishna's Best-Ever Fireworks Display.

THUS SPAKE ZARATHUSTRA

Gregor's choice of farewell performance was even more significant than it first appeared. It was Teller who brought my attention to the Zoroastrian doctrine underlying G's offering. His dance was not just a simple critique of bugbear Science, with a self-congratulatory coda of "cure" from its contrapuntal snare.

The religion of Zarathustra preached to pre-Islamic Persians a dualistic doctrine of struggle between light/good, and darkness/evil. Though equally balanced, it was two against one: the God of Light, Ahura Mazda, had as adversaries two demons, a good-cop/bad-cop, one-two threat against humanity. Humans were free to do evil or good — as they chose. The two tempters were Lucifer and Ahriman.

As we know even in Christendom, Lucifer whispered in man's ear: "You shall be like the gods, knowing good and evil." Lucifer, the master of delusion, tempting men to believe they are more powerful, more effective, more beautiful, more benevolent, more admired than they really are. Lucifer, appealing to man's pride and ambition, counseling disregard of limitations. Hence, the Tower of Babel, the Flight of Icarus, Fermi's uranium pile under the Stagg Field, the Birth of Dolly the Sheep, cloned from an adult somatic cell. Lucifer started men and women out on the path to freedom. Lucifer brought the gift of Art.

Ah, but then there is Ahriman, a character dutifully unmentioned in our covetous times. Ahriman whispers in the other ear, "You are *only* man with no divine element in you. But you can turn to your own use the entire world, and everything in it. There is no limit to the knowledge, goods, or power you can acquire. The material world is all there is, so make the most of it." Knowledge of the world is Ahriman's realm; he is constantly whispering information, suggesting new machines to invent. Ahriman wants humanity to advance at breakneck speed, long before ego and moral nature are ready. The future is already here, the sky's the limit, humanity's job is to create an earthly utopia here and now, crammed with sensual and intellectual enjoyment, and endless material possessions. Ahriman brought the gift of Science — the cold, razor-sharp intellect of Science, and death by a thousand cuts.

Gregor had danced an escape from *both* Lucifer and Ahriman that high-summer night in the blockhouse. His choice of Strauss and Nietzsche was designed to help us make that distinction. The twelve strokes of "*O Mensch, gib Acht!*" named for us our current marker in spacetime: midnight, and eternity.

I am now 88 years old. I am a philosopher and historian of science. I am dying of cancer.

Mine is lung cancer in a non-smoker. Why? Who knows? Perhaps from low-level plutonium contamination. Five years ago I had a six month cough. I thought nothing of it — winters in Princeton are cold and wet. Then it became hard to breathe. I thought it was just my payback for longevity — until I started spitting blood. My chest X-rays were negative but bronchoscopy showed a friable bronchial mass. My surgery was "successful", but Death's knock-at-the-door prompted me to finally start this biography of my friend. Last year, during a routine physical, Dr. Kitzmiller picked up some abnormal liver functions, and subsequently, a positive biopsy. Now I am developing bone pain, and last month had a positive bone scan. Metastasis. My doctors give me another year; three at the most with radiation and chemotherapy, but I have decided not to bother: fourscore and nine will be a more than adequate allotment.

As Gregor asserted his Jewish privilege to define a Jew, I now want to assert the increasingly maligned privilege of the aged — especially aged historians — to ruminate unmercifully on Life, Death and History. The surely fatigued reader, may skip to the end, though I can assure him that he will not find out who did it.

This world now seems to me a Kingdom of Death, a Death-World without antecedent. What is unprecedented is not simply the scale of mass destruction, but that its means are the unquestioned product of systematic rational calculation, and that its scale is expressed not only in numbers undone and areas destroyed, but also terms of the compression of time in which destruction is delivered. Gregor's second war, the war of the Manhattan Project, took approximately five years. Our last great "war" — some would call it "massacre" — took all of five days. Five days to slaughter hundreds of thousands of featherless bipeds who happened to live on top of oil reserves which took seven hundred million years to form, and will take less than two centuries to use up. Any residual complaint from survivors will also be dealt with.

In my lifetime, I have seen the crucial change from wars fought between armies — bad enough — to wars declared on civilians. Since the early '40s, with increasing cold-bloodedness, vast numbers of persons are simply marked for annihilation as part of an impersonal process of destruction. The adversaries are no longer humans, no longer even those humans of whom it is written *humanus lupus humani*. The struggles, such as they are, are between complex bureaucratic structures which control the technology of man-made slaughter to serve the ideological needs of civilization's death machine.

It may be that the world is truly doomed: there is too much competition for the Meanest Show on Earth. The mathematician J. Carson Mark once half-seriously suggested that all heads of state be forced to witness an atmospheric nuclear explosion once a year. Would he still propose such a tactic? Fallout issues aside, would such a demonstration not just produce euphoria and increased weapons sales?

Perhaps I'm being too cynical, but cynicism is the prerogative of age, and mine is well-earned. Surely the Nazi Heidegger was right: calculative thinking has replaced meditative thinking in the contemporary world — much to his despair. It is the manner in which nature is understood in modern physics. This truth alone will explain much. It will explain, for example, the technological society and the free market, a "totality of methods rationally arrived at," Jacques Ellul labeled it, "having as their sole interest the criterion of efficiency in every domain of life." This is not the rationality of the Enlightenment, but a modern, deadly, version embedded in the life-world like a cancer-causing virus.

To compound the pathology, we have recently witnessed a re-emergence of the qualitative at the heart of quantification itself, for numbers have become too large to accommodate quantity — their magnitude cannot be grasped. The qualitative is simply this, in Heidegger's formulation: the need for "unconditioned domination of the whole earth." Our current technology reveals the meaning of Being in our age. It manifests itself in devastation and the ravaging of nature, a process which continues to grow with no end in sight. The new rationality is divorced from any mythic or poetic consciousness: compare the killing described in Homer with contemporary extermination. In my childhood (forgive me, Gregor), only roaches were "exterminated".

Death has extended its domain even to the living. Auschwitz and its Brethren, not to mention Democracy and its Embargoes, encourage a new social form, a death-world of the living dead embedded in larger society. As we look around at the primo automata running the world, and the subsidiary automata taking their direction, we can't help but notice the next transition: from the death of body to the even broader death of spirit.

Where then is there hope, John?

It *is* possible that certain areas of our artistic, personal, and dream life may turn out to be secret laboratories in which to develop values on which our future depends. A radical new mode of self-consciousness may be in the making. The really "new frontier" of our age cannot be defined politically. It will be defined only by a revolution in our instinctual lives comparable to the industrial revolution. This is why Gregor's life, his example, held such great promise. Even though the trajectory of human history seems to be downward toward complacency, decadence, and coldness of heart, it has occasionally been the case that we are saved by the obscure, heroic efforts of individuals whose passion it has been to redeem the world, they who have lived a faithful life, and rest in unvisited graves. The lamed-vovniks, if you will. The second half of the century has not produced another Gregor, but I have not yet given up hope.

Ultimately, our "new frontier" will be a religious one. The overweening self-concern which fills fills the emptiness of the modern world may be modified towards a greater appreciation of Self. That's large-S Self, Brahman, not Atman. A new ground for transcendence will have to be discovered. The healing of hearts and the restoring of souls is the next great task. We will have to believe the future into existence.

****

I must end my effort, even as I began it, with a respectful, but non-apologetic critique of the master of Prague, Franz Kafka. What a serious misrepresentation of Gregor was Dr. Kafka's! Over the last eighty years, those who never knew him have used Gregor's name as the arch-symbol of alien-

743

ated man. Yet was there ever a being less alienated, more observant of self, more passionately connected to the world?

Of *The Metamorphosis* Kafka wrote: "I find it bad; perhaps there is no hope for me whatever," and later "Great aversion for *The Metamorphosis*. Unreadable ending. Almost radically imperfect. It would have been much better if I had not been disturbed at the time by a business trip." (Diary, Jan 19, 1914.) I would have to agree. Not only did Kafka's report miss the facts of the case, but the larger ending, the final use-value of that commodity has become more corrupt even as its exchange-value has skyrocketed. *The Metamorphosis* has helped to spawn cottage industries of nihilism, cynicism and despair on the one hand, and post-modern, deconstructive cool on the other. There is enough in the world about which to be cynical. Why add Gregor to this dismaying heap? I am hoping that, in some small way, my work may lighten — by one small part — the Angel of History's cleanup task, as the pile of debris grows skywards.

Kafka, in another note from his Diaries, makes a remark which bears reflection:

On my deathbed, provided the suffering is not too great, I will be very content. The best of what I have written is based upon this capacity to die content. All the good passages, the strongly convincing ones, are about someone who is dying and who finds it very hard, and sees in it an injustice. For me, since I think I can be content on my deathbed, such descriptions are secretly a game. I even enjoy dying in the character who is dying.

I find this intriguing, I who will soon have to submit myself to the same test — Kafka's art as a playful relation with death. Wherein lies the capacity to die content?

Is great fatigue or pain the sine qua non?

...for many a time
I have been half in love with easeful Death,
Call'd him soft names in many a mused rhyme,
To take into the air my quiet breath;

I think not. In Kafka's case, in Gregor's, and I hope my own, a contented death involves being able to find satisfaction even in supreme dissatisfaction. Kafka's heroes carry out their lives in death's space. His achievement has been to joyfully snatch his every sentence from that zone of insanity into which common sense has wandered in our time. I flatter myself to think that at the end I might share, in my own small way, that joy. We shall see.

It is understandable that Gregor, with all his omnivorous reading, would avoid the works of Kafka. Yet there is one work I deeply regret his not having read. It might have spared him so much confusion at the end, and perhaps have even altered his terminal plan. Why did his colleagues continue to build a needless bomb? Would that Gregor had encountered "The Great Wall of China", the great parable of our time.

****

In the inbox on Gregor's reading desk, under a pile of work-related papers, I found the following note, with its envelope, clipped to a musical score.

```
Cambridge, 13-04-45
Dear boy,
     Please accept a little present I couldn't help filching and
sending. R.S. has been a friend of the family since before the
(First) War - You may know he wrote two left-handed works for
my brother, Paul. This is his latest - just finished, as yet
unperformed. Looks meisterwerkisch to me, though I can't really
imagine the harmonies in the thicker parts. I persuaded him to
let me make a photocopy to send. Thought you'd appreciate it.
     The book on everyday language you suggested many years ago
is almost done. It will probably disappoint you. Truth is, it's
pretty lousy.
     These last years have been a dark time. I once wrote,
perhaps rightly: "The earlier culture will become a heap of
rubble and finally a heap of ashes, but spirits will hover over
the ashes." Yours likely will be chief among them. What more is
there to say?
     Come see me in Cambridge if you get the chance.
   LW
```

Who else could it be but Wittgenstein? Who else so commitedly unpolitical as to not mention the death of FDR the previous day? Under the signature, in answer to the question, G had scrawled:

7. WHAT WE CANNOT SPEAK ABOUT WE MUST PASS OVER IN SILENCE.

The score? Richard Strauss' late masterpiece, *Metamorphosen*, an elegiac streaming for 23 solo strings. On the 13th of February, 1945, the day before Ash Wednesday, a month before he put pen to paper, Dresden, the last German city standing, was firebombed by the British and U.S. Air Forces in the most destructive bombing raid in European history. Dresden's heart was demolished, and everyone in it was suffocated or consumed by fire. Something like 100,000 were killed, but who could count the bones and ashes? Cologne, Hamburg, Berlin, Weimar, Dresden — the sanctuaries of German culture — all were gone. Strauss wrote friends of his despair. *Metamorphosen* — with its quotations from the Eroica Funeral March — contains no metamorphoses, no theme with variations. What deeper changes then was the shattered old man invoking?

Strauss' long career had always seemed to me to be unconsciously, mysteriously dedicated to Gregor. Fools were his subject, holy and not-so-holy: *Don Quixote, Till Eulenspiegel, Don Juan.* Philosophy was his subject in *Zarathustra,* and transcendence. *A Hero's Life, Death and Transfiguration.* One of his very last songs summed up my impression of Gregor:

...the unwatched soul
wants to soar up freely
to live a thousand times more intensely
in the magic circle of night.

Tief und tausendfach zu leben. That was my friend.

I appropriated the score, and with Strauss' permission, *Metamorphosen* was performed in the Library of Congress' Coolidge Auditorium, conducted by Nicholas Slonimsky, on July 16, 1949 — the fifth anniversary of G's death. Very few in the audience knew the significance of the date. The 85-year old Strauss, fatigued from conducting his *Capriccio* in Munich, was flown over by a group of us to attend this U.S. premiere. Halfway through the work, he experienced an attack of dizziness and immediately afterwards was flown to Garmisch, his beloved home. He died three weeks later.

I shall follow him soon. And *apres moi? Le deluge?* Would it were not so.

****

What <u>is</u> there to say, when all is done?

Only this I feel, along with Emily D., dearest Emily, the sole true love in this bachelor's life:

I reason, Earth is short -
And Anguish - absolute -
And many hurt,
But, what of that?
I reason, we could die -
The best Vitality
Cannot excel Decay,
But, what of that?
I reason, that in Heaven -
Somehow, it will be even -
Some new Equation, given -
But, what of that?

Shantih shantih shantih

Princeton, N.J., April, 1999

WORKS IN THE MIX

VIENNA

Allen, Fredrick Lewis, *Only Yesterday: An Informal History of the 1920's*, Perennial Library, 1964,

Bangerter, Lowell A., *Robert Musil*, Continuum, 1989,

Davies, Norman, *Europe, A History*, Oxford U.P., 1996.

Gordon, David George, *The Compleat Cockroach: A Comprehensive Guide to the Most Despised (and Least Understood) Creature on Earth*, Ten Speed Press, 1996

Hughes, H. Stuart, *Oswald Spengler*, Scribner, 1962.

Janik, Allan, and Toulmin, Stephen, *Wittgenstein's Vienna*, Touchstone, 1973.

Kafka, Franz, *The Complete Stories and Parables*, Quality Paperback Book Club, 1983.

Monk, Ray, *Ludwig Wittgenstein: The Duty of Genius*, Free Press, 1990.

Musil, Robert, *Precision and Soul: Essays and Addresses*, U. Chicago Pr., 1990.

Nitske, W. Robert, *The Life of Wilhelm Conrad Roentgen, discoverer of the X-Ray*, U. Arizona Pr., 1971.

Peters, Frederick G., *Robert Musil: Master of the Hovering Life*, Columbia U. Pr., 1978.

Rilke, Ranier Maria, *Duino Elegies*, trans. J.B. Leishman and Stephen Spender, Norton, 1963.

Spengler, Oswald, *The Decline of the West*, trans. Charles Francis Atkinson, Knopf, 1926.

Wittgenstein, Ludwig, *Culture and Value*, trans. Peter Winch, U. Chicago Pr., 1980.

Wittgenstein, Ludwig, *Tractatus Logico-Philosophicus*, trans. D.F. Pears & B.F. McGuinness, Routledge & Kegan Paul, 1961.

NEW YORK

Allen, Leslie H., ed., *Bryan and Darrow at Dayton : The Record and Documents of the "Bible-Evolution Trial"* A. Lee & Co., 1925.

Brumbaugh, Robert, ed., *Six Trials,* Crowell, 1969. (Scopes, Sacco & Vanzetti)

Burkholder, J. Peter, *All Made of Tunes: Charles Ives and the Uses of Musical Borrowing,* Yale U.P., 1995.

Cowell, Henry and Sidney, *Charles Ives and his Music,* Oxford, 1969.

Davidoff, Nicholas, *The Catcher Was a Spy,* Pantheon, 1994.

electricchair.com

Fast, Howard, *The Passion of Sacco and Vanzetti: a New England Legend,* Blue Heron, 1953.

Frankfurter, Felix, "The Case of Sacco and Vanzetti", *Atlantic Monthly,* March 1927. (on atlantic.com)

Hoffman, Frederick J. *The 20's,* Free Press, 1965.

Irwin, Inez Hayes, *The Story of Alice Paul and the National Woman's Party,* Denlinger's Publishers, 1977.

Ives, Charles, *Essays Before a Sonata, The Majority, and Other Writings,* Norton, 1962.

Lanouette, William, *Genius in the Shadows: a Biography of Leo Szilard, the Man Behind the Bomb,* U. Chicago Press, 1992.

Ovid, *The Metamorphoses of Ovid, translated into English by Henry T. Riley, M.A.,* London, George Bell and Sons, 1898.

Perlis, Vivian, Charles Ives Remembered: An Oral History, Yale U.P., 1974

Sinclair, Upton, *Boston, a Novel,* Boni, 1928. (Sacco & Vanzetti).

Smith, Page, *Redeeming the Time: A People's History of the 1920's and the New Deal,* Penguin, 1987.

Swafford, Jan, *Charles Ives: A Life with Music,* Norton, 1996.

WASHINGTON, D.C.

Burns, James MacGregor, *Roosevelt: The Lion and the Fox,* Harcourt Brace & World, 1956.

Evans, Howard Ensign, *Life on a Little-known Planet,* illus. Arnold Clapman, Dutton, 1968. (Gregor's lab work taken from the experiments of Peg Ellis, as here reported.)

Friedel, Frank, ed., *The New Deal and the American People*, Prentice Hall, 1964.

Graham, Otis L., and Wander, Meghan R., eds., *Franklin D. Roosevelt: His Life and Times, an Encyclopedic View*, Da Capo, 1985

Hobsbawm, Eric, *The Age of Extremes: A History of the World, 1914-1991*, Vintage, 1994.

Lash, Joseph P., *Eleanor and Franklin*, Norton, 1971.

Miller, Nathan, *FDR: An Intimate History*, New American Library, 1983.

Smith, Page, *Democracy on Trial: The Japanese American Evacuation and Relocation in World War Two*, Simon and Schuster, 1995.

Sophocles, *The Tragedies of Sophocles in English Prose*, the Oxford Translation, Harper and Brothers, 1873.

LOS ALAMOS

Brode, Bernice, *Tales of Los Alamos: Life on the Mesa 1943-1945*, Los Alamos Historical Society, 1997.

Church, Peggy Pond, *The House at Otowi Bridge: The Story of Edith Warner and Los Alamos*, U. New Mexico Pr., 1960.

Coles, Robert, *The Old Ones of New Mexico*, U. New Mexico Pr., 1973.

Erdoes, Richard, and Ortiz, Alfonso, eds., *American Indian Trickster Tales*, Viking, 1998.

Feynman, Richard P., *Surely You're Joking, Mr. Feynman: Adventures of a Curious Character*, Norton, 1985.

Feynman, Richard P., *What do YOU Care What Other People Think?: Further Adventures of a Curious Character*, Norton, 1988.

Gleick, James, *Genius: The Life and Science of Richard Feynman*, Vintage, 1992.

Goodchild, Peter, *Oppenheimer, Shatter of Worlds*, Fromm, 1985.

Goudsmit, Samuel, *Alsos*, H. Schuman, 1947.

Groves, Leslie M., *Now It Can Be Told: The Story of the Manhattan Project*, Da Capo, 1983.

Hales, Peter Bacon, Atomic Spaces: *Living on the Manhattan Project*, U. Illinois Pr. 1997.

Jette, Eleanor, *Inside Box 1663*, Los Alamos Historical Society, 1977.

Jungk, Robert, *Brighter than a Thousand Suns*, Harcourt, Brace & World, 1958.

Lamont, Lansing, *Day of Trinity,* Athaneum, 1985

Los Alamos Historical Society, *Behind Tall Fences: Stories and Experiences About Los Alamos at its Beginning,* Los Alamos Historical Society, 1996.

Powers, Thomas, *Heisenberg's War: The Secret History of the German Bomb*, Little, Brown, 1993.

Rhodes, Richard, *The Making of the Atomic Bomb,* Simon and Schuster, 1986.

Rich, Adrienne, *The Dream of a Common Language, Poems 1974-1977*, Norton, 1978

Truslow, Edith C., *Manhattan District History: Nonscientific Aspects of Los Alamos Project Y 1942 throught 1946*, Los Alamos Historical Society, 1997.

Wilson, Jane S., and Serber, Charlotte, *Standing By and Making Do: Women of Wartime Los Alamos,* Los Alamos Historical Society, 1997.

Wyden, Peter, *Day One: Before Hiroshima and After*, Simon and Schuster, 1984.

The Author Thanks

— the many friends and family who ploughed through a Brobdingnagian manuscript with constancy, courage and comments.

— my then-agent, Dorian Karchmar, good-humoredly nurturing lifeforms crawling in her slush pile.

— the immortal Franz K. for his generous visit to Burlington, Vermont.

— the authors and historians who were my guides on Gregor's mountain path.

The book you have in hand is the elder, fatter relative, both ancestor and progeny, of *Insect Dreams, the Half Life of Gregor Samsa,* a book whose praises are quoted in the front matter of this one.

Insect Dreams was published in 2002 to great acclaim, in a version substantially shortened from this, its original, skillfully edited by Fred Ramey. Over the ensuing years, I had wondered whether the original version, the director's cut as it were, might not also be made available, of possible interest to ID fans, Kafka maniacs, and literary scholars.

Having recently founded Fomite Press, and by 2016 having published 80 or so other authors, I asked Fred how he might feel about Fomite bringing out the original, longer version to accompany *Insect Dreams* out in the world. He was supportive, generously helpful with the legal details of doing so, and further proposed an email dialogue about some of the questions raised by this prequel project: the editor's role in the life of a book, whether a published novel is a stable thing, etc., questions now relevant in a world changed by digital publishing. That discussion is now available as *The Insect Dialogues,* the first fruit of Fred's new imprint, Leaping Man. (leapingman.org)

About Fomite

A fomite is a medium capable of transmitting infectious organisms from one individual to another.

"The activity of art is based on the capacity of people to be infected by the feelings of others." Tolstoy, *What Is Art?*

Writing a review on Amazon, Good Reads, Shelfari, Library Thing or other social media sites for readers will help the progress of independent publishing. To submit a review, go to the book page on any of the sites and follow the links for reviews. Books from independent presses rely on reader to reader communications.

For more information or to order any of our books, visit http://www.fomitepress.com/FOMITE/Our_Books.html

More Titles from Fomite...

Novels

Joshua Amses — *During This, Our Nadir*
Joshua Amses — *Raven or Crow*
Joshua Amses — *The Moment Before an Injury*
Jaysinh Birjepatel — *The Good Muslim of Jackson Heights*
Jaysinh Birjepatel — *Nothing Beside Remains*
David Brizer — *Victor Rand*
Paula Closson Buck — *Summer on the Cold War Planet*
David Adams Cleveland — *Ashes of My Father*
Roger Coleman — *Skywreck Afternoons*
Marc Estrin — *Hyde*
Marc Estrin — *Kafka's Roach*
Marc Estrin — *Speckled Vanitie*

Zdravka Evtimova — *In the Town of Joy and Peace*
Zdravka Evtimova — *Sinfonia Bulgarica*
Daniel Forbes — *Derail This Train Wreck*
Greg Guma — *Dons of Time*
Richard Hawley — *The Three Lives of Jonathan Force*
Lamar Herrin — *Father Figure*
Ron Jacobs — *All the Sinners Saints*
Ron Jacobs — *Short Order Frame Up*
Ron Jacobs — *The Co-conspirator's Tale*
Scott Archer Jones — *A Rising Tide of People Swept Away*
Michael Horner — *Damage Control*
Maggie Kast — *A Free Unsullied Land*
Darrell Kastin — *Shadowboxing with Bukowski*
Coleen Kearon — *Feminist on Fire*
Coleen Kearon — *#triggerwarning*
Jan Englis Leary — *Thicker Than Blood*
Diane Lefer — *Confessions of a Carnivore*
Rob Lenihan — *Born Speaking Lies*
Colin Mitchell — *Roadman*
Ilan Mochari — *Zinsky the Obscure*
Gregory Papadoyiannis — *The Baby Jazz*
Andy Potok — *My Father's Keeper*
Robert Rosenberg — *Isles of the Blind*
Ron Savage — *Voyeur in Tangier*
David Schein — *The Adoption*
Fred Skolnik — *Rafi's World*
Lynn Sloan — *Principles of Navigation*
L.E. Smith — *The Consequence of Gesture*
L.E. Smith — *Travers' Inferno*
L.E. Smith — *Untimely RIPped*
Bob Sommer — *A Great Fullness*
Tom Walker — *A Day in the Life*
Susan V. Weiss — *My God, What Have We Done?*
Peter M. Wheelwright — *As It Is On Earth*
Suzie Wizowaty — *The Return of Jason Green*

POETRY

Antonello Borra — *Alfabestiario*
Antonello Borra — *AlphaBetaBestiaro*
James Connolly — *Picking Up the Bodies*
Greg Delanty — *Loosestrife*
Mason Drukman — *Drawing on Life*
J. C. Ellefson — *Foreign Tales of Exemplum and Woe*
Anna Faktorovich — *Improvisational Arguments*
Barry Goldensohn — *Snake in the Spine, Wolf in the Heart*
Barry Goldensohn — *The Hundred Yard Dash Man*
Barry Goldensohn — *The Listener Aspires to the Condition of Music*
R. L. Green When — *You Remember Deir Yassin*
Kate Magill — *Roadworthy Creature, Roadworthy Craft*
Tony Magistrale — *Entanglements*
Sherry Olson — *Four-Way Stop*
Andreas Nolte — *Mascha: The Poems of Mascha Kaléko*
Janice Miller Potter — *Meanwell*
Joseph D. Reich — *Connecting the Dots to Shangrila*
Joseph D. Reich — *The Hole That Runs Through Utopia*
Joseph D. Reich — *The Housing Market*
Joseph D. Reich — *The Derivation of Cowboys and Indians*
Kennet Rosen and Richard Wilson — *Gomorrah*
Fred Rosnblum — *Vietnumb*
David Schein — *My Murder and Other Local News*
Scott T. Starbuck — *Industrial O*
Scott T. Starbuck — *Hawk on Wire*
Seth Steinzor — *Among the Lost*
Seth Steinzor — *To Join the Lost*
Susan Thomas — *The Empty Notebook Interrogates Itself*
Paolo Valesio and Todd Portnowitz — *Midnight in Spoleto*
Sharon Webster — *Everyone Lives Here*
Tony Whedon — *The Tres Riches Heures*
Tony Whedon — *The Falkland Quartet*

STORIES

Jay Boyer — *Flight*
Michael Cocchiarale — *Still Time*
Neil Connelly — *In the Wake of Our Vows*
Catherine Zobal Dent — *Unfinished Stories of Girls*
Zdravka Evtimova — *Carts and Other Stories*
John Michael Flynn — *Off to the Next Wherever*
Elizabeth Genovise — *Where There Are Two or More*
Andrei Guriuanu — *Body of Work*
Derek Furr — *Semitones*
Derek Furr — *Suite for Three Voices*
Zeke Jarvis — *In A Family Way*
Jan English Leary — *Skating on the Vertical and Other Stories*
Marjorie Maddox — *What She Was Saying*
William Marquess — *Boom-shacka-lacka*
Gary Miller — *Museum of the Americas*
Jennifer Anne Moses — *Visiting Hours*
Peter Nash — *Parsimony*
Martin Ott — *Interrogations*
Jack Pulaski — *Love's Labours*
Charles Rafferty — *Saturday Night at Magellan's*
Kathryn Roberts — *Companion Plants*
Ron Savage — *What We Do For Love*
L.E. Smith — *Views Cost Extra*
Caitlin Hamilton Summie — *To Lay To Rest Our Ghosts*
Susan Thomas — *Among Angelic Orders*
Tom Walker — *Signed Confessions*
Silas Dent Zobal — *The Inconvenience of the Wings*

ODD BIRDS

Micheal Breiner — *the way none of this happened*
J. C. Ellefson — *Under the Influence: Shoutin' Out to Walt*
David Ross Gunn — *Cautionary Chronicles*
Andrei Guriuanu — *The Darkest City*
Gail Holst-Warhaft — *The Fall of Athens*

Roger Leboitz — *A Guide to the Western Slopes and the Outlying Area*
dug Nap— *Artsy Fartsy*
Delia Bell Robinson — *A Shirtwaist Story*
Peter Schumann — *Planet Kasper, Volumes One and Two*
Peter Schumann — *Bread & Sentences*
Peter Schumann — *Faust 3*
Peter Schumann — *We*

PLAYS
Stephen Goldberg — *Screwed and Other Plays*
Michele Markarian — *Unborn Children of America*

Made in the USA
Columbia, SC
24 January 2024

29973708R00422